Lone Star Ice and Fire

a novel by

L.E. Brady

oral press

ISBN: 0-9708293-3-7
Library of Congress Control Number: 2004100187
Manufactured in Canada
1 3 5 7 9 10 8 6 4 2
First Edition

Cover Design: Monica Fedrick
Cover Guitar Photographs: Robert Dunn
Author Photograph: Frank A. Schmitt
Fender Broadcaster courtesy of Dan Courtenay, Chelsea Guitars, NYC

www.coralpress.com
Coral Press
252 W. 81st Street
New York, New York 10024

To my friend Elizabeth Frank, who showed me such
a thing was possible, and to my husband,
Steve Brady, for once upon a time
insisting that I put on the headphones.

PROLOGUE: *LONE STAR*
Austin, Texas 1989

S ONNY BLAINE FELT raw dismay upon seeing the image reflected back from his mirror. Now he wore his daddy's face, instead of his own. Sonny had heard tell of people growing old overnight. Up until now, he hadn't believed it. He moved his nose within two inches of the mirror, peering, running sinewy fingers through his hair. Sluggish, he took a comb and smoothed his 'do into a pompadour. No signs of gray, no bald spots evident. His skin would never be as weathered as Daddy's had been. Big Billy Jay Blaine had labored hard all his life in the sun-baked Southern oil fields. Sonny earned his living mostly by night, playing blues guitar.

The real change showed in Sonny's eyes. Exhausted, haunted, they reflected the crush of responsibilities that had embraced him in the last five days. For an instant, he clutched a pendant he wore about his neck, and then dropped the necklace out of sight inside his collar—next to his heart. Cinching his bolo tie, he nodded grimly at the reflection. He turned away, walking toward a grouping of photographs on the wall.

Some of the photos were top line professional work. Others were pictures taken at home with cheesy cameras. Family photos of generations past and present were intermixed with performance shots and the proofs of music magazine covers.

Sonny gazed at each photo for a few minutes. One of his favorites was of his parents on their wedding day. Big Billy Jay posed in his Sunday suit, wearing the very bolo tie that now encircled Sonny's throat. Sonny's daddy had been tall and powerfully built. His deadly good looks were complemented perfectly by a sly, crooked smile. His bride, Ruby Crawford Blaine, looked unusually pretty in the picture. She wore a simple white gown, her auburn hair swept back under a veil. Plain, pale, and slight, Mama hailed from pioneer stock. She normally did not photograph as well as this. The photo, hand-painted in the old-fashioned way, captured the couple's love.

Next to the wedding picture hung a blown-up snapshot of Sonny, one arm slung around the shoulders of his little brother, Walker. The photo was now more than twenty years old. The occasion was Sonny's eighteenth birthday bash. Walker grinned at Sonny, his fedora pulled down on his forehead, a loaner guitar gripped to his chest. Sonny's younger self stared back at Walker, a real serious look on his mug. His favorite instrument to this day, a '65 Fender Telecaster, hung strapped to his shoulders. Only fifteen years old in the photo, Walker was as scrawny as a guinea rooster. Sonny, already tall and muscular, sported a tousled mop of hair. Even back then, they hardly looked like kin. Walker favored Mama's side as much as Sonny resembled Daddy's. In common, the brothers had their maternal grand-daddy's long-fingered hands, and Big Billy Jay's dark eyes and mighty arms.

The Blaine boys always shared one other thing: a soul-snatching devotion to the blues.

Soul-snatching. Already the rumors started—people were craving the supernatural. Things like this didn't just happen—at a crossroads, yet? Folklore had it that at the junction of Highways 49 and 61, in Clarksdale, Mississippi, Scratch had traded Delta bluesman Robert Johnson a black-magic guitar for his eternal soul. Not such a bad deal for a man who was likely to end up in hell anyways, what with the bluesy lifestyle he was leading.

And anyone who ever saw Firewalker Blaine play that damned guitar of his would tell you that he had worked it like something possessed.

It was a stupid folk tale, a good image to sling a blues or two around. It was a story Sonny had used to scare Walker when they were kids. He'd never before considered what Johnson's family must have thought of those gruesome rumors.

Feeling his throat tighten, Sonny made himself look away. He stepped carefully over cardboard boxes filled with reel-to-reel tapes, and crossed over to a window seat. Stored guitars, in various stages of assembly, littered the room. Sonny sat. The warmth of dust-speckled Texas sunlight pushed through the curtains. He picked up a battered blonde Fender guitar. He didn't bother plugging in.

Instead, he turned the instrument face down on his lap, running his callused fingertips across letters carved into the finish on the back. He flipped the guitar around, worrying the tuning pegs a turn or two. Second nature, Sonny tapped his foot three times and fell into a whispered shuffle run. He emptied his mind through his hands, letting for a moment the caress of music soothe him. Then he heard the baby start to fuss.

He put the guitar back on the stand and hurried into the bedroom next door. Cilla lay sleeping on her side, a cascade of long red hair hiding her face. She was already dressed in stockings and a low-cut black sheath. One of her breasts was pulled free of the neckline. Her infant son was mewling, struggling, beside her. The baby had lost his mama's nipple.

Sonny studied them, feeling helpless. He pondered how to take action. Finally, sensing Cilla was about to stir, he sat on the bed and gently rolled the baby toward his mama. He took Cilla's breast and guided the boy's little mouth back into place. The baby latched on and suckled furiously once again.

Sonny lightly stroked the baby's sweaty down curls. He whispered,

"That's the way, little man. Easy, now." The child's eyes closed as he fell into the rhythm of feeding.

Cilla stirred, murmuring her husband's name. Sonny hushed her, stroking her cheek with his fingertips. She seemed to fall back into a quiet slumber. Sonny crept from the room, shutting the door noiselessly behind him. He hoped mama and baby could both catch a little more sleep before it was time to leave.

Sonny went down to the kitchen. He wandered to the window and gazed out at the rose garden beyond. He lit a cigarette and from force of habit he switched on a countertop radio. The song playing, *Ghost of T-Bone*, was a take-no-prisoners instrumental. The guitar work was radiant—pure and true Walker.

Sonny reached to turn the radio off, but stopped short. Hand poised just shy of the volume knob, he let the piece flow over and through him. To listen to Walker's playing was like talking straight truth with him. Same as listening to him go nuts howling his raspy laugh, or fighting to still his frequent tears. Walker had never held anything back.

When the song finished, an uncharacteristically solemn jock said, "Of course, that was the inimitable Firewalker Blaine. We'll all miss you, man. Keep listening for more. We're paying tribute all day long to this unequaled Texas bluesman.

"And don't ya'll forget about the public memorial service this afternoon. Go on out and pay your last respects."

I TORNADO BLUES

1.

SONNY COULDN'T put it off any longer. He had to tell Walker that he was leaving for Austin at summer's end, heading south with the rest of the White Tornadoes. Maybe he'd show Walker his new guitar and amp, to soften the blow some. Sonny knew that the news of his leaving would shatter his little brother—and not simply because Walker thought Sonny was the best thing to come along since Muddy Waters invented electricity. Of the two of them, Sonny was by far Daddy's favorite whipping boy. Without his big brother around, Walker was bound to draw a lot more fire.

Sonny was riding shotgun, head lolling out the window of Floyd Montgomery's old van. Floyd drove, eyeballing the van's temperature gauge, muttering now and again that the jalopy was bound to overheat in this July sun. They were on the mirage-shimmered highway that led from Fort Worth to their hometown of Mingus. The band's drummer and bassist snored in the back, draped at odd angles over their music equipment. The night before, the White Tornadoes had worked a good-paying Sweet Sixteen party for a rodeo queen. Her old man had let them crash out afterward in his barn.

Such gigs were commonplace for the White Tornadoes. They had built quite a rep in these parts, playing everywhere—parties, school dances, weddings. Honky-tonks and roadhouses as far away as Dallas and Abilene turned a blind eye to the band's high school age, because the Tornadoes could pack people in. They played a tight mix of country-western and rock 'n' roll. They also peppered their sets with their first love, the blues, in the guise of British Invasion music.

Floyd had joined forces with drummer Eddie Finger when both were juniors in high school. Eddie was a fireplug of a kid with mud-colored bangs that flopped over his brow. He had a set of sparkly blue Ludwigs just like Ringo's that kept the beat sure and solid. As for Floyd, Sonny knew of his family long before the Tornadoes formed, because the Montgomerys and Blaines both attended Southern Baptist. Plus, Walker had long carried a torch for little sister Nancy Ruth Montgomery.

Floyd could blow a sweet and rough harmonica, working like an acolyte to master James Cotton's licks. He also possessed a gravel-pit singing voice way beyond his eighteen years, and had a squinty stare that made him look like a soothsayer. When Floyd bit into that harp and shook his Dylan curls, he could transform little girls into women.

Floyd and Eddie needed a bassist. They turned to a high-yellow kid named Johnny Lee Hogan. After graduating from the colored school in '64, Johnny Lee helped work his daddy's small farm, and picked up gigs when he could. Long ago, his granddaddy and Sonny's, musicians both, had played together some. Rumor was that Johnny Lee could pluck a mean stand-up bass. He was a goofball with Coke-bottle glasses and a haircut that resembled a poorly plowed field. He moved like a loose-limbed scarecrow next to the big fiddle. Sitting in, he fit right tight with their groove, and they hired him on the spot. Soon one of them rounded up a pawned McCartney-style Hofmann that, with a little TLC, sounded good. Though Johnny Lee was great playing either instrument, he came into his own with that electric bass. His walk turned into a soul strut, and his clear glasses were replaced by righteous Ray Charles shades. Sonny hadn't glimpsed Johnny Lee's eyeballs since.

At first they worried, mixing colored and white in the band. Johnny Lee couldn't even drink a malted with the rest of them at the Mingus Rexall lunch counter. But Johnny Lee turned out to help more than hurt the Tornadoes. With his hair processed, he was fair enough to pass when they played white only joints, and his presence helped land them gigs where normally only black bands performed.

Sonny was still in junior high when the White Tornadoes came to be, but the band didn't give a damn once they heard him. His tone was fatter than a Longhorn steer. No one could touch him for nasty, slicing rhythm licks. His crooked grin and black pageboy hair drove the girls crazier than even Floyd managed to. Just last night, Sonny was the one Sweet Little Sixteen had chosen for postparty romance. Johnny Lee spent the night standing guard, fearful her daddy would get wind of it and lynch them all.

Floyd and Sonny got Eddie and Johnny Lee delivered to their respective homes, and then headed to the Blaines' place. As they approached Sonny's rundown house, they spied a figure sitting on the porch steps. Floyd said, "Looks like Walker's waiting for you. He's going to love that new Fender you bought yourself."

"Yeah, he will," Sonny replied. "Leastwise Daddy's truck's gone. Must have got that job in Odessa after all."

"Looks like he left Walker a little reminder that he was home, though," Floyd sighed. "Poor little shit."

Sonny saw what Floyd meant as Walker jumped off the porch and ran to the driveway to meet them. His left eye sported a fresh shiner. Sonny felt anger and guilt surge inside him in equal parts. The Old Man would probably never have lashed out at Walker had he been home to take the heat—and here he was about to take off for good.

"Hey, ya'll!" Walker hollered, leaning into Floyd's window. "How was the party?"

"Not bad," Floyd told him. "Better yet, we went to a music store in

Arlington this morning that was having a sale. You should see what Sonny bought."

"Yeah? What'd you get, bro?"

"Give me two seconds to unload, Squirt." Sonny climbed from the van and went around back. First he dug out his old guitar case and amp and handed them to Walker. "You carry these in. I'll get the new stuff."

Loaded down, Walker rounded the van on the driver's side. As Sonny yanked out his new loot, he heard Floyd say to Walker, "Got two guitars in the house now, kid."

"Cool. Maybe Sonny will let me play one of them some." Sonny heard them smack palms.

"Don't hold your breath," Sonny growled, slamming the van door, his hands full of new gear. Walker wasn't ever supposed to fuck with Sonny's guitar. Sonny had beat the tar out of Walker when he'd caught him fooling around with it. Didn't seem to matter. Over and over he found Walker lost in the music, unaware of the trouble he was in until Sonny pounced. Walker swore he'd stop after each beating. He didn't. Even when Sonny couldn't catch him red-handed, he'd find evidence of tampering—weird tuning on the strings, the strap left adjusted to smaller shoulders, the case placed in the wrong spot—and he'd whomp him again.

Walker set down the amp to open the front door, waving back at Floyd. "Tell your sister I said howdy."

"Will do, Walker." Floyd yelled. He grabbed Sonny's arm as he walked by his window. "You really should let him play some, man, now you got two axes."

"We'll see. Later, Floyd." Sonny put down his new amp and watched as Floyd backed out. He heard the screen door slam behind him, and turned to see his mama, Ruby. Her arms were folded stern across her faded house-dress. She was frowning.

"Howdy, Mama."

"What's that you got there, Sugar-boy?"

"It's . . . just some gear I picked up in Arlington."

She clucked, shaking her head. "Spending your college savings on more music stuff? Honestly, Sonny. Money burns a hole in your pocket, don't it?"

"I got it for a great price, Mama."

Walker appeared behind her, patting her shoulder as he passed her. "Every guitar player needs a spare, Mama. Here, Sonny. Let me help you carry it downstairs."

He grabbed the case before Sonny could stop him. Sonny followed, lugging the amp. Ruby stayed put, continuing to give her boys the hairy eyeball. They tromped down the steps. The basement of the Blaines' house was their sanctuary. Unlike their room upstairs, Ruby didn't demand precise order downstairs. It was a good place to hide from her worries and from

Daddy's rages. They couldn't hear the sordid details of their parents' battles, or their equally loud, frenzied lovemaking. Their folks couldn't hear them much either and mostly left them to their bold talk and bolder blues records. They permitted Sonny his practice until his paws wept blood. Plus, the basement was the coldest spot around when the worst of the Texas summer settled in.

When he was small, Sonny stuck Dallas Cowboy pennants on the wall to decorate. As a teenager, he added posters of his favorite bands—the Bad Signs, the Yardbirds, Little Lord Mountbatton and the Royals. Ruby kept preserves stored on shelves tucked beneath the cellar stairs. Often, Walker and Sonny copped a Mason jar, sucking sweet jam straight off their fingers as they listened to records. When Ruby's father, Daddy Jim, passed on, the boys inherited a chintz couch and chair from his house, both too water-logged in a long ago flood to be parlor worthy. A sturdy record player sat on a milk crate placed between the two. The room was littered with pine boxes of 45s and LPs, some bought by Sonny, some left to them by Daddy Jim.

"Thanks for saving me from the college lecture, Squirt."

"No sweat, Sonny."

"Why'd you get the shiner?"

Walker shrugged, dropping his head. "I overheard Daddy on a phone call I shouldn't have. He wanted to make sure I didn't say nothing to Mama. Leastwise he'll be away on a job for a while."

Sonny felt his face grow hot with fury. He wanted to apologize to Walker for not being there to help somehow. Why bother? He was leaving him to more and worse once he split for real. Feeling bad about it, he asked, "You want to see what I got me?"

"Sure do."

Sonny pulled from the case a factory-fresh Fender Telecaster. The guitar was onyx black, with a virginal white pick guard and a slick maple neck. He'd talked his way, cheap, into a tweed covered Fender Vibroverb amp to go with her. The guitar and amplifier were a killer package and had only set Sonny back a week or so's roadhouse wages.

Walker was bowled over. "Oh, man, she's a beaut. Play something for me, Sonny. Please?"

"Okay. But this ain't going to become a habit, hear?"

Sonny plugged in and started fooling around with a little riff as he tried out the different effects. Walker started spewing questions like buckshot, asking about all the knobs and gadgets. Sonny tried to be patient as he answered. He didn't much let Walker hang with him when he played. He knew sometimes Walker hid under the stairs with the canning, spying on him as he practiced. Sonny ran him off when he noticed. But today Sonny played for him awhile, stopping to answer his questions, enjoying the feel of the new machine in his hands.

When he paused, Walker sighed, "That is just so cool, man. You sound even better than you do on your old Broadcaster."

"Thanks. Walker, look. We got to talk."

Walker looked worried. "What'd I do, Sonny? I been leaving your gear alone . . . well, pretty much, anyway."

"It ain't about that. Floyd and Eddie, they graduated in June, you know."

"Yeah."

"They need to do something to keep the draft at bay, leastwise until the war ends. They both got accepted at UT."

"That's swell."

"Johnny Lee, he's got flat feet, so he's 4-F. But he's heading for Austin, too."

"Oh." Walker said it real quiet. He seemed to know where Sonny was going.

"I've got to go with them, Squirt."

"But . . . you still got two years left of high school. If you drop out, Mama will just die. Daddy will probably kill you."

"I know. I really thought of dropping out and running away. But I don't want to do that unless I have to. I been talking to Uncle Charlie and Aunt Lucille about staying with them. I think they're going to take me in."

"Sounds like you got it all figured out." Walker said, his bottom lip quivering, fear jelling in his eyes.

Sonny looked at the new guitar in his hands. He wasn't ready for anybody else to touch his fresh new bride just yet. But he could do something to make Walker feel better. "Don't worry yet, Squirt. I ain't leaving for another month or so. Would it make you feel better if I let you play for me, on my old guitar? I know you been working her out when I ain't around."

Walker's face lit up. "I do got something I'd like you to hear."

"Go on, then. Plug that Broadcaster into the new Vibroverb. Let's see how she sounds through a real amp."

Walker sprung to Sonny's peeling vinyl case, fumbling to get the scratched-up blonde guitar connected. Sonny watched a serene smile creep over Walker's face as the tubes began to hum. The boy fiddled with the tone knob some, adjusted the tuning pegs with a precise twist, ear to the pickups. Hell and damn. Walker handled her like an expert—he must work out with the Broadcaster more than Sonny ever suspected.

Walker rubbed off his palms on his jeans. "Okay," he said, his changing voice cracking. "Here goes nothing." He grinned once at Sonny, and then dropped his eyes to the guitar, growing somber. Walker's fingers started moving through a minor-key blues ballad. His jaw went slack, and his eyelids dropped as he waded deep into the song. Sonny expected a few power chords, maybe a sharp little Brian Jones line. But no—it was a melody as rich as dark chocolate. He didn't say anything while Walker played. When Walker finished the piece, he let go a growling sigh. He seemed to shrink some as he folded his hands over the Broadcaster's waist, looking to Sonny. "So . . . what you think? You can tell me if it's junk."

"It ain't junk, Walker. It's . . . real nice. Don't think I ever heard that one. Where'd you learn it?"

"I didn't. I made it up."

Sonny hooted, "Balls, Walker. You did not make that up."

"Did too!"

Sonny didn't want to believe him. Too much that Walker could play something like that, with such feeling, in the first place, but that he'd composed it at all of thirteen years old was nearly crazy-making. "You made that up? With my guitar? That I don't let you play?"

"Uh-huh. It was wandering around in my head. I had to . . . let her out."

"Yeah. I reckon you did. Does it have a name?"

Walker's face reddened. "Well . . . it came to me in school one day. I was looking at Nancy Ruth, wondering what it would be like to kiss her mouth. It's called *For Nancy*."

Poor sucker. Walker was far gone over the girl. He could barely talk whenever she came around. No doubt, Nancy Ruth Montgomery was already a looker. Her blonde hair flowed like a Breck Girl's, and she had coltish legs and a butt you could place a coffee cup on top of and not spill a drop. From what Sonny could tell, Nancy Ruth didn't seem to realize Walker was alive. She had a bad crush on Sonny, though. A few times, after rehearsal in the Montgomerys' garage, she coaxed Sonny beneath a nearby weeping willow and pressed her mouth to his. The last time, Sonny had tried slipping her the tongue, feeling her up. She'd run off, shrieking giggles. He thought it best to leave her be after that.

"You ever play it for her?"

"No way. I couldn't."

Sonny pulled his new guitar tightly to him, a breastplate. Walker dropped his eyes back to the guitar in his lap. Sonny asked, "Does anybody know you can play like this? Does Mama?"

"Heck, no! She's on your side. Tells me to leave your stuff be. Quit being such a copycat, she says all the time." Walker looked back to his hands, stepping into a sweetmeat Texas shuffle. "Floyd caught me at it, though."

"Floyd? When?"

"Um . . . last week. Remember when you sent him back in for your weed when ya'll was going on that double date?"

Sonny didn't say anything for a minute. He finally managed, "Floyd *knows*?" Walker nodded, fear settling on his face.

Damn if it wasn't Floyd that talked Sonny into the new gear. Sonny wondered what gave when Floyd insisted they go early to Arlington before coming home, in order to hit a guitar sale he'd heard tell of. *Check this baby out, Sonny-boy. Don't it have a right nice tone, man?* Floyd was all excited about the guitars, hardly glancing at the sparkling chrome blues harps on display. Sonny said at first, No, I ain't in the market, the Broadcaster does good, despite a couple loose fittings. Pretty soon Sonny was swept along, though. He started laying hands on the things he'd pined for, untouched maidens not yet worked over by another player. After much trial, he'd settled on the black '65 Tele he now held on his lap. Floyd had been so pleased. That asshole.

"He never said nothing about hearing you play. Ya'll was in cahoots."

"I begged him not to tell you. I didn't want you kicking my butt again."

"Shit-fire. I damn well should kick it. Floyd's, too!"

Walker drooped like a basset hound. "I'm sorry, Sonny. Don't be mad at us."

Sonny crouched over and carefully laid his Tele in its velvet-lined case, snapping the lid closed. He stood, pushing his hair out of his eyes, staring hard at Walker. Walker cowed. He looked so pitiful it made Sonny laugh. "I ain't mad. I don't think. Hell, I don't know what to feel. It's complicated. It changes things."

"How? You're still leaving, right?"

"Yeah. But when I do, I'll give you that Broadcaster. And the little amp I bought with her. I was taking them with me when I split. As spares, like you told Mama. But I reckon I can't, now. It'd be like … like making you die of thirst when I had an extra canteen on me."

Sonny watched a stunned expression sweep Walker. The boy ran fingers over the Fender's varnished backside, where Sonny had carved a blocky S. BLAINE with his pocketknife when he first bought it.

"You . . . you mean it, Sonny? For real?"

"For real."

Walker started crying. "I wanted it so bad for so long. I don't know how to thank you."

"Quit bawling, first off. Don't ever play phony stuff. And take good care of her, hear?"

2.

SONNY HADN'T FOUND it difficult to convince Uncle Charlie and Aunt Lucille to take him in, despite the fact they'd never raised kids of their own. Sonny laid on the charm, promising he would be more help than hindrance.

It was Ruby that was the biggest obstacle. She thought he was too young to leave home. Sonny worked her, though, while Daddy traveled, while Walker slept. He tempted her with talk of a superior big city education. Bet University of Texas gives first crack to the hometown kids, he'd say. It wasn't like he was striking out on his own. Living with Uncle Charlie and Aunt Lucille would be almost like living at home.

Besides, though neither spoke of it, both Ruby and Sonny knew that he had to escape Daddy.

Big Billy Jay detested everything about his eldest—hair, clothes—and guitar, most of all. It rankled him fierce that Sonny often brought home more money in a week playing his "nigger music" than he could in a month of ball-busting roughnecking. Plus, Sonny was now big enough to look his Daddy eye-to-eye. Their last few battles had been less one-sided. Sonny was still enduring the blows and the venom of his old man's attacks. But he was fixing to strike back, and Ruby worried one of them would probably end up dead as a result.

At the end of summer, 1967, Sonny headed south with the rest of the Tornadoes. Sonny sussed out pretty quick how to keep his new guardians content. Charlie ran a funky little jewelry and leather shop called the Trading Post. He repaired and made cowboy hats and boots, and designed Western jewelry—bolo ties, buckles, and rings. Sonny spelled Charlie at the Trading Post after school and swept and dusted the place out come Sundays. He also did all the yard work and washed and Turtle Waxed the vehicles.

Lucille was even easier to keep satisfied than Charlie. She was a Texas glamour girl, all tailored suits and Cleopatra eyeliner, and worked as a secretary for some bigwig at the capitol. She was swayed by the things most women were—a tidy house, help with the dishes, sweet talk. Sonny buttered her up with chivalrous gestures. He was at her side, snapping his lighter before her cigarette ever met her lips. Or he'd drift a hand down to the small of her back and coo, Wasn't that dress fine on her! Flash the smile, say, Painful shame Uncle Charlie got first to the best looking woman in all of Texas. . . . Pretty quick, Sonny could have had the keys to the Governor's office, had he so desired.

It was weird, sometimes, having such a gentle home life. Sonny had spent a lifetime trying to avoid doing or saying something that would lead to hurt at the hands of his old man. Naturally he worried about how Walker was coping. The kid never complained much when Sonny called home once a week, though. Sonny could only hope that Walker was staying, for the most part, below Daddy's rage radar.

As for high school, it was to be endured—the price paid for his kinfolks' hospitality. They let him come and go pretty much as he pleased—just so long as he made it to school and kept passing grades. Sonny wandered the halls unmolested past the padlocked cliques. He was suited to wearing the badge of the outsider, though. The freaks thought he was cool, flattering him by keeping him in cheap Colombian grown weed and primo Dallas crank. The jocks didn't resort to pounding his ass much, so long as he left their cheerleader babies be. Football players sometimes hired the Tornadoes for their frat-boy-in-training beer busts, out on their folks' *ranchitas*. And schoolgirls, no matter their social circle, giggled and sent him hint-soaked glances. Sonny mostly ignored these silly virgins in favor of the syrupy tail that was always around after his gigs.

The teachers were like modeling clay. These were youngish to middle-aged ladies all, used to little more than fear and surliness from their male students. Sonny played them as slippery as an Earl Hooker instrumental. He drew passing marks despite staggering to class after gigs near unconscious with lack of sleep and chemical hangovers.

But the a la mode in Sonny's life was his music. Gone were the teeth-cutting nights, the Tornadoes grinding out Top 40 and country tunes, keeping the Dallas through Abilene honky-tonk customers dancing, drinking their sweat and piss weight in beer. Austin was a different animal altogether than his old stomping grounds. Here the band had to work hard to stand out from all the other fresh music that was pouring in from the Southwest. The band had to cook to satisfy the demanding musicheads that now made up their audience.

The Tornadoes' big break came in the form of a regular gig at a little piece of blues heaven called the Sugar and Spice Saloon. The joint was south of town proper. To get there you had to take the Old Road to a rutted dirt driveway. You had to know it was there to notice it, and once on it, had to ford a small creek. Two old black brothers, Prince and Shookie Brown, owned the saloon. They were locally famous for cooking the best barbecue in Texas. The bar had been converted from an early 20th-century wood-frame farmhouse. Most of the walls downstairs had been demolished save for ones surrounding the little backstage green room, kitchen, and the two-seater men's and ladies' rooms. The big room offered a vinyl-boothed restaurant and stone fireplace on the one side. On the other side, closest to a sweeping stairway leading up to the Browns' living area, sprawled a monstrous Old West–style bar. The bar flanked a sawdust-scattered dance floor and a decent wooden stage.

The liquor was cheap, and the music was as tasty as the food. A bar-side jukebox cradled a grand assortment of 45s. Folks found it well worth the drive, and if you got stuck in there by the storm-flooded creek, who the hell cared? There was plenty to eat and drink inside. There was plenty of cheap drugs and cheaper romance being consumed in the parking lot. World-renowned acts sometimes played the Sugar and Spice, bypassing the bigger Texas cities in favor of the spot. Any band that played there had to pass the Brown brothers' personal tryout.

"The White Tornadoes? Play on that Ajax ad?" Prince Brown asked the band, after they'd auditioned for him. The boys all nodded, not stopping to talk as they stuffed themselves with complimentary ribs. "Pretty good name, I got to say. Ya'll sound pretty damn good, too. Word has it around town that you make your gigs timely. We might could give you work."

"That'd be great, Mr. Brown," Floyd mouthed around his food.

"Just say when," Sonny said, after gulping. He already loved this place. Wasn't no cow town honky-tonk, no siree. The pictures on the walls, signed publicity shots and performance photos, were the Real Blues McCoy. He took his eyes from the head shots to flash a pleased smile at Mr. Brown. The man was scowling at Sonny, fingering his lip. Sonny's smile faded. Had he done or said something to offend Mr. Brown without knowing it?

"Now, this here guitar-man ya'll got might be a bit of a problem," Prince said after a minute of studying Sonny. "Not that you ain't good, son. But I got me a liquor license to worry on. See, the law pretty much leave us be out here. I always say they got to spend too much time with the politicians to bother with the hippies and us. But I try not to give them a thing to wonder about, under-age wise." He walked closer, peering Sonny in the face. Sonny dropped his eyes to his food. "How old you be, son?"

Johnny Lee answered before Sonny could, "Oh, he legal, my brother. Right, Blaine?" Sonny stayed silent and nodded.

Prince narrowed his eyes at Sonny. "Blaine's your name? Where ya'll from, now?"

"A little town between D/FW and Abilene called Mingus."

Prince let out a laugh. "Hold on! You ain't kin to a piano player named Daddy Jim Crawford?"

"Yes, sir. He was my mama's daddy."

"Well, damn!" He pounded Sonny a time or two on the shoulder. "I recollect his daughter up and ran off with a crazy boy named Blaine! No offense meant toward your daddy, son."

"None taken, sir. Fact is, my daddy is crazier than ever."

"That's one reason he's up here with us, Mr. Brown," Floyd said.

"That a fact?" The Tornadoes all nodded. "Well, well." He sat down by Sonny. "Your granddaddy, back before the war? He was a plain wild man on the 88s. Sat in with the colored bands whenever he could, too. He played here now and again."

"No kidding?" Sonny asked, looking around with even deeper respect for his surroundings.

"Uh-huh. Your granddaddy was one good, fair man, boy. Heard he passed a few years ago. Damn shame."

"Yes, sir. We miss him bad. Was him gave me my first guitar. And he left all his records to me and my little brother."

Prince Brown's eyes widened. "I heard tell of that record collection.

About the only one better than ours, I'll bet. You willing to part with it?"

"Even if I did have a mind to, my little brother would never." Sonny grew solemn. "Hope that's no condition of playing here, sir."

"No, sir, boy! That would hardly be fair. You say you have a little brother?" Sonny nodded. "Do he play piano like your granddaddy?"

"No, he plays guitar, too."

"Does he ever!" Floyd agreed.

"Well, maybe we'll see him here in a few years, too." Prince gave them all a stern once-over. "I just lost my regular Thursday night band. You think you boys can stay out of trouble, and be dependable, if I try ya'll out there for a spell?" They said they could. Prince looked at Sonny again, smiling and shaking his head. "Reckon it's the least I can do, for kin of Daddy Jim's. If ya'll do good this month, we'll put you on the mailer next." Prince then turned toward the kitchen and hollered, "Shookie, get on out here—and bring another platter of them ribs for these growing boys! Damned if one of them ain't Daddy Jim Crawford's grandson!"

3.

"ALL YA'LL RAISE your glasses, now! To Sonny Blaine, best damn blues guitar player in Texas!" Floyd declared, lifting high a tumbler full of whiskey.

"Shit! He ain't even the best in this room!" shot back one of the other gunslingers in the crowd, joined by loud hollers and laughter.

Sonny laughed, too, clinking a toast with Floyd. He killed it, and barely had time to set his glass down before someone refilled it. The Sugar and Spice was hosting his private party, a combination birthday, housewarming, and graduation wingding. Everything, from the whiskey to the jukebox, stacked solid with Sonny's favorites, was on the Browns, as their gift to him.

Sonny had managed to squeeze out his diploma a semester early, just before turning eighteen. Then he and the Tornadoes played through an unusually icy winter, padding their now regular house band gig at the Sugar and Spice with any other work they could rustle up. Sonny socked away enough to move out of his Aunt Lucille's and Uncle Charlie's house.

Now he and Floyd rented a run-down but well-built stucco house, close by the University. The place was what the band needed. The rent was bearable, and the neighborhood better than most that the local musicians haunted. It was a corner house with a vacant lot on the other side, so the Tornadoes could rehearse in the detached garage without pissing off the neighbors. Plus, the spacious yard, shaded in the back by a mighty oak, was great for parties. Even after first and last months' rent, Sonny was able to pay cash for a used midnight-blue Mustang. Diploma in hand, cash hidden in an under-bed cigar box, groovy wheels. . . . Sonny Blaine was set to conquer, man!

His party started late afternoon, with a bunch of Sonny's pals and folks he knew from the blues scene scarfing up the goodies. Everyone tried to give Sonny a night to remember, or forget, depending how foolish he became. The men plied him with intoxicants and bawdy stories, the women with sleazy dances and sloppy kisses.

Some hours into the festivities, Uncle Charlie and Aunt Lucille stopped in. They brought with them two wrapped boxes. "Well, Sonny, we've been right glad to have you with us," Aunt Lucille said. "I'm going to miss having you around the house."

"Now, I'll come by and visit! I loved living with ya'll. Especially you, Aunt Lucille." Sonny swept her into a vigorous hug. He boldly gave her a kiss that made Lucille blush and his buddies howl approval.

"Now, you stop!" she tittered, pushing away from him, wiping her lipstick from his mouth with a jittery finger. "Anyway, since you got your diploma—"

"—though I'm not sure how you managed, what with all them late nights guitar-slinging. What's the whole story there, boy?" Uncle Charlie asked.

"Extra credit, sir, extra credit." Sonny yelped, holding his glass to the sky. He sent silent thanks heavenward for those tenderhearted lady teachers and counselors at the high school.

"Extra credit, my ass!" Uncle Charlie snorted. "Well, anyway, you managed, boy, so we got a couple of gifts for you." They presented him with the boxes.

Inside the larger was a splendid custom-made pair of cowboy boots, black and gray, hand-stitched, the left one bearing a leather strap with small silver studs around the ankle. The other box held a belt to match. "Uncle Charlie, these are the coolest! Did you make them for me?"

"Yes, I did. I seen the ones you tried on down at the shop. Got your foot measurement that day I pretended I was training you how it was done. Seemed like these suit you."

"Hell, yes, they do. Thank you so much! Ya'll are just so sweet. I sure do love ya'll!" Sonny said in a slurred voice, pulling Charlie down with his forearm to hug the old man's neck.

"Oh, Jesus God! You know Sonny's damn drunk, be telling folks he loves them!" laughed Johnny Lee. Floyd and Eddie clinked glasses, drinking to that.

"I just hope you're done growing," Charlie said, eyeing his nephew's foot. "If so, these should last you a lifetime, you keep them soled and polished right."

"Someone else has a surprise for you, too," Aunt Lucille said. She pointed behind her. Sonny looked up from the boots to see Ruby and Walker, also holding a gift.

Sonny leaped to his feet, doing his best not to stagger for Mama's sake. He hugged and kissed her, then punched Walker's shoulder in greeting. "I'm real glad ya'll made it! Where's Daddy?"

"Sugar-boy, he's working in Louisiana, but sends his love. Look at this hair!" She brushed it out of Sonny's eyes. "Reckon any girl would kill for it!"

Floyd cackled. "The ladies been in some pretty nasty fights over your boy at times, Mrs. Blaine, but no one's died yet!" The others in earshot joined in the laughter.

"Small blessing. Walker Dale? Give Sonny his present. Your brother designed something special for you. Paid for it with his own gig money, too."

Inside was a guitar strap to match the boots and belt, with SONNY spelled in gray on black, silver studs between the letters. "Walker, man! I don't know what to say."

"You like it?" Walker asked. His voice no longer cracked. In fact, it was surprisingly deep. Deeper than Sonny's.

"It's far out! And you, Mr. Cool. You got yourself a secret agent hat."

Walker nodded, touching a hand to a black fedora that he wore at a rakish tilt. The hat added a couple years to him. So did his damn near shoulder-length hair and scraggly goatee. Daddy had to hate this look to pieces. Good sign. Walker must be holding his own.

Walker's build had filled out a tad since Sonny last laid eyes on him. Still skinny, he'd never be otherwise, but more wiry than scrawny nowadays. And the rest of this getup he wore? A couple years back, Sonny had handed him down a bright-red sweater. It had been too loud to suit Sonny, and was still too big for Walker. But he wore it anyway, cinched at his hips by a thick leather belt with a silver Lone Star flag buckle. Cheap love beads hung from his neck. He had on skintight Levi's, shredded out at the knee. Sonny probably wouldn't have recognized him on the street.

"Hey, little man!" called out a tall guy with a stringy chestnut ponytail and a floppy hippie's hat. He clapped Walker on the back, a big grin on his face. "It's me, Riley Goode, from the Cat's Claw? Good to see you again, Walker."

"Hey, Riley. You made it to Austin. That's great." Walker shook hands, grinning up at him. His head didn't even clear Riley's shoulder. "You got yourself a band yet?"

"Maybe. Trying to get started with this bunch forming a big review. Hot-looking girl singer, horns, soul kind of thing."

A slim, black-haired beauty, full-lipped and elfin-eyed, peeked up at Riley from around his shoulder. He didn't see her approach and jumped when she laid her hand on his forearm and leaned against him. She wore a short and clingy red dress, a chunky silver necklace, and a silver conch belt draped hip-high. "Really now, 'Really Goode'," she purred, tossing her curls. "You never let on that you think I'm a hot-looking girl singer."

Riley grinned down at her, reddening about two shades. "Well, I didn't reckon I had to tell you, Bee-Stung. And the name's Riley Goode, not Really Goode."

Sonny wondered if Riley hadn't blundered in correcting Bee-Stung Sanchez's pronunciation. She did have a trace of Tejana accent—"Really" might be as close as she could get to matching Riley's Dallas twang.

"I know how to say your name, Riley," she cooed back at the bassist, overmimicking his Texas pronunciation while pouting artfully at him. "All the same, I'll wager you *are* really good."

Sonny, Charlie, and Walker all went still and stood a little taller and straighter.

Leaving Riley blushing, Bee-Stung turned toward Sonny. He was still clutching his new guitar strap in his hands. She reached up and pressed her mouth to his. Sonny wrapped the hand holding the strap around her waist, letting the sliver-studded leather dangle riding crop–like down the back of her legs. She kissed him good and hard, leaving a smear of red on his mouth when they parted. "Happy birthday to you, Sonny-honey," Bee-Stung whispered, then walked slowly away toward the bar.

Charlie whistled slow and low. Ruby scowled and narrowed her eyes at Sonny like the kiss had been all his doing.

Aunt Lucille shook her head at Sonny, wiping lipstick off of his face for the second time within minutes. "Baby, we're seeing to it your mama gets fed before we go. We'll take her back in the kitchen to meet the Browns and get something to eat. Behave yourself, within reason, and look after Walker too, hear?"

"I will. Thanks again for the presents." Sonny kissed Lucille and Mama again, before dropping back into his chair. With effort he yanked off the scuffed, too tight boots that had served him throughout most of high school. The new ones formed to his feet perfectly. They were the most comfortable things he had ever worn. He pulled his jeans down over them and stood, wondering how he ever tolerated his old ones.

Pulling up his sweatshirt, he strung the belt through his Levi's loops, listening in as Walker visited with Riley. Seemed they'd met at a place in Dallas called the Cat's Claw that Walker got out to once in a while hitching. Riley said it was just a shitty little hole in the wall. "Great speed and pussy to be had there, though," he declared. "Met Walker at this Saturday jam thing they do. I walked in, what—a year ago? Two? Heard this guitar that stopped me in my tracks. It's this punk, manhandling a big blonde Fender. I damn near died!"

Walker was beaming, listening in at Sonny's side. Floyd managed to sneak up behind him, grabbing the boy's neck in his elbow and squeezing. Flailing, grabbing at Floyd's hammerlock, Walker grunted, "Turn me loose!"

"Fat chance, you little twerp!"

Still fighting back, Walker tried to talk. "Leastwise at the Claw, I could lay it down with some decent players—damnit, Floyd! Always a groove, playing with Riley."

"Hey, man, pleasure was all mine!"

Still gripping his neck, Floyd seized Walker's hat, messing up his hair, saying, "Sounds like you been working it with Sonny's old guitar, Squirt." Walker nodded, snatching at his hat, which danced in Floyd's hand, just out of reach. "Exactly like we planned that day in ya'll's basement, huh, Walker?"

"Sure enough!" He yelped, shooting a nervous grin Sonny's way. Sonny gave the wrestlers a harsh stare. These two had plain suckered him. Both of them, plotting to get Walker that Broadcaster from the word go.

"I'm glad to hear it!" Floyd declared, still tormenting Walker. "This little shit's got it going on, ya'll know it?" Riley nodded. Floyd added, "So here's a little advice, kid. Keep them paws of yours hard at work on that guitar—and not so hard at work on my little sister's goodies." Floyd released him. Walker reddened, stammering. Floyd slapped the hat back on Walker's head, and grimaced pointedly in the kid's face. Tossing his curls, Floyd swaggered toward the bar for another drink. Sonny and Riley laughed as Walker tried to adjust the fedora and regain his dignity.

"So, Walker, his sister?" Riley asked, nodding at Floyd. "That the lady you stayed with at my place?"

"Yeah. She's my steady now," Walker told Sonny, his face lit in a proud smile.

"That a fact? About damn time. She still got that fine ass on her?"

"You're talking about my girl, Sonny! Watch your mouth," Walker snapped, whopping him one on the arm.

"Simmer down. Didn't mean nothing by it." Sonny rubbed the spot where he'd been smacked. What a fierce look Walker was giving him—and the kid sure never raised a hand to him before. Poor thing—clear enough Nancy Ruth had made him her fool.

Riley stepped in between the brothers. "So, Walker? You bring your ax with you?"

"No, not this trip." Walker lowered his glare from Sonny, shrugging.

"Too bad!" Riley replied. "He's too damn much, huh, Sonny?"

Before Sonny could answer, Walker did. "Sonny ain't even heard me but once." He put on a tight smile, his eyes beneath the fedora now looking a little injured.

True, Sonny had not heard Walker since he had first played the Broadcaster for him. The brief moments they had spent together since, Sonny had avoided listening to him. This shamed him some, thinking on it now. "I'll give you a listen again right soon, Squirt."

"No time like the present!" Riley cried. "We got, what, all the best musicians in Texas right in this here room." Riley turned away from their huddle, letting go a piercing whistle. The crowd quieted, turning toward the bass player. "Listen up, ya'll! Sonny's hot-shit little brother's here! Ya'll won't believe what this punk can do with a guitar! Who wants to hear the Blaine brothers jam?"

The partyers let out war whoops, stomps, and pounded on the bar and tables until the beer pitchers jumped. Sonny pleaded, "Ah, Riley! Don't, now! I'm real wasted!"

Floyd was suddenly there, pulling Sonny to his feet. "Shee-it! Like you never been thataway at any of our gigs? Hey, Johnny Lee! Put this pretty new strap on Sonny's ax! We got all our stuff on stage already."

"But—Walker don't even have his guitar with him," Sonny protested.

Floyd snorted back, "Wonder if we can find one for him in this crowd?" Laughter rang out, and in a flash, several of the local strummers offered up their instruments to Walker.

"If this ain't hog heaven, I don't know what is!" Walker laughed, checking out the selections. He chose a pearl gray Stratocaster. "This'll do right nice. Thanks for the loaner, man! Come on, Sonny!"

Johnny Lee slung Sonny's guitar over his head. Sonny grabbed the neck, second nature. People chanted "SON-EEE, SON-EEE!" and slapped his back as he walked toward the stage. Walker had already scampered up there ahead of him. He reached out to give Sonny a leg up. Floyd, Eddie and Johnny Lee joined them. They fooled around for a minute or two, getting things tuned up and turned on. Clutching a harp, Floyd shouted, "Walker! Can you handle *Who Do You Love?*"

"I reckon so! Count us down, Eddie." Eddie did, and they lit into the Bo Diddley tune. Walker grinned at Sonny as they together strummed hard into the tempo. Sonny, though fuzzy-headed and unsteady, couldn't help but smile back at him. Floyd blew the harp intro, and growled out the peculiar lyrics of walking barbed wire and accessorizing himself with venomous serpents. Johnny Lee and Walker craned toward a second mike, joining in to chant the chorus.

The boys kept up the driving Diddley beat, backing Floyd as he snarled out the words. When the time came, Floyd bit hard into his harmonica solo, his shaggy curls flying. As Floyd's part finished, Walker pointed to Sonny—*Take it*—and Sonny did, wincing, bending at the knees and tipping the Tele's neck skyward to help squeeze out the notes. Despite the booze, his drug-addled bloodstream, muscle memory stayed with Sonny. He gave them a tasty, blistering run. Grinning, tossing his hair back as his friends cheered him on, Sonny passed the solo—"Go get it, Squirt!"

Walker went, all right. Head hunched, face hidden behind his fedora's brim, Walker's fingers danced, slid around the Strat's neck. Sonny watched, playing the rhythm to his brother's lead. Oh, he'd been plenty stunned by

Walker back three years ago, by the boy's splendid ballad, the smoothness and longing sweetness of the song. But here was another side of the kid's gift. Walker was . . . Smokestack Lightnin'! Confused, Sonny tried to keep track of Walker. He was wandering too far from the path. Showing his artistic immaturity—loads of flash, but no substance. He was pushing the envelope a little too far, would soon fly to pieces . . . but no! There, how the hell had Walker found his way home, back to the main riff?

Walker threw aside his hat, letting out a growl that came from real deep. He pulled the Strat over his head and onto his shoulders, literally playing over his head, upside down and backwards. He didn't miss a beat, just shot right true into another hot run. Sonny had a picture of this move on one of Daddy Jim's T-Bone Walker album covers. Maybe it came second nature to the Walkers of the world. Damn—now he'd have to master this trick himself.

Leaning over and scooping his fedora off the floor, Walker jumped back in with Sonny. Floyd blew another line, taking out the song. The crowd went fucking nuts! With a knowing nod to the assembled, Sonny pointed at his panting little brother. They screamed all the louder.

Walker tipped his hat, laughing with delight. "Sonny!" he yelped. "Let's do *Hideaway!*"

"I ain't working tonight! It's my damn party!" Sonny yelled back. Wiping his brow with the back of his hand, Sonny placed his guitar on a stand. Folks in the crowd berated him, a few flicked lighters at him. He held up his hands, shaking his head. "Ya'll entertain *me* for a change!"

"Groovy!" Floyd laughed. Then, into the mike, pointing into the crowd, he barked, "Someone get the guest of honor a chair, a drink, and at least one pretty girl! The birthday boy wants to be entertained, he tells us! After what you just seen, anyone got balls enough to take on Walker Blaine?"

A sax player and another guitarist hopped on stage. Riley's girl singer, Bee-Stung, climbed up too. She squeezed Walker's shoulder as she passed him while heading to join Floyd at the mike. Walker touched his hat in her direction, and then turned a pleased and silly grin on Sonny.

A yummy blonde grabbed Sonny's arm. She led him to a chair and plopped on his lap, cooing honey-drenched promises into his ear. Someone put a bottle of Southern Comfort in front of Sonny. He took a belt and settled in, not really certain he was ready to bear witness to Walker's jam session.

At that moment Walker caught his eye. The kid was sparkling with sheer joyousness. From the stage he silently mouthed, "Thanks for this, Sonny!"

✳ ✳ ✳ ✳ ✳

SONNY DROVE his brother back to their uncle's house the morning after the party. Walker was happy as all get out, hadn't shut up since they left. Sonny was miserable, his head and stomach like something long forgotten on the back fridge shelf, eyes aching as alcohol-hewn needles poked at them behind his shades.

Some woman had driven him and his car back to his apartment, followed by her roommate with Walker in tow. The ladies were off before dawn, heading home to get changed before work. Or so Walker told him, as Sonny had been deep under then. Floyd was still snoring hard in his room when the brothers left. Sonny didn't reckon Walker had yet slept. He was too bloodshot, wide-eyed, and jabbering giddy.

"Man, there's the coolest folks here," Walker babbled on. "And the crowd really liked me, huh? It's such a gas to play with this kind of talent."

"Including that talent that drove you home, huh? She was all over you."

Walker laughed. "She was nice, I got to say." His vein-striped eyes widened with concern. "Oh, shit, you don't think Floyd'll tell his sister about them, do you?"

"Nah. He's probably glad to see it. He tells me he frets about you and Nancy Ruth being so damn serious—his folks give him an earful, I guess."

"Well, it's a fact that there ain't no one I dig like I do her." Walker beat his fingers on the dashboard in time with the music on the radio. "How about that skinny girl with the sexy mouth? She's a good singer, huh?"

"Bee-Stung Sanchez? Yeah, she's pretty good."

"She's a stone fox."

"Oh, that she is. That's who your buddy Riley's talking about playing with? She's kind of wild and crazy."

"Yeah?"

"Yeah. I know her from high school. Her folks are from Mexico, but I guess she was born here in Texas. They got a little bar in the Palace, has bands some. We play it a few times a year. Bee-Stung's sat in with the Tornadoes on and off." Sonny turned the car onto their Uncle's tree-lined street, cruising slow. "She told me her daddy hoped she'd sing, what do they call it, *romanticas* and stuff, those border songs they do all emotional? Sad, full of passion. Kind of Mexican blues, I think of them as. She likes American blues better—more her style. That girl can outdrink, outsmoke, and outsnort just about any man."

"Oh, yeah? You ever date her?"

"Not really. We just, like, got it on after a few shows and stuff."

"Yeah? She seems right friendly."

Sonny grinned at him. "Right friendly!"

Walker was still for a moment, save for a wagging foot. "Bee-Stung, huh? What a strange name."

"It ain't her real name, dummy."

"So what is?"

"I . . . don't know."

Walker laughed, shaking his head. "Jeez, Sonny. You screwed the girl—more than once, too—and you don't even know her real name?"

"What can I say? Her nickname suits her. That's what you call those lips she's got, the kind God made just for kissing. Plus she's had her share of stingers, if you get my drift."

"That a fact?" Walker asked. Sonny nodded. "After she sang with me, she slipped me a vial, told me she'd see me later, and kissed me real good. I couldn't find her again when I was done playing, though."

"Probably left with some other guy. She gave you coke? No wonder your ass ain't slept!" Sonny said. Walker shrugged, smiling and nodding. "She must like you! That woman's a known glutton when it comes to drugs."

"Well, she's out of luck now. I did it all up with those two ladies who brung us home."

"You didn't share none with *me*."

"You was already passed out by the time I remembered I had it! Your girl was pretty disappointed with you, but the coke cheered her up. Did my level best to make up for your rudeness, too."

"So you got one fox chasing you, giving you her coke—then you chase two others with the same cocaine? All in one damn night, too. You more dawg than me."

Walker grunted, "Fat chance of that."

Sonny parked the Mustang in his aunt's driveway, behind his mama's old Rambler. Hopping out, he told Walker, "The hell with Floyd, I think I'll rat you out to Nancy Ruth myself!"

4.

SONNY WALKED to his corner liquor store to pick up a copy of the local weekly from a pile out front. He dropped onto the storefront curb and started thumbing through. He was anxious to read the review of Terry Joe McGowan and the Troubadours' new record. Sonny had a personal stake in the thing. He had played on it, been taken with McGowan's outfit all the way to L.A. to sit second guitar.

There he had spent a heady month cocooned in a glossy studio, laying it sweet and lowdown whenever McGowan called him in. The other Tornadoes had been a little freaked out when he left them behind for such a cush gig. Floyd had really tripped, though. First and foremost, Floyd fancied himself a blues purist, and didn't much cotton to "his" guitarist sitting in on a country album. Sonny argued that the country artist involved was more of an anti-Nashville hippie than all four Tornadoes put together—which was true. McGowan, with his long hair and peacenik rap, had all but been run out of Music City on a rail. Sonny did agree that the new bluesmen and the counterculture cowboys battled over the best clubs around Austin. But he also firmly believed the competition made them all better musicians.

Sonny's arguments didn't help much. Floyd was still giving him a bit of the cold shoulder over the session, but that wasn't all of his troubles. Eddie was spending less time with the band and more in college and with his girl. Johnny Lee had been moonlighting with some funk outfit on their nights off. And poor forlorn Floyd had a bad case of writer's block. He had dropped out of college completely. Now he was fighting a battle of wits with the draft board over shipping out to 'Nam. He was even thinking of high-tailing it to Mexico and hiding out down there. The whole thing made Sonny grateful his own draft lottery number had been so high.

Sonny had tried what he could to cheer Floyd. He had sent home rent and then some from the session money—also sneaking some cash to Walker to give Mama without Daddy knowing. And he'd taken tapes of the White Tornadoes with him to L.A., trying to sell the band to a label. He got a few scouts to sample them. Most that listened dug the band, but so far he'd gotten, at best, only polite dismissal. Blues belonged to the Brits was the twisted answer he kept getting. The record fat cats acted like Little Lord Mountbatton and his cronies had invented the blues out of whole cloth. Floyd had sunk into an even deeper funk over the news.

But the trip, man, had been a trip. McGowan's band was a hard-partying bunch—always had on hand good dope and beautiful, willing hippie girls. Seemed the band had known everybody who was anybody in L.A. music. At one soiree, Sonny had even shared a soul handshake, and a brief mystical rap, with Hendrix himself. He'd called home in the wee hours just to blow Walker's mind with that one. A cool ride, indeed. Icing on the cake was that the session and the jams around the sprawling city had given Sonny real street credibility in the business.

Sonny found the review of McGowan's record and folded the *Austin Chronicle* open to read it. They loved it, especially digging Sonny's work. Alongside the story was a picture of Sonny, a reprint of a shot from the album's cover. He was dressed in his birthday cowboy boots and belt, with tight black jeans and a University of Texas muscle shirt. He stood, weight on one leg, leaning on the neck of his Telecaster, the SONNY strap snaking around the guitar's body. His eyes peered from beneath his shaggy black mane, and he was giving the camera his finest crooked smile. Damn, he looked good, if he did say so himself. This picture was also going to be printed with a write-up about Young Turks in the business in *Musician* magazine. Another photo of Sonny jamming with McGowan and others at the Whiskey a Go-Go made the Random Notes column in *Rolling Stone*. Sonny felt in his bones that the Big Time was just around the corner.

He picked up an extra copy of the paper, to send home. He grinned, thinking how he could write to Mama that she could show the picture of him in the UT shirt to her buddies and pretend he was going to school. That would rile her up. Walker would bust a gut.

Sonny folded up the papers and stuck them under his arm as he got to his feet. He decided to pick up some smokes as long as he was out. Walking into the store, he was stopped by a young couple coming out.

"Hey! You're Sonny Blaine!"

"That's me." It pleased him to be recognized. Nice to be home in Austin, getting his props from the locals.

"My name's Mike." He extended a hand and Sonny shook it. Turning to his girl, Mike said, "Kitty, this is Sonny Blaine, from that band we went to see right after school started. The White Tornadoes, remember?"

"I sure do." Kitty gave Sonny a look that let him know she wasn't likely to forget him. He tossed his hair out of his eyes and gave her a slow smile.

Mike went on, "Word is ya'll and Terry Joe's band were going to do a show together out at the Sugar and Spice."

"Yeah. Better get your tickets quick, you going to come. They tell me that there's a real crush on for the things." Sonny kept his eyes on Kitty, and she on him.

"I bet! It'll bring in both the country and the blues crowd, after all. You playing with both bands?"

"That's the game plan."

"We'll be there," Kitty breathed.

Mike added, "You know, I play a little guitar."

Great. Here it comes. "That so?"

"Yeah. Maybe you can give me some tips, Sonny. On that one song you do—"

Sonny cut him off. "Look, the best tip I can give you is listen to a lot of music and practice, practice, practice. See you at the show." He hightailed it out of there minus the smokes. Being recognized and greeted by fans was cool. But he hated talking about playing with other stringers. Let them learn the hard way, like he had. Sonny wasn't about to help anyone cop his bag of tricks.

THE NIGHT OF the show, the Sugar and Spice was sardine packed with the biggest crowd it had ever hosted. Sonny felt like royalty. He pierced his left ear for the occasion. Uncle Charlie made the earring to Sonny's specs—a big brilliant-cut emerald encircled by a white-gold stud. He checked himself out in front of the mirror backstage, rubbing the still-smarting lobe. What a fit his piercing would give Daddy. He admired his other new purchase, a black leather motorcycle jacket like Brando's in *The Wild One*.

"My, my. Looky here. The boy's covered head to toe in studs," Floyd kidded him, catching Sonny in the act of preening.

Sonny let out a little chuckle. "Studs for a stud, see?"

Floyd shook his head. "Ain't you just something these days?"

"You think it's too much, Floyd?"

"When in doubt, say to yourself: 'Junior Wells, Jimi Hendrix, Little Richard!' You'll feel much better! You look cool, Sonny. It's your big night, man."

"Big night for us all, Floyd."

Floyd nodded, smiling. Still kind of sallow, he nonetheless looked better than he had in days. He smacked Sonny's back. "Too bad Walker ain't here. Could get you boys jamming. Then again, maybe it's best that hot dog ain't. Won't have to share the limelight with the little fucker, huh? You set?"

"Set as I'm going to be." Sonny felt the butterflies kick in just a tad. He could hear the restless audience hooting and stomping outside the door.

"I'll see if Johnny Lee and Eddie are ready to roll. The crowd's pretty wound up. We better get moving."

The house did rock that night. The White Tornadoes tore it up, keeping the pace straight ahead. Sonny and Floyd traded harp and guitar lines fast and fierce. Floyd nearly ruptured the rafters when he closed their set with a banshee-intense version of *Fortunate Son*.

The main attraction went over great, too. Sonny added his rockier edge to McGowan's C&W sound. On a few sweeter tunes he played a glittering National steel. McGowan had given him the acoustic to thank him for the session work. Sonny had worked out with it for the last few weeks, his hands remembering the broad neck of his first ax, the old Sears Silvertone that had been given him by Daddy Jim. No contest with his Fender, but the steel was cool for a change of pace.

About halfway through the first set, Sonny spotted a little guy dancing on a chair. The kid did a sharp two-fingered whistle at the applause, swinging his hat in the air. But he didn't recognize him as Walker in all the commotion.

After numerous curtain calls, Sonny was having a beer in the green room, buzzing on the postshow praise. Only a few minutes later, Shookie came and took him aside. "Your baby brother's in my office."

"Walker is? Are Mama and Daddy here?"

Shookie was too somber. "No. And something's wrong with the boy. Come on."

Sonny found Walker sitting in Shookie's big chair. He had on a fleece-lined Levi's jacket over a cheap white T-shirt, jeans, and boots. His fedora sat on the desk next to an untouched plate of barbecue. He stared blankly at the food. The fact that his forever-starved brother wasn't devouring the ambrosia was a bad sign, but Sonny was still too high on the performance to register the fact. "Hey, Squirt! Why didn't you tell me you was coming? Did you like us?"

Walker jumped at his voice. Then he was on his feet, hugging Sonny. "You were the best, Sonny. You had this place in the palm of your hand, man. And look at you, all decked out like a real star. That National is a real beaut."

"Well, come on back and try it out."

"I can't, Sonny. I just—oh, hell, I shouldn't be here."

"Sure you should, Walker. What, did Shookie and Prince give you a hard time about being underage?"

"No, they been real nice. . . . Sonny? I'm in big trouble." Dropping to the edge of the desk, Walker started to cry. Brokenly, he mumbled, "I stoled Daddy's truck and drove here."

Sonny closed the office door. "Shit, Walker. That was plain stupid. You wanted to come that bad, I would have got you here someway. Daddy's going to clobber you."

"I know he is. Tell you the truth, I forgot all about the show being tonight." Walker put his head in his hands and kept sobbing. Sonny noticed then how red and puffy Walker's eyes were. His dirty face was striped with old tear tracks, crisscrossed by fresh ones.

"Stop blubbering, man. When I'm through here, we'll go back to my place, call home and say—"

"No!" Walker yelped. "If Floyd sees me he'll—Sonny, Nancy Ruth says she's knocked up!"

Sonny covered his face with his hand. "Jesus."

"Bro, I was damn careful, I swear. Except for the first time, which just kind of happened—that was ages ago, not the cause of this. Ever since, I used skins. Always, I did. Never had one break or nothing." He shook his head firmly. "Man, I can't marry her."

"Of course not. Ya'll are sixteen years old."

"She don't see it that way."

"Well, she's going to have to. This ain't no good for either of you. Or the . . . kid. Look, has she been to a doctor?"

"No, but she's, like, three weeks late, and she never has been before. And she's puking before school. That's when she told me, yesterday morning. I went to kiss her and could tell she'd been sick."

"That could be nerves or whatever. You got to get her to a doctor. Then, if he says it's true. . . . Look, I know somebody here who can fix her up."

Walker furrowed his brow, shaking his head. "You mean . . . Sonny . . . girls die from that, or get all messed up inside where they can't never have kids. I don't want her hurt."

"This guy's a real doc, Walker. Takes care of the problem for a lot of the college girls. She'd be good as new. It's like $500, but I got money from the album I can give you. Don't panic yet, though. Ya'll are probably all worked up over nothing."

"You reckon?"

"Sure. This happens to chicks, especially if you ain't moving toward the altar fast enough to suit them. She's probably okay." He perched beside Walker on the desk, grinning at him. "Man. Bet you stole Daddy's truck over nothing."

"Well, I got to see your show. Good enough reason. Damn, ain't he going to be pissed?" Walker let out a nervous bark of a laugh that caught Sonny. Soon they were both howling with hysterics.

Shookie knocked gently, then peeked in. "You boys okay now?"

"We're fine, Shookie. Right, Squirt?"

Walker nodded, rubbing his wet eyes.

"Lots a folks asking for you, Sonny."

"We'll be right there." Shookie left. Sonny told Walker, "Floyd don't know a thing or he would have said something to me. Let's go raise hell tonight. Tomorrow, I'll follow you back to Mingus to help handle Daddy. And we'll deal with Nancy Ruth if we have to. One thing at a time, okay? Here." Sonny slapped the hat on Walker's head and dug a baggie full of pills out of a leather jacket pocket. He selected a fat white one and handed it to Walker. "It's a 'lude. It'll calm your ass down. Couple of beers and you won't feel no pain."

5.

SLEEPLESS, THE BROTHERS sped up U.S. 281 in the early-morning hours before the tractors and the trucks sneaking around the weigh stations on the interstate slowed their drive. Sonny followed the pickup in his Mustang. Mama's Rambler was not in the driveway when they arrived.

"Maybe they went to early church service or something," Walker whispered as they walked to the door. He looked like he'd died two hours past. Sonny could tell he was trembling by the quaver in his words. He added, "Thanks for coming with me, bro."

"You're welcome." Sonny was not looking forward to this himself. He had been away a while now, but the familiar queasiness of facing up to Big Billy Jay's rage sat coiled again in his belly. The weight of his shirt and jacket lay hard over his shoulder blades. His nerves were tingling, on red alert recalling the whippings he had endured until he left home.

Sometimes Sonny would jerk awake in the night, wild-hearted from beating dreams. Consciously he never remembered much more than the whispering slither of the belt leaving the loops of his daddy's work pants. When he fully woke up, his back often ached with the memory of the strap and buckle. Sometimes the dreams would be of Walker, screaming for

Sonny's help. In those dreams he was always frozen, unable to intervene or even to plead with Daddy to quit hurting the kid.

The worst dreams were straight from his old life. Shadowy scenes of Walker and him crying, sometimes bleeding, trying to comfort each other's pain in their darkened bedroom. These were always accompanied by the animalistic sounds of his parents' loving from next door. Walker terrified, so afraid Mama was getting hurt, too. Sonny, once he knew the score, soothing him: *Mama's cries are different. That noise means, for now, we're safe. Just go to sleep, Squirt. Might not hurt so much tomorrow. . . .*

Sonny drew in a shuddering breath, trying to push the dark past down, to deal with the here and now. Grabbing Walker's shoulder on the porch steps, he said, "Remember. Act like you decided to come see my show on the spur of the moment. Apologize like hell for taking the truck. Don't you say one word about Nancy Ruth. Ain't your problem yet."

"Okay, Sonny." Walker nodded. Some color was returning to his face.

They walked in to find their mama sitting up on the couch, dozing with her head hanging forward. She wore a wrinkled housedress. Her hair was disheveled, not wrapped tight in the pink foam curlers as was her custom at this hour. Walker hung back by the door as Sonny crossed to her, kneeling down to gently shake her awake.

Her eyes opened with a snap. "Billy Jay? Oh, Sonny. Walker Dale's run off. Took your daddy's truck and just run off, Sugar-boy."

"No, Mama. He's right here. He came up to Austin to see my big show last night."

Ruby jumped up and grabbed Walker, holding him tight in her arms. "Oh, baby! Why'd you go and scare me like that?"

"I'm sorry, Mama. I wasn't thinking."

She pushed Walker away arm's length from her, looking wide-eyed into his face. "You should have taken the Rambler, at least. Your daddy is fit to be tied." To Sonny, she said, "You got your car with you?"

"Yes, ma'am. I followed Walker home."

"Good. Put Walker's guitar, and them records you left behind, in there." Sonny headed down the basement steps. Walker started to protest, but Ruby shushed him. "You be still, Walker Dale Blaine. Your daddy is boiling mad. He already ransacked your room. When he hears you ran off to hear Sonny play, I wouldn't put it past him to bust your music stuff to splinters. We get him calmed down, we'll bring it back in, hear?" Walker nodded, hanging his head.

Sonny called from downstairs, "Where is Daddy, anyway?"

"He's been out half the night looking for your brother. Last I heard he was heading for the Montgomerys' place."

"Oh, Jesus!" Walker slapped a hand to his mouth. He shot a desperate look his big brother's way as Sonny shuffled by, toting the amp and a box of albums in his arms, the Broadcaster strapped on his back. He could still hear Walker and Ruby talking as he loaded the trunk.

"Walker Dale, you don't take the Lord's name in vain in my house. Oh, son. I hope you weren't fool enough to take Nancy Ruth with you to Austin."

"N-no, Mama. I didn't take her with me. What time did Daddy go over there?"

"I'm not sure, early though. He called and talked to Mr. Montgomery, asking if they had seen you. He asked Daddy to come over. Daddy left then, without a word to me."

The Rambler screeched into sight, barely missing Sonny's street-parked Mustang as it squealed into the driveway. Big Billy Jay leaped from the car. He didn't seem to notice Sonny as he stomped toward the house. Sonny could smell the whiskey on the old man from clear across the yard. Full of dread, Sonny followed him onto the porch.

He could hear Ruby saying, "Walker Dale, you look like you seen a ghost. What're you not telling me?"

"I'll tell you what he's not telling you! This moron got that tramp of his in trouble," Big Billy Jay screamed.

"S-sorry about taking the truck, Daddy," Walker moaned, slinking behind Ruby. She turned to stare at him, the pain all over her.

"The truck is the least of your problems. Damn, boy! I told you that girl was going to trap you." He staggered over and shoved Ruby aside, grabbing Walker's arm and shaking him like he was wringing a chicken's neck. "Got no brains at all, do you?" Walker shook his head no, fright stamped on his face.

"Let him be, Daddy," Sonny said from the threshold. He folded his arms in front of him. "Nothing's sure. She ain't even been to a doctor yet."

"Oh, looky what we got here," Big Billy Jay spat back at him, still gripping Walker hard enough to make the boy whimper. "Mr. Upstanding Example himself! What, he come running to you for advice?"

"Reckon he needed to." Sonny fought to keep his voice calm, firm. "This sure ain't helping any."

"Oh, you mighty big for your britches these days, Mr. Bluesman," Billy Jay sneered, giving his oldest a once-over, his mouth twisted. "Got that hair hanging halfway down your back like some girl. Big man in his leather jacket and sissy earring—telling me how to deal with my kid?" He tossed Walker against the wall like a rag and took a swaggering step toward Sonny, his work-scarred knuckles clinched for a fight. "This is my house. Don't you forget it, you good-for-nothing punk."

Inside, Sonny cringed, recalling past lost battles that ended in his blood being shed. Goddamn it, he was a man now. He'd spent too many years cowing to this bastard. Sonny growled back, "Like you'd ever let me forget, old man?"

Big Billy Jay roared, launching himself at Sonny. Walker was right on his heels. Sonny, slow of reflex with lack of sleep and partying, didn't even get his arms unfolded. He was hit square on the jaw and went down hard on the front porch. Groggy, he heard Walker holler, "Daddy, no—this ain't his fault!" Then came another bear roar from Big Billy Jay, a dull thump, and a loud wail from Walker.

Sonny sat up, shaking his head to clear the fist fog. Walker was lying on the floor, writhing, crying, and holding a hand over his left ear. He bore a sinister welt on the side of his face, and blood oozed through his fingers. Ruby was crying, screaming for them to stop. Big Billy Jay leaned over Walker, the anger visibly draining from him as he saw the damage done.

Sonny pushed himself upright, stalking over to Big Billy Jay. He spun his daddy around and punched, feeling the old man's nose break under his knuckles. He went sprawling, spraying blood and cursing. Sonny kicked him hard in the ribs with his pointed boot. Again he kicked, and this time Daddy bellowed in pain. Sonny screamed, "Come on, you evil mother-fucker! You want more? Fair fight now, Daddy! Or don't you pick on men your own size?" Sonny leaned over him, shaking his right hand out. Somewhere under the rage he knew it hurt like hell. He dimly hoped he wasn't injured bad enough to affect his picking.

"That's enough!" screamed Ruby. To Sonny's amazement, she slapped him hard across the mouth. She'd never once raised a hand before. But then, neither had he. Not to Daddy. "Get out of here!" she wailed in his face. "Take Walker Dale with you. Just go!"

Without another word, Sonny dragged Walker from the house. Stumbling after, the boy was choking out strangled sobs, gagging. He saw that the blood was coming from Walker's ear. Sonny shoved him into the Mustang's passenger side. "I'm taking you back to Austin."

Walker groaned, "I don't got none of my stuff."

"I got your records and guitar. It's everything you need."

"HOLD THIS OVER your ear. Mama used to do this for earaches, remember?" Sonny handed him a paper towel he had wetted down with hot water. Stopped at a gas station in Stephenville, Sonny bought Walker aspirin for the pain, and white soda for nausea. He'd pulled over several times already to let Walker vomit on the side of the highway. He said the bad ear was ringing something fierce and he was swept with dizziness. Though the pain was bad, the bleeding had subsided. "We'll get you something stronger for the hurt when we get home."

"Thanks. Oh, man, I hope I ain't deaf in it." Walker's voice was too loud. Yelling over the roar in his head, Sonny realized. "Did you know this is what happened to Beethoven? His daddy boxed his ears." He smiled weakly.

"Well, ain't you in good company. And he probably couldn't play guitar a lick." Sonny climbed back in the Mustang, glancing in the rearview mirror. His own jaw was turning purple and there was some swelling. His hand still smarted from the punch he'd landed, but he didn't think it was really hurt. He started the car, slammed her in gear, and gunned out of the roadside stop onto 281.

Things had become complicated so fast. Yesterday was the best day yet of his fledgling career. Now he had a kid to deal with—maybe a kid with a kid on the way. He couldn't very well take Walker home. By now Floyd would know about Nancy Ruth. His brother did not need another beating. He had to get Walker's ear looked at by a doctor. He had to get in touch with the guy to take care of Nancy Ruth's problem, too. Even if Walker couldn't, Sonny reckoned he could talk the stupid girl into doing what made sense. Uncle Charlie and Aunt Lucille just had to take Walker in. What about clothes for the kid? He was too small to wear much that was Sonny's.

Sonny lit a smoke, thinking what a pain in the ass all this was. But he couldn't just leave Walker in Mingus. Where could he go but to Austin? He glanced over, asking, "How's it feeling now, Squirt?"

"Don't know. I think the soda's helping. God, it's ringing so loud! I can't believe I'm the only one can hear this." He rode along for a moment, quiet. "Thank God, Mama had us get the guitar and records, huh? Daddy really would have torn them up by now. He just goes apeshit, Sonny."

"I know."

"Yeah, you do. You're really the only one who does know what the fuck he's capable of." Walker leaned back, his eyes closed. "Sometimes I thought he'd really take it all the way and flat-out kill me. Didn't think I'd make eighteen."

"You're out of there now."

"Yeah." Walker opened his eyes, his face crumpling. "Oh, man, poor Nancy Ruth. She must hate me. And Floyd? Jesus, Sonny, what am I going to do?"

"For now, just lay back. Sleep or something. You ain't doing anybody a lick of good getting all in a stew out here. You'll start puking again. And if you do, I'll kill you myself." Sonny laughed when Walker shot him a half-worried look. "Kidding, Squirt."

Walker did manage to fall into a doze, giving Sonny some time to plan strategies while driving. When they got back to town, he dropped Walker off at the walk-in clinic they all used. Sonny instructed the receptionist to do whatever was needed, that he would settle up with them when he picked up Walker. He then went to face Floyd.

Floyd was pacing in the living room of their house, surrounded by Lone Star empties. A full ashtray of Sonny's butts sat on the coffee table, next to the smoldering bong. Pot and cigarette fumes drifted in the air. Howlin' Wolf blasted from the stereo.

The second that Floyd saw Sonny, he started raving. "You know what those stupid kids gone and done? Yeah, you do. That's why the little fucker was acting so weird last night. Jesus God! Is he here?"

"Yeah, but—"

"I'll kick his fucking ass in!" Floyd stomped toward the door, heading out to find Walker.

"It's already been kicked pretty good by Daddy," Sonny said, catching Floyd by the arm and setting him on the couch. "Walker's over at that walk-in clinic on Congress. He may lose hearing in one ear. Simmer down, man. This ain't the end of the world."

"The hell you say. Bet you'd feel different if it was your sister."

"I know I would. But, look, she ain't even been to a doctor yet. If it's true, well . . . there's that doc who's helped more than a few college girls out. I'll pay for everything."

"God . . . damn," Floyd groaned. "I can't believe we're sitting here talking about my sister getting scraped out. No matter what else, she's my baby sister, Sonny." He lit another cigarette from his butt. "This is fucked up. I can't believe you had the balls to bring him back with you."

"Floyd, it was a real bad scene. I could not leave him there."

Floyd sucked on the smoke and started hacking. Shaking his head, trying to draw a clean breath, he sputtered, "Well, he ain't staying here. Even if I wasn't ready to wring his neck myself, my folks would disown me."

"I know, I know. Calm down." Sonny picked up the bong and took a hit off the remnants. Relaxing a little from the reefer, he picked up the phone to call Uncle Charlie. He said he'd already talked to Ruby. She'd just told her brother there had been a fight—hadn't mentioned Walker's ear getting boxed. That just figured. Sonny was able to at least get Charlie to agree to seeing them both over supper. He hung up the receiver and turned to Floyd, scowling. "That don't sound real promising. Have to try and work my charm on Aunt Lucille, I guess."

WHEN SONNY PICKED UP Walker from the clinic, he looked a little better. He was sipping a soda in the waiting area, his ear bandaged over. Sonny asked at the front desk to speak with the doctor who treated him. Instead, they sent out a slender brunette with sharp cheekbones and smoke-colored eyes. The nurse wore a lab coat over jeans and T-shirt, a stethoscope dangling from her neck. She looked like a teenager playing at Doctor.

In a soothing voice, she explained that Walker's eardrum was ruptured, and the inner ear had a concussive injury as well, causing the dizziness. "Hopefully, if no infection sets in, he'll regain most of his hearing. Walker, honey, we'll start you on penicillin as a preventative and give you codeine for the pain. The tinnitus, that's the ringing, may always trouble you, I'm afraid."

"Ain't there nothing I can do?" Walker said.

"Steer clear of loud noises, as best you can. It might aggravate it."

"Well, that ain't going to be easy, ma'am. I'm a guitar player," Walker explained, peering solemnly at her from beneath his bangs.

She gave him a warm, maternal smile, running a hand lightly through his hair. "You too? I guess it runs in your family. Then you better invest in some industrial earplugs, Walker. And absolutely no playing plugged in until we see you again. Understand?"

"Yes, ma'am."

"Now, you come back in three days—right away if you start running a fever. We'll take that packing out and take another look then." Walker nodded. Keeping her hand on Walker's head, she asked Sonny, "Where are you going to take him? Walker told me about what happened with your parents." She reached with her other hand and ran fingers over the spot where Big Billy Jay had landed the punch on Sonny's face. "Do you need your jaw examined? It's fairly swollen."

"Shook off worse in bar fights. Just smarts a little. And please, sugar— you call me Sonny. I promise I'll get Walker put up somewhere. Thanks for your concern."

"Of course." She dropped her professional manner and smiled coyly, gazing at Sonny with those pretty gray eyes. "Sonny, I love the White Tornadoes. Would you mind giving me your autograph?"

"Why, sure, sugar. Least I can do. What's your name?"

"Maggie. Maggie Clark."

She handed him a prescription pad, and he scribbled on one of the forms. "Next time you make it to a show, be sure to say howdy." Sonny kissed his fingertip and pressed it to Maggie's lips. She said she would.

Walker looked better, and was walking more steadily than when he'd entered the clinic. He whistled as he got into Sonny's car. "Wasn't you smooth with that foxy nurse lady?"

"Second nature, Squirt."

"Yeah? You get that much, the autographs and stuff?"

"Some." Sonny laughed as he glanced over and caught the awestruck expression on his little brother's face. "Look, I'm about starving. You reckon you can eat?"

"I better try. The codeine's kind of going to my head. Feeling good, but kind of queasy again, too."

They went to a little diner Sonny knew of on the east side. From home Sonny had brought a shirt for Walker. His own had a brown splotch of blood on the shoulder. Sonny happened to grab the UT muscle shirt from the photo on the McGowan record. Walker changed in the car. He emerged looking a little better. The shirt hung loose over his bony chest, but exposed were a pair of surprising arms, sculpted with sinewy, strong muscle.

"You got tough arms for such a little shit, Squirt. You should show them off more," Sonny told him a bit later, watching as Walker tore into a chicken fried steak.

"My one good feature. Nancy Ruth tells me I should show them more, too, that—" he stopped, mid-bite. "Shit, Sonny! I got to call her or something. She must think I ran out on her."

"Well, you did."

"I know, but . . . I want to help her. I just don't want to marry her."

"I hear that. Look, don't call her right now. Her parents will probably answer and it'll just be another big deal. Let it cool down a day or two. That much time ain't going to change things. Maybe she'll even get her period before then."

"I'm praying, man."

"Almost forgot." Sonny took a small brown sack out of his pocket. "Picked up something for you when I stopped by my house. This was going to be your Christmas present. But I'll give it to you now, since you had to leave town without hardly anything."

Walker turned the sack over and out fell a gold chain with a peace symbol on it the size of a silver dollar. "For me?" he said in wonder.

"Got it at Venice Beach. A genuine hippie souvenir, all the way from L.A. It's real gold, so don't go and lose it. You may have to pawn the damn thing before it's all over."

Walker dropped the charm around his neck. He held the pendant in his hand, his eyes going shiny with tears again. "I don't know what to say. You sure you want me to have it?"

"I bought it for you, asshole—was hoping it'd piss Daddy off. But I'll take it right back if you start bawling again. Now eat." Walker nodded, picking up his fork. Sonny pushed his own plate away and lit a smoke. "I don't know what the fuck we're going to do with you. Leastwise Uncle Charlie's letting us come to supper."

"You think they'll let me stay there?"

"Don't know. He already talked to Mama, and didn't sound thrilled to be caught in the middle. And look, they're real strict about going to school."

Walker frowned. "That's too bad. For sure, I'm done with that bullshit. Probably have to start my sophomore year over anyhow. I was flunking out. It's a damn waste of time. I mean, I know what I want to do with my life, and it don't involve algebra."

Sonny shrugged. "Look, I dig where you're coming from, but I don't know where you're going to go if they don't take you in. I can't take care of you. You know that, right?"

"I know, Sonny. You done too much already." Walker sat quietly for a while chewing, looking out the window at the passing traffic. Sonny drank his coffee, staring at his brother, mulling over their troubles. Suddenly Walker smiled, slapping a hand on the Formica table. "Hey, I know. What about those fellas ya'll play for out there at the Sugar and Spice?"

"Shookie and Prince?"

"Yeah! I bet they could stand some help out there. I mean, they could put me to work in the kitchen, cleaning up the place, in exchange for a meal or two. They live upstairs there, right? I bet they got an extra room in that place. All I need is some place to crash. Man, all them bands that come through that club?" Walker grinned. "Now, that's what I call a real education."

"I don't know about this, Walker."

"Come on, Sonny. Let's just ask them. All they can say is no. It'd be great if they let me. And you and me can play there together some."

Sonny's sandwich suddenly tasted like sand. He shook his head, washing down the food with his coffee. "The White Tornadoes are *my* gig. Got that?"

Walker looked a little taken aback. "I know that. I just—"

"We're the house band there. Worked hard to earn that, man. And if you do stay there, you'd best lay low when Floyd's around, anyhow."

"Yeah. That's true enough." Walker took a drink of water. He cleared his throat. "Do you think my playing's lousy? Is that it?"

Sonny sighed, shaking his head. "No, man, not at all. I mean, you're young and green, but you're . . . good. Real good, Walker. Just, the White Tornadoes, it's Floyd's and my thing, you know? I don't want to mess with our sound."

"Okay." Walker stretched, yawning mightily. He scooted his clean plate aside and dropped his face in his hands. "I got to either get some sleep or some speed soon. You got uppers in that baggie of pills you carrying?"

"First, let's drive out and talk to Shookie and Prince. Might as well see if they'd be willing to work something out," Sonny said. He didn't have any better ideas. Walker nodded, yawning again. "Maybe you should change back into that bloody shirt first, Squirt."

"Why? It's pretty gross."

"Yeah, but you look a lot more pitiful in it. We'll work on the old boys' heartstrings."

II   THE SUGAR AND SPICE SHUFFLE

1.

"Hey, prince. Can I borrow one of the trucks tonight?" Walker called out, trotting down the big staircase into the nearly vacant Sugar and Spice bar area. Prince was behind the bar, doing liquor inventory and babysitting a few mid-afternoon customers.

"That depends, Walker. You got all them onions minced, like I told you?"

"Yes, sir. You can tell by my eyes." Walker had chopped until he thought they'd melted clean out of his head from the pungent fumes.

Prince peered at him. "Could be. Then again, maybe you been upstairs toking." The barflies chuckled.

"Prince, I know your rules. Never in the house."

"Where you off to, son? Got a hot date?" one of the drinkers asked. Another let go a wolf whistle.

"Yeah, right!" Walker chuckled, ducking his head. "I got called for a gig. The bass player and guitar player got popped for drunk driving and concealed weapon on their way home last night, and ain't talked no one out of bail yet."

"Hmm. . . . Where ya'll playing?" Prince asked.

"Some place down toward San Marcos." He was being purposefully vague. Walker knew where the Cowboy's Sweetheart Roadhouse was. He had played the scary-ass joint before. As wild and ugly a crowd as they came, plus nudie dancing girls. Walker figured it was best not to worry Prince with too much detail.

"What's the place called, Walker?"

"Uh, I forget, Prince. Riley Goode got me the job."

Prince gave Walker a once-over that let him know he wasn't fooled. "You make sure all the beer mugs is washed and in the freezer first. Check the kegs, and change out any that are about done. Be busy here tonight, with your bro's band in the house. You can take my truck. It's got gas." He pulled a wad of keys from his pocket and tossed them to Walker.

He snatched them from the air, saying, "Thanks a lot, Prince."

"And you be careful out there, hear? I don't want to be bailing your underage ass out of the pokey, myself. Keep that new Zorro hat your Uncle Charlie gave you pulled low now, so they can't see you just a baby."

After finishing the chores that had been laid out for him, Walker stashed his gear in the pickup and headed out for the evening's work. The night was cold but clear as he drove along, struggling with the tuner knob to find something interesting on the old AM radio. Finally, hitting on an Isley Brothers' song, he settled back for the drive.

Walker found life to be peaceful with the Browns. They had been happy to take him in. There indeed was a spare room upstairs. The walls were covered in peeling flower-printed paper, and for furniture there was a little bed and an old cedar wardrobe. The best deal, as far as Walker was concerned, was his was the room the Browns used to store the bulk of their record collection. Mostly there was jazz and blues singles, randomly shuffled in and out of the Wurlitzer downstairs.

The Browns offered to move the records down to the basement, to give Walker a little more breathing room. He asked them not to. Would they mind if he explored their music? They agreed, and Walker went out and spent as little as possible on a used record player and a fresh phonograph needle. When time allowed, he retreated to his room, listening to the music, playing his guitar, often working until he fell out with the Broadcaster still clutched in his hands. No more school to distract him, no more Daddy on his case. It was right cool.

At first Walker was sure Prince and Shookie only let him stay as a favor to Sonny, and in Daddy Jim's memory. He made every effort to be useful to them, though. With no prompting he weeded an overgrown garden out front and helped plant rosebushes and ice plant. He started scraping the outside of the roadhouse, getting it ready for a badly needed coat of paint.

From growing up on Big Billy Jay's unsteady cash flow, Walker knew a thing or two about auto repair. He did his best to keep their two old trucks running well. In return the men let him use them most any time. They also made him an extra set of hands in the kitchen, chopping this and that, grinding pounds of fresh spices in an ancient pestle until the air filled with heady scents.

He had even thought up a couple of good ideas to attract business. One was the Jive Five Monday. On the first Monday of every month, Walker rotated five new records into the jukebox, row A, moved the others over a row and retired the last five, row F. The record heads in the area would come out and see what choice cuts that Blaine kid had put in the box. Usually folks stayed for supper.

Walker had also talked the Browns into opening Sunday nights for the first time. They told him that night of the week had always been too slow to justify paying the help. But he convinced them it could be easy and cheap, leastwise worth a try. They offered only bar service, and used up leftover barbecue making simple sandwich plates. These dinners were a great deal for all the musicians in town living the pauper's life. No band to pay, just have an open mike for all comers. Nearly always the scene turned into a killer jam.

When Walker wasn't working elsewhere, he was there, guitar in hand.

Word was spreading about this younger brother of Sonny's, as he was known around town.

Yeah, life was pretty fine, Walker thought, turning up the dashboard radio, singing along with *Nobody Like Me*. If only things were still good between him and Nancy Ruth, all would be a groove. Without will, his mind brought forth the feel of her teeth nipping on his palm as she fought to stifle her groans when they did it in the basement. He'd always taken care to smooth his calluses with Crisco so they wouldn't scratch her soft flesh when he loved her up. He pictured her under him on the old sofa, her long blonde hair haloed around her face, the clutch of her tawny legs around his hips, remembered the velvet squeeze of her inside.

Just as suddenly, it smacked him how much she must hate him. He deserved it, too. He never promised marriage, but he had told her he loved, *loved* her, and meant every word. And when she needed him most, he was gone. Left town. Out of touch.

Walker had steered clear of Floyd as long as possible. When he was home, and the Tornadoes were playing, he didn't dare leave his room. But not long after he'd hit town, Walker was upstairs practicing when there was a knock on the door. Into his playing, he'd said, "Come in," without looking up.

When he did finally raise his eyes, he saw Floyd in the doorway, squinting at him. He hadn't seen the singer face-to-face since moving to Austin. Walker put the guitar on the bed and backed away as far as the small room allowed.

"False alarm, Blaine," Floyd growled.

"Do what?"

"You're off the hook. My baby sister called—she ain't expecting." He shrugged. "Thought you might want to know."

Walker dropped like a dead weight onto the bed beside his guitar. He exhaled, feeling a vise slip off his soul. "Oh, man. Thank you, God." He extended his right hand to Floyd. "And thank you for telling me."

Floyd swatted Walker's hand aside. "I almost didn't. Let you know, I mean. You been such a dick." Floyd clinched his fist, taking a step toward him. "Damn, Walker. I know you had to split town because of your crazy old man, but why didn't you call Nancy Ruth? Leastwise drop her a line?"

Walker hung his head, mumbling, "I started to, a million times. I never knew what to say. I wasn't marrying her, and that's what she wanted. I just couldn't bring up a . . . an operation to her. She'd have gone apeshit on me."

"You still should have. Look, no one wanted to see you kids married. But you should have done something, man." Floyd walked within inches of him, scorn in his voice and eyes. "You always seemed more . . . decent than this, man. I expect this of Sonny. Not you."

"I'm real sorry. Do you think it would help now if I called or wrote?"

"Walker, I think you're the last person she wants to hear from. She knows where you are if she wants to reach you."

Sonny stuck his head in the door. "Hey, Floyd. We need to run our sound check." He flashed a grin at his brother. "Floyd tell you the good news? I ain't an uncle!"

Yeah, it was great news. Just great. But now Walker was so lonesome. He missed Nancy Ruth something fierce. She had been his first real crush, date, and lover. Now she was his first heartbreak. He didn't want to even be left alone with another girl. He missed *his* girl. Besides, the thought of being a daddy had scared him stupid. He couldn't think of causing and feeling the fear and pain of it again. Not now. The only thing he was getting close enough to caress these days was his sweet Old Broad, as he had come to think of Sonny's Fender Broadcaster. He laid his right hand on his guitar riding shotgun in its gig bag. No matter what he did to *this* girlfriend, she wouldn't be demanding his name on a marriage license!

Walker pulled into the dirt lot outside the Cowboy's Sweetheart. What a claptrap dump. He had heard that at one time the musicians played inside a chicken-wire cage to keep the beer bottles thrown in fights from hitting them. Walker wished that cage still existed. Of course, chicken-wire wouldn't stop bullets, which had on occasion flown along with the fists and bottles. And he knew to keep right on playing—and good, too—unless he wanted the shooters to turn the fire on him. He had learned the value of the solid-bodied Old Broad as both shield and weapon during these outrageous gigs.

There were a few Harleys and pickups parked out front, with lots more to come once the band and the girls got to work. Pulling his new broad-brimmed hat down and adjusting a fringed leather jacket he had scrounged up at Goodwill, he picked up his amp and slung the gig bag on his back. He swaggered in. Spotting Riley, he nodded, flashing a peace sign with his free hand.

"Here's Paladin now!" Riley said, grinning, coming to shake his hand. The blues community had taken to calling him that, after the cowboy from *Have Gun Will Travel*. Well, he did have the hat nowadays. His trusty Fender was his gun. Sure enough he'd go anywhere to work—this gig was proof enough.

The singer, probably twice Walker's age and half again his weight, stared down at him in dismay. "Riley! Who the hell's this ugly punk in the Roy Rogers outfit?"

"He's your guitar player."

"You said you got me someone good." The big guy looked extremely pissed off.

"I am good," Walker stated, tipping his hat at an angle and peering up at the singer. He hoped he sounded less scared than he felt. "I can play anything. You just name it, man."

Riley smiled, nodding, clearly amused by Walker's cockiness. "He can, Tony Ray. He's Sonny Blaine's younger brother, you know."

The singer looked even less happy. "Shit! His *younger* brother? I mean, Sonny Blaine plays like a motherfucker, but he ain't hardly dry behind the ears himself." Tony Ray put his hands on his hips, scowling at Walker. Walker managed not to drop his gaze. "Well, can't be helped now, I reckon. If Riley weren't vouching for you, man? Look, this don't work tonight, we'll probably get our asses kicked."

"It'll work," Walker assured him.

"If not, after the stompers and bikers finish, I'll kill you both myself."

"You won't need to," Walker said. "Now quit griping and fix me up a song sheet, so's I can see what I'm working with." He could still hear Riley trying to calm the singer down as he bent over to ready his equipment.

He was goosed from behind. A giggling voice said, "Tony Ray, you quit being so mean to our boy. Us girls just love little Paladin." Walker jumped up, blushing, to face a freckled girl not much older than he was. She had damn awful teeth but fine looking titties. And, small favor, she still had her robe on.

"Howdy, Suzy Q. Was that you poking me?"

"Howdy yourself, Paladin. No, I wasn't poking—only goosing. You'll sure enough know when you get poked by me, baby!" She laughed, as he looked at the floor, more crimson still. "Got you again, sweetie. Hey, ladies," she yelled backstage. "Paladin's filling in tonight. I already got him redder than a rooster's comb." Several other women stuck their heads out from behind the ratty curtain, greeting him with flirty, singsong voices. He waved, trying to concentrate on setting up. Suzy Q grabbed him and kissed his cheek. At least the fuss from the working girls put a more confident, less annoyed look on Tony Ray's ugly mug.

The dancers always made a big deal over Walker. They fed him whiskey and got him high in various fashions. They pinched and kissed him, teasing him until he thought he'd up and die. They liked it that he got so flustered. Plus, he was usually the only fella in the place that wasn't groping at them, talking dirty and everything.

Even more than barroom brawls, these women were the main reason he didn't like this gig. Girls were tough enough to hang with when they were fully clothed. These ones stood around shooting the breeze with him in nothing but teased hairpieces, spangles, and feathers. And most of them would do more than a nasty dance if the price was right. Walker knew this from the lewd stuff he witnessed after a little money changed hands. It scandalized him some. Even more so, it frustrated him to pieces.

But Walker never pursued the game at hand. Partly he left the girls alone due to nursing his heartache over Nancy Ruth—but also, these were scary, aggressive pros. He'd heard more than one guy bitching about picking up a social disease from the Sweethearts. So, rather than act a fool, Walker tried to concentrate on his playing, releasing his pent-up need through Old Broad. He worked at getting that low-down bump-and-grind lust into his tone, heating up the place. He made the naked ladies dance all the wilder. For him. For his guitar. Sometimes, up there behind Suzy Q or another young thing that particularly stirred him, Walker closed his eyes and imagined. Pretend it was she in his hands instead of the guitar, think of doing what would make her moan and shriek for him. This helped him tolerate the sweating flesh, and the mean nights, set after long, stoned set.

Walker glanced at the song sheet Tony Ray had handed him. Not bad—straight rock and country, simple chops. Maybe set two or three, after he'd won over Tony Ray and the crowd, he'd talk them into doing something to let him stretch. No Hendrix with this bunch, but something tough and surfy-flavored maybe, to show them he was every bit as good as Sonny. Wet behind the ears or no.

It worked out great. Tony Ray, and better yet all the shitkickers in the crowd, utterly dug Walker by night's end. Tony Ray closed with *Crosscut Saw*, letting Walker go for it. Walker lived for the solos, for that feeling that blasted through him when it all came together. It was like jumping off a cliff and plunging into a pool of mountain-cold water—scary, thrilling. When he nailed it perfect, he could feel that thrill reach out from himself, like he was stroking everyone in the room with his playing. The girls would stop dancing and stare back at him. The bartenders quit pulling beers; and better still, the customers didn't even care, being so caught up in his music. For a few magic moments, they all belonged to Walker.

Show over, he crept back home to the Sugar and Spice, chased by the sunrise. He was exhausted, and still horny from being near the Sweethearts. He crept up the stairs and fell into bed, out before he knew what hit him. A few hours later, he woke up and picked up Old Broad from his side. Time to practice hard, and wait for the phone to ring with his next temporary job.

2.

"IS THAT YOU UNDER there, Squirt?" Sonny was heading into the Sugar and Spice when he spotted a pair of skinny jeans and boot-clad legs sprouting from under the hood of a threadbare Red Impala.

Walker emerged, grease smeared on his T-shirt, face, and hands. "Howdy, Sonny. Heard ya'll tore them up last week at that Juneteenth festival in Dallas."

"Yeah. Walker, it was great. I came by to show you this." Sonny held up a newspaper for Walker to peer at, so he wouldn't grab it with his blackened hands.

Walker read silently, his lips moving. After a moment, he said, "Man, Sonny. What a cool lineup. You, Floyd, and Eddie the only white boys there?"

"On the bill, anyhow. Don't know if we would have gotten the gig without Johnny Lee in the band."

"Look at this, they quoted you." Walker read aloud, " 'The White Tornadoes' Sonny Blaine, a young, white Texas guitarist, was a standout. He possesses a rich style, solid as granite, not showy. He plays clean, with each note, bend, and vibrato sharp and defined. "There ain't a lot of foreplay needed with what I do," said Blaine. "I just deliver the goods." ' Sonny, that's so great, man."

Sonny nodded, folding up the newspaper and sticking it under his arm. "Yeah, I dug it. Got to jam with people you wouldn't believe. Folks I used to dream about as a kid. And—best news—we got a record deal out of it. Lone Star, out of Dallas, signed us."

"Lone Star? God, we got lots of records from that label, don't we?" Walker picked up a wrench from a pile of tools on the ground and ducked back under the hood.

Sonny leaned against the Impala. "Sure do. And Rollie Matthews, the owner, is cool. He's always done country for the whites and blues for the blacks. So he thinks we're real exciting. Said, 'Now I know how Sam Phillips felt when Elvis Fucking Presley walked through the door!' "

"Well, all right. Congrats, bro."

"Thanks. I'm real pleased. We all are—except maybe Eddie's girl. She's ready for the wedding. And we're gigging all the time." Sonny chuckled. "Glad that's his problem, not mine. Anyhow, where'd you get this heavy Chevy? You been making enough cash being Paladin to get your own wheels?"

"Nah, not hardly. It's that girl Vada's. She came by to drop off some audition tapes or something, and then her car wouldn't turn over."

"Who's Vada?"

"Shame on you, Sonny-honey—ain't like we never met." Down the porch steps clip-clopped a girl in high-heeled Candies, hips swinging, her thunderhead cloud of black curls bouncing. Jeans and a sleeveless shirt snugly hugged her whippet-thin body, and from her ears hung enormous gold hoops. She walked up and kissed Sonny's cheek with her crimson pincushion mouth, leaving a heart-shaped print behind.

"Well, howdy, Bee-Stung. Long time no see."

"Too long. Forgot your old friends, hobnobbing with the blues hoi polloi? Rumor has it you and those boys you play with got a record deal."

"That's so. How's things coming with your band, sugar?"

She frowned, waving a manicured hand in the air. "Oh, we had some folks split on us again. That's a problem with getting together what I want, aside from finding all the musicians I need. Question is, how to get them serious when I can't pay shit? No cash coming until we start gigging, but with the big sound I want, we got to work at it first."

"Reckon that's true."

She pulled a cigarette out of her purse, which Walker promptly lit for her. She kissed the air in his direction. He gave her a shy nod. "Got some good horn players now, and my rhythm section is real tight—I'd wager they're the best in town. Still waiting on word from a couple guitar players, though." She glanced at Walker. "You find out why my car won't go, Babydoll?"

Walker nodded, scooping cleanser on his hands and rubbing off the grease with a shop towel. "Just some crap on the battery cables. She'll start now." He finished cleaning his hands, checking them for cuts or scrapes. He grabbed his fedora off the roof of the car and put it on. "But you got a pretty good oil leak you better see to. Otherwise, you might burn up your engine."

Vada laughed, low and throaty. "It's what they all say." She bent over and tore off a towel from the roll. Wetting it with her tongue, she wiped the oil smear off Walker's face. "I do know about the leak. That thing drinks oil like I do mescal." She tossed the towel to the ground and sidled up beside Walker. "You been right sweet, helping with my car. I know how squeamish you guitar men are about doing things that might hurt your fingers." She took his left hand in her own, lightly stroking his fretter's calluses. "No harm done, huh? Nice, big hands you got."

Walker gently pulled his fingers away. He crossed his arms and buried his hands out of sight in his pits. "Uh . . . well . . . big hands help out . . . with, like, rhythm playing, vibrato, stuff like that there," he stammered, staring at the ground. "I can wrap my thumb over the top and . . . rock 'em pretty easy."

"Oh, I just bet you can." Bee-Stung laughed, winking at Sonny. He smiled back, shaking his head at her. Walker's face was scarlet. "So . . . Sonny's little brother? Heard tell from my bass player, Riley, that you're Johnny-on-the-spot if someone needs a gunslinger. Is that so?"

Still staring at his boots, Walker answered, "Yeah. But I want to get in a band regular. It's not that I ain't good enough. Mainly, folks worry I'm too young and that'll scare off jobs."

She stepped beside Sonny, tilting her head to study Walker. "Hard to tell his age with that hat on, huh?"

"That's a fact," Sonny agreed.

"Maybe we can work out an audition," she said to Walker. "You interested?"

"I sure am!" Walker straightened up. He looked her in the eye, all business now. "You mostly blues? No, more soul stuff, right? Riley says—"

She reached to lay a finger over his lips, causing him to both hush and flinch. "Slow up, Babydoll. We'll talk this over later. Now, do you like Mexican food—it's Walker, right?"

"Right. Sure I do."

"To thank you for helping me with the car, I'm going to have my mama make you something special. I'll bring it over Sunday afternoon, when ya'll are slow out here. Then you can show me what you're packing. Okay?" She laughed as he ducked his head again. She strolled passed Sonny, blowing him a kiss. "*Adios*, boys." She hopped into the car, which fired right up as promised. Revving the engine painfully, she sprayed them with dirt and gravel as she pulled away.

Walker held out his hand for a low five. "Can you believe that, man? I got me an audition!"

Sonny slapped palms, getting himself smeared with remnants of Walker's hand cleanser. He rubbed it off on his Levi's. "Go wash up, Squirt. We'll play some pool to celebrate."

"Maybe later, Sonny. Right now I just feel like playing my guitar some." Walker mimed a riff in the air. "Need to be sharp, come Sunday."

3.

WHEN SUNDAY CAME around, Walker was in a stew. He'd changed his clothes three times. He finally settled on scuffed cowboy boots, his tightest old jeans, and his leather belt with the silver Lone Star buckle. He yanked on a sulfur-yellow sweatshirt. A while back he'd cut the sleeves off, to show-case his arm muscles, like Sonny told him to. He added a leather vest Riley had given him. He topped himself off with his Zorro hat. Draping the peace symbol Sonny had given him around his neck, Walker checked himself out in his mirror.

He brushed out his auburn hair so it hung nice below his hat, then tried convincing himself that he was just looking the part of a cool player, right for the job. This had nothing to do with impressing sexy Miss Bee-Stung as a man. Couldn't deny she stirred him, though. She was kind of exotic, with her long black hair and that full mouth of hers. Back in Mingus, Mexican girls would sometimes come to town, following their folks north for harvest and calving season. But what little time they stayed, those girls kept to their own. Walker had never known a girl like Vada up close. It seemed like she even walked different from white girls—unhurried, the rhythm of her stride filled with tangy promises.

Small blessing his mug wasn't blooming zits right now. Couldn't do much about his crooked teeth except try not to smile too wide. And there was no hiding his big ugly nose. Drag was, he couldn't even claim that

Sonny got the looks and he got the brains, because big brother had it over him in smarts, too. Leastwise they both could play. He cocked his head, pulling on his brim, trying on a couple of tough guy faces, then a few come hither looks there before the mirror. Finally, he squinted, lifting his lip in a practiced Clint Eastwood sneer. He cracked up, glancing back to make sure his bedroom door was shut. What a fool he'd look to anyone walking in on him.

Vada arrived at the Sugar and Spice about two in the afternoon. She tottered in on her Candies, wearing a little nothing of a turquoise sundress, a squash blossom necklace encircling her throat. Waiting at the bar, Walker didn't know if the sight of her in that dress or the promised plate of Mexican delicacies she bore made him hungrier. He did his best to focus on the food, devouring it while she kept him company. She poured herself liberal doses of mescal and told him about her master plan for the band. Sonny and Johnny Lee came in, dragging a few instruments, about the time Walker was finishing lunch. They were there to lend Walker moral support and provide an impromptu rhythm section for his tryout.

With Johnny Lee on bass and Sonny thumping along on a snare and high hat, they took the stage and ran through *Hound Dog* and *Tell Mama* in front of the empty barroom. Walker pulled his punches a hair, not delving into his flashier stuff. Instead he served up solid music more typical of Sonny's groove. Bee-Stung stood straight in front of the mike, feet planted and hands on her tiny hips, belting the blues out *Mariachi*-style. Little as she was, her voice was big and round, Walker noticed, had real nice power to it. Her range was not especially high, so it wouldn't be hard for him to harmonize with. Walker nodded and smiled when she glanced at him. He hoped she liked his stuff as much as he liked hers.

After they had run through the tunes, she extended her hand. "You can surely play. You want the job, Babydoll?"

He pumped her hand, squeezing it hard enough to make her wince some. "I sure do. Girl, you can sing. When do we start rehearsing with everyone?"

"Let me make some calls and we'll see," she said, rubbing the fingers that Walker had just all but squashed.

Walker hopped off the stage and reached up to lift her down, holding her around the waist. Hands still on her, he asked, "Do I need to ask if the Browns will let us work out here?"

She shook her head. "My folks let us use their banquet room for rehearsals, so that's all set." She pulled away from his grip, heading toward the booths. "Grab that bottle, Johnny Lee. Let's celebrate."

The Browns were in the kitchen, assembling the plates for Jam Night. Walker was to call them should anyone come in needing a drink poured. No one did. The Blaines, Johnny Lee and Vada manned a booth, ripping through the Browns' mescal. Bee-Stung also had cocaine on her. They laid out lines behind the napkin holder and all sampled a little.

After an hour, none of them were feeling anything akin to pain. Bee-Stung shook the bottle. "Well, boys. I do believe we've finished all our party favors, 'cept for this here worm. How do we decide who gets it?"

"Count me out, girl," Johnny Lee declared. "I don't eat no bugs."

"I'll pass, too, sugar," Sonny said.

"Hold on. We been drinking booze the *bugs* got to?" Walker hooted in disgust. "Call the goddamn health department."

The others laughed drunkenly. "Babydoll, the worm's supposed to be in there. That's how you tell you got genuine mescal." Vada held up the amber bottle toward the light, so Walker could see the lifeless creature's silhouette as it rolled around the glass bottom. "See, it's made from the only type of cactus that the little fella lives in. Some people try to pass off tequila as this, but it's like mama's milk in comparison. Tequila's just booze. This is like drinking black magic." She leaned over the table toward him, her neckline dipping, nipples peeking at him behind her heavy necklace. Once Walker managed to return his eyes to her face, she added, "You eat the worm for that little extra fire, boy. You man enough?"

Walker wondered if they were fooling with him, but he took on the challenge. He grabbed the bottle and, squinting at her, downed the worm whole. Sonny whooped and applauded and Johnny Lee gagged and stumbled toward the men's room.

Vada gifted Walker with a slow smile. "I sure enough found my ax-man." She took a quarter from her purse and pulled Walker to his feet. "What you got cooking this month on the jukebox, Walker?" She swayed across the floor to the Wurlitzer, dragging him behind her. She turned him loose, considering the selections. After a minute, she punched a few numbers, murmuring approval. She turned, finding Walker not two steps away. He took her into his arms, looking her in the eye, leading her into a slinky two-step. Ruth Brown crooned about making time for loving.

"My goodness, Walker. You know how to dance. Most young fellas don't."

"Honey, I was raised right. And I ain't too young." He gave her a spin, then pulled her closer still. "You sure are awful pretty. Your nickname don't do you justice. Can I call you Vada?"

"I wish you would."

The record ended, but they didn't sit. Smiling, Vada put her hands around Walker's neck, leaned back, pushing her hips against his. He ran his eyes over her, seriousness locked across his face. The threatening horns of Little Willie John's *Fever* began, and they started dancing again as one.

Walker was barely aware of Johnny Lee returning from the toilet. The bassist dropped down next to Sonny. Running the back of his hand over his mouth, he whispered loud, "Ooo-wee. That girl's working her spell, ain't she?"

Sonny didn't answer, just laughed a little along with Johnny Lee.

Ignoring them, Walker joined in on the second verse of *Fever*, singing in a gritty, soulful voice. Sonny and Johnny Lee quit snickering.

Johnny Lee hollered at Walker, "Pipes ain't bad, kid." To Sonny, Walker heard him say, "Damn if he don't sound a lot like Floyd do, huh?"

Walker didn't hear Sonny's response, but he was pleased with Johnny Lee's comment. He'd been striving to mimic Floyd's tough vocal style since he'd first heard him sing with the Tornadoes.

Song over, Walker and Vada slowed to a standstill. She smiled at him, which made him unable to resist grabbing her chin and kissing that mouth of hers. She snaked her hands around his neck and clung tightly, kissing him back full force—sweet. They separated and Vada smiled again, sighing his name in a way that made him lose his mind. He needed to get her away from Johnny Lee's and Sonny's prying eyes.

If he asked her flat out to come to his room, she might say no. He couldn't think what would be the right thing to say now. Best to be polite, he figured. Dropping his hand to her shoulder, he whispered, "Thanks for dancing with me, Vada."

"Anytime, Walker."

"So. You want me to get some more quarters for the box?"

"Not really what I had in mind just now." She laughed that husky little laugh of hers when she said it.

"Yeah?" Her laugh and smile boosted his courage. Drunk and crazy high, Walker dared to scoop her over his shoulder. She grabbed onto the small of his back, still laughing low. She didn't order him to put her down, as he'd expected her to.

Walker staggered across the dance floor and carried her on upstairs to his room. Jam Night would just have to go on without the two of them.

4.

THE WHITE TORNADOES' album, *Storm Cellar Blues*, was in the stores. The cover showed the four of them posing with their instruments around an old cellar dug into the earth, doors hanging agape on rusted hinges. Behind them a cheesy image of a twister tore up distant flatlands. Rollie Matthews had called a few days before with the first sales figures for Texas. Thanks to a lot of play on college radio, it was on its way to being Lone Star Records' best selling disc yet. Floyd and Sonny thought it a great excuse for a party. Word spread for a Monday gathering at their pad. The clubs being usually dark that night, most of their compadres weren't working.

Sonny filled a plastic cup from a beer keg he'd situated on his back porch. He heard commotion from inside the house and stuck his head in the back door. It was his brother and Bee-Stung arriving together. Walker's bare arm was slung over her shoulders, keeping her close. "Hey, ya'll?" Walker hollered. "We got a pickup out there loaded with eats. Let's get a few of you boys to haul it in, hear?" A number of guys headed out the front door to hustle the trays of Mexican and barbecue the pair had brought along.

Sonny waded through bodies to greet the couple. Because that's what Walker and Bee-Stung were these days, a couple. Together. Sweethearts. Sonny never would have laid money on it. Walker shot from under the brim of his hat a dangerous eye to any man giving his woman too keen a once-over. And Bee-Stung, whom Sonny had known to appraise the male per-suasion like a Fort Worth auctioneer grading sides of beef, only had eyes for his little brother. In her relatively loose jeans and high-necked sweater, she was even dressed modestly.

"Welcome, kids." Sonny grabbed Walker's hand and kissed Bee-Stung's cheek. "Thanks for rounding up the grub." He pulled the wallet from his back pocket. "What do I owe you?"

"Don't worry yourself, Sonny. We got a good price from our connec-tions," Walker replied. "Lead us to the beer."

"It's out back. Come on." Sonny led them through the living room, barking at one kid to get his butt off a crate of records as they passed through. "I think the rest of your band is here, too," he added over his shoul-der. "I know Riley's out here, helping Floyd hook up some P.A. speakers, so's we can have some tunes outside. We want to keep folks corralled there as much as possible, to keep them from messing with the albums and gear."

"Good thinking, Sonny," Walker said. They went out back, and Sonny pumped the keg, pouring Walker and his girl foamy cups. He watched them toast each other, take a sip, then share a sudsy kiss. Bee-Stung reached up to hold Walker's hat in place as she pressed her lips to his.

The twosome's duets on stage, as lead singer and guitarist for Bee-Stung and the King Bees, had been causing even more talk than they did as the blues tribe's hottest couple. "Really" Riley Goode, as the lanky bassist had taken to calling himself, sat their rhythm section with drummer Jesse James Goddard. Jesse James was a foxy, muscle-bound Texan, blessed with great timing and a streaked-blond bird's nest of hair crowning impish blue eyes. He had bounced around Austin's blues scene for a few years. Rounding out the Bees were Ikey and Mikey Smythe, two horn-blowing brothers from Memphis, and an ever-rotating group of pianists.

Sonny hadn't had a chance to take in the Bees' show, but they were gig-ging pretty regular. Word was they had a solid, R&B-flavored set. Bee-Stung was said to still be her usual self on stage: hot wails, flirty rap, frisky dance moves. But Walker's playing was becoming the talk of the town. Not a week went by anymore without some asshole coming up to Sonny and just raving about the kid.

"Well, man, got a new record, and your first tour just around the corner," Walker said, lifting his cup to Sonny. "That's so cool. Wish we was out there opening for you, huh, honey?" he asked his girl, fingering one of her curls. She nodded, smiling at him.

"We don't got no opening acts," Sonny said. "We *are* the opening act, quite a few nights."

"Oh, yeah? For anybody good?"

"No one I ever heard of. This is a pretty low-budget deal. Our transpo is Floyd's van. We're staying in shit-hole motels. Might just camp a few nights and pocket the money we'd save on a room. But maybe we'll get seen, and the album will keep doing good. Then next time out will be better."

"There you go. Heard there's going to be a big farewell show at the Sugar and Spice. They was trying to get us to open for ya'll, but we got a good-paying frat party down at Baylor."

"Just as well, Walker. Maybe you didn't know it, but Nancy Ruth's coming to town that night."

Walker's lip quivered. "I didn't. That's a trip."

Bee-Stung scowled. "What's she coming to town for?"

"College," Sonny said. "Going to spend a few nights at our place until she finds somewhere to live."

"She's Floyd's little sister, you know," Walker said quickly to Bee-Stung.

"Uh-huh. And your old girlfriend."

"Honey, you know that's been over since I left Mingus."

"It had best be."

Walker cooed to her that she had nothing to worry about, then pulled her into a kiss. Sonny fought to suppress a grunt at Walker's pussy-whipped attitude. "You lovebirds make yourselves at home," he said. "Going to see to it that they haul the food back here, instead of leaving it inside to spill on my stuff."

He walked out front, directing the traffic toward the backyard. They started laying out the chow on card tables as the tunes kicked out of the P.A. Sonny spotted a pretty girl and asked her to dance with him—one of many tonight, no doubt. Tour time, soon, too, with a little sampling of what the ladies outside Texas had to offer. None of this "Yes, dear" shit that Walker and Eddie were slaves to.

Two-stepping with the girl, Sonny tried to imagine dating only her—or any one woman, for that matter. He was clueless about this ritual of monogamy. He needed hot action and a good night's sleep. Sure, it might be nice to have someone to cook for him, to help him pay the bills, maybe answer the phone when he was in the midst of working out something

inspired on his guitar. But along with those perks came nonsense, commitment talk. Women expected a man to be immune to a girl dancing just for
him, eyes full of promises. Even with the people around him mating up,
Sonny saw no reason to. Not once had he denied a woman he desired. He'd
never shed tears when they tired of his hound-dog ways and moved on,
either. There was always another pretty baby, literally waiting in the wings.

Late in the evening, tipsy and stuffed, Walker and Bee-Stung made to
leave. "Party's just getting started, kids," Sonny told them.

"Got to split now, Sonny," Bee-Stung said. "Mama needs me to work
breakfast tomorrow." She hugged him in a sisterly way. "Ya'll have a great
tour. Show 'em the proper way to do blues, now. Texas style!"

"I will, sugar. And you take care of yourself and Walker here."

"Will do. Babydoll," she said, turning to Walker, "I'm going to visit the
little girls' room before we take off. Meet me at the truck."

"Okay, Vada." Walker winked at her. The brothers watched her walk
away.

"You got yourself quite a lot of woman there, Squirt."

"I sure do. Another jealous one, though—just like Nancy Ruth thataway." He shook his head. "So, she's coming to your farewell show, huh? At
the Sugar and Spice—where I call home yet. Thank God I'm going to be
gone for the night."

"I think Floyd would have done his best to talk her out of coming if you
was going to be around."

"Don't that feel like it all happened a long time ago?" Walker sighed.
"When I think about what could have happened . . . jeez, there could have
been a little kid running around Mingus looking just like me."

"Pretty scary thought, all right. That poor kid." They laughed together.

"Well, I better hightail it, Sonny. I find it's best not to leave Vada waiting." Walker grabbed his brother and hugged him fast and tight. "You tear
'em up, man. I know you will. You the best I ever heard."

Sonny gave him a sharp slap across the shoulders. "Thanks, Squirt. I'll
get in touch when I get back."

5.

THE BALLROOM WAS Dancing Room Only when the White Tornadoes
played their last show before the tour. Not just fans, but many musicians
who weren't lucky enough to be working that night filled the house.
Everybody wanted to jam with Austin's hottest—voted Band of the Year yet
again in the local poll.

They worked until last call, and then the Browns' waitresses gathered up
all the glasses and locked the liquor cabinets. That way the police didn't wan-

der through and yank their license for serving after hours, and the musical fun could continue unchecked. The Tornadoes performed until almost sunrise.

After the show Sonny wolfed down some leftover ribs. He was wasted with playing and longing for a last night of sleep in his own bed before leaving town.

Floyd plopped down in a chair across from him, his eyes glowing. "Got a big favor to ask, man."

"So ask," Sonny yawned.

"Look who's waiting for me by the door." A cocktail waitress waved her fingertips at them. "You know I been chasing Patty on and off for two years."

"She finally lose that scary boyfriend of hers?"

"No. But he's out of town on business, and she's awful sorry to see me leaving on tour."

"Oh, man, please. I really wanted to sleep at home tonight."

"I'm not kicking you out. I'll go to her house. Just, could you take Nancy Ruth home with you? She's over there flirting with some lowlife. I want to make sure she gets back to our place okay."

"Consider it done." Sonny gave him a soul handshake. "And we'll see you when you come up for air. Make sure you're out of her bed before Killer gets home."

Sonny packed up what gear he had into his car and then returned to the bar to find Floyd's sister. He saw her laughing it up with two bikers. She had her blonde hair styled in a long shag now, and she looked smokin', decked out in a black-leather miniskirt, red halter top, and high-heeled cowboy boots. And no doubt about it, she owned one of the best butts this side of the Pecos.

"Hey, ya'll," he greeted Nancy Ruth and the badasses as he joined them.

A big guy Sonny knew only as Meatball clomped him on the shoulder. "Righteous show, my man! We going to miss your sound around here."

"Get on down to your local record store and buy a little of it for $4.99, Meatball."

"Already done it, Sonny. Maybe our motorcycle club can hire ya'll for a party or something when ya'll get back home—if you ain't too famous now."

"Hardly, man." Sonny turned to Nancy Ruth, noticing she was giving him a bold once-over. "Sugar, your brother's otherwise engaged. He wants me to give you a lift."

She sniffed, taking her eyes from his body to glare at his face. "Oh, so Floyd can go out and do whatever, but still wants an eye kept on me. Is that it?"

Sonny shrugged. "More or less. Look at it like this. After tomorrow, you got the place to yourself for a while. I'm too tired to argue, girl. Let's go."

She acquiesced but pointedly left their phone number with one of Meatball's buddies. Sonny opened the door to his Mustang for her and then climbed in and started off down the dirt road toward the highway. A beautiful sunrise, smeared with pink and silver clouds, accompanied their drive. Nancy Ruth spun the dial on the radio. She found an album show playing Hendrix's *Are You Experienced?* The psychedelic waltz time of *Manic Depression* roared out of the speakers. "Oh, God," she groaned. "I love this song and hate it at the same time."

"Yeah?"

"It's too much, you know? It's . . . *Hendrix.* But it reminds me too much of your brother." She spat the last out, like she was ridding herself of some gristle. "He was nuts about that song. Worked for hours on it, note for note. All Jimi's stuff. Tried to figure out his tone, his effects—everything." Staring at the dash, she listened for a few bars. "Guess Walker was pretty upset when Jimi ate it, huh?"

"I think every guitar player worth his salt was. Jimi was a rare genius. And it was a stupid, senseless loss. If those damn ambulance guys had just done their job and positioned him right. . . ." Sonny let the thought hang in the air, listening as the first threatening notes of *Hey Joe* wafted from the speakers.

"Only the good die young," Nancy Ruth mumbled, watching the climbing sun peaking through lacy clouds. "I almost called Walker. When Jimi died, I mean. But I came to my senses pretty quick. He's a creep."

Sonny wasn't sure how to answer but felt he should defend his brother in some way. "Walker's no creep, girl. He was a mess after he left."

"*I* was the mess," she growled. "He just up and split. Never heard another word from him."

They drove the rest of the way in silence. When they got to the house, Nancy Ruth helped Sonny drag his gear into the house. He thanked her and dropped to the couch. He stretched, propping his feet up on the coffee table, rubbing his aching left fingers with his right hand. Yawning, he said, "Sugar, look in the freezer and fetch me a joint. There's some already rolled, sitting in a baggie beside the ice."

"I'll only fetch it if you'll share." He heard Nancy Ruth open the freezer. He laid his head back and closed his eyes. He turned to watch her when he heard the crackle of a metal ice tray being loosened. She was pouring two whiskey rocks into jelly glasses. Then, smiling as she noticed him looking, she sashayed over. She handed Sonny the glass, cocking her hip as she lit the joint. He sipped the whiskey. She sat near him on the couch and handed the smoke to him. "Ya'll never used to let us girls smoke back home."

Sonny took a hit but choked bad on it, coughing frantically. Nancy Ruth pounded his back. He finally managed to utter, "Back then Floyd wouldn't allow us to give you any. Ya'll was pretty young." Sonny remembered well Nancy Ruth and her girlfriends hanging out when they practiced in the Montgomerys' garage. They'd giggle, whisper, and flirt, distracting the band with their teenybopper foolishness.

"Huh. You let Walker smoke, and he was my age." Nancy Ruth took the joint, inhaling. Unlike Sonny had, the girl managed to hold her smoke like an old stoner.

Coughing again, Sonny said, "I didn't like him doing it." He went and poured a glass of water. He took a sip and added, "I think he just did it to get me riled."

She blew out the smoke, hooting, "I doubt that, Sonny. Walker loves his drugs. Word is he's hanging with some coke whore and her band these days. That true?"

He paused to finish his water. "He's in a band with a girl singer that used to be pretty wild, sure. But I got to say she seems changed since he's been around her." He sat back down on the couch.

"Well, ain't that sweet!" She handed back the joint, her words oozing venom. "Little Walker has a way of changing people, I guess." Nancy Ruth didn't sip her whiskey. She tossed it back in one move. Nodding, she squinted, sucking in air to cool the burn of the straight alcohol. She added, "Sure changed me from a little girl into a woman. Later I thought into a mama. Word got out about that. Him splitting and all, leaving me, caused big gossip. People got nothing better to do in Mingus, I reckon." She laughed cold, without humor. "Everyone knew after he split that Walker's tramp put out. He changed me into the town bad girl. Remember what a cock-tease I used to be, Sonny?" She reached over and put her hand on his knee. "I never tease no more." Smirking, she rubbed his thigh.

Sonny removed her hand, closing his eyes. "Just pick out a record or something, huh? Let me kick back and unwind a little before I crash out."

Nancy Ruth got up and started flipping through one of many crates full of albums that were scattered around the room. "Here we go. Otis Rush." She put on the record, smiling, as the sizzling strains of *Blue Guitar* lilted into the room. She stood up, swaying before him in time with the music.

"You dance with me, Sonny."

"Sugar, I'm too beat." He didn't have to look up to see the storm brewing. It was in the air, plain as a pressure drop. "Make yourself at home. I'm going to bed." He made to push himself up from the couch.

"Come on. Just one little dance first, Sonny. I don't bite." She took the joint from him and dropped it into an ashtray. Then she grabbed both his hands and pulled him to his feet. "Well, not too hard, anyway," she added, wrapping her arms around him to grab his ass. He gripped her lightly around her middle. They began dancing slowly around the room, sidestepping the crates of records. She smiled up at him. "Ain't this sweet? You sure know how to lead a woman properly."

He watched her eyes as they went from playful to smoldering. He hoped he looked stern when he answered, "You're playing dangerous, Nancy Ruth."

"I know." Her tongue wet her bottom lip as she reached up to brush the thick mop of hair from his eyes. "I've always had a dangerous crush on you, Sonny Blaine. But the first time I ever noticed you, I was just a kid at the Velvet Sundae drive-in. Maybe eleven years old? I could not believe my eyes. What was that old song? *He's a Walkin' Miracle.* That's you, all right." She drew her fingers lightly down his jaw and across his lips. "I didn't even know what it was I was feeling, but oh, it was damn powerful." Nancy Ruth laid her head on his chest, humming.

The song stopped, and Sonny made a half-hearted attempt to pull away. She gripped him more tightly as *I Can't Quit You, Baby* oozed into the air. She whispered, "I was lying in bed one night not long after seeing you and being so thunderstruck. Thinking of you, touching. The very first time I got myself off I pretended it was you—"

"Stop it." Sonny firmly took her hands off of his butt, holding her wrists in front of her. "Little girl, you and me got too much history between us."

She pouted, but her eyes sparkled. "Won't dance with me no more, Sonny? Fine. Reckon I'll have to dance for you." She shoved him back to sit on the couch. Straddling his legs, she wiggled her hips in time with the music. She untied the strap to her halter top. Yanking it off, she threw it over Sonny's head. Beneath the musky fabric, he heard her skirt's zipper slide open.

Sonny wanted to leave. He didn't. He tossed her top aside, laced his fingers behind his skull and lay back, to better enjoy her lap dance.

Maybe in a minute he'd tell her: *Fine show, sugar. Sleep tight, little girl.* He'd go on to his room and lock the door. Bury his head under the pillows and sleep this particular hard-on off. He knew he shouldn't cross this line. She was Floyd's little sister. Only she wasn't so little anymore, was she? Surely didn't move like a child, wiggling that perfect ass of hers in his face. She smelled better every second she writhed for him, too.

Then again, she was Walker's old girlfriend. But Walker was off with Bee-Stung now. He probably wouldn't care. Nancy Ruth had admitted to becoming Mingus's latest bad girl, after all. Sonny would be another notch on her pistol—a simple vengeance fuck.

Nancy Ruth, hair tossed forward to hide her face, was squatting over him, still squirming. Only her boots were still on. She sang along with the record, close-eyed, in a low, rough voice. Sonny whispered, "Hmm. You something else, ain't you, girl?"

"Sure enough am." She dropped splay-legged onto his lap. She pushed back her hair, opening her eyes, and drew closer to his face. All at once the temptress was gone. She looked scared—young, lost, and a little desperate. Her voice was small as she breathed, "Sonny, please. I've wanted you for the longest—"

Confronted by her sudden vulnerability, Sonny felt something deep inside of him downshift. He stared back into her blue eyes, feeling her moist heat soaking him through his jeans. If he'd stayed on in Mingus, it probably would already have happened between them. Might as well quit fighting it. It wasn't like Floyd and Walker had to know it ever went down.

Rough and quick, he snatched her waist and threw her to the couch. Climbing on top of her, he grabbed both of her wrists in one of his hands, squeezing them hard enough to make her let loose a yelp. He shoved her hands over her head, pinning them to the arm of the couch. Her legs he parted with his thigh and knee. She moaned deeply, her eyes growing round as Sonny handled the wetness of her with his free fingers. He placed his mouth just a fraction away from hers and growled, "Brace yourself, girl. We ain't playing no more games."

6.

SONNY WAS AT the wheel, taking his turn piloting the van. His three compadres were snoozing hard as he drove them into the dawning sun over southeastern Arizona. The band had finished a two-night stand in Tucson a few hours before, yet another short hop on a three-month-long tour. They were now rolling the four-hour leg to Las Cruces for another night's work. The big orange sun hurt some even through his dark shades, clawing the hangover headache that was taking hold behind his eyes. The pain was less evil than it was on mornings when he wasn't chosen to do the driving. Last night Sonny had quit indulging early to be road worthy. When he finally got them to Las Cruces, they would all collapse vampirelike into a drape-darkened room and try to restore themselves before the next show.

He gazed in wonder at the unearthly landscape he was driving through, a place identified by a roadside sign as Texas Canyon. He laughed out loud at the name, causing Floyd's eyes to briefly flicker open in the co-pilot's seat. The singer was back under, though, before Sonny could share the view. Why *Texas* Canyon, he wanted to know? The Lone Star State held many a strange thing, but he'd never seen the likes of this. There were lopsided piles of enormous, smooth-edged boulders, looking like God had dropped a bunch of skipping stones all along the highway. Weird and wonderful place, Arizona, especially alight in the soft gold of this desert dawn. But then this whole state was straight out of a *Roadrunner* cartoon.

On their first swing through Tucson, some hippie chicks, generous with their weed and Purple Microdot, took the boys outside the city. They ended up at a desert picnic ground smack dab in the middle of a forest of gigantic saguaro cacti. There, watching a sunset the color of molten gold and fresh blood fade into a star-splattered night, they tripped and swapped flesh in a psychedelic orgy. Between gropes, Floyd scribbled lyrics madly in a little notebook he kept on him for that purpose. Once they came out of orbit, what words they could actually make out didn't make much sense.

Yeah, a long strange trip it had been, this first Tornado tour. They were getting a great response from audiences all over the Southwest. Sometimes they had more curtain calls than the bands they opened for. Good press, too, and Rollie's phone calls glowed about sales figures. Still, it would be good to return, reclaim the throne as Best Band in Town. Be good to play the Sugar and Spice for the hometown crowd, where they had nothing to prove.

Starting out, the band stopped over in Mingus. Everyone had wanted to see family. So did Sonny, as soon as he phoned Ruby from Eddie's parents' place, making sure Big Billy Jay was working out of town. His mama, bawling, begged his forgiveness for slapping him during the tussle. Sonny had no problem forgiving her. Not Daddy, though. Ruby had known better than to even ask.

She quizzed Sonny about his own work, and Walker Dale's, while she stuffed him with her down-home vittles. Ruby couldn't utter Walker's name without tears springing into her eyes. Sonny could see it clear that she missed her youngest something fierce. She was proud, and a little astounded, that Walker was also earning his keep with guitar playing. Most amazing was she didn't even hint at when Sonny might start college. Could it be Ruby was finally coming to terms with her boys' career choice? Probably she simply wanted to preserve their fresh peace treaty. Sonny was pleased not to wrestle with her either way.

He only dreaded one thing about getting home. He didn't want to see Nancy Ruth. Scary, that's what it had been at moments with the girl. Once that night, too caught up in screwing, he let her wrists go. She slashed his back with her nails before he restrained her again. Bit his neck hard enough to draw blood, even after she promised she didn't. A dangerous crush, sure enough!

He'd done all she begged for, and showed her a new thing or two. Still she wouldn't leave him be to get his desperately needed rest. He finally tossed her over his shoulder and dumped her unceremoniously into Floyd's empty bed. Then he locked himself in his room, burrowing under quilts and pillows. He'd finally drifted off to the sounds of her crying, cursing and scratching at his door.

When Floyd returned, swaggering and triumphant from his tryst with Patty, he took his sister out for breakfast. Sonny feigned sleep until they'd left. He rose and doctored his war wounds with iodine, praying the girl

would keep her mouth shut. Surely she realized the ruckus she would cause
if she blabbed. Floyd would be beyond pissed. He'd trusted Sonny to take
her home and keep her safe. Would be just as well if Walker never knew
about it, either. Bound to get back to them if she started talking, though.
Austin's music scene was like a hippie *Peyton Place*, its members always ready
to dish dirt about who was doing whom, and what song was playing as the
soundtrack.

When the Montgomery sibs came back from their breakfast, Sonny was
ready to leave. He wore a turtleneck to hide the love bites. With his gear
and bags by the door, he hoped to slip away quick. Floyd still seemed happy
and cool—a good sign Nancy Ruth had held her tongue.

They'd brought Sonny back a sandwich and coffee. Handing the eats
over, Floyd asked, "You about ready to hit it?" Sonny nodded. "Good. I'll
load your loot. Chow down and give Eddie and Johnny Lee a call, make sure
they're up and at 'em."

"Will do, Floyd." Sonny made the phone calls and then sat down to
bolt the food. Nancy Ruth perched quietly on the couch, the primary scene
of last night's crime. She made like she was reading the newspaper, but
Sonny could feel her eyes on him.

If only she were a groupie chick. Just say flat out: Sugar, we had us a
time, but it's over now. Simple and clean, no fallout. Finally, wiping his
hands on a napkin, he said, too cheerfully, "Got the place to yourself for a
while, Nancy Ruth. First time on your own, huh?"

"That's true. On my own." She met his eyes then. She looked hung
over, and real young. The young girl from Mingus had replaced the wild
woman he'd been fucking only hours before. That's what got him the night
before, that little-girl-lost quality she showed him under all the bluster. Her
eyes were bright with tears as she gazed at him.

Sonny peered out the front door, making sure Floyd was still out of
earshot. He sat on the arm of the couch. "We got to keep what happened
here secret. Talk can't lead to nothing but hot water for us both."

"I know. I'm not stupid, Sonny." Her voice broke and tears started to
spill down her cheeks.

Floyd honked for Sonny. He darted into his room and grabbed his
leather jacket. Her head was dropped forward, and her shoulders shook with
crying. Sonny figured she'd be fine as soon as he left. She'd forget all about
him and move on to the UT boys right quick. Unsure what else to do, he
mumbled, "So long, sugar. Have fun at college."

"Have fun on the road. And don't worry." She frowned, wiping an eye
hard with the palm of her hand. "I'll be out of your house when you get
home."

＊ ＊ ＊ ＊ ＊

"LOOKY THERE, Prince," said Shookie. "The mighty rock star's returned to stroll amongst us little people!"

"Hey, Sonny-boy!" Prince cried. The Browns were seated at the bar going over receipts when Sonny walked into the Sugar and Spice. The both slapped his shoulder in warm fashion. "When ya'll get back?"

"Yesterday, Prince. We're dog-tired. Good to be home. It ain't exactly glamorous travel in that van. The shows were fun, though."

"Well, that sounds good, boy. What brings you out here?"

"Three things. One, thought I'd see if Walker was here. Two, wanted to talk to you about getting back on the schedule. Most important, if I don't have some of ya'll's barbecue today, I ain't going to make it."

"Set yourself on down. Shookie, get this boy a plate of food. And a pitcher, Sonny, on the house." Prince poured him his draft in a chilled mug and sat it in front of him. "As to them other two things, Walker should be here any minute. He went to the Sanchez Palace for lunch, but I called him to come mind the store while we went to town. He's got to go back over there later. They play there at the cantina Saturdays, you know."

"Yeah. So, those two still pretty hot and heavy?"

Prince nodded, smiling. "Both them kids just walking on clouds. Never would have believed it of either of them. Boy seemed like he was scared to death of women when he first started living here." Shookie came out of the back with a steaming plate of ribs, greens, and cornbread. Sonny offered a grateful nod and dug in.

Prince pulled his date book from beneath the bar. "Now, as to the schedule. We'll be right glad to have ya'll back on Saturdays—starting two weeks from now? Be good to have ya'll back. Lots of folks have missed you."

Taking a second to swallow, Sonny replied, "Cool. What about Thursdays? That's been our day since we started here, what four, five years now?" The Brown brothers exchanged an uncomfortable look. "Well?"

"Well—that's our night now, bro."

Sonny turned around to see Walker strolling in from the front door, pulling back a bit when he saw Sonny. Walker was transformed from when Sonny left town—grown up. It was not so much a physical change. Sonny still had at least six inches of height on him. Rather, a new aura of cockiness enveloped him. His scraggly goatee was gone, replaced by a sharp hep-cat's soul patch under his bottom lip. He still wore the peace-symbol pendant Sonny had given him, and had added a big gold hoop in his left earlobe. The bolero hat bore a new red snakeskin band, and some new cowboy boots matched it, the toes tipped in silver. He wore black jeans and a vest of paisley over a red T-shirt, sleeves rolled up to expose his arms. His left biceps displayed a large tattoo of a Stratocaster sprouting the wings of a raptor.

Wiping his hands on a napkin, Sonny rose to meet Walker, slapping his back. "Just look at you, Squirt!"

Walker looked down at himself, holding his arms out. "Yeah, well. Vada kind of likes all this."

"Oh, shit, Walker. Like you don't?" Prince hooted. "You the *King* King Bee, after all."

They poured Walker a beer, and he pulled up a barstool beside Sonny. "So, anyway, Sonny, back to business. We took over Thursdays here now. Got quite a little following, too. Not that folks didn't miss you Tornadoes at first." He smiled. "We just won them over."

"Yeah," said Prince. "One look at these receipts proves it. This month we had the best Thursday ever."

"Ain't that something?" Sonny said. He knew that the Sugar and Spice could not exactly stay dark while the Tornadoes toured. He'd imagined there would be various groups filling in for the undisputed house band—not one band claiming their spot. Not the King Bees, at least. "The rest of the Tornadoes are going to be damned surprised by this turn of events. We still have the Saturday set?"

"Since we play at Vada's folks' Saturdays, I reckon you're welcome to it." There was an unexpected challenge in Walker's voice. He looked Sonny over like he was sizing him up.

Prince nodded at Sonny, a bit of apology in his eyes. "We look forward to ya'll joining the schedule again, Sonny-boy. No hard feelings?" He offered his hand.

Sonny shook it, and reached for Shookie's, too. "Of course not, man. Business is business."

"Well, all right." Prince picked up the bulging leather money bag. "Walker, we going to run this to the bank and pick up some supplies. Keep an eye on the place until we get back, son."

"You got it, sir." Walker watched the brothers leave. He and Sonny were left alone in the bar, though Sonny could hear busboys singing in Spanish, running water, beyond the kitchen door. Walker took a long sip of beer and said, "Thanks for writing me from the road, man. I called Mama, like you told me to. Should take Vada to meet her, I reckon—when the old man's out of town, of course. So, the tour went well?"

"Yeah. Made some good contacts, I think. It was pretty fun. Looks like ya'll done real well since we left."

"Real well's right. Just think. There's a whole new crop of college kids in town who think of me when they think of a guitar player name of Blaine." It wasn't friendly, the way Walker said it.

Sonny was puzzled. He thought Walker would be thrilled to see him—always had been before. If anything, Walker should be apologizing up and down for stealing their Thursday night spot. But he'd acted like he had a bone to pick since walking in the door. Sonny dug back into his food. Walker went and turned on the jukebox. He sat back down beside Sonny.

He pulled out his cigarettes, lit one, and dropped the pack on the bar. He drank his beer and smoked, mute. When he'd finished eating, Sonny helped himself to a cigarette from Walker's pack. Walker frowned at him, putting the smokes away in his vest pocket.

"All right. What gives, Walker? You're acting real strange."

"You think so?" Walker poured another beer, draining the pitcher.

"You know damn well you are."

He took a long sip off of his beer and squinted at Sonny. "You seen Nancy Ruth yet?"

Nancy Ruth! Sonny looked away, toward the jukebox. He hoped Walker hadn't caught anything in his eyes. "Why should I? You ain't seen her lately, have you?"

"Yeah." Walker smoked for a minute, quiet. Sonny felt the tension in the room rise. "She came around to a show about a week ago. Didn't even recognize her at first. Changed her hair. Looks real good, real sexy. Grown up. Filled out." Walker kept watching him. "She said right nice things about my band. She and Vada both managed to be ladylike and keep their fangs to themselves." Sonny chuckled a little. Walker didn't. "Funny thing is, she seemed real anxious to know when you were coming back. *Real* anxious."

"She is Floyd's sister, after all."

"Wasn't about Floyd. She wanted you, Sonny. Why is that?"

"Don't know," Sonny mumbled. It wasn't a lie, really. He didn't know what else she could want with him. He'd left her in tears—wasn't like they'd parted on good terms.

"She always had a bad crush on you. Didn't she stay with you and Floyd before ya'll left?"

"Just . . . for a few hours, really. So what?"

"So . . . nothing. I thought it was kind of funny she wanted to talk to you so bad. That's what she kept saying, she *had* to talk to you." Walker dug into his back pocket and pulled out his wallet. He dug out a folded piece of paper, tossing it to Sonny. "I told her I'd give you her new number. I knew Floyd would want it, anyhow." He stood up, tipping his hat brim almost formally. "Welcome home, Sonny. Why don't ya'll come by and see the Bees next Thursday? I got some new tricks up my sleeve. Now—I best make sure things are running smooth in the kitchen. The Browns depend on me."

7.

SONNY DIDN'T CALL Nancy Ruth. Far as he knew, she wasn't calling him, either. She'd probably found someone new and had forgotten him. The first week back in Austin, Sonny mostly stayed home practicing guitar and catching up on sleep. They let Floyd do the dirty work of getting them back on schedules around town. Seemed to do Floyd good, keeping busy promoting the Tornadoes. He'd lost some of the palpable funk he'd worn before the tour.

Floyd's problems weren't over, though. A letter from the draft board was waiting at the post office when they got back to town. It looked to be the dreaded "Greetings" notice, rather than the hoped-for deferment. Floyd left it unopened on the kitchen counter, as though by doing so he made it not real. Sonny couldn't say he blamed him for avoiding the news inside.

Walker called Sonny toward the end of that week, sounding more like himself than when they'd met up in the Sugar and Spice. He invited Sonny to meet Vada and him for Sunday brunch at the Sanchez Palace, Vada's folks' restaurant—on the house, of course. Sonny agreed and showed up about noon with the girl he'd brought home from his gig the previous night. She was cool brunette coed studying liberal arts at the U—pretty, bright, and enjoying her first year free of family curfews.

The place was packed as usual, but Vada and Walker had scouted out a good spot. Sonny and the girl joined them. Walker greeted Sonny with a warm handshake, and he tipped his hat and pulled out the chair for the lady. Things seemed cool. Hopefully Nancy Ruth's name wouldn't come up—not likely to, what with Vada present. They made small talk and nibbled chips and salsa for a while, and then grabbed some chow from the buffet.

"Might as well order that pitcher of margaritas, now you got someone of age to share with," Walker said as they sat back down, pouting at Vada. She purred at him, then kissed him, nipping his lip. Sonny spotted Vada's daddy, Julio, over by the cash register, white-knuckled, watching the twosome smooch, menace in his eyes. Sadly, Walker said Vada's old man could barely stand to be in the same room with him. Walker wanting things to go well, but Julio simply wasn't to be won over. He'd apparently hoped Vada would marry a nice Mexican Catholic—a mariachi, maybe. A white Baptist guitar-slinging cosmic cowboy matching up with his precious *mijita* was a plain nightmare for Vada's dad.

Vada signaled her mama, and Lupe Sanchez was soon rushing over with a sweating pitcher and glasses rimmed with salt. At forty, Lupe was still a looker—slim, dark, ripe-mouthed. Vada favored her considerably. Sonny's date didn't pass muster on the I.D.-ing. "None for you or Walker, I'm afraid," Lupe said, patting Walker on the shoulder. "The liquor board watches us awful close at brunch."

"It's okay, Mrs. S. We'll stick to water." He held up his glass in salute. Lupe smiled warmly at him. At least he apparently had a fan in Lupe.

"Need help hauling them heavy trays?" Sonny asked, touching Lupe's hand as she poured his drink. "Pretty thing like you, working so hard."

She pulled her hand away, blushing. "Goodness, no! Enjoy your food. I have to get back to the kitchen."

They watched Lupe hurry off. Vada narrowed her eyes at Sonny. "Teasing my mama like that. You should be ashamed."

"I just offered to help."

"Help, my ass!" Walker and Sonny's date laughed. Vada said to the girl, "How's your food, dear?"

"It's wonderful. I've always wanted to try your place, Bee-Stung. I've seen ya'll play here but never had the food."

"Yep, my folks can surely cook . . . sugar." Vada eyed Sonny coolly. He realized he hadn't introduced the girl. He couldn't—wasn't sure of her name. Vada had caught that. Vada looked back to the girl and added, "I much prefer to be called Vada offstage."

"Sorry. Vada it is, then." She smiled at Vada, and then turned toward Sonny. "I'm glad I came to see your band for a change last night, Sonny. Ya'll were on the road when I got to town for fall semester. I'd heard your record on the college station, of course. But I've been coming to see the King Bees every Saturday." She glanced toward Walker. "I didn't know Walker had a brother who played, too."

Walker shot Sonny a smug grin.

"Now you know where the real talent of the family lies," Sonny said, grinning.

"But I think you're both really good. I—" She broke off, looking past Sonny. "Hey. Isn't that your roommate, Sonny?"

They all turned to follow her gaze. Floyd was stalking toward them, his jacket hanging half off his shoulders. His Medusa curls were even more feral than usual. He pounded a palm on their table, hard enough to make the ladies jump. "Walker. Outside. Now."

"What's the hurry?" Walker asked. "Let me pour you a margarita."

"I said outside, asshole," Floyd spat, obviously fighting for control. People at the tables around them stopped talking and stared. Floyd pointed toward the door. Sonny followed his fingertip and saw Nancy Ruth, ghostly pale, hands clamped over her mouth. She was staring at him with tear-filled eyes. Her expression hit Sonny like a body punch.

"Okay. Take it easy, man." Walker grabbed his hat and trailed Floyd toward the door. He glanced back at the table, shrugging, looking confused. Vada's papa glowered at the two men as they walked by him.

"What's eating Floyd?" Vada asked.

"Not a clue," Sonny replied. He watched them stalk outside. Floyd grabbed his sister's arm roughly as he went past her. Nancy Ruth craned to keep her eyes on Sonny.

Seconds later, a muffled scream sounded from the parking lot. Vada and Sonny looked at each other. She was up and dragging him out of the booth and toward the door. "Wait here, sugar," he told his date.

She nodded, looking bewildered.

Walker was on the pavement, moaning and holding a hand over a bloody, smashed nose. Floyd was shaking out his hand and cursing at him. A couple coming up the walk gave them wide berth and darted back toward their just-parked car. Vada let out a shriek and ran to Walker, kneeling and pulling his head into her lap. Nancy Ruth was crying, groaning, "Damn you, Floyd—listen to me for once. It was Sonny, not Walker."

Sonny stood back by the door, feeling the other four people's eyes lock on him. "Sonny?" Floyd muttered the question, brows furrowed. As Sonny watched, he saw a look of reckoning slide over his best friend's face. "Sonny! She came over crying, you know? I thought she'd failed a test, or some college boy had broken a date or something. But then she said. . . . Man, when I asked her if it was Blaine, and she said yeah, I thought. . . . Damn it!" His eyes went to slits as he stared at Sonny. "That morning before we left town, ya'll was alone in our house. That must have been when, huh? Why, you fucking dawg! I'd been better off leaving her with them lowlife bikers at the bar."

"I. Uh . . . what?" Sonny stammered. Clearly Floyd now knew about that night. Walker was sitting up watching him with icy eyes. He ignored Vada as she whispered comforts in his ear and stroked his hair, the blood still draining from his nose.

"I'm . . . I'm going to have a baby," Nancy Ruth yelped, starting to sob. Eyes on her, Sonny heard Walker groan, followed by the soft thud of him collapsing against Vada's arms.

"No. No, you ain't, either." Sonny said firmly, a few seconds later. "You pulled this once before. You broke up our family over it. Then nothing come of it at all. You ain't pregnant."

Floyd threw a wadded paper at him. "Yeah? Take a look. Count backward, you sorry bastard."

Sonny picked up the paper from the ground and smoothed it open. It was a lab report from the clinic on Congress, a positive pregnancy test for Nancy Ruth Montgomery. Fourteen weeks gestation. She'd gotten herself knocked up . . . exactly when they had left town for the tour.

This couldn't be. He stared at the report, not daring to look at any of them. He could hear Floyd panting furiously and Nancy Ruth sobbing. Vada was talking to Walker soothingly again. Sonny's brother wasn't making a sound.

Sonny finally managed a cold-eyed squint. "Well, what do you want me to do about it? Go talk to your boyfriend."

"My boyfriend?" She asked him, small-voiced. "I don't have a . . . Sonny, you're the daddy."

"No way! I was standing right there when you gave Meatball's friend your phone number. I know how you college girls act your first few months away from home. I know it better than anybody does."

Nancy Ruth wiped her eyes with her fist. "Sonny, you know how I felt about you. . . . You're the only one I've been with here."

"I believe that like I believe the moon's made of cheese!" Sonny pulled out his wallet with shaking hands. "What, none of your boys going to give you the money? Here. Here's a hundred. I'll get you more later this week—and the name of a doc to fix it. You'll feel better in no time."

"*Mios Dios!*" This was from Lupe Sanchez. She stood outside the restaurant door, slowly crossing herself. Staring hard at Sonny, she said to her daughter, "Nevada, you get your friends out of here. They're chasing off the customers. Papa's calling the police this minute."

"I apologize, Mrs. Sanchez," Floyd told her. He grabbed his sister's arm roughly. "Come on. I'll take you back to Mingus. We're going to talk to Mom and Pop." He shut her up with a fierce glance when she started to object. He turned the same look on Sonny. "I don't know how I stood you all these years. You're one heartless fucker. Sorry for the bad language, girls. I call them as I see them, though. If you wasn't ladies, you'd tell him so, too." He turned his squint back to Sonny. "I'll be back for my stuff later."

"Your stuff?" Sonny whispered.

Floyd grunted. "You don't think I'm staying in that house, do you? With your sorry ass? Hell, no." Yanking his sister behind him, Floyd took a couple of threatening steps in Sonny's direction. Then he stopped, seeming to collapse into himself. "I can't do it no more. Can't keep fighting. The fucking draft board wins. I'll just let Uncle Sam have my ass, and get the hell out of here."

Sonny took a step toward him. "Floyd. No, man, don't—"

Floyd cut him off, tears in his eyes. "Don't you dare say nothing else. And you listen good. If you and Johnny Lee and Eddie even think about playing anything I wrote, I'll sue the balls off of you." He stormed off, trailing his sister. He hollered behind him, "Sorry I slugged you, Walker."

Mrs. Sanchez was holding her apron to Walker's bloody nose. Murmuring consoling Spanish sounds, she led him around the back of the restaurant to the Sanchez home. Walker was trembling, not looking at Sonny.

Vada came up to Sonny, hissing, "You get, before the cops arrive and bust you. I'll make sure the bill's taken care of and that your plaything from last night gets home." She shook her head, her full lips twisted in disgust as she stalked back into the restaurant.

Sonny managed to make it clear to his car before he lost his brunch.

8.

SONNY WAS WITHOUT a band for the first time since junior high.

Unemployed. Floyd was gone. Sonny hadn't seen him since the showdown outside the Sanchez Palace. Coming home one morning after a night of carousing, he found the house empty of anything that had been Floyd's. He didn't even leave a note saying, "Screw you, Blaine." Sonny called Johnny Lee, asking if he knew the score. He did. Seems after taking Nancy Ruth home to Mingus, Floyd made good on his promise. He ran to the Navy recruitment center, signing up for a two-year tour. Upped and handed himself over, after all his battling to stay Stateside.

That same day, Eddie came to see Sonny. The drummer told Sonny he'd been trying to think of a way to gracefully bow out of the Tornadoes. Graduation was right around the corner, after all. His girl had his ring, a wedding date, and a job set for him in Houston in her daddy's printing business. It had been fun and all, but time to start acting his age, you know?

Johnny Lee and Sonny called it quits officially then. Another Fillmore Divorce, as Sonny called it when a band dissolved. Johnny Lee had signed up for a couple of graduate courses, and was still doing session and substitute work. Sonny wasn't playing at all right now. He mostly felt sorry for himself, cross with everyone who dared come close enough for him to bark at—and there weren't many who bothered. He'd pretty much pissed off anybody he'd known.

Never a big spender, he had money enough to hang out and sulk for a time. He kept himself soused, focusing only on practice. He played until his hands cramped with spasms from overuse. Then he'd quell the ache in his paws with liquor and drugs, listening to records when he got too tired and messed up to play anymore. He tried his damnedest to not think about how he'd screwed everything up just by fucking that girl.

To avoid accusatory eyes, the liquor store was about as far as he ventured. While getting more Southern Comfort one night, he picked up the *Chronicle*. He squatted on the curb, staring at the rag and shaking his head. There on the cover, a cocky grin under his hat brim, was the blues sensation, Little Walker Blaine. For the first time in five years, since the White Tornadoes had first laid claim to the throne, there was a new best band in Austin. Bee-Stung and the King Bees were the reigning champs.

The next night Sonny decided what the hell. Time he made the drive to the Sugar and Spice, checked out Austin's new best band. Licking his wounds, Sonny stumbled in. The bartenders and waitresses were in the process of locking up the liquor. Sonny charmed his way into last call, ordering a double his mind and body had no need for. Just a hardy few remained, patrons who had convinced themselves that staying up all night dancing and drinking wouldn't ruin 'em the following day.

In a fringed minidress and spike heels, Vada was strutting her stuff. She wailed with hoarse abandon the old Etta James hit *Something's Got a Hold on Me*. Ol' Bee-Stung was surely more than pure scenery—Sonny would give her that. And the horns and rhythm section were grooving, mixed in well at the board.

Walker looked as preposterous as Vada did hot. He had on an ugly flowered Day-Glo polyester shirt. His jeans legs were stuffed into his boots—exactly like the pig sloppers back home in Mingus did! Walker grinned sweetly at his woman as she sang her playful love song for him. She shimmied behind him to slink an arm around his chest as he accompanied her on a luscious golden Stratocaster, stacked Marshall amps powering the sound. They must be pulling in good bread to afford all this hot new gear.

They finished the song with a flourish of horns and loud hollers from the small crowd. Vada bowed and said into the mike, "Boys and girls, ya'll got to be moving along, so the Browns can get the place cleaned up for lunch." The crowd groaned in unison. "Now, now. If some sweet thing out there'll find this girl a beer, I'll talk my Babydoll into playing a couple more for you all by his own self."

The other Bees retreated as two burly college boys lifted Vada from off the stage. Another man handed her what was left of a pitcher that a waitress had missed at last call. Sonny checked out Walker watching her drinking straight from the pitcher, one brow raised, frowning. He relaxed when she blew him a kiss and mouthed love talk in his direction.

He then sat down with the gold Strat and pulled up a chair, positioning the mike. "I want to play a couple of new ones I put together for ya'll." Walker's voice sounded different—gone a half tone flatter or something. It was because his nose had been kinked by Floyd's knuckle, Sonny realized. "This first song's for my sweetheart, Vada." He smiled at her as she sat down at the foot of the stage. She gazed back at her man with eyes tender. "I call this *Smitten*."

Walker hunched over the guitar and began an instrumental. Hewn from deepest velvet, no rough edges, the song had a plush, Hendrix-inspired tone to it. It was a true love song—words weren't needed to understand that. All was there in the playing: attraction, foreplay, building passion, wild release, and the afterglow of spent lovers entwined. Sonny cocked his head like a terrier, listening. He was floored. Walker had something timeless here. Something completely real.

Everyone in the room gaped at him as he played it, breaths all but held. He finished with a sweet glissando and a featherweight touch to the whang bar, blowing a kiss to Vada. Then, before the audience could react, up he sprung, kicking his chair aside. He unplugged the Strat, tossing it to Vada, and grabbed Sonny's old Broadcaster from the stand. Without the mike, he yelled out, "Now Old Broad and me going to give ya'll some gas to get you on home. This here's *Lickety Split*." With a growl he tore into a triple-time sonic shuffle, working the fretboard with light speed. The crowd whistled and stomped, egging Walker on.

Sonny downed his whiskey, slamming the glass on the table and stumbling toward the stage to better watch Walker's work. He eyed the fingering, trying to get his messed-up mind around how the tune was being played. His little brother's swift hands made this mystery seem effortless.

Walker finished playing, then doffed his hat and bowed. His long hair and ugly shirt were soaked through with sweat. The people yelled for more, but he shook his head no, clutching at his heart and grinning. He hopped off the stage, grabbed Vada about the shoulders and kissed her. The crowd descended on them, showering praise.

Sonny hung back, watching the King and Queen Bee holding court. Vada gripped Walker's big hand, which was clutched about her middle, and leaned in against him. She'd never looked better. And, face it, his old Broadcaster sounded tops, too. Maybe it was those Marshall amps. Like hell. That damn Midas touch on the fretboard was the reason, and Sonny knew it solid.

Walker spotted Sonny. They had not talked or seen one another since the shit came down at Vada's folks'. Sonny saw Walker's eyes darken for a fraction of a second, but then he broke into a smile, waving. "Come here, bro."

Sonny made his way over. A few people backed off, looking at him with disdain. Still, some greeted him warmly, expressing their sadness at the Tornadoes' demise. Sonny listened to Walker and Vada make conversation with their fans until the Browns turned up the lights, signaling the time for outsiders to make tracks. Walker grabbed Sonny by the arm, leading him to where the rest of the band was packing up.

"How long you been out there, Sonny?" Walker asked, his voice friendly. "Would have asked you up to play your old guitar with me."

"Ain't you generous? I just walked in, right before you took the spotlight for yourself."

"Oh. You been working tonight with someone?"

"Yeah. Hard at work with Jack Daniels."

Vada sniffed at him. "That all? Smells like Mr. Daniels brought along a compadre or two."

Sonny narrowed his eyes at her. Wasn't she just holier than thou, these days. "That's right, sugar. Like you used to party. In groups."

"You watch your mouth, Sonny," Walker said, low and cool. He took a stand in front of his girl. Riley rose from his bass's case, eyeing the threesome.

"Seems she's rewriting her past, huh?" Sonny could hear himself slurring. He didn't care. "Isn't that right Bee—oh, that's right. It's Miss Vada now, ain't it?"

She put her hands on her hips, tossing her curls back. Peeking over Walker's shoulder, she said, "Yes, it is. Now you better hush, Sonny."

Sonny knew he should hush—him of all people. But he was ripped up inside by envy watching Walker play those songs. If he didn't spit it out, the poison of it might finish him. He sneered, "Ain't fair, you keeping that stuff all to yourself, Walker. Used to, if Miss Vada was around, we was all as good as laid."

"You asshole!" Walker jumped, knocking Sonny backward to the floor. Sonny was surprised but unhurt. Quick, he grabbed Walker around the throat and squeezed.

Vada started screaming curses at Sonny, yanking hard at his hair. Jesse James leaped into the fray, prying Sonny's hands from Walker's throat, pulling his guitarist free. Riley dragged Sonny to his feet, leaving Vada clutching a ragged fistful of dark locks.

Prince ran out from the kitchen, a Colt .45 pointed in the air. "Break it up now, ya'll know what's good for you."

Coughing and gasping, Walker croaked, "Get the fuck out of my sight!" Jesse James supported Walker by the arm, warily watching as he was gripped by another ragged coughing spell.

"Calm down . . . breathe deep. It doesn't matter what he thinks," Vada cooed, rubbing Walker's Adam's apple with her fingertips. To Riley, she said, "Sweetie, will you do us all a favor? Take Sonny outside to cool off."

Sonny violently shook Riley off him. The big bassist glared at him, clinching his fists. "Fuck off, Goode! I know my way out—played here tons before ya'll ever did." Sonny stalked toward the door. Prince even eyed him coldheartedly, his .45 still at the ready, as he stumbled passed.

Sonny stopped just shy of exiting, turning to yell, "Take it from a real pro, Squirt. You ain't so damn hot. What's all that flashy bullshit? It's like you're jerkin' off for all the world to see." With that, Sonny ran outside. He could hear Walker choking bad still, and Prince quizzing Riley in an angry voice. Sonny made it only as far as the front-porch steps before he tripped up. Catching himself on the banister, he collapsed in a heap. He pulled out a cigarette with shaking, furious hands and lit it. Sucking in the smoke and rubbing the sore spot on his scalp where Vada had torn out a clump of hair, he tried to simmer down.

Staring at his boots in the moonlight, Sonny soon became aware of someone standing over him. He glared up, lip raised in a snarl, expecting Prince or Riley there to shoo him off. Instead, watching him in the bright moonlight was a man he had never seen before.

Sure as shooting this was not the typical Sugar and Spicer. His face was tawny, with a long nose, a full mouth, and wide-set, dark eyes. He was tall, slim, but he possessed the shoulders of a Longhorn linebacker. He wore an impeccably tailored dark suit, a deep maroon shirt and tie, and a red carnation on his lapel. His top lip bore a pencil-thin mustache. Golden brown hair was cut short in back but piled high in curls on top of his head, Little Richard–esque. From his belt hung a satchel of maroon rawhide, decorated with a crucifix and more cryptic symbols.

"What you staring at, asshole?" Sonny snapped.

The stranger smiled back. Playing it cool. Gesturing toward the bar, he said, "You would be the older brother of the firebrand in there? Sonny Blaine, is it not?"

Sonny nodded, still pissed but now intrigued. The guy sounded strange. He was a Southern boy, all right, but his accent was not that of the Texas plains. Something was foreign in the way he used his words.

"Beg your pardon. I have you at a disadvantage. I am Bonnell Devereaux. Late of Thibodeaux, Louisiana."

That explained the accent, and the doodad hanging from his belt. It must be a mojo charm. The man was one of the exotic, perhaps dangerous, French creatures from east of the state line. "Thibodeaux?" Sonny echoed. "Ain't that where Guitar Slim's buried?"

"*Mais, oui!* I knew I was on the right track with you. I'm here in your lovely state capital to complete the lineup for my new band—a most stylish blues band, Mr. Blaine. I am a very big fan of your record, *Storm Cellar Blues.* Rumor has it the White Tornadoes are no more—a falling out, of sorts?"

"Of sorts, yeah." Even more curious now, Sonny was starting to enjoy this dandy.

"Well, perhaps it is for the best. You and the bass player, Johnny Lee Hogan . . . you had words?"

"No. It's cool between Johnny Lee and me. He's been playing around and doing a few sessions. But I don't think he's got with no one regular yet."

"And you, Mr. Blaine? What are you doing these days?"

"Call me Sonny." Sonny let out a groan, thinking over his recent résumé. "Well, truth is, I been getting fucked up and fighting lately."

Bonnell let out a hearty laugh, saying, "That's rich! Points for honesty, I guarantee. Maybe we soon change your fortunes, Sonny. For tonight, I think I need to carry you home."

Sonny grabbed the banister, pulling himself up. "Man, you don't have to carry me. I reckon I can walk as far as your car."

"That's what I meant. How do you say, I'll give you a lift." Sonny trailed Devereaux to a vintage Cadillac convertible, sparkling in the moonlight. The thing was fire-engine red, satin-brush finished, with a white tuck-and-roll leather interior.

Sonny could damn near hear a heavenly choir wailing as he took her in. This was the machine of every Texas boy's dream life. He whistled. "Some fucking car you got here."

"She is very nice," Bonnell agreed, unlocking the passenger-side door for him. "I find it a comfort in my business . . . the road, essentially, being my home, you see. When I went to Thibodeaux College, my parents bought me this as a gift. A bribe, to keep me in school." He did the pouting shrug that Sonny had seen French people do on TV. "Of course, they were hoping their only heir would be a lawyer." Bonnell positioned himself behind the wheel, the V-8 thrumming as he turned the key. "If I had to be an artist, they hoped I would write stories—tawdry still, but more respectable than playing music. You know, William Faulkner. Tennessee Williams."

Sonny believed he had heard those names back in school. He sank back into the fine leather seat, closing his eyes. "Your parents just gave you this Cadillac? Must be nice!"

"Oh, indeed it is. The Devereaux clan is aristocratic Louisiana—from France, by way of Haiti, generations ago. Now—where are we headed, Sonny?"

"Back toward town, toward the University."

Bonnell nodded, easing onto the dirt road toward the highway. Ride was smooth despite the ruts they drove over. Sonny thought he might fall asleep if he didn't keep talking, so he asked, "Ya'll are French, huh?"

"True Creole, actually. The Devereauxs once owned a monstrous cane plantation. Many of our kind lost their holdings during the War Between the States. But Great-Great-Granddaddy Devereaux held on to the family fortunes. Immoral dealings with the Yankee devils, so it is still said." Bonnell chuckled, pulling onto the highway. He opened up the engine and let the fine old automobile soar.

Feeling himself drifting, Sonny mumbled, "Are ya'll still farmers?"

Bonnell shot him a sharp glance. "No longer are we plantation owners. We were never . . . *farmers.*"

"No offense meant. Where I come from, we got the farmers and the ranchers, and pretty much the rest of us didn't have a pot to piss in. Here, make a right at the next light."

"Plantation owners were more like . . . overlords." Bonnell let out another cool laugh as he followed Sonny's directions into town. "Daddy sold the bulk of our land, after the Second World War. To developers, you see. We still have a grand home in Thibodeaux. Full of tasteful antiques, and a couple of retainers."

Sonny blinked. "What's a retainer?"

Bonnell laughed. "A servant, more or less. We only still have a butler and maid, both old as dirt. I think anymore *Maman* takes care of Maybelle and Antoine more than they do her and my father. But then Maybelle's people have worked for mine since before . . . well, since we owned her people."

Again, he shrugged. "We're probably distant cousins, somewhere along the line. Of course, my parents would cut out my tongue for even suggesting it. Maybelle was my nurse, when I was small. She sang to me, mostly in Creole . . . our language, a special sort of French. Lovely voice, she. And Antoine, a fine *accordioneer.* Played their records for me, too—wonderful zydeco, swamp blues, *la-la* waltzes."

"You're a singer, right?" Sonny guessed. Devereaux exactly looked the part—slick and stylish as they made them.

"I am. A songwriter, too. And I play keyboards. But I am known best for my accordion playing. I've built a fine reputation as such recently in Houston's Frenchtown."

"Left at the stop sign. I'm the corner house, there." As the Cadillac pulled to the curb, Sonny said, "So, no shit, you play accordion, too?"

"Piano-key, mostly. In Louisiana, accordion is much like guitar in Texas. All about dancing."

"I know. Those boys from across the Rio Grande can get a crowd going with them things, too."

"They can! My—well, I hope, *our*—drummer is from Juarez, in fact. You know Cesar Rodriguez?"

"Sure. Rimshot Rodriguez. Good damn percussionist." They stepped out of the car. Sonny had to take a second to get his footing. "Here's home, Bonnell. I can probably dig up a Lone Star in the fridge. And I know certain I got a bong hit, if you're a partyer."

"Occasionally, I'll indulge. And this is an occasion, *n'est-ce pas?*"

"I think so." Sonny managed to get his key in the lock on the second try. He watched Bonnell's eyes light up when he saw the crates of albums lying about the living room. "Go ahead and pick something out and put it on." Sonny looked in the fridge, and pulled out two beers. He handed one to the Louisianan and proceeded to load up the bong. "So . . . what're you going to call yourselves, man?"

Bonnell took a sip of beer. He held out a Jackie Brenston record, smiling. "I was thinking of calling us the Rocket 88s. What do you think, Sonny?"

Sonny held up the beer in salute, handing Bonnell the bong. "Badass car. I like it, man."

"*C'est bon!* I'm hoping you're interested in playing with us, and that Johnny Lee will be game, too. Then, as we say on the bayou, we can *lassiz le bon ton rouler!*" Bonnell sampled a delicate hit from the water pipe.

"Do what, man?"

Bonnell blew a string of three nearly perfect smoke rings before he answered. "*En Creole*, Sonny Blaine. As you Texans would say—let the good times roll!"

9.

"MAN, THIS IS WEIRD, coming downtown just to practice," Johnny Lee said, as he and Sonny dragged their gear from Johnny Lee's pickup. They were meeting Rimshot and Bonnell for their first rehearsal as the Rocket 88s. "Ain't this what barns, garages, and basements is for?"

"I'm with you. But as long as Bonnell's paying, who cares?" Sonny replied. They went through some rigmarole with the secretary of the studio, convincing her that the likes of them really did belong there. They weren't quite convinced themselves. Neither had ever practiced in a rented rehearsal space. Even when Sonny recorded with Terry Joe, the band had gone right into the studio. But Bonnell would not hear of practicing in Sonny's garage, as the Tornadoes always had. He said he needed air-conditioning. He also wanted the privacy of the studio, to keep the overly curious away until they were ready for performance.

Sonny wasn't sure what to make of Bonnell. He was a strange cat, no doubt about it. Maybe he just seemed that way because he was so different from anyone Sonny had known before—rich and French, for starters. Still, he was too formal about most everything. When they talked music, though, Sonny liked what Bonnell had to say.

Still, Sonny had tried to dig up background on the singer but couldn't find out much. He asked around town all week—had anyone heard of this guy? No one local had seen him play. Eddie was now living in Houston with his new wife, so Sonny had sent him sniffing around Frenchtown. Eddie had discovered that Bonnell was known in Frenchtown as a top-notch pianist as well as a great accordion player. There were other stories, too, having to do with why he'd left Louisiana in the first place. Apparently something terrible had gone down in Thibodeaux, but Eddie couldn't find out any real details. Bonnell was leafing through the paper, waiting beside a fine-looking upright piano when Johnny Lee and Sonny arrived for the rehearsal. He was not in a suit, as he had been the couple of other times Sonny had met up with him. He was still dressed nice, country club casual–like. Rimshot had on chinos and a Mexican wedding shirt, with real gold chains and tattoos everywhere. He was relaxing on the couch, drinking a vessel of coffee. Johnny Lee and Sonny looked each other over—they had on their usual grubby clothes. No wonder the receptionist had hesitated.

Sonny introduced the bassist to the other two, and they proceeded to set up. When they were done getting plugged in, Bonnell tossed his newspaper to the floor and squatted on the piano stool. Without a word he gave one flourishing glissando down the keys, like Mozart. He then walked his fingers into a complex rhythm line, bopping his head in time. Rimshot fell right in with a polyrhythmic beat straight out of the Quarter. Sonny walked over to the piano. He observed Bonnell's hands, his changes, and then came in behind him. Johnny Lee jumped in, too. They all worked together off Rimshot's time. It was fresh, this addition of swampiness, joined to Johnny Lee's familiar bass line. They jammed it awhile, Sonny taking the lead at one point, grooving into the big sound of the piano. By song's end, Johnny Lee and Sonny were both laughing and shaking Bonnell's hand. He seemed pleased with them, too.

Bonnell then strapped on his accordion, fifty-some pounds of instrument. He needed his broad shoulders to give the thing perch. It was a lovely old instrument, finished in deep mahogany and gold, its leather bellows black and supple. He filled her lungs with air, a somewhat noisy process. Ready, he counted down in French. He let it loose with a strong, dance-inducing lead line. Again he nodded at Sonny to jump in, and he did, working tenderfooted off the unfamiliar instrument. It was Clifton Chenier's *Aye Tee Fay*—Sonny knew it from a Daddy Jim 45. The progression was basically blues, but it had a rich twist from the accordion's breathy tone.

Sonny felt musically challenged for the first time in a long time, and it was mighty exciting.

During the first couple of rehearsals, the band started working up some covers to get a feel of each other. Then they tried on a couple of Bonnell's compositions. He wasn't bad as a writer—had a provocative sense of percussive rhythm, and a good, funny way with words. Sonny offered a tough instrumental that he'd come up with during hiatus, and they came together to structure a great arrangement for it.

Within days, the Rocket 88s' sound was gelling. They sure enough didn't sound like anyone else. What they had was truly a hot hybrid of Louisiana and West Texas.

Bonnell's cash flow certainly simplified things. He had a definite vision for how his Rockets needed to look—wanted it as different as their sound in order to stand out from the pack. He presented the idea of a makeover to Sonny and Johnny Lee. Johnny Lee jumped at the offer. He'd always craved style but never had much of the means to implement it. Plus, he was a bit tired of his headband-cinched Hendrix 'fro and love beads. Sonny was a little less enthusiastic at first. He was who he was, after all. A haircut and a change of clothes wouldn't alter that.

But the more he thought about it, the more he knew he was ready for something different. The new and exciting work even had him partying less. He needed to show Austin that he wasn't the same kid whose wandering dick had broken up the Tornadoes. He felt almost grown, truly ready for the big time.

Bonnell set to work. First came the expensive haircuts. The salon that Bonnell sent them to was a long way from the Mingus barbershop, longer still from Sonny's back-porch swing. In the last few years the only scissors his hair had seen belonged to Eddie's girl. She'd trim the bangs out of his eyes and lop split ends off the rest, sweeping the mess into the backyard. Sonny had been fond of his long black hair—as had the women. It had been real scary watching big clumps of it hitting the salon's floor. He didn't dare check in the mirror while the hairdresser chopped away.

Johnny Lee got done first. His 'fro was cropped down close to his skull. He looked dead soul-cat cool with that cut and his wraparound shades.

Encouraged, Sonny finally dared to look at himself. The stylist had it short-er on the sides and in back, but kind of long still on top. She'd combed it up high over his forehead, with just a little pomade. Sometimes a few longer pieces fell forward, just above his eyes, but in fact that made the 'do work even better on him. For a few days Sonny's neck felt naked and cold, but he grew used to the haircut quick enough. It was far easier to care for than his former tangle-prone mop.

Bonnell's makeover of the two scraggly rockers didn't end at the hair-line. He took them to a fancy-ass tailor, having them measured for custom suits, silk shirts, and ties. By now Sonny was quietly scandalized by Bonnell's cavalier attitude when it came to money. Besides picking up the rehearsal room bill—no small chunk of change in itself—the cat had spent more on one haircut and outfit than Sonny had spent in years on clothing alone. But Bonnell had made one thing clear to them all. He didn't mind investing his own bread to get the look and feel of the band where he want-ed it to be.

The timing for the Rockets' debut could not have been better. Rollie Matthews was trying to round up new talent for his Lone Star label in the wake of the White Tornadoes' demise. Though Rollie was unhappy about the Tornadoes disbanding, he knew only that Floyd had lost his battle with the draft board. Being a vet himself he couldn't squawk too much about that. Not knowing the sordid details, he held Sonny no ill will.

Sonny tried to convince him to sign the Rocket 88s sight unseen. Rollie was intrigued but not about to risk it. No one was sure where music was headed anymore, least of all him, he told Sonny. It was almost 1973—the hippies seemed a dying breed, the grotesque war was bound to be drawing to an end, and the president himself was in hot water. Who knew what might hit the ears of kids in these troubled times?

So instead of signing any one of the young bands, Rollie decided to do a sampler album of the Austin Sound, paying a fair flat rate per cut. Matthews wanted to dangle the different talents as bait to the college sta-tions. Before making promises, he could test drive and see what might hook the ears of the record buyers.

Rollie did extend Johnny Lee and Sonny the courtesy of including their new group, despite the fact no one had really seen the Rockets perform. The King Bees, Austin's reigning Best Band second year running, were of course included, along with three other groups. All would play a couple songs at an Austin Opry House show to send off the record.

The Rockets did their best to stir up a buzz. They had professional shots taken in their cool-dude treads and plastered them around town. Bonnell arranged gigs at a few exclusive private parties to get tongues wag-ging. The press even came calling to Sonny. But they didn't want to do a story on the Rockets—not directly, anyway. They wanted a feature on the

Blaine brothers with a duo interview and a photo shoot at the capitol. Walker had said no. The writer asked Sonny to talk him into it.

Like hell. He hadn't spoken to Walker since the night he choked him, and didn't plan to anytime soon.

A week before the big show, Sonny overslept and arrived late for rehearsal. He was afraid the others would be pissed, waiting on him to start. But no, they were hanging out on the sidewalk with Vada when Sonny walked up. Bonnell was kissing her wrist, laying on the lines thick and deep. Rimshot and Johnny Lee watched on, silly grins on their faces.

"Here is the man you're looking for, *chère*. Sonny, you have a most enchanting visitor."

Sonny nodded at Vada. She smiled sweetly at the other Rockets, taking Sonny's arm. "Thanks, boys. We'll just be a minute."

"Consider Sonny yours as long as needed, you." Bonnell crooned.

She waved and walked a few steps away, pulling Sonny with her. The other Rockets went into the rehearsal room. "I've been trying to get a hold of you."

"I'm hard to catch these days."

"I reckon so. I'll get right to the point. You and Walker need to do that story for the paper. The pictures, too."

"I already told them no."

Vada shook a fist in the air. "*Aye yi yi!* You're both so stubborn. You think everything's about you? All us bands got big things riding on this album and show. You two fools do make an interesting story. Swallow your pride. Do the damned publicity, like a real pro would."

Sonny had to admit she was right. This was about more than any family feud. He nodded, staring at the floor. "How about I do this story for you, Bee- . . . Vada, I mean? It'll show you I really am sorry for being an asshole that night. I really am glad you and Walker are doing good."

"Well, thanks, Sonny. And just check you out." Her eyes went wide. "A new band, a new look?" She reached up and smoothed a stray lock away from his forehead. "Great hair. Can see your gorgeous face all the better. You look something like a fine young Elvis." She smiled. "Better, if such a thing is possible."

"Thanks, sugar. You look mighty fine these days, yourself." He wasn't merely returning the compliment in kind. Vada looked sleek, her hair and nails done to perfection, the dress she wore sexy yet tasteful. She was a radiant diva, by far the best he'd ever seen her.

"What about Walker?" Sonny asked. "That reporter told me he wouldn't do the interview. Asshole wanted me to talk him into it, in fact."

"If you get your own self there, I promise I'll get *him* there."

Bonnell stuck his head out of the door. "Almost through, you? We're ready now."

Sonny nodded. Vada waved goodbye and sashayed away. They watched her go.

"*Mon Dieu!* Is that one of yours, Sonny? Or is she for the taking?"

"Never was mine in any real sense," Sonny replied. "And these days she's spoken for. Don't even waste your time."

SONNY WENT ALONE to the photo shoot, gig bag strapped over his shoulder. He wore one of his new suits, a tailored black double-breasted wool set off by matching forest-green shirt, tie and pocket handkerchief. He had freshly polished the custom boots from Uncle Charlie. His only jewelry was the emerald and silver stud in his ear. He had spent a good deal of time getting his hair combed perfectly.

Walker showed up, gig bag in one hand, other arm locked around Vada. He was decked out in the bolero hat and boots, and a red suede jacket with fringe on the arms and back. His outfit was finished off with purple velvet pants and a sort of tie-dyed wrap tunic, held closed by a heavy silver conch belt. Along with his peace symbol he had three fat new gold rings on his fingers and a large lightning bolt dangling from his left earlobe. His hair was tucked behind his ears but otherwise hung loose, extra wavy from the damp weather. He was sniffing a little, as if he had a mild cold.

They met up on the western steps outside the rotunda. The brothers sized each other up for a moment, Walker pulling Vada even closer to his side.

"Shake, boys," Vada muttered, smiling at Sonny. "Folks are watching."

They shook hands once, quickly. Walker stared hard at Sonny—not unfriendly, just inquisitive. After a few seconds, he said, "I heard you looked different these days. That's a right nice suit. But even though I'd heard tell, I couldn't believe you chopped your hair off until I saw it with my own eyes. Seemed like keeping it long was a matter of principle with you. Man, the way Daddy and you used to go at it about that. Now? I swear you really remind me of that picture of him with Mama from their wedding day."

"I know what you mean," Sonny said grudgingly. "Only you could realize how weird it sometimes is for me when I catch a glimpse of myself unexpected."

"That's a fact." Walker smiled a little, real warmth in it.

Sonny smirked back, looking Walker up and down. "But they sure ain't going to mistake you for Daddy, Walker. That's quite some getup. Where on earth did you find them britches?"

"Last time Papa went to Mexico, he bought a mariachi outfit for Walker," Vada explained. "I don't know what he was thinking."

"But I don't wear the little jacket that come with it," Walker hurried to add. "It's a bit much."

"Yeah. You wouldn't want to go overboard or nothing." Sonny laughed, eyeing the velvet pants stuffed into the red snakeskin boots. Vada grinned at Sonny, patting Walker's chest.

"Ya'll, let's get going, before the weather really dies," the photographer hollered from his position. "Let's get one of ya'll posing with your guitars on the steps, here."

Sonny pulled his Tele from the gig bag. Guided by the photographer, he took a spot, making sure the SONNY tooled onto his strap was visible. Walker joined him, sitting at his feet, arranging his new gold Strat and coppery diamondback-skin strap to best advantage.

"Cool strap, Walker," Sonny said, as the photographer positioned them both.

"Ain't it sweet?"

"So's the rest of your new gear—that gold Strat, those awesome Marshalls you was using last time I saw you. I know Vada's folks ain't that generous."

Walker waited for the photographer to walk back to his camera before saying, "Vada's got a little side business, man."

"Doing what?"

"Tell you later," Walker whispered. He eyed Sonny from beneath his hat, gesturing at the onlookers.

Most of the photos from the session were too static. The frost between Sonny and Walker was still in thaw, and it showed in the final shots. The one of them on the steps was the best of the batch and was used for the story. They weren't looking at each other or touching, just focused out at the camera. Sonny grinned with cool self-assurance, holding himself tall and proud. Walker's smile was warm and open, his Strat snuggled to his chest.

The session was cut somewhat short by a sudden burst of hard rain, hail, and lightning. Onlookers scattered. The photographer grabbed his gear and ran into the capitol. The brothers had already packed their gig bags, so they grabbed them up and hightailed it to Vada's Impala. Walker stripped down to his tunic, and Sonny rid himself of the suit coat. Vada had been the only one smart enough to wear a raincoat. She drove them over to East Sixth, where they mercifully found a parking spot in front of a favorite pool hall. They dashed inside. Hardly a soul was there. Vada charmed her way into ample bar towels and a pitcher of beer. They dried off some and toasted each other.

On the second pitcher, things started to feel almost normal between them. When Vada excused herself to the ladies' room, Sonny decided he had better swallow his pride. "I already told Vada I was sorry, man."

"She told me you had. I wouldn't be here if you hadn't."

"Couldn't say I'd blame you for that."

Walker reached out his hand to shake. Sonny took it. Walker smiled, but added, in a cool tone, "Just remember what I told you then. Treat her with respect. She'll be your sister-in-law sooner rather than later."

"Yeah? That's great news, Walker. Congratulations." Sonny pumped his hand again, and Walker seemed to relax a little more. "So . . . you ready to tell me how Vada's making this extra bread?"

Walker looked around to make sure no one was listening. "We're turning a little coke. Not a lot, just so's we can get our own blow for free, plus pay for a few extras."

Sonny didn't say anything right off. "Sounds risky, Squirt."

"Oh, we're real careful who we sell to. Just our buddies. Small time, you know? Vada's got some shirttail relative bringing it across the line, so we know our source real well. You know how hard it is to make anything gigging, especially with a big band like ours."

"True enough."

"We never had what we needed, even with both of us living rent-free. Vada's folks don't pay her—she just gets tips from waitressing. And we really want to get a place of our own, get married. We needed to save up some money somehow."

"It's not like turning a little weed, though. Ya'll get popped and it's a heap of trouble." Sonny glanced over his shoulder toward the ladies' room, making sure Vada was out of earshot. "Besides—and I don't mean no disrespect, here, I swear it—but back when, your fiancée could do a lot of blow. Ya'll probably ain't making enough to make it worth the risk."

"No, we got it covered." Walker held up his hand, showing Sonny his new rings. "See? I got me some folding money these days! Besides, the girl don't do any more than I do."

Sonny found no comfort in his brother's last remark. Walker was sniffing constantly, but now Sonny was certain it wasn't due to any cold he had. He bore dark half moons beneath his eyes and was skinnier than ever, besides.

It seemed probable to Sonny that Walker was keeping up with Vada rather than the other way around.

10.

SONNY AND JOHNNY LEE'S new look and new band caused quite a buzz at the Lone Star concert. The tribe all gathered round, shooting rapid-fire questions at them. They played it cool—were about the only cool ones in the house, in fact. Sonny and Johnny Lee had played the Juneteenth festival and some other larger venues on the White Tornadoes Southwestern swing, and Bonnell and Rimshot were seasoned pros, but for most of the bands the big hall was a new experience. All managed to keep their egos in check, avoiding pecking-order skirmishes by drawing straws to see who played in what order. The King Bees had come up third, with the Rocket 88s getting the challenging but choice show-closing spot.

The whiskey and tequila flowed a-plenty, and Vada made sure everyone who wanted to could take an E-ticket to what Sonny called the "bathroom party." A person would approach her and after some discussion would follow Vada into the john. Moments later, out they came with boundless energy and their own mighty case of sniffles.

Sonny finally approached Walker and Vada himself. "Ya'll are being about as discreet as a train wreck."

Walker and Vada exchanged a wild-eyed glance and burst into laughter. They were flying, that was plain. Walker said, clapping him on the back, "We all friends here. Why don't you come into my office? Join the party, bro."

Still uneasy, Sonny followed Walker into the backstage bathroom and locked the door behind him. Walker pulled a baggie from his boot, removing one of many little origami envelopes fashioned from slick magazine paper. He tapped out fat lines on the chrome counter and handed Sonny a tightly rolled dollar bill. "On the house. Get that glum look off your face, bro. You worry too much."

No question Vada was turning dynamite shit. Sonny did enough blow to feel like he was Ming the Merciless by the time the Rockets took the stage to close her out. Bonnell started with a fast boogie-woogie on the piano, Sonny backing him up with a ripe-toned line. Then they took off on an old French waltz, jumped up a tad. Sonny loved being back in the saddle, working off the smoky splash of the sauce piquant that Rimshot and Bonnell added in to his Texas guitar drawl.

The audience gave the Rockets the loudest, longest applause of the evening. They left the stage, as was the custom, before taking their encore. The backstage folks heaped praise, backslapping them. Walker approached Johnny Lee, his gold Strat in hand, muttering something. Johnny waved Sonny over. "Let's bring on the Squirt to do *Hideaway* with us."

"I don't know. . . ." Sonny said, turning to find Bonnell, and pointing at Walker's guitar. Bonnell nodded, giving Sonny a thumbs-up. Walker shot Sonny a hopeful-puppy face. He couldn't refuse. Grabbing Walker by the scruff of the neck, Sonny pulled him onstage with the Rockets.

The hall's walls and ceiling shimmied from the stomping and whistling that erupted when the crowd spotted Walker. Rimshot counted it down, Bonnell laid a groove on the 88s, and Sonny opened Freddie King's mini-symphony. He did the first "movement," and then handed it off to Walker. They passed the song back and forth, playing catch, neither missing a change or a beat. Sonny kept it rough and stripped, feet planted wide, guitar's neck tipped toward the heavens. Walker, hunched over his ax, cruised out a little further, slip-sliding 'round the fretboard, showing off for the crowd. Sonny was tickled by how well they could work the song together, no rehearsal whatsoever. Beneath all the showboating, Walker had mastered the art of grooving true along with others. He was generous, too, encouraging the crowd to clap along when he handed over the lead lines, beaming especially proud at his big brother's work.

Vada kissed Sonny on the cheek and Walker on the mouth as they came offstage. While the crowd still howled for more, Vada and Walker dragged Sonny out the door, pushing him into the Impala. "Ready for a road trip, Sonny?"

"Road trip? Where?"

"Mexico. Vada and I are going to get hitched tonight. You're our best man."

Before Sonny could protest, Walker was ripping out of the parking lot, headed for I-35 South. Vada snuggled into Walker's side, whispering saucy words that Sonny could catch only a whiff of. Growling, Walker pulled her in close.

Not so long ago Sonny would have thought Walker was crazy to marry her. But it was clear she was devoted to Walker, and he to her. The kid had been a damned hermit when he first arrived in Austin, hardly daring to look at the girls who were drawn to him by his playing. And it was likely that Walker only cheated on Nancy Ruth the one time, during that surprise ménage à trois after Sonny's birthday party. Word was Walker was as faithful to Vada as she was to him.

Still, those spooky vows, that better and worse for a lifetime mumbo jumbo, were outright mind-bending to Sonny. Watching Walker jump in at the tender age of nineteen, only four women under his belt . . . it bordered on insanity. Sonny wished he'd had time to at least host a bachelor party for the kid.

Sonny was dozing when they hit the border. With the rising sun, they crossed into the different world that was Nuevo Laredo. Mexico was bright in color but faded, too, and poorer than even Texas poor. After some driving through the dirt streets, by plaster and corrugated steel buildings, they located the Mexican equivalent of the justice of the peace. The old man's wife, still in her bathrobe, stood up for Vada as the second witness. When the couple solemnly said their vows, Walker placed his golden pinkie ring onto Vada's hand. The band slid loose around her finger.

The newlyweds had Sonny take a couple of snapshots with Vada's Brownie. The bathrobed witness snapped one of Sonny and Walker, Vada in between them. On they went to a dirt-floored cantina that Vada knew about. She ordered a round of mescal, conversing in her fluent if Texas-accented Spanish. The barkeep saluted the newlyweds and dashed off to get the booze.

"You're the best man. You got to do a toast," Walker told Sonny, holding up his shot glass in one hand, a scurvy-looking lime chunk in the other.

"God. Can I toast with something else besides that shit? Water, maybe? Hot tortillas? I'm partied out, man."

"You can't drink the water here, Sonny. It'll make you sick."

"This mescal's going to make me sick, too."

The few men already in the bar, mostly farmers and day laborers, chuckled. They had wasted no time checking out Vada's black-stockinged stems sprouting from her red silk mini. She smiled back at them, telling them in Spanish to lift their glasses, too.

"Okay, okay. To Walker and Vada Blaine! Let's see . . . how about, May you always make beautiful music together?" Sonny looked hard at the mescal, then took it with a squeeze of the awful lime. He forced his mind blank to tolerate the burn.

"Well, I think that's just about sappy enough," Walker said, coughing down his own shot.

"I get to kiss the bride, right?" Sonny said, trying to stifle a gag as the foul liquor wailed in his gut.

Walker raised his eyebrow. "I guess it's traditional. Don't ya'll get carried away." Under Walker's watchful eye they barely brushed lips. And then there were hot tortillas, a big cast-iron pot of beans floating with melted cheese, a bowl of butter, and another round of mescal. The breakfast was superb, and the liquor didn't taste as bad on the second go-round.

Sonny remembered dancing once with Vada to a sad sounding waltz on the jukebox. Later, he found himself a bargirl. It went from there somehow, only getting hazier. The next thing Sonny knew, he was waking up in a dingy whorehouse room. It was miserably stuffy. The curtains weren't doing much to keep it shady as they had rotted into nothing from the burning southern exposure. There was a squeaky brass bed and a toilet that ran constantly. The bargirl was long gone. Sonny was grateful to find his wallet still intact, with just a twenty missing—payment for services rendered no doubt.

He hoped he could find the car and the new Mr. and Mrs. Blaine. He wasn't wearing a watch, but through the window the sun looked like it was thinking of setting. He found them back in the cantina, which was located conveniently across the street from where Sonny had crashed. Walker and Vada had spent the day together in another room of the hotel/brothel.

"You ready for an even longer road trip, Sonny?"

"Hardly."

"Come on now. We was talking about going home to Mingus so the two Mrs. Blaines could meet at last."

"I sure wish I had a change of clothes," Vada said.

"Me, too," said Sonny. He had lost his tie, and felt slimy with his own drunken juices, as well as the prostitute's.

"You look fine, Sonny, even if your suit's a bit wrinkled. I just don't want your mama's first impression of me to be this little, tiny dress," Vada said, smoothing Sonny's lapels.

"Then I just better buy my new bride an outfit," Walker proclaimed, pulling her to her feet and kissing her. "Come on, Mrs. Blaine. Let's go find somewhere that's still open."

They found a *turista* shop. Vada selected a modest yellow sundress, the yoke embroidered with red stitching. She changed in the car while the boys waited outside, standing guard. Flirting, Vada showed the border guards their marriage certificate, and they crossed back into the First World with amazingly little hassle. Walker jumped onto U.S. 281 in San Antonio. Sonny fell asleep in the back seat, lulled by the motor and the border radio.

He woke up with a start. Disoriented, feeling as though he were dreaming, he realized they were parked in his boyhood driveway, next to Mama's Rambler. He sat upright, hearing her holler, "My stars. It's Walker Dale!" Walker was picking up Ruby and swinging her around, kissing her cheek. Vada stood watching their reunion with a nervous smile on her face, spinning her make-do wedding band.

"Baby boy, look at you! You're all growed up now. But ain't you skinny? Come on in here and I'll fix you something good to eat."

"Okay, Mama. But first, you got to meet my wife, Vada. Honey, this is my mama, Ruby Blaine."

"Mrs. Blaine, hello. I've heard so many nice things—"

"Walker Dale. Did you say your wife? Lordy!" Ruby reached over to lightly touch Vada's shoulder, as if trying to decide if the girl were a mirage. "Why didn't you let us know you was getting married?"

"Because it happened kind of sudden," Sonny answered, stepping from the car, stretching. "We just got back from a Mexican wedding."

"Sonny! Oh, Sugar-boy. I can't believe you're both here." She ran to hug him, nearly knocking him over. Then she pulled back, gaping at him in amazement. "Your long hair's all gone. My lord, don't you look just like your daddy at your age? You're so handsome." She gulped once, and then burst into tears.

"Be still, Mama. Let's go on in." Sonny pulled her to his side and walked toward the house.

Ruby reached to kiss his cheek, whispering, "What in blazes is your brother wearing?"

"Oh, he ain't too bad right now. You wouldn't believe the getups he finds these days."

"Goodness me." She rolled her eyes at Sonny, watching her other boy and new daughter-in-law climb the porch steps. "He's worse than those hippie kids, ain't he?"

They followed the couple into the house. "Now, Vada," Ruby said, hurrying toward the kitchen, "you just set yourself down and make yourself at home. I'm going to rustle us up some leftovers."

"Mrs. Blaine—"

"Ruby, honey. You're family now. Call me Ruby."

"Ruby, let me help."

"Certainly not. It's nothing fancy. I know I got a spot of baked beans and potato salad, and there's plenty of fried chicken, too. Sonny, be a dear and go see if you can't find some of the family picture albums for your new sister-in-law. And Walker Dale, I know you don't think nothing of keeping that hat on in honky-tonks, but you'll mind your manners in my house. Hang it up on the rack by the door, hear?"

"Yes, ma'am," he said meekly, winking at his bride. "Is . . . is Daddy due back soon?"

"No, son. He's in Lubbock, on a job." Sonny came back in with the photos, exchanging a relieved glance with his brother.

They visited, enjoying the food. The women looked at the albums together, with Vada begging for a few copies of the pictures for her new home. Finally, in the darkness of the early morning, Walker stood, stretching. "Mama, we got to hit the road."

"Walker Dale, it's too late for driving that awful highway tonight. You know how them truckers get. You two lovebirds go sleep in my room. I'll gladly take the couch."

"Mama, we can't stay. We got to go and tell Vada's folks about getting hitched, too," Walker said. Vada winced at Sonny—it was clear she didn't relish breaking the news to Lupe and Julio.

"Oh . . . of course. Maybe ya'll can come for the holidays. Try!"

"Maybe." Walker looked at Sonny. They both knew the holidays would mean Daddy at home.

"It's hard to get away that time of year for us, Mama. Lots of parties to play," Sonny said in way of a quick excuse. Ruby said nothing.

She ran to get Vada a sweater to wrap around the thin yellow dress, to keep the cooled night air at bay. The threesome headed out to the porch, the girls laughing and teasing Walker. Sonny stopped in the bathroom before they headed out. He was about to follow Walker and Vada when Ruby came back in. She caught his arm firmly, her expression serious. "You hang on. I got something belongs to you rightfully." She reached over, pulling a torn and yellowed envelope out of a drawer in the hallway table.

A birth announcement . . . for Otis Rush Montgomery Blaine. There was a birth date, just over a year previous. Sonny shuffled over and collapsed into his daddy's easy chair. Out of mind, that's how he kept the Montgomerys. Too painful to picture Floyd on some fucking battleship, involved in a war that was daily making less sense to anyone. Worse, even, was Nancy Ruth, carrying his burden inside. Ugly trouble, and no denying it was his doing.

His mama whispered harshly, "Nancy Ruth asked me to tell you. I hadn't wanted to, not over the phone. And I didn't think it right to mention in front of your brother. When I heard the gossip, I assumed she and Walker . . . but she said no, *you*." Ruby folded her arms, scowling down at him. "Son, what was you thinking?"

"I don't know, Mama."

"What, wouldn't she marry you?"

"Marry . . . me?" Despite himself, he let out a short laugh. "Mama, it just happened that one time. We wasn't an item or nothing."

Ruby almost instantly turned tomato-red. Startled, Sonny recognized that she was as outraged as he had ever seen her. "I reckon once was enough to get a son on her. You kids these days, your free love? Used to, a real man would stand by any girl he got in trouble. To think my own firstborn. . . . Billy Jay Blaine Junior, I'd be *ashamed*!"

Sonny tried not to cringe. He did, though, hanging his head. He mumbled, "Have you seen . . . it?"

" 'It'? By 'it,' do you mean your boy?" She said it in a tone to sting and shame, and the aim was true. "Nancy Ruth brings him to visit some. He's a sweet and beautiful child. A dead ringer for your baby pictures. I only wish I had a picture of Otis to show you."

Sonny was tremendously relieved that she didn't. He closed his eyes, trying not to see the boy in his mind. "Mama, she told me she was—well, you know." He couldn't even say it, not in front of Ruby. "I reckon with her gone, it just didn't feel real until right now."

Ruby was about to say more when Walker stuck his head in the door, grabbing his hat off the hook. "Can you believe I almost forgot this, Mama? Sonny? You look a little peaked. Ain't too tired to drive, I hope. Vada's in the backseat, already out. I just got to join her. Your turn at the wheel, this leg."

DATELINE, AUSTIN

The bands on this choice collection album show a real energy, cutting a wide, colorful swath through Texas blues tradition. All turned in good solid sets at the showcase concert, leaving me hungry for more.

   Among the standouts were two bands, respectively featuring a pair of guitar-slinging Texas brothers. Sonny and "Little" Walker Blaine hail from Mingus, a tiny town outside the Dallas/Fort Worth area. They joined forces to close the show with a duet duel on Freddie King's *Hideaway*. This was pure poetry to watch and hear.

Little Walker, amazingly proficient for his tender twenty-one years, is part of the King Bee Review. This is a fairly large band, fronted by a magnificent powerhouse of a vocalist known as "Bee-Stung" Vada Sanchez. The younger Blaine plays with compelling volume and tone, his style crammed full of flowing runs and lightning fast licks. He seems to dip into a bottomless well of high energy, inspired passion. He is truly an original, with ample agility and honest feeling in his playing. Remember, you heard it here first. Go see this kid!

The Rocket 88s are a solid foursome. They have a tight, playful sound, fronted by lead singer Bonnell Devereaux, a Louisiana-bred vocalist who gives the band a fat swampiness with his accordion and keyboards. The Rocket 88s' Sonny Blaine is a name of some renown already. Sonny made a guest appearance several years ago on "Cosmic Cowboy" Terry Joe McGowan's second album, and is also known in regional blues circles for cookin' with his former band, the White Tornadoes. Sonny is more in the mode of the old-style rhythm players. He drives his band's sound with an understated, precise delivery that illustrates a real mastery of his instrument. He is a sharp-looking cat, too, with a compelling stage presence.

Musician brothers tend to play in bands together, or at the very least, have groups with similar sounds. This is a way men form bonds, not unlike playing sports or fighting in war. Not so with the Blaine brothers. No question, they're clearly both electric bluesmen. However, they tap into vastly different pools spring-fed by the same Texas tradition.

Twenty-two-year-old Sonny Blaine has a style that conjures up the cold deadliness of a Texas panhandle ice storm. The younger Blaine's style evokes searing heat that seemingly only he can master, bringing to mind an Indian mystic walking the bed of burning coals.

—Lurlene Luqadeaux, *Texas Blues Quarterly*, 1973

RUBY CLIPPED THE article slowly and precisely with her pinking shears. She glued the newsprint into a scrapbook she'd started when the Dallas papers reviewed the Juneteenth festival the Tornadoes played awhile back. She closed the book and read the cover—SONNY'S MUSIC. She needed to add Walker Dale's name there, too. Hard to believe her baby was grown, married to his pretty girl singer, yet. What would Daddy Jim say to that?

How she missed her daddy, and her boys. Fighting back tears of loneliness, Ruby pushed herself up from the table. She shuffled over to the wall calendar—Big Billy not due back for three more empty days. If only the boys had a mind to stay and visit. She peered out the window to make sure no one was watching her. Grabbing a stool, she climbed it and reached behind the canned goods to retrieve her half-full whiskey bottle. She filled a jelly glass and took two long draws, emptying it.

Pouring a second, Ruby vowed to sip more slowly.

III ICE AND FIRE

1.

EYES SHAPED LIKE a feline's, the color of Spanish moss—that was Sonny's first impression of Cilla Mountbatton.

The Rockets were playing a packed club in Santa Monica. Sonny saw her working her way through the dancing crowd to the edge of the stage. She watched him with those unreal eyes. He grinned, thrusting his hip for her benefit as he played a mean solo run. She didn't smile back, as women were prone to when Sonny pulled this maneuver. Rather she studied his hands, kept her gaze fixed on his Telecaster.

Great balls of fire, was she something. A mane the color of raspberry honey, tumbled in layers about a swan neck. Her skin was golden, luminescent, and surprisingly freckle-free, partnered with that red hair. She was dressed in second-skin 501s and a green satin leotard. No jewelry, no make-up that was noticeable, either. Petite, but with generous hips and breasts set off by an unusually tiny waist. Even if the rest of her had been unremarkable, her legs would have whet Sonny's appetite—lean and solid, with a perfect arch where her thighs became her groin.

Sonny craved this one, wanted to explore that delicate arch of hers, closer than close. He was sidetracked by an interview. But luck turned out to be with him. When people filtered backstage, he spotted the girl standing alone, looking his way. He smiled, motioning her over. She nodded hesitantly, scouting the other faces in the room before she came.

"Icestorm Blaine?" she asked. Sonny nodded. She had a slight accent. English, maybe? Not the ugly British Invasion twang, though. High tone, upper crust—like a princess. "I have your White Tornadoes album, and just bought your new one," she continued. "It's wonderful to finally see you play live."

"Well, thanks. Call me Sonny, will you?" He tried his best to annunciate. Today had been one long party. "And what's your name, sugar?"

"It's Cilla." He extended his hand to her. Her grasp was delicately boned with long, slender fingers. When she tried to turn loose, he held on. She frowned at his grip, continuing in a businesslike tone. "I'm quite interested in your technique . . . Sonny. You have a really clean, honest sound. I especially like that thing you do somewhere in between a bend and a vibrato." She jerked free, miming a chord pattern, rocking it right-handed in the air.

"That's a good description of that thing I do, all right. You must play a little, Cilla."

She smiled slightly, dropping her chin and gazing up at him beneath her bangs. "Just for the last couple of years. I'm beginning to move beyond the basics, though. Working on my style."

"Your style. Ain't that sweet." He slid his eyes down her as he spoke.

She paused and folded her arms across her breasts. "Anyway, I was wondering about your approach to playing. How did you develop your sound?"

"Just by playing a whole lot, fooling with gear until I found what I dug. Been at it since I was a boy, sugar."

"I see. I practice a great deal," she said. "I'm fortunate to have a pretty wide selection of gear available to me." Drag. That meant she likely had a guitar picker boyfriend. "Things are starting to come together for me—"

He slithered his arm around her waist, whispering in her ear, "Stay with me tonight. We'll talk more about playing and coming together."

Cilla stiffened. She pushed him off, her pretty face twisted in disgust. "Mr. Blaine, I wanted to discuss your music. Nothing else."

Sonny snatched up her hand again so she couldn't slip away. She gaped at the big paw enveloping her own. Her eyes grabbed his, flashing fury. He still couldn't seem to turn her loose. He tried to sound harmless, saying, "Don't be mad. We can talk about music all you want. But let's go somewhere quiet, just you and me—"

"Is there a problem here, Priscilla?" said a stern British accent behind Sonny. Cilla looked over Sonny's shoulder, her face awash in relief.

Sonny spun irritably toward the voice. He was going to tell the intruder to bug off. Instead he was dumbstruck. There stood Reg Mountbatton. *Little Lord* Mountbatton. Sonny dropped Cilla's hand, forgetting about her.

Here in the flesh was the undisputed High Lord of British Blues. He'd been a founding father, playing blues when even Brian Jones had yet to delve into the stuff. Alongside John Mayall, Mountbatton had poured the soulful foundation from which the British had conquered the world. One of the first solos Sonny busted open his finger blisters to had been from Mountbatton's first Royals record. Damned if he didn't look just like he did on Walker's Thunderclap album covers: skinny, with piercing green eyes behind little Lennon glasses, a thick Napoleon cap of brown hair, and deep olive skin. He was shorter than Sonny had imagined, though. No bigger than Walker, really.

"Mr. Mountbatton?" The man himself nodded, showing an uneasy smile. Sonny laughed nervously, extending his hand. "An honor to have you in the house. Thanks for coming, man."

"Please, call me Reg," said Mountbatton, firmly shaking the offered hand. "Your Rockets played a fine set. My daughter Priscilla is quite an admirer of yours. It was she who insisted we come."

His daughter! So she was royalty, after all—a British blues princess.

Sonny remembered the high points of the story of Reg Mountbatton. Reg himself was said to be the son of a black Mississippi GI. Story was his daddy never married his mama, and left her with child to fend for herself after the Big War ended. This daughter of Reg's was got on a flame-haired Irish model at the dawn of his music career. When her mama abandoned Cilla at birth, Reg claimed her for his own. Sonny never heard tell how pretty she was, though. He hadn't known she played guitar, either. Seemed he did remember reading she'd studied dance here in L.A. That would explain those exceptional legs of hers.

"Your daughter and I were just talking about music. I saw her watching us play." Sonny looked Cilla's way, now embarrassed by his attempted pick-up. She had to be just a kid. Sixteen, at the most. Her lips were pursed, her green eyes cool and narrowed.

"She's quite taken with the guitar," Reg said with obvious pride.

"A family tradition?" Sonny offered.

"Perhaps. But she's left-handed. Technique is nothing like mine."

"I started by playing Dad's instruments alone at home, teaching myself, Mr. Blaine. I wasn't aware when I began that guitars could be restrung for lefties."

"Oh. You play upside down, like Dick Dale and Albert King?"

"She does, indeed—and very well. Not that I'm a doting father." Reg smiled warmly at Cilla, placing a hand on her shoulder. "She shows great promise. But it's very late now, my dear. We should be leaving."

"You're right, Dad." She nodded curtly at Sonny. "I very much enjoyed your show. Thanks for taking the time to talk with me."

"I . . . my pleasure, Cilla. Thanks for coming, ya'll." Sonny watched them go, not knowing quite what to make of this Little Lady Mountbatton. Despite several people stopping to chat with her famous daddy, she never gave Sonny a second glance.

Her loss. He hated talking shop anyway. Started back when he was learning himself, with Walker always hanging around, asking endless questions. *How you do that bend thing and nail the notes true, bro? What you doing to get that there tone, Sonny?* Go figure it out your own damn self, Sonny used to scold. You teach yourself, if you got what it takes.

But a chick trying to pick up on his thing? Pretty weird. Never before had he thought of talking playing with a female. With rare exceptions, women sang, maybe played keyboards. A few strummed along with their love songs. Never had Sonny figured a girl for doing like Albert King.

Until Mountbatton walked up, Sonny had dismissed what Cilla was asking about playing. He'd been thinking other things. He winced. Probably still jailbait in California. Still, she did *not* look her age. How was he supposed to know? This was a nightclub, not a kiddy concert. Her daddy must have gotten permission to bring her in tonight. Sonny hoped she wouldn't mention his come-on to the Little Lord. He grinned, thinking of how nuts Walker would go when he was told about this chance encounter.

Cilla sure enough was heavenly to look on. Seemed smart enough, too. Down the line when she had grown up a little, Sonny might meet her again, take another shot.

"Hello, Icestorm," said a fine thing, reaching an arm around his shoulders. "You look like you need some company." This one was a typical blues babe—couldn't care less for guitar talk.

"Sure do, sugar," Sonny told her. He pushed Priscilla Mountbatton to the back of his mind.

2.

CENTRAL GEORGIA IN summertime is blistering and smells like swamp gas. The King Bee Review was performing at a little club in Atlanta. They were on their first tour outside Texas, promoting their first Lone Star Records release. It was about an hour before they should take the stage. Jesse James Goddard and Really Riley Goode were in an alley off the kitchen. Both sucked on cigarettes, trying to psyche up for another go. They leaned wearily against the sooty brick wall, sweating dank rivulets. The drummer and bassist listened as Vada screamed at Walker, the sound of her plain through an alley-side window.

"She's really going apeshit," Jesse James whispered. "What he do this time?"

"Does it matter?" the bassist said. "No doubt some girl's involved."

"I'm your wife, damn you," Vada cried shrilly. "You treat me with respect!"

"Honey, you know I got to make nice with the fans. She wasn't nothing, baby. We was just talking music."

Jesse James and Riley nodded at each other. "See? Here they go again," muttered Riley.

"Nice, you call that shit?" Vada snarled. "You really need to feel up her thigh to talk about music, Walker?"

"It don't never hurt," Riley whispered to Jesse, and they dissolved into muffled snickering.

"Now, it wasn't like that, honey," Walker protested, with his best make-nice tone.

"Don't tell me what I did or did not see. I slapped your hand right off of her *panoche!*"

Walker's voice was growing edgier. "So, fine. I'm damn sorry. Want to talk about you and your bucks?"

"Don't start, Walker."

"Problem is, where to start, woman? The biker bucks? The two dudes in Memphis, feeling you up between them at the bar?"

"Oh, here we go with Memphis again."

"You started this, Vada. We both know if I hadn't walked in, they would have been taking turns screwing you in about two seconds."

"*Pendejo!*" Vada screeched, accompanied by the sound of skin smacking skin. She broke into hoarse sobs.

"Uh-oh. Should we go in there, Riley?" Jesse James asked, not wanting to in the least.

"One of them will be out soon," Riley predicted.

And Walker was, right after. His face was twisted with fury, and a red slap and claw marks showed vivid on his cheek.

"You okay, man?" Riley asked.

Walker mimed for a cigarette, and Jesse James gave him one. "No. She's lucky she's okay." His hands were shaking as he lit the smoke. "Leastwise, I didn't deck her. Came real close, though." He touched his slapped cheek. His fingers came away wet. "Fuck, am I bleeding?"

"A little bit." Riley handed him a handkerchief.

"I don't know what to do with that woman," Walker said miserably, pressing the handkerchief to his wound. He took a long draw off the smoke, muttering, "She's gone nuts on this tour. Can't even take a piss to suit her."

He threw the bloody cloth back at Riley. Reaching down into his boot, Walker pulled out a black-velvet pouch. From inside, he retrieved a vial full of cocaine. With a tiny spoon that hung from a chain around his neck, he scooped a shot to his nose.

Riley glanced around, making sure no one was watching them. "Be cool with that shit, Walker."

Walker did another spoonful, eyes closed. He paid no mind to the fact that they might have an unwanted audience. "Sorry, Real. Where's my damn manners?" He passed around the cocaine to his rhythm section. "Man, everything's unraveling, ain't it?" Walker grumbled, rubbing his eyes. "Lost our pianist in Charlotte. I think Mikey and Ikey are fed up, too. Ya'll ain't thinking of bailing on us, are you?"

"No way, Walker," Jesse James said, taking the spoon. "Man, I speak for both Riley and me when I say we been real spoiled backing you."

"That's the truth, brother," Riley agreed. "No one else be nearly as fun to play behind."

"Well, thanks, boys," Walker answered, managing a smile. "The feeling's mutual."

"But, Walker?" Riley went on. "We're worried about ya'll. You and Vada got to stop this before ya'll kill each other."

Walker nodded, blowing smoke signals into the fetid air. The three bandmates stood, shifting restlessly, listening to the sobs coming from the window. "Here, let me have that toot back," Walker said, taking the vial from Riley. He whispered, "I better go act lovey-dovey to the old lady. Pour her a shot and give her some nose candy. We got, what, an hour to go before the show? Give her time to get primed."

The two remaining men lit another cigarette. Both tried to act like they weren't eavesdropping. Walker's voice wafted from the window. "Vada? Honey, I'm sorry I got ugly."

"Babydoll, I'm the one who's sorry. I don't know what makes me so bitchy. Oh, just look what I did to your face. Does it hurt bad?"

"It's okay, honey. Just do this up and you'll feel better right quick." All was quiet for a moment. "You look better already, girl. So damn pretty, ain't you? Come here. You're my wife, the only woman that matters. I love you, Vada."

"God knows I love you, too, Walker."

DARK ALREADY. Walker loped back toward East Sixth Street, alongside the viaduct. He was carrying his hat in one hand, shaking out his wet, Herbal Essence–scented hair. Best it was dry before he saw his wife. Under this clear Texas sky, Walker couldn't well claim he got caught in a cloudburst. Oh, well, better to smell like shampoo than reek of another girl, he reckoned. He might be able to work up some lie if Vada noticed the strange shampoo smell. He wished he had a flask on him, a little liquid courage. Or a little blow, maybe, to lighten his shame, to help him think. Straight, he didn't know if he could dream up a good excuse. He had to be careful here in town, no matter how tempting the offer. Talk spread like wildfire. Austin was not the same as the road. There you could literally cum and go.

He had begged the girl, Lily, to keep quiet. He hoped she would. He had told her that Vada would not hesitate to attack her, to be ready for a knockdown chick fight if she uttered a word. Vada would do it, too, and come at him with her claws ready, as well. His wife wasn't about to let him make a fool of her.

Earlier Walker had been in to case the new club. The vibe of the place felt good and bluesy. He took pride in the fact it would be the first club in Austin that he would gig before Sonny did. Granted, that was probably due to the fact the Rocket 88s had been on the road more than home in the last year. They were pushing their new album ...*And the Noises They Make*. Things were really starting to take off for Sonny's band.

Walker missed his brother, especially the day-to-day stuff. He liked to hang out with Sonny and get wasted, watch a ball game, maybe play pool. All the same, it had been a long time since he had been in Austin without Sonny around. Felt pretty damn good. He thought back to that first time when he was in town without his brother, when Sonny toured with the Tornadoes. That was when the Bees had really started to build their following. That was when he and Vada had fallen deeply in love, too.

Walker smiled, remembering. Things had been so new and exciting between them then, him learning all Vada's wily ways. Nancy Ruth had introduced him to sex. It had been fun with her, sure, but they'd both been pretty ignorant about things. Always they had to rush, scared of getting caught together. Vada, she taught him the art of soulful lovemaking. They could take it easy up in Walker's Sugar and Spice room, with no worry of interruption. Walker learned the rewards to be had by taking his time. He mastered other uses for his hands besides frantic fretting, learned mouth moves far beyond simple soul kisses. Vada gave him the subtleties, the skills to thrill. She had brought out in his loving what she called his poetry. "Can't be had if you don't got it, but can surely be trained if you do," she'd croon in his ear. "And you my A+ pupil, Babydoll!"

In return she had his unconditional, faithful devotion. Except for some early pangs over her former dalliance with Sonny, he had not cared a lick about Vada's past. It was just that—in the past. What they had together was the now and the future.

Plus, these days, the King Bee Review did all right for themselves. They were fresh off a tour supporting their first album, *Wild, Wild Young Men*. The record was doing well in Austin. They sold a lot at the gigs around the country, too. The tour had been no glamorous affair—fifty mostly second-rate cities in three months. All brutal bus travel, too, on a frail leased beast with incontinent air-conditioning.

The tour had taken a lot out of everything and everybody. But Walker's marriage had been hardest hit.

Walker was not sure why things had gotten so rough between them. Secretly, he wondered if she was jealous of the attention that he was getting. Lone Star Records was heavily promoting his contributions to their sound. On the album cover they had him front and center, standing on the Sugar and Spice's antique bar, holding a scantily clad Vada more or less as he would his ax. The other Bees were seated, flanking them, striking hipster poses.

The back cover had a portion of the *Texas Blues Quarterly* review of the Capitol Blues show, highlighting Sonny's and his duet on *Hideaway*. This was the very column that had graced the Blaine boys with their new stage names, Icestorm and Firewalker. The article was superimposed over a performance picture of Vada watching him going after it on Old Broad.

"After all, I'm just the pretty singer, not the person who masterminded this outfit," Vada would gripe. Rightly so, too—the Bees were her brainchild. Guiltily, Walker was having trouble with that very fact. He was getting bored with their big soul sound. He was ready to fly, strike out with his own sound, and let loose the rich tone haunting his mind. Perhaps his wife sensed his restlessness.

Whatever the cause, they had hit an ugly wall out on the road. The crowds dug Vada and all. She had a big beautiful voice, an earthy delivery—why not like her? Walker saw, however, that the die-hard guitar heads were becoming the core of their audience. And what press they attracted focused more on his playing and her good looks.

Then there was the constant battle against lack of sleep. Often the motels they roomed in were noisy dumps. At times the couple just stayed up and partied all night, hoping to doze on the bus ride to the next gig. But rarely was it cool or quiet enough to sleep onboard the beast. This led to exhaustion, short tempers, and bitter battles.

The real nastiness began suddenly, though. Vada was a shrew that day, about to go on the rag, she said. Her throat was raw, too. She was sipping slippery elm tea spiked with his whiskey, trying to gear up for the show. She kept bitching about how her costume looked on her while raking a brush through her hair.

Sure enough, her dress had been snugger than usual, but that was fine. Vada was so slender that a few extra pounds looked good on her. Most of the time she was too thin for Walker's tastes. He was always needling her to eat something. Looked lean and fine on his arm, maybe, but she sometimes felt bony and fragile when he held her close.

"Vada, calm down. There just more of you to love right now, you fine thing." Walker said it off-handedly, concentrating on carefully shaving around his soul patch. He had heard Big Billy Jay say the like often to Ruby. His mama had always handled it like a teasing compliment. Not so his lovely wife. No, siree.

Vada threw the brush to the floor. The clatter caused Walker to jump, nicking his chin. He swore and stuck a piece of toilet paper over the bleeding spot on his face. He turned to Vada to find her shaking, glaring at him.

"So I'm too fat for you, Walker? I hit twenty-five and blow up, is that what you mean?"

"I didn't say that. I said you look sexy."

"You said more of me. You know us Mexican girls, huge by thirty."

He put down the razor, wiping his face with a towel. "Vada, that ain't always so. Why, just look at your mama."

"Now you're saying I look like Mama?"

"Yeah, you look like her, lucky girl. She's damn gorgeous."

"Sure, for a woman in her forties. Sick of this older-woman thing, Walker?"

Walker was climbing a tower made of glass, void of purchase. "Honey, all I mean by that remark is that she's slim."

"You said I was old and fat."

He finally lost his temper and yelled back, "I did not say that, woman!"

Cursing quietly in Spanish, Vada started rummaging through her purse until she came up with her razor and stash. She violently cut up lines on a makeup mirror. She bent to inhale, her hair billowing in front of her. Sniffing, she offered her husband the last line. He took it, trying to make eye contact and look regretful. "Now be a good boy and pour me a drink," she grumbled. "Show me you don't think I'm mean as well as old and fat."

She'd gotten revenge that night at their show. Vada had been far more predatory than usual, practically doing a striptease during their performance. Walker normally was not bothered by her stage antics, as it was part of the job and part of her charm. But she was pushing it, finally down in the crowd, dirty dancing with a bunch of badasses. She watched his reaction, a smug smile on her heaven-sent lips. At that point Walker hadn't slept for about thirty-six hours. Exhausted rage filled his head as he decided that two could play at this game.

So he pulled out his seductive moves. He played it part Hendrix, part good ol' Lone Star stud. He mouthed the guitar, threw it to the floor, kneeling over it. He ministered to his Strat, cooing dirty love talk to her. Making the ax groan strangely, he ran his hand over the curves, meeting every woman's eye, his grin assuring satisfaction. He had them lapping it right up out of his big old paws. Vada loathed it. At the end of the night neither of them were speaking to each other. Both left the bar with someone else.

And so it went, with several improvs layered on their main vile riff. Sometimes they reconciled before the show ended, making out and whispering apologies between sets. Other times they would fight it out in the middle of the bar after their gig. They would howl curses at one another, showing off their by now reluctant conquests as they might a piece of fancy new jewelry.

A couple of times they had even been separated for the entire night, with one or the other staggering to the bus shortly before takeoff time. Once Vada had let a guy on a Harley drop her off at the bus, making a point to note Walker was paying full attention before she smooched her stud with that mouth of hers. Walker had not said a word to her during that day's road trip, but after the show that evening he stayed out the entire night. He'd come back, sans shower, purposefully ripe with the stink of another woman. The next day on the bus, Vada made some ugly remark. Back Walker came at her, saying vicious shit loud enough for their entire posse to overhear.

She totally lost it. Right there on the bus, in front of their band, she started sobbing and gagging—looking like he'd busted her heart into a million pieces. Walker felt like a world-class dawg then. Watching her retch into a plastic bag across the aisle, he realized she was bad sick. He'd made it worse by stinging her with his meanness. He tried to make up to her. After the grueling bus trip, he carried her into their motel room, bathed her, and put her to bed. Then he showered his own body with near scalding water, trying to wash away his guilt along with the scent of last night's fun. Dropping his towel, he sat naked beside the bed, pulling the Strat into his lap. He played *Smitten*, his song to her. He wanted to use the melody as a healing balm. She was trembling with silent weeping when he finished.

"Vada," he said, putting the guitar on the floor and taking her hand. "My sweet wife. I play that song for everyone, but it ain't meant for them. It's yours, Honey. I been acting stupid lately, but it don't mean nothing. I'm all yours, too. I promise." He took her in his arms. She felt weak as a sparrow. They both finally fell into a death sleep together.

Vada stayed ill for the next week or so, fevered and chilled, barfing violently on and off. Whatever she had seemed to make her period extremely heavy—Walker had to keep buying her Kotex and Midol in the night. It scared Walker, but she resolutely refused to see a doctor. She'd only gotten through the shows on sheer will and cocaine, lying down wherever she could find a spot between sets.

When she was finally well enough, Walker was happy to give her his ardent lovemaking. Seemed like they were cool. Then it came again, blindsiding him. Some mysterious deal upset Vada and she flipped out on him, and he struck back. Away they went, repeating the ugly unfaithfulness.

He hoped the marriage would right itself now that they were back home. Just now, things were sweet at their little house on the south side. Vada was being a doting wife—sexy as ever in the sack, driving him crazy, as he did her. Only problem right now was that they were real slim on both stash and cash. Well, this new gig would pay a little and Vada's cousin was supposed to have a new shipment of blow tonight. Walker couldn't recall if they were paid up with him or not. He'd front them anyway, most likely. Vada kept track of all that stuff—she was the one who dealt with the finances now. God knows she was a lot better at it. When Vada took care of such business, they got no threats of his fingers being smashed, or of her face being slashed.

The Bees were fast reclaiming their schedule around town. With Sonny gone, Walker could be top gunslinger. Not like he wasn't proud of Sonny's success. His big brother had earned every bit of it. But it was still okay that he was not *here*. Nice not to have Mr. Been There and Done That personified looming over them all. When Sonny was around, Walker always felt a little outclassed. *Man, I know you know who Walker Blaine is. Sonny's ugly kid brother? He's the dude wears all that flashy-trashy shit, plays them crazy-ass solos? Leastwise, you'd know his wife—we all had some of her back in the day.*

Walker shook his head slightly as he walked along, to rid his mind of visions of Vada with her other men. She was his. She meant everything to him. He had taken vows with her that he believed in. So why had he broken them so many times of late? He knew he better work harder to be a better husband. This wanderlust that gripped him was like smoking cigarettes or doing lines. He never noticed he was missing nothing when he stayed true. But once he started browsing, he couldn't seem to break the habit.

Like today. Just like a hungry stray, he'd followed that Lily girl home.

Couple hours past, up this little brunette Yankee had waltzed bold as brass, flirting hard as he checked out the bar. "Tell me somethin', Mr. Firewalkuh. Is your marriage one of them modern opun thangs?" She had asked this of him right quick, teasing him by mimicking his accent.

Lily had told him she was a coed newly arrived from Missouri. She'd asked to see his hands, of all things. Feeling a little self-conscious about his prominent veins and tendons on the knuckle-side, he held them out to her palm up. She puckered her lips, circling a finger on his left like she was telling his fortune. He'd fancied the feel of it to the point of arousal.

Then she'd said, dropping the fake accent, "I've been trying to imagine what these great big, talented hands of yours feel like. Hmm. Looks like your wife's not here right now. Why not come over to my place for a while?"

He'd tried not to, saying, "I really should start getting set up, darlin'."

"But I only live a few blocks away. We could go listen to some records together . . . or whatever."

Where had Vada said she was going anyway? Stopping by her folks? Walker sped up his pace, hoping he would still get back to the club before she arrived so he wouldn't have to explain a thing. In spite of himself, he thought again of Lily, her smile that was a gilded invitation. He'd told himself it would be fun listening to a few of her records. Maybe they could make out a little bit—no drastic sinning. Walker paused in his tracks to cup his hand around his lighter, firing up a cigarette. Yeah, right. He hadn't been at Lily's house twenty minutes before he was hard at work between her eager thighs.

Really Riley had seen him leave the club with the college girl. Walker could depend on his bassist to play dumb should Vada beat him back there. But it wasn't fair to put the boys in the middle of Vada's and his shit. It was even more of a reason for Walker to straighten out.

Walker saw a police cruiser's lights once he stepped onto East Sixth. Cops usually didn't park here until the wee hours, when they were trolling for drunk drivers. With growing panic, he realized they were outside the club the Bees were playing tonight. Then he saw his bassist talking to one of the cops. Really Riley caught Walker's eye with a warning glance as he approached.

Walker was clean, not a thing on him for once. Why sweat it? "Hey, Real. . . . Officer. What's going down?"

"Are you Walker Blaine?" the cop asked.

"Yes, sir. What can I do for you?" He smiled a bit nervously. "Free tickets for our boys in blue?"

The cop didn't begin to crack a smile. "Your wife has been arrested on suspicion of dealing narcotics."

Walker felt like he had been knocked upside the head with a hammer. "No . . . that can't be. Where's Vada? Where you got her?"

"She's been taken in for booking. We've already searched your vehicle with her permission. It appears to be clean. You can either ride with us or drive yourself. We'll have some questions for you at the station, but I think we're done here."

"Man, I can't believe this. We're suppose to play here tonight," Walker told him, pointing toward the bar. "I got to take care of some band business here first, Officer. Then I'll be right behind you. Please let my wife know." The cop shrugged. He told Walker exactly where to report for questioning and headed toward his patrol car.

Walker grabbed Riley's arm, pulling him into the bar. They went over by the stage out of earshot of everyone. Walker whispered, "What the fuck happened here, Real?"

"I don't know for sure, man. Vada came in not too long after you left. We had a drink, then we started to get stuff ready for tonight. Little while later, this dude comes up to her. I knew I never saw him before, but he's saying he was a friend of somebody's, and did she have something for him? She said yeah, but let's go outside. Didn't think nothing of it. But next thing I knew, I heard a commotion outside. When I looked out, the cops are dragging Vada away. She's yelling for me to get a hold of you, but shit, I don't know who that babe is you left with." Riley shrugged, frowning down at Walker. "Boss, I didn't have a clue where to start looking for you."

"It's okay, Real. Ain't your fault."

"You ain't holding, are you?"

"No, I ain't holding," Walker replied. "There's not a thing at home either, if they decide to search us there. Vada had all we had left. Even that wasn't much, less than a gram."

"That's good, leastwise. Less they have on her, the better."

"True. And we always do our weighing and packaging at her cousin's, so we don't have all that incriminating shit around, either." Walker rubbed his soul patch, scowling. "Suppose they're onto her cousin's ass, too? That'd be fucked—he's in deep, man. I reckon I better get a hold of him, let him know what's going down."

"I'd only call him from a pay phone. Not the one here, either. Stop at a 7–11 or something. And don't say nothing to them cops—it's your right not to. Act like you don't know jack about any of it, man."

"Yeah. Good thinking." Walker dropped onto the edge on the stage, woefully looking at Riley. "Shit, Real."

Riley reached out and squeezed Walker's shoulder. "What you going to do, Boss?"

"I don't know. Guess I'll call Vada's cousin and then head on down to the station. Once I see what we got to do, call Uncle Charlie and Rollie Matthews, and see if they can't help us out. We don't got no bread for lawyers and shit, that's for sure."

He pulled Riley onstage, up behind Jesse James's kit. Making sure no eyes were upon them, Walker swiftly pulled the velvet pouch out of his boot and tucked it inside the bass drum. He also pulled the tiny spoon on the chain from around his neck and placed it alongside the bag. "There ain't nothing in there, but I don't want it on me if they pat me down at the station. Wouldn't be cool."

"True. I'll take care of it for you. What about the show tonight, Walker? It's probably too late to get someone to sub for us. Sure hate to screw up things at a new club, especially after being out of town for a while."

Walker checked his watch. "We got about three hours. I'll be back for the show. Tell the bar manager that when he gets here, okay?"

"Sure enough will."

"I don't think Vada will make it back, but we'll make do. Most of the stuff we do I can sing okay. And we'll stretch out the jams a bit. Just keep everyone calm, Real. I'll handle everything from here on out."

3.

SONNY AND WALKER SAT in front of a roaring fire at Uncle Charlie's house, drinking heavily rummed eggnog. Sonny had made it back to town the night before, for Christmas Eve. The brothers spent it together at Vada's parents', with a small community's worth of her relatives. Everybody stuffed themselves with homemade tamales and real-deal beanless chili eaten by hand with Lupe's Sonoran paper-thin tortillas. Then all the would-be mariachis brought out their instruments and handed the brothers fat Mexican acoustic guitars. Feeling very gringo, the Blaines did their best to pick and strum along with the passionate music. Sonny took turns dancing with a dozen pretty cousins. Walker had eyes and kisses only for Vada. He had been exclusively attentive ever since her arrest.

Things looked like they were going to go okay for Vada. She would likely draw three years of probation instead of jail time, thank God. But there would be no road for her. No clubs. No band for three years, in any sense that mattered to her career. Sonny was startled when he saw her. Although Vada had always been small, she had her powerful presence, robustness illustrated in her big voice. Now she looked frail. In all the years he had known her, Sonny really never felt anything less than friendly or anything more than lustful toward his now sister-in-law. Seeing her this way gave him an unreasonable urge to hold her, to guard her from her troubles. He understood fully why Walker kept her so close.

Sonny and Walker tagged along to a Spanish midnight mass with a passel of Vada's kin. Having been raised Southern Baptists, now lapsed at that, neither had made much sense of the service. But the ceremony was a beautiful candlelit affair, with haunting a cappella hymns. Sonny felt a peacefulness creep over him that he had not known since his touring had begun four months before.

Vada lit a votive candle at some sort of shrine before they left. Tears streamed down her face as she kneeled, mumbling her Spanish prayer with closed eyes. Walker stood beside her, running a hand through her hair, shadows playing on his face from the many votives burning. From a few steps away, Sonny observed his brother and his sister-in-law. He was drawn for a moment into their closeness. An unsettling shiver raced through him. He couldn't imagine letting someone see him so vulnerable. Sonny escaped outside in the cold night, sitting on his Mustang's hood to wait for the couple.

Now Vada and Aunt Lucille were hard at work, making a monstrous Christmas Day feast. The women were big fans of one another. The brothers could hear their laughter floating in from the kitchen. Uncle Charlie had gone to the airport to pick up Big Billy Jay and Ruby. Sonny had bought the plane tickets for his parents. So many strange and lonesome towns in the past year had made him want to try and mend fences and be with all his kin this holiday. Walker agreed the time had come to see Daddy again.

"So what's happening with the Bees, anyway?" Sonny asked him, sipping in the rum's fire, watching the Yule log flicker.

"I told you our pianist had already bailed on the road, right?" Walker replied. Sonny nodded. "Well, the night of the drug bust Ikey and Mikey played with Real, Jesse James and me. Then they said *adios*. I heard they headed back home to Memphis. So that leaves us three dudes." Walker got up and peeked inside the kitchen. He heartily complimented the women on the aromas that were wafting their way. He came back with the rum bottle. "Just wanted to make sure the girls wasn't listening," he said quietly to Sonny. "See, I been feeling a little fenced in by the whole review thing for a time, but what can I do? I owe Vada and Lone Star Records bunches, you know? I been wanting my own thing, though, so I can stretch out. I'm ready for it now, Sonny." He poured more amber liquid to float on top of their nog. "I've played around with a few rhythm sections. There ain't none better than Jesse James and Real. We're going the straight power trio route."

"Yeah? You could probably pull that off tough, Squirt."

"Yeah, I know." Walker got a far-off squint in his eyes. "At first, when I starting playing out, I just dug playing anything, you know? I mean, I still like playing with Vada, with other people, too. But I got something cooking in me, Sonny. Like, there's this sound that's inside my head. It's hard to put into words, man."

"I know what you mean. Back when the Tornadoes started, we had to play lame clubs out in the sticks that didn't really let us rock it up or play blues. It was frustrating."

"Yeah, kind of like that. But it's something more, even." Walker smiled a little sheepishly. "I can't really express it right, I guess. Anyway, my wife ain't thrilled about any of this. At the same time, she don't want me to stop playing. She always says she's my biggest fan. Besides, she sure as hell don't want me finding another girl to sing for me."

"Still jealous, huh?" Sonny said, chuckling.

"I don't think *jealous* is the right word no more. That's the poison you feel when your lover gives you no trouble and you still don't trust them. It's a different thing, a heartache, when you give them cause. I gave her plenty of heartache that tour we went on." Walker took a big drink of the barely diluted rum, looking mournful. "Five years we were together before we got married, and I never cheated. Never even thought much about it. Here, even before my first anniversary, I'm out acting a fool."

"You? I can't hardly picture it."

"I know . . . but you know the road, Sonny."

"Oh, yes, I do."

"But it's not like Vada sat in the motel room alone and pining."

Sonny laughed. "I'll bet she didn't. Vada ain't going to stand around twiddling her thumbs while you're out messing around."

"That's the truth. I'm worried about her since the bust, though, Sonny. She don't have her same spark no more."

"No, she don't. She'll probably be okay now this trial is behind you." Walker nodded. Sonny stretched out, closing his eyes. "Tell me more about your power trio, Squirt."

Walker leaned forward in his chair, the enthusiasm glowing in his eyes. "Just want to do it balls forward, you know? Play rhythm and lead together. Cool instrumentals. Me singing some, too. I can sing pretty good, Sonny. Prince and Shookie been letting us practice at their place. We usually hit the jam on Sundays, too." Walker smiled with clear pride. "The Browns say I sing a lot like Daddy Jim did."

"I remember that voice that came out of you that first night you and Vada got together, when you danced to the jukebox and sang *Fever* to her. You reminded Johnny Lee of Floyd—not too shabby."

"Yeah . . . that was quite some day," Walker mumbled, gazing at the fire and tossing back his drink.

"You want the truth, Walker?" Walker turned his eyes back to Sonny. Sonny went on, chuckling, "Man, I could never get up there and sing. I had bad enough stage fright when I first started playing guitar in front of people."

"Well, I been doing backup and duets and stuff for a time with Vada, but it was still kind of scary at first. I'm getting used to it, though. Now, we only got two real problems. First, everyone acts like the power trio deal is done played. Like it's old-fashioned or something. People act like we're Cream or Thunderclap when we say power trio."

"You could have worse company, I reckon."

"Yeah, I know. And it'll be real cool to really touch on Hendrix's stuff more. But Rollie don't think it'll sell. He may not want us on the label."

"There's lots of other labels besides Rollie's, Walker. I mean he's a good guy and all. Treats us all right fair. But we're shopping for a bigger company. Get your groove solid and then make a demo. Shop it, if he ain't going to work with you. You need bucks to get the demo together, I could probably help you out."

"Yeah? Thanks, man. It's good advice, Sonny."

"No sweat." Sonny started to drift. Sleepily, he muttered, "What's the second problem ya'll got?"

"We need a name. Don't feel right about using the King Bees because I'd like to leave that for Vada if she wants to use it later. So we're Firewalker Blaine and the . . . well, the what? I tell you, it has practically ruined my life that James Brown's band got to the name the Flames first."

"So you sticking with that silly tag—Firewalker?"

"I kind of like it. Better than Little Walker. Don't want to give the ladies a wrong impression."

"So true," Sonny agreed, laughing. He managed to prop up on his elbow. "I hate them calling me Icestorm."

"Ah, it's cool, Sonny. Just like you. Just think: Muddy Waters, Howlin' Wolf, Lonesome Sundown—all them other dudes? It's the blues thang, Icestorm!"

"Spare me."

"Face it. You're just pissed because I got a hot handle and you got a cold one. Afraid I'll steal all your women?"

"You wish, you asshole. Now back to your band name. . . . Something hot's good . . . some fire imagery. . . ."

"Dig the high school grad at work!"

"Shut up, Walker. Let me think." Sonny lay back on his arms. He stared at the burning log in the mantel for a time, toying with names in his head. Finally, he said, "Hey, do you know what a salamander is?"

"Ain't it a lizard?" Walker asked. "I heard something about them ecologist dudes trying to save some damn salamander that lives only over by Barton Springs Pool."

"Yeah, I heard about that, too. That's what I'm talking about—they're kind of like a lizard. But mostly they live in the dark, in caves. Like ya'll haunt nightclubs? Legend is they can walk right through fire without getting hurt. They were a big deal with witches in the old days."

Walker laughed. "You're making this up."

"No, I ain't, Squirt. Knew a chick back when who was into magic and mojos and all that. She told me about salamanders."

Walker rubbed his beard, squinting. "That's pretty wild . . . Firewalker Blaine and the Salamanders. That ain't half-bad. Thanks, Sonny. You mind if we go with that? For now, anyhow?"

"Hey, as long as ya'll ain't the Rocket 88s, ain't no thing to me."

Lucille came in from the kitchen, toweling off her hands. "Uncle Charlie just pulled in the driveway with ya'll's folks. Ready, boys?"

"As we'll ever be, Aunt Lucille," Walker replied. He took his hat off and threw it on the couch, shaking out his hair as he did. He and Sonny shared an uneasy glance. "Man, I'm kind of scared."

"Me, too. Hey, Squirt," Sonny grinned, pulling out his wallet. "I'll give you a hundred bucks right now if you go change into them purple-velvet pants."

Walker cracked up. "Shit! Can you imagine what he'd do? I thought we wanted to make peace, not kill Daddy!"

Uncle Charlie opened the door, lugging in a couple of worn, tweed suitcases. He announced their arrival with a shout of "Hey ho!" which Lucille echoed, dashing to the door. Ruby followed behind, hugging Lucille and then kissing and embracing both of her sons. Ruby pushed the hair out of Walker's eyes with gentle fingers. A tear drifted down her cheek.

Last to come in was Big Billy Jay, holding a shopping bag of gifts by his side. His skin was even more leathered from the sun than it was in Sonny's memory, and there was a good deal of silver on his temples. Dressed in a sport coat and bolo tie, he stood strong, tall and tension-bound. Big Billy Jay smooched Lucille quickly on the cheek, and then turned to face his sons.

"Hold on. Ya'll can't be my kids. You all growed up."

"You look pretty much as ornery as ever," Sonny said. He held out his hand to his daddy, and Big Billy Jay took it, pounding Sonny on the shoulder as they shook.

"Well, well. Look at you! Mr. Bluesman himself. Leastwise you got a real haircut since I saw you last, even if you still sporting that sissy earring. We got us your new album. That's a suit I'd even like to own you wearing in that cover picture."

"Discovered a little style, I guess. Maybe I'll take you shopping while you here. Don't tell Mama, but we got some real pretty sales girls."

"We'll keep that between you and me, Sonny." Big Billy Jay turned his attention to his youngest. "Wouldn't know you if we met on the street, kid. Calling you 'Fire' these days, I heard tell."

"Uh-huh, Daddy," Walker said quietly. He held out his hand timidly, watching the floor. His daddy took it, looking as though he was fighting tears. He pulled his son to him in a tight hug. For a moment Walker froze, then hugged him back. "Real good to see you again."

"Good to see you, too, son. Still just a baby when you left home. Fire, that whole mess—"

"Forget it, Daddy. It's a long time gone."

"How's that ear I boxed? You need it in your line of work, I reckon."

"It's okay most of the time. Oh, if I play too many long nights in a row, it gives me some fits a-ringing." Walker stuck a finger in the ear, like he was digging for something. "The hearing didn't come all the way back, but I don't really notice often. I can hear out of it without no distortion or nothing. That's the main thing, playing." He shrugged, frowning. "Just from the loud noise we're exposed to, most musicians get the ringing some, anyway."

Big Billy Jay nodded, his face sad. He's old, Sonny realized. It was the first time he'd ever thought that about his daddy.

Walker shrugged, saying with a tight smile, "I look at it like this. It's this ear that kept my skinny ass from being shot out from under me in 'Nam."

"I reckon that's good, son." They stared at each other for a long time. Billy Jay nodded finally, clearing his throat. "You doing okay for yourself down here, huh, kid?"

"Not too bad," Walker said.

"We got both you boys' records—both of Sonny's from his two bands, and yours, too. And that pretty girl in next to nothing you holding on yours, Mama tells me that's your wife. Where is this Mexican bride of yours?"

"Daddy, please don't call her my 'Mexican bride.' She's just my wife. Okay?" Walker said it in a quiet, slightly edgy voice. When they'd talked about sending for their folks, Walker had mentioned to Sonny that he worried Daddy would say something hurtful, racist, to Vada.

"I don't mean nothing bad by it. Them's the most gorgeous women on the planet." He reached over to pull Ruby to his side. "Exceptin' your mama, of course. Why, didn't you know your great mam-maw on my side was full-blood Mexican? Where you think ya'll get these dark eyes from?" Big Billy Jay pointed to his own brow. "Not them pasty Irish Blaines or them redheaded Crawfords!"

"Hello there, Big Billy Jay. I'm Vada Blaine." She'd emerged from the kitchen, shaking her curls loose from a scarf. "Neither of your boys are near as handsome as you, now are they?" In a clinging sweater dress and boots, Vada strolled up to Big Billy Jay. She flashed him a smile that could melt granite. Sonny and Walker exchanged grins.

"Delighted, darlin'! Lord God almighty, boy. How'd you ever manage to snare this one?" Big Billy Jay asked Walker, kissing Vada's hand.

"Just plain lucky, I reckon," Walker said, beaming at her.

Vada came to her husband and cuddled into his side. "Oh, no, Babydoll. I am the lucky one. Now let's all go take a load off and get better acquainted. Dinner can handle itself for a time."

THANKS IN LARGE PART to the charms of the women in the family, Christmas at the Crawfords was a comfortable success. Big Billy Jay was on his best behavior, drinking just enough to sparkle but not sink into meanness. He kidded Sonny only a little about finding himself a wife in his travels. He had good-naturedly ribbed Walker and Vada about grandchildren. And naturally he couldn't leave Walker's flowing hair and pirate's earring be.

After dinner, Sonny had his aunt fetch the photo of the two brothers that had made the magazine cover a few years back. With unbridled glee he pointed out Walker's ensemble, the purple pants in particular. Even Walker's mama was reduced to tears from laughter.

"Well, I'm real glad ya'll are having such fun at my expense." Eyes narrowed, arms folded, Walker surveyed the table full of helpless people. "Some folks just don't know how to dress with flair."

"And thank the Lord for that!" Sonny cried before he resumed howling.

"I hope you die before me so I can bury you in them britches," Walker told Sonny, trying hard to keep up his indignation in the face of all the laughter. "And don't you doubt the casket will be wide open for all to see."

"Damn! Be spinning in my grave before I'm in the ground."

Everybody wound down in a minute or two. "Oh, man," Vada sighed, wiping tears of laughter with the back of her hand. "Thank you so much for including me today. I needed to laugh hard and forget things for a time."

"You are always welcome here, Vada," Aunt Lucille said, patting the girl's arm. "You know that."

"Thank you, Lucille. Look, if we can't help with anything else, Walker and I better get home. Sonny, we're dropping you off, too. Someone will help you get your car *mañana*. You been drinking too much to drive safe."

Vada had quit imbibing long before the brothers and took the wheel of the Impala. As they drove home, Thunderclap's overkill version of *Madison Shoes* came on the radio.

Sonny crowed, "Hey, I keep forgetting to tell ya'll this. I met Little Lord Mountbatton and his daughter in California."

"No shit?" Walker laughed. "How'd that happen?"

"They came to see my show." Sonny recounted his embarrassing introduction to Cilla.

"Sonny, you shameful pig," Vada scolded, scowling back at him in the rearview mirror. Much as Sonny had predicted, Walker was cracking up to the point where it was painful. "I can't believe you used that tacky come-on to anyone, much less that little girl."

"Ooh, he's Mr. Smooth, is our Icestorm," Walker cackled. "Sonny seems to think she was old enough to drive. Honey, that's plenty growed up where us hicks come from. The saying back home goes 'Old enough to bleed, old enough to breed.' "

"Aye! That's so sick, Walker." She slapped at him, but he managed to duck. "I should make both you *cochinotos* walk home."

"Man, Icestorm, we is in trouble now. My wife's calling us bad names in Spanish."

Vada ignored Walker, keeping her tone stern with Sonny. "Weren't you ashamed of yourself, Sonny?"

"Yeah. I was pretty drunk and stupid at the time. But I'll tell you one thing. She don't look like no little girl."

Walker gave him a curious glance. "What does she look like?"

"Walker, this was the best-looking redhead I ever seen. Big green eyes. Beautiful golden skin, too. Must be from her daddy's black blood, huh? And legs?" Sonny groaned. "You know, she looks kind of like Ann-Margret in *Viva Las Vegas*—real innocent, but real saucy, same time? That's Cilla. But darker, maybe even more gorgeous than Ann-Margret."

"Can't be. Ain't nobody more gorgeous than that." He ran a hand through Vada's hair. "Present wife excepted, of course."

"Good save there, Babydoll," Vada said coolly.

"Thing is, she plays guitar, too, Walker. That's what she wanted from me, to talk shop."

"You tell her you don't talk shop, not even to your pitiful baby brother?"

"Didn't have a chance to. Anyway, she ain't been at it very long, but Mountbatton says she's good."

"Well, then. There you go."

"And get this, Walker. She's left-handed, plays upside down."

"Damn! Like Dick Dale and Albert King."

Sonny reached over the seat, poking Walker's shoulder. "That's *just* what I said. Self-taught, I guess. I would have liked to have heard her, just to see what she was up to." They rode in silence for a minute. Sonny added, only half aware he was saying it out loud, "That girl sure enough was the living end."

"Dirty old man," Vada declared, reaching back to pop him one. "You finally find a girl you think's special, and she turns out to be just that—a girl."

"Don't get too bent out of shape, honey. Sonny thinks all girls are special. Don't you, bro?"

"Right, Squirt." He was thinking of those bottomless green eyes and those perfect legs rippling under her jeans. Just maybe, he thought, this one really could be more special than the others.

4.

SONNY WAS IN A nightclub. Even honky-tonk was too fancy a name for this joint. He felt about to perish from heat exhaustion and smoke inhalation. His back was to the wall, and he held just enough whiskey in his guts to take the edge off without going too far around the bend. A massive black guy played a huge old squeezebox, and he sang out in the scary-ass, ancient-sounding French these bayou dwellers used. The music was astounding, primal. The accordionist was playing a rhythm and lead combined, while a loose-necked kid kept time scraping a washboard molded onto him like a breastplate. His lead line was closer to a guitar's voice than a keyboard's.

Sonny didn't feel entirely welcome out here. He believed Johnny Lee, Rimshot, and he were only kept safe due to Bonnell's Creole pedigree. He was starting to long for the feel of dusty Texas earth beneath his feet. Spending the fall in Louisiana had been a gas, though. So cool to bop the French Quarter, hearing all sorts of jazz and blues pour into the streets, trailing along after Bonnell to tiny record shops. Under his native buddy's amused gaze, Sonny tried to search out stuff he'd been craving from Bonnell's collection.

Standing next to his Creole partner now, Sonny hardly recognized him. The normally impeccable singer wailed drunkenly along with the singer, swinging his fist in the air. Bonnell had let his high-piled hair at least proverbially down, making time with this home-folks crowd.

Leastwise, Sonny didn't have to worry about Bonnell getting too toasted to drive them out of here. Most of the way they'd taken a fucking *boat*. The water taxi was ferried by a toothless guy who looked straight out of another century. He spoke not a word of English, and laughed ghoulishly every time Bonnell said something to him in French. The boat itself looked like it was held together by duct tape as it cut a wake through the slime topping the black water. Sonny had huddled into a ball, making himself a smaller target for the beasts making such awful noise in the swampy night.

Certainly humans weren't supposed to live in this environment. But live they did. Lots of them were really talented, too. The Rockets were using a few choice old guys on their new record. During the daylight hours, the band was busy laying down tracks. Nice work, back in town, in a civilized, air-conditioned studio off the French Quarter.

The album was already named. The story of Bonnell's hometown was that native son General Thibodeaux lost one arm and one leg fighting for the South. When he came home, he ran for governor, and won, under a campaign slogan of Vote for the Rest of Me. The Rockets adopted the slogan as their album's title. They had a picture of General Thibodeaux's memorial statue on the front cover, and one of the band gathered around Guitar Slim's tombstone on the back.

The Rockets managed to stumble upon some unexpected work, too. They broke into the movie business in an indie filming in New Orleans, a hipster whodunit, *Bombshell*. The director was a Texas expatriate. He hunted down the Rockets when he heard they were in town. He wrote in a special part for Bonnell as a singing, swindling Cajun heavy. Sonny was amazed by his bandmate's acting skill. He looked so different; sounded different, too. A subtle shift of accent, a simple change of clothing, and the high-tone Creole became an evil ol' swamp rat.

The moviemaker stuck with the rest of the band playing themselves, adding their work to the soundtrack. Sonny got some extra screen time, two-stepping with the fine leading lady. Their dance had started out to be an incidental thing, but the director liked the way the couple looked on film. So he reshot, making the dance a centerpiece, background to dirty-dealings dialogue between Bonnell and the hardscrabble leading man.

Bonnell had a line, purred to the lead as a swamp-waltz played and Sonny stepped the actress around the room: "Don't mind that guitar picker dancing with your woman—he's harmless." Sure enough Sonny hadn't been so harmless the next few nights with that leading lady. It was the humidity she'd blamed, surrendering, no tussle. Despite the honkin' diamond on her ring finger, she avidly took to Sonny's bed. Didn't seem to matter that her husband was the money behind this film. Plus, she was right about the heavy air. It stirred the blood.

Sonny kept his eyes to himself in this stilt-top nightclub though. Wouldn't do to be dumped out in the swamps. Too many live things lurking out there. But it was stifling inside the club. There might at least be breeze off the water if he got outside. Through the smoke, he thought he could make out a screened-in porch beyond a door across the room. At least mosquitoes wouldn't devour him too much out there. He made his way through the sweaty dancers. The only others on the porch were two young Creole lovers, pitching a little woo. He crossed to the other side, away from the couple. It was indeed a degree or two cooler on the porch. He felt like wringing out his T-shirt, it was so wet. He took a deep breath—the swamp stank, but leastwise he'd left the smoke inside. And the full moon made the night look nearly daylight-bright.

He heard the sound of car wheels. Peering through the screen, he watched as the vehicle pulled into a small parking lot. So the Rockets had come in the backdoor. Bonnell had only been toying with them, making them take the damned boat, climbing up those slime-covered stairs from the landing. Shaking his head, Sonny leaned against a support post, watching as the insects brutally hurtled themselves at the screen. He wondered if the mosquitoes smelled their food—his blood—pumping inside of him.

Moments later, Bonnell stepped outside, crossing the porch to stand beside Sonny. Dressed in faded jeans that Sonny wouldn't have imagined the singer even owning and a sweat-soaked T-shirt, his hair falling over his face, he looked years younger than his usual polished self. He sipped a draft beer, following Sonny's gaze to the parking lot. "Oops. I am caught." He chuckled, his words mushy from drink. "Well, it was irresistibly amusing. Watching your faces in that boat? Every time a gator growled, you boys' eyes went big and round." He gazed up at the sky, losing his laughter. "Still, I apologize, Sonny. I shouldn't play such cruel games with ya'll tonight."

Sonny followed his eyes. "Because the moon is full? Let me guess. Some sort of bad omen among your people."

"This moon is, sometimes. It is a harvest moon.

"It's the prettiest thing in these bayous," Sonny said.

"It not just pretty. It has powerful *gris gris*."

"Let me guess," Sonny kidded. "Ya'll got fucking werewolves wandering these swamps, along with all them other monsters?"

"We don't call them werewolves. *Loup-garou* is what we call them." Bonnell said it without a trace of irony.

Sonny barked, "Creole werewolves. Shit, Devereaux. Ya'll are too much."

"Me, I've never seen a *loup-garou*. I've seen other things, though." Bonnell was quiet for a moment, finger-combing his hair up off his forehead. "Has Walker ever mentioned this moon—or something like it—to you, Sonny?"

"I don't know what you mean. As kids we used to lay on the front lawn and look at the night sky a lot, when it was too hot to sleep inside."

Bonnell acted as if he didn't even hear Sonny's answer. "Walker knows mysteries, Sonny."

Sonny rolled his eyes, keeping quiet. Bonnell was such a fucking drama queen.

Bonnell went on, his voice low. "No one really knows when the concept of the soul first occurred to us as a species—tens of thousands of years past, surely. But certainly, the idea of then bartering it away has to have followed right on its heels. The idea of the trade appears throughout the world, crosses almost all cultures. I've researched the subject rather thoroughly.

"Robert Johnson's tale, the one most of us know in America, that was an old story by the time he made his trade. The idea likely came over with the slaves—just as *voudou* did."

"How about that," Sonny said. He kept his voice neutral and his eyes fixed into the night. Where the hell was this nutcase going? Though he should probably just walk away from him, Sonny decided he'd hear him out instead, if only for the sport of it.

"Do they tell such a story about any of your great guitar players in Texas—that they sold their soul for music, I mean?"

"If so, I never heard tell of it."

"Here, we tell such stories—but it is skill with the accordion that is traded for."

"Huh. Is there some voodoo twist to it?"

Bonnell winced at the way Sonny said the magical word. Emphasizing the correct pronunciation, he said, "It's not *voudou*—though you can lose yourself to evil just as surely in that black art. No, what you do here is you find the biggest oak you can, come harvest moon. You wait there at midnight with your accordion." Sonny felt Bonnell's gaze fall on him as his voice dropped a half octave. "The devil, he comes to teach you how to play real fast."

Bonnell seemed to be waiting for Sonny to say something, but he wouldn't. He wouldn't even look at him.

The singer finally went on. "These swamps—strange things happening all the time, just like Guitar Slim said. You ever wonder why I left here, Sonny?"

"Who knows why you do anything, man?"

"You think I don't miss Louisiana—my ancestral home?" Bonnell took a sip of beer. "It's a deeply Catholic society, Thibodeaux. Fact is, people didn't much like me hanging around after."

Sonny finally looked at him, grunting, "You're drunk and talking shit, Devereaux. You forget you took us on that fucking boat ride just to freak us out. I ain't fool enough to believe you sold your soul."

Bonnell smiled then, a cold, preying expression that reminded Sonny of the gators outside. "Suit yourself, Sonny. But I'm not so sure you can dismiss Walker's situation as easily."

Bonnell's voice had a hint of danger in it now, an unwholesome power. Maybe it just felt that way because of where they were, and the strange, beautiful moonlight shining down on the swamp. Maybe it was the inclusion of Walker's name in this shit Bonnell was spewing. Whatever, this whole conversation was now starting to really creep out Sonny.

"I will tell you the truth now, Sonny. When first I came to Austin, it was not you I was after. Even then, word had spread as far as Houston about an amazing guitarist working in the capital. When I heard Walker, I too was utterly captivated. Doesn't it seem like other players can hit the same exact notes that your brother does, and yet their music just doesn't have the same effect on you?"

Bonnell was right about that. Sonny kept still, though.

"Then when I saw how he was after performing—raw, almost broken?

It was then I recognized what he was. I knew better than to put two of us in the band."

"Two *soulless* people, you mean?" Sonny forced a laugh, but his scalp was tingling in an unpleasant way. "You and your fucking ghost stories. Everywhere I go here, I see creepy little shrines tucked into corners, mojos hanging off everyone's belts or necks. Ain't a one of you who don't think their house isn't haunted."

"Most places are haunted by something." Bonnell kept his voice low, the eerie smile on his face, as he pointed to the porch's screen door. "Perhaps we Creole are simply more sensitive to spirits. You think you've got balls of brass, Sonny Blaine? Maybe we make you walk home tonight. You'll see things in these swamps that you'd wish you'd never—I guarantee."

"I don't even want to see what's supposed to be there—the quote-unquote normal wildlife. See, I can appreciate why ya'll are so superstitious, living in this weird-ass place. But me and Walker was raised Baptist in the western plains. Wasn't no devil walking the streets of Mingus, man."

"So you say."

Sonny nearly shouted, "Cut this shit out, man. Walker did not sell his fucking soul!"

At his exclamation, the necking couple on the other side of the porch turned wide eyes toward them. The woman crossed herself, huddling closer to her lover. Sonny overheard her whispering in Creole to her man. Sonny thought he made out Bonnell's name, and something about *le Diable*.

Sonny closed the distance between himself and Bonnell, dropping his voice. "I knew Walker before he could stand up and piss. You don't think I could tell?"

"Oh, but you can, Sonny," Bonnell whispered, looking him in the eye. "I've seen myself how much he frightens you when he plays. Only time I've ever seen you really scared—more scared than you were out on that boat ride. Even without knowing exactly what was going on, it's scared you when you've witnessed it take him over."

"Bull . . . shit," Sonny said slowly.

"Yes? Why then were you compelled to give him that old guitar, first time you heard him play?"

"He's my goddamned brother," Sonny snapped.

"Goddamned?" The gator smiled returned. "No pun intended, you?"

"I was leaving him to be beaten half to death by our old man, okay? He needed something to help him survive. So I gave him that fucking guitar." But Sonny remembered all too well that first time in the basement. Even then Walker had awed him . . . and frightened him a little, too. He waved his fingers at Bonnell, shooing him off. "You can't be saying that the devil took Walker's soul at all of thirteen?"

"Likely that was his God-given talent you witnessed that first time."
Bonnell's voice became a mere snakelike hiss as he added, "But that is what
the devil seeks—gifts from God that he can steal for his own."

Sonny suddenly was mighty pissed off. He grunted, "You're fucking
crazy, Bonnell, if you really believe a word of this."

Bonnell gave Sonny the French shrug, looking away. "Weren't crazy
people once said to be possessed by the devil?"

Sonny wondered now if Bonnell really wasn't dangerously insane. His
anger drained, replaced by a sobering, frightening emotion he didn't have a
name for. The feeling made a shiver course through him. For a long time
they didn't say anything. Finally Sonny had to ask it, in spite of himself. "So
how old were you when you did it?"

Bonnell reached for the mojo dangling from his belt, fingering it. He
was quiet for a long time, though his lips moved slightly, like he was mus-
tering up a prayer, or an incantation. The sight of it made Sonny open his
mouth to retract what he'd asked. Just as he was taking a breath to speak,
Bonnell grabbed his eyes again, dropping the mojo back to his thigh. He
still looked reptilian, threatening—but there was real horror in his expression, too.

"You're right about me being very drunk, Sonny. It is making me
stupid—talking too much, for your own good, and mine as well. But know
this thing. When you're very young, death doesn't seem real. Living, that's
what's hard."

Sonny nodded, thinking of his own boyhood.

"Later? With eyes wide open, you learn to be afraid—truly afraid. You
get watchful, feel it waiting for that one false move, one chance to claim
what's due." Bonnell's voice dropped all pretense of the previous gator
power trip. It was clear he had spooked his own self even more than he had
Sonny.

"I will probably pay an awful price one day for saying these things to
you. All the same, my friend, you need to be aware of what sort of *gris gris*
is at hand. You need to take care."

Turning his back to Sonny, he added, "Take a close, hard look at your
baby brother, Sonny. He feels it too—that hellhound's breath on his heels."
Abruptly, he stalked toward the bar's entry. The woman who had crossed
herself shrank away from Bonnell as he passed her by.

Letting out a breath he hadn't realized he'd been holding, Sonny
looked back into the night, at the bugs driven mad by the harvest moon.
They were battering themselves to death against the screen. The sound of
them breaking apart made Sonny want to puke. Despite the ghastly heat,
Sonny felt chilled to the bone.

✳   ✳   ✳   ✳   ✳

5.

VADA SAT IN THE living room, drinking coffee and waiting for Walker to return from the previous night's gig. She had hardly slept, finally deciding to part from the tangle of sheets once dawn had started to break. She rolled out of bed, threw on a terry-cloth robe and brewed a strong pot of Combaté. She went back to her room and opened a sachet-filled drawer, searching through her lingerie until she found a shimmery golden teddy. Walker's favorite. She pulled it on, and then covered it with the robe. She paused at her vanity, brushing and fluffing her hair, adding a touch of musk oil at her breast and throat.

Vada detested that her husband was out there making music without her. It would be three long years of not being able to even go inside a club and watch him, much less sing herself. She didn't know how she was going to bear it. She wandered out, poured her coffee. She left the cream off for her figure's sake but sniffed at it to make sure it was still fresh for Walker.

She dropped to the tattered old couch, mulling over what had gone down since her arrest. Certainly Vada was grateful not to have done time. She was also scared. She worried about her career, and more about her future with Walker. They had come to depend on the extra cash dealing provided, or at the very least the free drugs that came along as part and parcel. Dealing again was out of the question if she wanted to stay free. She was sure "they" were watching her every outside move.

The Bees album had taken a leap in sales after the arrest, proving the old adage that there was no such thing as bad publicity. However, their percentage was small. And, like the free blow and cash from dealing, the steady income of gigs they had once had with the King Bee Review had dissipated, too. The Salamanders had polished up a few sets and were gamely trying to build up bookings. Jobs weren't as easy to come by as Walker had assumed.

Problem was, when folks around town thought of Walker, they thought of him with the King Bees. They were used to him backing up the horns, piano, and Vada, occasionally stepping out with his solos or encore pieces. There were too many excellent players in this town, all laying claim to good clubs and good nights. Austin was a fan's paradise but a hard nut to crack for a new band. Walker was talking some about going and trying out the Salamanders' legs on the road. Vada hated that idea even more than his prowling free here. She didn't tell him so. She just wanted things to work between them.

She reached under her robe, rubbing the silk covering her svelte belly. Her mind fluttered back to when they were on the road last summer. Everything between them had fallen to pieces. It had been her fault, all her fault. If she hadn't gone crazy when she realized she was pregnant, she wouldn't have chased her husband into those other women's arms.

Walker didn't know she'd ever carried the baby. He didn't have any clue about her miscarriage, alone in their tacky hotel room. He'd been out all night that night, in a cold act of retaliation. The morning before, she had overslept in the bed of some horny, handsome biker and had to beg a ride to the bus. They raced up moments before departure. Vada straddled the back of his Hog, her stage costume leaving little to the imagination. She had tried to leave with polite thanks, but the fool grabbed her and kissed her hard right in front of her husband.

She was sure Walker hated her at that moment. He glared on with his hot-spring black eyes looking cold and hard as obsidian. She had been too sick, too humiliated to attempt to make amends. That same night, Walker made a great display of leaving with some corn-fed Midwestern virginal type under his arm. The tramp was about as different from Vada as he could go and still fuck a young female. Vada was already cramping brutally, and only got back to the hotel with Riley's help. The pain by then was so bad she couldn't stand upright. Riley offered to stay with her, but she'd sent the bassist off, hoping to sleep the misery away. Almost as soon as Riley had left her, vast bleeding began, sweeping her with weakness and panic. She spent the next few hours sobbing, bracing herself over the toilet. The life she tried to deny she'd been carrying tore loose from her insides and died right there in the bathroom. Once it was over, drained nearly to death, she cleaned up the blood and tissue. She took the reddened motel towels to the dumpster on legs she feared would give out from under her. Everything else she flushed.

The heartache she couldn't dispose of so easily.

Vada heard Jesse James's van pull up to the house. The engine cut out and the doors slammed. Jesse James and Walker were laughing, unloading in the driveway. Stopping only to check herself out in the hallway mirror and apply some lipstick, Vada went out the front door to greet Walker. He and his drummer waved. Walker handed her Old Broad's gig bag. As she carried the guitar inside, the two men began to haul in Walker's ever more cumbersome gear. He had managed to somehow beg credit for more amplification and effects. Damn straight, Vada's man did not take the term power trio in vain! The Salamanders had become near too loud for most of the clubs in town.

With Jesse James's able hands helping, they made fairly short work of getting Walker put away. A couple of neighbors, driving by on their way to day jobs, gave the rock 'n' roll threesome curious glances. Vada poured a little of her Mexican coffee into a travel mug for Jesse James and sent the depleted drummer toward home. She went into the house to find Walker flopped across the couch, his boots propped up on the armrest, his hat tossed to the floor. "Honey, I missed you last night," he declared when he heard her shut the front door. "How was work? Was your folks' place busy?"

"Very. Mama and Papa are going to work themselves into an early grave. Sometimes I wish they'd just sell that place." She brought him a sweet, creamy cup of coffee from the kitchen. "Then they could leave work at work."

He propped himself up and sipped it, opening and closing his over-worked left hand to stretch the muscles. "I know you worry about them. But I'm sure glad the courts are letting you work for them. We need the bread. And leastwise, you get to peek your head in when we get a gig in the cantina. You got something for me to eat, honey? I'm about starved."

"I brought you a dinner home. I'll go put it in the oven."

She did, and then came back and sat next to him on the couch. "It'll be warm soon, Babydoll."

"You're such a sweet wife!" He reached over, pulled her into his arms. With a big smile, he kissed her.

Right away Vada noticed he smelled wrong. Not like her musk oil. Expensive. She recognized the faint floral scent of Chanel No. 5. Fairly strong, too, likely real perfume rather than cologne. She never wore that particular fragrance, wouldn't even if they could afford it. Floral didn't suit her.

She pulled back, scowling. "What time did ya'll finish playing, Walker?"

"Just an hour or so ago, honey," he said, still smiling, playing with a lock of her hair. "You know how they do at the Sugar and Spice, lock up the booze at last call and let us rip! Why you ask?"

"Did ya'll take a long break or two? Visit the fans, maybe?"

"Uh . . . a few short breaks. You know the routine," he muttered, no longer smiling. She could see his eyes growing guarded.

"Lots of pretty things in the crowd last night?" Vada asked, after an uncomfortable silence. "Bet you did that nasty move with your mouth on the strings. Get them thinking?"

"Vada, stop. You don't got nothing to worry about. Who do I come home to when I'm done, huh?" He was looking at her lap now, not at her face.

"When you're done with what, is the question. What was it this time? Get yourself a stage door blow job from some rich cunt?"

Walker didn't answer. She must have guessed it dead on.

He changed the subject. He was becoming expert at this trick. "I brought you a present, honey!" He reached down into a boot, pulling forth his stash bag. "Got us some real good blow."

"Walker!" She pulled away from him, punching him hard enough on his shoulder to make him yelp. "You know we needed that gig money to pay insurance. Rent's due, too. And how about your payment on the gear? They'll come take all this shit—" she kicked at an amp "—right the hell back!"

"Calm down, girl. I still got the cash. Here." He tossed her a wad of bills, pulled from his other boot. He started chopping up lines on their chrome-and-glass coffee table.

"Then . . . where did the coke come from?" Vada asked as she counted his pay and tips. Of course, she knew where the blow had come from. Most likely it was another gift from Chanel No. 5. Still, she had to see what excuse he would find this time.

"A fan gave it to me. A dealer had a mess of it in his car."

A dealer's girlfriend was more likely, Vada mused. She grunted, "Just carrying a bunch with him, was he? How convenient."

"Told him I was broke, but he said no, never mind. I'd already paid for it with my killer set." He rolled up one of the bills and handed it to Vada. She looked hard at him. He reddened a little, but he managed not to drop his eyes again. "Come on, Vada. Let's enjoy our time together, huh?" He pulled her hair back out of the way with his hand so she could lean over and do up some lines. The drug really was splendid, hardly stepped on at all. Right away she felt choice. "Ain't that nice, my pretty baby? I miss having you with me at my shows. Miss you so, so much. . . ." Walker stroked and kissed, initiating their tender brand of loving. He started pulling the arm of her robe down her shoulder. "Oh, look at this," he purred, pulling on the strap of the gold teddy. "You put on my favorite nightie. Just for me?"

"Just for you, Walker," she sighed as he kissed her neck, her shoulder, and her breasts. For the time being, the coke and his touches drove the threats away from her mind.

A good while later, Walker fell into a restless slumber. She watched his chest rise and fall, rubbed a regretful finger over the growing bruise she'd left on his right shoulder when she'd struck him earlier. At her touch he muttered, tossing around in their bed. She almost woke him up, just to tell him it didn't matter what happened when he was out playing, so long as he kept coming home. Maybe this time she could work up the nerve to tell him about the miscarriage. She'd explain that that was why she went insane on the road, and how the pain of it still feasted on her heart. But what if he blamed her for it? She'd been keeping up with the boys, drink for drink and snort for snort. And, as disgusting as it was to think of now, she'd kept up with the boys fuck for fuck, too.

Walker had told her flat out he didn't care about her past. All he knew of it was she'd run around some with the guys she'd made music with, Sonny among them. She had to assume Sonny had spun tales to him about her, too, in the days before she had taken Walker for her man.

Vada knew for sure Walker didn't know about Angel, her cool second cousin from Arizona with the bad GTO and dangerous eyes—no one did, or ever would.

Years ago, Angel came to stay with them for a time. He was hiding from some "trumped-up" charges brought against him by some girl, her mama whispered. Vada's parents never seemed concerned when she took rides in Angel's muscle car—he was *carnal*, would keep the child safe from harm. He'd in fact never touched her on those rides, just drove hard through the Hill Country and talked to her about his dreams. It made her feel grown up to listen to his stories. She trusted him completely and had quite a crush on him, too.

On her eleventh birthday, everything changed. Her parents had a big party for her, loads of kinfolk, even closed the Sanchez Palace for the occasion. All day she'd felt like a princess, her hair teased up like the big girls', her new red-satin dress looking storybook sweet.

Late in the day, when the adults were drunk and singing sad songs of passion, a shit-faced Angel had lured her to the attic. There, among the dust and spiders, he had, at knifepoint, violated her in ways she'd never had reason to imagine before that moment. When she'd once tried to scream for help, he'd slapped her and sliced her in a tender place where no one would see the wound.

When Angel finally finished with her, he'd slapped her again hard and told her that he'd kill her slow if she ever opened those cocksucking lips and squealed on him. He'd said that she shouldn't bother. Even if anyone believed her, they'd tell her it was her fault for looking like she did. Vada still had never told a soul.

That night Angel left town. He died in a rollover on the Arizona–New Mexico border, not six months later. The secret of the rape went to hell with him. By the time he died, Vada's physical wounds from the assault had faded, even a shameful discharge that had nagged at her for a long time after the rest of her had quit hurting. The injury to her mind had never healed completely. When a man looked at her like Angel had in those moments before he put the blade to her throat, she didn't run and hide. She'd beat him to the punch. She'd fuck him and throw him aside before he could do the same to her. They might have thought her a tramp, but she knew she wasn't. She never let them get close enough to hurt her. She'd trusted no one, let no one come close to her heart, until Walker.

If she told Walker about the lost baby, she was scared he would accuse her of being pregnant by another man. Impossible. She figured she must have been nearly four months gone when she miscarried. That meant the child had been made before they'd ever left town. But maybe in town he hadn't trusted her, either. Until that tour, there had been no one but Walker in all the years they'd spent together.

She'd never forget how Sonny had cruelly denied being the daddy when Nancy Ruth told him about Otis. Vada knew Walker bore a deep wound from what Sonny had done, in part because he never, ever talked about it. She knew better than anyone that Walker was as different from

Sonny as candy was from caviar. He'd probably be heartbroken, but wouldn't he love her more for the hell she'd gone through alone in that hotel room?

She had just about built up nerve enough to wake him and tell him when he rolled toward her. Still out, he grinned, mumbling what sounded like a woman's name. Probably just harmless dream talk . . . but who knew for sure? Vada didn't want to. She crawled carefully out of bed, fearful of hearing more and worse.

Her nose and head hurt, and she was starting to feel queasy. She went to the coffee table and cut out another fat line. While sniffing in the drug, she smelled something burning. Jumping up and cursing, she remembered Walker's breakfast, still heating in the oven. When she opened the oven door, smoke billowed out. The food was dried out, charred. She opened a window to air out the kitchen. She took the mess to the bin outside, tossing the plate and all.

She came back in and dropped to her knees on the cold kitchen floor. Doing her best to keep quiet so she wouldn't rouse her husband, Vada wept until she was finally exhausted enough for sleep.

6.

THE SALAMANDERS WERE playing at the Sugar and Spice every Tuesday. Sonny had heard varying opinions on the band, from good to bad, and everything in between. Home for a break before the big tour resumed, he decided to check them out himself. He wandered in late and took a stool at the dark end of the bar. Didn't want to cause a stir.

Everyone had agreed on one thing, as Sonny did right off. The trio was loud as hell. Walker had a huge sound array now, as did Riley. Sonny could feel the music reverberate in his bones. They were running down an old surf tune of all things, *Walk Don't Run* by the Ventures. Jesse James, bird's-nest hair slinging sweat, was flailing away at his kit. Riley was thumping along, grinning at Walker. And there Walker was, a gazillion watts behind him, a new black-suede hat hiding his face.

He was spraying shrapnel with that old Broadcaster. After Sonny's mind adjusted to the volume, he had to admit they sounded pretty damn rich. This was vibrant stuff Walker was putting out.

Walker took his bows after the Ventures tune, wiping sweat from his brow. He took the mike. "Let's come home to Texas, now. This here's by Johnny Copeland." He blasted into *Down on Bending Knees*, one of his favorites from Daddy Jim's record collection. Sonny remembered Walker wailing along whenever he'd put the record on back home. Walker would grab a hairbrush as a mike and scream along in his high little voice. He so wanted to sound as tough and desperate as Copeland. There in the spotlight he read the lyrics in his silk-and-sandpaper soul shout, a perfect match to his robust playing.

The Squirt had come a long way from Mingus.

Sonny stayed through the rest of the performance. He soaked in liquor and danced with a girl or two. Mostly he listened and watched Walker and the boys. At times he lost himself in the music, let it take him, make him want to stand up and cry, "Preach it, brother!" like a Primitive-Baptist. Other times he found himself studying Walker's technique as a fellow player. He did this crazy deal with his thumb, using it looped over the neck on the low strings for rhythm lines. This method made his grip viselike and helped him reach for impossible notes when he barred. The sound he pushed along in the Texas shuffle tradition, but with an ingenious touch. And the solos? Sonny kept waiting for Walker's runs to tumble into nonsense. But back he'd come, right there, dead on, full circle.

Walker would pull some showboat stuff, behind his back or over his neck, throwing the guitar to the floor, kneeling and messing around, pulling bizarre, cool-ass noises forth. Sonny might have said that this was just hot-doggin', had anyone asked. He knew, though, as a player himself, many of the things his kid brother did while showing off would have been damned hard to manage playing straight.

Sonny couldn't make himself forget what Bonnell had said about the devil pact that strange night in the bayou bar. Impossible, of course—shit like that Robert Johnson story wasn't real. Still, Walker didn't even look like himself on that stage. He was big, powerful, as if a fiendish spirit could be glimpsed inside him as he ripped it up.

There was no denying one thing, watching him play like this. Walker had it, that essential something that made him more than a great musician. If he didn't blow it, Walker could be the best there was. More than the liquefaction volume pouring from the stage shook Sonny, right down to his core.

After the show, dazed with intoxicants and the mighty music, Sonny waited for his brother. He was busy courting the fans, talking music, and thanking them for their praise. Drenched in sweat, he looked used and sounded hoarse. When he saw Sonny, he pulled him into the fray. "Hey, big bro. Thought you was off in Germany or some damn place."

"Not yet. We hit the trail tomorrow. Thought I'd best come check out the commotion before I left."

"Hey, Icestorm! You should've sat in with the Salamanders," one of the kids with Walker said. "That would have been one to write home about." The crowd murmured agreement.

"Too much like a busman's holiday. I'm playing nonstop soon enough. Tonight I just came to watch my little brother, same as ya'll. Come on, Walker, show's over now. Let me buy you a drink."

Walker said his goodbyes to his fans, signing a few autographs, kissing a few girls' hands. They retreated back into Shookie's office. At Sonny's request, the Browns had left them a bottle of Crown Royal and two high-ball glasses. He poured the whiskey for Walker and himself. Then he pulled from his jacket a little wad of gold tissue paper. "Cheers, Squirt. Here. Brought you a New Orleans souvenir."

Grinning, Walker perched on the desktop and unraveled the paper. In it was a long string of cheap plastic beads. They were bright and shiny, like Christmas tree balls. Walker held them up to the light. "Ain't these gaudy? I totally dig them."

"Don't that figure?" Sonny said, laughing. "Them's Mardi Gras beads, Walker. Folks throw them into the crowd from the floats during the big parades." Sonny reached over and fingered them. "See these little gold ones shaped like babies? Bonnell says they bring luck."

"Take all I can get." Walker slung them around his neck. "Thanks, man. They look cool with the new hat and boots Vada had Uncle Charlie make me, don't you think? Cheers!" They clinked glasses, taking long draws from their cocktails. Walker winced at the burn. "Whew. That sure ain't the rotgut."

"No, siree."

"So, Sonny. What you think of my band?"

"Damn. Ain't ya'll loud?"

Walker laughed. "Well, yeah." He pulled an earplug out of his damaged ear. "Can't take it myself without this or it's hells bells in my *cabeza*."

"Jesse James and Riley are a real tight fit."

"Yeah, I couldn't be more happy there." Walker sipped his drink, nodding. "But what you think of my stuff?"

Sonny looked at Walker, who was smiling anxiously back at him. He knew Walker so wanted his praise, wanted pats on the head, and a you so fine, little bro—all that shit. Hell, Walker already knew how good he was. The word *genius* flirted with the edge of Sonny's mind. He furiously shooed it away. He smoothed back his hair, studying his brother. "We got different philosophies, you and me."

"What's that mean?"

"With me, less is more. With you, more ain't near enough."

Walker looked at his hands, frowning, his shoulders dropping. "You don't like it?"

"I didn't say that. It's just . . . a different school of playing, is all. Even on your ballads you're wild, all over the place. A little restraint might not hurt you none."

Walker nodded. He tugged on the Mardi Gras necklace, fingering a gold baby bead. "I play . . . what's out there. I don't think about reining it in. Don't know if I can. It's like music just pours out of, or through, me."

Pours through him—like it wasn't his music at all. That shit Bonnell signified bled through his consciousness again. He snapped, "Then why ask me? Do what the fuck you want." Walker looked down, trying to hide his hurt behind his hat. Feeling a little chagrined, Sonny gruffly slapped Walker's shoulder and refilled their glasses. "Cheer up. To our mutual success, little brother."

"I'll drink to that." Walker threw back his liquor and held his glass out for more.

As Sonny poured again, there was a knock at the door. Someone entered without waiting to be invited. Weird dude, looked like he had been preserved. His eyes were slits, his shoulders hunched. Tufts of hair stuck out every which way, deep brown, streaked purple. Skeleton-thin, he had his ostrich neck burdened by too many gold necklaces. He had his bottom half wrapped in leather pants. A LONE STAR RECORDS T-shirt hung loose on his bones.

The startled brothers looked at each other. There could be no mistaking Kyle Reagan, lead guitarist and head hedonist for the Bad Signs.

One of the London faction of the British Invasion, the Bad Signs had lasted long after most of the other bands of their ilk. They had lost a few members along the way to drugs, death, and incurable insanity. Somehow, despite being the biggest self-abuser in a kingdom of the same, Kyle just kept on going, playing his Chuck Berry inspired riffs. The Bad Signs admittedly had a timeless groove. Kyle and Jackie Higgins, the band's flamboyant lead singer, had even composed a few rock standards.

"We need to talk, Firewalker," the Englishman croaked in greeting. His accent made him sound like he was working around a serious speech impediment.

Walker peered closely at the creature. "Shit on a stick! You're really Kyle Reagan?"

"Who else?" Kyle asked, with wheezy laughter.

Walker poked Sonny, saying, "I saw him in the crowd. But I thought, nah, what would he be doing in Austin?" Walker extended his hand to Kyle. He then introduced Sonny.

"Pleasure, Sonny," Kyle said. "Do enjoy the stuff I heard of the Rocket 88s, though I haven't seen you yet live. I didn't put it together at first you were brothers. You don't look or play nothing alike."

"We get that a lot," Sonny told him. Walker nodded.

"Look, Walker, here's the deal. I heard about you through the grapevine—you might not know it, but you got tongues wagging. I came in on a whim to see you. You really are laying down *serious* shit."

"Thanks, man. That means a lot, coming from you," Walker replied, his voice going shy and boyish.

"Next month I'm throwing Jackie a birthday bash. I'm hiring out a club in L.A. for it. I want a fresh band to play for us, and I'd like it to be yours. You can name your price." He gave them his ragged grin. "I'm sure I can accommodate you."

Walker swung wide eyes to his brother. Sonny nodded, saying, "Sounds like an offer you can't refuse, Squirt."

"Do me a favor, Sonny? Get Kyle a glass." As Sonny went back into the bar, he heard Walker barking out a laugh and saying, "So tell me what you need, man."

7.

CILLA COULD SCARCELY believe she was in this club, waiting for Icestorm Blaine's little brother to play. Bored by the industry gossip at her table, her mind drifted back to the night when she had begged her father to get her in to see the Rocket 88s. She quite liked Icestorm's style, his cutlass sharp technique. He had a tight, rhythmic swing that made her curious. She couldn't deny he was also dead handsome. But what had it been, two sentences into their conversation when the lowlife Texan made his move? She shook her head. Typical musician behavior, really. Shouldn't have expected anything different.

She sat in arm's reach of her escort, the birthday boy, Jackie Higgins. As usual, Jackie had told her what to wear and how to do her hair and make-up. He sent her back twice for a different shade of lipstick before approving of the package. She was turned out in a gossamer green sarong. The dress, and men's stares, made her feel naked. Jackie wanted her hair piled up, just-out-of-bed Bardot fashion. She'd left it down, feeling somewhat less on display. Wear only earrings for jewelry, Jackie ordered. Then he gave her an emerald choker in a Tiffany's box when they were in the limo. She liked the necklace. Unlike the flimsy dress, the emeralds accented her eyes rather than her tits.

Appearances were everything to Jackie Higgins. Cilla was his most prominent accessory these days.

Jackie would be thirty-eight this birthday. Cilla had just turned eighteen. She had been more than a little flattered when Jackie had first courted her at one of her father's industry parties. Cilla was especially pleased when she realized how much Jackie's advances disturbed her father. She was still not above a little petty teenage pleasure when it came to annoying the unshakable Reg Mountbatton.

Her father had been a recovering alcohol and drug abuser for nearly ten years now. A big part of his clean philosophy was to let things roll on over him without ruffling his feathers. Cilla would now be the first to admit that Jackie could annoy even the most serene individual. Jackie thrived on conflict. And he was terribly vain, always jealous of her father's considerable talent and respect. Reg, in turn, despised Jackie's shallow pretentiousness.

Beneath the table, Cilla stroked a long, wide scar on her left kneecap. Jackie called it her one flaw. She thought of it as her fork in life's road, written on her by a surgeon's scalpel.

At fourteen she had taken a bad fall while studying ballet, tearing apart her knee. Her orthopedist assured her a full recovery. She could be a ballerina again after healing. She'd gone in a different direction instead. She had discovered, during her hip-cast-imposed layup, the pleasures to be had in her dad's Stratocaster.

Out of sheer boredom one day, she had picked up the guitar. It was lying, by chance, next to where she sat. At first, she couldn't make her hands cooperate in the least. Frustrated, she lay back in the recliner, letting her eyes wander. She gazed at a photo her father kept on the wall, there in his music room. It was taken back in the late '60s. Dad and Jimi Hendrix were playing together at some London happening. The photo showed Jimi playing his right-handed Fender flipped over.

A light went on in her head. Jimi must have held it that way to accommodate his left-handedness. Encouraged, Cilla turned Reg's instrument over in the same fashion, tuning pegs on bottom, high E string on top, along with the whang bar and knobs. That felt better—not good, but less awkward. She began to teach herself, playing deep into the night.

Never had it occurred to Cilla that guitar playing was something she had within her until her cast trapped her. Once she started, the need to master the guitar became addictive. Cilla submerged herself in learning while her leg mended, making steady progress.

When Cilla was healed, she sat down with her dad to talk about her future. She told him haltingly that she had decided she didn't want to return to the rigors of ballet training. She told him how much she had come to hate starving herself, and enduring the never-ending muscular and joint pain. She loathed the petty, competitive dancers who were her classmates. He nodded, poker-faced. She knew he must be disappointed. Reg had spent a fortune on her ballet training.

She told him about playing his guitar, and shyly performed a twelve bar blues she had composed. To her surprise, Reg was delighted by what he heard. Within the week, he escorted her to his friends at the Fender Custom shop in Corona. They made her a perfect Strat, to her specs, and painted it the same vivid green as her eyes.

Cilla had become friends with guitarist Kyle Reagan. He was a decent guy despite his crazy excesses. Kyle was one of the few men she knew who treated her with musicianly respect. He, like her father, thought she was damned talented, and encouraged her to join him and the boys at rehearsals. Those were the best times, just jamming with the Bad Signs.

From there, she had somehow fallen into this useless affair with Jackie.

He had been all flattery at first. She knew even then that he had a number of other lovers, men as well as women. But initially he treated her like something rare and delicate. Jackie didn't push the sexual side of things until he had asked her to move in with him. She had proven herself a failure then. She now welcomed finding evidence of his others in their house. It made her feel less guilt about rejecting Jackie's touch.

She hoped the show would be fun. Small favor that Jackie had not planned this party. He would have made it a discofest. Partnering with Cilla made him look like a hell of a hoofer. But the trendy dances bored her, and most of the music was lame enough to actually piss her off. She hoped that with the impending arrival of the '80s, disco would finally wheeze its last polyester breath.

Thank heavens Kyle had been responsible for this night's entertainment. He was raving about the Salamanders, claiming theirs to be the hottest urban blues he had ever stumbled across. "Like walking into a nightclub and discovering a twenty-three-year-old Howlin' Wolf!" Kyle declared. Cilla decided she should at least give this younger Blaine and his band a chance.

The lights went down. Cilla heard an amused buzz pass through the assembled guests. She turned to look at the stage and almost laughed out loud. She had once heard that you could always tell a Texan, but you couldn't tell them much. Hadn't anyone tried to talk Firewalker Blaine out of the ridiculous getup he wore? She could tell by the way he swaggered onto the stage that he thought he looked fabulous.

Yeah, right. Small, thin, he looked almost like a child dressed up as a movie-serial cowboy. He sported a flat-brimmed suede hat and cowboy boots. The boots glimmered with rose-gold straps, toe tips and heel guards, and the hat was decorated with a thick rose-gold band. His shirt could be most accurately described as a sleeveless kimono, splashed with bright colors. A silver chain belt, fringe hanging from the clasp, cinched the kimono closed.

Was that a bird, a crane perhaps, tattooed on his upper arm? No, a Stratocaster with wings! Around his neck was a red scarf and countless necklaces, including a peace symbol—perhaps they were still fashionable in Texas? And what the hell were these trousers he had on? Purple velvet. Metal buttons hooked with tiny chains up the legs. They were hideous enough to almost pass for cutting edge.

Cilla felt better already, just from looking at him. She sat back to enjoy the show.

Later, Cilla remembered something she'd read as a girl. Brian Jones, the founder of the Rolling Stones, said the first time he heard an Elmore James record, he felt the world shudder on its axis. She knew the feeling when, without a word, Firewalker Blaine hit the first unbelievably loud notes of *Lickety Split*. Everything faded away, except the man and his sound.

She left Jackie's table without a word to anyone and found her way over to the stage, standing just below the Texan, staring up, opened mouth. This was more than mere guitar playing. His sound was obese, a throbbing life force. She could almost reach out and catch his notes in her hand.

Firewalker saw her watching. He gave her a grin, winking, and started playing to her—for her. She could not even make herself smile back at first. And then someone, she never knew who, took her out on the dance floor. She didn't dance for show, like with Jackie. She didn't dance with discipline, as she had in school. She moved without even thinking about it. When the dance was over, Cilla didn't even thank her partner for asking. She pushed people aside to regain her spot just below Walker. Several more times she danced when asked, not caring whom she was with. After each dance she returned determinably to Walker's feet, soaking him in.

When the Salamanders finished playing, everyone—the barkeep, the kitchen help, and the star-studded crowd—came out on the floor. All cheered madly, begging for more. Firewalker pulled up a chair. He placed a finger to his lips. The people hushed. He said he wanted to play them something he'd written for his wife. Cilla wasn't sure what she'd expected, but certainly not the breathtaking ballad that he gave them. Instantly, irrationally, Cilla was swept with jealousy, her eyes actually burning with tears. It wasn't fair this incredible song belonged to another woman.

Once the show was over, the party descended upon the Salamanders. Cilla backed away from the stage. She turned to go to the ladies' room and ran right into Jackie.

He caught her about the arm, a little roughly. "So. You're back among we mortals, Priscilla?"

"Jackie! I apologize for ignoring you. I just never . . . never heard anything like that."

He nodded, all seriousness for a moment. "He's the real thing, all right. I can see why Kyle was knocked out. But I never expected to see you so affected by such sexually charged stuff." His tone became nasty again. "I think I'll hire him to play by our bedside. Melt your frost, maybe." He smirked. "That would be damned miraculous."

"Don't start with me here. Please." Cilla could feel her cheeks growing hot. Tears threatened to fill her eyes. She had thought herself beyond reacting like this to Jackie's cruel games.

Then Kyle was with them. He had the guitarist at his side. "Hey, you two. Meet Firewalker Blaine. Of course, this is my partner, Jackie Higgins. And this is Cilla Mountbatton."

Jackie shook the Texan's hand. "Cilla's my girlfriend."

"Lucky you," Firewalker said. He tipped his hat and kissed her knuckles.

Jackie cordially thanked the guitarist for performing at his party. Firewalker dipped his head, saying what an honor it was to perform for him. He then kept his eyes on Cilla's while he spoke to Jackie. When there was a pause, he said directly to her, "I saw you watching me."

She nodded, now embarrassed by her gee-whiz behavior during the set.

"You know, my brother, Sonny—Icestorm?—told me ya'll met awhile back." Firewalker smiled, shaking his head in wonder. "He tried to tell me how beautiful you was. I thought he had to be pulling my leg."

"Um ... thanks," she mumbled. Cilla usually found such comments unwelcome, but this time she was flattered. She felt herself start to blush, looking away from Firewalker's eyes. "You play really, really well."

"Well, thank you, Cilla. You don't mind me calling you Cilla, do you, ma'am?"

"Please do." She tittered. He called her *ma'am*! She glanced at Jackie's snide stare, and then turned to watch the guitarist as Kyle moved him on to the next clutch of admirers. Firewalker looked back at her, holding her gaze until he was surrounded.

Jackie squeezed her shoulder a little too hard, nodding after the slight Texan. "He's called 'Fire' for good reason. Guess I'd better take you on home, while the thaw's still on."

8.

HOPING NO ONE noticed her, Cilla ducked into the ladies' room of the hotel lobby, blowing her nose. She checked her look in the mirror, fixed her makeup a little, and then continued toward the elevators. Jackie had made her leave the party moments after they greeted Firewalker. Kyle stopped them at the door, saying the fun would continue at the penthouse suite he'd arranged for the Salamanders.

Cilla planned to rejoin them after changing into something more practical. Jackie had other ideas. As she was slipping on faded jeans over a leotard, he tried to bed her. She shook him off, crossly refusing. A screaming match like none they'd had before ignited. In the end Jackie told her if she went out, not to bother returning. He would have her belongings sent to her father's house in the morning.

She had driven to the hotel, crying furious tears. Now that the initial anger was passing, she felt relieved. The farce was finally over. She was past due to move on from Jackie. She just had no idea what to move on to. To hell with it tonight. She would join Kyle's party, have a good time.

When she knocked at the penthouse door, Firewalker answered. He looked like he had just showered, his long hair quite damp. He wore nothing but a pair of Levi's and his peace symbol necklace. "Howdy there, Cilla. Come on in. Be just a second—I'm on the phone."

She stepped in, watching him as he picked up the receiver. "No, they ain't back yet. Looks like Jackie and his girlfriend are here, though. . . . I know, Vada, it's a damn trip. Well, look, I should go. . . . I miss you, too, honey, so damn much . . . but I'll see you tomorrow. . . . I love you, too. Bye." He hung up, turning to smile at Cilla. "Had to call my wife and tell her all about the show."

"Of course. I'm surprised she's not here with you."

"She sure wanted to be. But she had a run-in with the law awhile back, regarding a little toot . . . probation, see." He shook his head. "No crossing state lines."

"That's a shame." Cilla had been wondering about the wife since he'd played *Smitten*, that stunning song. She knew Mrs. Blaine must still be in the picture somehow.

"Where's Jackie? Parking the car?"

"No, he's not coming. We had a . . . a huge argument." Embarrassed, she felt the tears welling up again. "It's over between us, in fact. He kicked me out."

Walker looked startled. "Are you okay?" He gently took her arm and led her to a couch and sat down with her. He seemed genuinely concerned.

She wiped her eyes with the back of her hand. "I'm fine. This has been a long time coming, believe me. Jackie's an idiot."

"If he kicked you out, he must be. There, I made you smile." He grinned at her. "I think you going to live, girl. Let me get you a drink. All I got is Crown Royal. Is that okay?"

"On the rocks, please." Cilla suddenly realized that she was alone here with Firewalker. "Where is everyone? I thought Kyle and some other people were coming over here."

"He did. But Jesse James was done played out and hit the sack. The rest of us partied a little, then ran out of blow. So Kyle, Riley, and some girls ran over to Kyle's place for some more. They should be back real soon."

"Yes. His house is just down the road from here." She collapsed into the couch, allowing her tension to drain away. She leaned her head back, looking out the sliding glass door of the balcony at the twinkling lights of the Hollywood Hills.

Firewalker sat down beside her, handing her the drink, sipping one of his own. "I'm glad you didn't let Jackie keep you from coming. I wanted a chance to talk more with you."

"Oh?"

He nodded. "My brother told me about meeting you and your daddy at one of the Rockets' shows awhile back. He was real jazzed about it. His first band used to do a lot of Little Lord Mountbatton and the Royals songs.

And I was way into Thunderclap when I started out. I guess you can tell I like the power trio thing." He smiled.

She smiled in return, nodding. "I can't say I spoke to your brother at length. I wanted to discuss music with him. He had something else in mind."

Walker rolled his eyes. "Yeah. He told me. He feels pretty bad about talking thataway to you. Sonny's okay, Cilla. Give him another chance someday. Anyway, he said you told him you played guitar. Left-handed, upside down, too. Is that for real?"

"Yes."

"Cool!"

She laughed to see the pleased expression on his face. "Not like I did it on purpose. That's just the way I started out with my dad's stuff. I didn't know about restringing and such."

"Do you like to play blues?"

"Well, blues rock is what I'm trying to do, anyway. I grew up with it."

"Would you play something for me?"

"I couldn't possibly."

Before she could protest more, he was up and bringing over his sweet gold Strat and a little Pig Nose amp. He plugged the guitar in and tuned it, then handed it to her, grinning as he flipped it over. She admired the guitar for a moment before pulling it into position against her body. "This is a truly lovely instrument."

"Yeah, she's right nice. She's a '57. Her name's Goldie. Now play her for me."

"Really, I don't think I should." She fingered a chord. Barely able to push the strings to the fretboard, she cried, "Good heavens, what have you strung Goldie with? Metal coat hangers?"

He laughed, patting her arm. "Heavy gauge string gives me my bold sound, darlin'. Your hands get used to it. Now, come on. It's just you and me here, girl. Show me how you do that upside-down deal."

"Well . . . okay. I don't know about these strings, though," she muttered, forming the first chords of a song. "Kyle likes the version I do of *Brown-Eyed Handsome Man*."

Firewalker laughed. "Well, he would. Ain't no secret he's obsessed with Chuck Berry."

"Quite. But I do Buddy Holly's version, or try to. Do you know it? It's a lot faster and tougher sounding than Chuck's." He nodded. Smiling nervously, she stood up, putting the strap around her shoulders, and added, "Buddy was from Texas, you know."

"First I ever heard!" Walker gasped, raising his brows, hand slapped to his mouth.

She huffed, "Of course you know that. How stupid of me. You even have that double-strum technique in common with Holly."

"Ah, it's just a basic shuffle, souped up a little."

"The attitude in your playing is similar, too. Texas guitarists are renowned for their cockiness, aren't they?"

"Seems I've heard tell."

Cilla giggled, then took a settling breath. Raking into the fast tempo song, she sang out, a little breathless. She didn't forget the lyrics, but wouldn't dare look up from her hands. She feared stumbling or losing her nerve. But Cilla waded through fairly error-free, taking the song out with triple-strum flourish.

Walker jumped to his feet, applauding. "That was good! You can really play that thing. And sing like an angel, too. Or maybe a devil." He stroked her shoulder. "You are something else, you know it?"

"Thanks for listening." She was thrilled that he approved of her chops. "Most of you don't bother to listen."

"Most of us? Us who?"

"Musicians. Guitarists are the worst."

"That a fact?"

"With my dad it's different, naturally. And Kyle's been great. But most of them . . . they tend to behave like your brother."

"That's a real shame. You're very good."

"You're most kind. I must say it wasn't easy to do that, Firewalker. I mean, aside from the strings being tough to play. You're pretty intimidating." She took off his guitar and handed it back to him. Sitting again on the couch, she watched him cross to his instrument's hard case.

"Intimidating? I'm a real sweetheart. Ain't I acting nice here?" he protested, putting the guitar in its case.

"That's not what I mean. It's the way you play. I've seen . . . I've never seen anything like what I heard from you tonight."

"Yeah? You heard lots of folks, too, I bet. You ever hear Jimi Hendrix play live?" He sat down next to her on the couch.

"I did, as a child. You remind me of him. Your playing." The bad taste in clothes, too, she thought, but didn't say it.

"He's one of my heroes," Walker confessed. "My brother met him once at a party, but we never seen him play live."

"I never saw a concert or anything. He'd just be fooling around at my father's house, you know." She was enjoying herself now. She felt relaxed, maybe even a little giddy with drink. "You want to know a secret? All the girls in my school had pictures on their walls of the Beatles or some of the other cute English guys. Some even had my father's pictures."

"We did, too. Sonny and I had a Royals poster when we was little."

"I bet I know the one . . . it was everywhere when I was young. Quite weird, for me. I had pictures of Jimi. I saw some film of him, playing *Like a Rolling Stone*, I think it was. . . . Well, I put Jimi's picture on my mirror. I had a terrible schoolgirl crush on him. He was wild, different from all the other players that came through our house. I was pretty young, but I knew his accent was unusual. I remember asking him where he came from."

Walker grinned. "Did he say Mars?"

"Yes! I believed him at the time. Perhaps I still do. I actually used to practice writing my name, 'Priscilla Hendrix.' Isn't that stupid?"

"Yeah," Walker agreed, laughing. "That's a girl thing, I think."

"I have one photo of me sitting on Jimi's lap. I was about ten years old. It's a favorite."

Walker shook his head, laughing in amazement. "What a trip. Growing up with such talented people in your own house."

"Well . . . you had pretty talented people hanging out at your house, too."

"Yeah, but we was all nobody back then. You got that picture in your wallet?"

"Sorry, no. It's framed at my house. But understand—it wasn't like I was at Dad's house all that much. I was usually at boarding school. First England, then here. I sometimes went home holidays—if he wasn't on tour. He and I have really just gotten to know one another in the last few years."

They both sat quietly—just shy of touching. They sipped their whiskey. Cilla was looking out at the city lights, thinking about nothing. She could feel Firewalker studying her.

She began to grow uneasy. Where were Kyle and the rest of them? She really should not be sitting here getting drunk with this strange Texan, no matter how mad she was at Jackie. She had learned the hard way from past experience that this was not safe behavior.

She thought of the worst time in particular now. She'd gone to a party, held at some rich boy's house, no parents around. She was still recovering from her knee surgery at the time. She was with older girls from her new school. She was trying to fit in, to make friends closer to her own age for a change.

After a bout of Cardinal Puff, a ridiculous and excessive drinking game, Cilla found herself in a bedroom, alone with a bunch of boys. Somehow they knew she was a dancer. Show us some moves, they said. She protested at first, as her knee was still tender. But she was drunk and having fun for a change. Then it had grown ugly. Suddenly they were on her, tearing off her panties, hands covering her mouth to prevent her from screaming. They all took turns with her. Once they let her loose, she ran away from that house. She fell a few times, afraid she would further injure her knee, but more afraid of them catching her and brutalizing her further. She finally found a main street and a pay phone to call for a taxi. Cilla never breathed a word about what happened at that party. She was ashamed at getting herself into such a stupid fix.

And here she was again, getting loaded in a room with a half-naked stranger.

He seemed a really pleasant stranger, though. He'd listened to her play. Cilla realized that she might not mind if he tried something. This was a frightening revelation. She jumped off the couch, moving away from him. "Hey, you know what? Right now, there's a radio show featuring great blues." She reached for the little clock radio on his nightstand, and tuned in the program, turning up the volume. Buddy Guy was singing *She Suits Me to a Tee*.

Walker smiled approvingly. "Well, hey! Sounds real fine to me already."

She stayed standing near the radio. She didn't want to go near him again. She felt lightheaded, and didn't think it was entirely due to the whiskey.

"Hey, Cilla. Since we got this nice music, would you do me a big favor?"

"It depends, Firewalker."

"Make it two favors. First, call me Walker. My close friends do."

"Is that your real name?" she asked. He nodded. "Very unusual. Is it a family name?"

"No, my mama said it just popped into her head when she held me the first time. Walker Dale. She's the only one calls me both names, though. My Uncle Charlie calls me Little T-Bone—always did, even before I started playing. Daddy tried to talk Mama out of naming me Walker. Daddy's Southern white trash, understand. Thought Walker was too black. But she wouldn't budge. And her daddy, my granddaddy, loved it. He was a real blues fan. Daddy Jim—that's what we called him—he used to say the ghost of T-Bone had whispered it in her ear."

"Surely T-Bone was still alive when you were born."

Walker waved a hand over his head, snickering a little. "I think Daddy Jim meant, like, astral projection or something. Trying to be poetic."

"It is poetic. Walker, then," she said. "What's your second favor?"

"There's just one thing I don't like about playing live. I'm up there working hard. All the pretty women are dancing with someone else." He stood up, holding his hands out to her. "You know how to two-step at all? Or *baisse bas*? That one's sort of like a waltz . . . what you'd call a three step, I guess."

"I've heard of the two-step. And the . . . *baisse bas*, is it? Sounds French. But I know my French dance terms—"

"It's Louisiana French, though, not France French. Kind of a nasty dance Sonny's singer taught us." Walker laughed, taking one of her hands firmly in his. With the other, he squeezed her waist authoritatively. "I was hoping you knew how to do it."

"Not me," She replied, placing her free hand on his shoulder. This was unwise. He had a nice shoulder though, surprisingly hot to the touch. "If we take it slow, I imagine I can follow you."

"I bet you can. Just feel the music, there, see? Quick, quick—now slow . . . slow—you got it, Cill. Come closer."

Walker was very fluid, easy to follow. Look into your partner's eyes. That's how she'd been trained to follow. Don't watch the feet. Read his next step in his eyes. And Walker's eyes were wonderful, such a dark brown they almost looked black. She could read his enjoyment, his longing, as plain as a billboard. Hopefully her thoughts weren't as obvious to him.

She wasn't certain what she found attractive about him. Could it be because she was furious with Jackie? She didn't think so. Walker had snagged her attention earlier, by his playing. His singing was appealing. His speaking voice was even better—rugged, with an honest Texas drawl, thick as clover honey. Dreadful grammar, yes, but he spoke to her with a blend of flirtation and respectfulness that was pleasing.

He was not much taller or even much heavier than she was herself. And forget handsome, by typical standards. Still, she felt drawn to him. She liked being held to his bare chest. Lovely, lovely arms, too. There was a phrase that described him perfectly—rustic charm. Walker was rustic charm personified.

She looked away, trying to pull herself back. "This is fun, Walker. I used to study dance." Her voice sounded too high.

"I know. You do the two-step like you been doing it all your life, girl." The song ended. Bobby Blue Bland's slow, sexy number *I'll Take Care of You* came on the radio.

"My mojo must be working," Walker whispered. "Playing us a slow dance." Cilla's knees gave a little as he pulled her closer. This wasn't dancing anymore. This was something closer to foreplay. She laid her head on his shoulder, and then suppressed a sudden urge to nip his tattoo.

She should leave here, and right now. She should, but wasn't about to. She held on tighter, enjoying the steady comfort of his heartbeat.

The song ended. The DJ was going down the playlist. Cilla didn't move. She waited, with her cheek against his warmth.

"Cilla? Can I just tell you one thing?"

She looked at his face, nodding.

"You are the finest thing I ever seen."

He kissed her. She heard a groan of pleasure. With distant surprise, she realized the sound came from her own throat. He was a thorough kisser, gentle. Took his sweet time.

Cilla was vaguely aware of the music resuming. Walker pulled away from her mouth, smiled once, and kissed her cheek. Pushing aside her hair, he licked and bit at her neck. Here came that groan again.

She felt his hands move to the fly of her jeans. She opened her eyes, coming back to herself somewhat. Stop him now. Run for safety. Go home to Dad.

Walker was married. He loved his wife. On the phone Cilla had heard him tell her so. She'd heard him tell her in *Smitten*, too. This was wrong. He dropped to a squat, sliding down the front of her, stripping her jeans along with him. Stop him. Jesus, his hands felt good on her thighs.

"Damn, girl! You got on one of these one-piece things. Any easy-open snaps down here?" He ran a finger over her crotch. She realized he was talking about her leotard. Walker buried his face against her belly. He breathed in the scent of her. He laid on heavy kisses to her inner thigh, muttering in between, "Just got to go a different route. Peel you from the top, like a banana." He reached up with callused fingers and rolled down a shoulder of the leotard. She couldn't tell him not to.

Someone pounded at the door. Cilla jumped free of Walker's grip, nearly tumbling to the carpet from the jeans around her knees. Kyle's muffled voice came from the hall. Walker shouted, "Hold your horses, man!" He grabbed Cilla's waistline, using her to leverage himself to his feet. Kissing her cheek, he sheathed her bare arm and breast in the leotard. He whispered, "Bad timing, huh?" Then he crossed to open the door. She swayed slightly where he had left her. He looked back before he yanked the door open and started laughing. "Girl? You might want to pull up your britches before I open up."

"Oh . . . of course. Thank you," she stammered. She fumbled with the button fly as he grinned on. She ran a calming hand through her hair. Kyle and the rest piled into the room, talking all at once. Cilla did her best to smile pleasantly, greeting everyone. Nothing had happened. Not really.

They partied until the Salamanders had to get to the airport. All the while everyone did Kyle's excellent stash and listened to the rich West Coast radio. Jesse James shuffled in sometime after dawn. He was cow-licked, sleepy-eyed, and half-starved. Kyle called room service and ordered a huge breakfast. Everyone but Jesse James was too wired to eat at first. But Kyle also had powerful weed on hand. They all managed to work up a fair case of munchies before time to fly.

Kyle told them he had made a tape of the show from the soundboard. He promised to send Walker the master. "But I want to keep a copy for meself," he added.

"I'd like one, too, Kyle," Cilla said. "Can we go make a copy before I head home?" Walker watched her from across the room, grinning. "I'll make sure we get yours to you, Walker."

"Thank you, darlin'."

"I want to see what I can do to shop it around," Kyle declared. "We got to get you signed. It's fucking outrageous you don't have a record deal."

"We'd be right grateful for any help you could give us," Walker replied.

Riley and Jesse James murmured agreement. "But for now, don't we need to think about catching our flight back to Austin?"

"Right. I'll call you a limo," Kyle said. He went into the bedroom to use the phone, trailed by his girlfriend. Jesse James and Riley went to their rooms to gather up things for the trip home.

Walker rose and came to where Cilla sat. He pulled her to her feet. Hands resting on her shoulders, he said, "Thanks for an enjoyable time, darlin'. I sure was glad to hear you play. Can't wait to tell Sonny how good you are. And I don't mean good for a girl. I mean plain good."

"Thank you, Walker."

"You work on getting a band together, now. I bet there's a million people in this town that would love to work with you. I know if you came home with me you'd have a group in nothing flat." He pulled her closer and whispered, "Crying shame we didn't have more time. Could have been real sweet."

"Sweet?" She moved away from him, avoiding his eyes. She managed to speak with a much chillier tone than she was feeling. Her heart pounded in her chest, and she knew it wasn't entirely due to the waning cocaine in her system. "Now you can still look your wife in the eye when you see her."

Walker ducked his head behind his hat brim. "Guess you got a point," he muttered. "I'm sorry." She nodded and started to leave. He caught her arm, his face serious. "I want you to keep playing, girl. You got talent. Do whatever it takes to get a band together. Use your daddy's connections, if you got to. Nothing wrong with that if it gets you heard."

She pulled her arm free, nodding. "Thank you, Walker." She stepped toward the door. Putting her fingers on the handle, she turned back to him. "And I promise to do what I can to get your tape heard. You're one of a kind. If people only get the chance to hear your music, there'll be no stopping you."

9.

DON'T LOOK BACK. *Someone might be gaining on you.*

Pitcher Satchel Paige had said that, years ago. Bob Dylan had given the same advice. Sonny blew a stream of cigarette smoke into the dark. Naked, he sat in his hotel room, his Telecaster across his lap. He wasn't plugged in. He didn't want the noise of it to wake up the woman in his bed.

With only the glow of his cigarette tip for illumination, his blind hands worked the familiar frets. He paused, stroking the guitar's smooth body. Sonny felt his way to the ashtray, snuffing out the cigarette. He then raced down the neck. Quick and slick as he was able, he tore into a complicated run, picked with the tips of his fingers.

(One . . .) He had to do it nine more times in a row, no mistakes. If he

messed up, he had to start over. Back when, that had been his unbreakable rule. Practice makes perfect, but only if you practice perfect. Sonny hit the lick a second time. He fumbled midway. Began again. *(One . . . two . . . .)*

He glanced across the room at the clock radio. Walker had called him maybe an hour ago. The fool said he forgot that Europe wasn't on Texas time. Sonny hated wee-hour phone calls. Mostly, they brought bad news. Not this time. Not from Walker's standpoint.

"Jesus, Walker, you about gave me a heart attack," Sonny whispered. He watched his bed buddy roll over, pulling the sheets with her. "I'll call you back later."

"Don't hang up, Sonny!" Walker hollered. The connection was muffled, buzzing. "Took me forever to track you down. Look, I got big news. Besides, Vada's at work now. Don't have to worry about her overhearing."

Sonny woke up another slice. "And what don't Vada need to hear?" He fumbled with a pack of cigarettes. "You been up to no good?"

"Damn near! You know that party I played for Jackie Higgins's birthday?"

"Yeah. Was it cool?"

Very cool, indeed, from the sound of it. As Walker told it, it had been a regular *Who's Who* of the too-hip-for-the-room crowd. And, of all people, Little Lady Mountbatton had been there. She had been the guest of honor's ornament du jour. Sonny heard tell that the girl had been dating the old fruity Bad Sign. What on earth women saw in that guy. . . .

Walker was on a brag. "Sonny, she ignored Higgins. She was listening to and watching *me*. Didn't know who she was at the time. Damn! Cilla's as fine as you said. That red, red hair? And them eyes. On top of being built like a brick shithouse." He paused. Sonny detected the high sound of ice cubes in a glass. "I played right at her the whole time, Sonny. Later, she came over to the hotel. Alone. I was alone, too. Kyle and them had to . . . go out. We went dry. Get me?"

"Sure. So, did you do her?" Sonny gripped the phone hard, waiting for the answer.

Walker hadn't. The others came back before he managed.

Damn. Sonny fumbled the run, sixth time through. Lost his flow, thinking about what Walker had said earlier. The idea of Walker and Cilla Mountbatton together ate at Sonny. He grimaced. How stupid was that? He had less than no claim on her. Determined to concentrate, he started his practice riff again. *(One . . . two . . . .)*

Cilla had played Goldie for Walker. That she'd managed to even produce sounds from the guitar's monstrous strings was feat enough. "She ain't bad," Walker told him. "Technically she's got it happening. Pretty tough little player."

"Be hard to sound pussy on that Strat, way you got it tricked."

"Maybe. But that girl played the hell out of *Brown-Eyed Handsome Man*." He paused, adding, "Buddy Holly's version, now."

Not too shabby. Upside down and backward, too, Walker verified. Just like Mountbatton said. Now Sonny wished he had taken time to listen to her. Been polite, like Walker.

Shit. He fumbled the run again. He was all the way up to eight this go-round.

"It was sure enough hot while it lasted," Walker had told him. "Leastwise, we got to slow dance and kiss some."

Sonny's fingers tangled again. "Fuck it," he breathed. He snapped his left hand out in a violent jerk, making the joints crackle. He adjusted a tuning peg, and started the run again *(One . . . two . . .)*. Focus on the playing, let it flow from his hands. Concentrate on the music, not on the girl: a hard, but doable, job. But the second bomb Walker dropped was more difficult to shake off.

Kyle had generously recorded the show. He and Cilla had taken copies, promising to circulate the tape. After one listening, producer Sterling Preston had signed the Salamanders. Sonny had been struck dumb for a minute by the news.

"Sonny! You still there? Hello?"

"I'm here . . . shit-fire, Walker."

"What? Man, our connection's going shitty." It was. Other garbled voices, and yet more white noise, cluttered the line. Walker was almost shouting. "Can you hear me, Sonny?"

"Did you say Sterling Preston? American Records' Sterling Preston?" Sonny asked, speaking slowly and clearly.

"Ain't but one!" Walker yelped. "Going to produce us, too. Man, I can't believe my luck."

Neither could Sonny. Sterling Preston's ear was twin to a bloodhound's nose. The man had an uncanny ability for unearthing new music of all kinds. He'd been nearly miraculous in doing it for half a century. All of Preston's finds were exceptionally gifted. Nearly every act was timeless, in fact. In the last decade Preston hadn't signed anyone—hadn't needed to, because of the library of music he'd secured for American.

After all this time, Preston had chosen Walker to add to American's legendary roster.

"Sonny? You say anything? I think I'm losing. . . ." The line exploded with crackling. ". . . hear me. . . ." One more big growl, and the connection came back a little stronger. Sonny caught Walker's words in mid-sentence. ". . . had to come out of retirement, get me recorded. He's going to release my stuff through Twelve Bar, American's blues division. Called me himself. I thought at first it was Real, like, fucking with me. Sonny? You still listening?"

"Yeah, I am. This is a miracle, Squirt."

"I know."

They both sat silent for ten seconds or so. Sonny finally said, "You can't mess this up, Walker."

"What? I can't hear you again."

"I said, Don't screw this up." Sonny spoke slowly. "Get someone to manage ya'll, now." Walker had never made enough to pay for management before. Few in the Austin Clan were represented. Management wasn't renowned for working its ass off for ten percent of nothing. "This is the big time for you," Sonny said.

"What? This connection's getting bad again," Walker said. "I hope you're hearing this."

"The big time, I said. Someone needs to help you with business." Sonny raised his voice. The sleeping girl groaned, but stayed out.

"Get me a manager, you're saying? Yeah, I got one. You know who Steven Taylor is?"

Of course, Sonny knew. He had been Reg Mountbatton's manager since the Thunderclap days—managed several other successful British bluesmen, too.

"We just squaring away the details now. We record in Reg's studio the first of next month." Another blast of static enveloped Walker's voice. Sonny took the phone away from his ear, slightly grimacing. The noise broke up enough to allow Sonny to hear Walker saying, ". . . wanted to be like you, because you're the best. Thanks for all. . . ." The end of the sentence ended up buried in fuzz tone that didn't seem to want to move on.

"Walker, you're breaking up too bad. I'm hanging up. Give Vada my love. Bye, Squirt." He put down the receiver before Walker squawked protests.

Sonny had gone back to bed but couldn't again find sleep. He thought about waking the groupie, seeing if he couldn't screw himself back down. She might want to talk, though. Instead, he took up his guitar.

Sonny yawned. He leaned over to a curtain within reach. Dawn was bravely peeking through a steady rain. England's weather sure enough was lousy—most of Europe had crappy weather. Sonny lit another smoke. He wished he was home in his own bed. He rested his head on the back of the chair, gazing at the sleeping stranger. He could not begin to recall her name.

He was happy enough, traveling the world, trusty Fender in hand. He was making good bread. He was respected in his field. Women were his for the taking. Except Cilla—but then she'd been too young when they'd met. Not like she was now, all grown up and playing house with rock stars.

Life was fine. He took one more drag off his smoke, and then crushed it flat in the ashtray. Time to start the solo again. (*One . . . two . . . three . . . four . . .*) Don't (*. . . five . . .*) look (*. . . six . . .*) back (*. . . seven . . .*).

(*. . . eight . . .*) Sterling Preston (*. . . nine . . .*). Producing Walker's debut. It seemed too good to be true. Maybe goodness and truth had nothing to do with it. Bonnell's insinuation, talk of dark barter, came slinking back into the forefront of Sonny's mind.

His fingers stumbled the tenth time through.

Someone might be gaining on you. . . .

10.

"SONNY!" BONNELL CALLED. "Come see who's on television."

The Rockets were in a hotel suite, unwinding after a festival performance. Sonny was at the wet bar, refilling his highball. He turned to Bonnell's voice. On the screen Sterling Preston was smiling like a proud daddy. On the other side of the suite, Rimshot and Johnny Lee hushed the girls they were chatting up and gathered round the TV. Bonnell leaned forward and turned up the volume.

". . . when I heard Firewalker's tape, I had to do everything in my power to help," Preston rumbled in his elegant Harvard dialect. "This young man's singing, much less his playing, struck a deep chord in me."

"Struck a chord, Sterling? Ain't you funny!" Walker barked. Preston and the interviewer laughed with him.

Sonny pulled up a chair alongside Bonnell. A woman in a red leather dress dropped onto Sonny's knee, wrapping an arm around his neck. Sonny took a long draw off his drink, mindlessly feeling the groupie up as he studied the screen. What a pair his brother and the producer made. Sterling Preston, nary a silver hair out of place, his dark suit cut to perfection, looked more like a stockbroker than a record executive. Walker was decked out in his typical funkiness. A new Texas-shaped ornament perched atop his hat brim. Red-gold, the size of a sheriff's badge, the trinket had a star ruby representing where Austin would be on a map. The face beneath the hat looked weary, road-worn. Likely, Walker would think the same of Sonny if he saw him now.

". . . a week after we started, we had the *Ghost of T-Bone* album all but completed," Preston continued. "Remarkable. What you'll hear on the record is what the Salamanders played live in studio. No overdubs, and very few takes."

"Yeah, well. They don't give you second takes in Texas clubs," added Walker. "Got to get it right the first time around, or it's hell to pay."

"You came up through the Austin club scene, isn't that right?" the interviewer asked. Walker nodded. "Who would you say were your big influences?"

"Musically? Well, there's lots. Hendrix, of course, and Buddy Guy. Hubert Sumlin's taught us all a thing or two. Nobody playing would sound like they do without B.B.'s influence. There's all the great Texas dudes I took in over the years. T-Bone, Gatemouth, Freddie and Albert King, all them guys. Everybody. Oh, man, I don't want to hurt feelings leaving no one out," he added, laughing.

"But I reckon my biggest influences was my late pianist granddaddy, Jim Crawford, and my big brother, Sonny. Icestorm Blaine, that is."

"Well, isn't that sweet?" Bonnell chuckled.

"You're Firewalker Blaine's brother?" the girl in Sonny's lap asked him. "I had no clue."

He pretended not to hear, staring at the screen.

"And they say no one remembers us little people," Johnny Lee cracked, punching Sonny's arm.

". . . Daddy Jim left us a talented gene pool, a respect of music, and a damn fine record collection," Walker continued. "Plus, Icestorm brought lots more good records home for us to try and figure out."

The interviewer asked, "Your brother, Icestorm, is a professional guitar player also?"

"Damn straight, you moron," Sonny said to the TV. The others in the room laughed.

Walker rolled his eyes. "Just one of the best. Lead guitarist for the Rocket 88s. Been playing professional since he was fifteen. He's the real reason I took it up." He looked into the camera. "Hey! You don't got a Rocket 88s album or two, do yourselves a damn favor."

"Ain't that considerate?" Sonny said.

"This cannot hurt us any," Bonnell commented. "Your brother, right now he is red-hot."

"Don't remind me."

"Red-hot," Bonnell repeated, giving Sonny a sidelong glance. "The great Sterling Preston coming out of retirement, just to work with Walker? It seems almost . . . preordained, *n'est-ce pas*?"

Before Sonny could answer, Johnny Lee waved them silent. "Let's see what else they say, man."

Walker continued, "I been real, real lucky. I had good music in the house since I was a little boy, what with the records, and my brother and his friends playing around me. Plus, God blessed me with a talent. I'm trying to use it to the best of my abilities, you know?" The interviewer and Preston nodded. "The Austin scene was so ripe when I hit it. There was great people starting bands all over. My brother was there, paving the way. My dear wife Vada, too, whose band Real, Jesse James and I played in before we put the Salamanders together. There's still a ton of talent there. They work their asses off, playing for nickels and dimes. Do it for the love of it. And that's where it's at, and why you stick with it. The pure joy it brings." Walker looked pensive for a moment. "But it don't always pay the bills, especially when times get hard or you can't work no more. There's a lot of folks, especially the older ones, who worked like dogs their whole lives, and due to crooked royalty deals and purely bad business doings, they ain't got a dime for later years. So, that's what Sterling Preston and me are trying to cook up next." Walker smiled at his producer. "Want to tell them about it, Sterling?"

"My pleasure. Firewalker has the idea for a fund to help artists in need, especially in their later years. Through the auspices of American Records, we are working to establish a Blues Artist's Emergency Fund."

"A charity?" the interviewer asked.

"I guess in the strict sense of the word, yeah," Walker answered. "But I look at it more as paying back what's owed, taking care of our own. Because I wouldn't be here without these people. I consider them my ancestors. And I feel like, if I do good, then I should spread the good." He looked at the camera. "Ya'll listening to my stuff and digging it need to go out and find other folks doing it, too. Look to the source."

"This is a pretty cool idea he has," Rimshot commented.

"It ain't bad," Sonny agreed.

"The first thing I want to do, to really kick this off, is have a big old show, with all the ticket profits going to this fund," Walker said.

Preston added, "The Salamanders would headline, of course."

"I picture having a bunch of home folks involved, too," Walker went on. "Kind of give ya'll a taste of the scene we sprung from."

"Where were you thinking of holding this show?" asked the interviewer.

"Maybe some cool place in L.A. The Wiltern or Pantages, something like that. Ain't folks in L.A. known for raising money for one thing or another?"

Preston laughed, patting Walker's shoulder. "And this cause is worthier than many."

The interviewer smiled. "Will your brother be involved with this?"

"Oh, hell, yes. Couldn't do it without him. But I haven't talked to him about it yet. We both been traveling, and we ain't been home at the same time in ages. But I think he'll dig this, and want to help." Walker peered into the camera lens. "Hey, Sonny! If you killing time watching us, listen up. You do this show with me, hear?"

SONNY WOKE WITH A jolt when he felt the plane touch down. It took him a minute to reorient himself and realize he was on his home turf, rolling down an Austin runway. The familiar blast of Texas humidity embraced him as he stepped out of the terminal. He felt relaxation begin to settle over him. He didn't have much time to let himself slide into true ease. He would barely have enough time to run by his house. He had to get down to the rehearsal space where Walker was putting together the act for the

Wang Dang Doodle Fund-raiser for the Sterling Preston Blues Emergency Fund.

What a Walker-like gesture, to name this charity he had brought painstakingly to life after Mr. Preston instead of himself. He caught a cab that took him down familiar streets toward home. Preston had put up the money from his impressive family fortune to get this show's expenses paid for, so that 100 percent of the pricey tickets could go directly into the fund. But the show was Walker's baby. He talked everyone involved into donating his or her talents. Sonny was excited to be a part of it. This truly was a good way to pay back the people who had inspired them both to make music.

Sonny put his Mustang's battery on the charge when he got home and went in to take a revitalizing shower. He called his management and arranged to have his mail sent around. He needed to spend part of the two days that he wasn't gripped in rehearsal taking care of home business. Then they would be off to Los Angeles for the big show.

Sonny wondered if his parents were staying with Walker and Vada. Perhaps they were all meeting up in Los Angeles. He wondered, too, if Vada had been able to get permission to travel out of state for the concert. She had kept pretty much to the straight and narrow since her arrest—at least as far as her probation officer knew. She only had one altercation, by all accounts defending herself against a drunken masher in her parents' parking lot last month. She still had a little more than six months to go on her probation.

Sonny hoped for his sister-in-law's sake that all would go well. From his brief talks with Walker, Sonny knew that his brother's sudden rise to fame had been trouble for the homebound Vada.

He pulled on boots, jeans, and a T-shirt and grabbed his Telecaster case. He'd carried it with him on the plane, instead of shipping it separately with the rest of his gear. He wanted the guitar handy for rehearsals. Two beers stood vigil in the fridge, next to an empty butter dish. Sonny popped one beer open for the drive and tossed the other into the car's passenger seat.

Chaos was pretty much the only one in charge when Sonny arrived. There was a group of horn slingers, including former King Bees Ikey and Mikey, blowing what sounded like random noise on stage. A bored-looking pianist Sonny recalled from nights on East Sixth Street tittered around on a grand. People he didn't recollect were running to and fro, barking orders to no one.

Sonny finally spotted a haggard Walker. He wore a BLUES EMERGENCY FUND T-shirt and raggedy jeans. His dirty hair was pulled into a ponytail. The tattered fedora he'd sported as a teenager was perched on his head. Several people surrounded him, talking in his face. Amid the confusion, Walker gripped a boy's hand. The child looked on, silent.

Sonny joined the group, waiting for Walker to give the different people instructions and send them on their way. Walker looked wildly relieved when he recognized him. "Man, am I glad to see you! I sure bit off too much this time. Here's hoping we get it all together by showtime."

"We will, we will. I'm at your disposal now, Squirt." Sonny turned a smile toward the boy, whose hand was completely engulfed in Walker's. "Looks like you got at least one helper already." Sonny automatically used his own daddy's standard small-kid salutation. "Hey, you. What's your name—and why?"

The curly-headed boy looked up at Sonny with deep black eyes. Sonny felt a tremor of recognition right before the little boy answered in a high, strong voice, "I'm Otis. You got to ask Mama just why, though. There's a guitar player with my same name." He gazed up at Walker, looking for approval. "Right, Uncle Firewalker?"

"Right as rain, Sugar-boy." Walker smiled down at Otis. He raised his eyes to Sonny's, giving him a sharp nod. "Surprise. Wasn't quite how I hoped ya'll would meet. But it's a crazy day."

Sonny's heart galloped as he took in the boy. Otis was a combination of Montgomery and Blaine if ever there was one. If he'd had any doubts about who was responsible for Otis, they had been wiped clean by those black eyes staring up at him.

Walker poked Sonny in the arm. "Heads up, man." To the boy, he said, "Looky there, Otis. Uncle Floyd's back to take you home."

Floyd Montgomery was charging up the aisle, scanning paperwork with his typical squint. He stopped below them in the orchestra pit, handing the papers up to Walker. "Walker, I got those mikes and stuff tended to. Thanks for letting Otis hang out—shit-fire!" He froze, seeing Sonny. He looked from his former bandmate to the boy.

"Hey. What a surprise to see ya'll . . . you and Otis here," Sonny said, trying to sound friendly despite his shock.

"Yeah. I just bet," Floyd said. His scratchy, rich voice and permanent squint were the only things that hadn't changed about him. Floyd had gone to war still a gangly, scraggly kid. He'd filled out, and his once wild array of curls were now neatly cropped close to his head. The formerly splotchy beard was plush, speckled with gray, trimmed smooth. "Looking forward to working with you again, Sonny. You been making some mighty fine, really original music since we seen each other last."

"Thanks, Floyd." Sonny was pleased to hear that his old singer liked his Rockets work. Floyd had been like an older brother to him before. . . . He looked down at the boy again, and guilt started to bubble up in him like a badly drawn draft.

Floyd held out his arms to Otis to help him from the stage. The boy reached toward Walker first, getting a quick hug. Then he let out a rebel yell and jumped from the stage to be caught by Floyd.

Floyd set him down, dropping a hand to the kid's shoulder, and they waded off through the rehearsal madness. Looked just like something out of fucking *Shane*. Sonny glared at Walker and breathed, "Why not just chuck an ice water balloon at me when I walked in, instead?"

"Sonny, please—"

"Please what? You could give me some fucking warning before springing them two on me."

"Didn't think you'd be here until after they left. Wasn't expecting Otis at all, but something came up and Floyd had to bring him with. And Floyd, I planned to tell you about him being involved before ya'll met up."

"So tell me now," Sonny shot back edgily. He wished for a smoke, trying to will his hands not to shake.

"Briefly, man," Walker said wearily. "We got so much to do. Come on, let's go grab the playlist. I'll show you what we got to whip into shape."

Backstage, they found a relatively commotion-free spot to sit. Walker offered Sonny a cigarette. As Sonny lit up, Walker said, "You know I put word out to the Austin crowd that I was putting this together, kind of a big band thing? Well, I knew we would have horns, and I got a hold of Ikey and Mikey. They're doing a big arrangement with some of their old cronies. Then I found a pianist and a B-3 Hammond player in a couple of local bands. So we was all kind of working arrangements, and who shows up but Floyd, harp in hand."

"Just like that."

"Pretty much. Guess he done a couple a tours in the Navy. You know, 'Nam was over before he got out from his first tour. Said it wasn't such a bad gig." Walker swept an arm through the air, imitating Floyd's squint. "Saw the world and all that shit. He's been back in Texas for a couple of years, helping his dad with the John Deere dealership. Came back to Austin a few months ago. He don't have a band just yet, but he's writing up a storm—real good songs, too.

"Anyway, he wanted to know if I needed a harpman. I said, sure enough, so long as we could all work cool together, you know? He don't have a problem. Seems Nancy Ruth and your . . . and her kid are doing real well now. She ended up back here at school. Not too long ago she married one of her professors. Girl's a regular faculty wife, Floyd tells me." Walker shrugged. He frowned at Sonny and took a long drag off his smoke.

Sonny stared back, silent. Finally, he growled, "This is a shitload to swallow, Walker."

"There ain't time to dwell on it now, Sonny." Walker held out a list. "Look here. I figure you'll work as my rhythm guitar, my second in command. Is that cool with you?"

"I reckon so."

"These are the songs I thought we'd do."

Sonny wrestled his mind back to the task at hand. He studied the playlist. The Salamanders were opening with some of the rocking songs from their record. Then the big band joined in for the rest of the set, which consisted of great blues songs penned by Walker's heroes. He had Willie Dixon's *Wang Dang Doodle* set up as Vada's showpiece, giving the concert its title. Sonny supposed Walker really wanted her there. And he had *Who Do You Love?*, the song that the brothers had first played together at Sonny's eighteenth birthday party, notated as a dual solo for himself and Sonny. Walker would take the encores alone, with *Smitten* and *Lickety Split*.

"This looks good, Squirt," Sonny said, nodding over the choices. "Real nice. You run through some of this stuff with these folks yet?"

"Really just the first three, the ones I do with Real and Outlaw."

"Outlaw?"

Walker rolled his eyes, laughing. "That's what Jesse James took to calling himself, our last tour. Felt out of it as the only one of us without a blues name, I reckon."

Sonny managed a laugh. "Like going through life as fucking *Jesse James* wasn't enough!"

"I know it. Anyway, I think just about everyone's here now. Let's see if we can find Vada, and when Floyd gets back from dropping Otis off, we'll see if we can get this thing moving."

They located Vada down the hall, in a room that had been set up for costume fittings. She was surveying herself in a full-length mirror, dressed in what Sonny later learned was a Bob Mackie original. The sleeveless second-skin gown was cut dramatically low in the back and was covered in sparkling mauve bugle beads. The neckline and hem were trimmed in black. Sonny whistled. "Damn. Sure a shame you married."

She tossed her curly head, her masterful pout in place. She glanced back to see who had given her the compliment. Seeing Sonny, she snapped out of her temptress act and dashed over to hug him. "Oh, my God! It sure is good to see you."

"You too, sugar," Sonny said, giving her a firm squeeze.

"We going to pull this thing off, Sonny?"

"It's going to be great, Vada." He held her at arms' length, grinning. "Girl, this takes me back. How long since we played in a band together?"

Her hands still on Sonny's shoulder, Vada gave a narrow-eyed stare beyond him. Sonny glanced back to where she was looking. Walker was taking her in, slouched silent in the doorway.

"Been way too long, Sonny-honey," she said, with a bitterness that took him by surprise. "Surely we went to your place and screwed like mad afterward, though."

Sonny pushed away, gaping, but Vada still clutched him. He turned to say something, anything, as an apology.

Walker had his forehead dropped into his hands, muttering, "Hush, girl. No ugly games with Sonny. He ain't had an easy day." He looked up to her face and shook his head at her. She stared back at him, eyes defiant. Walker added hoarsely, "You take my breath away in that dress, girl. Glad I picked it up."

Someone called to Walker down the hall, yelling something about a gruesome feedback situation. "Shit! Better go check." He asked Sonny, "Can ya'll be up for a run-through in twenty?"

"You got it, Walker," Sonny told him, watching as his brother raced off toward the stage. Roughly, he pulled himself free of his sister-in-law. "That was a shitty thing to say, woman. What's eating you?"

Her bottom lip started to tremble and tears filled her eyes. Swearing under her breath, she turned her back to him. "Give me credit for being truthful, at least. Mind undoing me?" She lifted her left arm, revealing a hidden zipper. Sonny hesitated a moment, then unzipped her dress. He turned his back as she started to slip out of the gown. He heard her say, "Developed some scruples in your travels? Or am I just not worth taking a peek at anymore?" She pulled a purple T-shirt dress over her head and put the gown on a padded hanger, placing it on a clothes rack. "You can look now, Sonny. Let's go share a little pick-me-up."

Sonny followed her into the attached bathroom, feeling utterly confused. "I came here, hoping to help Walker out with something real worthwhile. But since I got here, all hell's broke loose." Vada let out a mirthless cackle, bending over to pick up a big purse as Sonny continued to bitch. "Otis was with Walker when I walked in."

"Was he, now?" Vada straightened up, raising her eyebrows at him.

"Then Floyd walks in, for Christ sake. I ain't seen Floyd since that fucked-up day at your folk's place. Hell, I ain't ever even seen a picture of Otis before today. Now, here you go, stirring up ancient history."

Vada started furiously chopping up chunky cocaine rocks on a makeup mirror. "Poor Sonny," she sighed. "Your son is a gorgeous and sweet child. His mama's pretty darn cute, too. But who knows better than you, huh?" She snorted a fat line through a golden straw that was made for such a purpose. She pinched her nose, then said, "Uncle Walker has been real good to them two since they came back to town. He loves to share our good fortune. Naturally, that Montgomery girl looked us up. Damn well made sure she brought your little boy with her. Otis melted Walker's heart from the get-go. They're crazy about one another, that boy and my husband. Thank God that teacher married Nancy Ruth or I'd have killed her by now." She sniffed up another line and scowled at him, the back of her hand pressed against her nose. "Walker felt some obligation to them, you know. To him, blood is important. He figures one of you should help her out."

"I don't need this, sugar." Sonny broke for the door.

Vada grabbed his arm, waving the mirror in under his nose. "Don't go.

Please." She honestly did look sorry. "I shouldn't be so ugly. Take a peace offering?"

Sonny eyed her warily but did take the drug. Still sniffing, he asked, "Don't look like you and Walker are getting along so good."

"I've been stuck here," she practically whimpered. "He travels everywhere, women trailing him like flies on shit. It would be one thing if I had my own band here. No! I've just been hanging out for nearly three years." She reached back into the purse, taking out a fifth of mescal. She opened it and took a choking pull. She winced, adding, "I quit over at my folks when the money started happening. We bought a nice little place in the Heights."

"Well, that ain't all bad. It's real nice up there."

"Yeah, it is. And look." She held out her left hand. Walker's old pinkie ring, always backed with a little first-aid tape to make it stay on his wife's finger, had been replaced. Vada now wore a sparkling garnet and diamond eternity band. "Finally got a real wedding ring.

"But, Sonny? Can I tell you something? It doesn't feel like a real marriage." She dropped, cross-legged, to the floor like a little girl.

Sonny crossed his arms, leaning against the wall—not sure what else to do. "How do you mean?"

"I can't be happy as the big star's wife tending the home fires. In fact, I went back to work at my folks, to keep me sane. Keeps me from calling Walker on the road at three a.m. just to see if he's in his room." Tears started spilling from her eyes. She took another hit off the bottle, choking, gagging a little. "He's home so rare anymore. When time grows close for him to get back, I can't wait to have him in my arms. But when he's here, it ain't the same. We can't even go out to eat without people bugging us. I get so unsure of us that I start in on him. If I could only go on the road with him!"

Sonny took the bottle from her, pausing for a calming swig of the nasty stuff. He set the fifth down, squatting beside her. "Vada, you only got a little while more to go until you can travel. Quit pushing Walker away so hard. Make him happy to come back to you, instead of loving you better when he's gone." He turned her chin toward him and made her look straight into his eyes. "Don't let his best memories of you be when he's playing *Smitten* to a crowd a thousand miles away."

She nodded hard, her mouth firm, taking his hand from her chin and shaking it. "Sonny, you are right. Absolutely right." She took a shuddering breath, visibly trying to compose herself. "The court's just got to give me permission to go perform for this concert. If that fucker hadn't attacked me at work ... you know his lawyers tried to turn things around? Make it looked like I provoked him?" She laughed bitterly. "It's the story of my damn life. Men act like pigs, and it ends up my fault."

Thinking it best to avoid the conversation's turn, Sonny asked, "When will you know for sure if you can travel for the show? We only got two more days."

"I hope I know today," she cried in frustration. "I'm under an awful new judge who's stringing me along."

"Okay. We can't stew about what we can't help, sugar." Sonny swept Vada's hair aside. "You do make that dress he got you look reet petite, lady." She managed a smile. "That's what I call fine. Now save that smile for Walker, hear?"

11.

SONNY LEANED IN the doorway of a tiny make-do office out in L.A., watching Walker spit curses. His brother hadn't seen him yet. He was busy glaring and swearing at the phone in his hand. He threw the receiver at the floor. Then he started banging his head against a whitewashed brick wall, knocking the hat clear off his head. Sonny figured it was time to intervene.

"Whoa, partner! I know this is getting a bit real, but braining yourself ain't the solution," Sonny joked, grabbing Walker's shoulder.

Walker jumped at Sonny's voice and touch. His forehead was reddening where he had smacked it against the bricks. "Did you hear that shit? Did you?" Walker demanded. Sonny shook his head. "Sonny, they ain't letting Vada come! I can't believe those motherfuckers strung us along."

"Oh, man," Sonny groaned. "That's awful. I thought sure . . . I mean, it's just one night."

"You'd think, huh?" Walker stalked over to a surplus Army desk, where a bottle of Crown Royal sat. He cracked the seal and took in a good shot and a half in one pull. He winced, coughed, and shook his head. Slit-eyed, he gasped at Sonny, "That dick judge. He hates musicians. Told us so, flat out. Good thing we didn't have him from the get-go, or she'd be in jail, sure."

"This do suck, Squirt. But the show must go on in—" Sonny glanced at a clock on the wall "—about ten hours, now. We have to cut her number, is all."

"Call it the Wang Dang Doodle Fund-raiser, and don't do *Wang Dang Doodle*? Fucking brilliant, Sonny."

"Don't bite my damn head off! I'm trying to help."

Walker waved a hand at him. "I know you are. Sorry." He slumped into a chair, then tippled from the whiskey again. "God. This thing is way more complex than I thought it would be. Now this happens. You think Vada ain't losing her damn mind?"

"I reckon she is."

"Enough to worry about here, and I got to be scared she's going to do something crazy. She wanted to jump in the damn car and start driving out here. Can you believe that?"

"Even Vada couldn't drive from Austin to L.A. in ten hours."

"She don't care. She's freaking out."

"Walker. Just simmer down, now. You ain't doing us no good. Call Vada's mama. Have her pick up Vada. Then you don't have to worry over her. Get home tomorrow, quick as you can." Sonny knew that Walker had a couple of weeks in Austin before he was off to New York to record his sophomore effort. "You can do a lot to mend fences then. Right now, we got to worry about tonight."

Walker took a deep breath. He picked up his hat from where it had fallen. "Okay. That's what I got to do." He pulled a crumpled, heavily scribbled playlist from his pocket and mumbled, "Reckon I could sing *Wang Dang Doodle*. Howlin' Wolf did. I sort of do him justice. I really like Koko Taylor's version, though. Wanted it to be a chick thing." He jerked his eyes to Sonny's, wadding the playlist. He grinned, declaring, "I just thought of something. Sonny, you seen my manager here yet?"

"Yeah. Steven's upstairs somewhere."

"Do me a favor. Go try and find him while I call my mama-in-law. I got an idea." Walker picked up the phone and started dialing.

Sonny managed to locate Steven Taylor and escorted him back to the office. Walker was pacing, still sipping whiskey straight from the bottle. Two cigarettes burned in an ashtray.

"Good morning, Walker," Steven said pleasantly. "What can I do for you? Aside from suggesting you slow down on the booze, as it's not even noon yet."

"Right. I should put on the brakes," Walker agreed. He handed Sonny the bottle. Sonny took a sip before locating the cap on the floor and twisting it closed. "Steven," Walker said, "ain't Cilla your client now, too?"

"That's correct."

"Is she in town?"

"She is. She's coming to the benefit tonight, as a matter of fact."

"You got her home number with you?" The manager nodded, pulling a Filofax from his sport jacket. Walker dialed frantically as Steven read off the number. Sonny watched his brother transform from freaked-out mess to rounder as she answered.

In his smokiest drawl Walker cooed, "Hello, there, beautiful. Bet you can't guess . . . how'd you know? Yeah, I reckon not too many boys with a Mingus accent call you this early in the day." He winked at Steven and Sonny. "Look, baby. Our man, Steven Taylor, is standing right by me. He tells me you coming out to see our little fund-raiser tonight. Well, I was wondering if you could give someone else your ticket. Of course I want you here! But I need a favor. Do you happen to know the words to *Wang Dang Doodle*?" Relief on his face, he signed thumbs-up. "More or less is good enough. Get here as soon as possible, and we'll work on it together until you feel solid. And I want you to bring something fancy and real sexy to wear. Not that you couldn't make an old burlap sack look swell . . . yeah? One hour? Oh, Cill! I owe you big-time. Bye, darlin'." He hung up. "Vada's going to be pissed, but it can't be helped. Let's go run through our other stuff until Cill gets here."

STERLING PRESTON HAD reserved an exclusive nightclub for their post-fund-raiser VIP party. Sonny selected a table with a good view of the goings-on for his parents. Ruby wore her own mama's pearl brooch and a gaily flowered frock that Vada had helped her select. Big Billy Jay was striking in a suit fresh from Sonny's tailor. The old couple looked proud and happy, but drained, too. Sonny wanted them to relax and enjoy. "Let me go get ya'll a drink," Sonny said, squeezing Ruby's arm. "What'll it be?"

"Your Daddy will take a soda pop. And so will I."

"The booze is done paid for. Least we can do is drink up. Walker wants ya'll to have fun."

"I reckon he does," Big Billy Jay answered. "Look at that boy. Ain't he something?" His voice was filled with marvel as he stared at his youngest. Ruby and Sonny followed his gaze. Sterling Preston and Walker and his Salamanders held court, talking with handpicked press and a crush of well-wishers.

Preston cut a grand figure in his classic tux. His silver mane and Cheshire cat smile were both gleaming. Really Riley smiled on, too. He was one sharp-dressed cat, in narrow black pants and open-collar silk shirt. His jacket, cowboy boots, and Stetson hat were all brick red. Outlaw Jesse James was vibrating in place, like he was still thumping out the backbeat. He was outfitted in Central Casting drummer attire, a leopard-skin muscle shirt displaying his percussion-toned physique. Tight leather rock star pants and heifer-skinned cowboy boots completed his statement.

Walker did them all one better. He wore an updated, three-piece version of the gold lamé *50,000,000 Elvis Fans Can't Be Wrong* suit. The legs were tailored to fit beneath his rose-gold swaddled boots. The Texas ornament on his hat caught the light, flashing as he laughed with the boys. He displayed an outlandishly huge belt buckle, custom made with his F.W.B. initials, and a matching ruby-and-gold signet ring. With the suit, he wore a shiny purple shirt. A flowing black-and-gold scarf was knotted at his throat. Over it, he wore the Venice Beach peace symbol.

Sonny felt downright staid in comparison. He paired an exactingly tailored black suit with a deep-blue cashmere crew neck sweater. His custom boots and belt added a touch of Texas funk to the look. On his last birthday Uncle Charlie had given him a bejeweled '59 Olds Rocket 88 lapel pin. Sonny wore it to all his gigs.

Walker saw his folks and Sonny watching, and raised his glass to them as he bent his good ear to a newswoman's question. Sonny was relieved they had the concert successfully behind them. Every player had given the audience his all. This party was ripping along, too. A good crowd was dancing to the music mix thumping from the club's top-drawer sound system. Sonny and Walker had stayed up to all hours two nights before, tearing through their combined record collections. As they got loaded together, they bickered companionably over the making of the party compilation tapes.

Sonny clapped his old man on the shoulder. "You want something hard splashed into that soda, don't you?"

Billy Jay sighed and shook his head. "Be that as it may, son, your mama's laid down the law. She put us both on the wagon." His face was a mask of disappointment.

Sonny did his best to hide his surprise. "But this is a special occasion," he protested.

"This ain't my decision, Sonny," Ruby answered. "It's doctor's orders—your daddy's."

Sonny sat down beside his mama. Big Billy Jay didn't believe in doctors. In Sonny's memory, he had never been to one. "What's wrong with you?"

"It ain't nothing, Sonny. I just got to take a little better care is—" The old man broke off, looking beyond Sonny. He broke into his rakish smile, rising. "Well, hello, pretty one! I was hoping one of my boys would be polite enough to introduce us."

Sonny turned to see Cilla just behind him. Giving her a smile twin to his daddy's, Sonny said, "I have been rude. Allow me the pleasure, Daddy. Cilla, these are my parents, Ruby and Billy Jay Blaine. Folks, this is Cilla Mountbatton." Ruby rose alongside her husband to take the girl's hand.

"To be sure, it's my pleasure," Cilla said, smiling sweetly.

Sonny ran his eyes down her—impossibly charming tonight. She'd been pure fun during the long day leading up to the show, too. Even earlier than promised over the phone, Cilla rushed in, no makeup, hair on beer-can-sized curlers, wearing sneakers, gym shorts, and a leotard. "Don't flip, boys. I promise you a beauty queen this evening." Glamorous as a love spell, she came out at show time in a getup that should have been illegal. She wore a scooped-necked, bias-cut, flesh-colored slip of a dress, covered with a cutout lace pattern of deep green velvet. Her body appeared naked under the strategically placed velvet, and a slit in the slinky skirt rose high on her incomparable thigh. She wore stiletto heels and long velvet gloves that matched the dress.

She had made her entrance backstage right before everyone took the stage, walking purposefully slowly toward Walker. She paused, not a hair's width from bumping up against him, and did a pivot. "Will this old thing do, Firewalker?"

No one made a sound until Outlaw seeped out a low whistle. Walker did his best to look stern, growling, "Damn, woman. I know I told you to wear something sexy, but we don't want to set off the sprinklers!"

Sonny smiled, thinking back on it as he watched Big Billy Jay flirt shamelessly.

"Little girl, you are as pretty as a picture," the old man said, kissing her hand. "And you sure sing. Don't you think, Ruby?"

"Oh my heavens, yes. Walker Dale says you saved the day, filling in like you did for Vada."

"You are all too kind." She smiled at Ruby. "Walker tells me that your husband is quite a fine dancer. Would you mind if I asked Mr. Blaine for a dance?"

Sonny stifled a laugh while watching Big Billy Jay practically topple over with anticipation. Glancing at Sonny with shared amusement, Ruby said, "Don't imagine I could stop him if I tried, Cilla. Now, Billy Jay, don't tire yourself out, sweetie."

"I won't, honey. And thanks." He kissed his wife. Standing tall, Big Billy Jay offered Cilla his arm and strutted to the dance floor. Sonny and Ruby smiled at one another. Ruby sat down, sending her son after the drinks.

When he returned with two sodas, and a whiskey rocks for himself, he found Ruby watching Billy Jay making quite a show of two-stepping with Cilla. Her chin rested on laced fingers, and she smiled wistfully. "Look at him, Sugar-boy. To see him like that reminds me of when we was courting. Like yesterday all over."

Sonny watched as a tear formed in her eye. She tried to wipe it away without him seeing. "What's wrong with him, Mama?"

She shook her head, staring at her hands. "He don't want ya'll to know, but you will soon, anyway. It's his liver, Sonny."

"Is it . . . bad?" She nodded. "God, Mama. Can't they do something?"

"Not really." She tapped Sonny's highball glass. "Maybe if he quit drinking years ago, there'd be hope. You know he's always been hard-drinking. Can't say you boys is any different. There's drunks on both sides of your family tree. First your Daddy Jim drinks himself into the grave, now Billy Jay. . . ."

Sonny studied his glass. "Don't know what to say, Mama."

"Baby, I don't mean to sound like Carrie Nation. Make me the world's biggest hypocrite. I had my own problem for years."

"That's ridiculous. You just drank socially, parties and stuff."

"Shows how well I hid it from ya'll." Ruby looked away from her son, shame on her face. "Daddy Jim was a fine purveyor of the 'Do as I say not as I do' school of thought. Drank like a fish himself, but threatened Charlie and me with Eternal Damnation—and his belt—if we touched a drop. Fact is, I had my first drink the night I met your daddy. He carried a little hip flask in them days. I liked it a lot. But then, I liked him a lot." He saw her blushing, twisting the napkin in her hands. "The sauce takes away a lot of inhibitions, you know."

"That it do. . . ." Surprised, a little embarrassed, Sonny realized what Ruby was admitting. "My goodness, Mama. On your first date?"

She blushed more deeply, whispering, "Not even that. I mean it's not like he asked me out that night. We'd just met at a dance. I was so dumb. In fact, until that night, I'd only kissed one boy, and that was my third cousin that Daddy Jim made take me to the prom." They both let out a laugh. "I was in love with your daddy from the first instant I saw him, there by the bandstand, with those big arms and that crooked grin." Her eyes drifted to where her husband danced. She added, barely audibly, "I was so grateful when he stuck around."

She trailed off for a moment and took a sip of soda. It was clear to Sonny she wanted to tell him everything. Though it made him uncomfortable enough to want to squirm, she seemed to need to tell it. "Well. After we married in a fever, as Johnny and June Carter Cash say, your daddy started to travel. It left me lonesome, stuck at home. First you came, then Walker Dale. I started to use drink as a sort of companion. And then when he'd get back, we celebrated by getting good and drunk together." She shook her head. "It's been real hard to stop, Sonny. But I feel better than I have in years."

Sonny took her hand. "Did you get any help, Mama?"

"Just asked the good Lord for the strength to stop. Your daddy's doctor talked about that Alcoholics Anonymous thing. But he's out in Fort Worth. I don't imagine they have any of those meetings in Mingus, do you?"

"I don't know. Don't know nothing about it."

She flicked again at his glass with her finger. "Maybe you ought to find out something about that. I couldn't bear to lose my Sugar-boy to this stuff, too." She squeezed his hand in sharp fashion. "Be still, now. Here comes your little brother. Let's not ruin his big night." She stood to hug Walker. "Oh, baby? You played so nice tonight. What a wonderful job you did with this show, Walker Dale."

Walker kissed her cheek, smiling at Sonny. "Well, thank you, Mama. I could never have done it without Sonny's help. One more favor, bro?"

"Name it."

"Next time I start dreaming up grand schemes, stop me. Nowadays I pay folks to do my thinking."

"You got it, Squirt. I'll tell you straight out: Meat, just play your guitar."

"Good deal. You having fun, Mama?"

"I surely am."

"Would you dance with me, please? I'll even take my hat off. I know you hate it when I wear it indoors." Ruby started to beg off. Walker smiled, sweeping his hat toward the dance floor. "Can't let Daddy show us up, after all."

"Oh, I couldn't."

"Can't take no for an answer, missy. I'm a star. One of the perks is I always get to dance with the best-looking ladies."

Sonny watched as Walker two-stepped Ruby onto the floor. He looked back at the drink in hand. He had never thought about liquor as a problem. Considering it now, he could not recall the last time he had gone a day without at least a beer or three. He led a stressful life, what with the travel and so on. He needed a little something to unwind, was all. Everyone that he knew did some of this and that. He had his shit under control more than most. Hell, Walker drank and drugged a lot more than he did, and look at him. He was a regular Mr. Superstar. God Almighty! Didn't that sound like something Daddy would say? Sonny slammed down the rest of his drink and went to the bar for a refill.

When he returned to the table, his daddy and Cilla were back from their dance. They both stared at him, laughing hard together. "What?" Sonny asked.

"Your father is quite amusing. He was just telling me about the first time he let you drive his pickup."

"Not that story? Give me a break, old man," Sonny protested. Big Billy Jay cracked up all the more, pounding the table with a fist. Sonny shrugged at Cilla. "Despite Daddy's loose lips, will you let me have a dance?"

"I don't know. . . ."

"Be fair, girl. You done danced with all the other men in my family."

"I haven't danced with Walker yet."

"Maybe not tonight. But you did that night in the penthouse, after Jackie's party—leastwise that's what he told me." Big Billy Jay raised his brows, grinning. He looked from Cilla to his youngest, still cutting a rug with Ruby.

Cilla's eyes widened and her cheeks colored. "I can't believe he told you about . . . that."

"Sure enough didn't tell *me*," Billy Jay replied.

"Walker and I don't keep many secrets from each other." He jerked his head toward the other dancers. "Come on, girl."

As the Years Go Passing By, played by Albert King, filled the air as Sonny led Cilla to the floor. He pulled her close. "I'm sorry I made such a bad first impression, sugar. I hope you'll give me another chance."

"Isn't that what I'm doing now?" she asked. Cool, sure, but Sonny thought maybe she was flirting back a little.

"I can be real sweet." He used the smile on her.

She snorted. "I imagine plenty of women could vouch for that."

"Be fair, now! I'm a bachelor. Not like some other people that hit on you." Sonny nodded toward Walker, who was still dancing with Ruby. Walker watched them, one eyebrow raised.

"That's true," Cilla replied.

Sonny squeezed her. She let him, laying her head against his shoulder, not objecting. "You dance nice, sugar. Feel good, too."

"Thanks. You're not so bad yourself, Sonny."

"I'm staying in Los Angeles for a few days. The rest of the Rockets are meeting me here next week."

"Is that right. Are you playing here?"

"Uh-huh. And starting work on a new record, too. Anyway, I have a few days to kill. I sure would like it if I could take you out to dinner, Cilla."

"I'm sorry. I can't."

"Really?" She nodded, looking down at their feet. Sonny couldn't recall ever being denied a date before this. It took him aback. "You must be seeing somebody awful special."

She laughed, but there was no humor in it. "Hardly that. I'm just . . . not very good at that kind of thing."

The song ended, and Cilla stepped away. Sonny kept holding on to her hand. "Good at what? It's only dinner."

Pulling free, she answered with a smirk, "Now, Sonny. We both know there's really no such thing as 'only dinner.'" Cilla turned to leave and stepped right into Walker's arms. Almost like swearing, she said his name.

"Howdy, girl. I was fixing to ask you to dance after I was done with Mama. Looks like Sonny beat me to the punch."

She took Walker's proffered arm, glancing back at Sonny. "Thank you again for the dance. And for your kind invitation too, Sonny." Now was Walker's turn to shoot Sonny a smug look as he led Cilla away.

When making the tape, the brothers had followed Albert King with another slow dance, Roy Buchanan's instrumental version of *Sweet Dreams*. Sounded good. They both took pride in making compilation tapes that flowed. Sonny turned his back on Cilla and Walker and headed back to the bar.

Cilla didn't let Walker pull her too near. She glared, scolding him. "Walker Blaine, you have a big mouth. Sonny said you told him about our . . . dance. Fond of kissing and telling, are you?" She had to work at it to be angry. When Walker looked at her with his sorry dark eyes, she couldn't seem to summon the proper indignation.

"That ain't like me at all, I swear. I know it wasn't gentlemanly. But Sonny had talked and talked about meeting you." He was even blushing. "I guess I got to bragging. Reckon it's a dang guy thing."

She did her best impression of his accent. "I heard tell, darlin'."

He groaned and laughed. "I don't sound that hick, do I? Yeah? Am I forgiven, leastwise?"

"I suppose." She allowed him to pull her near.

"You sure was a trooper today, darlin'. Thanks so much for coming down and pitching in."

"I had a great time, Walker. And the cause is marvelous. Dad wished he could be here."

"Yeah. Would love to work with your dad one day. It's been great working with Sterling. A dream come true—beyond that. Never even imagined such a thing." Walker looked over at his producer. Sterling gave him an Okay sign with his thumb and forefinger. "Ain't he great?"

"He is. I'm so pleased it worked out for you."

"Got you to thank for it, in big part. Anyway, Sterling and me was just talking about your record a few minutes ago. I think it's great you got a band together."

"I wouldn't have tried without your kind encouragement. Believe me, that album didn't turn out the way I wanted. I had a producer that had a completely different vision than me. He bullied me."

"Shame on him."

Cilla shrugged. "He came highly recommended by Steven Taylor. I felt too green to fight him. I'm mortified every time I see the cover picture."

"I thought you looked hot." She did. In the picture she was barely dressed, windblown, straddling her Strat's neck.

"But did I sound good? No! Just like that tacky cover shot, the sound was way overblown. The whole focus was on my looks, not my playing. I wanted the sound stripped down, not me."

Walker nodded. He knew of her producer, mostly known for slick, layered dance mixes. He wasn't a good fit for Cilla. "Well, we have to change that. Maybe you'll allow me and Sterling to have a crack at your second outing?" Walker said as the song ended.

She raised her eyebrows, and seemed to be thinking it over. "I'll consider it."

"I'm going back into the studio for round two myself this month. Shortly after, I got to plan for a big ol' world tour. Sure would like it if your band would come along and open."

"I'll consider that, too." She smiled, winking. "Have your people call my people?"

Walker hooted, "Shoot! Didn't know you L.A. folks really said that. And since Steve Taylor handles both of us, don't that make them the same damn people?" He laughed louder. "Come on, darlin'. We need a drink."

"Not likely, boss," Outlaw protested, appearing out of nowhere. He stared at Cilla with famished eyes. "I sure enough would like a dance, too. What you say to that, you gorgeous thing?"

She smiled serenely at Walker, watching his expression cloud. "How can I refuse an Outlaw?" She let the delighted drummer wrap an arm around her waist and two-stepped away with him. She glanced back, wink-ing. "See you around, Firewalker."

Walker strode to the bar, joining Sonny. Sonny handed him his hat, newly fetched from their parents' table. Sonny ordered another whiskey, Walker's brand.

As Walker drew his hat brim down, Sonny commented, "Time for Jesse James to try his luck. Maybe that dumb-beast quality of drummers is more her speed." Walker offered him a low five, laughing. "You know what they call a guy who hangs out with musicians, don't you, Walker?"

"Sure do. A goddamn drummer!" Walker lifted his brow, staring as Outlaw and Cilla danced. Outlaw was grinning, whispering in her ear. She shook her head back at him, giggling. "She looks like she digs him, don't she?"

"It ain't him. It's the music. Whoever masterminded this tape done a brilliant job. Cheers, man." Sonny clinked his glass against his brother's. They drank together.

Sonny watched on, silent, as various people came up and spoke with Walker. He was, as ever, gracious to all. He listened to their silly stories with great attention. He talked up his musical heroes and signed autographs. He posed for pictures, arms around the fans like they were his oldest pals.

Sonny had to admit to loving this night, this experience. It was great to play with the old crowd. It was especially fine to play with Floyd again. Mama and Daddy were right proud, too. Maybe now they'd quit worrying that their sons were going nowhere fast.

Best of all, Sonny hadn't felt any jealousy or envy up there beside Walker. Their licks had fit hand in glove. When Walker soared off on one of his runs, Sonny watched along with everybody, filled with nothing but wonder. He'd had the true honor of laying down the groove for Walker to dance on. No question—this night, Sonny had been the best damn rhythm man for the best damn lead player anywhere.

The thought, and the whiskey, made Sonny feel woozy with affection for his kid brother. When there was a break in the well-wishers, he tugged on Walker's gold lamé sleeve. "Can I tell you something, straight out?"

"Go ahead."

"It's just. . . . This is good, this Blues Foundation you dreamed up. You done real fine tonight. I'm proud of you."

Walker dropped his head. His face was hidden behind a scrim of wavy hair and his hat brim. He sounded choked up when he answered. "Thanks, Sonny. Coming from you, that means a lot."

*   *   *   *   *

12.

WALKER HAD FLOWN straight home from the postbenefit party. He was worried about Vada. He knew she'd be pissed about Cilla doing "her" song. Seated in first class, Walker charmed the stewardess out of countless shots. He made too many trips to the can, using his stash to prime himself for the showdown with his wife. Walker was so ripped by the time they hit Austin, Riley had to help him off the plane. Good thing his folks were flying a different flight, or he would have shamed them.

Walker waited at the terminal nearly an hour. He paged Vada, but she wasn't at the airport. He tried calling home a half-dozen times—got nothing but a busy signal. Somewhat sobered up, he finally grabbed a cab. He found the front door standing open. The bedroom speakers were blasting out a platter from his old Duke/Peacock collection.

Something wasn't right. "Vada! Honey, you okay?" he called out, dropping his stuff in the hall.

When he saw her in their bedroom, he knew why she hadn't heard over the music. They weren't yet in his bed. A shirtless young buck in a broad-brimmed hat was kissing her, attempting to pull her panties off. What was left of Walker's cocaine was spilled on the top of his dresser.

"Well, well. Ain't this a sweet homecoming?" Walker growled.

The kid pushed himself away from Vada, gaping at Walker. After a second, he whispered, in a voice mixed with awe and fear, "Wow! Firewalker Blaine. I don't fuckin' believe it."

"That makes two of us," said Walker. He stared at the frozen couple for a few seconds, and then roared, "Get your goddamn clothes and get the hell out of my house before you're picking up teeth, you little shit!" Walker glared past the kid at Vada. She was trembling, hand over her mouth, her eyes feral. He could see she was stoned out of her mind.

Grabbing his shirt from the floor, the kid raced by Walker, gasping frightened apologies. Walker heard the front door slam seconds later.

"Oh, Babydoll," Vada whimpered. "I forgot about the airport." She backed away from him, falling onto the mattress when the back of her knees made contact with the bed.

"I can see that. Glad my flight wasn't late, or else I would have found ya'll. . . ." He trailed off, staring, stock still for a moment. Then he bellowed, "You stupid woman! Don't you know better than to shit where you eat?" He jumped her, grabbing her arms and shaking her ferociously. His hat flew from his head.

"Aiyee! That hurts, Walker," she screamed, trying in vain to push him away. Her words caused Walker to pull his rage back just a hair. He turned loose without striking her.

He kneeled over her, panting, clinching his fists for a moment and making her cower even more. He climbed off and stalked to the dresser. He pulled a credit card from his wallet and attempted to scrape the coke remnants into a heap. With his back to her he muttered, "Besides being rightly pissed off at what was going down in my own house, you forgot the front door is standing wide open out there, music blasting out. You can't do that shit in a decent neighborhood, woman. What if someone called the cops? We'd both be busted. You'd go straight to jail, with your record." He spun around, losing it again, raging, "My career would be fucked. You stupid, stupid bitch!"

She was lying curled into a ball like a cat, sobbing. "I'm sorry, Babydoll. So, so sorry. . . ."

"Hell, yes, you are. One damn sorry wife. Who was that punk, anyhow?" She couldn't answer for her sobs. "He your regular lover boy, Nevada? You making a fool of me every time I leave town?"

"No! He . . . he came into my folks' place, flirting. He plays guitar. . . ." She looked at him, still crying. "These kids come with their guitars to Austin like it's the Promised Land. They're always coming on to me. . . . It's like they think some magic will rub off onto them if they . . . if I. . . ." She broke down again.

He stood trembling over her, feeling like he was going to throw up everything he drank on the flight. He whispered, "That's twisted, Vada. I can't believe you play that game."

"I don't! Walker, you have got to believe me, this is the first time I ever brought home one of those . . . those wannabes. I just freaked out after I couldn't be with you in L.A. My mama came over and took me back to the restaurant. Clyde was there. He was concerned."

Walker returned to the dresser, scooping the cocaine pile back into a vial, as best he could. "Clyde? That's your stud's name?"

Vada nodded. "I spent last night at my folks'. When I left this morning, he was there in his car. He slept in the parking lot." She looked out the window, her voice dropping. "He followed me home."

Keeping his back to her, Walker shook his head. "And you asked him in and started to party?" He turned toward her while dabbing the last of the powder from the dresser and credit card edge with his finger. "Jesus, woman." He paused to rub his whitened fingertip over his gums. "He could have been an ax murderer."

"No . . . no. He's harmless."

"Oh, that ain't so," Walker snapped. "Maybe not dangerous. But he done plenty harm." Instantly, despite his numb gums, Walker felt bone-meltingly tired. All the struggle, all the work on the benefit overtook him. He collapsed on the edge of their bed, putting his face in his hands.

Vada realized after a minute that he was weeping silently, trying not to let it show. "Babydoll. Please don't." She reached her arms around him. He went rigid, but he didn't push her away. "I don't know why I did this. The local news had some footage of you talking before your show. So charming. I sat up all night thinking of the women that must be hanging on you. I called your room a bunch of times."

He interrupted her, glaring at her with tearing eyes. "I was late at the party. Had to be, to do the p.r. for the Fund. I wasn't with no one last night, Vada. I was worried about you. I was scared what you would think because I let Cilla sing your song. Got the first flight I could. I sat there the whole plane ride trying to figure out how to tell you."

Vada's lip pulled up in a snarl. "You let that Mountbatton woman sing *my* song?"

He sneered, "Yeah. Real betrayal, huh?"

Vada knew anger was the last thing they needed right now. She managed to shove her fury inside. She finally whispered, "You needed someone to do it."

"Uh-huh," he sighed. He folded into her lap, lying still. She said nothing, grateful he wanted to be near. She combed through his long hair with her nails, petting rhythmically.

"What the hell we going to do, Vada?" Walker said after some time had passed. "We can't keep at it thisaway."

"I know." She let out a long breath, pushing her hair back out of her face. "Maybe in a few months, when I can join you on the tour?"

"Don't you remember when we toured with the Bees? That's when all this shit started between us. The road is just bigger and tougher now, and a lot more . . . tempting. We went into that first tour crazy in love, newlyweds with no problems in sight. Look what happened. It was damn near over back then."

"Don't say that," Vada whispered hoarsely. "Don't ever talk about us being over." She bent down to clutch him. "You're the only good thing that's ever happened to me. Don't leave me behind."

He sat up and looked into her eyes. "I don't want to. But things got to change."

"I know, Walker."

"Maybe you can put a band back together when probation's up," he said. She nodded. "You and I did it on nothing but hope and guts, what, nearly ten years ago, Vada? This time around, you got the Blaine name, some money. We got access now to top-line equipment, studios. . . . I learned a lot from Sterling about producing and want a crack at it. I bet I can put a dynamite record together for you. Any musician in this town would be thrilled to play with you." Walker put a finger to her lips. "I only got one rule, hard and fast, when it comes to your band."

"What's that, Babydoll?"

He almost managed a smile. "No damn Clydes."

"All those poor boys are nuts, thinking they got a hope in hell of being a thing like you!" She hugged his neck, burying her face in his shoulder. "Walker, I'm so ashamed."

He hugged her back, stroking her hair. "Well, I ain't saying you shouldn't be. But look. You know full well that I ain't no saint, especially out of town. I got no right to get too bent out of shape. You know what they say about the goose and the gander, honey."

He kissed her then, long and hard, trying to block out the badness with the feel of her mouth. After a little time, and a few well-placed mutual caresses, it was working. He whispered in her ear, "I love you. Let's do something together. Something good for us."

"What? I'll do anything, Walker."

"I'm home for two weeks before I go to record, and then probably a month or so before I leave on tour. You got a little while before you can start working again. How about we throw away the birth control, see if we can start us a family?" He smiled. "A little black-eyed baby for you and me. Okay?"

Vada went sickly cold. She'd yet to tell Walker about her miscarriage. All he knew was that she'd been ill for a week, fighting fever. He hadn't seen how severely she'd bled. When she had later asked her doctor, he'd been concerned about infection. There had been other infections—first from her rape at the hands of her cousin, and later, too, during the crazy years before Walker. As Bee-Stung she'd jokingly called them her "childhood diseases." Things always cleared up with a little healing time, sometimes a shot at the clinic. She'd even taken a twisted pleasure in sending her faithless lays home with a little something extra for their sweethearts. But now the after-effects weren't funny. She had in fact not been taking the pill for over a year now, thinking also maybe a baby might be good for them. She hadn't told Walker this. There hadn't been a reason to, because nothing had happened. Not with Walker. Not with anyone. . . .

She felt her anger surfacing. She despised it, knowing it was the last thing they needed now. But Vada was too upset and wasted to contain herself. She yanked loose, spitting, "You want another little Otis? So go talk to that slut Nancy Ruth. She makes the prettiest babies, don't she?"

Walker's neck snapped back like she'd slapped him. He wrapped his large hand over his mouth, staring wordlessly for several seconds. When he did speak, his voice was soft. "I do love my nephew, honey. But you're my wife. I want a baby with nobody but you. Maybe a little girl, every bit as pretty as her mama."

The genuine sweetness of his words burned her like iodine in a canker. She shrieked, "So, you want to knock me up, then go make this amazing record? Then you head off on the biggest, most luxurious tour yet, all over the planet. Doing all the best drugs, drinking the finest booze. Bitches begging you for it. Meanwhile, I'm stuck home. 'Course, I got to clean up my act. I'm the damn incubator, right? I'm cold sober, getting fat, throwing up, miserable, going through a pregnancy alone. That's real damn fair, Walker!"

He gaped on with his jaw hanging loose. Finally he managed, "I got to work, girl. My daddy traveled for his work. It was part of his job. This is part of mine. You knew that when we started together."

She stalked to the dresser and laid out a king-sized rail from one of the vials Walker had just filled. She snorted it and then turned on him, new vindictiveness flashing in her dark eyes. "You forget. You hardly knew your ass from a hole in the ground—a shy little kid. Desperate for a job, and I handed it to you. You weren't nothing but a scared boy whose fine big brother I fucked whenever I got half a chance." The words were out of her before she could choke them back.

"Baby," he whispered, "I'm gone." He grabbed his hat and scrambled for his car keys, stomping toward the door. He paused, going back to grab the vial from the dresser. "And if you need more blow, Nevada, get one of your pathetic little boys to bring it to you."

She ran after him, yelling, "Walker, please, I didn't mean that." She chased him out to the Impala, holding on to the door with all her strength as he roared the engine to life. "Babydoll, don't leave like this."

Walker's face was livid when he spoke, his voice low and deadly. "Woman, you'll let go of this car if you know what's good for you."

She could see he meant what he said and backed up three paces. He peeled out, leaving rubber on their pleasant suburban street. Vada collapsed to her knees in their driveway, tearing her hair, keening.

13.

SONNY TOOK A long draw off his first-class airline cocktail as he flipped through the magazine he'd picked up at a D/FW newsstand. Wasn't it something what had become of the funky little *Texas Blues Quarterly*? Gone was its low-grade newsprint that blackened your hands as you read. The paper was now high tone, glossy. And the magazine came out monthly. The title, short and scripted in neon blue, was now simply *Texas Blues*.

Sonny glanced out at the inky sky speeding by his porthole window. He closed the magazine, gazing at the cover shot: Walker and his boys, windswept but commanding, posing tough in some ghost town. The same picture was on the cover of the Salamanders' new record. Walker had sent an advance copy around to Sonny's house prior to this latest tour of duty.

Sonny had liked it enough to make a tape to bring on the road with him. He predicted Walker's sophomore record would be even better received than *Ghost of T-Bone*. That first album had been outstanding, especially for a debutant effort by a "new" band. This new one, *Making the Muse*, was a blues-rock classic.

Sonny flipped to the Walker piece. Dallas girl, Lurlene Luqadeaux, was the interviewer. Luqadeaux was pretty cool for a journalist, despite the fact she had yoked Sonny with the Icestorm handle. Sonny scanned it. Same general bullshit. . . . Here was an interesting bit:

> **Firewalker**: I don't rightly know where it come from, Lurlene. Every time I grab my guitar, things happen. It's like something takes me. Out it comes. I mean, it's my music, but sometimes I'm not even sure where I'm going until I get there. I can start playing weird changes I didn't know I knew.
> **Luqadeaux:** Sounds as though you have your own personal muse out there.
> **Firewalker:** I ain't sure about that. What's a muse?
> **Luqadeaux:** Originally it refers to a Greek myth. Nine sisters presided over science, poetry, music. . . . They were the source of inspiration. They guided genius. . . .
> **Firewalker:** Greek babes, huh? Mighty fine! Then, yeah. I guess you could say when I'm really gettin' it, I'm making my blues muse. Bet I'm the best she ever had! *(Laughter)*

So this interview was likely the source of Walker's album title, and that of his latest venture, The Blues Muse World Tour. Sonny had been wondering where the hell Walker had discovered such a high-falutin' word as muse. He'd heard behind the scenes that Walker was prone to calling it The Beauty and Beast Tour. That was due to the fact that Little Lady Mountbatton, a stone beauty if ever there was one, had agreed to be the opening act.

Sonny reached overhead and pushed the call button. The stewardess, bearing auburn hair, tight legs, and a superior rack, came to serve. He gave her the now empty glass, ordering still another with his winning smile. He watched her go fetch his drink. He wondered if she was spending the night where they were headed. If so, maybe he'd spend it inside of her.

Where the hell *were* they going? Oh, yeah. Seattle. For a minute there, he'd spaced out. Anymore, the trips ran together in his mind—except for the occasional death-courting flights, where he was certain he'd end up in a million pieces on some lonesome pasture. Those rides Sonny spent praying, promising God he'd change his nasty ways and get a stay-home gig, if only . . . best not think on that. *Gris gris malfaire*, Bonnell would scold. This flight had been so far uneventful, exactly the way Sonny liked. He looked back down at the magazine and flipped past Walker's interview. He came upon an ad for the Blues Muse Tour. Cilla and Walker were facing off, clutching their Strats. Cilla, tousled hair like a bonfire, cat eyes flashing, that body hugged by a tiny dress . . . have mercy!

Walker, shooting her a sultry look, was draped in his latest tasteless threads. Liberace and Buck Owens better start worrying about the competition, what with the Squirt riding so high.

The stewardess returned with Sonny's fresh whiskey. She smiled and stooped over just right for Sonny to capture a peek of her black push-up bra. "Well, thanks, sugar," he drawled. "So, I was wondering. What you doing after ya'll land this bird?"

WALKER SLID THE KEY into his hotel room door, asking, "Cill, what did you tell that big scary cat, anyhow? He took off awful quick."

"I told him you were my husband, and you were delusional." She smiled at him. "Clint Eastwood complex, complete with .44 magnum. You're dangerously insane."

"Truth often works best, I reckon," Walker answered, laughing. "The insane part, I mean. Not the gun. Despite growing up alongside well-armed rednecks, my guitar's the only thing I know how to shoot. Thank God he didn't call our bluff." He stepped into his room, gesturing for her to follow. "Come on in, have a drink. I'll turn your Dodgers game on."

"In a minute. Let me stop by my room." Though no one was around, she whispered, "I'd like a little smoke. You, too?"

"Sure, darlin'. Bend one on up and bring it over."

Walker went in his room and pulled a bottle of Crown Royal out of a bag. He checked the bathroom and found two paper-capped glasses. He peeked in the hotel's ice bucket, happy to find a few unmelted cubes from an earlier trip to the machine, then he poured the whiskey over the ice slivers, stirring with a finger. He reached into his boot, grabbed his stash satchel, and tapped out just a dash of blow. Needed just a little, to feel frisky enough to entertain the lady. He checked himself in the mirror. Tired, sketchy. If he smiled, mouth closed, she might not notice how crooked his teeth were. Out of the blue, a bad old feeling surfaced: If only he looked like Sonny. He pushed the fretting aside by making a fair Spaghetti Western sneer at his reflection. Making faces in the mirror? Cilla hadn't lied to the big dude in the bar. He really was insane.

Minutes before they came upstairs, Walker had discovered Cilla in the hotel lounge. She was only trying to watch a ball game on TV. Walker was returning from a radio interview, and Cilla's unmistakable head of hair caught his eye as he passed the bar's entrance. A suit was hitting on her.

Eyes fixed on the TV, Cilla grumbled, "Again, no thank you. I buy my own drinks. I don't need another."

"Come on, baby. What are you doing here if you don't want company? Too pretty to be alone."

Cilla said testily, "I was watching the Dodgers and having a drink—get your hand off me!"

Walker sidled up between them, slapping the man's hand from Cilla's thigh. "You got a problem, mister? The lady said leave her be."

Looking incredulously at Walker, the suit rose from his stool—and kept right on rising. Shit. Where was Sonny when he was needed? He bellowed into Walker's face, "Not your business—" Stopping, the suit gave Walker a scornful once-over. "A fucking drugstore cowboy. Go home to the ranch, peewee. I saw her first."

"Sweetheart, I'm so glad you made it," Cilla cooed, brushing Walker's lips with hers. Walker dared to shoot a smirk up at the big, scary man. Cilla dragged Walker to a stool at the far end of the bar. She grinned, her eyes sparkling, and whispered, "Stay here. Try to look tough."

Cilla pulled the suit aside, whispering, gesturing frantically. Walker couldn't make out her words. The guy gave him a death-maker glare, but threw some bills on the bar and split.

Cilla rejoined Walker, grinning. "My hero."

"Oh, you saved the day, girl," he snickered. "Would have been nothing left of me but a greasy spot, had he not backed down. Let me buy you a drink for leaving me with my dignity, and for keeping me alive."

"After that bit of nonsense, I think I'd rather go up to my room, Walker."

"Well, why not come up to mine? Have that drink? Sonny's suppose to be here. I told him to come up to the room, but if I wasn't there, to wait in the bar. You ain't seen him yet?"

"No. I've been down here about a half hour."

Walker drew a gold pocket watch from his vest. "He's not suppose to be here for another few minutes. Sonny ain't unusually late, but he's never early. Let's go up to my room, so we don't miss him. I know he'd love to see you again."

Cilla wasn't entirely sure she wanted to see Sonny. It wasn't exactly that she disliked him, but she did dislike his sort—too cocksure, far too attractive. His smile alone was as tempting as milk chocolate. She finally said, "Perhaps I'll join you two for a minute."

Walker was still laughing at his own silly posing in the mirror when he heard a knock. He went to answer. No one was there. Walker looked side-to-side down the hall. Not a soul. Walker walked back into his room, puzzled. Maybe he was hearing things. He heard the sound again and realized it was coming from the door connecting the adjacent room—strange. He twisted the handle. Cilla smiled, holding forth a joint.

"Well how about that!" he said in greeting. "Discreet, huh? Didn't know you was right next door."

"Is Sonny here yet?" she asked, spotting the two whiskey glasses.

"Not yet. You like whiskey rocks, right?" He held out a glass to her, jerking his head at the TV. "Turn on the game."

"No. It's all over but the crying for the Dodgers." She took the glass from him, leaning against the wall. "I shouldn't mix my liquor, but what the hell."

"Let your hair down tonight. We earned it." He clinked his glass against hers. "Cill, I been dying to ask. How'd a little English girl like you get interested in baseball? Over there ya'll play with crickets, or some damn thing."

She laughed, sipping her drink. "That's *cricket*. It's an English ball game, goes on for hours."

"So does baseball."

"Not like cricket. They break for lunch, like a job. I never cared for the sport anyway. But, when I first came to Los Angeles, to dance school, one of my roommates was the daughter of a Dodger coach. The girl was a walking Hall of Fame. It was sink or swim living with her. And it was a nice diversion from all the crap that goes along with dance."

"What crap is that?"

"Oh, feeling shame if you so much as think about sweets. The dieting is endless. Painful injuries, too. And nasty competition for parts. It's a real catfight in the corps. I still love to dance for fun. I do it for at least an hour each morning. Keeps me in shape."

"And don't it work well." Walker smiled and drifted his eyes over her. She crossed her ankles, yanking up her jeans a tad to better cover her middle.

"Um . . . thanks. Ballet is an important base to have in any dance discipline. But I really like more lyrical, sharper stuff, though. You know who Bob Fosse is?" Walker shook his head. "He's a choreographer—maybe you saw *All That Jazz*?"

"Oh, right. That movie had some real sexy dancing in it."

"I would like to do more along those lines."

He smiled slowly. "Yes, indeedy. I'd like to see that. Um . . . can you do that one stretch where you go and pull your leg straight up alongside your body, clear up against your head?"

By the way Walker stared at her, Cilla thought it best to change the subject. "The Rockets are on the bill with us tomorrow, aren't they?"

"Yeah. It's going to be great." Rattling the ice in his glass, Walker sat on a love seat, propping his boots up on a coffee table.

"Maybe for you and Sonny. I have to open for you both. It's a bit frightful."

"How's that, darlin'?"

"We both know I'm out of my league. Walker, I just don't think I was ready for this tour."

"Cilla, you're a fine player. I wouldn't have asked you to come with me if you wasn't. You just got to relax a little more, let things flow, you know? Come on, sit. Let's talk." He patted the couch beside him. She joined him. He scowled, rubbing his soul patch, gathering his thoughts. After a moment, he said, "Now I been watching you for a few shows, I almost understand why that moron who produced your first record focused so on your voice. Blues is about emotions. You seem to express feelings pretty easy, singing. This sounds macho, but chicks can usually pull real feelings out vocally. Better than most men. It's why there's so many women blues singers. But you need to tap into your raw side with that guitar, too. Technically, you're there. But you're missing the heat."

Cilla laughed, staring at her drink. "This from someone named Firewalker? The rest of us have to worry about getting burned."

"They call Sonny 'Icestorm.' His style's more controlled, but it's still real lusty sounding. Don't you think?" She nodded agreement. "My bro says things with fewer musical words than me, but you know just what he means. I can't do what he does. I just go off." He laughed.

"He's sort of a Hemingway to your Faulkner, Walker."

Walker slapped his cheek. "Sure, I know them. Writers, right? I don't read books much. But I know my blues. We go for true love, or lowdown lust. Both. Rage, sadness, loneliness . . . all that's heavy. Real." Walker reached his hands into the air, like he was trying to capture something invisible. "What's the damn word I want, Cill? Like, of the earth, fire and water. . . ."

"Let's see—*elemental*, maybe?" she suggested.

"Yeah. Elemental. Unstoppable, juicy feelings." He laughed again, looking sheepish. "I ain't making no sense. Maybe I should read that Hemingway and Faulkner."

"Maybe so," she said, laughing. "But you do make sense."

"Now, that night when you came over after you had it out with Jackie. You played for me, and you was cooking with gas."

"I was . . . overwrought that night." She tittered, squirming slightly beside him.

"You got to learn to tap into that stuff." He brushed his fingertips across her breastbone, sending a tremor through her. "Got to, like, almost hook it to a switch right here. Think of it like an effect you plug into your amp. Learn to put it out there. Risk."

"Risk." She shook her head. "I don't know if I can."

"Well, I can try to piss you off royally every night before you take the stage. You'll go out there mean and tear them up!" He laughed and reached over to hold her hand. "Sweet girl, I hope this don't hurt your feelings."

"Not at all. I need to learn from you. This is the best classroom in the world."

"I'll teach you whatever I can. Glad to. Now, where's that smoke?" She took her hand from his and offered him the joint to light. He took a pull that choked him a little. "Can't hold my smoke no more. This reminds me of when Sonny and I was kids. We smoked dope a lot then. Guess it's true what they say. Leads to harder stuff."

"I don't know. I mean, I indulge in other things now and again, but this is my one real vice," she confessed, taking it from him and doing a toke. She held it for a moment, then said, on the exhale, "That's one reason I had such a tough time staying thin enough to make my dance instructors happy. I'm forever fighting the munchies."

"I wouldn't worry if I was you. Your pounds are in exactly the right places. Women stay too skinny these days. You're built like a lady should be." He leaned in closer to her, putting his arm around her shoulders, as he took back the joint. "Did you like that I put *I'll Take Care of You* on my first record?"

Cilla looked away, staring at the dark TV. Would have been wiser to let Walker switch on the game. "Yes. It was lovely, Walker. I always liked that song."

"It's the one we slow danced to after that party, you remember?"

"Of course I do."

"I think about that night a lot. I was hoping you would hear it and know I meant it for you." He put the joint in an ashtray and pulled her close. "Just to think of you makes me crazy."

She held herself stiff, but allowed him to kiss her. When Walker started to run his hands up and down her back, she shoved away and walked toward the TV. "Stop that."

He followed, grabbing her hand. "I didn't mean to upset you. I kind of thought you felt the same. Guess I let my ego fool me." Chuckling, he let her go, ducking his face down behind his hat. "Stupid, huh? You're such a refined and classy lady. What's the likes of me thinking? Nothing but a homely white-trash Texan."

She turned to him, her eyes shiny with tears. "Don't. You're not the only one who thinks about our dance. When I heard that song on the record, I hoped you were remembering me. But I can't do this. Walker, this may be my first big tour, but don't forget. I've been around musicians all my life. You've got a wife back home. I'm no groupie."

Walker protested, "Of course you ain't a groupie! I don't think of you like that at all. Come sit back down with me. Let's talk." She shook her head. "Come on, now. Just talk to me. I ain't going to try nothing."

She perched on the very edge of the couch, her knees tightly pressed together. He leaned back into the fabric, yielding space to her, emptying his glass. "Fact is, I ain't even been living with Vada since the benefit show. Got home and found her with some young buck who seemed to think he was me. They was nearly naked in my own damn bed."

"Is that the truth?" she asked, her voice wary. It sounded a little too convenient.

He nodded. "I swear it. I almost hit her—I shook her real hard. Then we calmed down, tried to talk it out. But then she . . . well, she said something ugly. She knows just how to hurt me."

"That's too bad, Walker."

Walker held up a hand. "I know what you're thinking. I'm trying to pull one of those 'my wife don't understand me' lines on you. I'm not. I don't know what's happening with my marriage. We been together a long time, and especially since we got hitched, it ain't been pretty at times. I know that's no comfort, Cilla, but it's honest as hell. I promise I'll be honest with you."

"Well, then. I should also be honest with you." She said nothing for a long time. She could feel him watching, waiting attentively. "I never talk about this. The truth is, I just don't. . . ." She paused, searching for words. She finally mumbled, "I don't date men anymore."

Walker's eyes widened. With a nervous laugh, he exclaimed, "Wow! You're a lesbian? I didn't have a clue."

She shook her head, laughing low, tears leaking from her eyes. The laughter quickly turned to sobs. He laid a hand on her back, telling her not to cry. "If I were a lesbian, I could *feel*. Look at me!" She stood up, running her hands down her body, as if modeling an outfit. "Men think I'm so hot. But it's a joke. It's like that part of me, my sex, is paralyzed." She shook her head, covering her face with her hands. "Nothing moves me that way."

"That ain't so. Have you—"

She cut him off. "I've tried everything. Read every book, watched every movie, tried all sorts of humiliating things. I've talked to shrinks and MDs. Nothing helps. It's always been simply horrible. Usually painful, too. A couple of times, I couldn't even . . . it's like I'm dead-bolted down there. It's way beyond not . . . you know, no orgasm. It's no wonder my playing is passionless. *I'm* passionless." She kept crying. "Frigid, is what Jackie called it. Too bad your brother is known as Icestorm. That would be a far superior name for yours truly."

Walker considered her for a time while she wept. He finally said, "Listen here. There's just no such thing as a frigid woman. All's wrong is you got yourself tied up with fear and shame."

She stalked into the bathroom, blowing her nose and wiping her eyes. "How would you know there's no such thing as frigid?"

"Because . . . I just do. I mean, the doctors say you got all your parts and stuff, right?" She nodded, her back to him. "Well, see? Might could be if someone's a psychopath and don't feel nothing, maybe they could be frigid, but not you. You're chock-full of feelings. Cill, it is like playing guitar. Learn to tap into that side of yourself, is all. Risk opening yourself up. Don't be so scared."

She grabbed a few clean tissues and sat back next to him. "I am scared. Scared of never feeling anything. Now I just avoid it. I haven't attempted anything in, like, two years. I keep busy with other things. But then I see couples together, happy?" She sniffed, voice low. She sounded more ashamed than sad. "It hurts to be alone, Walker. Really alone. Unable to connect on such a basic level with anybody."

She shredded the tissues, balling them up in her hands. "I swear, the only time I ever really felt anything at all was that night with you. I've wondered sometimes, if Kyle and the others hadn't come back just then. . . ."

"See? I knew it. Both of us was real turned on that night. The way you kissed, the way you looked at me, the way your body smelled, Cill. You wanted us to be together. You just need someone you're real attracted to taking his sweet time with you. And you need to not push. Feelings will happen at their own pace. I'm willing to bet you never told any of your lovers about this."

"God, no. And *lovers* is too strong a word for the men I've tried to . . . well. After the way Jackie reacted, I swore I'd never say anything again."

"Jackie sounds like a fucking prince!" Walker took the shredded tissue balls from her and threw them aside. Then he held both of her hands in his tightly and smiled at her tenderly. "But see, talking about it's the only way to get over it. Cilla, I ain't no prize. I never even graduated from high school. I ain't a high-class man, like you deserve. I know I'm married, and I can't tell you what's going to happen with Vada. Neither her or me have been faithful spouses, but, until now, our flings never meant nothing. This ain't fair to you or Vada either one, but the fact is I think I love you already."

Cilla opened her mouth to protest, but Walker shushed her.

"Girl, I think you are fun and super classy, and smart, and talented, and the most beautiful thing in the world. And a lady guitar player, too? I never even dreamed I'd meet such a thing. Now, I know I ain't nothing to look at." He winked at her. "I aims to please, given half a chance."

She smiled a little. "Well, Walker Blaine, you're not conventionally handsome. But you do have a certain . . . *je ne sais quoi*—"

"Oh, damn, I might as well give up now if you ain't even going to speak English. It's hard enough with you talking London and me talking Texan. There, leastwise I made you laugh." He dropped to his knees before her, still holding her hands. "Cill, I'll be patient. We'll just fool around some, if you want. I won't do nothing until you're begging me to. You understand? Let me help you—take care of you."

She smiled at him, laying a hand against his cheek. "Oh, Walker. You are such a great guy. God knows I'm tempted."

"Risk, Cilla. Come here." He led her to the bed. He lay down beside her, running a hand through her hair, giving her slow kisses on her neck. He whispered sweetness in her ear.

She was starting to enjoy the kisses and sweet talk, to relax somewhat, when there was a loud rap on the door. Walker buried his head in her hair, groaning, "Oh, shit! I bet that's Sonny. This is the story of our romance, huh girl? Knock, knock, who's there? Bad Timing!" The knock came again. "Hold on a damn minute!" Walker hollered, then dropped his face into the pillow, snickering.

Cilla struggled free of his grasp. "We can't simply leave him standing out there." Cilla got up, feeling off-kilter. Walker climbed off the bed, too. He grabbed his hat and poured another whiskey, shaking his head and muttering to himself. She stopped before the mirror and ran a hand through her hair. Satisfied that she looked presentable, Cilla opened the door.

She nearly whimpered when she saw Sonny. He was perfection. He was all decked out in black: leather jacket, touchable cashmere sweater, tight Levi's, his boots. One dark lock hung loose over his smoky eyes, falling from his otherwise flawless 'do. He leaned on the jamb, his emerald earring catching the light. Sonny's face lit up with his bewitching smile when he saw her. She had to look away, feeling the color rise in her cheeks. "Hello, Sonny," Cilla said to the floor. "Walker's been waiting for you."

"Hello yourself, sugar." Sonny entered, tipping her face to his with his finger, kissing her lightly on the mouth. She felt his eyes move over her as he purred, "You look heavenly. But you always do. You been getting a little sun?" He caressed the side of her face. "Got some pretty roses in your cheeks." He gave her another slow smile, and then spotted Walker. Raising his hand, Sonny cried, "Howdy, Squirt. How you doing?"

"Real good, Sonny." Walker slapped the hand and then hugged his brother, pounding him on the back. "Ain't you looking cool? Come in, have a seat. I'm pouring you a drink." Walker grabbed the ice bucket on the dresser and clinked tiny cubes into a glass.

"Say, Walker, you got any blow?" Sonny said. He grinned at Cilla. "I'm fighting the jet lag something fierce, don't you know."

Pouring the whiskey, Walker rolled his eyes at her. "Like he's got to ask? There's a bunch in Old Broad's case. Help yourself."

Cilla started for the door. "Walker, Sonny, I'll be going. You two have a nice evening catching up."

"It's New York City—party town, girl. Don't leave," Sonny pleaded, grabbing her arm as she walked by. He twirled her into his arms, waltzing her away from the door. "We are headed for a big wingding. I'll die if you don't come along. Later, Bonnell's taking us to an after-hours club that plays great old music. No one can dance as fine as you can, Cilla." He pulled her a little closer, whispering, "You spoil a man rotten. I been looking so forward to seeing you." He kissed her ear.

Cilla saw Walker watching, grinning. When it rains it bloody well pours. Her cheeks grew hotter still, and that wasn't all. Sonny hummed

Dance with Me, playfully stepping her around the room. In one smooth move, she twirled out of his reach and back to the door. "I think I'll pass. We have a show tomorrow." Walker extended an arm, holding a mirror with lines laid out. "No, thank you, Walker. That's the last thing I need right now. I'm off to a hot bath and bed."

"Okay. I'll stay and scrub your back," Sonny offered.

"Sonny, go have fun with your brother. Good night, Walker."

"Good night, darlin'. We'll talk more later." She left through the hall-way door.

Sonny slumped into the couch. "Lord God, Walker. Don't the road agree with her. Is it just my imagination, or has she gotten even prettier?"

"No, I think she has. Do up those lines, finish your drink, and let's get. I'm sick to death of hotel rooms already. I got more stash in my boot for later. Do we need to bring the guitars and stuff?"

Sonny slapped his hand to his forehead. "Take a damn night off, Squirt. Let's just go be two guys prowling. If we all go out to a club, we'll let some-one else play, hear? I got to take a piss. Call a limo, huh?"

"Will do." Walker waited until he heard Sonny close the bathroom door. He tore off a piece of the sanitary paper lid that had been covering his drinking glass and wadded it into a small ball. He opened the door adjoin-ing Cilla's room. Her side was still ajar. She was in the john, singing, run-ning her bath water. Watching to make sure she didn't see him in the act, Walker mashed the wadded paper into the latch-hole in her room's door-jamb. Now he wouldn't be locked out when he returned.

Grinning and proud of his ingenuity, Walker put on a coat and reached for the phone to call a ride.

14.

"I STILL CAN'T HEAR my guitar through the monitor, Jack." Cilla was run-ning through her sound check before the Austin show. They'd lived the road for a good three months now, and after a swing through Dallas the next night, would be winging overseas. Jack the sound guy fooled with something on the board, then waved at her to try again. She hit a Dm_7 chord. There it was.

She did a little run, checking the tone and levels. Satisfied, she gave Jack a thumbs-up. "You got it now. We're done?"

"Yeah," Jack answered over the P.A. "Ready to do the Rockets' check, when any of their bunch gets here."

"I'll keep an eye out," Cilla replied, lifting the guitar strap over her head. She placed her green Strat on a stand. She reached her arms over her head, groaning with the pleasure of the stretch. Scanning the auditorium, she saw lots of faces but saw none of the Salamanders or the Rockets. She figured Walker and Sonny would arrive together at any time now.

Cilla had been with Walker earlier that morning, waking up beside him as she had every night since New York. He'd left her under the covers, sloe-eyed and drowsing. Walker had gone to meet up with Sonny and take care of home business while he was in Austin.

As Cilla tuned her spare guitar, she tossed her hair forward to conceal her face. She wouldn't want anyone watching to see her foolish grin. She was a fool—a delirious fool.

Cilla understood now what all the fuss was. She appreciated why people didn't have sex exclusively for the manufacturing of more people. She grasped why the act was called loving. Thanks to Walker—sweet, wonderful Walker. He'd showed her, all right, the thing that powered their blues. She knew what sonnets and love songs meant. She was helpless, adrift in lust and love.

Stirring the morning after Sonny had dropped in, Cilla found a man in her bed, spooned against her backside. When she first awoke, she froze, feeling the slumber-rhythmed breathing on her neck. Panicked, she couldn't imagine what was going on, or how it happened that another person was in her bed. She wasn't certain where she was, or who was with her. She raised her head and recognized the Strat/raptor tattoo on the arm draped over her shoulder. She was relieved and annoyed at the same time. She lay quite still, trying to decide what to do. He felt rather pleasant pressed against her. Maybe she'd drift back to sleep, let him stay sleeping . . . but he wasn't entirely asleep. Not all of him. She tried to ease herself out from under his arm. Just when she thought she was clear, he snatched at her, yanking her back. He covered her protesting mouth with deep kisses until she quit fighting.

When he finally let her speak, she sputtered, "Walker, what on earth do you think you're doing?"

"Kissing you. Can't you tell? Better do more, until you notice. . . ."

She put her hand over his mouth. "I mean what are you doing in my bed?"

He peeled her fingers from his mouth, grinning. "I was sleeping. Leastwise I was until you tried to escape." He nibbled her neck.

"Stop that!" she groaned. He shook his head, chuckling, kissing her ear. She closed her eyes, keeping her voice neutral. "How did you get into my room, Walker?"

"Same way you came into mine last night." He paused in his kisses, pointing to the doors connecting the two rooms. "Got back about," he glanced at the bedside table clock, "maybe three hours ago. I was pretty wired. I found what was left of that joint you brought over. Smoked it and poured a drink to take the edge off. I peeked over here to see if you was awake. Fast asleep, though. So I sat here and watched you while I smoked, thinking how peaceful and perfect you looked."

"I'm glad I wasn't snoring," she laughed, a high sound that revealed her nerves. "That wouldn't have been very attractive."

He kissed the bridge of her nose. "I bet you even snore pretty. So, when I felt like I could sleep, I hated leaving. Why go to my big empty bed when I could cuddle up to such a fine thing as you? That'd be silly." He kissed her mouth again, taking his time. "You want me to leave now, Cill?"

"Um . . . I'm not sure," she answered truthfully.

"Then, I reckon I'll stay until you decide." He tugged at the neck of the XXL T-shirt, the only garment she wore to bed. "You surely don't sleep in much, girl," he teased.

"I wear more than you do, apparently."

"Naked's the only way to sleep, you got someone you love near. Skin feels real nice." In a smooth move, he yanked her shirt off, pulling her closer. He ran his scratchy left hand down her flank to her knee. "See now? Don't that feel good?"

"Walker . . . I don't think. . . ." She trailed off, unsure what else to say.

"That's the way. Don't think," he crooned. "Just feel good, girl. Easy. Remember, my sweet darlin', I won't do nothing without you wanting to, so bad. . . ."

He was a man of his word. They stayed in bed for hours that day. He was as patient as he promised. For the longest time, he only kissed her, gazed into her eyes, and said the sweetest things. When he finally reached for more of her, she was desperate for his hands and mouth. By the time they were actually making love, she was totally lost in him.

Afterward, she was moved to sobbing. She lay in his arms shaking, crying—happy. She couldn't quite believe how fast all of this had happened. When she caught her breath a little, she thanked Walker over and over like a silly little girl. He whispered back how it was his pleasure. He told her again he loved her.

And now she loved him completely. She didn't have a fraction of doubt remaining about her sexual appetite. She had feared, before that morning, that her passion didn't exist. Now her libido ruled her, a voracious, demanding thing. As long as she had her awesome lover man, that was fine with her.

As a bonus her playing improved dramatically. Her reviews were getting better with every show. She was learning to tap into that newly discovered passion to fuel her guitar work.

Walker was proud of her. He assured her that her playing was really better, that it wasn't only in her imagination. Sometimes, after loving, they sat on the bed without a stitch on, making music together. He was a patient mentor.

Perhaps most telling was the bill they'd shared with her dad, a few nights before Austin. After the show Reg was backstage, praising her abilities clear to the spotlights. He went on at length about how much she had improved on this tour. "As well as being intimidating, Mr. Blaine is quite an inspiration to us all," Reg had said. "He's obviously been a good influence on you."

"Dad, you have no idea how influential he can be." She let go a raucous laugh, sounding completely unlike her pre-Walker self. Reg regarded her with a puzzled expression that caused her to roar to the point of tears. She became more hysterical when she saw Walker fidgeting a few feet away. She could read volumes in his anxious smile: *Be cool, now. Don't spill the beans, girl.*

They didn't want Reg to know. Not yet. She didn't want any fatherly advice on the folly of loving a married man, not to mention another musician—and an abundant substance abuser, at that. She didn't care about any of those things. Cilla only wanted to *feel right now*, to love and play with her man.

They had agreed to keep their affair a secret just between the two of them. Walker was married, of course, at least for the time being. Plus, Cilla was still feeling a little shy about being so taken with him. She had spent her life more or less alone. She had never once met her mother. She knew what the woman looked like only from a few faded mod fashion layouts. Reg had tried to parent her, but she had grown up distant from him, in boarding schools while he traveled the world. Until now, Cilla preferred solitude to company. Now she had to have Walker near, missing him terribly when he was simply out of sight. She found the yearning as disturbing as it was joyous.

Also, Cilla didn't want the other people involved with the tour thinking she was just some foolish and starry-eyed groupie. She liked the respect she was receiving as a musician. For once, people were looking at her as more than a pretty face. She didn't wish to jeopardize her new status.

Still, Cilla felt like anyone could tell everything that was going on, if they just looked close enough. She was as changed as if she had suddenly grown ten inches or sprouted a third breast. People did comment at length on her new stage outfits. She had always dressed like a tomboy on stage— jeans, sneakers or boots, T-shirts or sweaters. Now she wore the body- conscious outfits that Walker enjoyed. He bought her skimpy tops and short, tight skirts so he could admire her legs from his spot in the wings. At first the new looks struck Cilla as too risqué. But Walker's reaction convinced her. Some nights he could hardly contain himself until they were out of sight.

Only Really Riley knew what was going down. In Santa Fe he'd had a room next door to hers, in a motel with thin walls. To her horror, the next day he sat beside her on the bus. Kidding, he'd mimicked her crying Walker's name in teasing whispers. Walker watched from across the aisle until he figured out what Riley was doing. He'd taken the bassist aside and put a stop to his razzing. Walker assured Cilla not to worry about Riley's giving them away. There wasn't anyone he trusted more. Riley apologized and never mentioned it again. From there on out, he treated her like one of the boys. He was even tutoring her on his four-string while riding the long lonesome highways between gigs.

A loud wolf whistle startled Cilla out of her reverie. "Hey, beautiful. Good to see you again," Sonny shouted, bounding down one of the aisles. He boosted himself onto the stage and swept her into an embrace. He kissed her more or less chastely. She peered over Sonny's shoulder as he squeezed her, searching for Walker. She spotted him, sauntering slowly down the aisle from the direction Sonny had just come. Her heart took it up a notch at just the sight of him.

She caught Walker's eye and smiled coyly, waving. He didn't smile back, just nodded at her. His jaw was clinched and his shoulders hunched.

Sonny said, "Sugar, you never met my sister-in-law, huh? Vada, come here a second."

That's when Cilla noticed her, following several steps behind Walker. Vada Blaine was stunning, and as different from Cilla as could be. She moved with languorous grace, and possessed a ballerina's build—well, how they were supposed to be configured, anyway. Her hair was waist-length, curly black; her makeup flawless; and garnets dangled from her earlobes. She had her boyish build sheathed in a tiny lapis dress. Once puberty hit, Cilla had failed miserably at maintaining such sleekness. It made her feel fat and sloppy merely to look at Walker's wife.

While Vada oozed chic and femininity, here Cilla was, her hair in a schoolgirl's ponytail. She wasn't wearing a speck of makeup and had on old jeans and a tour-swag tank top. She felt like one of the roadies in comparison. And those hands! Cilla always gazed at other women's manicures with envy, and noticed right off that Vada's soft hands had perfectly sculptured red nails. She glanced at her own, chopped to the quick like a workman's to be functional for fretwork, her fingertips covered in the thick calluses of her trade. If that weren't enough, Vada had the mouth most women used a gallon of lip liner trying to achieve.

Walker hopped up onstage, stooping down to pick up his wife after him. He stood apart as Vada walked up to join Sonny and Cilla. Vada extended her pampered hand. "Hello, Cilla. We finally meet. I have to say I've been awfully curious about you."

Cilla had what she hoped was a pleasant smile frozen to her face as she reached out to shake. "Why?"

Vada smiled, shifting her eyes to Sonny. "Reg Mountbatton's daughter, on tour with my husband, and holding her own, from what all the reviewers say? Reason enough. Besides, you are all that Sonny talks about anymore."

"Vada, stop it," Sonny protested. He glanced sideways at Cilla, somewhat ducking his face behind his jacket collar.

"Is that right?" Cilla asked politely. She glanced in Walker's direction. He was staring floorward, hiding his own face behind his hat.

"Yes, ma'am. And girl, if you'd known Sonny as long as I have, you'd know that was saying something. I'm sure there's plenty girls in this town who'd have bet the house you'd never see Icestorm mooning around over anyone."

"Vada, you quit teasing Sonny. You said you'd behave if I brought you," Walker grumbled.

"Babydoll, lighten up. I'm just having fun at his expense. He deserves it, God knows." Vada slunk over to Walker, hooked some fingers in his belt and pulled him in for a cheek kiss that left a scarlet imprint. Walker looped an arm around his wife's shoulders. He finally raised his head slowly, meeting Cilla's eyes. He looked tense, sad, and terribly guilty. Cilla was hard struck with nausea at the sight.

Sonny glanced Cilla's way, his face tinted red. "Don't listen to her, sugar. She likes to stir up trouble."

"Now, Sonny," Vada purred. "Is that fair?"

Sonny and Walker answered in the same breath. "Yes!"

Sonny chuckled, and Walker managed a small smile as Vada tossed her hair and offered a practiced pout.

Trying her best to keep her voice steady, Cilla said, "Sonny, they need your sound check. We just finished ours."

"Okay, sugar." Sonny took her hand and guided her over to where his road crew was setting up his stuff. "After Walker and them finish their check, you want to come have lunch with us? We're going out to pay the fellas who're hosting the after-show party, at our old stomping grounds. These two old guys fix the best food you ever had. I'd like it if you joined me . . . us. You could see where we sort of got our start. Plus, the Brown brothers got some real humiliating pictures of us hanging up in their club, when we was young'uns. Man—the things I used to wear!" Sonny looked over at Walker and Vada. Vada was hugging her husband around the neck, whispering in his ear. "'Course, Walker there's still mighty fashionably challenged."

"I'd better pass," Cilla said.

Sonny smirked. "Lunch ain't dinner, Cilla. Your virtue's safe. Walker and Vada will be with us."

"It's not that. I just don't feel well. I think I'll go back to my room and rest until tonight."

He looked at her closely, putting a hand on her forehead. "You're right. You *don't* look well. No fever. But you're clammy. You want me to take you? Walker can do my sound check."

"No, thank you. I'll be all right. Probably just the Texas heat and humidity getting to me." She managed a wan smile. "Or maybe the idea of opening for you two on your home turf has me rattled. I'll see you tonight."

Cilla hurried toward backstage. Sonny noticed Riley intercepting her. They talked for a moment, and Riley looked over at Walker and Vada, scowling. Cilla turned away, burying her face in her hands. Riley called out, "Hey, Walker. Cilla's feeling like hell. I'm going to make sure she gets back to her room okay. Handle the sound check for me if I ain't back in time. Okay, boss?" Walker nodded grimly at his bass player.

"Scared her away, Sonny? Lover boy's losing his touch, seems to me," Vada kidded him, walking over to him and dragging Walker by the hand.

Sonny plugged in his black Tele, laughing. "God, I hope not. Hate to think I make them downright *sick* these days."

"I don't think you had nothing to do with it," Walker said. His voice sounded so blue that it made Sonny and Vada stare at him. Walker looked up at Sonny after a moment, eyes flashing impatience. "Well? Get this shit done so we can get the Browns taken care of, huh? We ain't got all day!"

15.

SONNY WATCHED CILLA and Big Billy Jay on the Sugar and Spice dance floor. He was pleased to see Daddy having fun. The disease killing him was starting to show. Big Billy Jay's robust build had slackened, and his flesh had a vague yellow tinge. His threat was diminished, the black eyes lacking their typical daring. But tonight, Daddy was enjoying the party at the Sugar and Spice, bragging about his sons' accomplishments to all who would listen.

Ruby was still able to manage in Mingus, taking Big Billy Jay into Fort Worth to his doctor when scheduled. She had put the house on the market, however. Their doctor had recommended a specialist in Austin. Time would come when Big Billy Jay's condition deteriorated to the point that Mingus was too far from civilization to get him fast comfort. Although both her boys were on the road more than home now, Ruby had her brother, her sister-in-law, and Vada in Austin. She would soon need them.

The concert had cooked. Cilla's opening set was righteous hot. Sonny was impressed by her progress since seeing her in New York, early in the tour. He supposed she was getting over the initial stage fright the big venues could surely induce and was growing accustomed to the road. Her playing now felt packed with emotional intensity. Besides watching Cilla for the pure pleasure of soaking in her raw sexiness, it was satisfying to see her young talent blossom.

The Rocket 88s had a good run, too. Their old faithful fans were out in force, cheering them on. They did some of their older stuff and brought out a few new numbers from the soon-to-be-released album, *Woo You*. It was plain fun to play Austin. Strange to do it in such a big place, though. He felt, instead, like they should have done their set here, at the Browns' place.

Walker and the Salamanders had stolen the show. Sonny marveled at how success hadn't dimmed Walker's explosiveness one lick. He still played every show like someone held a cutlass to his jugular. But to see him when it was over, soaked with sweat, panting, and trembling slightly, was a little creepy. Playing at that level ripped away pieces of him. Sonny didn't like to be near Walker until he had recovered some.

His brother appeared fully revitalized now—with help from a few cocktails and medicinals. Walker was visiting a couple of small-time stringers, showing off Old Broad. Back when Sonny had picked up the guitar for a song, helping out in the Mingus junk store to pay her off, nobody knew how rare the Broadcaster was. Fender had only made a few before being sued into changing the name to Telecaster. Now the ax was worth more than an earl's ransom, and guitar freaks always wanted to check out Walker's special toy.

Sonny wandered over, listening in as a local house-band strummer oohed and ahhed. "Think you'd of upgraded by now, Walker," he teased. "Didn't Sonny dump that thing on you when he got a real instrument? Pass it along to me, man!"

"I ain't parting with Old Broad for love or money," Walker answered, laughing.

"But she looks like shit from your wicked handling."

"Yeah, but don't she sound great?" Everybody mumbled agreement. "Old Broad's my true love," Walker declared. "I had my tech tweak a few things to give her a little livelier tone, a little more vicious action, but she was always a real sound, basic guitar. Ya'll know how Fenders do. You can't kill them if you try. And don't even think of making off with her. Sonny and me made sure, long ago, that no one else could claim her." Walker turned the instrument over to show them the backside. There was now an ornate W & carved alongside Sonny's simple S. BLAINE. Walker grinned when he caught sight of Sonny looking. "Had to leave my mark on her, too. First girlfriend we ever had us in common, huh, Sonny?"

As if Walker had to ever sweat leaving his mark, Sonny thought. He was like a damn dog spraying piss wherever he went. He had brought forth this current blues renaissance practically single-handed. Incredible artists who hadn't played in ages were heading festival schedules and putting out records. And Sonny knew well that the Rockets' sales were up too, in big part because people were curious what Firewalker's brother was putting down. At least Walker was spreading the wealth.

Floyd stopped by backstage, bringing his new bride to meet folks. The White Tornadoes' former harpist/singer had been friendly enough. Sonny knew he and Walker were real tight these days, had even composed a few songs together for *Making the Muse*. And Floyd's wife, Julia Jean, was adorable. She was a petite ash-blonde, born and raised in the college town of Arkadelphia. She was, in personality and looks, the perfect Southern belle. Sonny thought Floyd had done real good in her.

Nancy Ruth had come along with Floyd and Julia Jean. Sonny had mumbled an awkward hello to the girl. She glared in his direction, not acknowledging him. He didn't blame her. At least they hadn't brought along Otis, too.

After a brief greeting to the Montgomerys, Sonny went ahead to the Sugar and Spice to make sure everything was a go for the after-show party. The Montgomerys didn't join the party at the Browns' club. Sonny was afraid it was because of him. When he got ready to go on ahead of the rest, Sonny had Walker walk him out to his car. He asked, "You think they'd come over if it wasn't for me being there, man?"

"That ain't it," Walker had assured him. "I mean, Nancy Ruth don't like you, but Vada hates her twice as much. So the girl was brave to come on backstage at all. As for Floyd—you ain't going to believe this one. He quit drinking. Heavy into that Alcoholics Anonymous deal, of all damn things. He's even a head Pooh-bah in the organization."

"No shit?" Sonny thought back to his conversation with his mama after the Blues Foundation show.

"Yeah. Says he got pretty bad in the Navy. He met his missus in the service. She told him no dice on the marriage unless he straightened up. So I guess that's why he quit. Anyway, he told me that's why he's writing songs for folks but don't have his own band. Don't really trust himself in the bars yet."

"I don't remember Floyd drinking all that much, do you?" He hadn't drunk any more than Sonny had—probably less, truth be told—when they'd lived together after high school. He shook his head. "Seems like coming by and raising a glass with us at a party wouldn't hurt him none."

"He said he couldn't. Said it might put him back to square one. Taking it too far, if you ask me. Ain't like he's sick."

Sonny had studied Walker, trying to determine if he was alluding to their daddy's illness. Walker's face had not registered any concern. Ruby still hadn't told him then. The damn Crown Prince of the Blues here, and she protected him like he was still her baby boy. Well, Sonny wasn't going to spill the beans. Walker would know soon enough, by the looks of Big Billy Jay.

Sonny turned to look at where his daddy and mama sat and saw his old man waving him over. Cilla was standing alongside Big Billy Jay. She looked damn fine, her golden-red hair loose and wild. She wore a cobalt-blue crop top revealing her tiny waist and flat belly, and a wee black-leather miniskirt. Today she'd bought herself a pair of Uncle Charlie's fine-tooled boots to match her outfit. Sonny crossed the room toward them, smiling at Cilla the whole way. She smiled back like she was awful glad to see him.

"Sonny," she said, grabbing his arm as he approached. "Your father is quite the dancer."

"Oh, stop now, girl," Big Billy Jay protested, grinning with pleasure. He mopped his brow with a handkerchief. He was winded, perspiring far too much for the amount of dancing he'd done. Sonny remembered a time when Mama and Daddy would dance all night, leaving Walker and him sleeping in their car outside some honky-tonk. He watched now as Mama stroked Daddy's arm tenderly. Seeing that small caress made Sonny blue.

"I can see why you were swept off of your feet by him, Ruby," Cilla declared.

"Charm and good dancing is a fact of life with us Blaine boys, sugar," Sonny told Cilla, shaking off his sadness. "You need another glass of champagne."

"I've had too much for my own good, Sonny. Still, I'll have more. It's a party, right?" She smiled back at his parents and headed off toward the bar.

Big Billy Jay caught Sonny's jacket, and he turned back. The old man mouthed, "She's a keeper." Sonny nodded agreement and trotted to catch up with Cilla. Shookie brought them another icy bottle of Moët that he had stocked especially for the occasion. Cilla was indeed drinking more than Sonny had ever seen her do. As long as she stuck close to him, he was not about to complain.

Except for dancing with Big Billy Jay and a few others in their crew, she had been at Sonny's side. Seemed she was starting to warm up toward him, so he was on his best behavior. Aside from a friendly word or two, he hadn't even bothered with other women this night. Maybe Vada's direct words this afternoon had turned his luck.

It seemed clear, at least to Sonny, that Cilla was keeping her distance from Vada and Walker. Well, they were sure wrapped up in each other tonight. Could be absence had made the heart grow fonder—this time. And Walker had likely warned Cilla to fear Vada's jealous nature. He'd told Sonny that Vada was uglier than ever about Walker's wandering eye. Cilla could surely make the most secure woman feel uneasy. Still, it was strange that Walker had not danced with Cilla, if only for show.

Now that Sonny thought about it, Cilla had not spoken to Walker all night. That seemed plain odd.

Cilla, slamming down another glass of Moët, wrapped her arms around Sonny's neck. She pulled him toward the floor, swaying in time with the music. "It's a slow song, Sonny. Quick, dance with me before Bonnell gets over here."

"Ol' Bonnell's pretty light on his feet. Nothing else, them Creoles can dance," Sonny said. He saw Bonnell, deep into the Moët himself, looking across the floor with a disappointed scowl. "You don't like dancing with my partner? How come?" Sonny said, leading her out to Otis Redding's burning *These Arms of Mine*.

"For one thing, your partner is awfully familiar with his hands. And for another," she paused, giggling. "It's hard to put into words. There's just something inherently untrustworthy about Bonnell." The laughter dropped from her voice. Her face went thoughtful. "He's got a lovely voice, but even when he's singing, his delivery just seems so . . . I don't know. Phony, maybe?"

"Phony, huh?"

"Something like that. Maybe because English is sort of a second language for him, because I get that feeling less when he sings with you in French." She giggled again, whispering, "The fact is, I think of him as the Used Car Salesman of the Blues."

Sonny hooted, "God, he would just hate that to pieces."

She tossed her hair off her sweating brow and laughed. "Jesus, I'm a bit drunk. I don't know what I'm saying. Please don't tell him I said that."

"I should. You know he thinks we named that hill west of town after him—Mount Bonnell? And just ask him—he'll tell you, straight out, that he's the only gentleman among us trashy Texans."

"Then he's wrong. It takes more than marrying generations of money to make a gentleman, Sonny." She pulled closer, laying her head against his chest. Closing her eyes, she added, "It's about how you treat a woman. Honesty. Tenderness. Patience. You know?"

"I think I do. Maybe if you'll give me a chance to prove I'm one—"

"Shh. Let's just dance, Sonny. These arms of yours feel so good."

Sonny did as she said, moving slow and sexy with her as Otis Redding bared his love-torn soul. He saw his parents looking their way, smiling.

Then Sonny spotted his brother watching them. The expression on Walker's face startled Sonny so much that he almost tripped over Cilla's feet.

Walker was standing at the other end of the antique bar beside his wife. Decked out to perfection in a leopard-print iridescent dress, holding hands with Walker, Vada looked every inch her husband's crown princess. She was laughing, simply aglow, visiting with Riley's latest girlfriend. She took no notice of Sonny.

But Walker was zoned in on Sonny's face, looking like he had murder on his mind. Sonny had never seen Walker stare that way at anyone. Sonny tried smiling at him. Walker sharply looked away, slamming down the rest of his drink. He pulled free of Vada, stalking off toward the bathroom. Vada called after him, a puzzled look on her face. Walker didn't acknowledge her.

When the song was over, Cilla said in a sleepy voice, "Sonny? Do you think the Browns would let us take the rest of that champagne bottle with us?"

"Sure, sugar. It's paid for. Where we going?"

"I don't want to go back to my hotel. Can we go to your house, please?"

Sonny was surprised by her request but did his best not to show it. He smiled and said, "Dandy by me, girl."

"WELL, HERE'S MY humble abode. It ain't much of a rock star's palace, but as they say, it's home." Sonny was glad he'd asked his management to send someone to scrape the dust off his place a couple of days previous. Heaven knows he had not been expecting such important company.

He'd made a number of improvements to the small house he had lived in for more than a decade. After purchasing it from his landlord to give him a much-needed tax write-off, Sonny had a carpenter build custom oak cabinets for his vast record collection and stereo system. He also tore out a wall in the living room and had a mason build on a big fireplace and mantle. There sat a few framed family photographs and one of the White Tornadoes, jamming with their heroes at Sonny's first Dallas Juneteenth Festival. There was the cover shot with all of the Rockets posing around Guitar Slim's tombstone. Secretly, he hoped for a couple of industry awards to display up there on his mantle. Maybe one day.

Recently, he'd had a brief affair with an interior decorator. She helped him redo his place with plush oriental rugs and heavy oak-trimmed furnishings, to complement the hardwood floors throughout the house. She found a wonderful antique bedroom set, with a sleigh bed, for his room. The second bedroom, Floyd's old room, was not redecorated. Sonny had shoved his old bed and dresser in this room for his rare guest. Mostly it was a storage space for musical equipment he used frequently. He kept the balance of his gear in the basement.

The decorator lady had selected for him an overstuffed leather couch and chair, placed in comfortable proximity to his fireplace. He sat Cilla in the chair and went to his kitchen to get champagne flutes.

She was up and rifling through his records when he returned. "I can't believe you actually have this old Solomon Burke album. Will you put it on for me, please?"

"With pleasure. Here's your champagne. And Walker told me one time that you love your doobie, so I brought you a joint, too." He put the album on, then turned to Cilla and lit the joint she now had hanging from her lips.

She pulled off her boots and fell into the couch. She eyed him strangely. "And what else has your little brother told you lately—you two who have very few secrets from one another?"

Her voice had turned cool. Had he made a wrong move without knowing it? He hoped not. "Hadn't talked much with him since New York, sugar. Even then, we just partied with a bunch of people Bonnell knew, cruising clubs and parties. Then today I thought we'd kick around town a bit, or hang out here and shoot the breeze. But he was home, I guess, until I picked Vada and him up." Sonny sat beside her on the couch. "I'm so glad you're feeling better. It would have been a real bummer if you hadn't made it to the Sugar and Spice tonight."

"I'm glad I did, in that case. Those teenage pictures of you and Walker are pretty funny. You two must've *lived* in obscenely tight bell-bottoms back then."

"Guilty as charged." Sonny nodded toward the White Tornadoes picture on the wall. "It was high fashion at the time. But, you think about it, bad as it was, Walker actually dressed more tastefully back then."

They both laughed. Cilla lifted her glass in salute. "I had a lot of fun with you tonight, Sonny." She downed her champagne and held it out for more.

He poured for her. "I told you I wasn't so bad."

"You did indeed. Oh, this is the song. I love this. *Cry to Me.* I was thinking of doing it on my next record." She closed her eyes and sang along with Burke, in a voice soft and husky.

Sonny listened to her, moved by the sadness in her singing. He wondered what the hell she could be thinking as she sang along. She'd always kept a distance from him before tonight. He should be thrilled to have her here—he'd fantasized about being alone like this with her so much lately that it was absurd. But he had a bad feeling about it. If he examined this feeling too closely, he was afraid he'd discover the last thing he wanted to.

Feeling the champagne, the weed—a romantic high, very unlike the mean horniness he associated with his usual whiskey-and-cocaine-shooter combo—he decided to risk it. He took her hand, tenderly touching his lips to her callused fingertips. Cilla stopped singing, opening her eyes and watching him kiss her hands. Tears streaked her face.

"Whoever put those teardrops in your eyes is a fucking fool, girl. Man, Cilla, I just wish I had the right words to make you feel better, but I don't have a clue where to start."

"I don't imagine you find yourself at a loss for words with women often," she tried to joke. She pulled her hand away, dropping her face into it.

"Your right. But I usually don't even bother with words." The champagne and the weed were making him feel a need to confess. He told her, "Me, I treat women more or less like I do guitars. I play with the fine ones until I'm wore out. Then I just put them down and forget about them until I get the itch again.

"I figured something that other people had inside them was missing in me. It never bothered me, though. It's kept life simple." He stopped talking, grabbing her chin and making her look at him. He took a deep breath and said, "I never loved anybody, never even came close to it. But Cilla, sweetheart, you—"

She put her hand over his mouth, shaking her head. "Don't say any more."

"But I need you to know." He tugged the hand he was holding, pulling her toward him, and wrapped his arms around her. He gazed into her eyes, feeling as though he'd drown in those sad green pools. "I been hoping I'd get this chance, and then, if I did, that I'd have the balls to tell you this. You got to believe I ain't just talking shit when I say I respect you. You spend the night with me tonight. If you don't want to screw me, it's okay. At least let me hold you near, girl."

She pushed back away from his chest, holding him at arm's length. "Oh, Sonny. You are deadly handsome. And talented, and cool, and. . . ." She paused, letting out a sound somewhere between a sob and a laugh. "You're even single. But you can tell I'm in love with somebody else."

"He ain't here." *Even single*, she'd said. "Your man's married. He's with her right now. I can read it plain, in your hurt. Let her have him. You stay with me." She tried to get up. He didn't let her. With one hand he pulled her chin to his and kissed her, nipping her bottom lip gently, tangling his other hand in her plush hair. She seemed to hold back for an instant, and then she began to kiss him back with gusto.

After a few minutes of burying her in kisses, Sonny reached under her top and began to run his palm over a breast. She grabbed the wandering hand as though she was thinking of putting a stop to it, but instead she held on to him. Just as this happened, Sonny dimly heard a car gunning up his street and squealing to a stop somewhere nearby.

Looking toward the noise outside, Cilla gasped and tried to pull away from him, but he wouldn't permit her to do so. He was about to tell her to just relax and not worry about whatever was going on out there when his front door was almost torn off the hinges from the pounding that shook it. Cilla let out a short yelp, staggering upright and yanking free from him. Every dog within a mile's radius started howling belligerently. Sonny jumped to his feet, striking a protective stance in front of Cilla.

Then he heard Walker's voice, screaming wildly. "Sonny! Sonny, you bastard! Don't you dare touch her. Let me in now. Now!" Walker howled along with the rest of the dogs, pounding again furiously, two-fisted.

Sonny swung around, locking eyes with Cilla. He groaned, "Fuck, no. I didn't want to believe it. Anyone but Walker."

She was shaking, a guilt plastered on her tear-streaked face. She begged, "Sonny, just make him go. Please."

"Sonny!" Walker wailed, now kicking the door, too. "I know she's in there. I ain't leaving."

Walker kept pounding and yowling at the top of his voice. Sonny told Cilla, "He's going to break the fucking door down if I don't open it. Go lock yourself in my room." He watched Cilla run down the hall, ducking into the bedroom, slamming the door behind her. He took a steadying breath and shot back the dead bolt.

Fist still poised to beat the door, Walker was trembling, snake-eyed with fury. He looked utterly dangerous. Sonny wished he had armed himself before opening the door. He pulled himself up to his full height, almost a head taller than Walker. He outweighed him easily by a muscular twenty pounds. In a sane fight Sonny could take him, no problem. Right now Walker was nowhere near sane.

"Where you got her?" Walker slurred in a throaty snarl. "They said you left with her." He pushed Sonny aside roughly, clomping into the living room. He spied her boots on the floor beside the couch. He picked one up and yelled, "Cill! Darlin'! Where's he got you?"

Sonny stared down, eyes full of icy hatred. "Shut the fuck up, Walker. She don't want no part of you. Get the hell out. Go home to your wife before my neighbors call the cops—before I do." He stalked toward the phone on the kitchen wall, lifting the receiver. "They'd have a good old time with that stash you keep in your boot, as well as the fact that you drove over here completely shit-faced."

Surprising the hell out of him, Walker popped Sonny solidly in the chest with Cilla's boot. The force nearly toppled him, and the receiver fell from his hand with a clatter. Walker raged, spit flying, "Yeah? You do it, and I'll have them search your goddamn freezer. We'll see who goes down quicker. Where is she, you fucker?"

Sonny gave Walker his twisted smile, full of malice. "In my bedroom, matter of fact."

Walker's eyes went round, his one brow jumping skyward. "You didn't—she wouldn't do it, 'less you forced her to. You fucking dawg, Sonny! Man, you never cared shit for no one but yourself." He pounded his own chest with a fist. "Cilla's *mine*. My woman. Don't you dare touch her with your heartless hands." Then Walker let out a banshee's howl and jumped his brother. They both tumbled to the floor. Like he was just a rag doll, Sonny tossed Walker aside. Then he pounced, straddling Walker, punching his face viciously, once, twice. Walker groaned, trying to turn over, to get his bloodied face away from Sonny's fists.

Cilla grabbed from above Sonny's arm, which was raised to strike again. She screamed, "Stop it! You'll kill him. I'll talk to him. I'll talk. Just don't hit him again!" Sonny allowed her to pull him off. He shook fiercely with the effort of squelching his singing rage as he rubbed his hand. Walker was moaning, his nose pouring blood and his lip split open. Cilla was down by him in an instant, crying over the sorry fucker. Crying over *her man*. "Oh, Walker, lover, are you okay? You're really hurt, aren't you?" Cradling Walker's head in her lap, she snapped at Sonny, "Can't you see he's bleeding? Get me a towel or something."

"Yeah, I best. He's going to ruin my new rug." Sonny stomped into the kitchen and wet a dishtowel. Walker was sitting up when he brought it back. The fight was gone from his eyes, replaced by pain. Sonny threw the cloth at him, deeply disgusted. "What you trying to do here, shithead? Prove to her what a badass, studly bluesman you be? Ain't looking too tough right now, lying there in your own blood."

Walker, still on the floor, held the towel to his bleeding nose. He looked up at Sonny, pale as chalk. He whimpered, "Give us a minute alone, man."

Sonny looked to Cilla, and she nodded. "Since she says okay, I guess I'll allow it. I'll be in my room if you need me, sugar." Just to spite Walker, he stooped over and kissed Cilla hard on the mouth. She didn't even seem to notice. Before walking away, Sonny turned a freezing stare on his brother. "You go nuts again, asshole, I'll bash in your fucking head with my Telecaster. I'll knock your brains clear to Houston. You dig?"

Struggling to his feet, Walker muttered through the now bright-red towel, "I dig, Sonny. Leave us alone. Now."

Sonny stalked back to his bedroom. He made a show of slamming his door. Hating himself for his weakness, he silently crept it back open, eavesdropping. He leaned against the jamb, trying to convince himself he was only listening in case Cilla needed his help.

"Lover girl, come here—"

Cilla's voice was outraged. "Don't you dare! What did you do, fuck Vada this morning still sticky from me? Variety is the spice, so they tell me. Another few minutes and I could have found out if that's the truth."

"Jesus. Don't even say that, Cill." Walker sounded wounded.

"Why not? You had yourself a black-haired and a redheaded lover today. What's wrong with me doing the same? At least Sonny and I wouldn't be breaking vows."

"You don't mean none of this. Come here to me—"

"Please don't. I think I'll lose my mind if you touch me." Sonny heard her break into wracking sobs. She choked out, "God, Walker! This hurts so much."

Sonny almost went to her then. But the sobs became muffled, and he heard Walker hushing her—holding her now, no doubt. Comforting her.

"Oh, Cilla, I'm so sorry. I thought you knew I had to see Vada when we came here. I wanted to tell her what was going on with us. But she was so glad to see me." His voice trailed off. "Okay. I promised you no lies. I ended up in bed with her today. We had just come from there when we saw you at the sound check. She was so happy to see me. I couldn't make myself tell her then. And then things got so busy, with my folks here and the show. Cill, you sounded awesome tonight. And you looked so damn beautiful."

"Really?" She'd stopped crying. She sounded surprised. "I felt like I was dying, with everyone watching me."

Walker let out a hollow-sounding laugh. "They don't call it blues for nothing, babe. Pain makes it burn, all right. And then, later? Seemed like you was flirting and dancing with every man but me. Especially Sonny. I watched him eating you up with his eyes. I hated that."

"It wasn't exactly a picnic for me, either."

"I know. Then you was dancing with him, against his chest close and tight. He saw me watching you. He smiled at me like—man, I almost tore you both to pieces right there. I had to go to the can and splash cold water on my face until I calmed down some. When I got out, you had left. With *him*. I just dragged Vada out of there and took her home."

"You fuck her again?" Cilla said, a hurt sneer in her quavering voice.

"God, no, darlin', I did not fuck her again. I broke her heart, is what I did do." There was a long pause, and when Walker resumed speaking, his voice shook. "I sat her down and told her—told her it was serious. I said I still love her, because I do. But I told her I love you, too. I told her I needed the time the tour gave me to decide about things." He let out a wrenching sigh. "Man, I can't figure this out right now."

Voice quiet, Cilla asked him, "What did she say to you then?"

"She asked me who, of course. I wouldn't tell her, though. Told her it didn't matter. What matters is it's the real deal."

"You wouldn't even tell her it was me?" Cilla sounded like she was going to cry again. "Are you that ashamed of me, Walker?"

"No, no, you got it so wrong. I did it to protect you." He dropped his voice nearly to a whisper. "Take it from me, Vada can be dangerous. She'd try to hurt you—I mean, like, beat you up. Worse, even. I don't want her fucking with you."

There was a long pause. Sonny had been holding his breath. He let it out slow so he wouldn't be overheard. What was going on out there? Had Walker left or—-. He heard Cilla then, low and sad, saying, "I guess it's official. I'm your mistress." She spat the word out. "I don't know how I can stand that, Walker. It goes against everything that I believe in."

Walker sounded panicky. "Cill, don't tell me it's over. Please, no."

"I wish to hell I could." He voice choked up. "I'm just not strong enough, though, to bear seeing you everyday, not touching you. Oh, Walker. You opened up something that's consuming me." She was weeping once more.

"Me, too. I know just how you feel."

Quiet again, except for the sound of Cilla's tears. Maybe this time Walker had really left. Sonny thought he should go out to her, to help pick up the pieces. He would apologize to her for hitting Walker thataway. He would offer her his own brand of sweet solace, show her she was right to stay here with him, instead of. . . .

Then Sonny heard her groan, an unmistakably sexual sound. She sighed out then, low and throaty, "I can't believe.... God, it's fire, you touching me like this."

"That's because you're mine. Ain't another man can love you like I do."

"I know . . . I should make you stop . . . but lover? I can't. . . ."

Sonny stood in the door for a few minutes more, his eyes and fists clenched. It hurt to listen to their erotic exchange of foreplay. He needed to pull Walker off her, finish beating him senseless, and throw him unconscious into the gutter. He'd do it, too, if it would change how Cilla felt about Walker. It'd be worth it, even if it made her hate him as well.

Finally, Sonny just shut his bedroom door. Turning the stereo in there up loud, he put on the headphones so that he could drown out the sounds of their lovemaking.

WALKER STRUGGLED TO on Sonny's couch. He could feel Cilla sleeping naked in his arms. A mothball-scented quilt draped them both. He lay still, unable to open his eyes for the wicked pain in his head. He felt as though his face had met up with the business end of a trash compactor. This was much worse than his usual hangover. He eased himself into a sitting position.

He opened his eyes gradually, looking down at Cilla. She was still sleeping. His heart jumped when he saw blood in her hair, on her neck and shoulders. Gently he ran a hand over the crusted gore, looking for a wound. There was not one he could see. It must be his own blood. Neither he nor Sonny had hurt her, thank God.

Sonny. On top of him, punching hard . . . that was the only image that flickered through hours of black fog. Everything after leaving Vada was . . . gonesville. He remembered running out of his house, his wife sobbing, begging him not to leave her. Clutching his felt-enveloped Crown Royal in one hand, he jumped into the car and tore out. He stopped at the first light to crack the seal on the bottle, taking a hard pull.

Then he remembered nothing until Sonny was pounding on him.

Walker stroked the quilt a moment, remembering it from childhood nights at Daddy Jim's. He grappled to get on his feet, nearly passing out from pain and nausea. Taking deep breaths to keep from vomiting on the floor, he pulled on his pants and went looking for Sonny. He was gone. Walker peeked out of the living room window and saw no sign of his brother's Mustang. Vada's Impala was parked damn near sideways, the front tires resting on Sonny's lawn. Walker shuddered, praying he hadn't hurt anyone on his way over.

His nose and mouth hurt the worst. He stumbled into the bathroom and performed his waking ritual of puking and peeing. The dry heaves went on longer than most mornings. Once the retching released him, he looked himself over in the mirror. Rust-colored blood covered his face. Both his crooked nose and split bottom lip were swollen, bruised. Raccoonlike, there were dark circles ringing his eyes. He knew he'd never looked worse, which was saying something.

What the hell had gone on here? Where was Sonny anyway? They needed to talk this out now that things were calmer, more clearheaded. Walker glanced into Sonny's room. The bed was made, or not slept in. The clock told him he and Cilla had to get ready to get to their flight. There was no time to find Sonny.

Walker went in the living room and pulled his stash from his boot. He returned to the bathroom, laying out lines on the countertop. Though it hurt badly enough to cause him to swear and sprout tears, he managed to inhale some of the drug through his broken nose. Once the burn subsided, the cocaine helped numb him, though his nose started bleeding again. Panting, Walker used a wet washrag to clean his face, and held it to his nose to stem the flow. He retrieved his whiskey from his car and poured two fingers into a glass, throwing it back in one gulp.

Feeling better, he went to rouse Cilla. "Darlin', rise and shine. We got to meet the boys and head out."

She stretched and her eyes eased open. They snapped wide at the sight of him. She sat up, grabbing his arm. "My God, Walker! We've got to get you to a doctor."

"Looks worse than it feels, baby."

"I should have taken you to hospital last night. But I was so very drunk, not thinking straight...." Cilla ran a finger gently over the gash on his mouth, causing him to wince. Jumping, glancing around, she yanked up the quilt to cover her naked breasts. "Where's Sonny?" she demanded.

"I don't know. His car's gone." She jumped up and grabbed her clothes, keeping watch out the window. "Cill ... what the hell happened here last night?"

She pulled her skirt on, eyeing him. "Nothing happened, Walker. I didn't do anything with Sonny."

"Well, good. Real good. But that ain't what I meant. I ... I can't remember nothing besides him decking me." Walker let out a sad little laugh, looking around the living room. More to himself than to her, he mumbled, "Maybe I grabbed his guitar. Sure used to make him pound me when we was kids."

"You truly don't remember?" Walker shook his head. Cill looked scared—but also somewhat relieved. "In that case, you can ask Sonny. I'm staying out of this."

"But, Cill—"

"No, Walker." Done dressing, she dragged a brush through her hair, heading to the bathroom. "I will not discuss this with you. Now, if I can't talk you into going to hospital, call the road manager. Have them send a car over for us. I have to pack. Besides, everyone's probably going nuts, wondering where we are."

16.

"THANKS FOR COMING with me, Real."

Riley nodded. He would rather be elsewhere. "It's okay, boss. Your bodyguard be a better choice than me, though. Hope no one mugs us down here. Just think, they probably can't even rob us in English!" Walker laughed a little but didn't sound amused. They walked through the shadowy depths of an underground garage below the concert hall where Cilla's band, the Rockets, and the Salamanders had finished performing. The two of them headed for a section cordoned off for the performers' limos and buses. The tour buses were being loaded with their gear. Walker headed over to the limos while Riley hovered a few steps away.

Riley's knowing eyes could tell Walker was petrified. The boss was shaking hard enough to make his many necklaces jangle. Some of it could be due to the choice shit they both sucked down right before this adventure. Riley had the blow shakes a little himself.

Leastwise, Walker's face was nearly healed from Sonny beating the crap out of him back home in Austin. Everybody had freaked when he and Cilla returned after being missing in action for hours. Walker's face had been mincemeat. Cilla wouldn't say a word. Walker volunteered only that it had been an old-fashioned bar fight. In fact, they should see the other fool involved if they thought he was a sight. While the wounds healed, Walker wrote a kick-ass shuffle and set it to hairy lyrics. He called it *Barroom Brawl*.

One snow-storming, drunken bus trip between Cheyenne and Salt Lake City, Walker finally confessed the truth to Riley and Outlaw. It was Sonny who'd hurt him so bad. Walker didn't remember why his brother did it, though. Too loaded when it happened, he told them. The bassist didn't even want to think about what that meant.

The Salamanders were on top, man! Living out their fantasies, traveling the world playing the greatest music possible. Everyone who knew shit from shinola said Walker was the best blues-rock guitar player on earth, maybe even that ever had walked the planet. The travel was exhausting, sure, but the perks! Jamming with their heroes, eating heavenly drugs, screwing top-drawer tail . . . they had it all for the taking.

Walker was always at the party, even though he was no more than pleasant these days to the babes. He had his own road girl, after all. Other people didn't know what was going on, or Riley would have heard the gossip. To Riley, Walker and Cilla's affair was as plain as the rebroken nose on his boss's face. Those two were crazy for each other.

No reason to worry, right? If Walker was drinking more than he ever had, doing more blow, more everything than even Riley could manage, it was his business. Walker sure seemed to love this girl. He'd gotten away from Vada's craziness, at least for the tour. Most of all, he was playing like his soul was ablaze—better then ever. Riley knew what a great hand fate had dealt him. He couldn't fathom backing any other stringer, and he knew Outlaw felt exactly the same. They were the greatest fucking band in the Milky Way.

Riley looked on, leaning against one of the cement supports, as Walker slipped one of the limo drivers some bills. That must be the car Sonny was supposed to take. Riley had tried his best to talk Walker into keeping out of his big brother's way. Lately, when the two bands crossed paths and played together, Sonny made it clear he didn't want a thing to do with Walker. Sonny wouldn't even do his own sound check, which he had always insisted on before. Johnny Lee took care of it for him. When Riley asked Johnny Lee the score, the Rockets' bassist said he had no clue what was up. All he knew was that Sonny was in a dark place right now.

Sonny would arrive shortly before show time, waiting his turn far from the Salamanders. He played his set and then stayed locked in his dressing room until the encore. He came out again for an encore and then split right quick.

Tonight, Walker had made a point to beat Sonny out to his waiting limo. Slipping a little farther into the shadows, Riley watched as Sonny stalked toward the limo where Walker waited. He was still dressed in his slick suit, and was wearing a black scowl. Riley peered inside as Sonny opened the door. Walker was lounging in the back, drinking a stout whiskey. Sonny balked, trying to close the door.

Walker grabbed his arm. "Get in here, Sonny. I'll pour you a drink. We got to clear the air."

Sonny snarled, "You turn me loose and fuck off, Walker. I got absolutely nothing I want to say to you. Get out of my car! I'm sure your adoring public, and your high-tone English tail, are pining for you."

"Stop it, Sonny. Look, I'm sorry about everything that happened that night at your house."

"Sorry, huh? Come busting in and. . . . Look, do I need to break your nose again to get my point across? Do I? I said fuck off! We see each other when business forces us to. Play nice for the crowd, and then go our separate ways. That's it, hear? Now get the hell out of the car." Sonny yanked his arm hard with Walker still holding on, throwing his brother to the ground. He raised a foot as though to kick Walker but stopped short of doing so. He climbed in and slammed the door. Walker sat on the pavement, staring at the tinted window, stunned. Sonny cracked the window open, and added, "I'm home next week for a spell, little brother. I'll go by and make real sure your wife ain't lonesome." Sonny made a filthy gesture. He sneered, "Keep clear of me, if you know what's good for you." The tinted window hummed closed. Sonny would not look back as he barked at his chauffeur to step on it.

Riley ran to Walker's side, hoisting him to his feet. He motioned the roadies, who were heading toward them, to stay back. Arm around his boss's shoulder, Riley asked quietly, "Walker, are you hurt, man?"

"Just my feelings." Walker stared after Sonny's departing ride. He groaned, "Jesus, Real. I can't believe he won't talk to me. What the hell did I do to him?"

Riley guided his boss toward one of the waiting long cars. Trying to shield Walker, he glared back at the curious security entourage. They turned away, pretending to go about their business. "Who knows? Probably not a thing you meant to do. What I think is, Sonny's jealous. He can't handle the fact that he ain't top dog in the Blaine house no more."

Walker climbed into the car, letting Riley scoot in beside him. Right away, he reached for the bar, pouring two large glasses of whiskey with shaking hands. "Jealous? Of me?" He snorted, slamming back the drink. "Sonny don't got reason to be jealous of me. He's awesome in his own right, his own way. People know that."

"That's beside the point. Sonny might not know it. That's all that matters to Sonny. I know you love your brother, man, but you got to face facts. Mostly, Sonny's a selfish dick. In my opinion, he always treated you like dirt." Riley saw anger flash for a moment in his friend's eyes. Better not to even think a bad thought about Sonny, as far as Walker was concerned. "Listen to me, okay, Walker? Stay away from him. Let Sonny work out whatever's eating him. He won't talk about it, anyhow. He's made that plain as day."

Walker downed his drink and nodded. "That's good advice, man. Even if I hate it." He pressed a button, opening the partition between themselves and the chauffeur. "Hey, buddy, do me a favor. Get on the horn and leave a message backstage. Have them tell Ms. Mountbatton to grab one of the other cars. Leave word we'll meet her back at the hotel." Walker closed the smoked glass and pulled out his vial of coke. "I can't go back up there and play nice tonight with the fans, Real. I feel sick about the way things just went."

Dear Sonny,
    Look, just read this, okay? Don't tear it up or nothing, please? I been trying to get a hold of you I don't know how long. I wish you'd just talk to me, let me apologize.
    As you probably know, my tour's been over awhile. I'm liv-

ing in California at Cilla's. For now, anyhow. Do me a favor and don't tell no one, though. People still don't know we're together. As a couple, I mean. Folks just think we're working together on her record. We don't go out much, unless it's like an industry thing, or sometimes we pretend we happened to meet up at a club. Mostly, it's the studio, and her house.

I feel pretty much like a fish out of water here, Sonny. I read once that folks out here rhyme "good" with "did"—and they sure as hell do! They all sound like Brian Wilson. And even when it rains the air don't get wet. Weird. I'm homesick as hell. But I don't want to come back and have to face Vada again.

I been home only once since the tour finished. Vada and me got real smashed. Ended up fucking, of course. That's always good with her, like playing an old guitar you hadn't handled in a time but know the feel of real well. But then she got pissed off about being used for kicks—like she wasn't getting her kicks, too? Anyway, we got into a knockdown drag out, and I punched her with a left hook. Knocked her damn near out. Bruised her pretty face real bad. Of course I felt like a complete shit. Even Daddy don't beat up women. But she drew first blood. You got to believe me about that.

Anyhow, I'm scared to see her. I get Steve Taylor to send her all the money she needs and stuff. Lone Star signed her again, at least. Don't know if you heard her new band, but they're pretty righteous. Small outfit for her, just rhythm section, sax, and guitar. Call themselves Vada Blaine and the Ballbusters. Ain't that just right?

Anyhow, Vada wants me to come home and produce her new record. Maybe you heard tell I been assisting Sterling producing Cill's latest. Going to do the same with Reg, too. Sterling's wife's been real ill, so he just ain't got the time, or drive, to do like he used to and camp out in the studio. So I camp out instead.

Been working some on my own record—kinda sorta, anyhow. Easier these days to work on other folk's stuff. The label's bagging on my ass for something new. No fun. But I have a blast making guest appearances on other people's records. Doesn't take no thought. Some of it's cool stuff, but some of it's lame as hell. I turn down more than I do. Don't mean to brag, but I think folks kind of see having me on their thing as a status symbol. Like driving a cherry Coupe De Ville in Mingus, or some shit!

I better go here pretty quick. Reg is coming to dinner. He's bringing a girlfriend who Cilla's worked with some. Reg's lady is a art director on music videos. She's gotten Cill some jobs dancing. The next video, Cill's going to be the one who comes up with the dances—what's that called, choreographer?

Tonight, I'm meeting Reg official, as his baby girl's man. She let him in on our secret a couple of weeks ago, over the telephone. But he just got back into town from tour. Going to ask me all about my intentions, no doubt.

Can you imagine Reg doing that shit? Pretty funny thought. Am I scared to death, though? Hell, yes! Don't have real good history in the girlfriend's daddy department. Nancy Ruth and Vada have daddies that hate me, after all. At least Reg and I are friends—or used to be, before this. I sure hope it goes okay.

I miss you, bro. Even if you don't never read this, I'm glad I wrote it. Sort of feels like we're talking, anyhow. I been thinking of maybe moving back to Austin, bringing Cill with. I don't know, though. Vada will do all she can to make life hell for us. Cill keeps dropping hints about us getting hitched, too. Shit, Sonny, I'm already married. I don't need another wife. I don't know what it is I need. I feel real confused lately. Hopeless, even.

Well, that's it, except for this. Find it in your heart to forgive me, Sonny. Please?

Walker

"LOVER, YOU KNOW we can't drink and party with my dad here," Cilla yelled out the sliding glass door that opened the kitchen onto her pool deck. Walker was sitting in a lounge chair. He had been scribbling away for the past hour, drinking whiskey steadily.

"Damn, girl. You mean I got to do like First Lady Nancy tells us and 'Just Say No'?" Walker grinned at her.

"Exactly. At least while Dad's here."

"But baby? I'm way too stoned to Just Say No!"

"Walker, please—just behave."

"I'll do my best." He winked at her and laughed, leaning over his notepad. His smile vanished as he began writing again.

Cilla hoped he was writing songs. She doubted it, because he just asked her how to spell "choreographer." She couldn't quite picture that word being in a Firewalker Blaine blues.

Walker seemed so frustrated with his own output lately. She knew he

was avoiding going in to do another Salamander thing right now. He needed to quit fooling with everybody else's music and work on his third album.

She peeked in the oven at a roasting goose, and then grabbed a joint
from the freezer. She tossed off her cover-up, joining Walker outside in her
bikini. He must have been writing a letter. He was licking closed an envelope. She glanced at it as he tossed it on the wrought-iron patio table. It was
addressed to Sonny.

She felt sadness and guilt starting to surface at the sight. She would do
anything to get the boys speaking to one another again. Anything, that is,
except give up Walker. That night had been so awful, with the two brothers both so gone, fighting like dogs over a bitch in heat. She'd been wasted
too, stupidly putting herself between them. She'd been using Sonny as the
perfect pawn to get back at Walker. She would never have had sex with him,
even as intoxicated as she'd been. Even as tempting as she found his looks,
she was sure she would have left before she actually went through with it.

She hoped so, anyway.

Walker pulled her onto his lap, covering her with smooches. She clung
to him, pushing Sonny from her mind.

"Don't worry, darlin'. Be on my best behavior for your daddy." He let
out a loud yelp of laughter as he lit the smoke for her.

"What's so funny, lover?" she asked on the exhale.

"It's dang weird, Cill. If you had told me, back in Mingus, that someday I'd be trying to impress the daddy of the English beauty I was shacking
up with, and he just happened to be *The* Little Lord Mountbatton, High
Lord of the Holy Six-String himself. . . ." He shook his head, laughing some
more about it.

"Well, I didn't exactly imagine ending up with the likes of you, either,"
she replied, wrapping her arms around his neck and burying her face in his
hair.

"I just bet!" He kissed her, and took a toke from the joint she passed his
way. They got high while watching the smog-shrouded cityscape lying
below them.

"This California living ain't half bad. Nice place to look at—when you
can get a good peek at it, that is."

"I've always liked it here," Cilla agreed. "Always good music to be
found, and fun things to do, too. Plus, there's natural beauty everywhere."

"Yeah. I got me a natural beauty." He snapped the waistband of her
bikini bottoms, peering inside. "And she's redheaded top to bottom, at
that."

"Walker!"

"Well, you are. But that neighbor of yours next door? I think she's completely man-made." Cilla laughed, kissing him as she struggled free from his
embrace. "Where you think you're going, girl?"

"To baste my goose."

He staggered in after her, grabbing her and heaving her over his shoulder and growling. He headed to the couch and threw her down, jumping on top of her. "No way! If I'm here, I'm going to be the only one basting your goose."

"Walker, let me go. Our dinner will be ruined."

"Should have deep-fried it or barbecued it, then. Proper way to cook, woman. You English don't know a thing about food preparation, do ya'll?"

"How dare you," she giggled, still trying to struggle loose. She was having a harder time resisting as his hands crept over her.

"How dare I? Like this!" She groaned, still laughing, as he went on. "And like this, too. See? You're helpless, Cill. How'd ya'll manage to conquer the world in the first place? Oh, yeah. Got ladies with these kind of charms on them. Make slaves out of us fellas, don't you?"

"Walker . . . cut it out. Oh!" She gave up struggling, surrendering to the heat of his hands and kisses. As a final protest, she moaned, "Lover, you really better stop. My dad'll be here any minute."

"Reckon he'll wait."

17.

"THIS IS GOOD stuff, Reg. Best you've done in years." Walker and Reg were in the sound booth, listening to the rough master of Reg's soon-to-be released album *Back on Track*. Walker rubbed his neck, achy from the cold air in the little room. These days it felt like he lived in artificially lit, sound-proofing-baffled rooms, surrounded by recording equipment, wiring, and high-grade gear. A high-tech cave dweller is what he'd become.

Reg's new album consisted of acoustic and electric blues, originals, and classics. They'd had a good time making the record. Reg was pleased to discover an enthusiasm that had been fading since Little Lord had, effectively, become his first name.

"I've really loved delving into this stuff again, Walker," Reg said, as they listened to an acoustic instrumental. "Thank you for the encouragement it took to get me started."

Walker sat beside him, smiling. Patting Reg on the shoulder, he said quietly, "Hey, man. My pleasure. My honor. You been such an inspiration to me over the years. Me and my brother both, you know? You have the real thing going on, Reg. We always respected your talent. We didn't cotton to the English guys much when we was growing up. They mostly sounded, I don't know, kind of phony when they played this stuff. You didn't."

"Thanks, Walker. I did strive for authenticity, especially as a boy. Wished so that I'd grown up American."

"So explain one damn thing to me. How can ya'll sing so damn American sounding but still talk like you do?

"Like what?" Reg asked, grinning.

"Like—like you was gargling marbles or something!"

"Hell, Tex! I can't believe you of all people are casting aspersions on dialect. You know, in most of the civilized world, the word *guitar* is accented on the second syllable? And another thing. Hear that word—*thing*? One syllable only, no 'a' in it, whatsoever."

"Point taken," Walker laughed. "But leastwise, I sing just like I talk. I remember Sonny and I couldn't believe our ears the first time we heard the Beatles speak."

"They're Liverpudlians. Northerners. What can you expect? Sort of our version of vulgar Yankees." They both chuckled. Reg reached to the board, fooling with the sound a little. "How is Sonny, Walker? It's been awhile since I've seen him."

Walker shrugged, his face darkening. "You probably seen him since me. We ain't speaking. We had this big blow up."

"What on earth could have been so terrible to keep you two from speaking?"

"This sounds so stupid. . . ." Walker lit a cigarette, closing his eyes. "Fact is, I don't know. Don't remember. I was way drunk. I know we had words—more than words. Sonny beat the shit out of me." He gestured at his crooked nose. "Re-realigned my face for me. Cilla was there when it happened. She was a part of it, I think. But she won't talk to me about it."

"You don't remember anything? You had a blackout?"

"No. Sonny didn't beat me up that bad. . . . I think I was conscious the whole time. . . ."

"Walker, that's not what I mean. A blackout is lost time, lost memory. It happens to people in trouble with alcohol." Walker's face started to grow indignant. Reg held up his hands. "Look, I won't lecture. Hell, when I was your age, booze was the least of it, though probably the worst of it. Finally it got to a point where I had to stop if I was going to have any kind of life, much less a career. I hope you don't wait that long."

Reg watched as Walker stared at the floor, huffing hard on his smoke. Reg switched off the reel to reel. "Listen to me, Walker. There's a tendency to think we have to live the blues we play. And I guess we do, in some ways. Life experience enriches the music, no doubt of that."

"Uh-huh. Got to live it to feel it," Walker mumbled, still watching his boots.

"Priscilla told me about your talking to her about tapping into the emotions that drive our stuff. You've helped her immensely that way. But, understand, chemicals don't pry inspiration open. Especially not for you."

Walker raised his eyes. "Why especially not for me?"

Shaking his head, Reg closed his eyes, as if he were meditating. "You don't know, really, do you? How amazing this gift you've been given is? It's unique, so very precious. I know. I've seen them all, seen them come and go." He leaned forward, peering intently into the younger man's eyes through his glasses, grabbing Walker's arm. "I've seen great talents live and die. I've watched people throw it all away because of drugs. But never have I seen anyone who can play with your intensity." Reg squeezed his arm. His voice was almost reverent. "I use that word to describe both your technical agility and the feel you put into your playing. What you have doesn't come from mere diligence. It's a gift. And I confess, you torment me at times."

"What?"

"You're so much better than I could even dream of being."

Walker was startled by such words—coming from Reg, of all people. "That ain't so."

"No false modesty needed, Walker. Please listen to what I have to say. The flip side of the torment is the inspiration you give me. That's the reason I had the courage to try this album. I wanted to see if I could still play this stuff. Frankly, I needed to know if I could play with real feeling, completely sober."

"It's the best stuff you done in years, Reg," Walker whispered. "Maybe ever."

Reg smiled and nodded. "I think so, too. I can touch on emotions that I deadened for a long time with self-administered anesthesia. Starting out, I was often paid in beer. Later, appreciative fans bought me drinks, got me stoned. I fancied myself as being very authentic—born English, maybe, but I had to prove I could tap into my Mississippi roots or some stupid thing.

"But eventually I learned to tread lightly, Walker. You idolize my old friend Jimi, yes? Just think what he'd be capable of today if he had taken care. His talents, so vast . . . just when he started to peak as an artist, he flamed out as a person."

"It wasn't his fault that he drowned on his own puke."

"So you say? Do you think he would have been in that ambulance in the first place if he had not overindulged on sleeping pills and booze? Do you actually think Brian Jones would have drowned in his own swimming pool if he hadn't addled his mind the way he did?"

Walker got up and stalked across the room, turning his back on Reg. He lit another cigarette. What he really wanted was a drink. Who was Reg to talk to him this way—compliment him, then tell him how to live his life? Where'd he get off? Walker turned to look at him. Reg watched him with calm, concerned eyes.

"Reg, why you doing this?"

"Because I'm scared for you, Walker."

"Like hell. This ain't about my partying at all, is it Reg? You don't like it that your daughter's mine."

Reg didn't say anything for a few seconds. Then he took a deep breath and replied, "This was not about her. But, since you bring up the subject, no, I don't like that she's *yours*, as you put it."

Walker stammered, "Yeah? Well . . . tough shit, Reg! She's happy. Can't you see that? She's playing great, she's dancing again, working on the videos. She ain't overshadowed by you no more. I know how that feels, because of Sonny. It feels great when you finally get recognized for yourself. Cilla's earned this respect, and this happiness."

"She has." Reg looked down to the floor, dropping his voice. "That is beside the point. Walker, even at my worst, I did my best to shelter my daughter from my excessive life. She's a naive girl. Even though she lived with Jackie, she didn't feel about him as she does about you. She's wide open for heartbreak by you."

"I treat your girl real fine, Reg. I don't want to hurt her."

"You already do. What, you think she forgets about your wife? Don't kid yourself, even if she doesn't discuss it. She discusses it with me."

"She does, huh?"

"She does. Did you know, every time she hears you play *Smitten*, it tears her up?" Reg nodded at Walker's surprised expression. "She was jealous the first time she heard it, and she didn't even know you. She said it is the kind of song every woman wishes she could inspire in a man. She's right, too. It's one of the finest love songs there is. That record will live on long after we do. It's classical, in the best sense of that word."

"Thanks—I think."

"Don't thank me. I'm not praising you now. The point I want to get across to you is this—Priscilla knows it's about your wife. It hurts her terribly."

"Fine. I won't play it no more."

Reg stood, slapping his hand over his eyes and dragging it down his face. "Christ, Walker. You miss my meaning entirely. Priscilla loves that song. But it threatens her." Reg's Zen calm dissolved completely, his voice rising almost to a shout. "To be blunt, what the hell are you doing, Walker? Are you divorcing Vada and marrying my daughter? Because if you're not going to do that, get the hell out of my daughter's bed! Break it off, sooner the better, before you fuck up both those women's lives."

Walker had no idea what to say to this assault of words from Reg. It was utterly unexpected, and it stunned and infuriated him. How had they come to this, from a pleasant listen of Reg's new work? Walker loved this man. He'd respected Reg as an artist nearly his whole life and wanted to do him honor as Cilla's daddy. Even though a part of him knew what Reg had said was dead on, he was still outraged.

"This ain't none of your business," Walker finally managed. "She's a big girl, now. This is between her and me."

"For now, yes," Reg said, his voice soft again, his arms folded like armor over his chest. "But I'll be picking up the pieces when you've moved on. And you will, Walker. I know you will, even if you don't yet."

They stared at each other across the sound booth, both seething. Thirty seconds of silent glaring passed before the door opened and Cilla hustled in. She was blotting rainwater from her hair with a towel. She kissed both men on the cheek, saying. "Hi, you two. It's pouring. I bet you didn't even know that, locked away in here. We had to stop our shoot on the video, before a dancer took a spill and Workman's Comp–ed the whole project." She trailed off in her chatter. "I'm sorry. Am I . . . intruding?"

"Of course not, baby," Walker said, taking her in his arms and kissing her. He held her to his chest, looking at Reg over her shoulder, his face pressed against her wet hair. "I missed you today, Cill," he went on. "The video going okay otherwise?"

"Well as can be expected, with these heavy metal idiots I'm working with." She laughed. "You should see the costumes—sword and sorcery pageant, set to three distorted chords." She shrugged. "But it's kind of fun, I have to say."

Reg smiled, pushing his glasses up the bridge of his nose. "Very good. Well, I must be off. I've got to deliver this master." He removed the reel, put it in its canister. He reached to stroke a hand over his daughter's cheek. "Take care, my dear. And Walker? Please consider all I've said today."

"Will do, Reg," Walker answered, not looking at him.

Reg departed without another word. Cilla pulled free of Walker, hands on her hips. "You were fighting. What about?"

"Nothing."

"No, it was definitely something."

"Oh, you know your daddy. Thinks he's got the world figured out. Trying to give me a little fatherly advice. I told him it wasn't his right until he was a father-in-law."

Walker regretted the words as soon as they left his mouth. Cilla's eyes lit up with such hope it made him feel worse than Reg's bluntness had.

She asked, a little breathlessly, "And . . . did you decide when he might become your father-in-law?"

"My present father-in-law hates me. I'm in no hurry to get Reg sharing Julio's point of view." Walker tried to pass the comment off as playful but could see it had wounded. "Hey, now. Don't get glum on me." He pulled her to him, kissing her soundly. "You my special girl. Feel better?"

"I suppose." She in fact sounded close to tears.

He squeezed her hard, saying, "You feel awful good to me, Cill. The best!" She gave him a forced smile. He turned away, facing the board. What an idiot he was—best to change the subject quick. "So, before your daddy came in and started lecturing me, Sterling was here. We went over your last week's tapes. He had a few right-on mixing suggestions, but he digs what we're doing. My darlin', we're so close to putting out an album you can be proud of."

This seemed to perk her up. "I think so, too, Walker. Did Sterling mention his wife's health?"

"Not good, was all. The worry's taking its toll on him, Cill. I hate to see him suffering so. Mrs. Preston's always been sickly, but she's a lot worse now. He's scared the end is near."

"Poor man. He always loved his work so, but now he's torn. Married nearly fifty years, did you know that?" Cilla asked. Walker nodded. She added, "A lifetime together. Can you imagine?"

She was watching him too carefully. He turned his head, putting the hat brim between them. "Pretty hard to imagine a lifetime with one person, all right."

The outside line rang. Saved by the damn bell from another heart-to-heart, Walker thought, relieved.

Cilla answered the phone. "Cilla Mountbatton." She stood up straighter, her eyes growing round. "How wonderful to hear your voice! Are you?—" She paused. "Yes. He's right here." She handed the receiver to Walker, whispering, "It's Sonny, lover."

Walker stared at the phone in disbelief for a second. He took a deep breath and said, heartily, "Hey, bro! I can't believe it's you. You in town? We—" He stopped mid-sentence, listening intently. "Where? Not at Fort Worth? How long has he been in Austin? Okay. Look, I'll get the next flight. Tell me where to reach ya'll. . . ." Walker gestured wildly for something to write with. Cilla found a pen and scrap of paper. He scrawled a long-distance number and extension. "Got it. Look, thanks for the call, Sonny. I'll see you soon as I can." He hung up slowly. Taking off his hat, he ran a shaking hand through his hair, his face going pale.

"Walker? What is it?"

"Daddy. Sonny said he's almost dead. If I want to see him, I got to go now."

18.

"WALKER! OVER HERE," Sonny called, watching his brother arrive at the nurses' station. Walker looked up, spotting Sonny waving him toward the smoking lounge. He thanked the nurse he was talking with and loped over toward Sonny.

Walker looked older, the lines around his mouth deep, some gray touching his uncombed hair. Even down the hall, Sonny could see the crook his fist had left in his nose. Though it was dark outside, Walker wore sunglasses. As camouflage, Sonny assumed, though the eternal hat made Walker as identifiable as his fingerprint. He also had on a full-length coat, fake-fur trimmed, the rest of it covered in a bright amoebic design. Only Walker, in this day and age, could have dug up a psychedelic pimp jacket. It hung loose off his shoulders. Walker's legs, wrapped in Levi's, looked like twigs. He was as thin as he'd been as a kid. Looked like a '60s teenybopper and a tired old man combined—bizarre, even for Walker.

He entered the lounge. They stood a few paces apart, staring. Sonny finally said, "You made it quick. That's good, Squirt."

"Hey, Sonny." Walker stepped forward, snatching his brother in a quick, tentative hug. Sonny permitted the embrace. "Where's Daddy at?"

"Down the hall, ICU. They only let us in two at a time. Mama and Vada are with him, now. You should know up front that Vada's been the best. Great to all of us."

"That right?" Walker removed his shades and stuck his head outside the lounge door, scouting faces. "That don't really surprise me. Does she know you called me?"

"She and Mama told me to. They need you here." Sonny grabbed Walker's sleeve, pulling him into a corner away from the few other weary souls in the lounge. He offered Walker a cigarette, which Walker grabbed gratefully. "Look here. We all got problems with each other. But we need to be cool," Sonny said. "Vada and I want things to go easy as possible for Mama."

"You won't get no grief from me, man," Walker snapped. "Who's been trying like hell to put this shit behind us? Huh?"

"Okay, okay." Sonny scowled over at a woman who watched them. She shrugged, turning her eyes away. Sonny glanced back to Walker, who was blowing smoke rings, still watching the people in the hallway. "So . . . how's Cilla?"

"Good. Did you ever get my letter?" Sonny nodded that he had. "Did you read it?"

"I read it."

"Did I mention she's been designing the dances in music videos?"

"Yeah. Being a choreographer. Couldn't believe you even knew that word."

Walker let out an annoyed huff, and then let go a grin. "Yeah . . . right. Well, she digs it. And we just about got her album in the can."

"Great." Sonny went quiet, thinking of Cilla. He wondered how she looked these days. He could easily conjure up her fairy-tale eyes and her goddess legs, the sweet smell of her neck. Was her hair long? Did she ever ask after him? How stupid, to think such sappy crap about Walker's woman.

Walker let out a burst of coughing, snubbing out the cigarette. He sighed, stretching his arms over his head. "Come sit with me, Sonny. Let's talk out something important, while we got the chance." Walker sat in a corner chair, shadowy under a burned-out lightbulb.

Sonny was too tired to protest much. He squatted on the arm of the chair, next to Walker. "Can't this wait?"

"No ... you need to know this. That night at your house, when we fought? I don't remember shit."

"Right." Sonny jumped up. He pulled his fighting stance, cocked his head, weight on one leg. "You want to pretend it never happened. I can't do it, Walker."

Walker chuckled, the sound of it high and jittery. "Well, I sure as hell can. It didn't happen for me. I woke up not knowing how I even got there, with my face all busted up. I remember you hitting me, but that's it. The last thing I knew was talking truth to Vada, feeling like a first-class dick."

Sonny dropped his posturing, sitting back down. "You really blacked that night out?"

"Looks like it."

"That's heavy shit, Walker. Does it happen to you much?"

"Don't know ... guess I wouldn't remember if it does, right?" Under his hat, Walker glanced sideways at Sonny, forlornly. Suddenly, he ruptured into uncontrollable laughter.

Sonny frowned, popping Walker's arm, as the raspy hysterics grew worse. "Stop that, Walker," he whispered. "I'd be ashamed. Daddy's dying, for chrissakes. We're in a hospital—behave yourself." Walker shook his head, rolling nearly off the chair. He mimed apology but was far beyond being able to utter the words.

Despite himself, Sonny was swept up in Walker's inappropriate laughter. Soon they were both helpless, tears streaming down their faces. They worsened when the other occupants fled the lounge. Any hope of regaining control was slapped away by fresh convulsions each time someone glanced in from the hallway, gaping at them with tight-lipped disapproval.

What a sight we must be, Sonny thought as he yelped. Walker was the high plains drifter gone citified pimp. And like he was any better himself? Leather jacketed, his hair slicked up—like some reject from a biker opera. They were both plain silly looking, in their poser outfits and cowboy boots. Why, neither of them had ever once sat a horse, despite spending childhood among saddle-bred rancher kids. Sonny had never so much as killed a cockroach with his boot's pointy toe. Some cowboy! He laughed all the harder, until he was afraid he was dying of suffocation, gasping and coughing along with his howls. Walker was at least as bad off as he was.

Exhaustion finally gripped them, forcing them to both wrangle some sort of composure. Wiping hysterics-induced tears from his eyes, Sonny heard Vada's stern voice. "Honest to God, boys. The nurses are sending someone from the crazy ward after ya'll. When I heard her say how weird one of the psychos was outfitted, I knew I had to claim you."

Walker panted, still bubbling with tired laughter. "Howdy, honey. I owe you a big thank you for all you done for my family." He approached his wife slowly, arms outstretched to hug her.

She folded her arms across her chest, leaning away from his grasp. She was gaunt, the circles deep under her eyes. The last few years had gained some on Vada. A broad streak of silver sprouted from her right temple, glowing bright among her midnight curls. She snorted, "I think they're still my family, too, Babydoll. Can't be rid of me without my consent, right? Or is it different out on the Coast? Folks change wives over there like they do their socks?"

"Of course you're family, sugar," Ruby said firmly, coming up behind her. She squeezed Vada's hand in passing, and then went into Walker's reaching arms, hugging him. "I'm glad you're home at last, Walker Dale. We've sure enough missed you."

Walker held her tight, saying, "I missed ya'll, Mama, something awful." He watched Vada with wary eyes. "Sorry if I'm ripe. Been in the studio for seems like days. I came here straight from the airport."

"None of us has had enough showers or rest lately," Vada answered, glancing Sonny's way. "Look, I'm taking your mama to my folks', to feed her properly. She needs to be away from here and hospital food. You go see your daddy, now." Vada moved closer to her husband, whispering, "Take your hat off for your mama's sake." Walker did, apologizing for it. Ruby nodded, looking too dazed and careworn to appreciate the small courtesy. "Better," Vada added. "You coming home after you leave here?"

"I would like to, Vada. If you'll allow it."

"Here, then," Vada said, dropping a key into his hand. "I had the locks changed after your last visit. Let yourself in, if you get there before me. Come on, Ruby."

Ruby kissed Walker once more then trailed Vada toward the elevators. Walker shouted thanks to Vada as she walked away. She didn't turn around, but waved curtly back at him. He said to Sonny, "That wasn't too ugly. I thought she'd make this messier."

Sonny nodded. "When push comes to shove, your wife is one class act, Walker. Come on. We better go see Daddy before visiting hours end." They started toward the room. Sonny warned, "Brace yourself, man. Daddy looks real bad. No liver left, really. Yellow as hell, wasted away. But bloated with bad stuff at the same time."

"Jesus God, Sonny," Walker said, putting his hat back on, shuffling behind. "This sure is sudden, huh?"

"No, it ain't. He lived longer than they thought he would. He was already sick at that L.A. benefit show, near three years ago. That's when Mama told me, anyway."

Walker grabbed Sonny's arm, stopping him. "You knew all this time and never told me? Why not?"

Sonny shrugged loose, saying wearily, "Mama said not to. First, you had that show, then the album, then the tour. Then this, then that." Sonny added a sneer to his voice. "Then, in case you ain't noticed, you forgot to come home."

Walker scowled, "I been working like a dog out there, you know."

"Sure you have. With Cilla. Nice work if you can get it."

Walker shook his head, protesting, "Not now, Sonny. Not the time or place for this."

Walker's comment made Sonny feel small with shame. "I'm sorry. You're right. It's not the time or place." Truthfully, he was glad Walker was here to share the load. He was burned out from feeling like an only child throughout this lingering horror. Their parents had moved to Austin eight months before, as things started getting too much for Ruby to handle. When Sonny traveled, which was more often than not, his parents stayed at his place. They went to Uncle Charlie's when he returned for his brief spells home. But even now, with Big Billy Jay out of his home and hospitalized for the past two weeks, Sonny could taste the death in the atmosphere of the house. He left every window open, even in the coldest weather, hoping the Reaper vibe would move on.

Vada had become Sonny's primary comfort. She kept his fear of death at arm's reach. She was a wonderful woman—dangerously so.

Vada knew Walker lived now with a mistress on the Coast. To Sonny's surprise, she didn't seem to know the other woman was Cilla—or didn't admit to it, at least. She knew Sonny wasn't speaking to Walker but never asked why. She'd yet to go try and drag Walker back home. Sonny believed Vada feared giving Walker an ultimatum.

Despite his own ache over Cilla's choice, Sonny wasn't tempted to tell Vada the facts. Much as with breaking the news of Daddy's illness to Walker, he didn't want to be the one responsible. He saw no purpose in cutting her deeper than Walker already had.

Something still pulsed between Sonny and Vada, remembered from back in the day. When the sun was shining they were pals, in-laws. But too many nights, after the trauma of a day at the hospital, they ended up loaded and alone together. Sonny wouldn't actually fuck her. His hard lesson with Otis and Nancy Ruth had taught him that much. Vada didn't force the issue, either.

Yet she was still desirable, adventuresome. Sonny enjoyed the sport of her, and it was clear she still liked his ways. He knew they were doing what they did as a way of lashing out at Walker, but there was more to it. The groping beat the lonely grief they both battled. Sonny could forget about death for a time with her mouth, her hands, and her sex. Problem was, when the buzz of the booze, the drugs, the "everything but" wore away, the guilt settled in, big-time. The next day he and Vada would have a hard time facing each other over Daddy's sickbed.

Vada had been anxious all day about seeing Walker. Despite their bawdy trysts and Vada's rejuvenated singing career, Sonny knew full well she missed Walker to the point of pining. Sonny was the only man she was fooling with. The hospital left time for little else. Besides, Vada told him, as Walker's wife, she had a certain status to uphold. Bee-Stung was a distant memory. Vada called herself—bitterly—the Exiled Crown Princess of the Blues. "Just hope Walker don't get a mind to chop my head off, like that Henry VIII did his leftovers," she once cracked while lolling in Sonny's arms.

Sonny shoved aside his thoughts of Vada as he and Walker entered Daddy's hospital room. Sonny had put up extra cash to assure a private room for Big Billy Jay's final days. Walker hung back as Sonny approached the bed. What was left of Daddy seemed to be dozing, but his eyes flickered open as Sonny took his hand. "Hey, Daddy. You ain't going to believe what I found wandering the halls."

"You didn't find Fire out there, did you?"

"He did, too," Walker said, glancing at Sonny with shocked eyes. He perched on the edge of the bed, masking his face with a grin, taking Daddy's other hand. "Sorry I didn't come sooner. Didn't no one tell me how sick you was."

"Don't blame Sonny or Vada, son. Your mama put her foot down about you knowing." Big Billy Jay stopped and rested before going on. "We know you damn busy, Fire. Got important work. Out there in the land of fruits and nuts, yet." He smiled wanly. "Who'd think a boy of mine would end up in California?"

"Mostly people think I'm nuts, too, Daddy. I even dress like a crazy person. You remember them purple mariachi britches?"

Remember? They still give me nightmares!" Big Billy Jay took his hand from Walker's, plucking at the pimp coat sleeve. "You're getting worse, too, ain't you?"

"Guilty as charged, Daddy."

Big Billy Jay rested again. Then he said, quietly, "But I know nuts, and you ain't that, Fire. You're a Texan. We got us lots of eccentrics and free spirits. It's what makes us the best." He took a shuddering breath. "Here's where you belong. Travel all you want, bless the world by taking it your music, but then come on home. This place holds the roots of your greatness. You come from a long line of noble Texas bluesmen." His eyes got a bit misty, and his voice cracked. "Your Daddy Jim was one. I'm scared if you don't get real Lone Star sod under your boot heels now and then, you'll lose what it is that's you, Fire."

"I think you're right, Daddy." Walker took up the old man's hand again, squeezing. He turned sad, curious eyes toward Sonny. Sonny knew what his brother was thinking, how surprised he was by Daddy's insight. Big Billy Jay had also talked to Sonny at length about staying true to his origins.

Such a speech, unusual for the old man even in healthy times, had taken a lot out of him. For a long while, Big Billy Jay lay quietly. The boys stayed beside him, listening to the beeps and whooshing of the machines hooked to him, ticking his life away. Sonny thought maybe Daddy had fallen asleep, and he was ready to take Walker and go. But again, his eyes half-opened, and out came his growl. "Boy? You been shacking up with that little red-head, ain't you?"

"Call her Cilla, Daddy. Yeah, I have. Don't tell Vada that's who, though."

"I won't dare. Or your mama, either. But I knew when we met Cilla that trouble was brewing. I said to your mama, that night: Ruby, that girl would be a perfect sister for the boys."

Sonny snorted. "Talk about trouble. Sisters ain't suppose to look like that."

"Well, some sisters do." Daddy said, grinning a little. "Ya'll come from a long line of redheaded women, after all. Cilla's got your talents, too. Way I figure, if that girl was kin to ya'll, you'd spend all your energy fighting the other boys off, instead of butting heads. Sonny's been bitter ever since you been gone, Walker.

"But I'll say this much. She's one worth fighting for. Hell, twenty years younger and I'd kick both your sorry asses to win her." He let go a wheezy chuckle. "Don't repeat that to your mama, now. Sonny, get me a little water?"

Sonny held the cup for the old man, to sip through a straw.

"Thanks, son."

Putting the cup aside, Sonny said, "Daddy, you're talking too much. You best rest."

"I'll shut up when I'm good and ready. Be quiet forever soon enough. And it don't hurt. They got me pumped full of even better than you two drug addicts can get a hold of. I been waiting to talk to Fire here, and I'm going to finish, if it's the last thing I do."

Big Billy Jay grabbed at Walker with startling strength. "You know how good your wife's been to us? No, you ain't even showed your face in how long? I know I couldn't have been so gracious to my pitiful in-laws, was my wife off with some other man. You think on that long and hard, son. You took vows with Vada. Been with her since you was a starry-eyed nobody, ain't you?"

"Yes, sir. That's so."

"Hell, it ain't like I can't see why you're torn. Not many men get a chance with one such woman. But you got to choose—for their sakes. And, if I was you, I would look to her who already wore my name. Vada's something else, son—and a big-hearted *Tejana* girl. Leave Cilla to a man who ain't already taken." He closed his eyes, his grip slipping from Walker. "Now I can sleep. Ya'll go do the same. Walker Dale, you smell awful. Go home, take a shower, and shave your whiskers so you don't scratch your wife's sweet skin. Sleep in her lonesome bed tonight and love her up proper. You know that's what needs doing."

A nurse came in with medication for Big Billy Jay. His sons left him in her care.

Walker pulled his hat low as they strolled toward the elevators. Sonny could hear when he spoke that he was in tears. "Man, he's about through, ain't he? Always such a mean s.o.b. I never pictured him going out so helpless."

"I know. Let's go do like he said, get some rest. I'll drop you by your house. I'm driving a new car you got to see. A cream-colored '58 Plymouth Fury. She's killer."

"I bet so. You didn't let go of your old Mustang, did you?"

"No, sir. Can't imagine I'll ever sell that one. Too many miles between us."

"I know what you mean. Like Vada and me. When I saw her, I felt like I knew where I belong."

They left the hospital together. Outside, there was a gaggle of teenage boys, smoking in the parking lot. Two of them wore black-suede hats, one with his jeans stuffed in his boots. They instantly recognized Sonny and Walker and started blabbering at them. Walker brushed the tears from his eyes and patiently listened to the kids talk music. Sonny stood, silent, a frozen smile in place, boiling inside at the intrusion. What they both needed was peace, quiet anonymity.

Finally, Walker managed to part with the kids, shaking hands with each. The brothers continued on to Sonny's vehicle. Out of the kids' earshot, Sonny grumbled, "How can you stand that? All the time, I mean? Folks bug me here in town, sometimes, but ain't as likely to spot me elsewheres. You get that everywhere you go?"

Walker shrugged. "Pretty much. Part of the big time, Sonny."

"Yeah, a shitty part. I don't get the way people think. Just because they like how you play, they think they know you, just come up and start jawing at you. We're leaving a goddamn hospital! It's like they don't have a clue."

"They're just excited kids, Sonny. Think how you felt, back when you was young and met Hendrix."

"But, Jesus, that was different. That was a party. I didn't corner him at a fucking hospital."

"True enough," Walker said. He flashed Sonny a weary grin as he climbed into the Fury's shotgun seat. "But I still get what those kids feel. They see their hero in the flesh. I try to be nice when that happens. Because I know damn well if I had seen Hendrix when I was a kid, even if he was leaving a damn morgue, I'd of been talking his ear off."

19.

BIG BILLY JAY LINGERED another two weeks. In his final hours he slipped into a coma, and he passed quietly as Ruby held his hand and hummed hymns of solace. Walker stayed with the family so that Sonny could rejoin the Rockets and make up the postponed dates. Walker and Vada took charge of the memorial services for Ruby. They took Big Billy Jay home to Mingus, burying him next to Ruby's parents.

Sonny arrived from D/FW a little more than an hour before the service was to start. He noticed, even before the funeral had begun, that his former hometown seemed full of strangers. At church, he found comfort in the old friends, the people he had grown up with and around. But Sonny was rattled by the amount of the curious also in attendance, and by the number of journalists. He nearly lost it when he realized what was going on. Strangers were flocking to a funeral just so they might grab a good picture of the two grieving guitarists. Only Walker's restraining hand kept Sonny from clobbering one particularly obnoxious photographer.

Walker pulled Sonny away from the creep, wrapping his elbow around his big brother's neck. He whispered, "Sonny, it's ugly, but don't give them nothing to feed on. It ain't worth the trouble." One of the ghouls got a shot of that moment, Walker holding Sonny, advising him to chill. The photo ended up being the most published picture of the event. Walker, weary, looked patient, like he was comforting a child. Sonny's face was angry, injured. Whoever caught this exchange nailed the truth of what had been happening, at least. Sonny figured it was a better shot than one of him tearing into the no-count sleazeball.

Both boys were off, back to the road, the day after they buried Daddy. There was no time to grieve, or to comfort Ruby properly. Vada was there for her mother-in-law, however. She stayed with Ruby, helping her close out the last of her Mingus existence. Vada eased Sonny's and Walker's minds, assuring them she would find Ruby a nice place to live down Austin way. Still numb, the brothers went their separate ways again—Sonny to Europe with the Rockets, and Walker with the Salamanders to a long-ago-scheduled tour of good-paying festival gigs.

Sonny heard more talk that Twelve Bar was hard on Walker's ass, pressuring him to finish the album he had promised before this festival season.

Now that Walker's mentor, Sterling, was distancing himself from work, Walker had no champion at the label. Business was business. The fans craved something new from their hero.

Come fall of that year, Sonny arrived home, resting a short while before jumping back into the studio. He discovered Walker had returned to Austin and was back with Vada, finishing up his third record in a hometown studio. Sonny decided to drop by the sessions.

When Sonny entered the booth, a lone engineer, with bags under his eyes and a joint in his mouth, was running an instrumental track, while Walker added vocals from the studio. Sonny nodded greeting at the occupied technician, then bent down to get an eyeful of Walker through the glass.

Walker looked seriously frayed at the edges. As he sang, his dark-circled eyes clamped shut. He gripped a half-empty bottle of whiskey in one hand. His hair hung in greasy clumps beneath his headphones, and his signature soul-patch beard, typically shaved sharper than a stripper's bush, was lost in scraggly overgrowth. He had on a T-shirt that was covered in stains, new and old, perhaps of coffee and Tabasco. And the grubby jeans Walker wore likely could stroll around town on their own accord.

Walker's singing sounded good, though. His voice was a bit rawer than typical, made from more grit and less silk. He was performing an old Unart tune, *I Found a Love*. They'd had that Falcons record when they'd been little things, listening to it together often. Walker hadn't been as interested in the vocalists, Eddie Floyd and Wilson Pickett, as he was in guitarist Robert Ward's work.

Sonny remembered what Walker had said about it back then, in his high youngster voice: "Listen at that, Sonny. That ain't lead playing or rhythm, neither one, huh? But both, too. He's using that guitar like another vocal."

Sonny didn't remember what his answer had been, only that he'd been surprised as hell by the kid's insight. Likely Sonny had sassed Walker, making fun of him—mainly because he hadn't thought of it first. Sonny never listened to the song in quite the same way again, though. Walker must have been about ten years old, if that. Now Sonny knew that Walker had been working out the thing note for note on the Broadcaster as soon as Sonny wandered out of earshot. Here they were, twenty years later, listening to the payoff. Walker was pressing his unique stamp on the song, yet wasn't destroying the texture of the original.

Walker finished the take. He took a pull off the whiskey, cleared his throat, and said into the mike, "Was that decent, Bobby? Roll it back for me."

"Break time first, Squirt. You got company," Sonny said through Bobby's mike.

At Sonny's voice, Walker's face broke into a tired grin. He yanked off the 'phones and bounded into the booth. "Sonny, man, so good to see you," he said, reaching a hand to shake. "What's up?"

Walker's hand was cold to the touch. He smelled far worse than he looked. Sonny tried not to wrinkle his nose up as he answered, "Just wanted to see what the haps was here. How goes the battle?"

Walker shook his head, scowling. "Not too hot. Not like the first two records. We had them all but in the can in days, single takes, even. This is more like squeezing blood from turnips." He turned to Bobby, still docilely smoking his doobie at the board. "Take twenty or so, my man. You need it. See if Real and Outlaw are about before you come back. Tell them I want to try *Walker's Walk* again."

The engineer pinched out the lit end of the roach, rolling his eyes. "Boy, those two are going to be thrilled about that," he muttered.

Walker slapped the sound-proof glass, making it shiver. "Is that right?" he barked at Bobby. "Better fuckin' well remind yourselves who's paying you here!" He glared after Bobby as the soundman slinked out of the booth. "Shit. You like that?" Walker asked Sonny. "I get attitude from everyone, anymore." He handed Sonny his whiskey bottle, then reached down, pulling a bulging baggie from inside his boot. Walker started laying out behemoth lines on a mirror that Sonny hadn't noticed before.

"Whoa, little bro," Sonny said. Each line contained damn near the amount Walker used to carry around in his little vials. "Where's your black stash bag?"

"It don't hold enough."

"For who? Keith Richard?"

"Oh, stop now. You ain't my mama. Who's got time to run home for more blow? I even sleep here sometimes. And if I leave the shit at home, Vada'll do it up with her cronies. Now, quit nagging and sample. It's real good."

Walker handed Sonny a silver straw. Sonny snorted all he could handle from one of the monster rails. It was so pure it about froze his face clean off. He washed it down with some of the whiskey.

"See?" Walker asked. "Ain't that a treat?"

Sonny felt the near pure cocaine's glow and the whiskey's warmth slip rapidly through him. "No doubt, man. Whew. Now, speaking of your partying better half, how is Vada? She's glad you're back with her, I bet."

Walker took the bottle back, taking a belt before he answered. "Sometimes she's glad. She's been working pretty hard herself. Her band is right tight. Good live, though I can't go see her very easy. People get all worked up if I'm there. It ain't fair to steal their thunder."

"True."

Walker leaned into the mirror. He did up an entire line, to Sonny's amazement. Pinching his nose, eyes squeezed tight and watering, Walker added, "I helped her lay down a couple a songs for the Ballbusters' record. I like the bunch she got with her."

"Do I know them?"

"I don't think so. They's kids who come along since our time. No punk guitar slingers with a hat, thank God. But you should see Buddy, her lead player." Walker turned loose his nose, grinning at Sonny. "Such a pretty boy. High black hair, tight T-shirts, leather jacket. I think he'd plumb fall out if he met you."

"That right?"

"Yeah. To impress me, first time we met, Buddy brought over his daddy's White Tornadoes album."

"Shit!" Sonny hooted. "His *daddy's* record? What a horrible thing to say to me, Walker. Makes me sound a million years old."

Walker laughed, "Good thing is, you'll always be older than me. And don't get glum. You was a boy genius, after all. What, eighteen when you stepped into the studio that first time, with Terry Joe's outfit?"

"Yeah. Long time past, huh?"

Walker nodded, taking another slug. He stumbled over to the board, rewinding the master. He played back the mix of *I Found a Love*. As Sonny knew it would, Walker's guitar line out-and-out tackled him. It echoed Robert Ward's piercing original, yet encompassed Walker's distinctive tone and style. Walker frowned, worrying his beard with his index finger, mumbling, "Pretty good take, huh? Can get Bobby to fiddle with it some, I reckon. I'd like Goldie forward a tad richer, maybe. Yeah, just a little. Don't she have an especially sweet tone there?" He looked back toward the studio, his expression a little lost. "Funny. I can't even remember what I was running her through."

"It sounds really fine, Walker."

"You think?" Sonny nodded, meaning it. Walker cocked his good ear, listening carefully again for a bar or so. He switched the tape off. He dropped into the engineer's chair, laying his face in his arms. His voice came muffled from under his elbow. "Sonny, it's so hard, anymore. I don't got the inspired feel at all. Sometimes we sit here, wasting all this expensive studio time, doing nothing but playing poker."

"Ain't you got nothing in the can, Squirt?"

Walker turned his head to gaze at Sonny, cheek still resting on his sleeve. "Some standbys, mostly, second-nature club stuff. Arthur Alexander, Howlin' Wolf. Even doing Buddy Holly's *Oh Boy*."

"Buddy Holly. Thinking of Daddy Jim lately, huh?"

Walker nodded. "Yeah. Remember how he called Buddy the Legend of Lubbock?"

"Sure do."

"Ol' Buddy, man . . . not only a great guitarist, but he was pure Texas, too."

"No doubt about it."

"But my own music?" Walker's shoulders moved up and down. "Nowhere. I got one flashy instrumental left over from the last record, the *Walk* you heard me and Bobby talking about. And there's this jazz riff I been messing with a long time, a little Wes Montgomery–type thing. If I can get it where I want it, the jazz deal would be a nice closer."

"See? Not so bad, Walker," Sonny assured him. Not that he believed it himself. He could see that Walker was in trouble.

"I got to write some lyrics, bro. Those get on the radio easier than instrumentals. Else the label's going to have my hide."

"Easy. Get Floyd's help. The songs he gave you for your last record kicked."

Walker nodded. "Way ahead of you. I called him to come in the other day. He did, but he split right quick. I told him, stay, play your harp." Walker sat up dancing his fingers in the air. "I begged him, man. Please, I asked him, leastwise squat long enough to leave your creative vibe here. But he wouldn't."

"How come?"

"He didn't approve of the booze and the blow."

"Floyd? Really? I mean, I know he don't indulge anymore. But I can't believe he gave you a hard time."

"I wouldn't call it a hard time, exactly. He said he'd get me some songs, said I could come get them at his house. But you should have seen the way he looked at me, Sonny. Not like he was judging. Like he was scared." Walker stopped the flapping tape reel with his palm. "If only you'd seen that look on Floyd's face. Daddy's gone, Mama's a mess with grief. I'm back with Vada. My life is just weird right now. Even Reg said a bunch of heavy shit to me before I left California, too."

"Reg? He's usually so damn mellow."

Walker stood, stretching to pick up the mirror. He did another monster line. Then he handed Sonny the mirror, sneezed, and shook himself off, head to foot, like a drying hound. "He's mellow, all right. But he was lecturing me all the same. About my talent. About me being high all the time."

Sonny set down the mirror without touching any more. He said, "Maybe that's what he said it was about. I bet really he was just pissed about you messing with his daughter."

The change was instantaneous. Walker looked like he'd sprung a leak somewhere vital. He fell back into the chair, laying his forehead in his hand.

"Reckon he had reason to be pissed, Sonny. Ain't no question I fucked up there." Walker let out a brittle sigh. "You heard her record?"

"Sure did. Whatever else, you and Sterling brought out some great stuff in the girl."

"I'm proud to have been part of it," Walker added, his hands still over his eyes. "So. You like the title?"

"Sure." She'd called it *Fool in Love*, after a powerful rendition she'd done of the Ike and Tina classic. The track was getting some good airplay. "What, don't you like it?"

"It's fine, I guess. But I thought she'd decided to call it *Real Deal Lovin'* after that slippery instrumental that's on there."

Sonny nodded. The song in question was his favorite on the record. Her playing sweated, swelled, was as soft and sticky as summer romance. "That *Real Deal Lovin'* cut is a classic, Walker. And she wrote it, too, huh? I had no idea she had something like that in her."

"Her stuff's real deep, Sonny. She just needs a little coaxing to pull it out." Walker took some smokes from his breast pocket, packing them against the soundboard. "Not surprised she changed the record's name, really. Less she's reminded of how I did her, the better." Still shaking his head, Walker pulled the cigarette box open and lit up. Before he'd hardly drawn a drag, he started coughing violently, gripped by hollow, rattling spasms. Sonny gave Walker a few blows between the shoulder blades with his palm, but it didn't help. He coughed so hard that he started gagging, finally retching nothing but bile into a nearby garbage can. Sonny spotted a glass of water in the studio by Outlaw's drum kit. He ran and got it, making Walker drink it, sitting him back in the engineer's chair. Walker was covered in sweat, panting as the fit slowly turned him loose.

"Jesus. Light up another fucking cancer stick, why don't you?" Sonny smashed Walker's cigarette down to a crumbling stub in the ashtray.

"It's nothing," Walker said, letting out another strangled cough. "It's a little lung infection. I'll fight it off."

"That what the doc says?"

"I ain't been to the doc. I'm fine."

"Fuck you are! Same thing Daddy Jim said, right before he bit it."

Walker pushed himself out of the chair. "It ain't like that, man. I'm just wore out. I don't sleep much. And lately, even when I do, I get really horrible nightmares." He rewound the tape again, stopping a little way into the solo. He cocked his ear toward the speaker, listening for a minute. He turned it off again, looking at Sonny with numb fear in his eyes. "You know how they say when you die in your dreams, you die in real life? It ain't true, man. I dream about dying all the time now—and I don't never go peaceful, either. It's like something is after me."

Hellhounds, Sonny couldn't help but wonder. Aloud, he said, "Maybe you better talk to someone about this shit, Squirt."

"Like who?"

"I . . . don't know, rightly."

"It's just this studio air's bad for me. I start coughing, and I can't sleep good as a result. It started when I was working on Cill's record." He drew in a congested breath, turning his gaze on Sonny, one brow raised. "You seen her since I left?"

"Nope." It was the truth. He didn't add that he had tried to. When he got wind that Walker had split, Sonny had called her a couple of times. The first time, he'd lost his nerve and hung up when she'd answered. The second, her machine had picked up. He left a stuttering, formal message that he regretted miserably as soon as he disconnected. Cilla never called him back.

Sonny didn't like the way Walker was staring at him. To shift focus, he said, "I heard something about Cilla, though. She's going on the road with Grey Alonzo and the Stallions."

"No kidding?" Walker sounded startled. "Opening for him?"

"No. She's with his band for the tour. His old lead player quit to do his own thing. So, there's a filly among the Stallions this go-round."

"Well, how about that." Walker rubbed his chin, scowling.

"Yeah. You seen that video of his, that she's dancing in?"

"Made a point not to."

"Yeah . . . well, anyway, that's how they met. I heard Sterling introduced them, telling Grey to audition her for the gig." Sonny shrugged. "Reckon it'll be good exposure for her."

"Maybe. Grey ain't exactly a bluesman, though." Walker's voice oozed sudden contempt. "He's one of them Yankee Dago crooners!"

Sonny let out a guffaw, popping Walker in the shoulder. "Nice redneck talk, boy. You sound just like Daddy."

"Come on, though. He's no Texan, is he?"

"No, but that don't mean he's all bad."

Walker let go a small grin. "Or all good, neither. Not like us Lone Star boys."

"Can't everyone be so lucky." Sonny laughed again. "Yankee Dago crooner? He ain't Dean-fucking-Martin. The Stallions are tight as hell. Grey's one of Sterling's magical finds—you know *he* ain't going to be backing no lame crooners."

"I never seen them," Walker said, a little defensively.

"I did, before they hit it big. Grey's got tone a-plenty—plays an old blonde Tele, not too much newer than Old Broad, matter of fact. Simple rock licks, but solid enough. He's a real showman, too."

Walker nodded, looking like he'd coughed up his soul during his spell. Sonny knew he should try to talk with him about that night with Cilla. However, the only reason Sonny had been able to leave behind their feud was Walker's blackout of the events. Any talk could surely grow ugly, threatening to reopen the fragile scars.

Sonny was brought out of his musings by a gunked-up sniff that came from Walker. "Oh, man," Walker groaned. "You got a hankie? Mine's played." Walker tilted his head back, pinching his nose. Blood dripped down his arm, mingling with the other rusty stains already on his T-shirt.

Sonny handed over the handkerchief. Walker took it, pressing it to his tilted-back face. The handkerchief started reddening at an alarming rate. Sonny grunted, "Enough of this shit, Walker. Let's get you to a doctor right now."

"This ain't nothing," Walker said nasally. "Don't think I'll even need ice to stop it this time."

"Ice? This time? How often you get this?"

"Not too much. It's part of the lung thing. And hay fever, too. These dry studios—"

"Hay fever my ass. It's those monster lines. That's why you won't see a doctor, ain't it?"

Walker pulled the handkerchief away, facing Sonny. "See? Stopped already. Ain't no thing." Walker wiped his ghostly white face with the blood-and-snot drenched cloth. Sonny went queasy at the sight.

Riley and Outlaw opened the door. They greeted Sonny noisily as Walker jammed the disgusting handkerchief into his already filthy jeans pocket. While his Salamanders chatted with his brother, Walker cut up some more lines, offering it all around. Under Sonny's scrutiny, he didn't do one up himself.

"Gentlemen, start your engines," he said cheerfully to his rhythm section. "We going to try the *Walk* again."

Outlaw did a smidgen of the coke, whining, "Man, leastwise let's try and put it to bed today." He grinned at Sonny. "Curse whoever invented that Louisiana 3/4 time. What Walker needs is to borrow Rimshot from ya'll's band to...." Outlaw trailed off, eyeing his boss. "Man ... you got blood all over your face again."

"Where?"

"Your cheek—up here, Boss," Riley said quietly, demonstrating where on his own face. "Your top lip, too."

They all watched as Walker wet his fingers and rubbed most of the smears away.

Sonny asked Riley and Outlaw, "This happens to him all the time, don't it?"

"Often enough," Riley mumbled. He and Outlaw exchanged a worried glance.

"Stop it, boys," Walker barked. "You're going to get Sonny spooked over nothing. I'm just rundown."

"Whatever," Riley sighed. He shot Sonny a frightened glance. Outlaw cleared his throat, like he wanted to say something more, but he held his tongue.

They want me to do something about this, Sonny realized. Why? They ran with Walker. If something needed doing, the Salamanders were the ones who should act. They had the most to lose if something happened to his brother.

Walker interrupted Sonny's grim reflections. "Heard you Rockets are back in the studio this week."

"Next week, officially. Going to do it in Austin this time. I'm pleased, really. Be good to sit still for a time." Sonny stretched his arm over his head. "This constant touring's got me wore down."

"Yeah? I'm just the opposite." Walker tapped his fingers on the soundproof glass, gently at first, then hard enough to make it flex dangerously. "This place is a tomb," he growled. "Need to make tracks, do some gigs."

Sonny caught Riley and Outlaw exchanging a haggard glance. He could see they were exhausted, certainly not yearning for another tour. For their sake, Sonny chided Walker. "Don't be such a road whore, Squirt. It won't hurt you none to be home for a spell."

"So *you* say."

"Now, bro. Take some time to heal and enjoy yourself. Go out on the town, even. Remember why you moved here in the first place, man."

Walker narrowed his eyes at Sonny. He looked really pissed now. "I remember," he muttered. "Do you? We all came here for the music. But it ain't easy no more. Can't drop by the Sugar and Spice jam, or sit in with Vada's band, like I used to—causes too much of a fucking scene. I can't even go out and watch somebody else play. Things get too nuts when I do." He glowered hard at all three men. They hung back, silent.

Walker looked at the cocaine on the mirror. Sonny grabbed the straw off it, shaking his head sternly.

Walker swore under his breath but didn't argue with his brother. Instead he padded a little up with his fingertip and rubbed it on his gums. Grimacing, he added, "Ya'll know what I'm saying is the damn truth. The road's the price we got to pay. It's the only way anymore." Another thick drop of blood rolled down his lip. He swiped it off angrily, stalking back toward the studio. "Come on, boys. Sonny, go find that slacker engineer Bobby and tell him to get his ass back in here. We got work to do."

20.

THE BROTHERS MET UP next at Christmas time. They made it home to Austin, both determined to help Ruby through her first Christmas in a strange city without their daddy. Vada took charge of the holiday, doing all she could to make it a cheerful occasion. She covered the outside of her house in tiny, colorful lights. She bought the biggest tree she could find and swathed it in scads of tinsel and ornaments. Glowing luminaries lined the driveway and front walk. On Christmas Eve, Vada took Ruby along to the Sanchez Palace for the annual mega tamale wrap and steam. The Blaine boys stayed behind at her and Walker's house. They gave their word they wouldn't get too trashed to join them later at the Palace for a nighttime feast and Midnight Mass.

Sonny pulled a curtain back, watching what was for Austin an unusually heavy snowfall. It was starting to stick to the pavement. The clouds had been heavy all day but hadn't begun to drop their load until after the women left. Sonny hoped he and Walker would be able to follow later and scarf up all the savory Sonoran eats. He was having fun with Walker in the meantime, getting pie-eyed and playing guitar.

Sonny had brought along his National steel. Walker was handling a seasoned honey-colored Martin that he had picked up during his travels. Sonny dropped the curtain and sat back down on the couch, next to Walker's Martin. He ran his palm over the guitar's silky hip. Walker strolled back in from the can, saying, "She's a sweet thing, huh, Sonny?"

"A beaut, Squirt. Sounds real tender when you hit a note, too. Like tinkling bells."

"Yeah. Found her in an English guitar store. So pretty, I had to make her mine. But I never play acoustics. Really don't feel sure-footed. Figured it was time for this old dawg to learn a new trick." He picked up the Martin and handed it to Sonny. "The guy who sold it to me charged me a fucking fortune."

"That ain't right. You know he'll milk the fact he sold Firewalker a guitar to every picker who walks in his store," Sonny cracked, tuning the Martin.

Walker laughed, nodding. "The blues version of 'George Washington slept here.' "

"Exactly. Here, try the National on for size," Sonny said, nodding toward his case.

"You ain't going to clobber me if I do?" Walker asked, grinning.

"Not this time. Must be that damn Christmas spirit in me. Go on, check her out." Walker took the steel up, running a few practice scales for feel's sake. Sonny watched his brother's paws at work while sipping at his eggnog-splashed rum. He said, "Hey, Walker, you remember that old record of Daddy Jim's? A Lightnin' Hopkins thing. Something about betting the ponies. . . ."

Walker hit a strum and sang out a few bars. "That the one?" Sonny nodded that it was. Walker grinned, tossing his head toward his record shelves. "I ended up with that record. Hid it from you on purpose, when you moved to Austin. Let's run it down, Sonny. And one and two. . . ."

They flailed their way through the song, laughing at their mistakes.

Walker sang it, recalling nearly all the words, inserting his own bawdy lyrics when he spaced out. Then they jammed for a little, mixing bits and pieces of different things, trading licks. It felt good playing with Walker. Sonny never got a chance to play alone with his brother. At the very least, some-one from the family would be their audience. And these days if they were playing together, it was almost always as part of an encore for thousands of strangers.

Walker shook his head, letting out a good-natured curse as his fingers fumbled on the acoustic's stout neck. Sonny felt shamefully pleased at the sight. He had a definite edge in acoustic play from his years working with the steel.

"Harder than it looks, huh, Walker?"

"Yes, sir. And it don't *look* easy!" Walker shook out his fretter and reached for a pack of cigarettes. He offered Sonny one. "Man, this is fun. I like hanging out with you. We don't get much of chance anymore, you know?"

"I know."

Walker paused, then added in a softer voice, "What I really hated was when you wouldn't talk to me, bro."

Sonny lit the smoke, shaking his head. "Let's not get into that."

"Okay." Walker lit up but took to coughing pretty quickly. He snuffed the cigarette out.

"You need to quit them things, Walker."

"You, too. Now let me be. Leastwise, I cut back a lot since that lung thing." Walker sat back into the cushions, letting Sonny's guitar rest against him. "Sonny? I been thinking. How about we do a record together? Not a Salamander or Rocket thing. An *us* thing. A few handpicked cronies maybe. Do whatever feels right at the time."

Sonny took another sip of his drink, shaking his head. "Be too hard. Besides all the scheduling bullshit, we're on different labels."

"It'll take a little doing, sure. But I've guested all over the place. The labels don't give a damn. It's free advertising for them—you know, Firewalker Blaine appears courtesy of Twelve Bar. Like that there."

"I'll think about it, Walker." Sonny narrowed his eyes at Walker's hope-ful grin. "What if I say yes? What you going to do to level the field? Tie your right hand behind your back?"

Walker let out a raucous raspberry, putting the National away. "Oh, cut that shit out. Don't you buy into that Clapton is God–type crap they try to lay on me. You know damn well I wouldn't be doing what I do without your bad influence. Hell, I'd probably be a lifer in prison."

"You do have that crazy-white-boy thing going on," Sonny snickered, putting the Martin back in its case. "You know that famous photo of Billy the Kid? Looks just like you."

Walker threw his head back and cracked up. "God, I wish I could deny that! Wasn't blessed with that pretty mug that you got, that's for damn sure. You ready for another drink, Sonny?"

"If you'll drive to your in-laws, I am." Sonny handed Walker his glass and stretched out on the couch. Vada kept a little TV in the kitchen on almost always, and Sonny could hear the news droning from the set. He hollered to Walker, "See if you can't get a weather report, Squirt. This storm looks like the real thing."

"You got it," came Walker's answer from the kitchen. Sonny rolled onto his elbow and pulled a joint out of his guitar case. He toked on it, drifting in his mind, considering the album with Walker. Might be fun if, as Walker said, they left both their bands out of it. Maybe they could do stuff that fit neither combo. Explore their roots, Daddy Jim's stuff—jazz, Western, rockabilly, blues like the Lightnin' piece they were messing with today. It would be a good seller for whichever label decided to put it out, from fan curiosity alone. . . .

Sonny jerked awake to the sound of something breaking. The sound of Walker lowing came from the kitchen door. Sonny pushed himself up and staggered into the kitchen. Walker was in the middle of the room, staring at the small television. There were chunks of glass scattered at his feet. A jagged half of a heavy highball glass was clutched in his right fist. Blood dripped from his grip into a growing pool.

"Shit, Walker. What you gone and done to yourself?" Sonny scooped up a dishtowel from the counter. With it he took the sharp shards from Walker's hand then tossed them into the trash. Holding Walker's wrist, Sonny tried to blot up enough blood to see if any glass was still in Walker's wound. He couldn't see anything obvious, so he started pressing down with the towel. "How the hell you manage this?"

Walker kept staring at the TV. He whispered, "She really went and did it." He winced as Sonny pressed harder on the cuts, looking down at it. "Jesus," Walker whimpered, sinking to his knees. "My hand."

The towel was reddening quickly. Sonny held the cut hand above Walker's head, keeping his voice gentle. "It's bleeding pretty bad, Walker. Leastwise, it's not your fretter."

Walker didn't answer. He was staring up at the TV again. Sonny turned to look. He jumped with a start at the image—Cilla dancing close to Grey Alonzo on a rainy magenta-lit street scene. Grey's latest hit played under the announcer's voice. ". . . Publicist said that the wedding was private, with only immediate family and closest friends in attendance. Due to Alonzo's rocketing fame, the couple kept their relationship a secret while on tour together."

"What in hell?" Sonny said.

"That fucking *Dago Yankee crooner*, Sonny. She went and married his ass." Walker moaned. "I didn't believe her."

Sonny suddenly felt like puking. The drink in his guts, the wet heat from Walker's blood on his hands sickened him, as did the news. Taking a deep breath, he pulled Walker up by his armpit and led him, stumbling, into the bathroom. "Here, sit on the floor and keep your hand up, over the sink." Walker did, leaning against the washbasin cabinet. Sonny turned the faucet on over the cuts. He asked, "Vada got gauze and iodine in here?" Walker didn't answer. Sonny glanced down and saw Walker's blank stare, his ghostly pallor. He reached down and slapped Walker briskly on the cheek with his damp hand. "Walker? Don't you zone out on me. You're too drunk to be losing blood like this. Where's the gauze and iodine? Even if I take you to Emergency, I got to wrap this thing up."

"Under the sink, maybe. How did I cut myself, Sonny?"

"Fuck if I know. You still had the glass in your hand when I walked in. Might could be you just squeezed it too hard." While he talked to Walker, Sonny found the first-aid kit. Washed clear of the bleeding, the cuts didn't look very serious, and they didn't have the telltale pulsing squirt that meant a torn artery. "Can you move your fingers? Yeah, that's good, Walker. It don't look like you cut any nerves or tendons or nothing." The movement had made it bleed hard again. Sonny rinsed it some more. He decided to wrap it tight and watch it for a little, see then if they had to resort to the hospital. There might be a bit of a scene there, and too many questions, what with Firewalker's precious paw injured. "Looks like you ain't hurt yourself too bad. But Vada's got nothing but Merthiolate here in this kit. It's going to burn like a motherfucker."

"Daddy's cure-all," Walker said weakly. "You remember?"

"Too well. I got to use it, though, Walker. It's better than ending up with fingers gone like Daddy Jim or Django Reinhardt. Now don't pass out on me." Sonny gripped Walker's wrist hard and dumped a good portion of the iridescent orange firewater over the cuts.

Walker let out a shout somewhere between blasphemy and pre-language as he tried to jerk free of Sonny. He didn't faint, though. In fact, his color grew better as Sonny started wrapping the hand in gauze. "What would Daddy say?" Sonny dropped his voice down gruffly, into a dead-on Big Billy Jay impression. "Means it's working, don't it, boy? Be more careful next time, I reckon."

"Stop it! That's too creepy," Walker said, laughing feebly. He sat still as Sonny finished winding the bandage and taped him. He let out a long breath and sighed, "Can you believe Cill married that asshole, Sonny? She's only known him, what, a few months? I figured she was bluffing."

Sonny dropped the first-aid tape. "Bluffing? She told you about this?" Walker didn't look up as he nodded. "When? Was she here?"

"No . . . I was there. When I played the Greek last. She was in L.A., on a little hiatus from the Stallion's thing. I found out she was playing a club on Sunset. I went to see her after my gig. Didn't want to attract attention, so I dropped off my show jewelry at the hotel, hid my peace symbol in a plain black T-shirt. Pulled my jeans down over my boots. No hat, even."

"No hat? Bro, you was righteously *incognito*." Sonny washed his hands and shoved the first-aid kit aside, to be stored later. Grabbing a towel to dry off, he slumped to the floor beside Walker.

"It worked, too. No one paid me any mind. Had to show my license to the bouncer to prove I was me even. She was on her last song." Walker let the injured hand drop into his crotch and rapped his head once, hard, against the sink cabinet. "Sonny, she sounded awesome. And she looked gorgeous."

"I believe it. Look, keep your hand up, above your heart. It'll help the bleeding stop." Sonny pushed Walker's loose arm up onto the counter.

"I'll try, Sonny." Walker winced but kept his arm elevated. "So I waited for her after her show that night. Her security knows me, from when we toured together. They let me backstage. I was scared, but fucked up enough to not let it stop me. I got about five minutes alone with her." Walker stopped talking for a few minutes. He closed his eyes and rested his head. Sonny thought he might be asleep until he noticed a tear run down the side of his nose. "I promised her everything, Sonny. Told her I'd divorce Vada and marry her, I'd leave Texas . . . told her I'd stop playing my guitar, even."

"You did not."

"Oh, yeah, I did. Whatever she wanted, long as she took me back. She didn't say shit. She stared at me like I was something vile, man. 'You're too late. Far too late, Walker,' she went, real bitter like. So, since words wasn't working, I tried to be her lover man again. I grabbed her, wouldn't let her go. Told her, you know we're made for each other—no one can make you feel like I do. Kissed her then, for all I was worth. She didn't fight. She kissed me back." He stopped talking again, dragging his good hand over his wet eyes. His voice broke when he spoke. "Then she shoved me off. She told me, 'You can't. Not anymore. I'm getting married.' I didn't believe it, though. No way. I grabbed her again, told her she just wanted to make me hurt, feel jealous, like I had her. I was her man. Her *man*. Not that . . . pretender. She loved me like I did her. We're soul-mated, I told her."

"Jesus. Did she tell you who she was marrying?"

"Yeah. I believed her even less then. I could tell how she felt about me. Then fucking Reg shows up." Walker managed a strangled laugh. "He actually picked me up and threw me outside on my ass. Must have looked so stupid, the two tiniest dudes in the joint, tussling by the stage door. That's it between Reg and me. He hates me now, for certain. Fuck it all, Sonny." Walker slapped his forehead. "Honest to God, I thought she was shitting me. Never dreamed she'd go and do this."

"It's a shock, all right," Sonny said, fighting to keep a level voice. The unsettling news was starting to sink in. To distract himself, he heaved himself up and gazed at Walker's injury. The gauze was staying white. Sonny was fairly certain the bleeding had stopped. "Looks better, Squirt," he said. "But maybe we should swing by the hospital. Can you act straight enough that they won't give us the third degree?"

"I reckon so. I'm okay, though. Let's just skip it."

"No. Even if they don't want to stitch you, a shot of penicillin couldn't hurt. You can't take a chance with your hand, Walker."

"Well, like you said, leastwise it ain't my fretter," he said, wiggling his uninjured left hand and whimpering out a sorry excuse for a laugh. "And fortunately, I also uses my left paw when pleasuring the ladies. Besides, didn't you say you'd do the record with me if I tied a hand behind my back? Will this do?"

"We'll see," Sonny said, pulling his brother to his feet. It made Walker go dead-white again. He nearly toppled. Sonny steadied him. "You're shaking like a leaf, man."

"I feel real c-cold, like I got chills, and my hand's throbbing like a b-bitch," Walker managed, his teeth chattering.

"Hang on. Lean on the sink for a second." Sonny darted into the master bedroom. He yanked a colorful Mexican blanket from the foot of the bed and took it to wrap around Walker's shoulders. "Steady, there. We'll pretend you're James Brown doing *Please, Please, Please*." He patted Walker between the shoulder blades.

Walker nodded, smiling wanly, pulling the blanket close with his good paw. "Do me one m-more favor?" He nodded toward the sink-side drawer. "Look in there. Vada has a little medicine bottle. Bring it into the kitchen for me."

As Walker shambled out of the room, Sonny dug into the drawer. He found it, a cobalt-blue antique bottle filled with powder. He hollered into the kitchen, "You don't need fucking blow, Walker! You're drunk, lost blood . . . it ain't going to cut the pain."

Walker stuck his head back into the bathroom, scowling. "It ain't blow. Give it here." Sonny handed it over and trailed Walker into the kitchen. With chattering teeth, he managed to pull the cork out of the bottle with his mouth. He placed the open bottle on the counter and opened a drawer. He pulled out a cleaning tray, scattered with marijuana stems and buds, a Zippo, and a little clay pipe. He packed the bowl with a red-gold *colitas*, and then sprinkled a salting of the powder on top. Dropping the cork from his mouth, he put the pipe to his lips and took a deep hit. He was able to hold it for about five seconds before going into a wicked coughing fit. When his choking let up somewhat, he repeated the draw, holding the smoke a little better this time.

Sonny watched with slow comprehension. One time or another, he himself had done just about everything. He'd really only drawn the line at one thing, and it was what Walker was doing in front of him right now. Sonny muttered, "Christ on crutches, Walker. You're into smoking heroin?"

Walker was already a little slack-jawed and glassy-eyed. "So what if I am?" His voice was low and thick. "It's medicine in most countries. Helps the cough a whole lot once it's in me. My hand feels a lot better already. And I don't do it much."

"Sure you don't."

"No, really. It makes me too lazy." He paused for another toke. "I ain't shooting or nothing. I can't stand getting stuck—went out cold when they tattooed me, even. But Vada don't mind needles a lick. Got a golden arm these days, with her cocaine-heroin cocktails. Says she likes how the smack takes the edge off the coke crash."

Sonny's head throbbed. Vada was doing speedballs now? "Walker, this is fucked up. If your wife don't flat out OD, she's still playing dangerous. Hepatitis. Even . . . AIDS. . . ." It hit Sonny that only minutes ago he'd been covered in Walker's blood. Almost in slow motion, he brought his own hands up to inspect them. What if he'd cut himself, taking the glass from Walker's hand? What if one of his playing calluses was ragged, pulling loose down to open, pink skin? Sonny spotted no sign of a threshold to infection. He was nearly sick with relief.

While Sonny examined his hands, Walker strolled in slow motion toward the living room. He stumbled once over the dragging blanket, then he pulled it up on his arm like a toga, collapsing onto the couch. Sonny followed him, standing over Walker's prone form.

His eyes closed, in a dreamy voice, Walker muttered, "Vada says she don't share needles. And I seen her soak them in bleach. But it's still bad. The woman goes totally crazy when I try and talk sense to her. Want to help her—told her we'd try and clean up together, even. She won't hear it. Says I don't know shit. I ain't never home. If I push it, she really loses it . . . starts breaking shit, throwing things at me, hitting, scratching. I try not to hit her back, but sometimes I can't help it. I try my best to run from her when it gets to that point."

Sonny had seen bruises on Walker. He had a pretty good one right now, left of his chin. But he never dreamed that it was Vada's doing.

Walker went on, "She's so sorry after she loses it like that, especially if she draws blood. Says it'll never happen again. But it always does."

"So get the hell out."

"Can't, Sonny. She'll kill herself if I try and leave her again." Walker's head fell forward as he nodded off. Alarmed, Sonny sat beside him and shook him back awake. Walker continued, as if he hadn't just fallen out while talking. "She'll take me with her, too, I reckon. But she'll let me tour, to make enough bread, to keep her high."

"And what about you, Squirt? You gotten real bad, too. You even realize it?"

Walker didn't answer. He mumbled instead, "You see why I'm such a sucker for the road? It's fucked-up here. And I don't have the first clue how to fix it."

DATELINE, LOS ANGELES

In the big Grammy category of Record of the Year, Gray Alonzo is the odds-on favorite. He's never had a nomination before this. He told me recently, "It helps to have a pretty bride in the Stallions, pulling in her own nomination."

Alonzo is, of course, referring to his new wife and touring guitar player, Cilla Mountbatton. She garnered her first nomination in the Contemporary Blues Album category for her sophomore effort, *Fool in Love*, recorded prior to the Stallions record-breaking tour.

Here's where the nepotism comes into play. Cilla's father, the legendary Brit guitarist Reg (Little Lord) Mountbatton, is nominated opposite his daughter, with his rootsy *Back on Track*. Delving into mainstream pop for too long, Mountbatton père has returned with great verve to the music at which he most excels. This first nomination is long overdue.

There's more. Proud to say, two releases from my hometown label Lone Star also grabbed nominations in the same category. The two are *Swamps Meetin' the Plains*, by the Rocket 88s, and *Loving You Too Long*, by Vada Blaine and the Ballbusters. Vada Blaine, a longtime fixture as a vocalist on the Austin club circuit, is the sister-in-law to the Rockets' guitarist, Icestorm Blaine. Though both talented in their own right, these sibs-in-law are both best known, respectively, as brother and wife to guitar deity Firewalker Blaine.

Don't strain yourself trying to figure out who's the final and shoo-in entry of the category. With his monster seller, *Shadows A-Fallin'*, Firewalker and his solid Salamanders have the ace in the hole. Place your bets on this one to take it all. Firewalker Blaine has a hand in three of the other four records nominated. He was co-producer, with great record man Sterling Preston, on *Shadows a-Fallin'* and *Fool in Love*. Blaine had his first executive-producer shot on Mountbatton's and his wife, Vada's, fresh-sounding wax. Also, he plays on all three efforts. This has to be some kind of first, an artist involved with four fifths of the nominated efforts in any category—and blood kin to one of the play-

ers on the fifth, yet. The Texas Steamroller seems to be working
25 hours a day lately. I wonder how Firewalker manages without
flipping? Must be that confounded blues power. . . .

— Lurlene Luqadeaux, *Texas Blues*, 1985

21.

SONNY DIDN'T HEAR about Walker's collapse until three days after it happened. He was with the Rockets overseas, doing a series of grueling one-
nighters. None of the Rockets knew until the host of a German entertainment show asked Sonny about Walker.

Sonny gave his rote answer: "Firewalker's touring again, doing great.
He's happy about the Grammys and other awards *Shadows a-Fallin'*
received. We hope to get our bands together for some shows this go-
round."

"Has he left the hospital?" the interviewer asked.

The other Rockets all turned surprised stares to Sonny. What was
Walker doing in the hospital? It couldn't be real bad or someone would have
called. Sonny found his voice and said, "I'm not sure. But don't worry about
Firewalker. He's tough as they come."

Sonny let Bonnell take charge of the balance of the interview. As soon
as they were done, Sonny took the others aside and said he had no idea what
was going on but to cover for him while he tried to find out. He searched
out an office phone, managing to get across in broken German that he
needed privacy. He reached neither Vada nor Ruby. Only a recording
answered at Walker's management firm, since it was the middle of the night
in California. Sonny paced, smoking, wracking his brain for someone else
he could call. Uncle Charlie!

Charlie was dead asleep when he picked up but assured Sonny he was
glad for the call. "Better you get the truth before ya'll hear the snow job
they're putting out to the public. Because they're playing this down, Sonny.
Saying Little T-Bone's got a nasty case of flu. He canceled the tour."

"Canceled it?" Sonny knew now that it *was* bad. He'd seen Walker go
on half-dead from illness and pull out a great performance. "What's happened, Uncle Charlie?"

"Your little brother's nasty habits caught up with him, Sonny. They say
Walker's been having a rough one this time out. But the show's been great
as ever. Most folks didn't know how bad things were—even his entourage.
Anyway, he barely got through the St. Louis show. He finished the set, took
a few steps backstage, and fell out. Couldn't rouse him, couldn't even find a
pulse, it was so faint. Rushed him to Barnes hospital."

"Did he . . . OD?"

"Not exactly. Walker had a nosebleed earlier that day—a hemorrhage, actually. After they hospitalized him, Riley found blood-soaked towels in Walker's hotel room."

"Christ."

"His nose is all eaten up inside. And the alcohol? His blood ain't even clotting right because of the damage done to his insides. They're still giving him blood. He's also got bad walking pneumonia that they think he's carried around for ages, now. Your mama's with him. She says he cries like a baby when he's conscious."

Sonny couldn't speak for the shock. Suddenly anger swept him—why hadn't the Salamanders done something? Why hadn't somebody? Why hadn't he? He knew how bad things were when he saw Walker last, broken and blitzed beside the Christmas tree, hurt but too afraid to go to seek medical help because he was so stoned. Sonny finally managed to mutter, "Poor mama."

"What was that, Sonny?" Static was bouncing around the connection.

Sonny raised his voice. "Is mama okay?"

"She's fine, son. This ordeal's given her something to make herself feel useful. Helped her out with her grief over your daddy. It'll be good for them both, once he's stable enough to get home."

"Stable enough? Shit."

"Yes, sir." Charlie paused. "You know where his wife got to?"

"Vada? No. Maybe on the road?"

"Yeah, she is. But we can't seem to catch up with her. She don't return calls."

Sonny said nothing. Who knew what kind of shape the woman was in? Hopefully Vada was merely distracted with some silly stud and not in dire straits herself. He didn't want to tell Uncle Charlie about Vada's problems, too. "Tell me what to do, Uncle Charlie. Head home? Go to St. Louis?"

"No. Sit tight. Take care of business. You can't help now. Walker's still in ICU."

"ICU. Jesus Christ. He fucked up big-time, huh?"

"Sure enough did. This here's a wake-up call for Little T-Bone. He's got to change if he wants to live. There ain't a thing you or me can do about that, Sonny."

Dear Sonny,

  Sorry you had to hear of my troubles the way you did. I'm getting better now, slow but sure. I was feeling bad for a long time. And this tour it got a whole lot worse. I coughed constantly, puked a lot, nosebleeds and, what do you know, had a real bad case of . . . THE BLUES! Wrote it off as too many smokes, too much junk food, allergies, and, well, if you gonna walk the walk. . . .

Knew I was in deep when I got the nosebleed that morning, after snorting my morning wake-up. For once, I had no girl with me, so I was dealing with it alone. Freaking out big-time. Kept telling myself it wasn't so much worse than usual. But it was. The bleeding never really stopped all day, just slowed down enough for me to act like my nose was running. I was too scared to tell anybody. We had a show. Everyone was counting on me. So I started drinking to calm down. Seeing as I was about a quart low, it was the worst thing I could have done.

Don't remember a thing about playing that night. Next thing I knew I was in the hospital with all these tubes and monitors, the doctors telling me that even though I might bleed to death, they had to operate and shit. I wished then I had gone ahead and died. All I could do was cry for mama, like a little kid. What a shameful feeling. But she came—she said that's what mamas are for.

I stayed in the St. Louie hospital awhile. They had to fix my nose (a horror story—but hey, they even straightened it out where you and Floyd popped me). Plus they had to get me past the DTs, and get my lungs cleared and blood clotting right and all. Touch and go, man. But now I'm back in Austin, in a rehab place, getting my head on straight. Real's home with his folks in Denton, doing the AA and NA thing. Outlaw's fine. He ain't never been as bad as Real and me. Always had to keep semi-straight to keep up with us on the drums. Gene Krupa and Keith Moon aside, I guess drummers do get a lot more of a workout than us stringers. *Lickety Split* do put the boy through his paces!

This place is pretty rough, Sonny. Thought I'd just sit around and be clean, smoke cigs, eat donuts, drink coffee. Maybe try out my sober rap—"Hey, pretty mama! You detox often?" Hah! No, sir. It's work. Lots of therapy. Got to look back at shit I don't want to. You know some of it, growing up with Daddy and all. They say I got to deal with that stuff if I'm going to stay clean.

I'd like to see you. They don't allow visitors, not even Mama. Won't let me make phone calls yet—might be calling my *connecta*, or something. They did say Vada could come. But she won't. Too busy on tour, she says. My ass! But ain't that a strange twist? Who's stuck at home while their spouse is on the road this time? Anyway, heard tell your paths would cross at the Mesquite Festival in a couple weeks. Talk to her, Sonny. See if she's okay.

This ain't fair of me, but I'm asking you to tell Vada this. Tell her I can't be with her no more if she don't get help. Tell her I love her, and I'll do whatever it takes to help her kick. But I can't go back to her while she's using. She'll listen to you. She's told me how close ya'll got again while Daddy was dying. Don't freak out. She told me you wouldn't actually screw her. Didn't know you was capable of such restraint. But who am I to get pissed at ya'll? I was shacking up with Cilla at the time, after all.

I ever say how much I hate the way these women of mine get a sweet tooth for you? But it's natural. You're the type of coldhearted fucker women swoon over, right? Never do give a damn about them, do you? And how about your kid, Otis. You seen him, lately? I gave him a guitar awhile back. It made him so happy. You should stop in. Show him a lick or two while I'm out of the picture. Yeah, right. That might show you care about someone besides yourself.

LATER ON ... whew! Feeling much better now. Back from the head-shrinker session. Was your ears on fire? I wanted to throw this letter out—didn't mean for it to get so bitter. But she, my doc, that is, thinks I should send it. Wish you and me could talk, face-to-face. Not about this ugly stuff, but just shoot the breeze. Well, work, work, work. Got my chores and a group thing shortly. It helps to get in the right mental space before the group session, to deal with other folks trying to pull it together.

Take care of yourself. Be careful. Trust me, you don't want to walk a mile in these boots.

I love you, Sonny.

Walker

22.

ONSTAGE, WITH MAKEUP and the lighting lending theatricality, Vada was as alluring as ever. Even up close, the ravages of hard living and speedballs wasn't all that obvious. Yet Sonny could see the change. She didn't dress in her jungle-queen minis and stacked heels anymore—hard to hide the track marks in her old King Bee getups, and even harder to walk in those stilettos when she was hyped. Vada now favored velvet cat suits, hip-draping belts, ornate cowboy boots, and leather bolero jackets. Tonight she was head-to-toe in crimson and copper, and she was gettin' it. The crowd loved her.

Her range had become deeper—heroin dropped vocals down a step. Walker had invested in vocal coaching for her before she resumed her career. As a result, her singing had more control and power than ever. She sounded better than ever. In her art, if not her personal life, Vada was still in command.

Bringing it down from a hard-rocking set, she launched into her encore with her record's title track—a song of love worn out. She gripped the mike as if she were using it to pry the words loose. Sonny couldn't stand watching her sing the lyrics of a love gone dead. It was too close, too revealing. He stepped back into the dressing room and did a quick blast of blow before it was time for him to go on. A spark of shame hit as he got high, thinking of Walker locked away in the hospital. The drug smothered his guilt quick enough. Any remaining residue washed away with a shot of Southern Comfort.

Vada was already offstage and gone by the time Sonny got back to the wings. Just as well. He didn't want to talk to her about Walker, especially right before playing his set. He pushed Vada from his mind as he swaggered into the limelight with the other Rockets.

After the concert, there was a party at one of the promo men's house. His sprawling estate was absurdly overblown, even for Texas rich. The grounds and house were jumping with talent, support workers, and hangers-on. Mr. Promoter had bought the spread with his folks' oil money, so said the buzz. The blues crowd was certainly making the most of the accommodations. People frolicked in various stages of undress in the Olympic-sized pool and nearly as large spa. Everybody stuffed themselves on a luxurious spread of food and liquor. Folks were getting high on everything, right in plain sight.

Sonny partook, too, but not with complete ease. Gossip about his little brother was everywhere he turned. Word was out that Walker was hospitalized, but the publicity mill's attempts at whitewashing had pretty much backfired. Wild rumors abounded: Walker was a blithering idiot, mind taken completely by abuses. He'd suffered a coke stroke, left side totally paralyzed, and would never play again. His hands had been crushed in a freak stage mishap—the doctors were trying to teach Walker to use his fingers for simple tasks. Sonny thought it ironic that every bogus scenario ended with Walker unable to play. Probably, hopeful stringers started the tall tales, gunning for the Crown Prince's throne.

The gossip pissed off Sonny. How dare these blabbermouths invade Walker's privacy and with packs of lies at that? Besides, Sonny doubted Walker's sobriety was permanent. His little brother liked the high life far too much to put it down. Sure, he'd been forced to stop for awhile until his body healed. But once those wounds were closed, Sonny figured Walker would be hungrier than ever for his kicks.

Sonny could tell that people were watching *his* every move, too. As if they were just waiting for him to take a spill. Fuck them, he thought, tossing back another shot. He had no reason to stop using. He wasn't hemorrhaging, or hacking himself to death with pneumonia—nowhere near it. He was aces.

Sonny moved on to the next group of revelers whenever the questions began about Walker. Tonight he drank and drugged with impunity, just for effect. He was doing like Walker used to when he was a kid, hanging with the Tornadoes—proving that he could hold his own with the big boys. Feeling primed and a little pissed about the scrutiny, Sonny considered joining the naked fun in the hot tub, take on a few babes at once for all to see.

Then he saw a flash of red hair across the pool. His heart jumped. The girl rose from a chaise lounge—too skinny and flat-chested to be Cilla—but not bad. She wore a flowered bandeau and sarong, and sipped on a pastel drink with a paper umbrella poking out the top. Sonny lit a cigarette and went to her.

Her roots were brown, and her eyes gray instead of green. The shrill voice that issued from her hibiscus lips was pure Texas hillbilly. But if Sonny squinted just right, she looked enough like Cilla—for his purposes, anyway. Sonny soon discovered her sole reason for being at the party was to entertain the promoter's guests. Far be it for him to refuse a little Southern hospitality. He didn't waste any more small talk on the call girl, but he grabbed her arm and went inside the massive main house. They searched around for an empty room. Sonny found one finally with the door ajar. He peeked in and saw an empty bed. He pushed the girl into the room. Without a word he smacked her up against a wall and kissed her hard.

"Hey," she said, pulling her mouth off his. "Take it easy, Icestorm. That hurt."

"This ain't the prom, sugar," Sonny grumbled, filled all at once with drunken fury. He yanked her skirt aside and jammed his hand into her panties, purposefully rough.

"Leave, Sonny," a familiar voice said from inside the room. "We were here first."

Sonny then noticed the couple on an easy chair that had not been visible from the doorway. Bonnell sat facing him, his pants around his ankles. With her back to Sonny, a woman straddled Bonnell. Sonny recognized her ebony curls and the way she moved. Holy shit! Completely forgetting the redhead, Sonny grabbed Vada off of his bandmate and tossed her to the floor.

"Christ, Devereaux," Sonny growled. "We got every whore within a hundred miles of here. You got to be doing Vada?"

"She left me little choice," Bonnell replied indifferently, trying to retain some dignity as he put himself back in his pants. Vada lay curled on her side, pulling her cat suit to her. She was either laughing or crying hysterically. Sonny couldn't say which for sure. Bonnell zipped up, adding, "Poor 'tite fille, all alone." He turned his eyes to the redhead, who gaped on in scandal. "Understand, chère. Vada's husband is locked away in the insane asylum—"

The girl squeaked, "Firewalker really has gone crazy?"

"Shut your damn mouth, Devereaux," Sonny hissed. "Walker ain't in that kind of place."

"Don't be so defensive, you." Bonnell stumbled, picking up his rough silk jacket. Sonny could see he was extremely plastered but was fighting not to show it. "I spring from Southern aristocracy." He missed the sleeve the first time he tried to slip on the jacket. "My kind is rife with unbalanced relatives—in and out of—what's Maman call them? Sanitariums? Count your blessings it is Walker that is committed instead of you."

"Get the fuck out of here," Sonny yelled, slapping the door jamb. He caught sight of the call girl's eyes, saw how thrilled she was to be a witness to such dirt. Stupid cow. "Take this whore with you."

"Hey!" she objected. "I'm no whore. I'm a escort."

Sonny rubbed his tired eyes. "Sugar, if the shoe fits—"

"Why, you mean fucker!" the girl shrieked, surprising them all into silence. "What about your shoes, Mr. High-and-Mighty Icestorm? They don't fit at all. You call yourself a guitar player? Firewalker's the real talent in your family. You should just hang it up."

Sonny might have belted her if he hadn't been so floored. Bonnell gasped, then roared with laughter. The girl grabbed Bonnell's arm, turned on her strappy shoe, and flounced out. Sonny slammed the door nearly hard enough to unhinge it. Rage stopped his breathing as he listened to Bonnell's French babble and laughter fading down the hallway.

He finally sucked in air, blowing out hard. He turned to deal with Vada, whom he'd plain forgotten for a minute. She'd crawled up into the luxurious bed, her breasts wrapped tight in a yellow silk sheet. She smiled, her eyelids heavy. "Didn't know you cared so, Sonny-honey. Come on, sweetie. Won't even be sloppy seconds, you interrupted so early. . . ."

When Sonny found his voice, he spat, "This ain't no teenage game, girl. Bonnell of all people?"

Vada displayed herself, leaning on her elbow. "Bonnell's pretty and exotic. Every woman wants a Frenchman at least once."

"Vada, it's practically incest!"

"Uh-uh. Bonnell and I share no family ties. You and me now. . . ." She smiled, crawling off the bed and dropping the sheet. "Come on, Sonny. Let's finish up what we started before Walker came back to me."

His attention on Bonnell when he had caught them, Sonny hadn't taken note of Vada's body. Now he saw she was emaciated—breastless, her hipbones like doorknobs, her ribs like piano keys. Her head, her full lips, looked too big for the rest of her. If he squeezed her, Sonny thought, she might crumble to dust. She reached toward him. Against the papery skin of her inner arm, fresh blood still dripped from a track mark. It was one of countless others running her limb like a road map written with needles.

Sonny grabbed her wrist, touching a finger to the mark. Vada, her temptress expression swept away by shame, tried to pull free. Sonny kept her in his grip. "Ain't this sexy? Hope you at least did Bonnell the kindness of using a rubber. You're probably a regular Typhoid Mary. But can't they cure typhoid? Not a real good comparison, I reckon." He let her go.

She turned her back on him, snatching her cat suit off the carpeting. Stepping into it and covering herself, she grunted, "I got enough bread to get clean kits, Sonny. I don't share my needles."

"Thank God, for all your boyfriends' sakes. Not to mention your husband's."

Pulling up the shoulder of her suit, she whirled on him, her long hair flying. "Fuck off! I'd bet the bank Walker ain't safe every time he plays house with some groupie bitch. Are you?"

"This ain't about me, Vada."

"Of course not. Nothing's ever about you." She picked up a belt off the foot of the bed, buckling it around her hips. She slipped on her jacket, pulling her hair out of the collar, and dropped into the big chair. "You are so slick, ain't you, Sonny-honey? So fucking cool. Untouchable—don't let a soul get too close, or some of that permafrost might melt! Right, Icestorm? To think my name, Nevada, means *blizzard*. Been a much better name for *your* ass." Pulling on her boots, she added, "Actually, you and me make quite a pair. Probably better than your brother and I ever did."

Shod, she leaned back, draping her fleshless legs over the arm of the chair. "Fire and Ice, the Blaine boys. What a genius that reporter chick from *Texas Blues* was, dubbing ya'll that. Ya'll are polar opposites. You—too cold to give a shit. And him . . . he's so hot-blooded, it robs him of sense."

Vada clapped her hands together, wrapping her red nails across her knuckles. "Be good to throw you two into a blender. Then I could mix me up the perfect man." She stared at Sonny, gripping her hands so tightly together that her fingers went bone white. She added, her eyes growing desperate, "As it is, I don't think I can stand either of you no more." She released a choking sob, tossing her hair forward to hide herself.

Sonny was unsure if he should stay or leave her alone. Finally, he dropped to his knees, leaning on the chair arm. "Vada? You know this is fucked-up. Let Walker help you."

She wailed, "Walker don't want to help me. He wants to leave me!"

"He'll have to, if you don't stop using that shit."

"I can't stop, Sonny." She was slurring slightly.

Sonny was scared he'd say something to make things worse. Then again, they couldn't get a lot worse. He took up her limp hand. It was death cold. "Go see your husband, sugar. Just talk to him."

"I can't set foot in that hospital."

"Don't listen to that asshole, Bonnell. It ain't a crazy house, girl. It's a place for people to go clean up their act."

"I know that, Sonny." Vada pulled her hair back from her face with her free hand. Her eyes were growing glassy, unfocused. The heroin portion of her needle cocktail was sliding into position. "Don't you get it? That's what scares me. Scares me to death."

23.

SONNY DID HIS BEST to leave the party discreetly, his wasted sister-in-law in tow. Vada was so out of it by the time they were back at the hotel he had to carry her to her room. He laid her down on the bed and tossed the bed-spread over her. He sat down next to her, lighting a cigarette, watching her sleep. No, this wasn't sleep. She was nodding, miles from nowhere. Now her face looked peaceful—young, absolutely beautiful.

With two fingers, Sonny separated the silver strands at her temple from the rest of her mane. He gently pulled the hairs straight, releasing them to bounce back to the pillowcase. Her youth in sleep brought to mind the tough teenage *mamasita* Vada once was, the girl with the wicked laugh who danced and loved with everyone. Pounding her mescal, she never gave a damn. After a violent clutch in the back of the van, it never mattered to her if Sonny ignored her during the rest of the night. She had no need to walk back in under his arm—had she? How suddenly she'd changed when Walker became her man. The party girl transformed into serious chanteuse in the beat of a heart.

Sonny laid a hand across Vada's bony chest, feeling her slowed breathing. What might life be like now, if, just once, Sonny hadn't ignored her the second set? Bold as love, if he'd had Walker's balls and taken Vada for his girl? Strange fantasy. He didn't need a woman of his own. He had all he needed, right there in his music. His black Telecaster was wife enough. Demanding, yes, but never needy, like a woman of flesh. Sonny knew he didn't have the warmth it took to keep such a woman as Vada happy—to keep any woman happy. He was too much kin to his Telecaster. Both were hot-looking, great-sounding instruments, capable of producing powerful emotions in others. But, like the wood of the guitar, he didn't feel anything himself. Not like other people seemed to.

Sonny wondered if he should stay with Vada tonight. He could watch over her, make sure she managed to wake up tomorrow. He decided against it. Instead, he rolled her limp form onto its side. She grumbled unintelligibly, a dead weight against his palms. He propped the pillows behind her back. Now if she got sick, too stoned to rouse, she wouldn't choke to death like Jimi. Savior-wise, it was as far as Sonny could go for her. He paused at the door, looking at her once more. Swiftly, he left her room before somebody saw him. Sonny didn't want any untrue gossip to get back to his brother. It wouldn't help Walker's recovery any.

SONNY DEPARTED THE HOTEL the next morning without seeing Vada. He headed over to the Lone Star offices, where the band had a scheduled business meeting. Rollie Matthews was finally convinced of the marketing power of music video and wanted to have the Rockets be his first talent to do one.

When Sonny arrived at the corporate offices, the sleek receptionist led him into a snug conference room. The other three Rockets were already there, drinking coffee, browsing through the *Dallas Tribune*. Johnny Lee and Rimshot lifted their coffees and mumbled howdy as the receptionist fixed Sonny a large mug of French roast with cream and sugar. Smiling, she seated Sonny, wrote down his breakfast order, and hurried out. Bonnell said nothing in greeting. Despite his opulent, carefully pressed attire, his neatly styled hair, Bonnell looked hellish—pasty yellow, horribly hungover. He kept his back to the other three, eyes out the window, sipping daintily at the chicory-flavored brew. Sonny didn't mind the cold shoulder. He had nothing to say to Bonnell, either.

A few minutes late, Rollie came bustling in, followed by two creative types who were working on the video. The receptionist and two assistants carried in steaming Styrofoam food boxes, right behind the bigwigs. The assembled group dove into the rich Southern breakfasts.

Rollie puffed on his Havana, drawling, "Boys, I was expert in handling the wax, before this MTV bullshit reared its head. Knew my way backward and forwards in the radio market. But I see times, strategies, changing. Ya'll's albums never sold like I thought they should. I think a video could be the answer. With you two heartthrobs in the band—" Rollie pointed with his glowing cigar to Bonnell and Sonny "—this will be great exposure. You done your best work yet on *Swamps Meetin' the Plains.*

"I think we all agree with you," Bonnell replied, dabbing at his mouth with a napkin. His voice sounded raspy, but he was looking improved. He glanced at Sonny for the first time that morning, adding, "Except for our chances being spoiled by a certain . . . *indisposed* guitarist, I think the record might have pulled in any number of honors. But then, that thorn is probably far less hurtful for me than it is for you, yes, Sonny?"

"Shut up, Bonnell," Sonny grumbled. He hated when Bonnell pulled this high-caste-superior act. Today he laid it on extra thick, no doubt to save face from Sonny finding him literally with his pants down.

"What's up with ya'll?" Johnny Lee said, tipping his shades down his nose to get a better look.

Bonnell raised his chin at Sonny. "Sonny's understandably uptight. Perhaps fearful of a breakdown also, you?"

Sonny shot his chair back, slapping his palms on the table. "I ought to beat some manners into your high and mighty ass." Bonnell leaned back in his chair, smirking right at him.

Sonny would have gone over the table at the singer had Rollie not scolded, "Ya'll act like adults, for Christ sake! We got company." He nodded toward the creatives. Sonny slowly eased down into his chair, staring Bonnell down. Bonnell finally looked away, busying himself with buttering a biscuit. Rollie said, "That's better. God knows Walker's a thorn in all our sides. Had him in the palm of my hand and let him slip right through. We can't worry about him. Let's get the details of this video settled."

The video was going to be of *The Girl Can't Help It*, a vintage Little Richard tune from the album. The song had come from a movie by the same name. They had all loved it as kids. In the film there had been many performance bits by pioneer rockers. Plus, it had starred blonde sexpot Jayne Mansfield. The Rockets' remake was even more raucous and raunchy than the original. They were filming the video in Austin, with a retro feel. The Sugar and Spice would be used in the performance portion. The plot, such as it was, would have Bonnell lovesick, following a goddess all over town. All men were her slaves. With a sidelong glance, she could toast a loaf of bread. A side of beef would roast, as Prince unloaded it from the freezer, with a mere thrust of her divine hip. Quick cuts, bright-colored costumes, and lots of lowdown dancing would be included.

Everyone was pretty excited by the concept—even Sonny and Bonnell thawed enough to exchange a few staging ideas. They worked everything out on paper, except for one final detail. The writer-director said, as he tapped his pencil rapid-fire on his notes, "All that's left is the biggie—our dream girl. We need a spectacular babe, maybe someone a little familiar to our audience. A Kim Bassinger–type, you know? But she needs to be able to dance her ass off. We want that part really punched up. Any ideas, gentlemen?"

Sonny grinned. "I got the perfect girl. Let me make some phone calls, see if I can't sweet talk her into helping out."

SONNY LEANED AGAINST the plate glass windows that looked out onto the runways. As people began to emerge from the gate, he glanced at his face, reflected back in the night-darkened glass. He ran a hand over his hair, satisfied with his appearance. Sonny leaned against his mirror image, cocking his hip, posing in black-leather jacket, boots, and tight jeans. Cilla liked him dressed in form-fitting black—he used to read it all over her, back when they'd played shows together.

It was trouble, to pull off his provocative Icestorm act, while cuddling a huge bouquet of long-stem roses. He felt the other people at the gate watching him with the tolerant smiles bestowed on lovers about to be reunited.

Cilla walked right up without him noticing. She tilted a pair of cat-eyed sunglasses down, revealing smiling green eyes. "Lovely roses. I do hope they're for me."

Sonny gaped at her for a moment before handing over the flowers. "Sugar, I plumb didn't recognize you." Her hair, hidden mostly under a scarf, was gamine short, and black. Her figure was hidden under an ankle-length Burberry's. But Sonny did know the boots uncle Charlie had made for her, peeking from beneath the raincoat. "What happened to your red hair? Don't get me wrong. You still look good enough to eat."

"Well, thanks—I think." She grinned, handing him her carry-on. "It's just a rinse for the video. We decided to go with a sort of *Cat on a Hot Tin Roof* look." She glanced around. "No press here, right?"

"I don't think so," Sonny said, surprised. "Here in Austin, they don't exactly stalk us. Not even Walker. You been in L.A. too long."

"More like married to the rock star cover boy too long," she muttered. "Let's get out of here, okay?" Sonny led her by the elbow to his nearby Fury. He opened her door and gave her a hand in, then put the bags and flowers in the trunk. By the time he climbed into the driver's seat, she had struggled free of her coat and shades and was rubbing her temples. Sonny started the engine, letting it warm up for a minute while he looked at her. She was wearing jade-green leggings and a drop-shouldered cropped sweater to match. She was heavier than the last time he'd seen her, back on the tour as Walker's woman. Her waist was still tiny, but her belly rounded slightly. Her ass and tits were fuller, too. The girl wasn't fat, but she'd softened—her torso was less dance-toned. Not that Sonny was complaining.

Her face was altered, too—matured now, from budding sex kitten to womanhood in full flower. The faint smile lines around her mouth and eyes, the more defined features, only enhanced her looks. Despite his best efforts, Sonny felt deep longing surfacing. Better get in gear and drive before he did something foolish.

He decided to talk shop. "We need to film part of our show at the Sugar and Spice tonight. We'll use some of the footage in the video. We need you there, too. We're all hoping you'll sit in some."

"I'd love to, Sonny. But first I need a shower, a little rest. I've got to unpack a few things. Where am I staying?"

"I got you a pretty little suite right near the capitol building. You can see our sexy Lady Liberty perched right on top of the rotunda from your window." He reached over, casually picking up her hand. "Hotels are pretty impersonal, though. You're welcome to stay with me."

Cilla eased her fingers from Sonny's. "I think I'll be safer in my suite, thanks anyway."

"My neighborhood's plenty safe, sugar."

Cilla hooted. "You know damn well I'm not worried about the neighborhood. Nice try, Sonny."

Sonny saw to it she was checked in, then escorted her upstairs. As previously arranged, there was a chilling bottle of Moët and a Baccarat vase for the roses. Cilla dropped her coat on the bed and went to putting her flowers to right in the crystal vase. "Oh, these smell like heaven, Sonny. I adore the way roses brighten up a room." She turned, smiling, breaking most of the stem off a bud she had pulled free of the bouquet. She slipped the flower into Sonny's leather lapel. "How did you know I loved yellow roses so?"

"Dumb luck. A florist I once knew told me that yellow roses meant joy and friendship. I'm overjoyed to see you and so hoping we're still friends." He'd longed to buy her eleven blood-red blossoms joined by one virgin white—the bouquet of lovers. He was glad he'd restrained himself. The safe choice had worked splendidly.

She smoothed his lapel. "There—a little color. A yellow rose for my Texas friend—friends we are, Sonny." She started humming, going back to toy with the flowers in the vase as Sonny opened the champagne. "Did you know Walker used to have a bouquet delivered to my dressing room before every show? Unusual tangerine roses. They all but matched my hair. Gloaming Nocturne was what they were called—such a sensual fragrance." She leaned in, burying her face in the petals. "So nice, roses. No one has given me flowers since that tour. Thank you, Sonny."

"My pleasure, sugar." He walked over to her, laying an arm over her shoulders. "What else do you need?"

"Rest, if we're working late." He kissed her chastely on the cheek and made to leave. She stopped him at the door with a hand on his arm. Her brow was furrowed. "Sonny . . . Walker won't be around for any of this, will he?"

"No, baby. He's still in rehab. I did like you asked. Only the people directly involved with the shoot know you're here." He squeezed her hand. "He ain't going to bother you."

"Good . . . though I'm sorry for his troubles." Her eyes clouded further. "But I saw it coming, I suppose."

"Yeah. I think we all did."

✳   ✳   ✳   ✳   ✳

THE SUGAR AND SPICE crowd, paid nominally to stand around in their cool cat and kitten getups, responded with gusto when called on. The Rockets had a red-hot run, fueled by the howling faithful. For encores, they called Cilla up, still outfitted in her bombshell couture, to sit in with the band. Bonnell introduced her as "Mademoiselle Venus." Sonny was pretty sure she had gone unrecognized in the getup and dye job. She and Sonny played a couple of duets together. He liked watching her work, left-handed and upside down, off his lead. And she looked just too fine, dressed in the frisky little video number. Neither the boys in the band nor the men in the crowd could think straight.

Last call, she put down her guitar and hopped up on Bonnell's piano like a dance hall babe. She sang a smoldering version of Aaron Neville's *Tell It Like It Is*. Sonny was mesmerized, hardly conscious of the chords he played behind her. He tore his eyes away and scanned the crowd. Every man in the place was being rocked to his foundation by her performance. Damn right, this girl couldn't help it. Cilla was a natural-born Venus.

Early morning, after a few celebratory drinks with the band, Sonny escorted Cilla back to her room. He was thrilled when she invited him upstairs for a smoke and a nightcap. She'd changed back into jeans and a T-shirt before they'd left the club. Once in the room, she kicked off her shoes, poured him a glass from the champagne he'd had delivered earlier, and lit a joint. She opened the curtains of the balcony. Blowing out the smoke, she swept an arm toward the view. "Just as you promised. It's a great view of the Lady Liberty statue. Doesn't it look like she's standing atop a little girl's birthday cake covered in cherry frosting?" She turned to grin at him. "You'd think Texans, of all people, wouldn't want a *pink* state capitol. Kind of sissy, you ask me."

"It ain't really pink," Sonny grunted, sitting on the room's loveseat. "It's just the way they got it lit."

Cilla about choked on her drink. "Sonny, you know very well that building is as pink as a Mary Kay Cadillac, night or day." She laughed. "Texans just won't admit the truth of the matter. Plus, you dare to call that little rise out west of town *Mount* Bonnell."

Smirking, Sonny narrowed his eyes at her. "Quit making fun of our lovely state capitol and our big-ass mountain and set yourself down here beside me, girl." He slapped the couch seat.

Still chuckling, she took her place beside him, tucking her legs beneath her like a cat. "Sonny, I enjoyed this evening so much. This video's going to be fun. I've worked out some great dance steps—nothing too difficult, but it'll look really cool." She handed him the smoke, stretching her arms overhead, yawning. "I'm exhausted. But I'm so glad I had a chance to play live again."

Sonny took the smoke from her fingers, saying, "I would have thought you got your fill, playing that mega-tour with your husband's band."

She frowned. "That's over, you know. Grey liked me in the band before we got married. But now, I'm the wife, not the guitarist."

"No kidding?"

"Oh, yes. He's a good Italian Catholic boy. Wanted me home, having babies as soon as possible. We were pregnant right off." She paused, her head jerking down to stare at her lap. "I managed to stay that way a whole three months."

"Aw, sugar. I'm so sorry." Putting the roach in an ashtray, he put his arm around her shoulder and pulled her into his side. She didn't fight it.

"It was awful, Sonny. But I was afraid it might happen." She paused for a long time, allowing Sonny to run a hand through her short hair—soft, like a cat's. She was losing herself in sad thoughts, Sonny could see. Closing her eyes, she leaned into the scalp massage, asking, "Sterling never told Walker, did he?"

"Told him what?"

"What happened to me after he went home to Vada? I'm sure he didn't say a thing. Sterling is old school, a man of his word." She leaned forward, putting her drained champagne glass on the table. She turned to look him in the eye, her face solemn. "You mustn't ever tell Walker this."

"I promise I won't."

She got up from the couch, picking up the roach. She relit it, pacing. "Two weeks after Walker left me for Vada, I realized I was pregnant. I had no idea what I should do. There was never any question I would have the child. But when he left, it was a nightmare. Did he tell you how I behaved?"

"No, sugar. He never did."

"I went crazy! I begged him not to go. I clung to him like a dishrag when he tried to get in the cab, screaming and crying. . . ." Tears started down her face as she took another calming hit off of the joint. "It sounds so foolish," she said, exhaling the smoke. "Walker wouldn't look at me. Just kept saying he was sorry, he had to do this. I think the taxi driver nearly called the cops on me, I was making such a spectacle." She rubbed her eyes with a fist, smearing mascara beneath. "Probably partly the pregnancy hormones, I realized later. When I found out, I vacillated between telling him and just keeping mum. I fantasized about showing up at some music awards show, huge with child, springing it on him that way. Or perhaps just sending him a birth announcement."

"Trust me—the birth announcement method's quite a shocker."

She stopped pacing, looking surprised. "That's happened to you?"

Sonny was quiet a moment, then said softly, "Yeah. A long time ago, it sure did." He could still see Nancy Ruth's yellowed announcement, given to him by Mama on the day of Walker's wedding. He still felt Ruby's fury, sharp as a poke in the eye. A wave of guilt threatened to submerge him, but Sonny pushed it under. Cilla needed his attentive ear. "You never told Walker? So what happened to . . . the kid?"

She laid the smoldering roach in the ashtray and rejoined him on the couch before answering. "It died. Inside of me." She leaned into his side again. He hugged her as she continued. "I was working on my album, struggling to finish it through a haze of heartbreak and shock. I told Sterling one day when we were finishing mixing some duets. I broke down. He made everyone leave the room, and I told him what was wrong. He was very supportive. No one else but my doctor knew." She stopped talking again, gripping hard around his wrist. "Finally, we were done, save for choosing the cover art. Sterling met with the photographer and me in his office. He wanted to lend me moral support. I'd felt like hell all the night before, but I chalked it up to having to face all those pictures of Walker and me, when we were happy."

Sonny kissed the top of her head. "That had to be rough."

"Yes. But that wasn't the problem. I started bleeding, right there in Sterling's office. Horrible pain . . . they had to take me by ambulance to hospital. I was suffering a tubal pregnancy. Neither the mother nor child can survive if it's allowed to continue. I nearly died. I don't remember anything until I woke up. Dad and Sterling were with me, breaking the news."

She cried for a long time, clinging to Sonny. He held her, making comforting sounds, truly sorry for her pain. When she managed to slow her tears, she told him more and worse. The ectoptic pregnancy had left scarring behind, limiting her fertility and her ability to carry to term if she did manage to conceive. She didn't know how bad things were until losing not one, but two, of Grey's children. She had miscarried again only two weeks before. And now Grey had another woman and wanted a divorce.

"He told me about her when I called him on the road and told him I'd miscarried again. If that weren't bad enough, he said some paparazzi took photos of them that really leave no doubt. They should be all over the tabloids in the next few days."

"Oh, baby. I can't believe he was such a dick, going and telling you about the pictures."

"No . . . that was for my own good. That's one reason I'm here, and want things kept quiet. I want the press to leave me alone as long as I can manage it. They'll never look for me here." She ran her fingers through her hair, managing a small smile. "Plus they won't be looking for a brunette."

"You do look different. But still real beautiful."

They sat together, silent. She let Sonny hold her close. He watched her desolate face, staring out at the lighted capitol. Should he kiss her? He wasn't sure.

Soothed by the feel of her nearness, he was just starting to doze off when he heard her say, "Oh, Sonny, I'm a mess. I can't do anything right where men are concerned. I'm such a failure as a woman."

He couldn't believe she was saying such a thing. How dare Walker

leave her in such a horrible fashion, after stealing her right out of Sonny's arms? And Grey, that cheating bastard, treating her like damaged goods. Sonny was even mad at Cilla, for seeing herself as no more than breeding stock. "Don't talk crazy. You don't have to make babies to be a woman. If you want kids, there's plenty needing homes." He pulled her chin around, making her look at him. "You want the truth? You're more woman than anybody. And I've known a lot, too many. Not one ever shook me like you do.' "
He did go to kiss her then, doing his best to put all his unfamiliar compassion into the act.

She pushed at him, finally pulling free. "Stop that, Sonny."

He grabbed her face, looking her wildly in the eyes. "But I love you, Cilla. I'm wild for you. Can't think of anyone but you. I sleep with women that favor you just so I can pretend I'm loving you."

He tried to kiss her again, but she shook her head, keeping his mouth off of hers. She struggled in his grip. "Don't Sonny . . . you don't know what you're saying, you're so wasted—"

"I'm always wasted," he declared. "It never makes me say stuff like this. Might make me brave enough to admit it to you, but it don't change the feelings that are always there. Let me show you just how much I love you."

"You don't know me well enough to love me."

"That ain't so," he whispered, trying to meet her lips again.

"This is ridiculous. You know I'm married."

"Your asshole husband damn well ain't."

She jerked her eyes to his, wounded. "Quite true," she replied coolly. "But that doesn't make my sleeping with you right. Sonny, after what happened with Walker, I swore to myself that I'd never break another wedding vow. That includes my own."

Sonny jumped up, stalking around the suite like a caged cat, thinking. He watched Cilla studying him, her eyes a little frightened, sorrowful. After a minute, he dropped to his knees at her feet. "Okay. I care too much to make you do something you think's wrong. Besides, you're probably still hurting from losing the baby and don't want no man like that." He rested his cheek on her knee, eyes closed. "Still, I can't let you walk around feeling less than the incredibly womanly thing you are. We can do stuff that don't technically break vows. I know lots of ways to make you feel good, girl." He kissed her hands.

She considered his offer. She'd always found Sonny to be stunning to look at. But she'd never had delusions, not from the first time that she saw his cocky smile on the White Tornadoes album cover. He was rake to the core. She still wasn't sure she even liked him much.

But here he was. His need to please her made her feel desirable for the first time in too long. How lovely to be held in those perfect arms of his, arms that he insisted wanted her and no one else. Pressed against that nice, strong body of his, touched by his big callused hands, by his black eyes. . . .

Hands and eyes so much like Walker's. No—drawing that comparison wasn't fair to any of them.

Knowing she was messing with fire, she decided what she'd do. "You know what I really need?"

He quit kissing her hands and looked solemn. "Tell me."

"I need to be held. And I want your kisses, Sonny. Can you manage only that?"

"Well, yeah. But—"

She stopped his words with her hand. "No buts. I mean this. If you force the issue, I'll be gone. I'll quit this video and make you look like a fool."

24.

BEFORE CILLA WENT OUT to the Sugar and Spice's sawdust floor for a dance sequence, she stopped in the hallway to adjust her costume. She felt so prefab, painted up in tart makeup, her body wrapped in extreme support garments, draped in a pinup's dress, her hair teased stiff with spray. Wasn't she *supposed* to look invented for this bawdy little film? The video was perfect for the Rockets—ribald and fun, just like their shows. She bent down to pull up the T-strap on her heel, unable to breathe from the grip of the merry widow she wore. She straightened up and had to readjust her cleavage, to make the push-up device she wore feel a little less armorlike. As she cupped her breasts, another set of hands grabbed over hers and yanked her into a storage closet lit only by a 30-watt bulb. Sonny's clutch was too fast to escape. He covered her protesting mouth in a kiss.

When he finally pulled away, she scolded him. "For heaven's sake, at the very least you've smeared my lipstick. They're waiting for me on the set."

"I been waiting for you in this closet," Sonny returned. He kissed her again, slowly, the way she liked it. She didn't struggle, locking her arms around his neck. When he let her go, he whispered, "Wild thing. Keep a whole crew waiting while you grab me for a make-out session."

"Sonny, you are such a bad one." She giggled, running the fake nails, pasted onto her fingertips for the shoot, up his biceps. He had on a tight cobalt T-shirt, with the sleeves rolled up to expose his arms and hold his pack of smokes. They also had him in skintight faded Levis and his boots. Sonny was the bad-seed greaser of the video. The look suited him so well it made Cilla breathe hard whenever she saw him. She whispered, "How did you sculpt these pretty arms, boy? From holding up all the weak-kneed women you accost and bury in kisses?"

"How'd you guess?" He nibbled at her earlobe. "The rest of my work-out is even better, but I really need a partner for—"

They heard shouts calling from the hallway for Cilla. Sonny opened the door and pushed her out before they were caught together. A second later, he heard the crew fussing, calling for makeup, as they whisked her out for close-ups dancing with Bonnell.

Sonny slumped onto a box of beer, laughing at his lovesick self. He was lost over a woman who wouldn't even deign to sleep with him. Why, a snap of his fingers would summon a bevy of beauties to his bed. But, crazy as it felt to him, Sonny wanted only this woman.

A few nights back, Sonny had broken the rules—and nearly lost her. They were drunker and higher than usual after the shoot. It was hot in her room, and humid, even with the air cranked. A thunderstorm lashed wildly outside. The tapes she'd made from his record collection, loaded with serious make-out music, were pulsing from the boom box. The vibe was too much for Sonny. As Cilla returned to the couch from refilling her champagne glass, he'd tackled her to the bed.

The cold splash of her champagne on his chest made him crazy. He grabbed the glass from her hand and smashed it against the wall. Before she could react, he was on top of her, stopping her words with his tongue. She pushed, two-handed, at his face. Easily he snatched both Cilla's wrists and pinned them over her head. With his other hand, he urgently fondled her.

She managed to jerk her mouth away from his. "Let me go this second!"

"You don't want me to. Can't hide that," he growled in her ear, working his hand under the fabric of her soaked leotard and panties. He stroked with his thumb, sliding two fingers inside of her. She was all set for loving, no doubt about it. "These lips ain't telling me to stop."

She groaned, her hands trying to break free as he petted her and kissed her neck. If it weren't for the damn leotard he'd have her naked from the waist down and be getting at her proper, with his mouth. She'd be lost, then. Wouldn't be long, even this way. He could tell she was about to cum to his fingering.

"Sonny, no!" she cried.

"You want kisses only? I'll give you a kiss, girl, you ain't never going to forget if—" Sonny stopped talking when he pulled far enough back to see her face. Honest terror shone from her eyes. Surprised, he let go her hands and pulled his fingers from her. Sometimes he found it thrilling, spooking a woman a little before fucking her. But he didn't want to scare Cilla. He wanted to love her right.

He shoved himself off, stomping to the other side of the room like a furious toddler. After a few fuming seconds, he growled at her, "Ain't another woman on earth I'd take this from."

She had pushed herself into a sitting position, yanking the skirt down over her knees. She made a whimpering noise. Sonny realized she was struggling not to cry when she finally looked up at him. Her expression outraged him. He made an obscene show of smelling his fondling hand, licking his fingers clean. That did it—Cilla dropped her head and started weeping hard.

Sonny was mad at her for not surrendering and at himself for breaking her rules. He didn't want her quitting the video over this, more for his own sake than the band's. He went and sat at her feet. She shrank away, so he didn't touch her. "I'll tell you the truth. First time I kissed a girl, I was barely fifteen. She was at my first Tornadoes gig. She was begging me to fuck her, not half an hour after we met."

Cilla sniffed, peering over her hands. "Isn't that lovely. Aren't you the hopeless romantic?"

He jumped up and poured another glass of champagne and downed it too fast, causing a stab of pain in his head. Wincing, he snapped, "What I mean is, I ain't never played these stupid games."

Cilla was on her feet in a slash, stomping her way to the door. She smacked her fist against it, her chest heaving. "Fine—the stupid games are over. Go home. Take a cold shower. Better yet, go manhandle someone else."

Sonny saw plain enough that her fear was now gone, replaced by fury. He dropped his voice, approaching her with his head down. "Cilla, please. Don't say that."

"It needs saying. This is stupid." She threw the door open. "Forget about me."

Sonny slammed it, grabbing her shoulders. "I can't forget you. Not on your life am I leaving like this." He kissed her as tenderly as he could manage. She allowed it. Good sign? He pulled back before he wanted to, asking, "Please forgive me?"

"Only if that never, ever happens again. It's not that I don't want . . . to. I can't. Not now."

"Okay. I know you won't until you ain't married no more."

"At least until then."

He stroked her cheek. "Let me stay a little longer? Just hold you for a little? I'll be good as gold."

She nodded. "For a few minutes."

He hugged her, rocking her side to side. He whispered, "Even though I hate waiting for you, I love it you take marriage so serious. It shows me when we take our vows together, I'll have me a true and faithful wife."

Drinking the lukewarm beer in the storage room now, Sonny couldn't believe he'd said it aloud. Thing was, he meant it—he wanted to marry her, soon as she'd allow it. Right after the words had slipped out that night, he'd shoved her away and dashed into her bathroom. He'd almost been sick, had to rinse his face with cold water for a long time until he quit shaking. When he'd come out, he'd said a quick goodbye and left her gaping after him.

She hadn't said yes to marriage. But she hadn't said no, either. She hadn't told him a woman of her caliber would never marry the likes of him. Neither brought it up again. They continued their sexy little waltz—the necking, and the pining. Pure torture. Pure bliss!

The shoot would wrap today. After tomorrow night's wrap party, Cilla had to leave and meet Grey in L.A. to finish dissolving their marriage. She'd asked only for what she brought to the union—Reg's trust fund, the Hollywood Hills bungalow, the E-Type Jag, and any musical equipment and records that were hers. Grey was trying to give her a whole pile of cash, too. Sonny figured he was coughing up due to guilt—and well he should. Grey owed her, if nothing else, for the tabloid pictures of him cavorting with his mistress.

But Sonny feared she would think he was after her cash. That was bullshit. Sonny already had more money than he'd ever imagined when he'd picked up the guitar. He'd never expected to go further than Daddy Jim had, traveling around to honky-tonks, playing his own brand of blues, living hand to mouth but loving his life because of the music. If he didn't eat out nearly always, and party so damn much, he'd be better off than comfortable. By Mingus standards, he was sure enough wealthy.

Cilla would leave him day after tomorrow, the morning after the party. Sonny hoped she'd come back to him quick. But since she had to go anyway, the timing was good. Walker was getting out of rehab in three days.

Sonny had talked on the phone to him a time or two. Walker seemed to be doing well, and sounded determined to keep up his good behavior on the outside. He'd vowed to attend daily Narcotics and Alcoholics Anonymous meetings. It seemed to Sonny that Walker was taking this being-clean shit to the extreme, even trading one set of addictions for another. He prayed his brother wouldn't become a soberer-than-thou creep. Sonny thought he'd steer clear for a spell, just in case. Besides, he was afraid he wouldn't be able to hide his feelings for Cilla.

Sonny hadn't told Walker that Cilla was working on the video, much less what was happening between the two of them. He didn't like to think about what Walker would do when he did find out. Sonny would say nothing yet, he knew that much. Sighing, he took another hit off the hot beer. Here was another secret for his sizable stockpile, but at least it was his own, and a cherished one. Sonny was starting to hope he might find the kind of happiness with Cilla that he never believed was possible.

He finished the last sip of brew and tossed the empty into a corner. He managed to free the vial of coke from his snug jeans pocket, doing a blast as he went over in his head the steps he had to do in the next shot. Music videos were so dumb—and expensive as hell. When Sonny was a boy, they could have lived for years on what this thing would eventually cost Lone Star. No wonder Rollie resisted making a video for so long. At least this one had a major babe in it. His babe—a lot to be said for that. When they were old married people, they'd have this video to remember their courtship. Besides, it was a good song to shake those blues away—the Rockets' mission statement, after all.

He left the storage closet and went into the restaurant portion of the main room. Here he could watch the filming of the dance between Bonnell and Cilla. They looked very hot, moving together in a Creole-flavored tango. Bonnell had on tight velvet dancer's pants with pointed-toe Italian boots and a loose red-silk shirt. Bonnell's wavy brown hair tumbled forward, and his ever-present mojo swung from his hip suggestively. Cilla moved like oil in his arms, her clingy red gown and black fishnets complementing Bonnell's costume. Sonny, amused, watched Bonnell's eyes feasting on her. This wasn't merely good acting. Sonny knew Bonnell's inability to charm Cilla out of her skimpy costumes was maddening to the singer.

A slender brunette, pony-tailed, dressed in sweats and a midriff-baring UT shirt, approached Sonny. "Hi, I'm Betty, an intern with the makeup crew? They want me to add a little sheen to your arms. It'll show off your muscles on film." She blushed and looked a little flustered. "Do you mind, Icestorm?"

"Of course not, sugar. Go for it." He extended an arm and let her apply the massage oil with a foundation sponge. Felt nice and sensual, this rub-down. The girl let go a little laugh as she applied the warmed oil. Sonny grinned at her, saying, "Sound like this tickles you more than it does me."

"Sorry if it tickles. I'm new at this—body makeup, I mean. You have, um, real nice arms."

Two weeks ago, Sonny would have replied, *All the better to hold you with, my dear*, and proceeded to do so at the first opportunity. But now he only answered pleasantly, "And you got a real nice touch, sugar. You'll make a fine makeup artist."

Sonny turned his eyes to Bonnell's hands, making sure they stayed where they were supposed to for the shot. He wouldn't put a sneaky feel past the arrogant bastard. Ever since the thing with Vada, Sonny was having more trouble than ever stomaching Bonnell's uppity bullshit. He even was considering leaving the Rockets behind. But he'd been here since 1972—almost fourteen years now. Change was hardly in his vocabulary. He still primarily played the second electric guitar he'd ever owned, and lived in the same house he'd moved into out of high school. He mostly wore the boots Charlie had made him for graduation. He was a creature of habit, and the Rockets were just that—a comfortable, and profitable, habit.

The director called the dance a take. Cilla disengaged from Bonnell's arms. He kept her hand, kissing it as she wheeled away. Bonnell leaned in, whispering something in her ear. She smiled back, nodding ever so slightly. The smile the singer gave Cilla in return made Sonny's scalp tingle and his heart bang. Might be high time to beat some manners into the dirty French boy.

Cilla pulled free of Bonnell's hand, grabbing a towel and water bottle from a set assistant. As she headed by Sonny, she stopped, gazing with a small frown at the unguent-applying female. "Having fun?"

The girl turned deep red, dropping Sonny's arm. She stammered, "I just—they told me I had to."

Sonny grabbed Betty's shoulder, squeezing it in a friendly fashion. "She's just doing her job, Cilla—and doing it well. But I was fixing to ask Betty, here, for the first dance at the wrap party. How about it, sugar?"

"Love to, Icestorm." The director beckoned to her, and she excused herself.

Cilla took a long pull off the water, staring hard after the makeup girl. "First dance, huh? Sonny Blaine, ever courteous to the ladies."

Sonny dropped his eyes, staring into Cilla's. "Swear I was just being friendly, girl. You know you got my last dance that night. Ain't no question about that."

25.

CILLA WASN'T SURE why she'd agreed to meet Bonnell at the Driscoll Hotel's bar. In part she supposed she was feeling somewhat sentimental. With the filming done, her time in Austin with the Rockets was drawing to a close. Plus she was still miffed at Sonny. He shouldn't have groped her. She couldn't get over his backhand proposal, either. She'd never dreamed he was actually thinking of *marrying* her—not Sonny. Maybe meeting Bonnell tonight was a way of proving to herself she was under no obligation to Sonny. All the same, she didn't think she'd tell Sonny about this rendezvous. She'd told him instead she needed a night alone to pack.

The Driscoll was a relic from the early statehood days, when Texas was still chafing from the fact it hadn't managed to go sovereign. Now dwarfed by surrounding buildings, the hotel offered old-fashioned Texas elegance. Cilla loved the grand lobby, the stairs sweeping from either side of the front desk up toward the lounge. Only the front deskman and another fellow checking in presently inhabited the lobby. They stopped talking, smiled, and followed her with their eyes. She saw no recognition in their glances—only admiration. Good on both counts.

She'd dressed for impact. Bonnell just wasn't the jeans-and-T-shirt kind. Her teased black hair was wrapped in a scarf, and she wore shades, despite the late hour, for that extra air of mystery. Her fire-engine lipstick was of a shade she'd never dare wear as a redhead. The cocktail dress she wore had a low neckline and a wide belt that accented her waist. The emerald collar given to her by Jackie Higgins was at her throat.

Cilla paused at a bronze statue outside of the bar proper. It was a disturbingly real likeness of a toppled cowboy, his foot hopelessly entangled in the stirrup of his galloping horse. She noticed, too, above her head, a mounted set of enormous longhorns. How had any bovine's head supported such monstrosities? She glanced behind, then to her left. She laughed a little, relaxing. She felt certain that the press weren't following her. They blessedly still hadn't seemed to realize she was in Austin.

In the lounge there were only five people, plus the barkeep. One was a suit—a politician from down the street, probably. He was sharing wine with a much younger woman. There was also what could only be a wealthy rancher drinking margaritas with a stunning, buxom Latina. Bonnell waited at a table far from the others. Champagne chilled in an ice bucket in front of him. He'd already poured himself a glass. He was smartly dressed in black Armani. He rose as she approached, turning her wrist over to kiss the pulse point.

"*Mon Dieu*, Madame. You are a vision. I thank you for joining me." He pulled out her chair, then poured her a flute. "Have you eaten?"

"I have."

"Perhaps something chocolate and indulgent then? I know you are fond of the stuff."

"Really, no." She'd never mentioned her love of chocolate to him. He'd probably seen her toss down a Hershey's Kiss between takes. She removed her sunglasses, and then sipped. Drinking stars, as Dom Perignon declared about this very sparkling wine. "This is just lovely, though. You shouldn't have."

"*You* are lovely. This?" He gestured at the ice bucket, nearly purring. "Merely a small token. You wonder why I invited you here this evening."

She had some inkling of why. She had a less clear idea of why she'd accepted his invitation—especially dressed so, since she wasn't going to grant him his wish. She only nodded in answer.

"*Ma chère*, I know your love life is currently . . . complicated. I am sorry the tabloids have become so ugly."

"Thank you. It has been quite difficult."

"I can simplify things for you." He topped off her flute. "I am a rich man, you know. It is a result of family money, of course, not the money I make playing music. And my name, it means something, especially in my homeland."

Homeland, he'd said—as if he were a prince of Czarist Russia. She unwound the scarf from her head. The other two women in the bar were impeccably turned out, too. The rancher's woman was fabulous in a slinky red dress, her hair big and her diamonds real. The politician's girl was more subdued, a classic Grace Kelly sort—suit, small gold pen, pearls. Cilla and Bonnell blended in with the scenery. Turning her attention back to him, she said, "Then your name must be a great comfort to you, Bonnell."

He showed his teeth, pearly against his tawny skin. "Sometimes it is a blessing—sometimes a curse. For instance, I could never ask a girl outside of one of the old families for their hand. Marriage, it's not something I can offer. I make that clear up front."

She rolled her eyes. "That news is bound to break some hearts. Not mine, seeing as I'm already married."

"A tenuous circumstance at best, no? Your divorce will be final as soon as it is legally possible."

He wasn't asking. But the tabloids hadn't yet suggested divorce, and would have screamed it had they known it was in the works. Only one person, bedsides the lawyers and Grey, knew. "Sonny?" she breathed.

Bonnell waved a hand in the air, eyes narrowing. "That idiot? Please. I have better ways of finding out what I need to." He sipped, eyes still squinted. Leaning closer, he said, "Alonzo was looking to bring forth a dynasty when he married you." He cocked his head, looking at her under the small table. "You were blessed with hips made for *bébés*, certainly. How unfortunate you can't carry to term."

The hair rose on the back of her neck. *He knew about her miscarriages.* She felt positive Sonny wouldn't tell him such a thing.

Bonnell nodded, seeing her confusion. "Even well-guarded secrets leave traces. Medical records, for example—not anywhere near as confidential as you might think."

She stared at him, feeling nauseated. He didn't drop his gaze. She finally asked, "Why . . . why would you pry into something so personal?"

He shrugged. "Because I can. My money and connections make such things doable. I needed to impress that fact upon you."

"How dare you," she whispered, rising. She took up her scarf, twisting it in her hands like a garrote. The rancher, his woman in the powder room, tipped his hat to her. The bartender smiled at her, scanning her body with subtle greediness.

Bonnell eyed the necklace resting on her throat. "Do sit, *ma chère*. Finish this bottle. Hear me out. You'll be glad you did."

Not sure what else to do, she eased back into the chair. She let him refill her flute, and drank deeply. It hit her then, what the station was of the other women in this room. These powerful men had wives elsewhere. Tonight they were out drinking with their *trophies*.

"Cilla, you and I, we're actually much the same. Though you were born in Great Britain, you are Creole in the true sense—an epic mixture of bloodlines. Women of your kind are highly prized in my culture."

"My kind."

"One-quarter black—father's father. That particular mixture produces our greatest beauties." Quick as a wolf spider, he grabbed her right, her fretting, hand. "Like some priceless golden idol, you." She tried to pull away. When she did, his grip turned painful. Bonnell was leaving no doubt as to who was in charge here. She knew instinctively that if she didn't acquiesce to being held, he'd try to injure her. He'd do it for the same reason he'd dug up the details of her miscarriages—*because he could.*

"Everything would be laid out legally, I assure you. You would be taken care of for a lifetime so long as you played by my rules, *ma chère.* You'd have freedom my wife would never be allowed. You'd have your music, your dance—even your lovers, if they did not inconvenience me, and you used discretion." He squeezed her fingers a shade tighter. He was really hurting her now, but she tried not to show it. He noticed the effort, looked pleased. "Strong too, you. And unlike Grey, I am thrilled you are barren. I'd likely insist on sterilization if you weren't."

Barren. Her face flaming with shame and hurt, she almost threw her drink in his face. She was stopped by a certainty that he'd break her knuckles if she did. Plus, if she had missed something, if they were really being watched, the paparazzi would have a field day with such a shot.

"If you'll stay to hear me out, I'll turn you loose now," he whispered.

She nodded. He let go. She rubbed her aching hand. As she did, he reached inside his jacket. For one terrible instant, she thought he was pulling out a pistol. Instead, he brought forth a manila envelope. He slid it across the table to her.

"Go on, open it."

Cautiously, she did. Inside were two five-by-sevens. The first showed an elegant woman. She had sunglasses on, and the picture was a bit grainy—taken by telephoto, it appeared, making her features indistinct. Flame-red hair brushed her shoulders. She walked alongside a horse. She wore jodhpurs, riding boots, and a cable-knit sweater. The second photo had the same telephoto look to it. Its subject was an older, golden-skinned gentleman, seated on a park bench or bus stop—it was hard to tell which. A cane rested at his side. He wore a sweater and slacks, sensible shoes, a fedora. Neither subject appeared to know they were being photographed.

Bonnell pointed at the man's photo. "Despite some effort, your own father has never located him, doesn't even know his real name. But see? Something alike in them—you can see even in this single photo, no?" He reached for the picture of the woman. "A great beauty in her day, she—brief though her day was due to foolish choices. Hard to tell from this how well she has held up. But no question. When your hair is its natural shade, you are blessed with your mother's hair color."

Cilla studied the photos, trying to commit some detail to memory. Almost as a thought aloud, she asked, "Where did you get these?"

"Not important. I have them, that is what is important."

She looked at the people in the photos—strangers. "How do I know they are—"

"They are who I say they are, *ma chère*."

She believed him. She looked back at the man's picture. There was indeed something of Reg in the square of the shoulders, in the shape of his forehead.

Bonnell leaned forward. "Imagine. I can give you *family*. Mine, to an extent—but, more important, yours." He picked up the photo of the old man. "You can give your father something he's wanted forever. How touched Reg would be—how pleased with you, child." He reached over and touched her cheek with the tip of a finger. "I have more of them—photos, names, addresses. Preliminary contact indicates they'd be interested in a meeting."

In silence, she studied the photos. She drank a bit more—she could feel the champagne going to her head. A drop of sweat dripped down her forehead, and her heart pounded in a confused rush of feeling. She said to him, "And in return?"

"As I said, a simple arrangement between us. An understanding."

She huffed, "You've gone to an awful lot of trouble just to fuck me."

He growled with dark laughter. "You like a little dirty talk? I like that in my women. Bluntly, yes. Whenever I fancied, I'd fuck you, do whatever I wanted to with you, in fact." He dropped a hand under the table, pushing her skirt up, feeling her thigh. "In return you'd have protection from scrutiny. Family. You need both, especially now, with your recent public losses, no?"

His fingers ventured to her crotch. She violently shoved his hand away. Head cocked for the view, he watched as she tried to discreetly maneuver her dress back over her knees.

Bonnell smiled then—an awful, menacing expression that scared her more than anything he'd done so far. The smile made his handsome face brutal. She knew she was now seeing the real Bonnell. She also knew she would learn to dread such a smile from him, were she to accept what he offered. "Of course, you must attend to your divorce first. Then I can arrange the meetings with your mother and grandfather." He paused, that grin still on his face. "That is, after I've sampled something of what's due me, made sure it's worth the price."

She took a deep breath and said. "If this is true ... worse, if it's some kind of sick joke ... you're crazy."

He took the photos and put them back in the envelope, pocketing them again. "Think how disappointed Reg would be, did he know you'd refused to help him find his long lost father? You may not know it, but Reg has tried repeatedly to find the man. He never will without me. Money alone, even rock star prestige, won't make it happen. My connections—especially in the South—run deeper than you can possibly imagine."

Bonnell folded his hands on the table. The terrible smile finally left his face, replaced by a puzzled look. "Cilla, it's not like I'm asking you for something sordid, a one-night stand. You've much to gain from this arrangement. Please tell me you aren't resisting because of those fool brothers?"

She looked away, watching the bartender shaking another margarita. Had Bonnell's mysterious sources dug up dirt on her relationship with Sonny and Walker as well? Maybe she was just more obvious than she realized. Didn't matter. She should never have come tonight. She wanted to forget everything that had happened here. She wished, this instant, that she was wrapped in Sonny's arms, listening as he pledged himself to her—maybe even pledging herself straight back at him.

Again, it was as though Bonnell read her thoughts. The cool control he'd been showing disappeared, and his voice was low and angry. "They are not good enough, neither of them. To Sonny Blaine, you are only another in his endless line of cunts."

She flinched at the word, tears springing to her eyes. She trembled with the effort it took to not cry.

"As for Walker. . . ." Bonnell reached for the mojo dangling at his side. "No question, powerful *gris gris* surrounds that man, a deep and dark luck. But no matter what he did to get you into his bed, he's long finished with you. He abandoned you when you became inconvenient. With us, that wouldn't happen. We'd have a legal contract." The awful smile returned. "Call it a pact, if you like. Even if I tire of you, you'll always be provided for."

She rose then. Her knees nearly buckled, her legs shook so with rage and the effects of the champagne. She carefully rewrapped her scarf and put on her shades. She hadn't felt as violated when she'd been raped as she did at this moment.

The other people in the bar went silent, watching. They could not have overheard, Cilla was sure if it, but that something terribly wrong had happened between them was drifting in the air like stale cigar smoke. The bartender opened his mouth as if he were going to ask after her, but he shut it and busied himself washing glasses when Bonnell glowered in his direction.

Loud enough for the bar folk to hear, Cilla said to Bonnell, "You can go to hell." Everyone in the room looked on as she walked deliberately back toward the lobby.

Just as she passed the statue of the cowboy being dragged to death, Bonnell called after her. "Think hard on my offer, *ma chère*. You know no one else can give you the things I can."

26.

EVERYONE AT THE video wrap party was flying high. The rough cut looked great—sexy and funny, everything they'd hoped for. Trusting no one else with the task, Sonny had taken on the chore of making music tapes for the party. He had stuck to mostly danceable soul stuff, heavy on everlasting-love songs. The tapes were being well received by the hundred or so revelers in the Sugar and Spice.

Sonny watched from the corner of the bar as Cilla danced with Johnny Lee. She looked delectable. She had spent much of the afternoon washing the dark rinse from her hair. She now had a tousled cap, light auburn, still a shade darker than her natural color. She wore an outfit that the band had given her when they'd wrapped. Sonny had had it made for her by his tailor and Uncle Charlie. It was a green suede dress that fit her like a kid glove, cut low, front and back, slit up her leg so she could dance. She had a wide belt and boots, also in suede, made to match, accented with intricate black stitching. From Cilla's ears hung diamond drop earrings, Sonny's personal gift to her. He had bought them impulsively the second day of the shoot, spending a stupid amount of money on them. With them she'd worn her emerald choker.

He'd saved the earrings until tonight to give to her, when they had managed to steal a moment alone before the party. Kissing her neck, he'd told her, "First of many such gifts, sweet girl. Can't wait to drape your naked body in jewels, for my eyes only."

They were still pretending to be no more than pals, not yet even sharing a dance. Sonny flirted shamelessly, typically—this time all for show. He wanted the whole world to know how he felt about her, wanted to declare it tonight. But Cilla insisted that for now they must play it cool. Sonny agreed, but really only for Walker's sake. Dealing with Vada's addictions would be enough of a challenge to Walker's recovery. He didn't need to know yet about Sonny's romance.

With satisfaction, Sonny noticed that when he had been away from her for long, Cilla scanned the crowd, looking for him. She'd give him a sweet smile when their eyes connected. She was drinking scads of champagne, and indulging privately in Sonny's coke stash every so often, too. She needed to cut loose before she left to finalize her divorce.

He'd put a song on the final tape of the night that was especially for Cilla. Bobby Moore's *Searchin' for My Love* had cornball lyrics, but they summed up how he felt about her. During the song that came before it, he did search out his love. She'd finished dancing with Johnny Lee and was visiting with him at the bar. Bonnell hunkered over his drink nearby, watching over his bassist and the girl as if he were a vulture.

"Howdy," Sonny said.

"Hey, Sonny. This girl can sure cut a rug, huh?" Johnny Lee said, smiling at Cilla.

"That she can."

Bonnell looked down his nose at Sonny. "Been dancing with many *'tite filles* as usual, you. Who'll be the lucky lady tonight?"

"Hard to say, Bonnell," Sonny said. "Maybe you and I got to draw straws."

"Hey there, gorgeous," Cilla yelped, hugging Sonny's neck. She stumbled into his side, and he steadied her. She turned her gaze to Bonnell. "Your guitarist is bloody gorgeous. A flawless beauty."

"I'd say flawless is taking it a bit far," Bonnell grumbled. Johnny Lee nodded, laughing.

Sonny squeezed Cilla's waist, asking, "Wondered if you'd dance with me now? I'll probably head out after this one."

"Sure, sugar," she slurred, doing a pretty lame imitation of him. "Didn't I promise you the last dance?"

As Sonny led her toward the dance floor, he heard Bonnell say after him, "We salute you, Icestorm. Enjoy your pas de deux with the lovely lady." Sonny glanced back to see Johnny Lee and Bonnell holding up their glasses. Johnny grinned and winked. Bonnell watched with lidded eyes, rubbing his mojo with his free hand.

Sonny took Cilla to a semiprivate, darkened spot on the dance floor, just off the backstage hallway. She gripped him tightly, flowing sweet with him in rhythm to the scratchy soul ballad. Sonny was a man who sang only when completely alone to accompany his tape deck while driving distance. He left public singing to the soulful-voiced dudes, to the Walkers and Bonnells. But now he earnestly crooned the love song into Cilla's ear, enraptured by the smell of her perfume mingling with her sweat.

All at once, a wicked déjà vu engulfed Sonny. This was too much like last time, when Cilla had left this place to come home with him. The night of the ugly fight with Walker returned full force. He shook it off with no little effort. Really, that was then. Ancient history—a different world.

When the song played out, he held Cilla at arm's length, admiring her. "Thanks, sweet girl. I put that one on just for you. I better head home now, before I'm too loaded to drive. You ready to go back to the hotel?"

Cilla said nothing for a moment, staring at him with desperate, unfocused eyes. "Not yet," she whispered. To Sonny's surprise, she shoved him into the hallway, away from the other revelers. She grabbed the back of his head, pulling him to her, her tongue mingling with his in a kiss. She pulled away again just as suddenly, urgently whispering, "You really do love me, don't you, Sonny?"

Her asking outright caught him off guard. She'd always tried to stop him from saying it before. Glancing around to make sure no eyes were on the two of them, he nodded.

Tears springing to her eyes, she whimpered, "I'm not just another cunt to you?"

"What a thing to say." He took her face in his hands. "Of course you're not. Girl, what's gotten into you?"

She whispered, in a tumbling rush, "I shouldn't be here. Shouldn't do this. Can't help it. I need you though. Make love to me."

Again he nodded, pulling out his car keys. She grabbed his hand, shaking her head, "No. Let's not drive anywhere. I don't want time to change my mind." She rubbed up against him, her eyes slitted, a sleepy kitten's. "Here, someplace. Right now."

This wasn't right. It could surely wait until his house or her room. He'd ask her on the drive why she'd changed her mind so quick, and what had made her say such a nasty thing about herself.

Then she started fooling with his belt buckle, purring into his shoulder. The feel of her hand against him broke Sonny's resolve. No one seemed to be watching, so he took her hand and led her through the kitchen. It was vacant now, as Prince, Shookie, and their crew had joined the party. In back alongside the pantry was a heavy wooden door. Behind it was a remnant of the bar's former life as a farmhouse. Sonny tried the knob. It was stiff, but he forced it opened onto a slim servant's stairway. Cilla smiled, stumbling against him as she started to take the stairs.

Sonny climbed aft of her. She was pretty much gone. He was nearly carrying her. She leaned back against him, squeezing his arm. He hoped this wasn't taking advantage. It wasn't in the same class as holding her down and trying to force her to yield—she was insisting this time. Still he bore an ominous feeling in his gut. No reason to worry, was there? Tonight was the beginning of a new life for them both.

It didn't occur to Sonny that he was trespassing in the Brown's living area until he actually stepped into their apartment. He hadn't been upstairs since he'd helped Walker move out. He'd just have to apologize, explain himself to the Browns later. He did have enough respect for the old men not to take her into one of their rooms. Only one place to go, then—Walker's old room. He led her to the door, uneasy with the thought that Walker had likely told her about his time here.

The small room was unlocked, though a bit musty. The light switch worked. The room looked pretty much as it had when Walker lived there, less Old Broad and the accompanying gear, and the old record player. The flowered wallpaper remained, in worse shape than ever. The Browns' boxes of records were everywhere. The twin bed was still in the corner, covered by an old chenille bedspread.

Sonny left the light on so he could see her while he loved her. He made sure the shade was drawn, and sat her Cilla down atop the bedspread. He took off his jacket and tossed it over one of the record boxes. He'd worry about the rest of his clothing later. He was too impatient to see Cilla naked to waste time undressing himself. Accompanied by the music pulsing from the party below, Sonny unzipped her and stripped the dress down to her waist, kissing her shoulders and neck.

Soon, between slow kisses and strokes, he had her unclothed except for thigh-high black stockings and the heavy earrings and necklace. He ran a finger between the elastic of the hosiery and the soft skin of her inner thigh. He'd leave them on this first time. She groaned, eyes closed tight, parting her thighs. "Woman, you're so gorgeous."

"So are you," she answered, in a far-off voice, "and you feel so good." She hooked her arms around his neck and pulled him down to lie beside her. She purred, a deep sound in her throat as Sonny ran his hands over the curves of her, kissing her breasts.

He mumbled things to her between kisses—the best things, meaning them all. He'd never felt anything close to this before—like he was a drowning man. He didn't want to pleasure her just to bend her to his will. He needed to please her, for love's sake. He wanted Cilla for his wife. He told her this. Swore devotion, words of love, as had never left his lips before. Any other woman he had bothered to speak to during sex he'd only done so to instruct—or debase.

He was compelled to kiss her sex, to make her lose herself to him, the first time, with his mouth. He journeyed down her body slowly, teasing her with nibbles, with licks, telling her that he'd be back up in a minute. She was sopping, salty-sweet. She clutched his head, pulling into him, groaning, kissing him back with her musky essence as he skillfully worked her.

He was delirious, happier than he'd ever been, as he felt her starting to climax. She grabbed his left hand, squeezing hard, starting to pant, gasp out, "That's it. Oh, Walker!"

Sonny jerked free of her, jumping to his feet, staggering back as far as the blocks of record boxes would allow. He felt like she'd dumped a bucket of dry ice over him. He stared at her, laid open to him, her head still arched back, her hands grasping to pull him back.

She opened her eyes after a second or two. The moment she saw the look on his face, she closed her legs, pushing herself up to a sitting position. "That felt amazing . . . what?" she asked, panting out the words, still teetering on the edge of her orgasm. He stared at her hatefully, unable to summon his voice. She dropped her feet to the floor, brushing a hand through her bed-mussed hair. "Was I doing it wrong?"

It took him a second to manage words. "You were doing it just fine, girl," he said, deadly quiet. "Just not with me."

She looked at him with confusion on her face, swaying slightly where she sat. He saw realization hit her like a karate kick. Her eyes went wide, face flushing, hands to her mouth. "Sonny. *Sonny.* Oh, God. I'm so sorry. I didn't mean that!"

"Like hell you didn't." He spat the words like a cobra. "Here I thought we was being true to your husband, all this time. Instead, we been playing a sick little game, and I didn't even know it. No wonder you always close your eyes when we kiss."

Tears spilled down her face as she pleaded. "I'm not playing! I—I'm just really wasted. Got my wires crossed." She staggered to her feet, grabbing his arm. "I made a mistake, Sonny."

"Not as big a mistake as me." Sonny jerked free of her grip, causing Cilla to tumble over one of the record boxes. "Best find yourself another ride to the hotel, bitch." He grabbed his jacket, grateful he still had on the rest of his clothes. Fumbling with the lock, he could hear her behind him crying, struggling to dress. Sonny yanked open the door and darted down the hall. He could hear her begging him to come back. Part of him wanted to return, desperately. But if he did go back, he was scared of what he would do to her.

Sonny had never been moved to hit a woman. But he wanted to now, to beat and violate her, wanted to try and hurt and humiliate her as she had him. Once he started, he didn't think he could stop before killing her. And even murder wouldn't drive Walker out of her heart. If he thought it would, he'd be in there pummeling her this second.

Sonny careered down the narrow, hidden staircase and dashed unseen out of the kitchen entrance. He managed to get a good ways from the building before the sick burning pain and the taste of her juices, still in his mouth, forced him to his knees, retching.

When the heaving turned him loose, he reared up, looking around. No one had witnessed his humiliation. He dropped his hands back down, crawling like an animal away from the stink of his vomit. He fought back tears through sheer will, groaning, going farther away from the building, into the shadowy wild grass. A knife twisted in his chest, making it hard to take a breath. For the first time in his life he understood why this was called heartbreak.

He was grateful Walker was in lockdown still. If he weren't, Sonny would tear him to bits without so much as a howdy-do. He knew Walker would still have that idol-worship look on his face even as he died by Sonny's hands. That was the problem with Walker. If only he were a son of a bitch, it would be so easy to hate him. Even before they started playing—certainly since—Walker had adored Sonny. Not an interview passed that Walker didn't rave about Sonny's talents and influence on his own. The kid was decent to a fault.

No wonder Cilla still kept him in her heart and mind. What had Vada said about them both? If she could only combine Walker and Sonny, that man might be ideal. Yeah, Sonny had the looks the women liked, the cool. Walker had what really mattered though, what made love a lasting thing.

Sonny crouched, shaking, staring at his hands in the moonlight. Daddy Jim's hands. Walker's hands. If Sonny were to place Walker's signet ring on his bare finger, their hands would be twin. Same calluses, same ribbons of vein and specialized gristle that had come from their years playing Texas blues guitar.

Sonny didn't dwell much on his gifts, but he knew what he had was real. He had an ear for song, and a lifelong devotion to his instrument. From the first time he had picked up a guitar, he'd had the dogged dedication it took to master the ax, the ability to play the music as he felt it. His music was what made all of life's other bullshit bearable.

Didn't matter what his life's work had been. Be you gunfighter, pitcher, steel-driver, guitar player—there was always that someone somewhere that held the edge. This time, this place, it was Firewalker Blaine. Everyone knew. Reg had talked of it once to Sonny, about what it was like to play with Walker on the same bill. Reg said he had to pretend that Walker didn't exist beforehand, drowning him out with headsets set to anyone else's music. He'd told Sonny, "Otherwise, my ego would melt. I might pack it in for good."

And this was from one of the premier guitarists of their time. Would T-Bone have been so intimidated? Would Hendrix? Sonny knew that they likely would have been. What Walker had was that precious and profane. Sonny was grateful for them all—T-Bone, Reg, Jimi, Albert, Jeff Beck, B.B., Robert Johnson, the other names lost to time who'd left their licks to build on—the gifted, innovative cats who had come before. They had laid the groundwork, blazed the trail. Some were cursed—like Bonnell said of himself, like he had said that he knew Walker was—some likely blessed. All were geniuses within their art. Without these forefathers, there would be no Icestorm. There would be no Firewalker.

But none of those names that were legend had Sonny's blood in their veins, nor had they sprung from the same source. Whatever it was, demon or archangel—perhaps something so terrible that it had no proper name— why had it chosen Walker for its sublime vessel? Why had it not chosen Sonny? He'd given his whole life to playing. He'd give everything, anything, to play with Walker's soul-flaying depth. Maybe It didn't think Sonny was ever worth it. Maybe his soul was already fucked from the get-go, never worthy of such a trade.

Sonny managed to struggle onto his feet, brushing the dirt off his palms. He had no idea how long he'd been out here, staring at his hands in the moonlight, dwelling on the loathsome truths that haunted him. It was time to go, before Cilla, or someone else, found him in this pathetic state. He located his leather jacket, dropped when he ran outside, and pulled a vial from an inner pocket. He did a big blast of coke to both clear and numb his mind. Darting toward his car, he realized he didn't want to go home. But he couldn't stay here, no way in hell. Right now, there wasn't anywhere Sonny wanted to be.

27.

SONNY TOOK ILL, which trapped him in Austin for weeks after the video wrapped. He was sicker than he'd ever been, too sick to make it to a doctor. His body shook with chills, and he had wretched nightmares. He puked anything he consumed, other than slugs of codeine cough syrup and baby sips of whiskey. Sonny convinced himself that this illness must have coincidentally come on the night of the party. Must have been starting when he'd puked so violently in the weeds outside the Sugar and Spice. That's why he hurt inside like someone had seeded his chest and guts with Red Devil lye. A nasty flu—nothing more. It had nothing to do with that faithless bitch.

After ten days of being dog sick, Sonny improved somewhat. He managed to eat a little and get out to his dealer and the liquor store, his stash of booze and drugs gone dry. He didn't feel healthy, but at least he didn't still think he would die. He got it together enough to take care of what business he had to, shuffling off as much as possible onto his manager and the other Rockets.

Inevitably, too soon, tour time came around again. Weak, still feeling like a zombie, Sonny struggled through rehearsals. He was grateful that at least they were still pushing *Swamps Meetin' the Plains* so that he didn't have to wrestle with any new stuff. *The Girl Can't Help It* video premiered right before tour time began again.

The morning he was to leave, he was slumped glum-hearted on his sofa, having a last cold beer before he had to meet the Rockets at the bus. He stared at his equipment, dreading the work ahead it represented, really dreading the long hours to be spent in Bonnell's company.

He was roused out of his funk by a noise outside. An unfamiliar muscular engine—Chevy, maybe?—was pulling onto his street. He got up and glanced out a side window. A wet dream was parked in his driveway. A Chevy, indeed: '61 Corvette, two-toned in copper and burnt sienna. Sonny was so enchanted by the beauty of the thing that he opened the door without considering whose it could be.

Walker was standing on the front stoop under his old blue bolero, his fist poised to knock. Sonny resisted the temptation to shut the door in his face.

"Hey, man. I finally caught up with you," Walker said, smiling just a little.

"Almost didn't. I got to leave in just a minute." Sonny made a show of looking at his watch.

"Tooled by to show you the new wheels. Come see," Walker said, pointing at the car. Sonny took the opportunity to give Walker the once-over as they went to check out the car. He looked a hell of a lot better. Of course, the last time Sonny had seen his brother, Walker had been bloodied, smoking H, confessing Vada's abuse. Now he carried more pounds than he ever had, and it suited him. The doctors had done good work on Walker's nose, straightening all the bends Sonny and Floyd had added, plus improving somewhat on God's original plan. But the change in him was not only on the surface. Walker had aged. It was more than deeper crow's feet or new gray salting his hair. He had the same look in his eyes borne by men that Sonny knew who had seen battle.

"It is a beautiful machine, Walker," Sonny admitted, running his hand over its satin haunch. "How'd you come across it?

"A car restorer located it for me. It's a sobriety present to myself, for getting to ninety days. Nearing one hundred now."

"How about that?" Sonny said, staring pointedly at the car's interior, feeling Walker's eyes on him.

"Mind if I come in for a sec, Sonny?"

Sonny did mind but didn't say it. He walked back toward the house, leaving the door open behind him as he entered. He grabbed his half-drunk beer off the coffee table, taking it to the sink and pouring it out.

"Don't do that on my account," Walker said, nodding at the bubbles foaming down the drain.

"No, it's okay. It's too early to be . . . you want me to make coffee or something? Don't got no cream here, though."

Walker held up a fancy blue bottle of imported water. "Nah, I'm good. I just wanted to see you for a minute before you left town again."

Sonny held his arms outstretched. "Here I am."

Walker didn't say anything for a few seconds. Then he nodded, answering, "Sure enough. Here you are." He sat on a stool in the kitchen. "But where you been? I'm surprised I hadn't seen you since I got out."

"I been real busy. Plus, I was sick there for awhile, a real bad bug. I told Mama to tell you."

"She did." It was Walker's turn to give Sonny a once-over. "You look like you been sick."

"Gee thanks, Walker."

"Don't mean to be ugly or nothing. You just look, like, drained. Skinny, too. Hope antibiotics helped?"

"No, it was like . . . viral, I reckon. I been on the mend for a few weeks now."

"Good. Anymore, there's viruses out there you don't recover from."

Ah. Mr. Clean had come to pontificate. Sonny threw a quick verbal jab in return. "Speaking of such things, how's your wife?"

Walker's face darkened. Sonny could tell he'd gotten the point. "You seen her since me, Sonny. I ain't laid eyes on her since before I ended up in the hospital. Talked to her a time or two on the phone, but she's avoiding me. I can't go to our—well, really her—house. I don't trust myself around her stash."

"Too bad," Sonny said. He meant it, too.

"Yeah. Sure enough is." They stared at each other a minute, not speaking. Walker finally broke the silence, making his voice lighter. "How about you? Got some new lady that's kept you distracted?"

"Is that your goddamn business?" Sonny snarled. The instant anger, the venom in his words, surprised him at least as much as it did Walker.

"Jeez, Sonny." Walker flinched, throwing up his hands. "I just wondered what's been up. I ain't seen you in ages. Word is no one has, really."

Sonny nodded, feeling himself cool down a snatch. He muttered, "Just been keeping to myself, is all. Been steering clear of broads, too."

"Yeah? That ain't like you at all."

Sonny didn't answer. He didn't know what possessed him to say that much. This was so damned tiresome. He needed Walker to go—to never have stopped by in the first place.

Sonny glanced again at his watch. Walker didn't seem to notice—or if he did, ignored it. He got a real somber look on his face, saying, "I was thataway for awhile, too—with the girls, I mean. The booze and the blow, it was wicked on my circulation and shit. Got to where I couldn't do nothing with the babes even if they was around."

This was the last straw. Sonny slammed his fist into the counter, bellowing. "Shut the fuck up! The last thing I want to hear about is your limp dick."

Trying not to look scared, Walker jumped off his stool, backing out of the kitchen. "Sorry, man. Didn't realize it'd be a sore subject with you."

"It ain't a sore subject." Sonny drew himself up over Walker, taking small pleasure in seeing that familiar old fear on his brother's face. "I ain't *never* had that problem."

"I didn't say you did. I was just telling you some of what happened to me, before. . . . Sonny, please. I don't mean to piss you off, man. I just been wanting to talk to you. We ain't even talked on the phone since I got out, you realize that?"

Of course he did. He'd made a point of avoiding Walker, just so they wouldn't get into this touchy-feely kind of bullshit. Grumbling, Sonny stalked toward the freezer. He pulled out a carton of cigarettes, shaking a pack free and throwing it on the counter. The rest he busied himself slipping into one of the suitcases parked by the door.

Blowing out held breath, Walker took a draw off his blue water bottle. He went back into the kitchen and picked up Sonny's cigarettes, packing them against his palm. Perking up, he said, "I saw *The Girl Can't Help It* video a couple times this week."

"Hard to avoid these days. Heavy rotation, as they say."

"Well, it should be." Walker enthused. "It really shows off that kind of sexy fun the Rockets do so good. Your playing on there is dynamite, too—fat toned and shit? Nice, Sonny." He paused, just ever so slightly lowering his voice. "And man, don't Cill look fine in it—as a brunette, no less? Didn't even know it was her, first time I saw it—not until she started dancing."

Sonny didn't answer. He concentrated on working the cigarette carton into the contents of his suitcase.

"Didn't know ya'll had plans to use her in a video, Sonny."

He zipped the bag, still avoiding Walker's face. "We didn't plan it, exactly. We needed a leading lady who could dance, and she was available. Austin was a pretty good place for her to hide from the press. Didn't want nobody knowing she was here."

"I can understand. I saw them awful stories about her and Grey after I got out."

Sonny grunted, righting the bag. He pulled his itinerary out of his pocket and studied it.

Walker opened the pack of smokes and lit one. "You heard Floyd and Julia Jean had a baby girl?"

Sonny stood, dusting off his hands. "I didn't even know she was expecting. Is everyone doing good?"

"Real good—except maybe the grandparents." Walker snickered. "Floyd and Julia went and named her Caledonia Blue."

This bit of news wrested a smile out of Sonny. "What, the grandparents don't recognize this as a fine blues name?"

"Too blues for them, I reckon—like Daddy felt about my name."

"Well, that's great news. Please pass along my congrats."

"I sure will. I was over there just yesterday, and they were asking after you." Walker paused, taking another gulp of his water. "Otis happened to be there, too. I brought a guitar along, so we was able to work together a little."

Sonny saw clear to what Walker was doing now. He was using the new baby as an excuse to bring up Otis. Sonny slouched on the counter, closing his eyes. He said nothing.

"He played for me some, Sonny. Hard to say yet whether he has any real talent. Still, it's fun showing him new licks—he really seems to want to learn." He stopped. Sonny could tell Walker wanted him to at least acknowledge what he was saying. Sonny kept his eyes shut, silent. After a minute, Walker went on, in almost a confiding tone. "Sonny, Otis favors you. So

much like you at that age—except curly, like Floyd? I was correcting something he was doing yesterday—took the guitar from his hands to show him
a better way? And he gave me this sort of pissed off look when I took it."
Walker let go a nervous laugh. "Scared the hell out of me, that look. Took
me back to being little, and you whipping me for touching your gear."

He rambled on a few minutes about Otis and the new baby. Sonny tried
not to listen too closely. He didn't like thinking about Otis.

When Walker paused again, Sonny looked up, saying, "I really have got
to get gone, Walker. Tell Mama I'm okay, that I'll check in from the road.
Give the Montgomerys my best, too."

Walker put his empty water container on the counter. "I'll leave this
bottle here. Cut it off right here." He indicated a point about three inches
down the neck. "Sand the edges smooth and it makes a real warm-sounding
slide. Pretty color, too, huh?"

"Sure enough. Maybe I'll do that."

Walker pointed to the gear and suitcases. "Leastwise let me run you
over to the airport?"

"No . . . it's fine. I still got a few things to take care of. I'll just call a cab
when I'm ready."

"Suit yourself, man." Walker went to the door, Sonny following him.
Quick, he grabbed Sonny in a hug. Sonny gave his back a slap and pushed
free. Leaving Sonny on the threshold, Walker pulled his keys from his pocket and climbed into the restored Vette, revving the engine. He grinned at
Sonny from behind the wheel, honking once. Sonny smiled back, waving as
the car backed into the street.

As the car tuned around the corner, Sonny's smile faded completely. At
least that was over with, seeing Walker for the first time since everything.
Maybe it was good to be getting the hell out of town for awhile after all.

28.

"JESUS WEPT, SONNY," Bonnell snarled. The rest of the band petered into
silence as Bonnell dragged a finger across his neck in the sound booth's
direction. Sonny saw, through the glass, the engineer slapping his own face
with his hands. Tearing off his headphones, Bonnell stalked toward where
Sonny sat with the Tele across his lap. "Where the hell's your head? Follow
Johnny Lee's $3/4$ groove, you. Wasting all our time, are you not?"

"Yeah, I am not, you phony-ass Frenchman," Sonny shot back. "This
stupid song is what's a waste of our time." He knew he should be apologizing for blowing the rhythm riff yet again. He would have, in better days. But
he was sick of Bonnell's constant nitpicking. He might as well have a nag of
a wife as work with this asshole.

Usually Sonny welcomed recording time and the accompanying break from travel. He hoped the familiar hometown studio would stir his artistic juice, and becalm his mind. But it wasn't happening. He was agitated, restless—flirting with insanity, he sometimes thought.

After laying down tracks, he'd hit the bars, cutting a swath through the local watering holes and bar babes just like he had on the recent road trip. If there was a party, or a stoned-out all-night jam, Sonny was there, emperor of the revelers. What was once fun was just joyless excess, though. And people talked—even a few of his fellow hell-raisers chided him to slow up. Worse was the growing pool of recoverers, friends, and associates who followed in Walker's sober bootsteps. Shaking their heads, tsk-tsking. Fuck 'em. They only made Sonny want to push it rougher, further. Just because Walker was mugless didn't mean Sonny was doomed to fall.

Sonny was fine and dandy. Felt better than ever. Yeah, man.

It was all a big black lie, and Sonny knew it. But he needed to drive Cilla from his mind. He tried his damnedest to erase her with chemicals and a long line of frightened, roughed-up redheads. She wouldn't leave him, though. He'd seen her recently, purely accidental. Sonny was in a sports bar, somewhere, ready to watch a National League playoff game on TV. Suddenly, there was Cilla, a clinging Dodger-blue dress setting off her grown-out Titian tresses. Sonny thought at first he was hallucinating. But no, she was singing the national anthem, looking for all the world like a bona fide goddess. Every fucker in that bar made some nasty comment about her and what he would do with her if given half a chance. Thinking he might keel over, or worse, kill some horny smart-ass, Sonny walked out before the game even started. He purposefully missed the rest of what he heard was a great series, terrified he'd be surprised by her again.

Later, he'd heard how she'd scored that singing gig. She was dating one of the Dodgers, a handsome southpaw pitcher named Mickey Canttoni. He was the Dodgers' latest Italian hope, a bad boy with wicked heat in his left. Canttoni and Cilla had met at a charity event, a Jocks versus Rockers thing one of the L.A. rock stations held to benefit charity. Wouldn't you know, Canttoni was starting pitcher the night Cilla sang the anthem. Sonny knew Cilla must have loved opening that game, baseball fan that she was. Sleeping with the right men sure had its perks.

Bonnell started yelling at him again, bringing Sonny's fuzzy mind back into the studio. "Stupid, my song is, you? Fine words from this drunken Texas trailer trash. Can you still put two chords together and give us something superior to work with? I won't hold my breath. You can hardly tune that thing anymore."

Sonny could feel all eyes on him. He looked around hard enough at the other Rockets to make them busy themselves with their instruments. Not Bonnell. He was breathing hard, glaring, smirking—truly pissed off, Sonny could tell. Silkily, Sonny replied, "I ain't never lived in a trailer, you French cocksucker."

Bonnell tossed his hair back, affecting his oh-so-bored patrician laugh. "But see, my friends? Sonny does not deny being drunken or trash. Ignorant Texan, though French speaking, I am not French. I . . . am Creole."

Sonny jumped up and let his Tele hit the floor in a nasty cacophony of notes, causing the sound guy to jerk off his 'phones in pain. He took a second to put it right on its stand. Then he took a fighting stance, waving his fingertips—*come get me*—saying, "Crap-hole, did you say? Couldn't quite make it out in that stupid accent of yours."

"Look who's talking about stupid accents? I speak two languages fluently, and flirt with two more, while you completely mangle your own native tongue."

"That's enough, ya'll," Johnny Lee barked. Rimshot grunted in agreement.

Sonny and Bonnell ignored their rhythm section. They had taken to circling around each other in the studio. Bonnell's face was now masked with the gator look. Sonny was sneering pretty damned cold himself, still beckoning the singer. "Come on, rich-boy. Let's see what you got."

"I got more than you can even imagine, you pussy. You, on the other hand, can't even deal with a little heartache."

Sonny stopped circling, cocking his head. "What did you just say?"

Bonnell smiled through the gator gaze, hissing, "Trust me, that loose English cunt isn't worth your grief."

Sonny staggered, dazed for a moment. Bonnell's words had struck harder than a Foreman left hook.

"Devereaux, that's enough, man," Johnny Lee shouted, grabbing at Sonny's arm to restrain him.

But Johnny Lee's shout had worked to bring Sonny around. He lunged, but Bonnell just managed to dodge him, laughing in his face, upsetting Sonny's guitar with a loud crash. Knocking it over was probably accidental, but the sound kick Bonnell then gave the instrument wasn't.

Sonny screamed, "You chickenshit fucker, lay off my gear!"

"Why? You can't do anything with it anymore." Bonnell had worked his way behind the drum kit, causing Rimshot to swear in Spanish, doing his best to push the singer away from his equipment.

"Too bad you don't have your servants here to fight for you," Sonny yelled back, "same way they fuck your mama for your daddy."

That did it. Bonnell snarled like a rabid dog and sprung, grabbing at Sonny. Sonny still had enough reflex to duck him, landing a sound punch in the singer's mouth before Bonnell managed a fist. The singer went down hard, wailing, blood pouring from between the fingers he held to his mouth. Rimshot, still spitting out Spanish curses, leaped from behind his kit and ran to the heap on the floor that was Bonnell. Johnny Lee grabbed Sonny from behind and dragged him from the studio. Sonny could hear Bonnell cursing at him in a mixture of English and Creole. Sonny made out a few words, something about the lunacy of losing your mind over a classy piece of ass.

Johnny Lee shoved Sonny into a nearby lounge and tossed him onto a sofa. When Sonny tried to rise, Johnny Lee smacked him back down hard. "You set right there, boy, until you settle your white ass down. Don't you move, don't you even say jack shit. And listen up, hear?" Sonny sat back, folding his arms, staring into the hall. He felt like a school bully sent to the principal's office. Johnny Lee went on, his voice quieter. "Ain't no front-page news that we all get fed up with Devereaux's shit. I know he been riding you especially hard lately, too. But you can't be popping that s.o.b. in the mouth. He's likely to go get some of his Louisiana heavies to smash your hands up, Sonny." Glancing back at the door, Johnny Lee dropped his voice, adding, "Worse, he'll get that hoodoo servant of his mama's to put some badass hex on you. I wouldn't put nothing past that man."

Johnny Lee paused, scowling. The fluorescent lights reflected off his ever-present shades. He looked exactly like a gigantic, scornful beetle. The thought nearly made Sonny laugh, and helped cool his rage a few degrees.

"Shit-fire, Johnny Lee," Sonny sighed. "I know I shouldn't have popped him, even if he had it coming. Worse, he was right—I was fucking up the rhythm line, over and over again."

"Yeah. Better admit that to Bonnell, not to me, if you want to keep your damn job."

"Like that asshole would try and fire me."

"Been making noises that way. Rimshot has, too. And I hate being in the middle of the hurricane ya'll got spinning around this band. Don't push too hard, Sonny, less you ready to jump ship. Plenty of kids right here in Austin can be taught to fill your boots, we need them to."

Sonny gaped at his bassist. "He . . . really said that? Rimshot, too? They want me out? But . . . I'm a huge part of what makes the band go."

"That was true in the past, my man. But anymore? Your last name's been more valuable to this band than your playing has."

Sonny's anger started to fester again. "Fuck is this shit, Johnny Lee?"

"Shit that been a long time coming, boy."

Angered and shocked as the words made him, Sonny knew they were true. He couldn't remember when he had last zeroed in on inspiration, feeling it push him to soar. His standard interview line about delivering up the goods . . . well, the goods had been left to rot on the dock of late.

Johnny Lee dropped to the couch beside Sonny. "Used to be, Sonny, people checked out Walker because they'd been impressed with your stuff. They wanted to see if his chops measured up. He was, like, the challenger to the champ, you know?

"Then his career took off. Never no shame in that. Don't take nothing from you—honors you, in fact. Folks that found his music came looking for yours. They'd find something different in you, but always real good, Sonny." Johnny Lee paused, watching as Sonny lit a cigarette with shaking hands. "Ain't really there no more, Sonny. You falling to pieces before my eyes. I knowed you since you was a little shit, wrestling with that banged-up Fender you willed over to Walker. I ain't *never* seen you like this."

Sonny smoked in silence for a moment. He wanted his hands to stop shaking before he answered. Finally, he mumbled, "I know."

"That English girl, she be the reason behind all this trouble in the band."

Feeling a cold wave flow through him, Sonny turned his eyes to Johnny Lee. He couldn't tell much what the bassist was thinking, nodding behind his shades. "I don't know what you're talking about."

"Sonny, please. That Cilla's driven you and Bonnell both batty. Him, he's just pissed because I don't reckon he got his way with her. But you? I can't quite get my mind around what's happened to you."

"Nothing's happened to me."

"Bullshit. I knowed you too long. I knew something had changed in you when we was doing the video. You walked around with a shit-eating grin on your face, all dreamy-eyed and sweet-natured. I remember thinking if it was anybody but Sonny, I'd say they was in love. Not you, though. You play with the ladies like they're your toys. More I watched you, though, more I knew it had to be.

"I sure enough didn't figure it for Cilla, though. You two hid it pretty good. Not like when she was your brother's woman. Talk about heat—they tried to play it cool, but the damn thermostat would jump ten degrees when they was in the same room together. . . ." Johnny Lee saw Sonny wince at the words. "Oh, man. Now I see the writing on the wall. She told you she still loves Walker?"

"You could say that."

Johnny Lee nodded. "Could be she do. Tell you this, though. I saw her coming from the back of the Sugar and Spice, the night of the wrap party? She was a mess, just bawling, slumped against the wall in the hallway by the johns. I hurried her out the back way so no one would find her so troubled. She begged me to take her back to the hotel. So I put her in my car.

"She looked bad—real drunk, her hair crazy, makeup all smeared. Her leg was bleeding, stocking ripped, like she just barked her shin on something. Truth? Looked like she been roughed up. Sonny, you know as well as I do that if some redneck Texas Ranger had pulled us over, seen a messed-up white girl crying in my car . . . well. It made me a little nervous. But I had to help her. The way Bonnell been acting all night—weird and, I don't know . . . dark? I thought he assaulted her or something."

"It wasn't him," Sonny admitted.

"Cilla told me so. She was looking at the cars in the parking lot as we pulled away. 'Sonny left?' she asked. Far as I know, yeah, I tell her. She really started wailing then. That's when I put it together—put ya'll together. I asked her if you had hurt her. You know what she said?"

"No idea," Sonny whispered. He wasn't sure he wanted to know. He felt like he was going to puke—must be that flu rearing its head again.

"She told me, in the saddest voice you ever heard, 'I hurt Sonny—not the other way around. I was cruel to him. Please tell him how sorry I am.' Word for word, that's what she said. And then she started crying again, all the way into town. She was shattered." Johnny Lee got to his feet, walking toward the door. He leaned against the jamb, removing his shades. His dark eyes, the eternally hidden flesh around them framed by the pinch marks from his glasses, looked sympathetically on Sonny. "I ain't told you what she said before now because you been so crazed. Didn't want to hurt more than help. I thought you'd start to come around, sooner or later. But you ain't. It's been, what, eight months since we finished that fucking video? All the drinking and drugging and shit, it's fucking up your work, man.

"Look, you can talk to me about it, anytime. Swear to you, little brother, it won't go no further. But I think you need more help than I can offer. You need a pro."

Sonny jumped up, stalking away from his old friend to glare out the window at nothing. "Fuck you, man. I don't need nobody."

Johnny Lee approached Sonny and gripped his shoulder. "Simmer down, Sonny. You do need somebody—us, your friends and family. Got lots of folks who care, man. We don't want to sit around and watch you burn out, faster every day. It don't show weakness to ask for help, you know. No, sir. What it shows is balls, man."

With those words, Johnny Lee put his shades back on and walked out of the lounge, shutting the door behind him. Sonny sat back down on the sofa, rocking back and forth. He had to go back to the studio and apologize to Bonnell—to everyone. Even now, just a few minutes gone, he could scarcely believe he'd up and socked Bonnell. Hell, he'd thought about punching Bonnell plenty of times—who hadn't? But to actually do it—man, it was a surefire sign that he was out of control.

It had been self-defense, though—Bonnell had come at him. Nevertheless, it had been a foolhardy move. Johnny Lee was right about Bonnell. With all of his creepy connections, he was a dangerous cat to fuck with.

Sighing, Sonny got to his feet and went back to the studio ready to eat some humble pie.

* * * * *

BONNELL'S LIP WAS SPLIT and he had a chipped front tooth. Finding him in the studio with an ice pack held against his mouth, Sonny had laid back his ears, begging forgiveness. He swore to all of the Rockets and recording crew that they'd have no more bullshit from him for the balance of the sessions. To Bonnell, Sonny pledged a meal accompanied by vintages fit for a king the next time they hit the Quarter. The singer seemed to accept his apology. They called a hiatus from recording for a few days. By the time they got back, Bonnell bore no more than a faint scab on his lower lip, and looked to have already had his tooth repaired. No permanent harm seemed to be done.

From then until the album's finish, Sonny made every effort to show up at sessions on time and reasonably straight. Maybe he'd start the day with a few lines to wake up, and whet his sore finger tendons with a shot or two of Southern Comfort scattered throughout the day. Anymore, it was as close to sober as he could manage.

Sonny turned the other cheek when Bonnell inevitably picked on him, on his playing. He kept his cool and would do his best to deliver what the singer was asking from him. When he'd feel his temper start to bubble, he reminded himself that Johnny Lee, Rimshot, and the fans were depending on him to act professionally. He'd spent too much time lately playing the part of a spoiled brat instead of acting like the seasoned road and studio man he was. He wouldn't allow Bonnell to again push him into that corner.

The sessions weren't very demanding of him, really. This was the first Rockets album they hadn't done straight-up live. Sonny knew that in large part this was so that they could cull his rough edges. Mostly he sat around and waited until time to pop in with his twelve bars here and there, like George Harrison on the early Beatles stuff. He did do his rhythmic magic to some extent, but Sonny knew better than anyone he wasn't up to his old standards. He kept his lines simple—out of necessity more than artistic choice.

Soon enough the album was in the can. They'd decided to call it *Tickling the 88s*. The name suited it. It was much more Bonnell's album, swamp-pop piano-and-accordion heavy, than any of their previous records. The photo they decided to put on the cover even reflected the band's change in dynamics. Bonnell was front and center, flanked by Rimshot and Johnny Lee, all of them dressed to kill. Sonny stood off to the side and behind them. He was in his black jacket, T-shirt, and jeans, a brooding look on his face that might easily be mistaken by the casual observer for tough-guy cool. Nothing of his trademark grin, present on all their other covers, was anywhere in evidence.

Sessions behind him, Sonny once more lost himself in the big party. Until he left town, he steered clear of Mama and his aunt and uncle, making excuses, returning few calls. Walker wasn't a problem, at least.

Thankfully, he was on the road, traveling farther and longer than he ever had. From all reports, Walker was sticking to, and proclaiming loud, his new clean lifestyle. He was playing the biggest venues of his career. The music press was head over heels in love with him and his Salamanders. Even the straight press was talking. Walker was fast approaching a B.B. King, household–name kind of fame.

The Salamanders had just released their studio opus, called *Harder Than It Looks (And It Don't Look Easy!)*. Walker had a copy sent to Sonny through Rockets' management. Sonny got a small kick out of the title—it was an old joke between them. It began when they were kids, watching some maestro chasing it down on Ed Sullivan or Steve Allen. Despite being pleased by the title, Sonny wouldn't listen to it at first. He left it atop his stereo sealed in shrink-wrap.

A day or so after getting the album, he'd heard the title track on the radio. It rocked indigo, all right. With Floyd's help, Walker had put another spin on Sonny's and his pet phrase. The song expressed the day-and-night struggle to keep straight. Sonny couldn't help then but open the album. He didn't put it on at first, though, just read through the credits, looked over the pictures.

One shot of Floyd and Walker working together in the studio stirred something akin to jealousy in Sonny. His own first bandleader/former best friend and the little brother had become a first-rate songwriting team. *Harder Than It Looks* was one of several lyrics that Floyd had penned with Walker for the record. The exposure had been great for Floyd's career. His band, The Texas Sidewinders, was even opening for the Salamanders this tour. Sonny heard through the grapevine that the big venues were an important step for Floyd. After achieving sobriety, he had finally admitted to, and recovered from, hellish stage fright.

Among the acknowledgments was a note clearly meant for Sonny: "For everything I know, big bro." Sonny stared at the message a long time, not sure how it made him feel. Tired of trying to decide, he put the album on.

It was an inspired piece of work, no way around it. The classics Walker had chosen to redo blistered with new life. Lyrically, his new stuff was the most thoughtful material he'd ever delivered. All of Walker's playing roared with intensity. Sonny could actually hear the tubes in Walker's amp sizzling on a few spectacular runs.

Then there was the closer, an instrumental called *Gloaming Nocturne*. Sonny knew it was for Cilla—that was the name of those roses Walker had sent to Cilla before their shows together. Just seeing that title had kept Sonny from listening as long as he did before now. To hear it, though, was to be flat-out mesmerized. *Gloaming Nocturne* was crafted from the same plush fabric as *Smitten* had been before it. Yet it was more mature—a full-grown man's work of true-blue love and truer, bluest loss.

Cilla would know Walker meant the song for her. It hurt Sonny just to know that, made him wish he had it in him to create such a sublime piece. Even if he could master it note for note—and once upon a time he'd had the technique to do just that—it wouldn't come out of him the same. His version—anyone else's—wouldn't have Walker's soul meshed inside the melody.

When the album ended, Sonny sat in silence for about ten minutes. Then he was compelled to again drop the needle onto *Gloaming Nocturne*. Standing by the stereo, eyes closed, he rubbed his upper arms to quell the gooseflesh that grew there. Players held aloft Walker as the reigning guitar speed demon—and he was, no doubt. When Sonny witnessed Walker play one of those speed-of-light runs, inhumanly fast, Bonnell's stories of dark dealing rang truest. But Sonny knew him better than anyone, and knew that at least his raw-sweet instrumental side, as unearthly as it felt, was made entirely of Walker. Somehow, his brother managed to take his muscles, his guts, his jism, his heartbeat, his very essence, and transform them into these aching, poignant melodies. Surely something so transcendent could not be demonic.

Sonny dropped his head as the song ended again. It felt like his heart might explode with the crazy pride he felt for Walker at this moment, nourished by the furious love he had for him, too. The fierce feeling only made Sonny's own misery keener.

He sure as hell didn't want to tour again, but he was stuck. He didn't know how to bear the next few months trapped in a bus with Bonnell. It was worse to stay in town, though. Everyone watched him. But the anonymity of the road was growing dangerous—and less anonymous besides.

Sonny's lust had gone twisted ever since he took sick after the video. He'd always dug the fact that he could take the most self-possessed bitch and with a few well-rehearsed moves turn her into his fucking machine. Sure, there had been times in the past when he'd liked rough stuff, but really only if the lady was into that scene, too. Truth told, now it was better for him when they didn't want it rough. That's how they were going to get it. To get off, he needed to piece out his hurt and fear.

Sonny could tell the groupie grapevine was buzzing about the detour his tastes had taken of late. City to city, he felt fear in the eyes of the ones he considered after a show. Despite their tough reputation, the groupies were really just a bunch of star-struck romantics. They needed something of you, wanted a share of what they imagined Icestorm to be. More and more, he even left the groupies alone, resorting to real pros, to call girls. Actual whores had no expectations except cash. You could order up a redhead to specs, hand her a stack of bills, and pretty much do what you had to with her. Extra money generally bought silence when things got too out of hand even for the girls who specialized in his sort of trip.

Toward the end of that tour even the other Rockets were giving Sonny funny looks when they thought he didn't see. He was sure they'd heard stories about him, too. A few mornings, when he woke up not remembering much of what had gone down beyond bringing a pro back to his hotel room, there would be wreckage around him. He'd find broken lamps and furniture, pieces of violently shredded underwear, defense wounds on his face and body. He might remember a blurry battle of flesh and fetish, flashes of useless cries for mercy from his victim.

The further he went with it, the more degraded he felt himself, and the less it pleasured him. Then, while in Ireland last time out, he'd spotted a flame-haired young woman walking alone late one night. She had the look of a young coed, probably out late studying. He followed her a long ways, unnoticed by her on the darkened streets. He fantasized about how easy it would be to grab her from behind and drag her off. He'd be back on the road, out of the country, before she'd even have time to report the assault.

Realizing what he was contemplating doing, Sonny ran from the girl clear back to the hotel. Safe in his room, he admitted the truth to himself: If he'd followed her even a few minutes more, he would have stopped imagining the act and followed through with it. What sort of monster he was evolving into finally stabbed hard at him through the numbness he'd encased himself in. He had to break this cycle of misery. He needed someone to set him straight. A faceless innocent wasn't the answer—Jesus, no— but neither were the seasoned pros. He needed someone who cared, yet who wouldn't expect too much from him. She had to be someone who couldn't be too shocked or sickened as she helped him set his mind back to right.

Was there such a woman? . . . Maybe one.

Tough and tender Vada might be the answer; in her own way, she was every bit as broken as he. She wouldn't judge him. God knew they shared history. She hadn't been his first lover by a long shot, nor he hers, but their youthful encounters were still in his mind—overdriven, pedal-flooring encounters. Even as a girl she'd been able to practically fuck a man to death. They'd blistered each other again when Daddy had been dying, when Walker had still been in La La Land with that woman. What they'd had between them had not really faded away with time, despite both of them doing their best to steer clear of it because of Walker.

Sonny knew he probably could never love her, not like a man was supposed to his woman, and not like even Vada must need loving. But Vada knew him better than he'd ever let any other woman know him. She might accept what little he had to offer. If she could only handle him in this deranged state, she might be able to rein in his madness enough to make him want to live again. Two old warhorses might just surprise the hell out of everyone and even find something like contentment together.

Before he got to Austin again, Sonny had convinced himself that Vada was his chance at salvation. He tried unsuccessfully to call her once he was home. Unable to get her by phone, he'd gone so far as to go see her band on East Sixth the night before he left town again. He thought he'd wait for her after, explain what he had in mind, and see if she was game. He'd chickened out though and fled after only one song, grateful to have gone unrecognized.

Later, while touring, usually after doing something wretched to some poor whore, he'd muster up the balls to call Vada. He tried his best to plan it time-wise so that he would catch her home before or after a gig. Somehow though, he never managed to reach her. Nowadays Sonny's timing seemed to be off in damned near everything.

29.

VADA SAT ALONE at her kitchen table, still in a robe, letting the steam from the mug of Combaté coffee moisten her face. It was nearing sundown, but she only recently stumbled from bed. She'd flipped on the kitchen radio, set as always to the community station.

Of all the damned things—they were doing a tribute to Muddy Waters. Jimi was playing *I'm a Man*. She groaned at the too familiar Hendrix licks, but didn't turn it off.

She poured a little mescal into her coffee from a half-empty bottle on the table—a hair of the dog. She'd been on a bender for two days. Her heroin supply, which should have lasted twice as long, was completely gone. She'd already called Nicky. She was waiting now for him to bring her more shit before she started jonesing in earnest.

The bender had started after a meeting with Walker at his lawyer's office. She'd met with him to go over and sign their settlement agreement. In sixty days, give or take, their marriage would be dissolved. No more Walker-and-Vada, after all these years. No more Mrs. Walker Blaine. Vada Blaine she would remain, at least professionally. She could hardly go back to Bee-Stung Sanchez at this stage of the game. Bee-Stung was dead and gone. Vada Blaine, goddamnit, was still out there fighting.

She glanced at the fat settlement agreement, still sitting on the table where she'd dropped it after returning from the lawyer's office. On top of the documents lay a yellowed snapshot. Walker had given it to her when they'd met with the lawyers.

The photo, taken with her old Brownie, was of her as a bride, flanked by best man Sonny and groom Walker. The wife of the man that had married them had taken it right after the quickie across-the-line ceremony. Sonny, smiling over the couple, was in a rumpled but costly suit—his uniform as a freshman Rocket 88. Walker and Vada, also in their stage attire of that era, gazed with great joy and hope into the camera's lens. She'd been wearing a tiny red dress, her track-free arms and legs on display. A blue handkerchief, loaned to her by the woman who took the photo, covered her head as a makeshift veil—something borrowed and blue in one fell swoop. Vada had been wearing her *abuela's* copper bracelets for something old, and had considered Walker's pinkie ring, her temporary wedding band, the something new. What a makeshift deal that wedding had been. It hadn't felt that way at the time, though. She'd been so happy to at last be Walker's bride.

"Used to carry this picture in my wallet on tour," Walker had said as he'd handed it to her when the lawyers gave them a moment alone. "When I'd get to missing you, I'd take it out and think about the sweet times. I think you should have it."

"Why now, Walker?" she'd asked him, with more irritation in her voice than she actually felt.

"I don't have a home no more, girl. I'm too much gypsy. You keep track of stuff better, always have." He'd tried to smile through the tears that had been filling his eyes. "Besides, it's one damn thing the lawyers ain't got a hold of first, huh?"

She hadn't wanted the picture—not right then. But she could sense that Walker needed her to have it. Fine, then. It would be the last thing that she'd ever have to take from the bastard.

No, that wasn't fair. Walker might be any number of things, but he wasn't a bastard. Even these days, gone as straight as a missionary, he seemed more pained by her lifestyle than judgmental of it. And his settlement had been more than generous—way more. With the solid lineup of the Ballbusters—her best band since Walker and his Salamanders had been part of the Bees—she'd been making bread enough to live frugally. What Walker had bequeathed her with the divorce would enable her to live a lush life.

The house, paid for, was hers now. She'd never have to worry again about how she'd settle up with Nicky or any other lowlife dealer. Never have to compromise on cheap junk or have to milk the good stuff just to keep the demons at bay. It would be one long, smooth ride from here on out.

Scratching her arms, her stomach squirming, Vada drained her coffee. She'd burned her mouth but didn't much notice. She stalked into her bedroom, throwing clothes aside to locate her purse. She fumbled inside it until she found a packed vial of cocaine and tapped a little onto one of her long fingernails, sniffing it. She wished she had some Robitussin AC to gulp— not that it was strong enough to get her off, but it at least eased the sickness. The coke didn't help the heroin itch either, but it woke her up and would make the wait for Nicky more bearable.

Might as well start getting her outfit ready for tonight. She went to her closet, raking through the hangers. Most of her old costumes now swallowed her, and the majority showed too much needle-scarred skin besides. She finally settled on a long-sleeved blue unitard. It wasn't a proper stage costume, rather something an adolescent cheerleader type might wear to aerobics class. But it was Spandex—it didn't just hang on her. Paired with boots, big jewelry, and some sort of jacket, it would do.

Holding the costume up against her body and assessing it in the mirror, Vada again considered her new financial situation. She didn't have to account to anyone, could spend her divorce money any way she saw fit. Maybe she'd do some costume sketches, work up stage outfits with a real designer. Like Cher, she could collaborate with someone cool like Bob Mackie. She'd loved the Mackie gown that Walker had once bought her. Sadly, it was one of the things she could no longer wear—now too loose, too revealing.

Problem was, having someone design stuff for her would mean stripping down in front of fitters. There would be no way to hide her track marks from them. She didn't think she could take the humiliation.

She took off her robe now, staring for a hard minute at her nakedness. *Mios dios*, she was a living wraith. *El espectro*, Papa had seethed in her face the last time he'd seen her. Papa remained blind to her real vices, though. He still blamed Walker for everything—that faithless *Americano* louse of a son-in-law, causing his *mijita* to wither from heartbreak. But Mama, she was wiser to her daughter's ways. She'd never blamed Walker. She loved Walker, respected him, at least as much as she did Vada.

Better just to steer clear of the lot of them, so as not to see the fear and concern in their faces.

Her eyes misted up now with longing for her parents, blurring her ghastly reflection. She bit her lip, forcing the tears back. No denying the life she'd led was now showing all over. Maybe a good plastic surgeon, one who wouldn't ask too many questions, could conceal the needle marks, if not actually repair the damage done to her veins. While she was at it, she might get the big boobs nature hadn't seen fit to give her. She didn't need a facelift yet, but she could do with an eye job and get a few scowl lines filled in with a little collagen or something.

A new start—sky's the limit. Maybe she'd even start eating healthy.

Hell, maybe she'd start eating again, period.

Sighing, she tossed the unitard onto the bed for later and pulled on a sweatshirt and a pair of baggy-assed jeans that had once fit her figure like they'd been painted on. She stalked on back into the living room, looking out the window. No sign of Nicky yet, damn him. He'd told her he had shit handy. So what was taking so long? She watched the road, as if by doing so she could conjure the dealer up out of thin air.

The next Muddy Waters tribute song that came on made her whirl, eyes narrowed, toward the radio. It was Walker's bouncing overture on *I Can't Be Satisfied*, dating back to their King Bees album. Why today, of all days? She hadn't heard the damn record in years.

Heart fluttering, she listened to herself sing the menacing lyrics of violent breakup with a critical ear. She'd been an okay singer back then, nothing special. At that point she'd not quite found her voice. The same wasn't true of Walker. He'd been barely a man when this record had come out, and yet he had it already, that tone of his. It was raw, virile, a countrified innocence mixed up with something wise, almost sinister.

His sound wasn't always sinister, of course. At its most loving, it was the sweetest rush Vada had ever known. She remembered the feel of him pulling free of her body on the day he'd proposed. Groggy with his loving, she'd protested, trying to draw him back into his little bed at the Sugar and Spice. He'd shaken his head, hushed her. He'd dropped to a knee, grabbing up his then-new treasure, the Goldie Strat.

"I ain't going far, girl. But there's something I got to do right now, before I chicken out." Voice skittish, he'd kicked on the amp, gazing at her adoringly. "You're the best thing ever happened to me, Vada. You even let me get this here guitar, no complaints, instead of what you deserve—a ring. I hope what I'm fixing to give you instead will be enough to make you to marry me."

Then, for the first time, Walker had played *Smitten* for Vada. The song was better than any engagement ring. With that melody, Walker had given their love immortality. She'd really thought then they'd always be together. She'd believed it anew every time Walker had used the ballad to make amends to her. More than anything else in the world, *Smitten* was hers. It was *theirs*.

She looked at the garnet-and-diamond ring that had, once the money came, been given her to symbolize their union. She still hadn't been able to make herself remove it from her left hand. Though the ring had been given to her after the American Records contract, it still brought to mind young, prefame Walker. She could picture him, returning home from some two-bit gig, clutching in his fists a fresh-picked bouquet of black-eyed Susans.

But the ring made her think of another Walker, too—one whose fists had given Vada black eyes of a different sort.

Vada gave Walker his due. He'd never struck her first, no matter how mad he'd gotten. He'd rarely hit her even when she'd labored to goad him into it with her own words and blows. She, on the other hand, had left him repeatedly with shameful injuries he'd had to explain away with invented bar fights.

The first time Walker had briefly returned to Austin from his California sojourn, he'd stopped by to see her. He said he was there to clue her in on the arrangements he'd made for her to more readily access his expanding earnings. The atmosphere between them was viscous with tension. To ease the pressure, Vada had poured them a couple shots, and Walker had broken out his rock star–grade cocaine.

At first their intoxication had brought out the good kind of heat between them. They'd ended up taking their pleasure in each other on the living room rug. But almost as soon as they'd finished, Walker had gone quiet, moody. With hardly a word, he'd dressed and made to go. Vada hadn't stood for it. *What did he think she was*, she'd screamed in his face, *some groupie bitch he could just up and leave? Maybe that was how he treated his California slut, but here it wasn't going to fly!* She'd blocked his retreat, striking him hard enough to knock his hat from his head. Wordless, he bent to retrieve it. When he rose to face her, she hit him again. Eyes narrowed, but still silent, Walker had attempted to push past her. That was when Vada had grabbed an empty mescal bottle, smashing it upside his head.

It did the trick. Bloodied, Walker decked her good, almost breaking her neck with his blow. Her shoulder muscles still sometimes seized up from that punch. He'd left her face in a state where she'd had to resort to pancake makeup and dark glasses for weeks.

He'd been instantly remorseful. Bursting into tears, he'd tried to gather her up in his arms, begging forgiveness. Crazy with pain, she fought free and staggered into the kitchen, grabbing a butcher knife. She'd chased him into the night, fully intending to stab him to death. If there'd been a gun handy, Vada knew for certain that Walker would be dead now.

Vada's heart throbbed from the sordid memory of it. She whimpered with the effort not to cry. Even after that awful fight, he'd come back to her when he'd learned his daddy was dying. He'd moved right on back in, becoming a husband to her again. He'd worked hard alongside her and the band on their first Ballbusters record.

He'd truly tried to make it work.

So why hadn't it? Too little too late, she supposed. Things had conspired against them. Her drug bust, her secret miscarriage, had caused irreparable harm. Both incidents had bred ugliness in their life together. Maybe if she'd ever found the courage to let Walker share with her the pain of that lost child, it might be different now. If she'd only been able to later give him a child when he'd asked her to. Instead, she'd pretended she hadn't wanted his babies. The truth was, Walker, his children, that normalcy and security had been what Vada had wanted most of all.

Too late now. He'd changed too much. He was, as those pious AA assholes liked to parrot, *clean and sober*.

Starting to shiver, Vada again picked up the faded wedding photo. She touched a fingernail to her soon-to-be-ex's youthful face. She still loved him. She had no doubts that Walker had really loved her once—maybe still did. But he'd moved on. It was time for her to follow suit.

She moved her fingernail over to Sonny's beautiful smile. The boy he'd been could get a girl off as rough and nasty as a shot of 'shine and a blast of bathtub speed. What had happened between them had meant nothing. Not back then. Not until Big Billy Jay had been dying. From her vantage point now, Vada realized she and Sonny had more in common than she and Walker did. They bore similar scars, similar fears.

In the end Sonny might have made her a better match.

Grimacing, Vada chased away that insane thought. She'd learned one thing for sure from all of this. If she ever did allow another man to come close, it wouldn't be another fucked-up Texas ax-man.

She tossed the picture back to the table and took another belt of the mescal. She gagged but kept it down. Raking her hair from her face, she at last heard Nicky's beater pulling into the driveway. Vada dropped the bottle to the floor, not caring that she'd spilled its remaining contents onto the carpet.

She was waiting with the door open when Nicky came shuffling up the walk. This cat didn't even try to pass for a straight. Nicky always seemed to be in the same pair of greasy black jeans and shades, with a rotating wardrobe of about five long-sleeved swag shirts. His limp ponytail and breath smelled rotten. But he dealt the best stuff Vada had found since the *Federales* had waylaid her smuggler-cousin.

As always, he grabbed Vada for a kiss as he came in. When Walker had lived in California, she'd once made the mistake of fucking Nicky in trade when she'd had no ready cash. Ever since, the fool had always made a show of trying to get her into bed instead of taking money for his dope. With all the shit Nicky did himself anymore, he probably couldn't do anything with her had she permitted it.

She pushed him away. "Not now, Nicky. You bring it?"

He sat on her couch, smirking. "Hi to you, too." He pulled out a parcel, laying it on the coffee table. "Doesn't have to cost a thing, baby. You know that."

Sighing, she went into her bedroom, returning with a wad of twenties. "Here's your money."

"Cool. I should get some more soda in a few days, too. You got enough of that to last you until then?"

"Yeah. That I got still."

He sniffed the air. "How about a cup of that fine Mexican coffee, *señora*?"

He said it in a Frito Bandito accent that Vada found degrading. She kept her cool, though, pulling him playfully to his feet, guiding him toward the door. "Not this time, Nicky. Got a show tonight. I still have a million things to do to get ready."

"It's still early, mama. Let's cook up a little treat, huh? Get a buzz on together." He ran a fingertip down her arm. She did her best to quell a shudder of revulsion.

"I really shouldn't. I don't want to get too high to sing." Vada knew she couldn't risk being too nasty to him. She didn't want to chance losing such a solid *connecta*. "But listen, Sweetie. I appreciate you coming by. Next time, I'll make us that coffee." She smiled, bright and fake, hoping he'd read into it something that wasn't there. "We'll party down then. Promise."

Nicky stopped on the front step, counting the money. While doing so, he said, "Heard you and Walker finally called it quits for real."

"You heard right."

Shoving the money in his pocket, shuffling his feet, he mumbled, "Maybe you and me could go out sometime, now you're single?"

Vada didn't detect any of Nicky's usual bluster in the question. He even looked a little shy, asking. His offer strangely touched her. "Nicky, I am flattered," she replied honestly. "But I really don't think I'll be dating for awhile."

"Yeah. I dig. Oh—." He glanced around, making sure no one was in earshot. "Baby, they tell me that shit's straight from Afghanistan. It's barely stepped on." He grinned, showing his bad teeth. "You be extra careful."

"Always am."

He grabbed her again before she could close the door. She fervently hoped none of her neighbors had seen them.

After Nicky was gone, she turned up the radio loud. Little Lord Mountbatton and the Royals were blazing through their version of *Find Yourself Another Fool*. Pacing, scratching, Vada wailed along with the lyrics, no warmup. Unhealthy for her vocal cords, but she didn't give a damn. The act of losing herself in the song helped her manage to resist the heroin's pull for a few minutes more.

But as it ended, Vada snatched the baggie from the coffee table. She retrieved her vial of coke—a pinch mixed in would keep her from getting too lowdown. She'd be straight enough by showtime. In the kitchen she took her works out and turned on the stove.

Normally what she'd told Nicky was true. She didn't bang this close to showtime. But she hadn't been able to earlier because he'd been out. And with all this blues in the air today . . . well, as Muddy had said best, she just couldn't be satisfied. But she could envelop herself in her bitches' brew, the one thing left her that made the loneliness bearable.

Done cooking the speedball, Vada took everything she needed to fix and laid it on the kitchen table. Sitting, she leaned over to thump the veins in her foot, trying to find one that would still do the trick. Straightening up to load the syringe, Vada once more took note of the old snapshot. She studied her hopeful young face, her unscarred arms, and the two men who'd meant so much to her. Why had Walker given her this damned picture? Couldn't he understand that it would hurt her too much to keep it?

She ripped the photograph to shreds, letting the tears she'd been fighting for days break through.

Loading the syringe, Vada realized that perhaps she had cooked up a little too much. Maybe it was a sign. She could make the pain disappear for good. No, no, she thought, wiping her eyes with her sleeve. She had that gig tonight. She'd just do up a tiny . . . little . . . splash.

30.

ASTRIDE A PEELING vinyl barstool, Sonny ordered another shot to follow the last bunch. The bartender, Jonesy was his name, eyed him coolly. He was an ugly fucker, hollow-cheeked and cockeyed, arms tattoo-strewn—but then, his bar was no palace. Jonesy held out a scaly palm. "Sonny, I need your keys first."

Sonny started to snarl back, but he let it go. He fumbled in the leather jacket's pocket and handed Jonesy the means to his ride. They could pour him into a cab when they had to. It wasn't like anyone would come and fetch him here, would even know to look. Not a living soul besides these barflies knew that he ever came to this place.

He hadn't been here in what seemed like ages. Vada and he used to drink here together when Daddy was dying. They'd agreed it was the sort of place that Big Billy Jay would have liked. It was situated on a lonesome crossroads almost smack on the Blanco/Travis county line. The clientele was made up of laborers, truckers, roughnecks, ranchers, and the women of their ilk. It wasn't like Austin's blues bars, which were quickly changing character, becoming almost trendy. There was no mechanical bull as there was in the counterculture C&W clubs. And these patrons would make short order of the punkers that for half a decade had been trying to take Austin for their own.

No, this was a real Texas bar, as proud as the Alamo and mean as a gunfight at high noon. A warped pool table and a jukebox were the only nod to luxury in this nameless joint. Sonny had liked the fact that he could come in and be just another drinker. He wasn't saddled here with his Texas Icestorm rep. Most of these folks hadn't likely known that Sonny was who he was—and anyone who had wouldn't give a shit anyway.

Most of the barflies here tonight had seen Sonny and Vada drinking, maybe dancing to the jukebox, in those weeks before Walker came back from California. Sonny imagined they were thought of as a couple of cheatin' hearts, stealing moments together—which was close enough to truth. He remembered now that on one occasion here, he had hinted to Vada that maybe this was the very place where Walker had sold his soul for music. It had been the only time he had ever uttered aloud the idea that Bonnell had planted in his brain.

Vada had stared at him a moment, wide-eyed with surprise. Then she'd

asked him what the hell he was going on about. He mumbled something
about the bar being on a crossroads. You know, Robert Johnson had sup-
posedly met the devil and sold his soul to play guitar. And Walker's shit,
after all, was just too much . . . didn't this seem like the kind of place the
devil himself might toss back a few?

Vada had looked around, starting to snicker almost immediately.
"Personally, none of these guys look like my idea of Evil Personified," she'd
whispered. "You can't mean Jonesy? Satan would at least have himself a better venue than this. Or is that the devil, Sonny?" She'd pointed out a blub-
bery guy smoking a Kool butt they'd seen him scrounging up in the parking lot when they'd arrived. "Or him, maybe, the dude with no left arm and
the busted eyeglasses?"

She'd then started roaring with drunken laughter. He'd joined her
quick enough. They'd had to beat it then, staggering out still shrieking
under the surly gaze of Jonesy and his resident drunks.

Sonny didn't remember much of driving home that night, just a blur of
lights and lines and laughter. But he did remember, once they'd miracu-
lously managed to get to his place without killing themselves or getting
popped for DUI, that he had thrown Vada to the rug beside his fireplace.
Laughing and wrestling with her, Sonny had pantsed her, then eaten her out
for a sweet long time. After screaming herself hoarse with pleasure, she had
vigorously returned the favor in kind.

These barflies hadn't cared who'd they'd been, what their story was,
back then. But tonight, everyone seemed to recall Sonny's nights here with
Vada. They'd seen her picture in the paper or on the news, and maybe seen
the film clip one station had shown alongside her story, featuring Walker
and him playing together. Even Jonesy had told him, "Sorry for your loss,
man. She was something else. What a shameful waste of woman."

Vada's corpse had been loaded with cocaine, alcohol, and heroin.
Evidence was that the heroin had actually stopped her heart. She was
already cold to the touch by the time Walker found her. Her guitar player
had called Walker that night, after Vada failed, for the first time in her
career, to show for a gig. Sonny had been on the road with the Rockets
when it happened. He had come back to his hotel room, too gone to even
notice the phone message light's blinking. He hadn't gotten word until late
the next morning

Johnny Lee was hit almost as hard as Sonny was by the news. Bonnell
and Rimshot had not known Vada as well or as long, but they were still
shocked. In haste, the band rescheduled a few shows and headed back to
Austin.

Since coming out of rehab, Walker had lived with Ruby during his rare
moments off the road. Vada had apparently been avoiding Walker like he
was radioactive. Finally, when Vada's frightened parents begged their son-

in-law to intervene, he'd resolved to do what he could. Walker had later told Sonny how he had one night laid wait after her gig. She'd tried to flee when she saw him standing beside her car. Walker had managed to grab her, forcing her into his own vehicle as she screamed for help. Recognized, no one stopped his abduction—everyone knew they were a crazy couple.

Vada clawed Walker's cheek once, good, before he managed to pin her arms. Even now, he bore a faint final scar thanks to her nails. But Vada was so emaciated and stoned that she couldn't fight him for long. Still in Walker's restraining arms, she'd let him speak. He whispered in her ear his fears, trying to force her to see the damage she was doing to herself, to everyone she loved. Panting, trembling, she wouldn't look at him, her hair hiding her face.

After she'd died, Walker told Sonny, "She didn't say nothing for a long time after I finished talking. Then she asked me to turn her loose. She got out of the car, leaning in the window, telling me to get to one of my fucking meetings and leave her the hell alone. I told her flat out: Then this is it, honey. I can't go back to this life. She just nodded, told me to hurry up and get the papers ready to sign. Sonny, man, always before then, she'd tell me, 'Babydoll, you can't ever leave me. It'll kill me if you do.' "

Sonny knew that for Walker, the doubt of how was the worst of it. Everything was pointing to an accidental overdose, but Walker would never quite believe that finding.

Her family would bury their Nevada Magdalena Maria Sanchez Blaine with a Catholic funeral, once the police released her body to them. Walker knew that Vada's grief-crazed daddy, full of misplaced blame and ebony hatred, wouldn't allow him anywhere near her actual funeral. So Walker had arranged his own service, held earlier this very day. Sonny hadn't been able to stay long.

He stared at the golden shot that Jonesy had just poured. Someone put a Freddy Fender song on the box and cracked the cue ball against the stripes and solids. Sonny took the shot all at once, needing something to take his mind away tonight. But he didn't feel the relief of being drunk yet, just hot numbness overlying his anger.

They'd had the memorial at the Sugar and Spice, closed to the public. Despite his green sobriety, Walker decided that the old bar was the best place for the service. It had once been his home. He and Vada had first kissed there, on the night of Sonny's eighteenth birthday. He had passed her audition for the King Bees on the Sugar and Spice's stage. They had fallen for each other in their little upstairs love nest.

For Walker's sake, Shookie and Prince made the liquor available only from a make-do bar in their office, keeping the bulk of the stock stored behind the after-hours cabinets. Sonny set up camp behind Shookie's desk, drinking more than his share, making up for the time he'd lost since he'd gotten home. Sonny had spent as much time as he could stand at Mama's, doing as she ordered, listening to Walker's woes. And what with Mama and Walker being AA disciples these days, there wasn't so much as a bottle of cooking sherry in her place.

At least Mama kept her TV tuned only to her stories, turning off at the news hour. Plus, she wouldn't allow Walker to watch "that vulgar MTV" in her house, which was a great blessing for Sonny. *The Girl Can't Help It* was on all the damn time. Biggest hit record they'd ever had, thanks to that stupid video. Sonny had never even watched the finished product all the way through. He knew he couldn't bear it, having only glanced at a portion of it: Cilla, moving like a harem girl, tarted up like a doe-eyed whore—tempting yet untouchable. Dark-haired Cilla who had been his. Almost his. Never really his.

Sonny forcibly twisted his mind back to Vada, back to the memorial. They had enlarged a stunning photo of her, shot at the height of her beauty. In the picture she was dressed in the red Bob Mackie gown that probation had not let her wear to the first Sterling Preston Blues Emergency Fund show. Her hair was tossed to the side, her dark eyes bewitching, and her magic crimson lips were smiling. Vada's left hand, perfectly manicured as always, was at her throat. That first purchase made from Walker's budding stardom, her wedding band, was clearly on display.

The Browns had placed a microphone and chair beside Vada's portrait. Walker's Goldie Strat was on a stand on the opposite side of the chair from her picture. Many friends and family came up to read, sing, play, and tell stories about Vada that made the assembled laugh and cry.

Last of all, Walker had taken his turn. Dressed in Johnny Cash black, he wore the suede hat and boots Vada had long ago had Uncle Charlie make for him. He'd picked up Goldie and sat down, adjusting the mike. He was still for a minute after he plugged in, attempting words a couple of times before he actually managed to speak. Finally, in a voice grief-broken, he rasped, "I always felt, Vada, that I never knew how to say what you meant to me. Good and bad times . . . I only had one way to show you. This is how I remember you, honey. It's how I always will."

Walker then played *Smitten*. He'd played it for Vada many times, when she'd stood below, watching him on this very stage. He'd played as foreplay, when they were alone. He played it for hundreds of thousands of fans a world away from her. But those who saw him at this memorial agreed—the classic love song, always moving, never was as Walker played it then. This time it was to honor his lost wife, and he poured his grief into the notes. He played it deeper than the darkest blues. Tonight, *Smitten* was a requiem—Vada's dirge.

Riley had to help Walker offstage when he was finished. Everyone in the house, except Sonny, was lost to tears.

Sonny had been desperate to split the service. He had made a lame excuse about getting something from the car. Once outside, Sonny had fled before anyone could stop him. He ran for this dive, where only Vada would have known to find him.

Sonny wanted to cry for Vada, for his loss. Since the day of Daddy Jim's funeral, when he was twelve, Sonny had not shed a tear. He was now convinced that he'd lost the ability to cry. Otherwise, Walker's heartbreaking version of *Smitten* would have surely done the trick.

The song on the juke changed to one of Sonny's favorites, the original of *Pancho and Lefty*. But this night, Townes Van Zandt's plaintive warble hit him like a grenade. He'd never before noticed how much the first verse described him—iron-skinned and kerosene-breathed, a free and empty road whore. He listened, seared by the high lonesome of Townes's tale of outlaws and losers.

He had to have another drink; oblivion had to be just around the corner. Jonesy had stepped into the back room to change kegs, so Sonny had to wait for another. The spooky ballad ended, and for a fleeting moment, Sonny felt relief flood through him. Something, anything, would be better than that mirror of his wasted life. But when the needle dropped, he heard his own, all-too-familiar lead line. Shit—the record was officially everywhere. He tried to hit the floor at a run, to get away from *The Girl Can't Help It*, from this bar and the memories it held of his dead sister-in-law.

Instead, Sonny tripped on the barstool, knocking himself cold. He learned later that he'd cracked a hairline fracture on his cheekbone as his face made contact with the filthy floor. Going down, he could have sworn he heard Vada's throaty laughter.

Later, he vaguely remembered Jonesy pouring ice water on his head to bring him to, telling him that he'd arranged him a ride. Did he want to go to the hospital? the trucker heading back toward Austin had asked. He'd hit the floor damned hard, after all, and he sure didn't mind dropping Sonny there. No, just home please, Sonny managed. He'd left Jonesy a fifty for his trouble. He'd done the same for the nameless Samaritan who'd gotten him to his house.

Once there, Sonny had passed out on his couch. It was dark—still? Again, probably. When he'd come to, his face was swollen and throbbed insanely. He'd eaten some painkillers, put an icepack on his cheek, and started to drink again. After a time the sharpest of the pain receded. He picked up the remote and started channel-surfing cable, jumping clean over MTV so he wouldn't dare see Vada's face on a news clip, or Cilla's in his video.

He stumbled upon something extraordinary as he ran through the channels. A station was showing *Bombshell*, the film that the Rockets had performed in at the start of their national career. He tuned in just as the opening credits started to roll. Seemed like a lifetime ago they'd done it.

Sonny leaned back and watched his young, vital self—the then recently christened Icestorm. He was little more than a boy, strong and supple in his killer threads, his best come-hither grin in place.

Sonny drank hysterically while he watched, not caring a lick about the dangerous combination of downs and booze he was brewing in his innards. He could scarcely believe that it was him dancing with the leading lady. Here was the proof, preserved for posterity. There had been a time when Sonny Blaine had been utterly confident. When Bonnell, his accent shrouded in deep Cajun, assured the hardscrabble leading man, "Don't mind that guitar picker dancing with your woman ... he's harmless," Sonny broke into crazed laughter. He felt a fool, all alone in the house, raving away like a madman until even through the numbing downers his body ached from it. Icestorm hadn't been harmless back then, no siree. He was ready to conquer the world. And his playing sounded sharp as a tack as he propelled the band along with his bone-cold Telecaster work.

When the movie ended, Sonny felt it had been sent to him as a sign. Despite the hour, and the fact that he could barely talk, what with his swollen face and drugged and drunken state, he'd called Bonnell. It took him a moment to make the sleep-slowed singer understand his mushy words, but he'd finally gotten it across that the band needed to start auditioning new guitarists for the tour. Bonnell didn't sound surprised, obviously protesting only to be polite. They both knew the time had come to part ways.

That done, Sonny stumbled off to his bed. He couldn't sleep. He lay awake, wondering what the fuck he was going to do now? He'd worked in music for close to a quarter century, plying his trade with uncompromising Texas blues. He might sit session work. Just here in Austin his living could be good. It had been a treat when he'd worked on Terry Joe McGowan's record many years ago. He could delve into other styles besides blues. Study with somebody, even.

Or maybe he'd hang it up instead. No reason he had to play. Let Walker do it for them both. Maybe he would go over to Walker's, next time the little maestro hit town. Sonny would dump all his gear on Mama's doorstep, then just walk away without a word to either of them. Hand all over to the worthier opponent. Long live the Crown fucking Prince.

But then what would he do with himself? Sonny lit a cigarette, considering the options. He was damn near forty, with little more than a compromised high school diploma and a few good recordings made. There were no big awards on his mantel, and certainly no pictures of a loving wife and kids. What he did had been more than enough for a good long time. Then he'd flown apart at the seams, over a stupid bitch, yet. Sonny knew that he had to find a way to pull himself back together or soon there would be nothing left to reassemble.

He woke up the next afternoon bearing a deep cigarette burn on his fretting hand. He'd been too far gone to rouse when it happened. The sheets and mattress beneath his hand had been scorched, too. Pure luck the whole house hadn't burned down around him.

31.

THEY WOULDN'T STOP knocking. Sonny finally surrendered, stumbling off the couch and dragging on a dirty pair of jeans. He opened the door to Ruby and Walker. Ruby clutched a big cooking pot in front of her like a shield. Walker was carrying a bag of groceries and his bottleneck-slide blue water. They smiled pleasantly, acting as though they hadn't been pounding at his door for a good ten minutes.

"Hey ho, Sugar-boy! Your little brother and I was visiting Uncle Charlie and Aunt Lucille, and we said, Why don't we drop by? I hope we didn't wake you."

Walker snorted, pushing Sonny aside and walking in. "Look at him. 'Course we woke him." Walker set the groceries on the kitchen counter, then handed Sonny the bottle of water. "And if you believe that Mama always carries an emergency ration of chicken and dumplings in my glove box, then you can believe we just happened by."

Ruby reached up and kissed Sonny's unshaven cheek. She blushed, slipping by without looking him in the eye. She headed into the kitchen, turning on the oven to preheat and putting the soup pot in the refrigerator.

Sonny noticed the state of his house for the first time in days. He'd always been a neat bachelor, even more so as he approached middle age. He never had much of a mess, in part because he never generated one. Even when home, he usually ate out. If he did entertain, it was green salad in walnut bowls, corn and steaks on the barbecue, and the mess created was vanquished right after dinner. Any chaos he produced was extinguished with an hour's tidying.

Now his place was the pits. Remnants of the sparse food he'd consumed of late were scattered everywhere, spoiling in oily wrappers. Ashtrays overflowed with cigarette butts and roaches. Sonny's dirty clothes lay where he dropped them, mixed in with a few things women left behind in haste, fleeing his postcoital meanness. The room was littered with beer bottles. Three empty whiskey bottles were on the kitchen counter, alongside a partly full fifth.

Sonny knew he must look at least as awful as the house. He hadn't been outside for a number of days, or showered, or shaved. He couldn't remember when he'd last changed clothes. His head was muffled with partying. He was beyond caring what Ruby made of his appearance—bad mannered of her not to call first.

Walker cocked his head sideways. He gave Sonny a long once-over.

"Truly hanging out, huh, bro? News caught up with me on the road that you up and quit the Rockets before the tour."

"Been a long time coming, Walker."

"Didn't say I was surprised, particularly. Heard they got Vada's old guitar player, Buddy."

"Yeah. I heard, too."

"Buddy's a good boy. Got to be tickled pink at finally playing at being you for real. He thinks you hung the moon by your own damn self." Walker stepped over the crap in the hallway and on into the living room. He held up a roach from an ashtray. "So, what's next for the Icestorm? More fine living? Better check with your service—I think *Lifestyles of the Rich and Famous* been trying to reach you."

"Why don't you fuck off?"

"Sonny! Uh, uh. Don't be ugly to your brother," Ruby reprimanded from behind a clatter of pans in the kitchen.

"Sorry, Mama," Sonny said. He pulled Walker into the hall. "No one asked you to come. Take her and get out."

"I can't. I came by to ask you a favor."

"What kind of favor?"

"Need you to come somewhere with me, in just a few minutes. I got to give a speech at this thing. But I hate public speaking."

"You're a goddamn performer. You'll handle it."

"It's different with my guitar, Real and Outlaw riding shotgun. This is a smaller, much tougher crowd than I'm used to." Walker laughed a little. "Ain't a soul going to hold up lighters for an encore."

"What, are you doing a guitar clinic?"

Walker shook his head. "Not quite. Now look. Go get a damn shower, get presentable. Mama's going to cook dinner while we're gone."

"I ain't budging until you tell me where we're off to."

"Ah, come on, Sonny. Where's your sense of adventure? Not like you can claim to be rushing off on tour this time."

"Asshole."

Walker smacked Sonny's back. "You hear Mama—don't be ugly to your brother. She'll wash that mouth of yours out with soap, you don't watch it." Walker sniffed. "Way you smell, you could use it." He laughed loud, pushing Sonny toward the john.

Sonny felt better after a shower and a shave. He managed to find some clean jeans and a T-shirt. He combed his 'do back—his hair wouldn't set up quite right, as it was a lot longer than usual. He let a good portion of it fall over his brow. Feeling a little guilty about it, he slipped out a vial, doing a couple of blasts to wake himself up. He stashed the rest in his boot for later, just like Walker used to. Now he was ready for nearly anything Walker could throw at him.

When he came out, Walker had made some progress straightening the living room. He had the clothes dumped into a pile on the chair, the empties and food wrappers tossed, the roaches preserved in a discreet ashtray on the wall unit, the cigarette butts trashed. In the now-shiny kitchen Ruby was cutting vegetables for a chop salad. On the stove a pot of chicken broth simmered. Sonny could also smell something brown and rich baking.

"Mama, you did not make a Karo nut pie while I was in the shower." She nodded that she had. "You're too good to me."

"Wasn't nothing, Sugar-boy," she told him, coming out from the kitchen to hug him. "I miss you so. You didn't even call and tell your own mama that you'd left the band—Walker had to. But, never mind that. You look better after bathing." She pinched his side. "But you're skin and bones, baby. Good food's cooking, though. Now, you run along with Walker." She waved Sonny away, the way she'd dismissed him as a child. "We'll have a nice supper fixed when ya'll get back. Just show me how to turn on my stories on TV. I'll be happy as all get out."

Walker was whistling, strutting as they headed for his Corvette. Sonny slid into the freshly waxed car—comfortable ride. He watched Walker amble around to the driver's seat. His hair had grown nearly waist length but was fluffy and clean, shining auburn in the sun. He wore a smartly tailored corduroy jacket in maroon, with black slacks and a matching crewneck sweater. He had on the black suede hat and boots that Vada had given him. His appearance now made Sonny realize how accustomed he'd grown to Walker's former self—filthy and stoned.

Sonny turned his face skyward, wanting to feel the breeze on his skin. "Put the top down."

"Nah. My hat'll come off."

Sonny laughed. "So take it off, fool! Damn, what you want? A chin strap like we had when we were kids?"

"That'd do. Still, I hate the way your hair flies forward in a convertible. I know I dropped out of high school, but I don't get the physics behind that."

"I solved the problem," Sonny said, slipping his comb out and dragging it across the side of his head, *Route 66*–style. "A little dab'll do ya."

"Yeah, well, not all of us is blessed with your artful bone structure, Sonny. They'd break and run if I tried your 'do. Plus, my hairline ain't getting any lower."

"You going bald, Walker?"

"Didn't say that. But I ain't getting a lot hairier, neither."

Sonny slapped at the hat on Walker's head. "Maybe you should let your head breathe. It'd reseed if it saw sunlight."

"Sound theory," Walker cracked, pulling up to idle at a stoplight. "I feel naked without the *sombrero*, anymore." Two girls in the next car peered admiringly at the Corvette. Then they glanced up and saw Walker and Sonny. They mouthed Walker's stage name. He touched the brim with his hand toward them, smiling. "Besides, you think I'd get that kind of reaction without this? Just be another homely Texas boy. Also a good reason to keep the convertible. The women dig it."

"Making time these days, Walker?"

"Pretty much just with one lady. Now I know you ain't been talking to Mama. She'd tell you flat out my girl's way too young for me."

"Well? Is she?"

"Yeah, probably. She's eighteen." Walker glanced over, and upon seeing Sonny's grin, held up a hand, blushing. "She's older than her years, Sonny."

"Sure she is. Cradle robber."

"It ain't like that. She's like us. She's been working since she was, like, fourteen. Traveled the world."

"Oh, yeah? She a singer?"

"No . . . a lingerie model."

"Well, damn, Walker! Why didn't you say so?" Sonny laughed hard and real. He realized it was the first time anything had struck him as funny in weeks. "What's this model's name?"

"Salome Ross. You probably seen her pictures one time or another. You'll meet her in a few. She should be where we're headed. Look but don't touch, you hear?" Walker pulled the car into the lot of a convenience store. "Pit stop first."

Sonny watched as Walker walked in, pausing to toss a couple of bills to the homeless guy stationed at the door. He wished he could ask Walker to pick up a "road kit"—what they used to call a six-pack drunk in transit. Out of the question, of course. He instead bent down, making like he was looking for something on the floor. Stooped, he snorted a stout blast from his boot vial. He sat up, checking his lip in the rearview mirror for tattletale traces of coke. He rubbed the residual powder onto his gums. He was starting to feel a little human, his edge and energy scooting into place. If only he had one beer. . . .

When Walker returned, he threw a paper bag at Sonny. No beer. Cigarettes, a pint of half and half, and ten packs of Sweet Tarts. "Jesus, Walker. We expecting trick or treaters?"

"That's for me. I crave sugar all the time now I'm not drinking. Alcohol turns to sugar in the blood—it's a common side effect." Walker tore open a pack with his teeth. He held out the bag to Sonny. "Want some?"

"Never been too keen on candy."

"If you stopped drinking, that'd change." They headed uptown, finally pulling up in front of their Mama's church. "Here we be, Sonny."

"Church? It ain't even Sunday . . . is it?" Sonny realized he wasn't certain what day of the week it was.

"It's Wednesday, man," Walker said gently, touching Sonny's shoulder.

"Wednesday. Sure." Sonny shrugged him off. "Seems to me you'd be one to steer clear of churches."

Walker frowned, putting the car in park. "What makes you say so?"

"I just . . . I don't know. I mean, you ain't exactly Pat Boone."

This made Walker laugh. "Nowadays, some folks might think I am. Come on in, Sonny."

Sonny trailed Walker across the lot to a fellowship hall. When they walked in, Sonny saw they had it set up for a class. A number of people sat around visiting, drinking coffee and smoking. A few faces Sonny recognized. He spotted the Serenity Prayer painted on the wall, next to a banner, with the Twelve Steps and AA outlined in cheesy silver paint. He grabbed Walker's arm, pulling him back toward the door. "No you don't," he hissed. "No, sir. I didn't say I'd come to this."

"Yeah, you did," Walker said mildly. "This is where I got to do my talk. You said you'd lend me moral support, right? Well, that's all you're here for. Now, come back in. Meet my girl, Salome."

Sonny could feel the coke bouncing around his bloodstream, making his flared anger and wild heartbeat worse. He felt as if every one in the room knew he was loaded and holding, so he didn't make a scene. He followed Walker back in, staring at the floor. Several people greeted Walker, shaking hands, applauding when he held up the pint of cream like a beacon. Walker glanced back at Sonny, saying, "They kid me about putting on airs, bringing half-and-half when we got Cremora. But I can't get into the powder stuff. Looks too much like one of my bad old habits." A guy pouring coffees laughed, giving Walker a high-five.

Walker tapped the shoulder of a tall, splendid woman leaning on the coffee table. "Look who came with, Salome."

She cooed, leaning over to kiss Walker. Her complexion was a tasty desert brown. Perfect cheekbones were high and sculpted, framed by a straight Cleopatra bob. Her eyes were wide-set, giving her an innocent air, and her mouth was heart-shaped and full. She had a figure, voluptuous but slim, that revealed her trade. Sonny had indeed seen her picture, believed she was once even in *SI*'s swimsuit issue. After greeting Walker, Salome extended a hand to Sonny. "Welcome, Sonny. Your brother told me so much about you. We're all supposed to act cool here, like we don't know each other from Adam. But I have to confess that I'm a big fan of your music."

"Told you we had a lot in common," added Walker, grinning.

Salome linked arms with Sonny. He surrendered to her expert manipulation—what the hell. "You come sit by me," she told him. "Together, we'll give Walker moral support. He hates when he has to speak at these things." She eased down into the chair between the brothers, her thin cotton jumpsuit hugging every one of her curves. With her moneymaking smile she advised, "Just relax, baby—go with the flow."

Relaxing was out of the question. Sonny did do his best not to attract any attention to himself. Even coked out, distanced, he could feel palpable warmth among these people. Some had known each other since the bad old days. Some had apparently met first in meetings.

One other man was new to the room—bloated, broken, and ragged. He told them that his wife and kids had walked out the day before. He didn't know where else to turn. The others assured him he was welcome here.

They began with a chapter from the Big Book, written by AA co-founder Bill W. Except for Sonny and the other new guy, they all took turns reading the opening chapter. It outlined Bill's own trials, and the origins of the program. After the readings, several people took the floor, telling their stories, or a portion thereof. Sonny was surprised to find himself moved by some tales. Other stories were darkly funny enough to make him laugh.

Walker was the last of the speakers. He stood up, tipped his hat, and took a deep breath. "Hi. I'm Walker, and I'm an alcoholic/addict." He smiled at them all before going on. "I'm not very good at this. How to start? Where I started, I reckon. Stealing sips from Daddy's whiskey back in grade school. I dug the buzz, can't lie about it. I also liked that drinking made me feel less shy. Less like a geek beside my perfect older brother. Them days, no one even saw me if Sonny was in the room. That went double time for the girls.

"Then Sonny started playing guitar. He was really amazing, right off the bat." Walker gave Sonny a nervous smile. "Pretty quick I knew—hey, that's what I want to do, too. But Sonny wasn't one to share." People laughed. Some turned to smile at Sonny. He stared down at his own clenched hands. "Sonny thought I was just getting his gear to mess with it. Everybody did. He'd beat the shit out of me for playing his guitar." More laughter. Salome squeezed Sonny's arm. Walker went on, "Man, them beatings pissed me off! But what was I going to do? I was too little to do more than just squall about it—still am."

As the chuckles subsided, Walker paused. He went on in a quieter voice, low and serious. "I wasn't just fooling with his stuff, not even the first time I picked it up. I knew I could be as good as Sonny." He put his fist to his chest. "It burned in me, like nothing else ever has. What Sonny didn't get at the time, what no one got, was this—I didn't have a choice. I had to play—had to! Plus, it was my only way to compete with him. But still, he stayed a step ahead. Wherever I went, he'd been, he'd played. Folks treated me like a copycat for a long, long time."

Walker scowled, holding his hands out in front of him, as if he were kneading bread. "So ... I had to push it—to the max. Trickier, louder, tougher, I strove for it, big-time—but not just in my music. Sonny can party hard. I wanted to show I could keep up. I even married the hardest-partying woman in this town. My brother'd been there first, too. I didn't care. Not too much, anyway.

"I loved my wife. Her and me fed off each other, good and bad. Good, with our music. Bad, with the drinking and drugging. I stayed at the party until I broke to pieces, far away from home. I almost bled to death, body and soul. And I know most of ya'll know where the party took Vada." Walker's voice cracked. He paused, dipping his face behind the hat, hand over his eyes.

Salome reached out a hand to his. He took it, beginning again, his voice slowly regaining strength. "I still feel the pain of losing Vada—always will, I guess. I couldn't stop her from killing herself. Sometimes . . . lots of times, I want to drink that pain away. Or numb it through my nose. But if I kill the pain thataway, I'll reap more and worse later. Thanks to all of you here, and to all the groups on the road, and Floyd, my sponsor, I'm making it. So far, so good."

Walker looked directly at Sonny. "Let me tell you something. Simple as this sounds, it's not. But it can work—if you give yourself over to it, admit how powerless you are. Turn it over to God. Reach out for help. It don't come easy at all." He turned his eyes to the other new guy, the broken man. "You ain't going to like a lot of what you have to face up to. But you can do it. A day at a time is all it takes." Walker took off his hat, shaking out his hair. He held up the hat, pointing to a small pin on the crown. "I was so proud the day I got this. Meant more to me than all the gold records and awards littering my house. It's my one-year pin. My first 525,600 minutes of sobriety pin—not that I'm counting." People laughed again. Walker smiled, dropping the hat back into place. "I'm working on year two. And I want to reach out to anybody that needs help. They come to me at shows, sometimes. On the street, too. I try to tell them how this helped me, how ya'll did. Anyway . . . thanks. That's all I got to say."

Walker sat. Salome kissed his cheek. Sonny tried to catch Walker's eye, but Walker wasn't buying. The meeting rounded up quickly afterward. Walker made his way over to the broken man, sitting with him, talking in a serious, soothing tone. Someone came up and started chatting with Salome. Sonny scurried to the bathroom and did a little more blow. He put on his shades and wandered out to the coffee table to wait, sucking up a cup with Walker's cream. Dropping a few dollars into a donation basket, he turned to the wall and read the instructions on the fire extinguisher to avoid talking to anyone. Someone tapped him on the shoulder anyway.

He turned, expecting Walker. Instead, he was facing Nancy Ruth. Her hair was a lighter blonde, dyed now, and pulled up in a scarf. She wore an expensive pair of navy slacks and a matching sweater set, with a strand of pearls at her throat. She was heavier through the hips and bottom than Sonny remembered, but she was still quite pretty.

"Hello, Sonny. It's been a long time. Good to see you here." Her voice sounded less country than he recalled. She extended her hand to him. Sonny took it tentatively. He had not touched her since the night they had made Otis.

"I didn't see you come in, sugar."

"Oh, I was running late, as always." She arched her brows, smiling. "Better late than never, don't you think?"

Sonny smirked, shaking his head. "Bet that's one of them sayings just full of meaning for ya'll teetotalers, ain't it?" She smiled back, more warmly than he, not answering. He went on, "Walker brought me. He didn't say where we were going, or else I wouldn't be here. I thought we was headed to a guitar clinic or some shit."

"That so, Sonny?" Nancy Ruth said, a little of Mingus slipping back into her voice. "Well, Walker brought me to my first meeting, too." She shrugged. "Next thing I knew, I was doing ninety meetings in ninety days. I get my one-year pin, God willing, next month. I'm a better mama to Otis these days, that's for sure." She checked her watch. "Speaking of Otis, I've got to pick him up from school." She turned to go but paused, studying Sonny's face. "He looks like you, my boy. You should come see him. He is very curious about you. He has all of your records." She nodded goodbye, heading toward where Walker and the pony-tailed coffee guy counseled the new man. Walker paused in his ministering, kissing Nancy Ruth's cheek.

A few minutes later, Walker gathered up his brother. He walked outside ahead of Sonny, quick, nervous, like he was trying to keep cool knowing a mugger shadowed him. Walker opened a pack of candy before he started the car. He put a tape in the deck, some harmonica-driven juke. Sonny couldn't recall the song's name. Walker finally spoke after he drove a few blocks. "Thanks for coming with, Sonny. Hope I didn't pick on you too hard."

"Not too hard." Sonny watched Walker chomping candy and bopping to the tune as he drove. He looked like a kid again. "You didn't really feel like that back when, like you had to compete with me all the time?"

"It ain't so strange. It's typical brother stuff, right?"

"Yeah. I reckon. But it's . . . silly. I wasn't trying to show you up."

Walker glanced over, nodding, grinning. "I know that now. Might listen to your own self now and then. You make good sense, Sonny."

Soon they turned into Sonny's driveway. "Let's go in and eat. I'm starving," Walker said, jumping from the car. The food waiting for them was down-home gourmet. Ruby seemed happy, better than she'd been since Big Billy Jay died. She was waiting on her sons to the point of absurdity, laughing and talking trivialities. She didn't mention the meeting. The coke had pretty much worn off, and Sonny ate himself nearly sick. He didn't realize how much he missed good food until he tasted some. When they finished, Ruby wouldn't let them help clean up. She shooed them into the backyard.

They sat together on the porch swing, both pushing off with their right leg in a slow, even rhythm. Walker stretched, groaning, "She's a hell of a cook."

"Sure enough."

"So . . . what you been up to, bro? Looking for a new band? Time come for you to lead one?"

"I burned my fretter with a smoke, night I left the Rockets." He held it up, showing Walker the still-red scar on his index finger. "It's okay now, but. . . . I ain't touched my guitar since."

Walker swung his face to Sonny's. He looked genuinely stunned. "No kidding? I can hardly believe it. Why, as kids, you played whenever you got a chance."

"Yeah. Back then. Now, I can't seem to. . . ." Sonny trailed off, unsure what he was going to say. Can't seem to play? More like he couldn't seem to do much of anything.

Walker sat still for a moment, waiting to see if Sonny would finish his thought. He finally said, "Everyone needs a break. Even if we love what we do. I didn't touch my ax the whole time I was hospitalized. Mama brought Old Broad to me in rehab, but I just stared at it. And then I got scared that maybe I couldn't play anymore. But nope, it was like riding a bike." He cupped his hand to his left ear. "Sounded better straight. My bad ear don't bother me as much as it used to either, buzzing and all."

"Great."

"So, what's it going to be, Sonny? What's happening with you? You thinking about writing music? Catching up with friends and family? Fixing up your cars?"

"None of the above."

"Maybe it's time to take a little inventory, bro."

Sonny let go a short, bitter laugh. "Trouble is, ain't much to inventory."

"Probably more than you give yourself credit for." Walker stood in front of Sonny. "Sonny, look. I don't know what happened to you while I was in rehab. You changed, though. I don't think you just seem different to me because I'm straight. Something really left marks on your soul." Walker leaned over to look him in the eye. Sonny pushed himself back into the bench. He wanted to keep as far as he could get from this probing stare without actually picking up and bolting. "I know you won't talk to me about it. But you could. Ain't nothing I would judge you for. I been there and done that—worse and more, in fact."

"Pretty safe bet."

Walker straightened up and walked down the porch steps. He searched around the overgrown backyard for pebbles. He picked up a handful and started tossing them at the monster oak that grew in Sonny's yard. "Just don't let the scarring tear up your good parts. That's what you got to be careful of." Walker paused, aimed, shot a rock at the tree. "So . . . I think we should make plans. I finally got time home, a good stretch, come December. Let's have some fun."

"Fun."

"Yeah. Let's get in the studio, lay some stuff down. Start on our record."

"No."

Walker scattered what he had left of his pebbles into the grass. "No? Just like that, no? How many times are we both going to be home, able to do this? I bet we don't have to fool much with the label. Rollie will cut you loose, since the Rockets got Buddy in the band. I could get you a sweet deal with Twelve Bar. Same label, no conflicts."

"Don't do me no favors."

Walker turned from the yard, his face surprised. "I'm doing the label a favor, if I'm doing anybody one. Rewarding Sterling's kindness over the years by hand-delivering a great talent to him. They get you in transition. Then, once you decide what to do, they get all your great new stuff. Meantime, they got us both on the same record. What more could they want?"

Sonny thought back to the Christmas, almost two years gone, when they had sat alone in the home Walker had shared with Vada, playing together for the pleasure of it. They'd had fun until Walker hurt his hand and spilled the nasty truth about Vada . . . and Cilla. He couldn't bear thinking about either woman. Just so their faces wouldn't float into his mind, he looked back to Walker's hopeful eyes and said, "Maybe we could do a few songs. Don't make me decide this second."

"Fair enough." Walker sat back down on the swing. He lowered his voice when he spoke again. "How about this idea, Sonny? Why not try doing the record straight?"

Sonny jumped up, heading toward the door. "Fuck you, Walker. Don't think because I sat through that stupid meeting I—"

Walker caught Sonny's arm, stopping him. "Cool your jets. Just listen. Man, you ever played a show sober, could you help it? I know I didn't before I stopped. See this?" He pointed to his one-year pin on his hat. "Before this I didn't think I could perform straight. Now it's like I rediscovered everything I loved. Feels like my fire's been stoked with new and better fuel."

Walker led Sonny back to the bench and went on in a quiet voice. "The first time I started a performance without a thing in me, I about died. Scared shitless. I thought I might jump ship. But when the lights came up, I could make out a joyful face or two, hear them cheering—not just some wasted roaring blur. I can't begin to tell you how good that was—beyond the best.

"Look, the meetings, like we went to today, are great for keeping focused. But you been at it a long time. Let's get a doctor to help you dry out. The place I went really helped me. Now, it's rough—no doubt about it.

They make you not only get clean, but want you to talk about the crap that helped feed your addictions. It hurts a lot. But you get rid of some of that pent-up pain. Trust me on that."

Sonny sat quiet for a long time, a snatch of Townes Van Zandt's poetry circling inside his iron skin, the hard and bitter shell in which he'd encased himself. He whispered, "Them places cost an arm and a leg. I don't got insurance, and I ain't exactly gainfully employed. Who knows where my next paycheck comes from?"

"From our record!" Walker laughed a little, then added, nearly whispering, "Don't worry about the money, bro. I got money enough."

"I can't let you pay for this."

"Why not? Remember back when I was a kid, you wanted to give me money to fix it when I thought I got Nancy Ruth pregnant? You didn't worry about it—you just wanted to help me. 'I got money from the record,' you said to me. Only thing different this time is I'm the one with money from the record."

Sonny jumped when Walker took his hand, trying to pull away. Walker didn't turn loose, only gripped tighter with his mighty left fretter. "Sonny, getting clean takes guts. You got them in spades, man. You just don't realize it yet. I love you too much to sit back and watch you kill yourself." Then Walker's hand pulled away, like a benediction. "Please, man. Let me help you."

IV CROSSROADS

1.

CILLA WAS STILL in her stage clothes, postperformance sticky and hot, when there was a knock at her dressing room door. Her assistant Trudy poked her head in, a big smile on her young face. "Hon, you have special guests asking after you. Floyd Montgomery and his wife are here. Eddie Finger, too."

"Floyd Montgomery?" Cilla sat, yanking off her cowboy boots.

"Don't you know who he *is*?" The girl shut the door behind her, whispering, all aflutter. "He was in Icestorm Blaine's first band. Eddie was their drummer! 'Course, Floyd co-wrote some of the best Salamander songs with Firewalker."

"Trudy, I know who Floyd is," Cilla replied, turning to let the girl unzip her green leather dress, the one given to her by the Rockets for dancing in their video. She slipped it off and gave it to Trudy to hang up. "I just wasn't expecting anyone to come back tonight." Certainly she hadn't expected Eddie and the Montgomerys. Why were they in Dallas?

"They just want to say howdy and give you compliments on the show."

"Invite them in, of course. Offer them drinks and some of those sandwiches the kitchen sent us. I'll be out just now."

Grinning wide, Trudy raced out of the small room. She was a sweet kid, a Dallas native who knew her way around both the city and an appointment book. Cilla took off her bra and toweled down as best she could—it would have to do until she got home and showered. She doused herself with powder before she pulled on a pair of jeans and a TEXAS RANGERS T-shirt. Might as well pull the green cowboy boots back on, too—when in Texas, after all.

She'd been in Dallas for a couple of months, having followed her fiancé, Mickey, when the Rangers optioned him. She had spent most of the time since unpacking and acclimating to the oppressive heat and humidity. She'd begun to adjust to the climate, even if her hair still hadn't. She now understood fully why the slicked back 'do and the helmet head hadn't gone extinct hereabouts. Other than the dampness, she rather liked the change Texas offered her. She loved the people, especially the ones who'd made up her audience at the few high-end club gigs she'd played. Tonight had been the best of the shows yet. The band had really been on fire. The crowd had been filled with dancers who could have been extras in an Alan Freed musical.

Cursing the insubordination of her sweat-drenched hair, Cilla pulled it tight into a ponytail. As she applied lipstick and perfume, she remembered the drive she'd taken to Mingus recently. When Mickey went off with the ball club, she'd grown bored with unpacking. On pure impulse she'd jumped in her Jag and hit the road, map in hand. Once she'd left Fort Worth's suburbs on I-80, there was nothing but wide-spot-in-the-road towns and great expanses of flatness taken up by ranches and farms. Only low-slung buildings and insectlike water towers broke the horizon. The vast sky spooked her somehow, made her crave the cradling mountains of the West.

The old, buckshot MINGUS CITY LIMITS sign bore an addendum—*Birthplace of the Blaine Brothers*. She'd stopped to snap a picture of it, as she was certain others had before her. A little heart-heavy with the thought of Sonny and Walker, she wondered if they knew of the sign. She doubted they'd been to the place since they'd buried Big Billy Jay.

Mingus was a dying town, if it had ever been fully alive in the first place. It was the kind of place a person was born planning to leave. She'd driven around some, wondering which of the rundown houses had been the Blaines' boyhood home. Downtown, she'd spotted the Montgomery's John Deere dealership, and had come across the Velvet Sundae Drive-In, a burger stand Walker and Sonny had both cited as their teenage hangout.

She'd gone inside the restaurant. It was long after lunch rush on a school day. All that was there was a bored-looking soda jerkette, her frosted blonde bangs stiff with spray. A young and lanky wrangler, the counter-girl's sweetheart, was chatting her up, perched on a stool. They both said howdy. Cilla ordered a Fudge Velvet Sundae Deluxe—the specialty of the house.

While the girl built the treat, Cilla spotted two pictures on the wall. One was of the White Tornadoes. They were schoolboys still, posing in front of this place with silly grins, having not yet adopted the requisite rocker's pout. A slicker, signed shot from Walker's first days of national fame—pout in evidence—hung next to the Tornadoes picture. As she picked up her sundae, the boyfriend gave Cilla a meaningful once-over and a slow smile that reminded her of Sonny. The kid received a smack from his little queenie for his trouble.

While Cilla ate, a couple of real cowboys came in and ordered burger baskets, tipping their Stetsons to her. No one seemed to know who she was, other than not one of them. They didn't even seem curious as to why she was there, as did people in some of the small towns she had passed through on tour buses. She realized people probably stopped through now and again because of the Blaines' connection to this place.

She finished the ice cream and left. Driving back toward Dallas, she'd suddenly been overtaken by tears. Seeing Mingus had made her ache for the brothers—made her long to have known them as the driven boys they'd been, full of the talent and ambition that had taken them far from home. Maybe she cried too for something less tangible—for a birthplace that celebrated her, as Mingus did the Blaines.

In the dressing room Cilla took a deep breath, bracing herself for the unexpected company. She emerged into the club's green room to find her band hanging out, eating and flirting with a couple of giggling girls they'd asked backstage. Julia Jean, Floyd's pretty wife, and a slightly balding, pudgy fellow she took to be Eddie Finger were talking with Trudy. Julia Jean greeted Cilla like they were long lost sisters, full of compliments. Eddie praised her, too, dipping his head in shy fashion, shaking her hand. Cilla didn't see Floyd, though. She asked after him.

"He's out in the hall still," Julia Jean said. "We got more company with us, but they didn't want me telling."

"Oh?"

"Sonny and Walker are waiting, too," Eddie told her.

Her legs turned buttery at the news. "You're . . . kidding."

"Sure as shooting, we're not!" Julia Jean exclaimed. "This trip was their idea. Came all the way here just to see you play." Leaning in and lowering her voice, she added, "Frankly, hon, they both seem nervous as cats in a roomful of rockers. That's why we left Floyd out there, to keep them from stampeding. Walker said that they'd leave, no fuss, if you didn't want to see them. Be sad to disappoint them, coming all this way just to say howdy, huh?"

"Of course. Please—ask them in."

Cilla's heart pounded like a bass drum pedal as Floyd and the brothers entered. Floyd greeted her warmly, taking her hand and smiling broad. The brothers hung back behind him. Cilla glanced toward Sonny, taking in his familiar biker jacket, worn open over a FREE CHUCK BERRY T-shirt. She avoided his eyes. She was still haunted by their last face-to-face the night of the video party, and the black hatred she'd seen in him.

She turned her attention instead to Walker. His head was lowered, hidden by his hat brim. He wore a gray and white serape that she'd seen on him in the cover shot of *Harder Than It Looks*. Clinching her teeth, she tried to smile as he raised his head.

He smiled back. It was wrong, the smile. It wasn't Walker's. There was no mistaking that sidelong high-calorie grin. Even though a trimmed goatee framed his mouth, and his hair was almost to his shoulders, Sonny was under that hat. Startled, she swiveled her eyes to the man she'd mistaken for Sonny. She saw now that he was too small, all but swallowed by the biker jacket. The FREE CHUCK BERRY T-Shirt he wore hung loose on his slim frame. Plus, she saw now that he wore a Black Panthers–style beret that Sonny wouldn't be caught dead in.

If that didn't beat all—they were dressed as each other.

"Hey, Cill," Walker said. His voice, nearly a whisper, was tremulous. "Ya'll sounded great tonight."

She let go a high-pitched yelp. Words tumbled out of her. "Walker! Are you trying to be Kyle Reagan in that horrid old shirt and . . . that is Sonny's jacket, isn't it?" Walker nodded, smiling a little. Cilla let go a real laugh. "Sonny—good God, look at you! If that damned getup is any indication of what sobriety and leaving the Rockets has done to you, you'd better reconsider!"

The others in the room joined Cilla in her laughter. Scowling, Sonny snatched the beret from Walker's head and slapped the Zorro hat back where it rightfully belonged. "There. The universe is back in balance," he muttered.

"Thanks, bro. Do feel more natural." Walker was still talking in a soft, quaky voice. He dropped the beret with useless fingers as Sonny handed it back to him. Walker hadn't moved or taken his eyes off Cilla.

Cilla nodded. "That does look better." Still shaken, but aware she had an audience, she took a step toward Sonny. "Clint? Do you perchance have a six-gun under that poncho?"

The crowd busted up again with laughter. Red-faced, Sonny stripped off the serape, throwing it on the floor. In short order he'd reclaimed his leather jacket. He darted into the dressing room that Cilla had recently occupied. She could see him before the mirror, back-combing his long hair into something vaguely resembling his trademark pompadour.

Cilla peered at Walker, muttering, "You know, you're a very strange man."

"Now, girl. We just didn't want to cause a stir at your show. No one recognized us got up like this." He smirked in Sonny's direction. "Just thought Sonny was another Firewalker wannabe, you know?"

Sonny rolled his eyes. "You and your stupid ideas."

"Hey, Cilla?" Eddie yelped. "Ask Sonny if he's buying tonight! I think he's got—" here Floyd joined him "—*a fistful of dollars!*" They high-fived each other, laughing their fool heads off.

"Ya'll quit teasing Sonny, now. I think he looked cute," Julia Jean cooed.

"Cute. That's what I strive for, you know—cute," Sonny growled, eyes narrowed at Walker. Walker kept his eyes on Cilla, but he chuckled a little in response.

"If you would only leave your hat at home, Walker, no one would have looked twice at you," said Cilla.

"Like I didn't try to tell him that?" Sonny said.

Shaking her head, Cilla went to the little refreshment table, pouring a generous glass of wine. Eddie joined her in one. The other visitors grabbed sandwiches and soft drinks. Floyd and Eddie sat down with Cilla's bassist, Danny. Sonny wandered over near them, shaking Danny's hand. They apparently knew each other from Dallas clubs, back in Sonny's White Tornadoes era. Julia Jean talked with one of the girls.

Cilla took a deep breath, drawing closer to Walker. "What the hell are you doing here?" she asked, straight out.

"We like your new album," he told her. "Just wanted to see what you was putting down live."

"If that was all, you'd have waited until I played Austin. Neither of you would have come all this way, dragging along Eddie and the Montgomerys, if you didn't have an agenda. Care to enlighten me?"

"You can see right through us, huh?" Walker answered, his voice still mild. He glanced at Sonny. Though standing near his fellow Tornadoes, Sonny's gaze was fixed on them. He was listening in. He gestured at Walker to continue. "Maybe you heard a rumor Sonny and me was making an album?"

She had heard something to that effect but had written it off merely to rumor. "People have been saying that for years—wishful thinking again, I figured."

"Not this time, girl."

"Really? Congratulations to you both." She smiled at Sonny. He gave a short nod in return, his eyes guarded.

"Yeah. It's been really cool," Walker said. His voice rose a little, showing his excitement with the project. "So far, we just been choosing material, rehearsing and writing together. But we're ready to lay down stuff right quick. We want to include old friends—" Walker nodded at Eddie and Floyd— "make a thing not Rockets or Salamanders, but just whatever the hell we're feeling now."

"Sounds really great. I can't wait to hear it."

"We hoped you'd say that—huh, Sonny?"

Sonny nodded at her again.

"See, we want some nice female vocals on a cut or two," Walker went on. "Need a bassist, too—don't want to have to do everything ourselves. You did some of the bass work on your latest, right? And sat bass on your daddy's new record, too?"

She nodded. So here was the answer—they'd driven all this way just to talk to her about playing on a record. A little ball of disappointment settled in her belly—strictly business. Draining her wine glass, Cilla listened carefully as Walker revealed more details about the project.

2.

"SHE'LL DO IT," Walker said as he drove Sonny's Fury southbound on I-35. "It's like a job interview. She got to play kind of coy at first."

Sonny hooted, "What do you know about a damn *job interview*? You never went on a job interview in your life."

Walker laughed sheepishly. "Ain't it the truth? But Salome goes on interviews, for shoots."

"Right. Like they actually care what Salome's got to say. They just want to see if she's got the goods."

Walker didn't say anything for a minute. When he did speak, he sounded cross. "I hate her job. Posing in her *chones* like she does? Guys jerk off with them catalogs she does, you know."

"No shit?" Sonny chuckled, making a crude motion with his fist. "Never occurred to me."

Walker grimaced, but then let go a snarling laugh. "She don't like what I do for a living much, either."

"Sounds like trouble in paradise to me."

"No, it ain't like that, Sonny. It's just . . . women, you know?"

Sonny nodded—acting like he knew shit about women. He muttered, "It was damn convenient Salome wasn't with us tonight."

"Salome's on a shoot in New York, Sonny."

"I know. Just convenient timing, is all I'm saying."

Walker lit a cigarette, smoking half of it before he spoke again. "Cilla ever tell you about when I walked out on her?" Sonny didn't answer. Walker took another drag off the cigarette. On the exhale, he said, "When ya'll did the video, ya'll hung out a lot, right?"

"Yeah. But she was married then, remember?" Sonny lit his own cigarette. He cracked his window, letting the chilly wind blow into his face. "She needed a friendly ear. And Bonnell was coming on to her like crazy."

Walker grunted, "That fool always bugged the hell out of her."

They drove in silence for a few miles. Sonny tried not to think of Cilla. It wasn't easy. Walker had on a stupid cassette—full of longing love songs that Sonny wished would end. But car rules were solid between them—whoever drove got full tune-choosing privileges.

"You seemed pretty uptight tonight yourself, Sonny," Walker said at last.

"Maybe because I was dressed so goofy," Sonny snorted. Walker didn't answer, or laugh. Sonny was about ready to tell him that he was just kidding, not to be hurt, when Walker spoke up again.

"You slept with her."

Sonny let out a sigh. He filled his voice with a threat so subtle that his little brother was likely the only person on earth who could catch it there. "Walker? Just drop it, man."

Walker didn't answer right at first. Finally he said, "Okay." Soon he started singing under his breath. When the tape ended, he reached around in the dark for another. "Changing the subject—what do you make of that pitcher she's with?"

"He's a real dick."

"Ain't he? I mean, he ain't no crooner, but she got herself another damn Dago Yankee. Goddamn jock."

Cilla's sweetheart had arrived in the green room a few minutes after the brothers' entrance. Mickey Canttoni was fresh from a late-inning game, crowing his victory. Undeniably handsome and well muscled, Mickey towered over everybody in the room and moved with a panther's grace. Cilla seemed happy to see him, giving him a sound hug and kiss. Mickey treated her decently enough from what Sonny could tell, but kept her barely a hand's reach away: his property. Typical athlete, Sonny thought. Used to strong-arming and competing his way through the world.

They had gone over to Mickey and Cilla's house for a small after-show party. The couple had just rented a place in Highland Park until the end of the baseball season. Canttoni had on display a number of his awards and pictures, but there were none of Cilla's. It looked as though he had rented all of the furnishings—the vibe of the place was heavy, masculine. Trying to wander away from the others without being obvious, Sonny had come across a crate of Cilla's records. They were placed on the floor in a little alcove, next to her stereo. He was squatting, flipping through the albums, when he sensed someone come up from behind. He turned his head, expecting Walker. It was Cilla.

"Find anything worth putting on, Sonny?" she said. "Most of my stuff's still in L.A. And my collection never ranked up there with yours, certainly."

"Oh, we got a few fun things here." He straightened up, handing her a sleeve, holding a couple more. He looked at the records in his hands, not at her. "Nice dress you wore during your show, sugar."

"Wasn't it? It's a favorite of mine. It was a gift."

From an old flame? Aloud, he asked, "How you liking Dallas?"

"It's is a nice enough city." She touched his arm. He had to suppress a flinch. He finally looked at her face. She smiled, drawing her gaze down him. "You do look marvelous, Sonny—though I can't decide if I like your hair that long. But you should definitely lose that beard. Your face is far too pretty to hide."

Sonny sighed. " 'Pretty'? Julia Jean calling me 'cute,' earlier. What the hell am I doing wrong?"

Cilla's laugh sounded strained. "Hmmm . . . how about dashing?"

"*Dashing*'s better," Sonny said, managing a small grin.

"Save for the beard, though, I'd say you look better than ever. That's no small thing."

"I even been working out some, if you can picture that." It was true. Walker had been right about the sugar crave that hit when you got straight.

Sonny had to hit the gym five times a week to keep at bay the candy bars he now ate with the gusto of a PMS-afflicted woman.

"Cleaning up your act obviously agrees with you."

"Reckon I'm feeling a lot better. Pushed it pretty hard and far there for a while." Sonny bent over and started studying the records again. He wished he could avoid this small talk, but it needed doing. Best to get this first awkward conversation out of the way before work began.

Cilla put on the record he'd handed her, Magic Sam's *Black Magic*, while Sonny kept browsing in the crate. When the music started, she dropped beside him, grabbing his arm. He started to pull away, but she held tight. He focused on the hand that gripped him: her right paw, her fretter. Smaller than his own, but coarsely veined, callused, strong—like his left. An artist's hand. "Sonny," she whispered, barely audibly, "I've needed to apologize to you for such a long time."

"Forget it." Sonny yanked free. He pulled an album from the crate, pretending to read the back cover. He hated her for doing this, here, with everybody a few footsteps away.

He hated her mostly because she made him feel cowardly. He should just grab her, wordless, and toss her into the Fury. He'd drive her fast and hard out into the country, not speaking until they were far from everything and everyone. He'd confess to still battling the worst kind of hurt. Admit to her how what had happened between them had messed him up in a way he'd never imagined. But fuck if he could. Instead he added, "Better this way. You're a nice girl, Cilla. Once I'd done you, I wouldn't have been interested no more."

"Sonny, I know how you felt." She said it in a soft and caring whisper. Too close to the way she'd talked to him before, during the video days.

He knew he was no actor. One look in those devastating eyes and he'd blow it. He kept on peering intently at the liner notes as he stood up from his crouch, turning his back on her. "Girl, you're too used to making men act stupid. Won't work with me."

She stood beside him, laying a hand almost weightlessly on his back. She whispered, "Sonny, I know you're not as heartless as you make yourself out to be—"

He slapped the record against his palm with a loud pop. Cilla jumped back a step. He spun and managed to give her startled face a cold squint. "I'd bet the bank you're a great fuck. But if you think we would have amounted to more than that, you're kidding yourself."

Cilla shook her head at him, her eyes beginning to grow bright with tears. He squatted back down by the records. Thirty seconds later, Cilla's fiancé peeked into the small room.

"People were wondering where their little hostess had gotten to, sweetheart," Mickey said to Cilla, in his harsh Bronx accent. "Hiding out with one of your musician buddies?" He held his hand out to Sonny. By the tight-lipped squint on Canttoni's face, Sonny knew he was being sized up. "Hi. Mickey Canttoni."

"Sonny Blaine," he replied coolly, shaking the offered hand. Mickey tried to pull an athlete power grip to one-up him, but with his own big hand, Sonny gave as good as he got. Pity we don't shake lefty, he thought. Then Sonny could mess up that million-dollar southpaw with his own mean-ass fretter.

Mickey laughed, ripping his hand free from the power shake. "Oh? Also known as Icestorm, right?" Sonny nodded. "Or Dom DiMaggio."

"Who?"

Cilla glared at Mickey, saying, "Don't start."

"Next she'll tell you I'm always an asshole after a big win and a few beers."

Sonny nodded. "Legendary jock mentality, I heard tell."

"That's a good one, Dom."

"Call me Sonny." He looked to Cilla, who was in turn eyeing Mickey frostily. "Who's 'Dom'? Ain't it Joe DiMaggio?"

"The brother they remember is."

"Mickey, please."

Mickey smiled unpleasantly. "Sweetheart, he asked. I'll educate you, Sonny. Dom was a professional ballplayer, back when. Real good hitter, not a bad fielder, either. If you follow baseball you might have even heard of him . . . if it hadn't been for his brother, Joe. Even you musicians heard of Joltin' Joe. Must have been real tough on poor Dom. Always living in the shadow of his little brother's talent." He laughed. "You can just imagine how tough that was on him, can't you, Sonny?"

Sonny was struck dumb by the asshole's gall. If Cilla weren't right there in the room with them, Sonny would bust the pitcher's straight, white teeth clean out of his pretty face. And when Mickey bent over to pick them up off the floor, he'd take his boot and stomp his talented southpaw to mush.

Mickey just smiled, his arm circling Cilla's shoulders.

Cilla was red-faced, embarrassed. She yanked free of her fiancé, snapping, "How dare you speak to Sonny that way? Go upstairs if you can't be polite to my friends."

"Baby, I'm talking baseball, like everyone always wants me to," Mickey commented, mildly. He started to exit, tossing over his shoulder as he did, "See you around, Dom."

Cilla dropped her face into her hands. "Sonny, I apologize. He usually gets a little testy around my musician friends, but he's never been that horrible."

"Ain't none of my business who you run with." Sonny dropped the other records beside the stereo and went to find Walker. Cilla followed him, silent. She walked them to the car. As Sonny sat stewing in the front seat, Walker and Cilla stood outside the car, talking more about her working on the record. They had left with Cilla saying she would call Walker within a week and give them her final answer. Sonny watched as Walker escorted her back to her doorway. Before she ducked in to retrieve Floyd and his missus, the twosome stood on the threshold, gazing at one another. They looked as though they were on a first date, both wondering if a goodnight kiss was appropriate. Then Cilla went in, leaving Walker staring after her. Floyd and Julia Jean came out moments later, with a flourish of Southern farewells. Floyd and his wife decided they would overnight at Eddie's in Dallas, rent a car, and head over to Mingus to visit his Montgomery kin in the morning. The brothers wanted to put the pedal to the metal and head back home that night.

Sonny didn't tell Walker about Mickey's insult until he asked, on the drive, for Sonny's take on the man. After Sonny finished telling him, Walker damn near swerved off the freeway, he was so outraged. "Jesus God!" Walker proclaimed. "Where does he get off? Ain't like he's Joltin' Joe—or even brother Dom, for that matter. He's just a pretty pitcher. Sorry-ass American Leaguer, now, to boot. Too much a pussy to even stand up and hit the damn ball for his own self."

Sonny was touched by Walker's indignation on his behalf. He cracked, "Well said, Joltin' Joe."

Walker smacked him on the arm. "Sonny, don't let that asshole get to you. He's full of shit. I bet he don't know vibrato from a curve ball."

"Like we do?"

They laughed together. Walker added, "But I ain't accusing him of lame licks. Too bad Cilla's his girl, huh? She'd be better off with . . . someone else."

"Better off alone. Oh, well. Nothing we can do, Squirt."

"I don't know about that," Walker said thoughtfully. "First of all, we make her come to Austin to record. Keep her there, much as we can. This whole love affair's got to be about that big, muscle-bound body of his. We keep her away from him, she might come to her senses. Plan, bro? Maybe it'll leastwise stop her from marrying the fool."

3.

CILLA SAT IN the recording booth alongside Eddie Finger. They sat off-camera, watching the Blaine brothers being interviewed by one of the cable channels. They were starting their second week of recording the album they'd dubbed *Lone Star Ice and Fire*. The atmosphere so far had been relaxed. Everyone involved was there for the sheer pleasure of working together. This time they weren't working under the contract requirements of Twelve Bar or under the heavy hand of a producer's personal agenda. The brothers themselves were producing. Their label, pleased to see them at work on a surefire hot seller, stepped aside and gave them room to wander.

Most of the week had been spent experimenting with material they were considering putting on tape. The jam sessions helped Cilla settle in, and reacquainted her with the brothers' diverse styles. She was also learning how to work off Eddie's groove, to fit him as his bassist. She had been nervous about working with Eddie. Bass playing was fun, like dancing through a guitar. But it was the area in which she was least sure of herself. Eddie was cool, though. He had none of the rocker affectations. Instead he looked like the Texas print shop owner he'd been until recently. Immediately, he had proved himself to be another charming, talented Mingus boy. Must be something special about the tap water of that town.

Eddie's divorce was fresh, the wounds of it still open. Though glad to be back in the music game after having set it aside for years for his wife's sake, he was still smarting fiercely from loss. He was staying at the same hotel as Cilla until he found a decent place to rent. Nights, after they'd left the studio, Cilla and Eddie met for a cocktail in the hotel lounge—sometimes dinner, too. Cilla enjoyed his company, the uncomplicated relationship, and knew that Eddie did, too. He was never fresh with her. He just needed a sympathetic female ear that would listen as he talked about his failed marriage. She was more than happy to listen, and to offer what insights she'd gained from her own broken marriage. She did her best to make him feel better about his fresh start.

As for fresh starts, Cilla was thrilled to have one with the Blaines. It had hurt deeply when she believed she might never work with them again. As guitarists, they had both inspired and educated her. She really had been duly honored when they asked her to work on their long-awaited album.

But it wasn't easy on her. Her feelings still ran river deep for Walker and Sonny.

Sometimes she found her situation laughable, smack in the middle of these two, playing such sexually charged music. Sonny—well, he was perhaps the handsomest man she'd ever laid eyes on. But Walker, plain though he was, was the one who stirred Cilla to the boiling point. She had to handle the tension of it all by bursting into unexplainable fits of laughter now and again. Not that she wasn't behaving professionally—she was. But she was also having fun for a change.

"Rhythm section. Get over here!" Sonny ordered. Walker was gesturing for Eddie and Cilla to join them in the studio. The game plan was to play a little live for the cable show, as a promotional thing. They decided to perform a bit of *Boogie Stop Shuffle*, a full-tilt piece composed by the great jazz bassist Charles Mingus. The brothers had been huge admirers of

Mingus's since discovering him through Jeff Beck's sumptuous version of *Goodbye Pork-Pie Hat*. They thought it only fair that two cats from Mingus, Texas, give Mingus, Charles, his rightful nod. Besides, *Boogie Stop Shuffle* absolutely cooked.

The song went so well that they ended up calling it their take. At least they recorded one thing this day. After the video crew left, the album photographer arrived. The sessions came to a standstill yet again.

"Glad we making session wages for nothing today, huh, Cilla?" Eddie kidded her. "I got a deck of cards. You know how to play gin?"

Walker hollered over from where he and Sonny were posing with their guitars. "Hey! No gin allowed here. You got to play some nonalcoholic card game."

Cilla and Eddie killed a few hands while the photographers took various poses of the Blaines. The shot that finally ended up as the album cover was a close-up of the backside of Old Broad, the carved W. & S. Blaine clearly visible. The brothers clutched the guitar's neck between them, fist over fist, as if holding a baseball bat and trying to decide who would hit first in a sandlot game.

Then they called Eddie and Cilla over last, including them in a few of the photos. The men sarcastically checked their watches as she quickly brushed and fluffed her hair and put on lipstick. "No more war paint," Sonny chided her. "Ain't no question you the best-looking thing in the room. Don't show us up too much."

Gracie, the photographer, was instantly entranced with Cilla once she saw her through the lens. She looked her over with a practiced eye after taking a few shots, exclaiming, "I can't tell for sure until these are developed, but I think my camera is in love." Gracie touched Cilla's hair, and brushed an educated finger over her cheekbone. "You have amazing coloring. I've never seen a redhead with such dark skin . . . it isn't hair dye either, is it?"

"Sure ain't," Walker confirmed before Cilla could reply. She was grateful no one asked how Walker was so certain.

Gracie went on, peering into Cilla's face. "I hope we captured the green of your eyes. And your body—I don't think I've ever seen such dramatic curves on a subject. I work too many fashion layouts, you know. Most models are as straight as sticks."

Cilla dropped her eyes, feeling the blush creep into her face. The room went quiet as she felt the men join in the appraisal. "Thanks, I guess," she mumbled. "Don't expect too much from the shots. I'm, like, out of proportion. I'm okay from the waist up, but my butt and hips look huge in pictures."

"Oh, stop, Cilla," Walker chastised her. "Your ass is perfection."

"I'll second that," Sonny commented. Eddie smiled at her, nodding, as did Gracie's young male assistant.

"See there?" Walker said. "You still think like a bulimic ballerina. Gracie? You still got film?"

Gracie picked up one of her Nikons. "Sure do."

"Get this shot." Walker suddenly grabbed Cilla from behind. The fingers and thumbs of his large hands met easily around her waist. He scooted up the light undershirt she wore to grip her. Walker's warm palms and fingers tightly squeezed her flesh. Aroused by his sudden touch, she gaped back over her shoulder at him. She could feel his breath on her neck as he whispered in her ear, "Remember this?"

"Unhand me, Walker. Literally," she ordered.

Walker kept his eyes and clutches on her, cracking up. She couldn't help but laugh, too. The camera flashed. Gracie crowed, "Cool. I wanted another picture of your magnificent hands, Walker."

"Magnificent, huh?" Walker snickered, acting like he didn't notice Cilla was trying to pry loose from his grip. "Looks like big, ugly paws to me."

"Don't be silly. Your hands have been shaped by your skill into something fine," Gracie shot back. "Like Cilla, they're uniquely lovely." She turned her camera toward Cilla's face, observing her through its lens. "Have you considered modeling, Cilla? You're small, but long-legged. And you have a certain sensuality that I think some agencies would go nuts for. We could do a portfolio—"

Cilla cut her off. "No thank you, Gracie. I spent too many years in front of walls of mirrors in ballet school fretting over my weight. I've been asked to model before."

"Maybe if the right situation presented itself?"

"Really, no," she said firmly, holding up her palm. "It's a simple-minded and degrading profession."

A contemptuous voice from the studio doorway declared, "Girlfriend, like Walker's song says, it's harder than it looks." A regal woman, her head tilted sideways, gave Walker a hard stare. He let go of Cilla's waist at the sound of her voice and bounded over to her. He grabbed her, pulling her face to his for a smooch. She let him kiss her, keeping her eyes on Cilla. When her mouth was free, the woman added in the same nasty tone, "Not everyone's lucky enough to have a rich daddy who's a great guitar player."

"Ouch!" Sonny coughed. Eddie stifled a chuckle, heading for his drum kit and out of the melee.

"Please forgive me—that came out all wrong," Cilla responded, walking toward the beauty at Walker's side. She recognized the woman now— she had seen most of her in expensive lingerie catalogs. Cilla extended a hand.

"My name's Salome," the beauty said, taking the proffered hand after a moment. "You must be Cilla. Walker does prattle on about you."

"I say only nice things, Cill," Walker said, laughing too forcefully. He hugged Salome again. She finally turned her eyes to his, scowling.

Walker addressed the others in the studio. "Good time to break, huh? Ya'll got enough photos of us?" Gracie and her assistant nodded, beginning to pack her gear. Walker said to the other musicians, "Let's get lunch while they're packing up the cameras and stuff. See ya'll in an hour or so." To Salome, Walker cooed, "I'll take you someplace nice to eat, baby." Walker waved and headed for the door, pulling Salome along. She turned and smiled smugly, right at Cilla, just as her face disappeared around the door's frame.

Cilla stared after Salome and Walker, swept with outrage. She jumped when she felt a hand fall on her shoulder. "Whoa, sugar," Sonny said. "Knew you was plenty limber, girl, but never saw you put your foot clear in your mouth before. Didn't exactly make a pal of Salome, there."

"*Salome*, of all things. Does she at least have a last name?"

"I think it's Ross," Sonny answered. "Why?"

"I once had a stepmother—Mimi, Simply Mimi—for about five minutes."

"Oh, yeah. I remember seeing pictures of your dad with her. Some French clotheshorse, right?"

"Yes. Not much older than I was at the time, and a vain bitch if ever there was one. Simply Mimi made a real fool of Dad and took him to the cleaners. My charming birth mother was a model, too, you know."

"Uh-huh."

"Got pregnant to nab Dad, but when he wouldn't marry her, she sure didn't want me. If she hadn't lived in Ireland, I'm certain she would have aborted me. I heard she made herself puke all the way though her pregnancy just so she wouldn't get stretch marks."

"No wonder you hate models."

"I'm just glad Dad quit fooling with those pretty, empty heads once he got sober and sensible." She raised her brows at Sonny. "Better have him give Walker a little sage advice, don't you suppose?"

"Meow, woman!" Sonny said, grinning at her. "Leastwise, Salome don't call Walker's friends 'Dom DiMaggio.' "

Cilla winced and dropped her head. "Touché. That was horrid of Mickey. I'm so sorry."

Sonny smirked. "I looked up his stats. Dom wasn't bad, you know."

"No. He wasn't. Just under-recognized, because. . . . Anyway, I am sorry about Mickey acting like that."

"Me, too. Sorry to see you hanging out with a jerk like that."

"To be honest, I'm glad to be away from him right now. He's in the midst of contract negotiations. He's a real bear."

"Probably won't hurt you none to spend some time alone. You go from one man to another too quick."

She snapped her eyes to Sonny's, scowling. "That's rather an awful thing to say."

Sonny took his hand off her, smiling unpleasantly, imitating her accent. "I'm rather an awful guy. Remember?"

"You like people to think so," she answered.

They gazed at one another until the photography duo and Eddie left the room. Then Sonny headed into the sound booth. She followed him after a minute. He sat in the engineer's chair, rewinding the tape they had been working with. He pointedly ignored her. She twisted a piece of her hair, watching the booth's door. "May I ask you something?"

"Hmmm?" He acted engrossed in his project.

"Did you ever tell Walker?"

He glanced up from the deck, his eyes still unfriendly. "What? About us? No need to. Nothing happened."

She could practically feel the mercury drop as his cool veneer slipped like a needle into its groove. "That's not true," she managed to say.

He shrugged, switching off the rewound reel. "What would I say? All I ever really did was kiss you." Sonny leaped to his feet surprisingly fast and darted within inches of her. He gave her body a visual fondling. "Of course there was that last time, when I didn't stop at just kissing your face."

Startled, she was doused with the memory of Sonny's skillful mouth. And he was remembering how she tasted. She could read it like print on paper as his eyes took her in. She stumbled back toward the door, mumbling, "I'll go grab lunch now."

"Good idea, girl."

"D-do you want anything, Sonny?"

"Not lunch, I don't." She looked up at him with flustered eyes. He held her stare for a few seconds, then gave her a smile. "Easy, now. Just having a little fun at your expense. Go. I'll do some fooling around with the thing we laid down today. Walker said something about one of his friends stopping by. I better stick around, in case they show."

Cilla nodded and scampered away like an animal escaping a trap. Sonny allowed himself a tense laugh when she was out of earshot. Satisfying, her reaction. Now, at least, he was facing the real woman, not just pining for his lost dream girl. And she was a terrific, solid rhythm behind them. Walker had been right about that.

Sonny started the tape, trying to focus on work, but it was difficult. Cilla had distracted him. He could stir her up with a glance, a few well-placed words, just as he could other women. But she was the only one who could do the same to him, though he hardly admitted it even to himself.

Cilla had a soul held prisoner by the blues. She had that in common with Vada. But Vada had been only a singer. Cilla was a guitar player, like

Walker and him. Just like other women? Like hell she was. If he kept telling himself often enough, though, maybe he'd believe it someday.

Sonny put his mind back to the soundboard, focusing on *Boogie Stop Shuffle*. He was fooling with the mix when he heard someone come in. He looked up, expecting Cilla. A tall teenage boy, hidden behind Ray-Bans, wearing the latest Salamanders T-shirt, jeans, and cowboy boots, had shuffled in. He had an unruly head of dark-brown curls that brushed his shoulders. A smudge of a soul-patch darkened his chin.

"Um ... sorry to interrupt. Is Walker—or Floyd—here?" the boy asked. He shoved his hands in his pockets, glancing around.

"Haven't seen Floyd today. Walker just stepped out for a few. Wait in here if you want. He should be back pretty quick." Sonny extended his hand. "He told me he had a friend coming by. I'm his brother, Sonny."

The kid coughed, not taking Sonny's hand. "I know who you are."

Sonny figured the boy for a fan. "You know Walker from meetings?"

"Hardly." The kid took off his sunglasses. Sonny looked back into bootleg copies of his own eyes. "I'm Walker's nephew, Otis Montgomery."

"Otis. . . ."

"Surprised, huh?"

"Reckon I shouldn't be." Sonny stood up slowly, letting the tape continue to roll. "Otis. We met once, years ago."

"I remember. At a rehearsal for the Emergency Fund Uncle Walker helped start. I didn't know who you were then. After we left, Uncle Floyd told me you were Icestorm Blaine, but I didn't know ... well, you know." They stared at each other. Otis finally broke the eye contact, nodding at the rolling tape. "Sounds pretty tough. That's a Charles Mingus deal ya'll are playing."

"Good ear."

"The Prof, my ... dad is a real jazz snob. He has all kinds of jazz records—some compact discs now, too. The Prof doesn't think anything else is—" Otis held up his fingers in quote signs, changing his voice in a clear imitation "—'a valid American art form.' "

"Is that right?" Sonny said, smiling.

Otis nodded, his own mouth twisting into a lopsided grin. "I think jazz is real cool, too. But there's a whole big musical world out there. Got to keep my ears and heart open ... well, that's what Uncle Walker tells me."

"He's right as can be. What kind of music do you like?"

"I like everything, as long as it's good." Sonny laughed with him. "Really, I'm pretty open-minded about stuff. I've kind of grown up with electric blues, what with Uncle Floyd and Uncle Walker. That's probably my favorite. And there's lots of good blues to hear in this town. Thank God, Mama came to her senses and brought me here to raise, instead of that one-horse town she's—ya'll—are from."

Sonny nodded. "Mingus ain't such a bad place to grow up, but it do get boring when you hit your teens. I was lucky enough to meet up with your Uncle Floyd and his band and get out young, so I did all right. Your Uncle Walker about blew a gasket before he left, though."

"He's told me so."

They exchanged a nod, then went silent, gazing across the small room at one another. We're both picking out how we favor each other, Sonny realized. Otis's eyes and mouth were all Sonny, and he was about the same height and weight that Sonny had been in his mid-teens. But his stance was more Floyd's than Sonny's, as was his mess of curls. His nose, something in his jaw, was vaguely Nancy Ruth's.

There was no denying this was his son, a part of him walking around independent, thinking and feeling, living his own life. The idea of it was nearly overwhelming. Sonny hadn't felt anything but raw shock that first time, when he'd seen Otis as a kid. Back then he'd had a buzz on all the time—he did his best not to feel much of anything in those days. Now sometimes it was like there was just too much to feel out there. Sonny finally got out, "Walker tells me you been playing a guitar he gave you."

"A little bit, yeah." Otis dropped his eyes.

"What he start you on?"

"Um . . . pentatonic scales, little shuffle rhythms."

"No. I mean what sort of guitar?"

"Oh! A nice old Strat. Pretty sunburst finish."

"Cool. You bring it with you?"

"Nope. I'm here to listen to the pros work today."

Sonny walked past Otis and held open the door to the studio. "Problem is, today we ain't working. Le me show you what we got in here. See which one you like." Otis hung back. Sonny grabbed his arm, pulling him along. "Leastwise take a look."

Otis wandered about the studio, studying the different guitars, saying, "I don't like Uncle Walker's gear much. I mean, he has great guitars. But he's always got that heavy-gauge string on it that's just hell to deal with."

"Don't I know it," Sonny agreed. "But you know how he is about his ballsy tone. No room for compromise with Walker."

"I guess." Otis was admiring Sonny's faithful black Telecaster. "Got a picture of this thing on a few of my records. You had it a long time, huh?"

"Since I was sixteen. Just a little younger than you are now, right?" Sonny said. Otis nodded. "Bought it brand-new, a '65. Finish is chipped in a bunch of spots now, but it sounds better than ever. Go ahead and try it out. I just do medium-gauge string. Piece of cake compared to your uncle's shit."

"You really don't mind?"

"My pleasure, Otis."

Sonny watched the kid as he sat down and put the SONNY strap around his shoulders. Otis flipped on the amp, hitting a little distortion, and pulled the toggle forward, to get a clear, rough sound. He made sure he was in tune, and then dug into the beginning of the high single-note solo from Otis Rush's *All Your Love*.

"That ain't half bad," Sonny praised him. "Did Walker teach you that?"

"Nope. I taught it to myself." He smiled. "Figured I ought to know something by my namesake."

"Good for you."

"Yeah, well, that part's pretty simple. Some chords, but mostly one note at a time. I have more trouble when I get into rhythm shit, and the chord stuff? Hard to get all my fingers in place in time and keep it moving at the right pace."

Sonny grabbed a spare Strat he had lying about the studio, then sat down opposite Otis. "It's all the same, really. Speed comes with practice on your finger work. Getting your muscles, as well as your brain, to memorize where to go. Repeat the scales and chords over and over until you can put them together, in the right order, in your sleep. Rhythm playing and chord solos are just a matter of keeping the cadence going instead of letting the single notes talk for their own self. Watch, now." Sonny hit into one of the well-known Rockets' rhythm lines to demonstrate. "Just some simple noting here within the chord. You don't have to let the whole thing go each time . . . and then you tag a few little bends and wiggle your wrist a bit on the end. You're driving the song, and everyone thinks you bad. Easy."

"I don't know about easy."

"But not as hard as it seems, either. Let's take the Otis Rush thing you just played. That's a real rhythm-driven deal. Lots of muting and shaped phrasing is what makes it cook. You know the opening?" Sonny demonstrated what he meant.

"I kind of know it by ear."

"Let's slow it down and take a look at it." Sonny walked him through it at half speed. "See? Let me pick it up now and show you. Now, this song, you really just play in between the singing, sort of B.B. King style." And, forgetting himself in the lesson, Sonny did the unheard of, and sang the first line. "Now here's the rhythm line." He sang again, adding, "Repeat it . . . and so on. It really is just repetition, Otis. Then you give it a little variation, for style's sake."

Over the intercom from the booth came Walker's voice. "Hold on there, Caruso! I ain't cued up. We got to get you on tape warbling, Sonny. Making history today for sure."

Sonny glanced up, embarrassed. He had been so involved teaching Otis that he had not heard the others come in. Eddie, Cilla, and Walker hunched over, grinning at him through the sound booth's glass.

"Ya'll just leave us be for a few more minutes. And for damn sure leave the tape off. I'm giving the boy a little lesson, is all."

Walker spoke into the mike again, giving Sonny a thumbs-up. "And about damn time, too, Sonny. Otis, this is unheard of. Sonny don't show no other players his thing. Take it as a genuine gift from your old man, hear?"

4.

SONNY STOOD ON his front porch, sniffing the air, watching the sky. No good could come of what he saw and felt. Though still daylight, it looked more like nightfall, with green clouds and a tangible pressure drop in the air. Austin was experiencing a very late Indian summer, with balmy temperatures well into the part of fall when normally the town woke up to chilly weather. Today the air had been hazy and still at noon. The temperature had dropped drastically in the last hour, with spurts of wind that shook the windowpanes. Jagged cracks of lightning and rumbling thunder filled the sky. Being a plains-raised boy, Sonny knew the signs. To him it felt like a big one was coming. He stepped out into the driveway, peering down the road. He trotted back up onto his porch, shaking the rain off. He heard the phone ring and dashed inside to answer.

"Otis?"

"No, it's Walker. You watching the sky, man?"

"Yeah. Bad stuff coming. Hail, at least. But with all the heat this month. . . ."

"I know it. You still waiting on Otis?"

"Yeah. Look, we better just skip coming out your way tonight."

"Absolutely. Stay put. Floyd and Eddie already called and said no dice. And Salome's flight out of Dallas was canceled. I told her just to get a room and sit tight until tomorrow."

"Should I call Mama, make sure she can get to shelter?" Sonny asked. "Does she even have a basement on her condo?"

"No, but she and Aunt Lucille was going to be doing something at church this afternoon, and then she was having supper with them. Uncle Charlie's got a regular storm cellar on his place." Sonny heard a big thunder crack not far off, and right after a woman's scream sounded from Walker's end of the line. "Hear that? It was real close to us. Hang on—" Walker's voice was muffled, comforting sounding. Sonny could hear crying on the other end of the line. Turning back to the mouthpiece, Walker said, "Cilla did make it over from the hotel, about thirty minutes ago. She's scared shitless." Quietly laughing, he added, "The woman breezes through earthquakes and mudslides, but this storm's too much on her. It don't hardly even thunder in L.A., Sonny."

"Well, go try and calm her down. I'm glad she ain't stuck alone on the tenth floor of the hotel. She'd really hate that. Look, we better get off the line anyhow, with all the lightning. Ya'll be safe. Oh, here's Otis now."

"Good. Talk to you tomorrow, Sonny."

Sonny hung up and went to the door. The wind was howling now, and the sky was all but black. Otis hopped from his car and tore into the house, soaked from his brief sprint.

"I didn't know if I was going to make it," Otis declared. "The radio said there was already trees and telephone lines down all over town. It's a full-fledged warning now. Guess they spotted some huge funnel clouds on the Southside."

Sonny tossed Otis a towel. "I'm just glad you got here in one piece, son. Needless to say, we ain't headed to Uncle Walker's barbecue." As Sonny spoke, a huge crash of thunder hit, and the electricity went dead.

"You got candles or flashlights, Sonny?"

"There's a couple flashlights in the kitchen, I think—I know I got candles in the basement. Wait and—" Sonny clammed up as the long single-note wail of the tornado siren sounded. The signal meant they better take cover, and fast. No time to dig for the flashlights. Sonny, halfway into the kitchen, said, "Downstairs, now!"

"I can't see a thing, Sonny." Otis sounded terrified. He was across the living room, hunching by the door. "Where are you?"

With the surefootedness of having lived in the same house for years, Sonny bolted over to Otis. "Give me your hand. The basement's just back of the kitchen."

Sonny held his left hand out in front of him, heading swiftly to the basement door. He started down, saying behind him to the boy fiercely gripping his right, "Now, careful. These old steps are skinny. You got your footing?"

"I think so."

Sonny could hear his son's less-sure tread. "Walk careful. There's no handrail. Count to twelve, and you'll be on the foundation." Once they were both down, Sonny led Otis to the southwest corner. "Here's where they say to sit, Otis. Though I never quite got that part of it. Seems like twisters jump all over anywhere they want to."

"I always wondered about that, too," Otis said, his voice tiny.

Sonny rummaged around in the dark corner, hoping that in his search for light he wouldn't place a hand on top of a black widow. He finally grasped some candles stored there, and lit a couple. The small flames broke gently into the heavy fabric of the underground darkness. Sonny could now see Otis clearly, sitting with his hands gripped around his knees. He was trying to maintain his composure, but his expression was wide-eyed with fear.

"We're okay, Otis. We got it made down here," Sonny said, hoping he sounded comforting.

"I know. . . . It's silly, I guess. As many of these things as I have gone through growing up here, you'd think I'd be more used to them." He laughed nervously. "But they scare me to death, man."

"Twisters are damn scary. But we're right where we should be. Wish I'd brought my steel down here. You ever played one of those?"

"Can't say I have. The very idea would probably send Prof into a tail-spin."

"Why?"

"Steel guitars are country. Jazz only, man."

"Is your old man really that hardcore against other types of music?"

"He's a good guy, but a die-hard jazz snob. He says country is for ignorant people. Classical is boring, mostly songs penned for kings who had no musical sensibilities. He barely tolerates Mama's old rock and blues records being around the house, even though she doesn't play them when he's home. He even acts kind of superior toward Uncle Floyd, because he plays a harmonica."

"And plays it damn well, too."

"I know. It isn't an easy instrument. But it's too country for the Prof's tastes."

"Huh. How does he treat Uncle Walker?"

Otis laughed. "Mama makes sure they don't run into each other. Prof would deny it, but he's jealous all the way around of Uncle Walker. He admits Uncle Walker is talented. But Prof really wishes he would concentrate more on that Wes Montgomery–flavored stuff. 'He wastes his tremendous talent on that blues,' he says."

"Balls to that. I mean I love when Walker delves into jazz, myself. But blues is his mother tongue."

"Exactly! I think what really gets Prof's goat is the fact that Mama and Uncle Walker used to be sweethearts. He'd never admit it, but it's a sore spot. He shouldn't worry. They're just friends, now."

"I'm glad to hear it. Long time ago, they were hot and heavy," Sonny said, grinning, "I think they spent quite a few hours alone in our basement in Mingus—didn't have nothing to do with twisters, though."

"Why did they split up, anyway?"

"They was just kids. Walker moved to Austin to play music. Your mama wisely stayed in high school." If Otis wasn't aware that Nancy Ruth had once thought she was going to bear his half-sibling/cousin, Sonny sure wouldn't spill the beans. "Walker didn't really have a band in Mingus. So he dropped out of school and split. He hated school."

"I love school. I want to go to UT in a couple years. I don't know what I'll study yet. Maybe history. Or civil engineering."

Sonny felt proud of the boy, of his enthusiasm. "Imagine loving school! I stuck it out through high school but can't say I liked it. You take after your mama. She was a good student."

"I guess." Otis sat quietly for a minute, watching Sonny. "You and Mama . . . never dated, huh?"

Sonny wasn't sure what to say. "What's your Mama tell you?"

"Not much. I mean, she told me you were . . . the dad. But not how it happened. She said to ask you."

That figured. "Um, your Mama always liked me. Even before I was as old as you, she flirted and stuff. But she's three years younger than I am. That don't matter much once you're grown, but it's a lot younger at your age." Otis nodded slowly.

Sonny paused, thinking what to say about that night. He didn't want to make Nancy Ruth sound bad. That would hardly be a fair thing to do to her, or to Otis. No one liked to think of his or her mama as a sex kitten. The short time span between Ruby and Big Billy Jay's wedding date and his own birthday always ate at Sonny. At least Daddy had bothered to give him his name. It was more than Sonny had done for Otis. "When she was a little older, when she came up here for college, she stayed at this house for a few weeks. Back then, your Uncle Floyd and I shared this place. One night, your mama and I was here alone . . . it just happened once, Otis."

Otis nodded, quiet for a minute. Sonny hoped he wouldn't ask any more details. He didn't want to invent a prettier story, and he didn't want to say more about the wasted, half-mad tryst that was the reality of Otis's conception.

"Tell me just one more thing? Was Otis Rush really playing in the background when ya'll were . . . when it happened, Sonny?"

Sonny snorted. "Exactly what I would have asked, in your place. Yeah. Otis was on the stereo—when we started, anyway. . . . After the storm blows over, I'll even show you which record." Sonny pointed over their heads. "Hell, I'll give it to you. You came to be right up there in the living room."

Otis gazed toward the ceiling, his face solemn. "I had no idea."

Another huge clap of thunder shook the house above them. Both of them jumped, and the raw fear returned to Otis's eyes. Sonny patted the boy's arm. "Just noise, son. My daddy used to say as long as thunderheads was overhead, funnel clouds couldn't be."

"For real?"

"I don't know if it's true," Sonny admitted. "We never got hit dead-on when it was thundering, that much is fact." Otis smiled wanly. Sonny wanted to make him forget the storm as best he could, so he kept talking. "Your Granddaddy Blaine was a piece of work."

"I knew him a little before he died. He was always real nice to me."

"You don't say?" The old man must have turned over a new leaf with this grandkid. "That's good. How do you and the Prof get along?"

"Pretty well, Sonny. He's treated me like his own, good times and bad."

"You are his own. The one raised you is your daddy. Sex don't make a man a father. Leastwise your mama did good by you. I'm glad you had the Prof, a good man, in your life."

Otis didn't say anything.

"I know I can't undo it, the years not seeing you, Otis. I'm the first to admit I'm real selfish. I hope you understand it wasn't nothing you did that kept me away. I never let no one come close—especially when I was drinking and drugging. And having a kid's about as close as it gets. My own daddy . . . I'm glad ya'll got along. But he and I didn't. He was pretty unhappy with his lot in life. He was a real serious alcoholic, too. He beat us up, me and Walker. I really don't know how to even begin being a daddy. I hope it's not too late for us to be friends, at least."

"We're becoming friends, I think." Otis smiled, looking a little less fearful. "It's been cool to hang with you while you worked on this record. I mean, I've known who you were to me since I was about ten. But you were always gone. I quit telling my friends after awhile, because no one believed me." Otis laughed, adding, "At least not until they'd come over to find Firewalker playing guitar in my living room. It's just a weird part of my life, having my birth dad be this local legend."

"Me, a legend? Hardly that."

"But you are, Sonny," Otis told him. "People hereabouts drop their voices when they speak the name of Icestorm Blaine. Just the other day I saw these two people shopping in that record store over on Guadalupe? They were jumping all over this lady's case, merely because she said you had been 'replaced' in the Rockets. They set her straight. They were going on and on about how you can't replace our Icestorm. He's this national treasure. They were practically on their knees to you."

"I'll be damned. That's the funniest thing I ever heard."

"It was funny, but it was also very cool. For years I've been going in that same record store and staring at this old poster they have on the wall of the White Tornadoes. I think it was an ad for your shows at the Sugar and Spice, back in the Sixties. You know the one I mean?"

Sonny nodded. "Yeah, I do. It's one of our first promotional posters, from 1967. They left off the 'e' at the end of my name on that thing."

"That's the one. Anyway, you were about my age now in that picture, weren't you?"

"Let's see . . . yeah, I guess I was."

"And Uncle Floyd has my hair on there." Grinning, Otis grabbed at his own curls. "Anyway, the other day I was in there looking at the poster. I could feel someone watching me. I looked over, and the clerk was looking from me to that picture of you. He said, 'Jesus, kid. You know you look just like Icestorm?' And I was . . . well, jazzed."

"Jazzed!" Sonny laughed. "How proud the Prof would be by your use of that term. Well, maybe not, attached to the likes of me. He probably thinks of me as just some blues bastard."

"Nope. I'm the blues bastard, if you think about it."

They both laughed together and then sat quietly in the candlelight, listening to the storm raging outside the house. Sonny put a hand on Otis's shoulder, giving him a comforting squeeze whenever the boy jumped in reaction to the house's groans, the mad winds, the thunder cracks.

As the worst of it passed, Otis said, "Thanks for being so cool about me acting so pussy over a silly storm."

"You are acting just fine, Otis. And this storm ain't a silly one. We'll stay down a little longer just to make sure. Want to play a game, make the time pass?"

"What kind of game?"

"When it stormed bad and we was little, Walker and I used to play this game called *The Ed Murrow Show*."

"Who's Ed Murrow?"

Sonny chuckled, feeling a million years old. "He was a big-time interviewer when we were kids."

"Like *Sixty Minutes*?"

"Yeah, like that. Walker and me would pretend to interview each other. You go first."

"How?"

"Well, who do you want to pretend to be? Mike Wallace, maybe?"

"Maybe so. He'd ask the tough questions."

Sonny laughed. "You asked some pretty tough fucking questions already tonight, kid."

Otis grinned. "True enough. No, I'll be the cool one—Ed Bradley? Let's see. I know. Walker started playing music because of you. But what made you pick up the guitar?"

Sonny thought for a minute, remembering Daddy Jim. His stories, his very voice, had so soothed Sonny as a child. Walker, too. Maybe he could get a little of that calming cadence into this story for his own boy. He'd sure try. "I had this granddaddy—your great-granddaddy—Jim Crawford. One of his hands was maimed in World War II. Before that happened, he was one of the best stride piano players in Texas. Went by Daddy Jim in the clubs. That's what Walker and me called him, too. Daddy Jim's the one that dubbed me Sonny."

Otis looked startled. "So you're not actually named Sonny?"

The question made Sonny grin as he answered, "I'm Sonny, all right—through and through. But my Christian name is Billy Jay, just like Daddy's was.

"Anyhow, when I was twelve, Daddy Jim bought me this cheap little guitar. . . ."

✳   ✳   ✳   ✳   ✳

"HOLD THE BOARD right there, Otis. Watch your fingers." Sonny took a nail from his mouth and placed it against the piece of plywood Otis pushed against the sill. The board was warped, had likely been lying across the rafters in his garage, with other various scraps, since the house was built. But it would serve, keeping the wind and rain out of his bedroom until he could replace the window. He'd lost the glass to the storm. Part of the ancient oak in his backyard had been cleaved away. The tree didn't look mortally wounded but was in need of a little surgery. Sonny's neighborhood, as a whole, had fared well. Neighbors walked around, greeting each other, checking for damage. Windows were broken here and there, garbage was strewn about, and there was a doghouse smashed through a street-parked car's windshield. Luckily, the dog hadn't been in it at the time. The phones and power were down. Talk was of throwing a street-wide barbecue, pooling together the food thawing in their dead freezers.

As Sonny was pounding the last nail into the board, he heard Walker's voice. "Managed to do a home repair without smashing a fretter with the hammer, huh? Ain't as soft as I thought."

"Hey, Uncle Walker!" Otis trotted down the back steps. Walker gave him a hug. "You okay?"

"Weathered it fine." Walker put his arm around the boy's shoulders. Sonny noticed Otis was already taller than the crown of Walker's hat. "What about your mama and stepdaddy, son? You talked to them?"

Otis nodded. "Already been by the house. No damage. Mama said none at Uncle Floyd's either. Came back to give your brother a hand cleaning up."

"Good boy. Ya'll excuse me a minute?" Walker disappeared around the side of the house. They could hear Walker speaking with someone in a quiet voice but couldn't make out his words. A moment later Cilla rounded the corner, Walker following behind, frowning, his hat in his hand. Cilla walked with mincing steps, hugging herself as though she were cold. Her face was drawn and pale. Her hair looked dirty, matted in the back. "Thank God you're both okay," she sighed.

"Are you?" Sonny asked.

"I suppose. . . . Walker's taking me to the airport. I want out of here." Her eyes shifted to Walker. She frowned, adding, "I'm going home to my fiancé. I was scared shitless last night."

Walker nodded, saying gently, "I know, Cill."

"He's picking up Salome while he's at the airport," Cilla continued, still staring accusingly at Walker.

"She called this morning from Dallas. Got booked on a flight about an hour ago," Walker explained.

"You're lucky your phone works," Otis said. "Sonny's is out. So's ours. I guess a lot of them are around town."

"Yeah. Lots of roads are closed because of downed wires and debris. Mama's and Uncle Charlie's are out, too." Walker pushed his hair back from his face with his hand, replacing his hat. "Cilla and I stopped by Uncle Charlie's—Mama was there, just like we thought. They came through fine. Mama's Rambler didn't, though. A tree fell on it."

Sonny came down the steps, joining the others in his backyard. "Oh, shit! Is Mama grief-struck?"

Walker laughed. "She'll live. Uncle Charlie's already trying to talk her into one of them pretty Ford Tauruses."

"Good. I'll pay for it myself. That fucking Rambler was a death trap." Sonny went to grin at Cilla. He noticed she was swaying slightly, and looking paler by the moment. He grabbed her elbow. "Girl, sit. You want some water or something?"

"No. I'm fine. Really." She collapsed on the stairs and put her face in her hands. "I just want to be home, in my own bed. But before we go, Walker needs to tell you about Prince Brown."

"Yeah, I do. Man, he had a heart attack—"

"Jesus! Is he—"

"No. No. He's in the hospital, though. Going to be okay."

"Thank God," Otis breathed. Sonny nodded, dropping next to Cilla on the steps. He lit a cigarette. Cilla snatched it from his fingers, taking a long drag.

"I didn't know you smoked, Cilla," Otis said, sounding a little shocked.

She smiled at the boy. "Otis Rush Montgomery, today . . . I smoke!" She turned to Sonny. "I'm assuming you don't still have a bottle hidden around here?"

"Fresh out, baby."

She nodded. "Just as well. Shookie called Walker from hospital. The club is a mess. The whole Southside is . . . direct hit, they said on the car radio."

"More than one twister hit, I guess. But that one that got the Southside was a big fucker," Walker added. "Some places the damn pavement was even sucked off the ground. They think scores of folks are dead—just digging through rubble, mostly in the newer, cheap-ass-built suburbs. I'm going to go give blood later and see if they need volunteers. Shookie says the Sugar and Spice's roof is pretty much gone."

"Damn shame. I'm just glad the old men made it through. Is Shookie holding up okay?"

"Uncle Charlie's taking Mama over to sit with him at the hospital. I'll go over later, too." Walker lit his own smoke. He shook a butt loose from the pack, holding it toward Otis. Otis took it, holding it awkwardly as

Walker lit it. He coughed like he had TB the instant he inhaled. Everyone started laughing.

Walker beat on his back. After he recovered, Otis gasped, "I—don't smoke much."

"Then don't start now. As if you're mama don't already think of me as a bad influence," Sonny declared, snatching the cigarette from his son's fingers. He stomped it under his boot.

"I don't know how kids ever get hooked on those things. Speaking of kids, Uncle Walker, Sonny taught me a game last night he said you played when you were little.

"You remember that interview game I used to make you play during storms?" Sonny said.

Walker's eyes lit with recognition. "Hell, yeah. I recall one time Sonny almost beat me up over that game."

"Why?"

"I asked him, If he were a crayon, what color he'd be."

Otis burst out laughing. Sonny grumbled, "Isn't that the stupidest question? A damn crayon, of all things."

"Oh, you never had no imagination," Walker chided him. To Cilla he added, "I always wanted to be the gold one."

"How surprising," she replied, managing a tight smile.

"You finally got your wish, with that silly gold lamé suit you wore first at the Wang Dang Doodle concert," Sonny pointed out.

"You are so right. I bet that's why I love that suit so much."

"That, and a general lack of taste," Sonny cracked.

Walker ignored this, saying to Cilla and Otis, "I always asked Sonny silly stuff. Back then I read a lot of teenybopper magazines. *Tiger Beat* and that there. Bad interviews with the likes of Little Lord Mountbatton about his favorite food and color? But Sonny here, he asked me ugly stuff. Like, he'd ask which horrible death I'd rather go by."

"He did not," Otis said, laughing.

"Did, too. Like, do you want a mine to cave in on you, so you slowly suffocate, or fall out of an airplane and go splat? Or would you rather burn up or freeze to death?"

Cilla was on her feet, shaking a finger at Sonny. "Sonny, shame on you." She laughed a little, despite her apparently blue mood.

"I did it just to mess with Walker's mind. He'd try and be tough, so I'd get more and more gruesome until I made him bawl. That was the whole point of the game. But Mama would get so pissed at me, I had to quit doing it."

"I should think so," Cilla added.

"Shit, that ain't the worst of it, not by a long shot. I could turn ya'll's hair white, with the stories of things Sonny did to me."

"You won't, because I'm still bigger than you," Sonny added, with mock threat in his eyes and a clinched fist.

"My eternal cross to bear, for damn sure. Anyway, Cill, we better get you to the airport if you want to catch that plane. And I don't want to leave Salome waiting."

"No. That would never do," Cilla grunted. To Sonny and Otis, she simply said, "See you soon."

5.

THE STUDIO DIDN'T get its power back for a whole week. Everybody had clean up and insurance to deal with anyway, so it wasn't such a bad thing to take a recording break. Prince left the hospital, and he and Shookie moved into a house in town. They decided to sell the Sugar and Spice, once they brought it back up to code. Both knew if the heart attack had been any more serious, Prince wouldn't have made it, so far from town, on the other side of the rain-swollen creek. They talked of opening a smaller place on East Sixth, smack in the music district.

Sonny spent some of the downtime helping Ruby car shop, fixing her up in a new Taurus. Though she whined a little about the price and showiness, Sonny could tell she loved her new wheels. They dropped by once to show Walker, but no one was home. Once Sonny got his phone service restored, he gave Walker a call. The answering machine picked up:

"You've reached Salome Ross. If this is regarding a job, please leave the agency name and number, and I'll get back to you. If you're looking for Walker Blaine . . . he doesn't live here anymore. Don't leave him a message here, if you want him to get it. Peace!"

Sonny hung up, puzzled. Didn't sound like it would do to leave questions on the machine. Mama hadn't said anything about Walker's moving out of Salome's. She surely would have crowed about the break up, did she know—she hadn't approved of their age difference.

So where could Walker have gotten to?

On the day they were to meet back at the studio, Sonny arrived early. Walker's Corvette was already in the lot. Sonny found his brother alone in the studio, playing Goldie. Walker looked grungy, decked out in gear befitting his homeless status. He wore a black 'do-rag wound around his head and an old festival sweatshirt with the sleeves lopped off. Hole-riddled Levi's covered his skinny legs. A scuffed boot tapped out time. Walker was real gone in the song he was playing. Sonny recognized it instantly as *Gloaming Nocturne*, the closing ballad from the last Salamanders album.

Unnoticed, Sonny listened in as Walker immersed himself. It was riveting. This was the perfect way to hear him play, when there wasn't even a pretense of performance. He was doing it only for the pleasure, for the feeling. He sparkled, sounding sharper than ever these days. Sonny realized suddenly that Walker was still growing as a player, that his talent had nowhere near peaked. What was he going to play like when he was in his fifties and sixties? The thought struck Sonny as both exhilarating and fearsome.

Finishing the song, Walker saw Sonny watching him from the booth. Looking distant, still embraced by his muse, he waved him in. "Good to see you, Sonny. Guess we beat the rest of the crew here."

"Guess so. I tried to call you. Got new digs?"

"None permanent, yet. Talked to Mama today. She's going to let me move in with her awhile until I decide what to do." Walker smiled. "Figured you didn't need a roomie."

"You got that right." They nodded at each other. "You been sleeping here, Walker?"

"Some. Stayed a night at Floyd's, but didn't want to be an imposition on his family. I could have taken a room, but I just didn't feel like it." Walker looked down at this hands, fingering a mournful minor run.

"So you going to say what happened with Salome?"

"Usual shit. She's awful young. Mama was right about that. Sometimes she just acted like a spoiled child, wanting her way, and right now. And I got my hang-ups with her job. I really didn't like her modeling all that sexy stuff. But I'd drive her crazy, too—working the same song over and over, or just wanting to play or compose when she wanted to go out shopping or to dinner. Just stupid stuff."

"Too bad."

Walker nodded, not saying anything for a minute as he fooled with the song. "You know I met her at an NA meeting? It's a good place to meet sober women. But then, you got to worry about attending the same meetings and having to pull your punches. Your gripe's with them, you can't really talk about that. Plus, we both always was traveling with our jobs."

He went into the song again for a bit, scowling slightly. Just a snatch of *Smitten* appeared in the middle as he added, "I probably shouldn't of gotten involved so quick after Vada died. But I hate being alone. After Vada OD'ed, I lay there at night and thought about the real good times . . . the ugly shit, too. I felt empty. Guilty, too."

Sonny nodded. There was nothing he could think of to say.

Walker stilled the strings. "You still go out chasing tail, Sonny?"

"Not since I quit getting fucked up." He didn't elaborate how things had been way crazy before he got clean. What it was he wanted from women, now that he didn't want to hurt them or fuck mindlessly, wasn't quite clear to him yet.

Walker said, "Me, either. I ain't real interested in meaningless shit—I done sowed my wild oats, you know?"

"Yeah, I do."

"And if I do meet someone," Walker went on, "I always got to wonder if it's the real me she's digging. She might just be into Firewalker. Or maybe it's the money she thinks he's got."

"You decided all this after Salome got home the other day?"

Walker gave Sonny a sidelong glance. "I been thinking these things about Salome and me for a time. Needed something to force my hand, I reckon."

"That storm scared you that much?"

"No, but it scared Cilla. She went stark crazy. When we lived in L.A., there was a drought on, so it never rained much. When it did, it was only pouring rain. None of the dramatics of a Texas thunderstorm."

Walker paused for a minute, again playing the beginning of *Gloaming Nocturne*, the ballad he had written for Cilla. Sonny saw clear to what was coming. He lit a cigarette, hoping he was wrong, and just as certain he wasn't.

"When the siren sounded, we got downstairs. Salome and I stuck a futon in the basement this summer so we could just head on down and crash if the forecast sounded bad." Walker stopped playing and lit his own cigarette, a faraway expression in his eyes. "Cill was clinging to me, crying and screaming every time the thunder hit, begging for God to make it stop . . . I never seen anyone as freaked out. My heart really went out to her."

"Ain't all that went out to her, right?" Sonny said, turning his back on Walker and pretending to fool with one of his amps. "You fucked her on Salome's futon."

Walker was silent for a long minute, then said, "You don't get it, man. It ain't just fucking with Cilla. It's the most intense loving I ever known. That either of us ever known." He paused, then added with great emphasis, "We're the real deal together."

Sonny sat, pulling his Tele into his lap. "Ain't that sweet."

Walker didn't seem to pick up on Sonny's sarcasm. He kept right on playing and talking. "I tried to forget what it felt like with her. I want to spend time with Cill without those memories making me feel sad. I like her as a person and I enjoy her as a musician, too." He paused, playing the main melody again, saying better with his notes what he was feeling than he possibly could with words. Sonny was compelled to insert a light rhythm line into Walker's lead. Walker played it sweet against him, looking into Sonny's eyes as they finished, both laying hands over their strings together to still them. "She ain't like other women, Sonny."

"No shit."

"I thought maybe I made what we had before too perfect in my mind. You know, because I left it behind? And I sure always regretted that."

"Why'd you leave her then?"

He paused again, watching his hands as he started to play again. "I thought it was the right thing to do. Daddy said so, right before he died. That's mostly what he talked about with me, was Vada, and doing right by her. It kind of brought me back to what was real, seeing him dying, talking to him about stuff for the first time in my life without being scared to death of him. I was flying high right then, careerwise and every other way. I couldn't think straight at all, man. I spent a king's ransom a day on good shit. And all the time, people turned me on so they could hang with Firewalker."

"Stop talking about Firewalker like he ain't you."

"He don't feel like me, though. He's something I hide behind. But when I was high, and drunk as a fucking coot, messing with Cilla, slapping and getting slapped by Vada? I believed I really was him." Walker put Goldie on a stand and cracked his knuckles. "The night of the storm, I tried to show Cill how different I am now."

"You are different." Sonny put his guitar on a stand and picked up Goldie. He squatted on a stool a few paces away, shaking his head at the feel of the thick strings.

Walker followed, taking a long drag off his smoke and blowing rings. "She told me things that night. About the tour with Grey and being married to him, about being with this Mickey asshole—"

Sonny hit a fat lick, dragging his left down the neck in imitation of Walker. "Oh, please tell me she called him 'Mickey Asshole.' It'd do my heart good."

"Don't I wish! She knows deep down he's no good. Even though she wears his big old rock on her hand, she ain't in no hurry to tie the knot this time around. For one thing, she's worried about him later on wanting kids. She has female problems." He sat quiet for a minute, closing his eyes. "Sonny, Cill had my baby in her when I left. I swear I didn't know. That would have changed everything."

Still intent on Walker's guitar, Sonny replied, "She didn't know she was pregnant when you left. Else she would have told you, just to keep you there. There was nothing you could do, anyway, even if you stayed."

They didn't say anything for a long time. Sonny focused on playing a song he was working on, once he got the feel of the fat frets and strings. Into it he jumped when Walker spoke again. His voice rang with shock. "Sonny, you knew she lost that baby, and never even said one *word*?" Growing visibly angry, he snapped, "Why the fuck not?"

Sonny turned to face him. "She made me promise not to. I knew she'd tell you if she ever wanted you to know."

"When did she tell *you*, for chrissakes?"

"When we did that video together. Her marriage was breaking up, remember? I guess she told you about losing Grey's babies?" Sonny was relieved when Walker slowly nodded, his anger shifting to sadness once again. "I told you before, she needed a friend to talk to."

"All the same, why'd she tell you something like that?"

Sonny put the guitar back on the stand. He walked over to Walker and stared down on him. Walker narrowed his eyes and stared right back up at Sonny. "Look Walker, I know you got every reason to believe I'm a dick. You surely think they call me the Icestorm for things other than my playing style, too, right?"

Walker wouldn't answer.

Sonny went on. "Who you want her to talk to, her husband who was making a public spectacle of them both? Bonnell just wanted in her pants. She ain't got no girlfriends to speak of. And I know you better than just about anybody does. I did my best to be kind, even if that's too tough for you to picture."

Walker finally dropped his eyes. Quietly, he said, "I don't mean nothing against you personally. I'm just having a hard time with her going through this and not telling me. Reg and Sterling knew, too, yet ya'll never said boo about it. That's hard to swallow, is all."

Sonny picked up his black Telecaster again, comforted by the familiar neck. Walker pulled a stool up across from him, watching Sonny's hands. Sonny stopped playing and offered Walker a smoke. Walker took it, nodding, saying nothing.

"So what now?" Sonny finally asked. "Where ya'll go from here?"

"Damned if I know, Sonny. Things was magical when we finally fell asleep the night of the storm. We'd made love, talked things out.... I thought we'd be together again. I guess I was being a fool. The next morning, the phone woke me up. I dashed upstairs, naked as a jaybird, to grab it. Thought it might be Mama or you, with trouble from the twister. It was Salome, making sure I was okay and telling me when her flight would be in. Sonny, I know how tacky this sounds, but I had forgotten all about Salome. When I hung up, I just stood there for a second, thinking, got to deal with that bad breakup stuff now."

Walker smacked his forehead with his hand. "I did like this and said, 'Ah, shit!' or something aloud. That's when I heard Cill let out this sad little laugh. She was standing in the basement doorway, already dressed, holding her purse. She was royally pissed. She starts squalling, saying she don't know what had come over her. She couldn't go down this road with me again. She wanted me to just take her to the airport so she could get home to Mickey. I tried to talk to her, to kiss her, but she wouldn't even look at me. Told me she'd wait out front while I got dressed. So I did. But I couldn't believe she was acting like that—after being so close the night before?" He shrugged, looking mystified. "Before she left, she insisted we stop by and check on Mama and ya'll. We'd gotten the call about Prince, and she thought you needed to know. But fuck if she'd deal with me. She said, 'No talking or touching.' She just stared out the car window, taking in the storm damage, crying some.

"She made me drop her curbside at the airport. She split without another word to me. Then I picked Salome up. I was sore, no doubt about it. And pretty quick we got in a stupid argument. Some petty shit, I can't even remember what. So I broke up with her, just like that. Man, was she pissed!" Walker paused, managing a sorry smile. "I really suck at breakup stuff."

"Leastwise you got the balls to tell them. I do my best to just disappear."

"That is worse, I reckon."

"They think so."

Walker shook his head. "She's probably gone for good."

"She left most of her stuff at her hotel, right?" Walker nodded. "She'll come back for that shit. Girls don't leave stuff behind easy. I had them come by my house when they couldn't stand me no more, just to pick up ugly shoes or some other silly shit they forgot."

"Still, she could just have the hotel send—" Walker stopped short as the studio door opened.

"Boys, your rhythm section has arrived," Eddie Finger crowed, strutting in with his sticks held high. Cilla followed him a few footsteps behind, head lowered like a geisha's. "The beat do go on, ya'll. Hey, Sonny, during our downtime, I was thinking—"

"Did you hurt yourself doing it?" Sonny deadpanned.

"Very funny," Eddie shot back. "Look, let's borrow Johnny Lee from the Rockets and do a benefit show with all us original White Tornadoes. We could donate the cash to help folks rebuild and stuff."

"That ain't a half bad idea for a drummer, Eddie."

"Ah, screw you, man," Eddie sneered, laughing. Floyd and Otis strolled in, catching the tail end of their exchange.

"What, Eddie, they making drummer jokes again at your expense?" Floyd asked, dropping his harp case on Sonny's amp.

"They're fixing to, Floyd." Eddie beat a silent tattoo in the air and commented to Cilla, grinning, "The sad thing is, half the time I really don't get them jokes."

Everyone else laughed. Sonny noted Cilla raising her eyes, gracing Eddie with a warm smile. Floyd pointed at the brothers, saying, "Hey, Eddie. You know how many guitar players it takes to screw in a lightbulb?"

"Can't say as I do."

"Just one . . . but fifty more of them will say they could have done it quicker and with more feeling!"

They all cracked up, then turned their gaze in Walker's direction. "Why's everybody staring at me?" he asked.

Eddie said, "Because all of us was thinking only a fool would say he could do that lightbulb better than you can, kid."

"Shut up, man," Walker said, starting to blush. He grabbed his nephew's arm. "Hey there, Otis. You going to sit in today? We're going to mess with an old Ted Hawkins soul thing and one your Uncle Floyd helped me write this week called *Sugar and Spice Shuffle*. You could try out some of that rhythm stuff your daddy's been showing you." Walker gave Sonny a proud grin.

Otis held up his hands in surrender. "Forget it. Just here to dig on ya'll. I've never seen Uncle Floyd and Sonny play together."

"Suit yourself," Walker said, patting Otis on the back. He turned his eyes to Cilla, nodding greetings. To Sonny, Walker sounded nervous. "Real glad you made it back to town, Cill."

She wouldn't look at him as she answered. "Did you really think I wouldn't come back to finish this project? Granted, I behaved childishly the night of the storm. But I do pride myself on my professionalism."

"I never doubted you for a minute. It scared us all. Don't forget, though—they got them bad storms up Dallas way, too. You live here in Texas, you deal with it." Walker paused, waiting until she looked up at him. He then said in a more gentle voice, "One thing I sure enough learned, darlin'. You can't run off every time things gets real."

6.

WALKER ENDED UP buying the Sugar and Spice from the Browns. He didn't want to run a club—not by a long shot. He was instead looking for a house, which is after all what the Sugar and Spice had been in its first incarnation. The Browns would open a smaller place in town on East Sixth. Walker gave them the money needed to make it happen. "It ain't a loan," Walker assured them. "It's five years back rent, plus interest."

It was the perfect solution. The Browns were closer to town, in case more medical help was needed in their later years. They were both tired of the grind of running a nightclub but weren't quite ready to leave the music and restaurant behind. The place they'd open would feature their solid-gold jukebox and food, maybe a little acoustic music a few evenings a month.

For Walker, the purchase was symbolic. In part he'd done it, and invested in the new joint, to help out the old men, to pay off his debt to them somewhat. It was under Prince and Shookie's roof that Walker had his first taste of a sane life away from Big Billy Jay's abuse. There was also the fact that, long before the Blaine brothers were born, their Daddy Jim had played the club. Most of their heroes had trod the stage, at one time often as not backed by Sonny's first band. Walker confessed to Sonny that he believed the place to be some sort of family power point, a Blaine Chaco Canyon. Besides, once he fenced in the multiacre property, he'd have a sweet retreat from public life.

The first order of business had been replacing the roof and damage in the upstairs living area, bringing it back up to code. As for the downstairs bar portion, there was one last thing that needed doing before Walker dismantled the barroom. Hundreds of people in the area had lives devastated by the tornado. Walker had jumped right on Eddie's suggestion they have a fund-raiser for the storm-ravaged. They'd do the thing as the farewell concert of the Sugar and Spice. They'd all agreed it was a great idea to reunite the Tornadoes for the gig. Johnny Lee had been contacted on the road. He'd been thrilled with both the cause and the idea of playing again with his old band.

Walker used his clout to make the concert happen ASAP. He'd started the donations himself, selling the antique bar to an El Paso outfit for a tidy sum. He'd made a big production of announcing the gig on local news, having the check from the bar sale blown up huge like a sweepstakes winning. TV stations around the country picked up the story, and donations began to pour in. The White Tornadoes Reunion Tornado Fund-raiser had officially begun.

It was a small, well-heeled crowd, limited in number by the size of the place and the minimum $200 donation per head. For the price they got to feast on the Brown's Texas gourmet and hang with, as Vada had liked to call them, the blues hoi polloi.

Before the actual performance, Sonny and Johnny Lee had gone out into the crowd. Many people they knew from the old days. It struck Sonny as funny that many of the now well-to-do contributors had been starving, drug-addled hippies when they had first come here to see the Tornadoes. It was a pretty apt description of the band at that time, too. Sonny saw that even though very nice champagne was being poured for those who still imbibed, many of his former party partners were sticking to the cappuccino and Walker's blue-bottled water.

After a few minutes mingling, Sonny had retreated to ready himself for the show. He stepped out back of the kitchen for a smoke and found his brother and a clutch of roadies doing the same. Walker stood off by himself, bouncing from foot to foot, puffing madly—downright twitching. He was dressed in his usual heinous manner: scads of gaudy jewelry, a kimono that looked like it was sewn from a pop-art painter's drop cloth, skintight crimson leather pants. Walker's feet were clad in three-toned cowboy boots. A new magenta hat topped him, encircled by a band of golden eagle dollars.

Sonny touched Walker's shoulder, causing him to jump nearly out of his skin. "Hey, little bro. You okay?"

"Couldn't be better," Walker answered in a decidedly grim voice.

"You look ... well, like Firewalker should. But you're acting like—" Sonny cocked his head down so he was looking right into Walker's jittery eyes.

"Like what?" Walker snapped.

"Squirt, you been behaving yourself today?"

"What the hell does that mean?" Walker gazed hard back at him, taking a drag off his cigarette, exhaling smoke right in Sonny's face.

"Ain't been putting shit up your nose, have you?"

Stunned outrage swept Walker's face. Sonny understood that whatever was eating at Walker, it wasn't cocaine. "Hell, no!" Walker all but roared back. The smoking roadies stopped talking and looked their way, causing Walker to drop his voice. "You think I'd do that right before this thing? Jesus, Sonny."

"I guess I just hadn't seen you before a show since you been straight. You always act like someone's poking you with a cattle prod?"

Walker kept glowering at him, visibly trying to simmer down. "Is that what I'm like right now?"

"Pretty much."

He nodded, lighting another cigarette from the last. "Won't deny I get more edgy than I did when I was loaded all the time. You know how brave and stupid booze and toot make you." Sonny nodded. "But ... I guess it's just Cilla I'm worrying on. She's sick as hell, ain't she?"

She was. She had been sick for weeks now. It was hard to get through a morning without having to abort a take or two as she dashed to the bathroom. Sonny tried not to concern himself—she wasn't his problem. All the same, he couldn't help worrying. He'd lie awake at night, seeing her green-tinged complexion in his mind's eye.

Sonny had found her tonight, a few hours before show time, crouched on the ladies' room floor. He'd heard her dry heaving in there, and had steeled himself to go check in on her. He'd barely recognized the bedraggled girl, smelling of puke, her hair stringy and soaked with sweat. He suggested that maybe she'd gotten dysentery from drinking the water after the tornado—they'd been told to boil it for days on end, and a few people who didn't had taken ill.

Having seen her in the bathroom, Sonny wasn't sure she could go on tonight. But he'd spotted her just a few minutes ago from a distance, in the house, at Mickey's side. Her hair was floating around her carefully made-up face. She looked unearthly gorgeous in a fiery orange-gold sheath and matching amber jewelry. She'd smiled and given him a strong thumbs-up. If he hadn't seen her sick earlier, he wouldn't have known anything was the matter.

She had pulled out a great, sexy performance. Everyone had gone above and beyond. Egos were checked at the door, and all seemed to have a blast—performers and audience alike.

After a long and generous encore, Sonny had headed back into the crowd. Dinner was being served. He was invited to sit with a couple of former party girls for dinner. Somehow he'd parted with them on relatively good terms. He was having fun catching up, telling them about the new record, when Bonnell strolled over and asked to join them.

"That is, if you fine ladies do not mind?" he cooed, kissing their wrists in his usual manner. Charmed, the women made room for him.

"Man, you been way too pleasant to be around today," Sonny said to him, only half kidding.

"You know I love this town. I'm glad I was able to offer a small amount of help." Bonnell had arrived unannounced late this morning, bringing around boxes of éclairs for all. He'd made a point of praising everyone on his or her worthy charities. He even wrote out a shockingly generous contribution check of his own. Then he offered any services he could provide as a performer and master of ceremonies. Ever stylish in delivery, everyone agreed the singer was perfect for the emcee job. He was welcomed aboard. Bonnell had labored hard throughout the day fitting his piano and accordion to the groove, enriching several numbers. He worked especially diligently with Sonny and Walker, adding a great stride line to *Daddy Jim's Walk*, a cooking ¾-time tribute tune from their album. He even agreed to lay it down on tape for them before he left town again. Sonny was nearly as mistrustful of Bonnell's generosity as he was pleased by it. But then disasters were said to bring out the best in people. He decided to accept his old bandmate's actions on faith.

"There's a small bit of compassion left even in me," Bonnell assured the women, flashing a practiced smile. He turned the grin to his old partner. "Found a singing voice, you? I confess to being pleasantly surprised."

"That makes two of us," Sonny said, embarrassed but still pleased by the compliment. He'd made his public vocal debut at the benefit. Walker insisted he do it. He wouldn't rest after he overheard Sonny singing while demonstrating his lesson to Otis that day in the studio. He talked Sonny into singing lead on a couple of songs.

Sonny had protested initially. "You and me both may be able to play guitar, but I ain't got that voice of yours."

"Sure, it's different from mine, Sonny—not better or worse. Just like our playing," Walker had answered. "You actually got pretty good pipes. Got sort of that sweet Irish tenor thing happening. Here we all thought the music came through Mama's side. Them Leprechaun Blaines must have had a few crooners back in the day, too."

Sonny wasn't crazy about the results, but they were keeping the songs on the record. And he hadn't chickened out tonight. He sang one of the songs at the concert—and hadn't made a fool of himself. Right before he'd stepped up to the mike, Walker strolled over and said in Sonny's ear,

"Pretend you're all alone, tired as hell, driving I-10 across the belly of the state. You're keeping awake by singing along with the tape deck."

It had worked.

Now here was Bonnell, telling him, "Who knew you could carry a tune? To think when last we met, you were in such upheaval. I do wish you well, Sonny."

Sonny thought he sounded sincere—and could usually tell when Bonnell was bullshitting from past experience. He offered his hand. "Thanks, Bonnell. I'm glad everything worked out for the rest of ya'll."

Floyd approached the table then, his squint more pronounced than usual. "Excuse me, folks—Sonny? You know where Walker's got to? There's all kinds of folks asking to see him."

Sonny quickly surveyed the crowd again. Sure enough, no sign of Walker. He remembered their brief conversation before show time, and it made him uneasy. Something wasn't right.

Where was Cilla? Sonny spotted her, seated left of Mickey. At least she hadn't run off with Walker, leaving all the folks who came tonight to get their picture made with the guitar god shortchanged. Mickey was eating with one hand and talking full-mouthed with the person on his right. His other arm was gripped solidly around Cilla's shoulder. She seemed to be ignoring the conversation altogether. Her body leaned away from Mickey's as much as he would permit. The fork still lay beside her plate of untouched food. With a lost expression, she seemed to be scanning the crowd herself.

Sonny excused himself, leaving the girls in Bonnell's capable hands. He followed Floyd into the kitchen. Floyd took him into the pantry, out of the kitchen help's earshot, saying, "Walker's been acting weird all day. Been uptight for awhile, really—you noticed?"

"Yeah. I thought he was high before show time. But I asked him flat out, and he denied it. I don't think he was lying, neither."

"Yeah, he seemed straight onstage, didn't he? I ain't never seen anyone handle sobriety as well as Walker has, Sonny. But I do wonder, with the way he's acting up, if he ain't headed for a slip. I mean, where the hell is he? He knows how important his hanging out and talking to people at this thing is."

"Yeah, he does. Let's see if we can't round him up."

As Sonny followed Floyd out the kitchen door, he thought about the show. Walker couldn't be sulking about his performance—or anyone else's, for that matter. They'd done sweet justice to the full range of their careers—from stuff Sonny hadn't done with the Tornadoes in ages, right up to the new stuff from *Lone Star Ice and Fire*. But Floyd was right—something was eating Walker bad.

It had to do with that damned redhead, no doubt about it. Sonny had been watching Walker and Cilla during the show. When she wasn't on,

Mickey had her close at hand, sometimes kissing her neck. She didn't seem to notice her fiancé. She was watching Walker's every move. Sonny realized now that the two were still caught up in each other, even if they were trying to play it cool.

Walker's Corvette was still in the lot, so, after a quick walk around the grounds, they hit the upstairs. There was the various flotsam and jetsam from the remodeling project. No Walker, though. Again, they made a walk-through of the crowd, asking a few people if they had seen Walker. No one had. Cilla caught Sonny's arm as he passed her table. "Sonny? Are you looking for your brother?"

"Uh-huh. You know his whereabouts, girl?"

"No ... I've been wondering what happened to him, myself." She looked into Sonny's eyes, the worry evident in her own.

.As Mickey snatched her closer to him in a bear hug, her expression changed to one of annoyance. "Don't sweat over Joltin' Joe, Dom," Mickey slurred. "That fool'll turn up sooner or later."

"Shut up, Mickey," Cilla hissed under her breath.

"You better listen up to your woman, asshole," Sonny growled, leaning over to whisper in Mickey's ear. His voice was deadly, but he showed a pleasant expression on his face for the assembled guests. "I don't see a hard ball for miles around, so I reckon my head's safe enough," Sonny continued. "But I see plenty of solid-body guitars. And I can swing one of those a lot better than you could, judging from watching you when you still had the nuts to stand at the plate with a bat in your hands."

Mickey registered the threat slowly. His face grew more outraged by degrees, and he removed his arm from Cilla's shoulders. Free at last, she hurried toward the restrooms. Sonny stalked off before Mickey could gather his wits and come after him, verbally or otherwise.

Floyd was motioning from the kitchen. "Found him, Sonny. Downstairs."

"Downstairs? The cellar, you mean?"

"Uh-huh. You better talk to him, man—he ain't too cool. He listens to you better than the rest of us. Come on." Sonny followed Floyd through the kitchen and down the cellar steps. The old basement was in reality little more than a cavernous root cellar, with just a few bare bulbs cutting into the darkness. Much like a cave, its temperature stayed fairly constant. As well as offering sanctuary during twisters, it was a good place to store liquor and dry goods for the saloon.

Walker was sitting on a beer keg, lost in the shadows beneath the stairway. He still wore his stage costume. His wild clothes overpowered his smallness here in the darkness. He looked crushed, like a kid on Halloween who had lost his candy through a hole in his goody sack. He held a still-sealed bottle of Crown Royal in his hands. He was staring at it intently. Tracks from tears streaked his cheeks.

"Hey there, Squirt," Sonny said, pulling up a beer box to sit on. "Don't go freaking out just because they didn't boo me offstage when I sang. You still the one in the family with all the chops."

"Man, you got the chops too, Sonny. You need to cut that shit out," Walker said distantly. "Besides, you're a goddamn hunk. That's real important. Ain't no doubt that the person who first said beauty's only skin deep was born pretty."

"You sitting down here staring at straight poison because you ain't Charles Atlas? That's plain dumb." Sonny put his hand on the bottle. "Ain't a woman up there that wouldn't bed you in a New York minute. You know that. Now give that bottle to me and we'll go on upstairs."

Walker shook Sonny's hand free of the liquor. "Oh, yeah. Any woman up there, mine for the taking. But for the keeping, that's another thing altogether, ain't it? No, they got husbands and fiancés and shit to go home to. Can't stay with me. I'm just Sancho, Sonny."

"Sancho?"

"That's what the Mexican girls call their backdoor man. Shut up and fuck me, they tell Sancho. As for talking, they do that with someone who really matters."

He raised the bottle, looking at it, swirling the whiskey around. "Lot of balls in this thing, you know it? They say the girls get prettier at closing time? Well, I always felt a lot prettier, too. Made me feel like I really could walk on hot coals, get enough of this shit in my gut."

"Hey! Walk on hot coals. Might could be a blues name for you in there somewheres," Sonny said, trying to keep the fear from his voice. Walker just kept staring at the liquor. Sonny grabbed his arm and shook it once. "Let's cut through the bull, here. This is about you and Cilla, ain't it?"

Walker kept swishing the amber fluid around, studying it. "Everyone on the record knows?"

"No one but me, Walker, I'm sure of it. That's just because you told me about the night of the storm. Even I didn't know for sure that something was still happening until I saw you singing to her tonight, and her watching you with that desperate look on her face."

"Huh. I sing songs to her soul, while that big Dago of hers is playing with her body. Bet she dug that. Have me doing what I do best while he does what he do best." Walker cracked the bottle seal open, tossing the lid to the floor, and took a big whiff of it, closing his eyes. He stopped just short of drinking.

Sonny was stern. "Don't you get it? The girl never forgot about you, all those years you been gone."

"Right. That's why she married Grey and is getting set to marry this jerk."

"My point exactly! She's just searching. She don't come back to no one like she does you. Can't get you out of her head and heart."

"Bullshit," Walker said.

"No it ain't. Look, you know you hurt her real, real bad. She's a proud woman."

"I know it. And that's why I gave her all the power this go-round. Thought it was only fair we kind of traded places. I'm the secret this time—she's the boss." Walker slammed his empty hand into the basement step above him, spilling some of the whiskey. "I can't take this shit no more!"

"So, what? You're going to drink poison? What's that going to change? Two years and more of hard-earned clear-headedness, is what. You just going to feel like hell when you come down, and the stuff that's eating you's still going to be the same. Give me that bottle." Sonny stood, holding out his hand.

"No."

"Walker—"

"I said no. I—I don't want to!" He sounded like a petulant child. He clutched it to him, shoulders slumped. After a minute, he hollered up at Floyd.

Floyd's voice floated down to them. "Right up here, Walker. Sitting on the basement steps, listening in, just like I used to when you was a kid playing Sonny's guitar."

Sonny saw a satisfied smile skate across Walker's lips. Sonny hollered back, feigning outrage. "And I told him not to ever touch my gear. You damn well knew that, Montgomery. And just look what come of it."

"Sonny, don't you ever let nothing go?" Floyd yelled back, laughing low. More gently, he added, "What you need, Walker? Just say the word."

"Go get Cilla. No one else, though. Tell her she's got to come talk to me."

"You got it, man." They heard Floyd clomp up the wooden steps overhead.

"That's the way, Walker," Sonny told him.

"Might still drink this whole damn thing," Walker said, glaring at Sonny in the dim light.

"Well, at least you ain't yet," Sonny said, lighting them both a smoke.

"That's so," Walker agreed, taking the cigarette with his free hand.

They sat together for several minutes, not speaking. Walker put the open bottle to his nose now and again. Sonny wasn't sure if he really smelled the whiskey, too, or just imagined he could. He had to admit he wouldn't mind sharing a belt. He knew now wasn't the time to be thinking that way. He had to be the strong one here. If he could get through tonight sober, he could maybe keep Walker that way, too. At least Sonny could get him out of here and away from the humiliation and the gossip that would surely follow if he lost it at this thing. If he did, Walker would be mortified when he came to his senses. More than himself, he would feel he had failed all the people he had helped inspire to seek the sober life. That, Sonny knew, would crush him.

They heard someone walking down the stairs, a lighter tread than Floyd's. Cilla's heels. Sonny met her halfway up the steps, taking her hand and guiding her down to keep her from stumbling in the unfamiliar gloom. "Walker? What are you doing down here?" she said.

"I'm thinking," he said with a touch of surliness. "I know no one believes I actually think, but I do, every so often."

Cilla's expression changed from puzzlement to fear when she noticed the whiskey bottle. "No, Walker. Please don't drink that."

"I ain't yet," he told her. Sonny helped her sit on the box where he had been, and made to leave. "You stay put, Sonny," Walker told him, in a voice that brooked no argument.

Sonny tried to pull free of her hand. Cilla didn't let go. She mouthed him a silent *Please stay*. He snatched free, but did drop to the bottom step, lighting another cigarette.

Walker said, "This won't take long." He added, his voice oozing disgust, "We don't want your handsome sweetheart wondering where his pretty baby's got to."

"Let him wonder." She sat on the box Sonny had pulled up beside Walker. "Tell me what's wrong."

"You and me. I know I said you could call the shots, that you could do whatever you wanted. But it's driving me crazy." He coughed out an empty laugh. "You know, I think every man fantasizes about being some unbelievably gorgeous woman's love slave or some damn shit. And I'll admit it was real hot at first. But Cill, I need to be your partner, not your slave or master. I can't stand hiding my feelings for you. And all I do all weekend when you go back to Dallas is picture you and that big jerk. . . ." He stopped, rubbing his eyes and grimacing before he went on.

"I been down here, trying to decide a few things. First is, how much I want this here drink?" He shook the bottle at her. "I remembered earlier today that I had this bottle hid down here. Stashed it years ago. Stoled it from a liquor delivery when I still lived here. Was like it called out to me."

"Lover, you don't want it," Cilla whispered.

"Hell, I don't!" he snapped at her. "I want it all the time. It never stops, the crave. You don't got the problem I got, so you just don't get it. Hey, Sonny?"

"What?" Sonny sighed.

"You want a drink?"

"Oh, yeah," he said, glancing back between the wooden treads at the two of them. Cilla's head was cocked to one side so she could peer under the hat brim into Walker's eyes. A beaded shoulder strap slipped down one arm.

She and Walker weren't touching—but just barely. Looking away, Sonny added, "But, Squirt? I ain't going to take one. Not right now."

Walker nodded. He turned the bottle upside down and let the whiskey splatter on the dirt floor, filling the air with its smoky scent. "Not right now," he echoed, handing Cilla the empty bottle. She stroked his arm, nodding encouragement. He said to her, "It's also been tough, seeing you go out drinking with Eddie—"

She interrupted. "Eddie and I are only friends. You know that."

"I know—that's not what I meant. But he can have a damn drink with you. I can't do that. Can't even share a great bottle of champagne with you like we used to do. Not ever again."

"It's not important. You taking care of yourself is what matters. I'll do anything to help you."

Walker nodded. "Okay, then. I can't go on like this. I'm going back on the deal we made. I need all or nothing from you. I want you to go home and think about us, Cill. Think real damn hard. Because you only got two choices." He held up two fingers. "I wish I could say that if you don't want to be with me, that's cool, we'll be friends, we'll play music and hang out and all. I'm usually real good like that. I'm friendly with almost all the girls I used to see. After she cools off, I bet Salome and I will be pals even. But with you, that won't fly. It's too much, too deep and strong between us. We just got to keep our distance, or I'll mess up." He pointed at the empty whiskey bottle.

"Oh, Walker," Cilla said, starting to cry. "I don't want to lose you."

"Then here's your second choice. But go home with Mickey and think about this real hard before you decide. You got to be sure." Walker looked down at the floor, and dropped to his knees, carefully avoiding the booze soaking into the dirt. He grabbed her hands in his. "If you come back here, you marry me. Soon as we can manage. No shacking up, not this time around. We're wasting time. You got to be my wife if you come back. Only way it can be. Death do us part."

She pulled away and fell back against the stairs' support beams. "Walker . . . my God. I—"

"Don't say nothing. I told you. Go home to Dallas with him tonight. The record's practically in the can, anyhow. Sonny here can play a bass like nobody's business. If we got anything to fix or overdub, he'll handle it." He dropped his head. "I need you out of my sight while you're thinking things over. You been the master of the game long enough, ordering me to shut up and just do you when I come to your hotel room. Ball's back in my court now, girl. Get out of here." Walker, still on his knees, shooed her toward the steps.

"Walker—"

"Shut up, woman," he growled. More gently he added, "Get, now."

Sonny got to his feet, leaning against the banister, giving her room to climb past. She stopped at the top of the stairs, turning back. The bulb at the top of the stairs flickered off her eyes, making them look catlike. One leg was bent, foot resting on the top riser. Her hair was a fiery halo. Her illness-slimmed figure was graceful and vulnerable, shimmering in her lamé gown. She locked her gaze with his. Cilla had never looked more wondrous than she did now, standing above him, eyes glowing, the rest of her backlit from the kitchen. Whomever she chose, it hit Sonny in that instant that he'd forever lost his Golden Girl.

She pulled up her dress strap. Her face twisted rapidly with distant hope, confusion, and remorsefulness. Then she seemed to hone back in on Sonny. He thought he could see an apology in her eyes. He nodded once at her. She returned the gesture and darted back into the club.

When the kitchen door slammed behind her, Walker asked, "She gone, Sonny?"

"Yeah. You staying down here all night, Squirt? I can say you took sick or something."

Walker stood up, brushing the dirt off his knees and boots, coming over to Sonny. He rubbed his eyes and smiled slightly. "Reckon I could do just that. It's my basement now. Smells too much like booze down here, though. I better come up and do right by all these big spenders. Been sulking down here like a little boy long enough."

7.

AFTER CILLA HAD LEFT Sonny and Walker in the basement, they stalled only briefly before joining the party. Walker was greeted by loud applause as he strode in, waving like a Rose Bowl queen. He apologized for his tardiness in a strong, saucy voice. "Let's just leave it at unavoidably detained, ladies and gents." The crowd's impression was that a woman caused his delay. True enough.

The throng descended on Walker, wanting to talk music and old times with Austin's Favorite Son. Sonny searched the room, verifying that Cilla had indeed left with Mickey. Walker stayed to the bitter end, being gracious to even the most obnoxious, dancing with every woman who asked him to, posing endlessly for pictures. Sonny was amazed by his brother's poise. Walker knew well how to handle his public. He sure had the shit it took to play the celebrity game—smiling, despite his broken heart.

But the very next morning Walker was back to counting days. Though he had not actually taken that drink, he'd come within a fraction of doing so. He had fallen off the wagon mentally. "Got to get focused, or I ain't going to stop at just smelling the stuff the next time around," Walker told

Sonny. He asked Sonny to go to the meetings with him. Sonny obliged for the first couple of weeks.

After meetings, they'd head to the studio, tweaking the recording for *Lone Star Ice and Fire*. Sonny felt the master was ready for delivery. He warned Walker they had to be careful not to mess with it too much or it would lose its spontaneity, its loose quality. But Sonny soon saw that Walker was mostly farting around, changing very little.

The record was a project Walker could work with hands-on. Remodeling the Sugar and Spice occupied Walker's mind, but there was little he could do to help. He would go by and approve the work and the budgets, but the labor had to be done by the experts and their crew. Growing up with Big Billy Jay had taught the Blaine boys inexpensive, quick repair work but nothing of quality remodeling. Besides, Walker distracted the young guys doing the grunt work. Most of the crew were of the perfect age to be his biggest fans. Lots of them, like so many others in the music-crazed town, were pro-am stringers themselves. It quickly became a safety issue when a true-blue guitar god stalked into their midst.

Walker sat in all over town, with huge acts playing the big venues on down to the tiniest holes. Not since his days as Paladin, the shy baby ax-man, had he jammed with so many diverse acts. Occasionally he dragged Sonny along. Sitting in with old friends admittedly was a gas.

Walker was in-house signing autographs for the paying customers the day Sugar and Spice, Too opened. For old time's sake, Walker took over the jukebox selections. He brought back Jive Five Mondays when his touring schedule allowed. In turn, this helped the record stores in town, as the disciples would then try to search out the stuff that had Firewalker's stamp of approval. Austin's hipster economy boomed, thanks to Walker.

The other Salamanders were lying low, enjoying their downtime from touring. But Sonny knew Walker was antsy, ready to hit the road. Walker wanted him to come along. The idea of touring only made Sonny weary and nervous. Sonny had acted like a marauding pirate his last couple of tours with the Rockets. He knew there were hotels and bars that never wanted his sorry ass back inside their establishments. At the time, Sonny thought they had a lot of nerve. Now he was deeply shamed by his drunken, drugged-out shenanigans.

Sonny was scared he might drift back into his bad old ways on the road. At home, it was harder to slip. Austin was small enough for people to watch out after each other. You could always call someone to lend a hand when the old demons came scratching at the door. Walker tried to assure Sonny that he had found a meeting in every city. He ran a clean tour. Those who still imbibed kept house separately from the sober folks.

Walker tried to talk up the tourist angle. "This ain't going to be them nightmares of one-night stands, like before. I'm going to do some sightseeing, too. Just think—we could get a snapshot of you, me, and the Seattle Space Needle. The Washington Monument. Sears Tower. We'll call it the Stud's Scrapbook."

"Maybe I'll join you boys for a date or two. I just don't want to get out there for real just yet, Squirt. Did it for what, twenty-plus years? Still need to cool my jets."

Walker finally relented, but he talked Riley and Outlaw into a pre-Christmas tour. The boys could be home for the holidays, then resume their road trip in February. They left town after a honkin' farewell show at the Auditorium. Sonny joined him for a couple of songs from the new record. Walker played with his usual string-shredding intensity and seemed pretty happy with life in general. Sonny hoped this tour signaled a new beginning for his little brother.

While the Salamanders toured, the remodeling work was completed on Walker's new abode. He called to ask Sonny if he would check out the job. If everything was cool with the place, Walker wanted to arrange a small Christmas housewarming winging for old friends and family.

Sonny felt strange, a little bothered, by the Sugar and Spice's transformation. At least it was still in the "family." He whistled, turning off the highway onto a smooth, one-lane paved road. Always before, two dirt-lined wheel ruts made up the driveway. Except for repairs and maintenance, Walker had changed the exterior building little from what it had been back when he moved in. The old gravel lot had given way to a small paved area, with easy parking for about five vehicles. The balance of what had been the former parking lot was now festooned with rose bushes, their bases covered in redwood chips. The chips crunched beneath Sonny's feet as he walked to the rear of the house. There was a patio now, a small lawn, a big spa, and a rock-hewn pit barbecue. The rest of the large property was left to abundant oaks, cottonwoods, wild grasses, and flowers that naturally flourished near the creek-dug ravine.

Inside was a different story altogether. If Sonny had been blindfolded, brought in, and asked to identify where he was, it would have taken him time to figure it out. Entering from the front porch, Sonny found himself in a beautiful, high-ceiling living room, cooled by lazy Casablanca fans. Walker kept only the hardwood floors and the huge stone fireplace on the ground floor. The fireplace was at one end, well-made, with brightly colored mission-style furnishings huddled around it and a large woven Mexican rug lying in front of the hearth. Sonny shook his head and laughed as he spied a truly ugly wooden clock shaped like Texas hanging on the fireplace. Walker had told him about this clock. He'd spotted it at a D/FW airport gift shop. Sonny had made such fun of him when told about it that he could hardly believe Walker still had the balls to buy it. Paid an idiotic price for it, no doubt.

Just below the clock was a wooden mantel. Displayed were all of Walker's Grammys. Sonny took one down, choosing one that the Rockets had been nominated for, too. The statue was heavier than he had expected. He felt a twinge of envy bubble to the surface as he rocked the Grammy in his hand. Be nice to have one or two of these living at his house.

Sonny replaced the award carefully, turning his attention to the stereo and record shelves made from cherrywood, crafted by the same cabinet-maker who had designed Sonny's similar oak shelves. A large picture window had been installed on the garden-side wall, framing the rose garden and the creek's ravine beyond.

Where Shookie and Prince's offices had stood now was a spacious dining room, abutting the kitchen. Sonny peered in at the *House and Garden* kitchen. When Walker showed Sonny the rendering of the kitchen remodel, Sonny teased Walker about all the fancy chrome appliances, the butcher-block counters. "What a waste of money, Squirt. You ain't cooked since you married Vada."

"Leastwise, now I won't be embarrassed to hire me a pretty little chef," Walker had laughed back.

Where the Sugar and Spice stage had been now stood a recording studio and rehearsal area, with Walker's other awards on display. Alongside the studio was a guest room. The former bar's small men's and women's rooms had been combined into one large clay-tiled full bath. The wall to the outside was glass bricked. In the middle of the room was an antique claw-footed copper bathtub. Walker had found the tub at a garage sale for a mere twenty-five bucks. He'd had it polished to sparkling red-gold. Sonny had to fight an urge to strip on the spot and take a long soak. He instead headed up the freshly varnished staircase.

Upstairs, Walker stayed with the original three bedrooms and two baths. The plumbing had been upgraded, and the bathroom walls and floors were retiled. The bedrooms bore new carpeting and paint. The two larger bedrooms, Prince's and Shookie's, were nearly identical, except the one without a private bath had a niche built over the front porch. Walker had dubbed it the Guitar Room. There was a window seat in the niche—a great spot to sit and play. A couple of the instruments here were sinful temptations, though most were in pieces, missing a component or two. Old Broad and Goldie were on the road with their master.

Sonny was gazing at the case holding Walker's old Martin, thinking he might sit and play for a little while. Then he noticed a group of photos on the wall, near the foot of a futon couch. There were various performance shots and many family photos, too. One of Big Billy Jay and Ruby, from their wedding day, hung next to a snapshot that Sonny had taken with Vada's Brownie camera the night she and Walker got married. Hard to believe any of them had ever been that young. Even harder to believe was a Blaine family portrait, taken at the Dallas Olan Mills when Sonny was all of ten.

Then Sonny's eye caught a picture that made him lightheaded. He'd never seen this photo. Him and Walker, clutching guitars—the scene was unmistakable. It was taken here, at the Sugar and Spice, at Sonny's eighteenth birthday party. They had just finished playing *Who Do You Love?* That had been the first time they had ever played together, the first time Sonny ever witnessed Walker play with a band.

His own hair hung below his shoulders, a Jim Morrison mane, framing a face grim with apprehension as he looked on Walker. Walker smiled radiantly below his then-new fedora. Peach-fuzz bearded, scrawny—still such an awkward little kid.

Sonny, all alone in the big house, cracked up as he looked at that freaked-out expression on his own Young Turk face. Had the boy he'd been even suspected what was to come? The sound of his laughter echoed lonesome off the emptiness of the building.

Still chuckling, Sonny went to inspect the last bedroom—the room that had been Walker's for five years. Sonny's laughter died in his throat as he opened the door. The record collection had moved on with the Browns. The little room looked fresher—the old flowered wallpaper gone, new paint and carpeting in place. Otherwise, it was much the same—too close to the same. The night of the video wrap party came hurtling back. The memory of Cilla in this room returned through sense memory: the yielding softness under his fingertips, the taste and smell of her cooze, the sight of her lying on the bed, in stockings and diamonds, open and willing . . . and the sound of her saying the wrong name. Sonny didn't linger in the room for a minute longer. The walk-through was now officially over. He dashed down the stairs and out of the house. He was panting when he collapsed into the Fury's driver's seat. He closed his eyes for a minute, taking a deep breath or two to calm his stupid panic.

He got over it.

He called Walker that night, telling him the place looked ready. Walker arranged for catering through his management and had Sonny make calls to invite people. Uncle Charlie, Aunt Lucille, and Ruby were coming. Otis was, too. Sonny also invited everyone who had been involved with *Lone Star Ice and Fire*. Except for Cilla. Walker didn't say, "Don't call her," but then, Walker hadn't so much as uttered Cilla's name since she had left the tornado benefit with Mickey.

The day of the party, Sonny and his mama arrived early. Ruby figured her boys could watch bowl games together while she stole a rare moment with both of them. Since Walker had only just gotten back to town for his break, Ruby wanted to help him get the vittles together, and put his place in order.

"Relax, Mama. I had the housekeeping service come over yesterday," Walker told her.

"What for? I could have cleaned up."

"Don't be silly, Mama. You're my guest."

"I'm your mama. Silly is letting a bunch of strangers clean up after you."

The concept of catering was even more mysterious to Ruby. "I can't believe my baby's turned into such a city slicker. Why, back in Mingus, we might do a potluck at the Elk's Club or church, but if you invited friends and neighbors, you did great big farmhouse dinners, put a big side of beef on a spit. You'd cook for them your own self. That's what a party is. Walker Dale, this newfangled kitchen is just going to waste. It's a shame."

"We'll see if you still feel thataway after you see how good the food is, and how the mess disappears with the caterers," Walker replied. He grabbed Ruby's coat off the sofa and held it up to her. "Tell you what. I'll take you to town, and you can get stuff to make me a Karo nut pie in my fancy new oven."

"Balls, Walker! She makes that pie, it's all mine." Sonny laughed, stretching out on the couch.

"I'll make two!" Ruby declared, slipping her arms into the offered wrap. "You want to come with us, Sugar-boy?"

"No. I'm going to stay put on this couch, watch football, and dream about my pie," Sonny said. He did fall into a light doze right after they left. He surfaced from sleep when he heard a knock at the door. Sitting up, he checked the Texas clock. It was pretty early yet for guests to arrive.

Opening the door, Sonny was nearly knocked to his knees to see Cilla leaning heavily against the jamb. If not for her hair color, Sonny might not have recognized her. She was dressed in oversized black sweats and running shoes. Her hair was limp, and her face bore no trace of makeup. Her lips looked dark against the decided pallor of her complexion. A few pimples even bloomed on her chin. Cilla's eyes were puffy and red with crying. Sonny glanced beyond her. She'd driven up in her old Jaguar, the California plates still in place.

"Sonny?" she breathed. She pushed herself off the jamb, swaying a little. "I don't have his phone number. I rang your mother's, but no one answered."

Sonny found his voice—a voice. It sounded high and unnatural to his ears, like he'd been kneed in the crotch. "Um. There's a bunch of people coming over. Walker's having a housewarming thing. Family, folks from the album, Riley, Outlaw . . . they'll be happy to see you. Did Walker invite you?" Sonny knew that he sure enough hadn't.

"No. I only knew that Walker was back from the road." She slumped again against the door frame, dropping her face into her hand. Her voice sounded teary as she added, "My timing sucks. I can't believe I hit town the very day he's hosting a stupid party." She wiped her eyes with her palms and tossed her hair out of her eyes. "Sonny, please don't say anything. I have to talk to him, but it can wait a day. I'll get a room and come back tomorrow." She turned to go.

"No you don't." Sonny stepped onto the porch, grabbing her wrist as she started back down the steps. Her hand felt frozen, lifeless, in his palm. "Walker would kill me if I let you leave. Come in, girl. I'll get you some water or something. You look like you been through a wringer."

Cilla opened her mouth to answer just as Walker and Ruby drove up in the 'Vette. Walker peered through the windshield, looking to see who had arrived so early. Sonny saw his brother's face register astonishment at the sight of Cilla. He climbed cautiously out of his car, ambling toward them. Within arm's reach, he asked, "Girl, what's wrong?"

"I clearly had no idea you were having a party." She motioned to her sweats, and ran fingers through her messy hair. "I'm sorry to just drop in like this."

"Don't be. I was expecting company. We can fit in one more, easy." Walker moved closer. "Where you coming from?" He cocked his head at her car.

"Dallas. Walker, I left Mickey today."

"No shit?" She nodded. Face growing hopeful, Walker grabbed her free arm. Sonny turned her loose, shuffling inside the house behind them. Ruby trailed in last, clutching a bag of groceries.

Ignoring his mama and Sonny, Walker led Cilla into the downstairs bedroom. He left the door open, giving Sonny and Ruby a clear view. Sonny couldn't make out their words over the drone of the football game on TV. Cilla was crying again. Walker wiped a tear off her cheek with his fingertip as she spoke. He scowled, eyes burning beneath his hat brim.

Ruby handed Sonny the bag of groceries, her face a puzzle. Great. Looked like Walker hadn't told her about what had gone on with Cilla. Sonny shrugged, rolling his eyes. Dollars to donuts, Ruby would be pissed at him, instead of Walker, for not clueing her in.

"Is that Cilla?"

"Who else, Mama?"

"I couldn't tell, right off. She looks so poorly. She and your brother? . . ." Ruby let the question hang in the air. Cilla nodded firmly at Walker, laughing through her tears. Letting out a whoop, Walker gathered her up in a bear hug and kissed her soundly. His hat was knocked to the floor by the force of their embrace.

Seeing them clinch, Ruby exclaimed, "Oh, my stars. Walker Dale must have been with her, all them nights after supper when ya'll was recording." Blushing, Ruby shook her head, hand to her mouth. She continued to watch the couple. Cilla's back was to them, her arms reaching to squeeze Walker's neck. One of Walker's hands was laced in Cilla's hair, the other rubbing the curve of her hip. Ruby whirled on Sonny. "Billy Jay Blaine Jr.! Did you know about them two?"

Sure enough, she was mad at him, instead of Walker. "More or less."

"How long they been carrying on?" she demanded.

"Forever, seems like." Sonny couldn't stand watching them kiss another moment. He walked past Ruby's glaring face toward the couch, adding, "Only this time, I thought she was gone for good."

8.

SONNY DID HIS BEST to stay clear of the happy couple. News spread like a drought-fed brushfire that Walker and Cilla were to be married, even before their management firm made an announcement. The news caused a flurry of press in the music magazines (TWO MUSICAL DYNASTIES UNITED) and the tabloids (LONE STAR SCANDAL: MOUNTBATTON'S DAUGHTER LEAVES STRIKING STRIKEOUT FIANCÉ FOR HOMELY HILLBILLY GUITARIST). Sonny knew that quick nuptials had been Walker's plan. Knowing still didn't make the ache any easier to bear.

Ruby ordered Sonny to make an appearance at a tree-trimming party at Walker's. They were forecasting a freeze that night, and she said she didn't trust herself driving her new car over in the weather. As soon as they arrived, Sonny saw that Cilla had regained her sparkle. Her smile and laughter came readily. Her pallor was replaced by a golden glow. She was dressed in a green, oversized knit tunic, black leggings, and ballerina flats. She danced around the huge spruce they had installed by the stairwell, tossing tinsel like it was fairy dust. Walker hovered ever near, keeping one hand always on her. Every few minutes the couple seemed to forget that family and friends were there with them, and gave way to not-so-chaste smooching. Sonny drank an entire cup of virgin eggnog, then hung his own contribution to the tree—a fourteen-carat golden ball, engraved with the year and the couple's names. He sat with Otis and Floyd and exchanged spare pleasantries. He monitored his watch. An hour's worth of good cheer was all he could muster without getting ugly.

At the stroke of sixty minutes, he stood, handing his empty glass to Cilla. "Well, it's been fun, but I got another thing I got to get to. Otis? Get your grandmama home safe for me, hear?" Otis nodded, patting Ruby's hand. Ruby smiled at her grandson but shot Sonny a bothered glance. Sonny waved, darting into the downstairs bedroom, grabbing his leather jacket from the heap of coats on the bed. When he stepped through the front door, Walker and Cilla were on the front porch waiting, holding hands.

"Get back inside to your company," Sonny said. "Ya'll don't have to see me out."

"If you're leaving already, I reckon we do," Walker said. Sonny thought he sounded ticked. "What's the big rush, Sonny?"

Lying was easy enough. "Just got another . . . thing, is all. Another Christmas party—you know how it is, this time a year. Thanks for having me." Sonny trotted down the steps to his car, his back to the couple. He could hear them coming down the steps after him.

Cilla stopped him from climbing into the car with a hand on his arm. She said, "Sonny, one reason we asked all of you here was to announce our wedding date. We're getting married in two weeks."

"Two . . . weeks? You eloping?"

"After all the rude ruckus in the press?" Walker grunted. "Fuck no. I want to make it official."

"Ya'll can't get a wedding together in two weeks," Sonny said, coldness creeping from his gut to his limbs.

"Sure we can," Walker insisted, pulling Cilla to his side. "The house just got fixed up. We'll do the thing here. Mama already sweet-talked her preacher into performing the ceremony. Reg is back from the road then, so he can give his baby girl away." He shrugged. "Just order up the flowers and food, buy rings, and we got us a wedding."

"You don't got to go back on the road until February, Walker. Slow down. Make this easier on everybody, especially Mama. This'll make her a crazy person."

"I thought of that," Cilla said. "Ruby and I've had a talk. I've convinced her she doesn't have to do a thing. Besides, we've waited long enough as it is."

A grin slid over Walker's face. "Little too long, as it turns out."

Cilla hit him playfully. "You said you wouldn't say anything, Walker!"

"To no one but Sonny, I meant."

Cilla looked exasperated. Walker just kept his Cheshire cat grin fixed on her. Too precious. Sonny had to will himself not to sneer as he said, "Look, I got to fly. Congrats. I—"

"Wait! Walker's right. I want you to know." Cilla took a deep breath. "I took your advice after the tornado fund-raiser and finally saw a doctor."

"And you had dysentery, right?"

"No, no." Laughing, she declared, "I'm pregnant." Cilla turned sideways, pulling her loose sweater tight across her belly. She held a pose, smiling coyly, showing off a definite bulge between her hip bones.

Walker reached a hand around her, stroking the swell. He added, in a voice filled with pride and wonder, "Looks like the little dude came to be during the tornado."

The frost that had crept over Sonny threatened to stop his breath. He managed to ask, "You feel okay?"

She nodded, her laughter joyous. "Never better. The doctors say we're both doing great. My dangerous first trimester is behind me. Now we'll do just fine."

"A baby . . . that *is* big news." Even at his most lovesick, Sonny had not imagined making a family with Cilla, due to her fertility problems, so he hadn't even considered how watching Walker and Cilla having a child would feel. Poker-faced, he watched Walker smile down at her, rubbing her belly—in a world of their own. After a moment Sonny regained his composure enough to smile and extend his hand to Walker. "Congratulations."

"Thanks, Sonny." Walker shook firmly, beaming.

"But this is even better reason to hold off getting married. You don't need all that stress in your condition. That baby's health comes first."

"It'd stress me out more to wait. I need to be married before he's born," Cilla said. "And I'm finally over that dreadful all-day morning sickness, yet I'm not showing much yet. With the tour break, Walker's actually at home for a little while—we can honeymoon."

"Sounds like your mind's made up," Sonny said. "Good luck."

"I need more than luck, bro. I need a best man."

Sonny took his time answering. How could he say no without blowing his cool? "Been there and done that already, Squirt. It's likely bad Karma to have the same cat twice."

"Bullshit. We both want you to stand up for us. We're asking Julia Jean to be Cilla's matron of honor."

Sonny looked to Cilla. "You really want me up there?"

Sonny saw sadness behind her smile as she answered, "Of course I do, Sonny."

"What do I got to do? This'll be a real wedding. Last time we just blasted to Mexico, got you hitched and snockered, and blasted back to the States after sleeping and fucking our buzz away."

"Would you mind making compilation tapes for the reception?" Cilla asked.

"I reckon I can manage that. What else?"

Walker gave him a sly grin. "Bachelor party?"

"Look out!"

Cilla frowned at them. "Not on your life. I don't want you guys chasing a bunch of naked ladies around while I'm pregnant."

Walker deadpanned, "So you don't care if I chase naked ladies around when you ain't pregnant?"

She smacked him playfully. "Just try it, buddy. No, I was thinking instead we'll invite everyone to the rehearsal dinner, and have a prewedding party. We could have everything ready for a jam session. Anyone who wants to play together can. I bet a lot of people would dig it."

"Be an awesome jam, with your guest list," Sonny said.

"Exactly. Nobody has to participate that doesn't want to." She grinned. "But I know I will, because soon I won't be able to hold my guitar, with my big belly."

"You just got to master those T-Bone moves, darlin'," Walker said, playing air guitar behind his neck.

"And the big belly thing can be done," Sonny added. "B.B. King seems to manage."

"Sonny! That's wicked," Cilla scolded. Quietly she added, "Add B.B. to the invites, Walker. I'll talk late-term technique with him."

Walker scratched a tally mark in the air. "Here we go. This is how small weddings get huge. One guest at a time."

"I really should invite him, lover. He's been friends with Dad for years."

"That's true." He shrugged at Sonny. "The guest list shows what an odd couple we two be. I got obligations to Second Cousin Heady Jeb Joe and Great Aunt Teddine Jewel. She's got obligations to B.B. and Bad Signs. I mean, my God—my daddy-in-law's going to be Little Lord Mountbatton!"

Sonny laughed in spite of himself. "Heady Jeb Joe. I forgot about him. Maybe you shouldn't send him an invite. That head of his will make Cilla here worry too much about the birth." Walker joined in the laughter.

"Heady Jeb Joe? You're kidding, right?" Cilla asked.

"We ain't. Looked just like Charlie Brown as a kid, didn't he, Squirt?" Walker nodded. "Head like a goddamn pumpkin."

"Dear God. Too late to avoid your gene pool now."

"Welcome to the South, girl," Walker snickered. "Always thankful when new blood splashes into the inbred stew."

"How's Reg taking the news?" Sonny asked, finally managing to climb into his car's seat. He'd observed Reg's treatment of Walker at the Tornado show—polite but distant. It had seemed to Sonny that Reg still resented the hurt Walker had caused his daughter.

"He's coping," Cilla replied. "He wasn't thrilled when we called him and told him about the wedding."

"Can't say I blame him," Walker said. "I hope he don't flip out when we tell him about the kid."

Cilla hugged him, smiling radiantly. "Dad loves you like a son, lover. If he freaks out, it will only be because he thinks he's too young to be a grandfather."

WHAT SONNY GOT roped into doing was mailing a few invites and picking out the groom's suit. Walker threw around wads of cash to get ready in time. They had the invitations printed and out the door in two days, with the generous help of Julia Jean and Ruby. They made phone calls to those on tour,

inviting them verbally. Walker's tour wardrobe managers all but instanta-
neously created Cilla's wedding dress. Two floors of the Driscoll were
reserved, to assure their well-known guests some degree of privacy.

Once the big day arrived, things were all set to run smoothly. There
was some worry of a paralyzing ice storm hitting town, but it cooperated
and stayed in the Panhandle. The weather was crisp and clear. The house
looked spectacular, covered with tiny Christmas lights. Luminaries glowed
from the main gate all the way up to the house. The whole indoors was
heady with scent from a huge Douglas fir Christmas tree. The evergreen's
fragrance was layered with a top note provided by hundreds of Gloaming
Nocturne roses used as decoration. Countless candles lit the downstairs
with their romantic light. Cilla and Walker would be married in front of the
mantel, with a Yule log brightly burning.

Sonny went to his tailor to have their suits made, keeping Walker's
weird taste completely out of the process. He chose deep-blue double-
breasted silk. His tailor cut the suits a little loose and hip to prevent them,
as Walker put it, "from looking like a couple of Texas Republicans." They
both wore narrow, crimson ties. Walker managed to keep his jewelry to a
minimum, a small hoop earring and his signet ring. His peace symbol was
worn over his old-school tie.

Sonny did what he could to talk Walker out of wearing a hat for the
occasion. It was futile. Cilla had found one she simply could not resist and
bought it for Walker as a wedding present. He insisted it was just right for
the ceremony. The broad-brimmed hat was dark red, a fine match for his
tie. The band was a thick gold braid, featuring a large and beautiful fire opal
over the brow. What made it a hat only Firewalker Blaine would dare to
wear was the addition of an actual red fox's tail dangling from the band
down the back of the brim.

Sonny thought he was immune to the sight of Walker's flashy hats, but
he laughed himself into convulsive tears watching his brother posing in it
before the mirror. Walker smirked at his reflection, cocking his head this
way and that. "This is one righteous sombrero, huh, Sonny?"

"Fuck, no! It's the silliest damn thing I ever seen," Sonny howled, flipping the tail forward to cover Walker's face. "Make up your mind, Squirt.
You want to be Clint Eastwood or Daniel Boone?"

"Both!" Walker said, taking the ribbing in high spirits. "Besides, this
here tail matches Cill's hair damn near perfect."

Cilla's bridal dress was dilly-dilly lavender blue, with three-quarter
sleeves and a scoop neckline. It was made to fit snug at her still small waistline, but had petticoats and a full knee-length tulle overskirt, camouflaging
her pregnancy. To complete the look, and to keep her already swelling feet
out of heels, she wore pointe slippers, the long laces tied at her ankles. The
ensemble was reminiscent of something a prima might wear as the princess

in *Swan Lake*. Her hair hung loose. In lieu of a veil, she wore a silk scarf looped around her head and neck, trailing down her back. She pinned Ruby's mama's pearl brooch over her heart, and carried a bouquet of Gloaming Nocturne and baby's breath. Julia Jean wore an identical dress, in a shade matching the Gloaming Nocturne.

Sonny held the matching rings. They were too flamboyant, as Walker had designed them. He'd paid Uncle Charlie big to have them finished in time. The bands were thick rose gold, with alternating channel-set sapphires and diamonds, and one large brilliant-cut ruby in the center setting.

As Sonny took his spot at the mantel, fingering the ring box, the full impact of what was happening hit him. He waited with Walker for the bride's entrance, watching the firelight play off of his brother's happy features. Sonny tried not to be obvious as he sucked in a couple of deep, steadying breaths and turned to watch for Cilla with the assembled guests. Otis, acting as usher, seated Ruby, and the ceremony began in earnest. The air filled with Walker's playing. It was a piece he'd recorded for the wedding march, a bop instrumental version of Gershwin's *They Can't Take That Away from Me*. The poignant lyrics of eternal love flitted through Sonny's head as they waited for the bride to make her entrance.

Cilla came to the top of the stairs, clutching a nervously smiling Reg's arm. Sonny's legs went slack at the sight of her. Her skin shimmered in the firelight. Her eyes sparkled, near tears. She graced Sonny with a radiant smile as Reg released her at the mantel—a smile like a kiss—like a knife. The joy on her face, the sound of Walker's gorgeous take on Gershwin— Sonny knew that this moment would forever haunt hm. Even so, he managed to will a smile in return.

Then Cilla gave her full attention to Walker, and he to her.

During the ceremony, Sonny let his mind stray. He went back to that nightclub in Santa Monica years before. He remembered vividly the girl in the green leotard, intently watching his hands as he played guitar. Once, for a few days, he believed that he would be the one to marry Cilla. He thought Walker would be in his boots now, eating his heart out.

But Walker was a better match for her. His little brother had that dose of tenderness a woman needed to be happy. Had Sonny married Cilla, she likely would have soon left him, driven away by his distance. Knowing this made it no easier on his ego. He had failed without even enduring a trial of proof.

What would Daddy Jim make of all this? He would have been so tickled by his grandsons' careers. No doubt this fine redheaded musician joining the family would delight him. Perhaps most amazing to Daddy Jim might be Walker now calling home to this honky-tonk where he and his grandsons had each made music over the years. Sonny believed the old man's spirit was with them tonight. Feeling foolish for it, he nevertheless sent an appeal to Daddy Jim to give him the strength to make it through this nightmare with his grace intact.

Sonny did make it, played it as cool as custard. He signed the license with his fan-autograph flourish. He posed with a practiced smile for the wedding pictures. He was certain no one could see the toll this ordeal was taking.

Once the ceremony wrapped, the caterers removed the seating and moved in dining tables. During the transition the crowd enjoyed hors d'oeuvres and drinks on the patio, a large fire in the barbecue pit keeping the cold at bay. Once everything was set up, all moved back in to dinner.

Sonny made the expected best-man toast before they dined. He had agonized over his speech for days. He finally decided to keep it short and sincere. He didn't trust his composure enough to draw it out. "Walker, Cilla, I can honestly say I never thought I'd see this day. Yet here ya'll are, joined for a lifetime." He raised his glass of sparkling cider to the couple. "To my brother and his exquisite new bride: May ya'll have many years of joy and happiness together." The toast was well-enough received. No one kidded him about its brevity. The people here knew Sonny to be a man of few words. It was filled with honest sentiment, too. It would be unfair to wish this couple anything less, the way they felt for each other.

After the dinner, the dance music tapes were put in place. Walker and Cilla had their first married slow dance to Albert King's version of *The Very Thought of You*. Thereafter the party became much more unstructured. People danced and mingled. Some wandered about the large house and grounds. A few of the famous stringers present holed in on the upstairs Guitar Room, retreating to play with Walker's outstanding toys.

Sonny had drafted Otis to man the reception tapes. Confident the music was in good hands, he headed to the front steps, craving the outside's cold. He wanted a smoke and a moment's reprieve from the happy scene inside. Lighting up, he dropped his head into his hand and tried to empty his mind.

Quickly, Sonny sensed he wasn't alone. A heartbeat later he heard a familiar voice. Bonnell was singing an old Chuck Berry song that the Rockets 88s had made their own, a jumping little ditty about a Creole wedding that had taken the old folks by surprise. The singer let loose his high-tone chuckle. "*C'est la vie* indeed! Apropos song for this night, *n'est ce-pas?* Sonny, *mon ami ancient*. Did we not meet in this exact spot, more years ago than either of us would care to admit?"

Sonny looked over to the far side of the darkened porch. Bonnell sat in a fan-backed chair. "Sure enough. I had just got done strangling Walker within an inch of his life."

Bonnell laughed again. "Ah, yes. Well, Walker is bound to inspire strong emotions in you." Bonnell paused. *"Que'lle surprise*, hey Sonny? Even I couldn't have guessed it would be little Firewalker to land that delectable girl."

"Me, either." Sonny wished the man would leave him be, but could think of no way to dismiss him without upsetting their recent truce.

He heard the ting of things crystal tapping together, followed by Bonnell's footsteps creaking toward him along the porch's old boards. "I ran into a bit of a dilemma deciding on their wedding present. I know that Walker no longer imbibes. But I understand his bride hasn't his problems with liquor."

Sonny nodded agreement, still looking out into the night. He paid Bonnell's words little mind.

"So I went to my parents' wine cellar, searching for a special gift for the bride," Bonnell drawled. "We have bottles dating back to before my family had even arrived in Haiti." He held out an antique glass vessel with a red wax seal displaying an ornate N. "This is Napoleon Brandy, a century-and-a-half old, maybe more. Sonny, it is art in a bottle."

"I just bet." Bonnell had his attention now.

"But I've heard rumor that Mrs. Firewalker Blaine is in a family way. Is this true?"

"I don't think they want it spread around just yet. So keep it quiet."

"My lips are sealed. But as that is the case, I won't give her this brandy. These days, don't they say drinking might be unhealthy for the unborn? And of course I wouldn't want to tempt Walker, leaving such a treat around the house for months on end."

"Mighty thoughtful of you, Bonnell," Sonny said, intently watching the bottle.

"Instead I purchased them a silver platter." The superior laughter bubbled forth again. "I'm sure Walker will miss out on the intended irony entirely, but me, I thought it a fine joke. Perhaps I'll go with a silver spoon for the little tyke's baby shower."

"Good one, Bonnell. Maybe you could pass on the one you was born with."

"I see that sharp wit hasn't been wounded by circumstances, you," Bonnell said as he held the brandy bottle up to glisten in the moonlight. "One of the last of its kind, this brandy." He dropped to the steps alongside Sonny, setting two snifters between them. With his palm Bonnell cracked the bottle's brittle seal. He handed Sonny the pungent cork to sniff. "Lusty as a woman's scent, eh?"

Sonny held it between his fingers and took a long whiff. "Damn. Smells even better than most of the women I've run with."

Bonnell chuckled, nodding. He poured the brandy into one of the glasses, taking it in his palm and swirling it. "Have you ever drunk brandy, Sonny?"

"Can't remember. Nothing like this stuff, at any rate."

"Right you are. This *stuff*, as you call it, is almost not of this world." Bonnell took a tiny taste, inhaling as he did so. He kept the brandy in his mouth a few seconds before swallowing it. He sighed, an almost sexual sound. "Certainly not your usual poison, Sonny."

Poison. Boy, Bonnell had called that one just right. It had been damn near a year since Sonny had touched such poison. It was time to go inside, get away from this asshole. Sonny needed to find Floyd, someone, in the program. He had to turn his back on this temptation, tonight of all nights.

But . . . would it hurt to sniff the cork again? It smelled so damned fine that it made Sonny's eyes tear up. Reluctantly, he handed it back to Bonnell. "I better go check in, see how Otis is doing with those music tapes."

"Don't be silly. You can hear for yourself—Otis is doing just fine. It's not like anyone is going to miss you, Sonny." Bonnell handed him the other snifter. Sonny took it by the stem, like a wine glass. "No, cup it in your palm, as you would a breast," Bonnell said. "You want to warm the brandy with your body's heat." He poured a small amount in the glass.

Sonny swirled it as he'd seen Bonnell do, sniffing it. He'd likely never have another chance like this one. Who in their right mind would turn down booze made for an actual emperor? Besides, there probably wasn't even a whole shot poured in the bigass glass. It wouldn't be a real slip—just a little sip.

"A simple toast, to take the edge off," Bonnell whispered. "It'll do us both good, before we go back in and have to watch Cilla dancing in your little brother's arms."

Sonny looked at the glass for few more seconds. He came very close to throwing it on the ground. But it would be like tossing gold dust into the wind. "Um . . . well, now you poured it for me, it'd be a sin to let it go to waste," Sonny said, clearing his throat.

"Exactly. A *sin*."

"Not like one's going to hurt me." Sonny glanced about, making sure they weren't being watched. "Still, I don't need to get the hairy eyeball. Let's go around to the kitchen door and head downstairs."

They circled the house unseen. Once they adjourned to the cellar, they drank the entire bottle of brandy in short order. Sonny could not believe how marvelous it was—like drinking satin coals. He couldn't stop at a taste of the stuff. Bonnell kept instructing him that he needed to slow down in order to savor the scent and flavor. Sonny had to consciously not gulp it. Though Bonnell in no way objected, Sonny knew he was downing more than his share.

For a time he didn't feel the buzz. Then it came, and all at once.

The brandy slammed Sonny hard upside the head. He felt himself go from clean to wildly drunk in a breath. Bonnell was loaded, too, yakking away mostly in Creole. Then the toasts began: to the unlikely couple; to bluesmen and women, whether they burned in hell or partied upstairs; to wild women found and sweet women lost. They went so far as to sing the maudlin Etta James tune *Stop the Wedding*, punctuating their performance with laughter and belching.

Sonny was mind-blisteringly drunk, hitting the place where he felt like his eyes were rooted to the sides of his head rather than facing forward. He was able to see too much at once without being capable of focusing on any one thing. And as had often happened in his drinking days, Sonny felt his spirit slide from joyous to hard-edged in nothing flat. This shift had been an attribute when facing a rough crowd in a tough room, but it had also caused him grief time and again.

"Alas," Bonnell said with a slur, peering into the now empty bottle, "our cupboard is bare. Perhaps they have some more of that mediocre champagne which they offered during your touching toast for the few here who still imbibe." He paused, giving Sonny a dark smile. "Imbibe regularly, I suppose I should say. Why not continue our fun, Sonny? Should we go a-hunting?"

"I better just keep my ass right here for now. Don't think I can even stand up, much less do the stairs without killing myself. Sure don't have the tolerance I used to."

"Suit yourself. I shall venture out alone in search of more nectar and a worthy woman or two. Cheers!" His tread stumbling, Bonnell took the cellar stairs.

Sonny heard a burst of raucous music as the basement door opened and closed. He sat in the near darkness, the festivities apparent only as a muffled vibration overhead. He was glad Bonnell was gone. Alone, he started to realize what he had just done. Remorse crept into his soggy brain. He remembered the recent night he had sat here with Walker, talking him out of drinking the whiskey. Sonny believed then that he was completely in control. Yet the first time he had ever been seriously tempted he had gone flying into the abyss all over again.

He felt his temper starting to solidify. He shouldn't be at this damn wedding, much less playing best man. Standing up for them? If there was one woman in the world he didn't want to see Walker married to, it was Cilla.

It wasn't fair. Whether it was a gift from above—or below, as Bonnell believed—Walker had it all, courtesy of those miracle worker paws of his. He had made Sonny into a footnote. *His brother plays, too?* Walker had the whole world in his hands. Did he have to take the only woman Sonny ever loved, to boot?

He heard the door at the top of the stairs open. "Sonny? You down here?" Fuck, man. It was Walker. Sonny didn't answer.

"I know it's you down here," Walker said, his boots clomping down the wooden steps. "I smell your nasty brand of cigarettes. No one here knows about this place but the Browns, me, my wife, and Floyd. They're still all upstairs."

"Bonnell knows about it now, too," Sonny said, fighting to sound coherent. "We been down here chewing the fat."

"You and Bonnell playing nice? Didn't think you two hung out at all now you ain't forced. . . ." Walker's voice trailed off as he caught a good look. He glanced around, finding the empty brandy bottle near Sonny's feet. "Oh, I see. Bonnell decided to sabotage you with some of his fancy-ass booze. That sounds more like him."

"Bonnell didn't do this to me. *I* did this to me. You know what the program says about owning up, little brother."

Walker sat down on a box, not saying anything. Sonny thought he might spontaneously combust if Walker didn't go away. Finally he snapped, "Leave me be. Get back to your guests and your new bride, Walker. Ain't nothing you can do here."

"I can be here for you."

"Like I need you here."

"You do. Wish you had come talk to me before you drank that shit. I could have been strong, like you was for me, last time we was sitting down here."

Sonny laughed bitterly. "Oh, that is rich. I sat here that night and listened to you talk about Cilla. Listened to you propose to her, in fact. Tonight, we could have the groom listening to me whine about my useless feelings for his wife?" Sonny pointed at Walker's wedding band. "That's beyond pathetic. Talk about water—" he leaned forward, dropping his voice "—and some damn great brandy, under the bridge."

"What?"

Sonny yelled at him, spitting, "You're such a dense piece of shit. You're like one of them idiot savants. Clueless, except when it comes to your music."

"I'm not so dumb. I know you used to have a little thing for Cill—"

"A little thing, he calls it!" Sonny slapped a hand over his face, erupting in empty laughter. "Little thing, yes, sir. Tell me something, dickhead. You ever ask her to marry you before you did here, in this basement?"

"Uh . . . no."

"So I beat you to the punch. I asked her, when we shot that video together. I mean, I never dropped to my knees and said, Marry me, Cilla— like you did. But damn sure she knew I wanted to make her my wife as soon as the shit with her ex was settled."

Sonny could see the words collide with Walker's psyche. Good—but was there still a grain of doubt in his eyes? "You don't believe me. Ask your hot little wife about it. She'll tell you. 'Course, she never said yeah to me, but she never said no, either. I never gave her that chance." Sonny looked up, seeing fear on Walker's face—and a stout dose of jealousy, exposed by his cocked brow. "Oh, get your damn eyebrow down. I told you before I never fucked her. But I did come . . . this . . . close." He held up his finger and thumb, nearly touching, right in Walker's face. "Then I blew it. Jumped out of her bed when she went and said—"

Sonny caught himself, choking back his deluge. Drinking made you stupid, all right, made you blurt out unspeakable shit. He stared hatefully at Walker. His brother stared back, pale, wide-eyed. When he managed, Sonny added, "You never escaped her mind. We'll leave it at that. I think your bride feels pretty bad about messing with my head. She don't think I'm some big joke—that's the one thing makes it bearable." Sonny lit a cigarette. He felt he was going to lose the brandy any second now. He thought he'd do his best to puke on Walker's boots if that came to pass.

Walker kept gawking at him. He finally mumbled, "I don't know what to say, man."

"Ain't nothing to say. Better you than me. You'll make her happy. I'm clueless about that shit." He took a few dizzying puffs off his cigarette before he spoke again. "Besides, ain't no way I'd marry her with that damn kid in her. Whose is it, really? Not mine, God knows. But there's a good chance you going to be raising little Mickey Asshole Jr." Sonny chuckled. "Maybe even little Eddie. You know that animal magnetism them drummers got. Your woman sure spent a lot of time drinking with him, about the time she got herself knocked up. Don't stop at just kicking up her heels, do she?"

Walker stalked to the far side of the room. Good—he'd struck a hurtful chord at last. Sonny could see him shaking with fury, and it was deeply satisfying.

Soon Walker turned back around, trembling slightly, struggling to keep his face neutral. "It didn't matter none to me who the daddy was. The baby is Cilla's, so that makes it mine. But they have to run all kinds of tests, because of her past problems. And one of the tests told us it's for sure. It's a boy, and he's definitely mine."

Sonny said in a low, cold voice, "Good news just keeps on coming. Lucky boy wins again. Too lucky, always seemed to me. Tell me the truth, Walker. Was it a standard contract? You have to sign in blood?"

"What contract?" Walker asked, clearly puzzled. "You mean my contract with Rollie? Or Sterling?"

"Shithead, I'm not talking about a *recording* contract. Talking about the one that got that record deal for you, though—and everything else you ever wanted."

"You're talking crazy now," Walker said, his voice really shaking.

Sonny watched him about ten seconds, then asked, "Is it crazy? Was Vada's soul part of the trade, too?"

Walker walked back toward him. There was something odd in his eyes—menace, fear—hard to place what it was exactly. Real quiet, he replied, "You should know better than to ask such things. Shut up *now*, Sonny."

Sonny staggered to his feet. Swinging at Walker—missing by a country mile—he nearly fell over, ramming his arm into the steps. He hit it hard, but couldn't feel it just now. "Fuck off, Walker! Ain't I done everything you asked?"

"Sonny—"

Sonny spun, collapsing back onto his crate. "Go upstairs. Here's your wedding present—I won't blow everyone's good time with drunken bullshit. Tell them I took ill. But if you don't leave now, I'm going beat the shit out of you."

Walker laid a hand on his arm. "I never meant to hurt you—"

Sonny yanked his arm away, spitting, "Don't you dare touch me. Never meant it? So what? It hurts anyway, having you as kin to me."

He watched as Walker took the steps with leaden boot treads. Sonny had no doubt Walker would strap on his swaggering public persona by the time he reached the revelers. His simple mind would probably forget this whole pathetic conversation when he hit the honeymoon suite with his little mama. *That's it, Sonny-boy. Make yourself feel better by dumping your grief— on the groom, for chrissakes!* Only a really worthless piece of shit would do that to his own brother on the man's wedding day.

Sonny may have fallen asleep, or may simply have passed out. All he knew for sure was that when next he knew anything, Floyd was sitting across from him, squinting at the empty brandy bottle. He heard Sonny stir, and looked up smirking. "Hey, Sleeping Ugly. Boy, you fall off the wagon in style. No Thunderbird or Night Train Express for our Icestorm."

"If I'm going to fuck up, I figured I'd do it right. Did Bonnell announce he got me drunk, say I was crying in my brandy?"

Floyd let go a wheezy laugh. "Bonnell's got his own problems. He came staggering in from the kitchen about an hour ago. He dragged some unwilling girl out for a dance, stepped on her foot, grabbed her tit, and got slapped to the floor. Then he started babbling and crooning in that weird language of his—"

"He goes off in Creole when he's loaded—and expects you to understand what he's talking about."

Floyd laughed, nodding. "Loaded's right. Talking shit, he grabbed another woman, kissing her and feeling her up. She happened to be the wife of Houdini Jones, Cilla's gigantic saxman? He let Bonnell have it good, right in the kisser." Floyd mimicked a right hook. "Bonnell went down like he's made of glass. They carried him into the guest room and left him there. Last I heard he was passed out cold on the bed. There's some talk of dressing him up in women's lingerie and taking photos for the *National Enquirer*, just to teach his ass a lesson."

"So there is some justice in the world, after all," Sonny slurred. "Sorry I had to miss that."

"Yeah, so was everybody else. Lot's of people were asking where you went. Walker told them you didn't feel good."

"Guess everyone figured that meant I was wasted."

"Not at all, Sonny." Floyd grinned. "I think all the men double-checked to make sure their wives, daughters, and girlfriends was all account-ed for. People figured you was getting a little, is what I heard. Like that other Sonny in the *Godfather* movie."

"Would have been better off." Sonny dropped his head in his hands. It now hurt like a washerwoman was wringing out his brain case. He was going to be sick for real, and very soon. "I fucked up big-time. Almost a year clean. Now look at me. I said shit to Walker I shouldn't never have."

"Don't sweat Walker. He's already at the hotel. But before he left, he asked me to give you a hand, if you would let me." Floyd held out his palm. "You going to let me, Sonny-boy?"

Sonny stared at the offered hand for a long time. Finally, he hit it with a low-five, saying hoarsely, "Okay. But I can't go upstairs. All those people, seeing me like this? Mama'll be so ashamed. And Otis? It really ain't right he should see me thisaway."

"Give me your keys. I'll go pull your car around, and we'll scoot unseen out the back way." Sonny handed him the keys. Floyd headed upstairs, paus-ing to add, "Let me just go tell Julia I have to get you home, because you're too ill to drive. Then I'll spend the night in my old room. Just like old times."

"Old times, huh?" Sonny whimpered. The room was starting to spin like a midway ride.

"One important change. When you wake up all hungover and remorse-ful, we won't take a hair of the dog and start all over again. I'll drag your mournful ass to a meeting. Maybe you're finally ready to start dealing with the truth that's tearing at you. Get yourself a sponsor—like maybe me, even. Quit being a sober drunk, huh, Sonny? Try really getting well this time around."

9.

SONNY SPENT MOST of the night with his head in the toilet, certain he would never feel whole again. At dawn Floyd scraped him off the bathroom floor and dragged him to a sunrise breakfast club meeting. The regulars there included businessmen, politicians, teachers, and homemakers, but, at that ungodly hour, certainly no musicians. Sonny knew that at one time he would have thought himself far too hip for this room. Now he was grateful not to see a familiar face in the bunch. No one here had any idea who he was. Caught in his incestuous little music world for so long, he forgot sometimes that there was a whole 'nother city that paid no more attention to his scene than he did to theirs.

Once Floyd saw he was settled, he left, so Sonny could do the work he needed to. The true anonymity with these people made it much easier to open up. Haltingly, Sonny confessed to having his last drink only hours before, after nearly achieving his one-year anniversary. And for the first time he talked about, instead of around, his feelings for Cilla. He wouldn't name names, and referred to his brother as his friend. Other than that, he told the story much as it had happened. He did leave out the ugliness of Cilla's calling him the wrong name. After nearly spilling that detail to the one person he couldn't bear knowing it, he hoped to keep the shame of it locked away for good.

After the meeting, the difficult testifying, he understood something of the comfort the Catholics found in the confessional. Carrying the burden of his hurt around for all this time had left him wasted. He had not even recognized that fact until he had parceled some of the load out by talking about it to others. These people, so different from the ones he usually ran with, had been kind and supportive. Many took the time to congratulate him for climbing right back on his horse after taking such a nasty spill.

After, Floyd picked him up and took him home to sleep. Sonny woke up late afternoon, just as the winter sun was setting. Floyd was still there, watching a bowl game on TV with the sound turned down, listening to a Los Lobos album on the stereo. "Feel better now?" Floyd asked him.

"A little. Thanks for dragging my ass out of bed and making me go to that thing before I had time to reconsider."

Floyd nodded. "Best way to do it, after a slip. I been there, too, Sonny. Don't beat yourself up too bad, is all. Just move forward."

"Okay." Sonny pretended to listen to the music while he tried to find the right words. "Thanks a whole lot, Floyd."

"What are friends for, Sonny-boy?"

"That's just it. You are a real friend to me—my oldest friend. I ain't been one to you. Your little sister. . . . I'm sorry I took advantage of Nancy Ruth."

To Sonny's surprise, Floyd started to laugh hard. When he finally was able to speak again, he cried, "Man, you really do think you is the greatest cocksman in the world, don't you, Sonny? Don't no one 'take advantage' of my little sister. And you? She's always had a real bad case of hot pants where you was concerned. I got a real strong feeling you didn't exactly start what produced Otis."

"True enough. But I should have left her be that night. Leastwise, I should have been better to her after."

Floyd held up a hand. "That's a fact, Sonny. But there's no going back. And you are doing nice by Otis now. You know how happy you made him, just by hanging out and talking, showing him some licks on the guitar? He's a different kid. Got new confidence. Did you meet Sally, his date for the wedding?"

"Sure did. Gave me a real scare."

"Do what?"

"She looked so familiar. So I talked with her a minute, and realized I'd nailed her mama a time or two back in our White Tornadoes days."

"Oh, shit! Don't tell me they're kin."

"No, no chance of it. She's a whole year younger than the demise of the band. Came to be while I was playing hermit and hating myself, after you joined the Navy."

Floyd laughed. "Thank God. You old whore. Amazing you ain't daddy to half Otis's high school."

"You telling me."

"Anyway, Otis has been trying to get up the courage to ask Sally out for months. I think he finally did it in big part because he feels better now about where he comes from."

"Let's just hope he's got more sense where the ladies are concerned."

"Oh, I think Otis has got his head on pretty straight. Won't even touch liquor because of all the drunks in his family tree. But he's always been too quiet, never challenged a soul about anything. That kind of worried me. He's starting to come into his own, though. I was over at their house the other day when he put on our *Storm Cellar Blues* record with the Prof sitting right there in the living room."

"Yeah?"

"Yeah. Nancy Ruth and I just watched this look of disbelief come over the Prof's face." Floyd pulled himself up straight, looking down his nose. " 'What is *this*, Otis?' he asked the kid. Otis grinned that smart-ass smirk you two both got and said, 'That there is a valid American art form, Daddy-o!' "

Sonny laughed. "Oh, ain't he the cool one. What did the Prof do?"

"That's the best part. The Prof nodded, and then he sat there and actually listened to our record. After the side ended, he told Otis, real serious and scholarly, 'It may not have the intellectual appeal of jazz, but you are correct, Otis. It is American. Valid? Questionable. But you may be right in calling it . . . an art form.' And he got up, patted Otis's shoulder, kissed Nancy Ruth, nodded at me, and left."

Sonny whooped, "Another boy for Jesus! Next Saturday night we'll see the Prof out shakin' a tail feather at the Embers Club."

Floyd chuckled. "I don't think I'd go that far, but maybe he'll quit treating me like I'm Li'l Abner." He stood up, turning off the TV. He picked up his coat off the couch and pulled it on over sweats he had borrowed from Sonny. "Grab your jacket, Sonny. Julia's expecting us for supper."

Floyd and Julia Jean didn't live far from Sonny. He had been to their house once or twice during the recording of *Lone Star Ice and Fire*. They had a small but elegant home in an older, very respectable neighborhood. Royalties from Floyd's contributions to the Salamanders' records made the location possible. Their place had a down-home, kick-off-your-shoes feel to it.

Julia Jean greeted Sonny using all her Arkansas beauty-queen skills while hostessing. "Why, hello, baby! I'm so glad you're here tonight. You look so good in this leather jacket, I hate to take it off of you." She helped Sonny from his coat, kissing his cheek.

Sonny smiled at her, "You're a treasure, girl. All the good ones really are taken. Thanks for letting Floyd give me a hand last night, sugar."

"Don't be silly, Sonny." She hugged him. "The day may come when we need you to put us back on the right path. That's what we're all here for."

"Good deal. Now, put me to work fixing supper."

"I've got it under control. You can best help me by going into the living room and seeing that my other guests are happy. One of them is a record collector."

"Sounds like my kind of people."

"I believe you're right." Julia Jean drew him into the living room. Otis waved to him from the sofa, his arm slung securely around his girl, Sally. Otis's cousin, baby Caledonia, wriggled and babbled on his knee. A woman with a thousand-watt smile was rooting through the records, chatting with Floyd. She had big hazel eyes, long brown hair, and a figure just the right side of plump. Holding him by the arm, Julia Jean said, "Sonny, I'd like you to meet Annabelle Lange. She works with me over at the Chamber of Commerce."

"Well, well. The infamous Icestorm himself," Annabelle said in a deep and honeyed voice. She extended a hand. "Besides hearing all the tall tales around town, I got you playing on a record or two. Of course, Julia Jean's told me all about you, too. Some of what she told me was even good." Julia Jean and Annabelle laughed together, as if the joke was definitely on Sonny.

He smiled, shaking her hand. "You're the record collector?"

"You bet your life, hon. I live and breathe it. When I divorced my mean old drunk of a husband, I let him have it all: house, car, dog, savings. Everything but my music. I had my lawyer put that in writing."

"Now, that's what I call a dedicated music lover," Sonny said.

"I knew you'd be impressed," Julia Jean told him. She hustled back toward the kitchen, calling out as she did, "Otis, put Caledonia down, and you and Sally run to town for me. I'm going to need milk for the gravy. Ya'll can take my car."

"Sure, Aunt Julia Jean." Caledonia squawked when Otis placed her on her blanket. She climbed to her feet and toddled to her mama's side.

"And Floyd?" Julia Jean said, hoisting the baby to her hip. "Come with me in the kitchen and do some chopping for the salad, hear?"

Annabelle kept flipping through the records once the others had left. "I do believe this is a setup, Sonny. Julia Jean has been saying forever she wanted us to meet."

She settled on a King Curtis collection and put it on the turntable. As the robust strains of saxophone soul filled the air, she went over and sat on the couch. Sonny still stood in the middle of the room. She patted the couch beside her. "Am I that scary? We'll talk over rare imports or something. Set yourself down here, Sonny."

"Don't mind if I do."

They talked record collecting until supper was on the table. The breadth of Annabelle's musical knowledge took Sonny by surprise. Her tastes were varied, and more important, her own. She didn't like stuff because a boyfriend told her to, or have her tastes shaped by commercial radio. She listened to the left side of the dial. She scoured record stores for cool loot in the same way that most women sniffed out shoe sales. Sonny had never met such a female before. Divorced, and, what luck, no battle-scarred kids. Best of all, she was a recovering alcoholic, too.

"Got sober a year before I finally worked up the nerve to leave Chet. We met in a bar, of course. He's a big handsome cowboy. Mean as he was good-looking. Nice as he could be until he got the ring on my finger. The screaming and yelling came first, then worse."

"I'm sorry, Annabelle."

"Me, too. But it's finally in the past. You just got to keep going forward." She held up her left hand, wiggling a ring finger that still bore the faint impression of a band. "Free and legal at last. Got almost three years sober under my belt now. Don't know if I'll ever take another drink, but I do know I won't end up with a crazy man again."

"You're a nice woman. Real pretty, too, if you don't mind me saying so. A man would be a fool to treat you thataway."

"Chet *was* a fool. But so was I, for putting up with it all that time. The booze was a big part of it."

"I know. I had almost a year myself . . . until last night."

Annabelle nodded gravely. "I hope you won't be mad that Julia Jean told me you had a slip at your brother's wedding. Weddings, funerals, those emotional times, they're always a challenge. But you did just right, getting back to a meeting today. You'll be okay, Sonny." She patted his arm. "There's a meeting I like to go to. It's tomorrow afternoon. Maybe you want to come along with me?"

That was mighty nice of her. He probably should start going to other groups besides his usual. Maybe he'd grown a little too complacent. "I'd like that, Annabelle. And maybe we could go grab a bite after?"

She smiled at him. "Are you asking me for a date, Sonny?"

"I'm not sure. Guess I shouldn't be . . . um. . . ." Sonny didn't know what else to say. He was rusty as hell. "Don't feel like you have to because you invited me to a meeting."

"I won't. Anyhow, you seem a whole lot nicer than you're reputed to be, Sonny." But she kept right on smiling when she said it. "I'd be a damn liar if I said you weren't the most attractive thing I've seen in a coon's age. Plus, I can hardly wait to see your Johnny Copeland records."

FOR THE FIRST TIME in his life, Sonny was *dating*. He had taken women out before, but that was mostly a means to an end, or just for show. Before Annabelle, dates were the ritual a man had to sometimes perform before he could get his rocks off. Cilla had been right when she had once told him that dinner was never just dinner. And Sonny rarely had to bother with even dinner. Someone fine was always hanging around, wanting to screw the guitar player.

His time with Annabelle was different—strange for him, but fun. They shared evenings at the movies or simply lingered over a fine meal, talking. Strolls alongside Town Lake and picnics at Lake Travis or Barton Springs Pool became a regular thing with them. He even took her with him sometimes when he worked, a thing he had never done with a lady before. Strangest of all was the way evenings ended at Annabelle's front door, sealed with only a friendly kiss—which was the way he wanted it right now.

Tonight, after a great time at the movies, he again walked with her to the door. He gave her a quick embrace and started to go. She stopped him with a hand on his arm. "Come on in, have a cup of coffee."

"It's late, Belle. If I drink coffee now, I'll be up all night."

She grinned, starting to say something, but her words were lost in laughter.

"What's that, girl?" he asked, following her inside.

She was blushing, looking away from him. "Sit down. I've got decaf, for heaven's sake."

Sonny settled into her couch as she put on some music and ground the beans. He watched her working. Pretty woman, no doubt about it. Tonight, when he'd greeted her at the door, she'd tried to hold on to him a little longer than he'd allowed, gazing at him like she was hungry. Then at the movie, she'd run her nails gently up and down his thigh, never looking away from the screen.

She came back in with his mug, fixed in the way he and Walker always joked they liked their coffee and their women—sweet, hot, creamy. Sonny took a sip, studying her as she took a seat across from him. Shapely legs, pumps crossed at the ankle, on display in a short leather skirt he really liked. Titties looked good, too, pushing against her touchable soft sweater. Like a ripe peach, her flesh gave slightly when he hugged her. She always smelled tasty, with something cinnamon in her aroma. Very sweet, no doubt about it. He knew she could be hot and creamy, too, if only he would do something about it.

"Don't gulp that so fast. You'll burn your tongue, hon."

"Well, I don't want to stay too long. You must be tired, after a long day at work."

"Oh, don't be silly. Stay as late as you like." She set her cup down and leaned back into the overstuffed cushions of her chair. Her skirt rose higher on her thighs. Running a hand through her hair and giving him a smile that could liquefy diamonds, she said, "I'm not tired. And I can sleep in tomorrow. Most likely, I'll lounge around in bed all morning long."

Sonny nodded, taking another near scalding sip. Why not go right over there, wrap her hair in his fist, pull her lips to his for a long soul kiss? Run his hand between those fine, full thighs, make her purr like a kitten? It was clear enough that was what she wanted him to do. He must be losing his mind. Only his mind—God knew the rest of him was armed and ready. "And you deserve a morning to lounge," he finally mumbled. He put the half-drunk coffee down and picked up his jacket. "Sugar, I'm beat. I better go."

She pulled her skirt down, her vamp face vanishing. "So go," she sighed. Looking at the floor, she busied herself picking up the mugs.

He wanted to tell her he'd like to stay, feel and taste her, inside and out. Instead he walked toward the door. He heard the cups clatter a little too forcefully into the sink. He walked back into the kitchen. She was near tears, though trying not to show it. "Belle? Friend of Floyd's wanted me to sit in on a song or two for his record tomorrow. You want to come?"

"Maybe. Call me." She put a smile on her lips that Sonny saw wasn't in her eyes.

"I will, around noon. I hope you'll come along." He scooted out the door. Once seated in his car, he banged his head hard on the steering wheel. What the hell was wrong with him?

Annabelle made it clear that after ten years in a boozy, bloody marriage, she wasn't in a hurry for a commitment. She was only a little younger than he was. She was an ideal woman to be with at this point in his life. Damn it all, those soft thighs of hers, peeking out at him under her leather skirt.

He should go back there, give her a night she would never forget. But he couldn't. He wasn't sure why. Maybe in part he resisted because his last encounters with women, before he'd gotten straight, had been so brutal. He didn't want to treat Annabelle like that. He wasn't sure what he wanted.

After sitting in his car for a long time, he started the engine. Almost as an afterthought, he drove over to Floyd's house rather than his own. He got out of the car, sitting on the hood until he shivered with the cold. He could see Floyd's shaggy hair silhouetted against the living room window shade. Finally, Sonny knocked.

Floyd opened the door. The TV, sound turned off, was the only light on in the house. A flushed-cheeked Caledonia Blue slept on Floyd's shoulder. He motioned Sonny in without speaking. Sonny helped himself to some water while Floyd mounted the stairs with his daughter.

Sonny sat himself on Floyd's couch, watching the newly elected U.S. president's face flickering on the TV.

Floyd came back downstairs, sans Caledonia Blue. Stretching, he said, "Poor kid felt rotten. Think I finally got her down, though. I made Julia go to bed early. She and the baby both got some sort of nasty bug. Ain't got me yet. Lucky you caught me here and still awake, Sonny, instead of out gigging."

"Uh-huh. Best part is, now I can give you shit. I caught you redhanded, watching your hero." Grinning, Sonny pointed to the image of George H.W. Bush, orating silently on the muted screen.

Floyd grunted, grabbing the remote control to get rid of Bush's face. "Man, I was just channel surfing and stumbled over him. That asshole ain't my hero."

Feigning shock, Sonny said, "You mean to tell me you didn't vote for a Texan for president?"

Floyd smirked. "Texan, my ass. These days, he's from Maine—a bona fide Yankee. Besides, you forget. The last Texan we had in the White House sent me over to Vietnam."

"That's true, huh?"

"And leastwise, despite his other faults, Lyndon Johnson supported Civil Rights reform. Bush had his campaign manager, that asshole Lee Atwater, play the race card in the worst way just to win."

"Ain't it a damn shame that Atwater plays a fairly mean blues guitar?"

Floyd shrugged. "Just goes to show you, Sonny-boy—who the Good Lord chooses to bestow his talent on is a big damn mystery."

After they sat in silence for a time, both staring at the quiet TV, Floyd cleared his throat. "But you didn't come over here to talk politics at damn near midnight, did you Sonny-boy? Not that you ain't welcome, but we both know you never just drop by. Your resistance slipping a little?"

"No, my resistance is fine, man. It's too good, in fact. I can't even indulge in my girlfriend."

Floyd listened wordlessly, channel surfing the silent TV as Sonny confessed. After Sonny stopped talking, Floyd kept nodding for a minute. He turned on a lamp. Turning off the TV, he asked, "So tell me, Sonny. How many girls you balled since you went through rehab?"

"Well . . . none."

"No shit?" Floyd looked genuinely startled. "Congrats, Sonny. You're working the program better than I thought."

"But I swore off drugs, not women." Sonny stood up, pacing. "At first, I thought, well, I just ain't around those girls anymore. You know, groupies, bar babes . . . hookers. And the shrinks tell you not to fool around for awhile, right?"

Floyd nodded. "That's true. Let me ask another . . . you ever gone to bed with anyone when you was straight? In your life? I mean, absolutely nothing in your system. No hangover, no nothing."

"I don't think so."

"There's your answer, Sonny-boy. You really like Annabelle, huh?'"

Sonny nodded. "I really like her. For more than . . . sex. She's a nice girl."

Floyd smiled. "Nice girls like sex too, you know."

"Of course I know." Nice girls. Cilla was a nice girl. He let himself feel with her, and look where that had gotten him.

"Sonny, it's a real trip to feel, without a barrier of drugs between your heart and your dick." Floyd stood up, stopping Sonny's pacing with a hand on his back, sitting him down. "But when it happens? Dynamite! It's a lot like the first time you step into that spotlight without all that shit in your head. Scary, sure, but what a rush."

Sonny nodded. "I remember Walker saying something like that, the day he convinced me to go into rehab. About playing his music clear-headed, I mean."

"Yeah. It's great, ain't it?" Sonny nodded. Floyd flipped back on the silent TV, adding a little too casually, "Walker says howdy, by the way. He and Cilla want to see you."

Sonny nodded, keeping his own eyes on the show. "They doing okay?"

"Real good. Cilla's getting big now, uncomfortable. But she's happy. Let me call them tomorrow, so we can get together."

"I don't know, Floyd."

"So, you fucked up. Walker forgives you. You kept your nasty scene in private. It's that idiot Bonnell that Walker don't want back in his house none too soon."

"I reckon not."

"We'll go over there. You bring along Annabelle. They'll think she's great. Don't you think so?"

"Uh-huh."

"And Sonny?" Floyd added, flashing a knowing grin, "Talk to your woman. Tell her it ain't her fault. Otherwise, she'll start blaming her imper-fect butt."

"Hey! Her butt's great."

"Hell, yeah, it is. But tell her that, not me. You'll wonder why you didn't sooner."

10.

"JUST LOOK AT that rose garden. Didn't it used to be a parking lot?" Annabelle asked as Sonny drove the Fury up to Walker's house.

"Sure was. You think this is cool, just wait till you see what he's done inside." Sonny pulled the Fury beside his mama's new Taurus. Floyd's and Uncle Charlie's pickups were out front, too. Good. Lots of folks were around—better than facing Cilla and Walker two on two. Sonny put the car in park but left it running, pretending to listen to the radio.

Annabelle scooted over next to Sonny. "We going in?"

"Not sure yet," Sonny mumbled, trying to smile at her.

She ran a hand over the side of his face. "I know this is scary, Sonny. For me, too. I'm meeting your family for the first time, after all. Let me give you a taste of courage." She pulled him over for a kiss. "Feel better now?"

"Oh, yeah. Belle, you keep that up and you'll be combing the rats out of your hair again."

"I like a rat in my hair . . . long as that rat's you." She kissed him again, more slowly this time.

Sonny heard a rap on the driver's-side window. Floyd was hunched over, grinning at him. "Break it up in there," he barked. "Ya'll are too old for necking in cars."

"Speak for yourself," Sonny told him, leaving the car and going around to open the door for Annabelle. She winked at him as she stepped out, fanning herself with her palm.

Sonny noticed Walker watching them from the porch steps. He was dressed down, in jeans, boots, and a ratty old Rocket 88s sweatshirt. His one stylin' touch was a classy black bolero with a silk band. Smiling slightly, Walker raised his chin sharply at Sonny, in *paisano* greeting. Sonny returned the gesture, taking Annabelle by the arm and leading her to his brother. "Walker, I want you to meet Annabelle Lange, the only woman I ever met who owns *Born under a Bad Sign*—autographed, no less."

Walker kissed her hand, purring in his best ladies'-man voice. "You're a knockout—and you have an autographed Albert King record to boot? You are too good to be real, sweet thing."

"Oh, I'm real enough, all right," she said, giggling. "I'm glad to finally meet you in person. I'm the one had the Chamber of Commerce put your picture in the city brochure."

Walker grinned at Sonny. "Imagine that. Me, a damn tourist attraction."

"I can't believe what you've done with the old Sugar and Spice," she said, gesturing at the grounds. "Back when, I used to come out here and see all of ya'll play."

Walker shook his head, looking her over. "Can't believe I never introduced myself to someone fine as you."

"Watch him, Annabelle," Sonny warned. "He thinks he's real smooth."

"Think it? I know it." He took Annabelle by the arm. "I'm going to give you a tour of the place. We'll talk. You like Sonny? Wait'll you hear about what I had to put up with, growing up with him. We'll see what you think about your boyfriend then."

Annabelle looked over her shoulder at Sonny, a question in her eyes. He realized she was checking to see if he minded her going off with Walker. Touched by the gesture, Sonny smiled, waving her on. Watching them go in, Sonny lit a smoke. Floyd drew up beside him. "So far, so good, Sonny."

"Yeah. Got to say, I'm glad Belle's here with me."

"I bet. Looks like you two worked things out."

"Oh, yeah."

"Well, all right, man. Now, put out that cancer stick and quit stalling. You got ladies wanting to see you." Sonny stomped out the smoke in the driveway and followed Floyd inside. Uncle Charlie was laid out on the couch, an arm slung over his eyes, dozing. Floyd saluted Sonny and took the chair next to Charlie, picking up the newspaper. "You go face them alone, Sonny. They done picked on me already."

Ruby, Aunt Lucille, and Julia Jean were in the kitchen, drinking coffee and cooking. They all squealed when they saw Sonny, petting him, handing him a mug. Ruby started trying to pry out choice information about Annabelle while he added cream and sugar.

"Mama, let me be."

"Sugar-boy, you can't blame us for being curious. You never brought no one home before."

"Or to our house, either, when he lived with us," Lucille added. "She must be special."

"She is. She. . . ."

He stopped when he saw Cilla watching him from the back doorway. Silently, he took in the sight. Her hair had grown longer and thicker, hanging in loose tendrils almost to her waist. She wore Walker's gray-and-white serape over leggings and ankle-high flat suede boots. The round swell of her pregnancy was obvious beneath the cloak. Her face was puffy, weary but still lovely.

"I'm so glad you've come. We've missed you terribly, Sonny." Her eyes were tearing up as she reached her arms out to him. With the other women watching, smiling, he crossed over and hugged Cilla carefully.

"Missed you, too." Almost as quick as he embraced her, he turned her loose. He stared at her middle. "Did that kid just kick me?"

She rubbed her bulge, grimacing slightly. "I'm afraid so. He's quite rude that way. If it's any consolation, it feels even worse from the inside. Walker thinks we have a future placekicker for the Longhorns in here."

"I think he's right," Sonny answered. He turned to see Walker and Annabelle stride in, his arm tight around her waist. He was whispering in her ear, and she was laughing so hard she had tears streaming down her cheeks. Sonny narrowed his eyes at them. "Don't believe a word he says."

When she was able to stop laughing, Annabelle declared, "But I have to. It all sounds just like you. I don't know how this poor boy is as sane as he is."

"Which is not very."

"Uh-uh, Sonny. Be nice," Ruby said. She gave Annabelle a smile. "Introduce me to your friend."

Annabelle dried her eyes with her fingertips, trying to regain her composure in order to meet Ruby with dignity. Sonny saw Annabelle didn't have a thing to worry about. Ruby gave Sonny an approving nod, already taken with his girlfriend. Walker poured his own mug of coffee.

"Come on, Sonny," Walker said, slapping his brother's shoulder. "Let's get out of this hen house so they can give your lovely lady the third degree. Don't know about you, but I need a smoke."

"You don't 'need' one, lover," Cilla scolded.

"I know, darlin'. What I need is to quit the damn things," Walker replied, running his free hand gently over her pregnant stomach as he passed near her. He winked at her, and her stern expression softened. To Sonny, he said, "Cill don't allow smoking in the house no more, with those little lungs growing inside her." He tipped his hat to the ladies, leading Sonny out the back door and onto the patio. Out of kitchen earshot, he added, "She's freaking out about the weirdest things, and the kid ain't even born yet. She's done got him choking to death on guitar picks and all sorts of other terrible scenarios." He chuckled. "Turned into quite the little mama. Nesting, they call it."

They sat in two metal chairs. Walker propped his feet up on a table, lighting up. "I can sure enough smell spring in the air, can't you? New life busting out all over. Won't be long now before we got a new life in there, too." He pointed a thumb back toward the house.

"That's so. Your wife looks good."

"Yeah, she does. Leastwise, she's gorgeous to me. Little Buddha Girl, I call her. She's sure ready to have that kid, though. When people ask if she wants a boy or a girl, she tells them, 'I want it OUT!' " They laughed together. "We been trying to decide on a name. I thought about Billy Jay, after Daddy? But that's really your name. I thought we'd leave that in case you ever had another son."

"Don't worry about that. I won't have no more kids. Do it, if you really want to name him after Daddy. I don't even think of it as my name anymore."

"Me, either—you been Sonny too long." Walker took another long drag, carefully blowing smoke rings as he breathed out. "Plus, I don't want to speak ill of the dead, but my memories of Daddy ain't too great."

"I hear that. Any other ideas?"

"Well, I liked Sonny Jim, myself. You know, after you and Daddy Jim?"

Sonny stared in stunned silence for a moment. "No kidding?" Walker nodded. "Jim's right nice. But Sonny? I mean, I was never a small-kid Sonny, not to anybody but Daddy Jim. Just a cool teenage Sonny. Maybe kids would tease him."

"Nah. This state's lousy with 'Sonnys.' All the same, he'd have some mighty big boots to fill, named for you." Walker said. "I don't think we'll name him that, even though I'd like to. Do you remember my favorite scene in *A Hard Day's Night?* It's the one where George Harrison wanders into that obnoxious TV producer's office?"

"I kind of remember . . . don't they show George some ugly shirts?"

"Yeah, that's the one. That's what the jerky producer keeps calling George—Sunny Jim! Cilla just cracks up every time I bring up that name, and starts spouting lines from the thing. Seems she was raised up on that movie like it was mama's milk."

"Well, good—she's got an out. Now she ain't forced to name her boy after me." The words came out more embittered than he'd meant them to.

Walker was quiet for a few seconds. Then he said, his voice gentle, "It ain't like that, Sonny. Cilla thinks the world of you. We've both missed you something awful, bro."

The conversation had been pleasant so far. Sonny hoped they weren't veering into rugged country. He did his best to get them back to the main road by asking, "So, what's the wife want to name the little cat, Squirt?"

"She'd really like to follow our family tradition of juniors and name him for me."

"Yeah? That's cool, Walker. I think you should."

"I don't know. It's confusing. I ain't never going to be thought of as Big Walker, what with me being so fucking puny. And you know I never much dug Little Walker."

Sonny rolled his eyes. "Yeah, yeah, I know. Because it gave the ladies the wrong impression. So, how about Walker the First and Walker the Second, like royalty? They do call you the Crown Prince of the Blues."

"Oh, please!" Walker said, throwing back his head and laughing. "That ain't in the least bit big-headed, is it? I don't think so, Sonny. Anyway, we pretty much settled on naming him for me, but calling him J.R.—short for Junior, you know?"

"J.R. Blaine." Sonny nodded, approving. "That has a right cool sound to it."

"And easy to spell, too. Hopefully he'll have Cill's brains instead of mine, but you never can tell." He pointed a trigger finger at his head.

They sat still for a time, listening to the birds singing above and the creek babbling down the bluff from where they sat. Closing his eyes, drifting a bit, Sonny drawled, "Peaceful as hell out here, huh, Squirt?"

"Oh, yeah. It's so good after the craziness of the road. Be glad when this tour wraps up and I can stay home with the wife and kid for awhile. Maybe I'll get us a dog. Need some kind of hound around this place, I reckon."

"Won't be peaceful once that baby comes out squalling. I bet you'll be itching to go again in no time."

"I don't know, Sonny. I can't wait—squalling, diapers, nights walking the floor, all that stuff." He shook his head, gazing at Sonny with an expression of pure joy. "It's a miracle, man. I can't believe I'm going to have a son with her. I still can't really wrap my mind around the fact that Cilla married me. Me, Sonny, of all people."

Sonny finally said, "She loves you. Like nothing else there is."

"And I love her like that. And my little boy growing in her . . . hell, he shouldn't even have a shot at being here, what with Cilla's problems. Gets me thinking, seeing the way everything fits just right, you know?" Walker laced his long fingers together, his face solemn. "Everything that's happened has had to. We been put right where we have to be, so the things that are suppose to be, are. Sometimes, I believe the whole reason that storm hit when it did was so we could make little J.R. together. And because Shookie and Prince had to move into town, I got Cill and my boy a real special home to live in."

Sonny hooted, "So Prince gets a heart attack, and a bunch of folks lost their loved ones and property, just so your life can finally come together."

"I know it sounds dumb, and maybe even a little selfish. But it's strange how things happen sometimes. Ain't that so, Sonny?"

"Maybe." He studied Walker as he leaned back in the chair, smiling and shaking his head beneath his black hat. Sonny could hardly see a trace of the shy little kid that he once had been, or even much of the strung-out guitar superstar that had come along later. Walker now positively shone with contentment. Of all the things that Sonny had envied in Walker's life, he never imagined that this settled quality would be one of them. Then again, he himself was far more settled than ever before.

Now it was time to take care of business. "Walker. I'm here for a reason."

Walker turned to him, his expression still peaceful. "Reason is, we missed you. Don't say nothing, bro."

"I got to. I acted like a dick at your wedding."

"Bonnell acted like a dick," Walker replied. "You hear about his antics?"

"Yeah. Must have been something to see."

"Makes a good wedding story. He ain't going to live that one down none too quick."

"Ain't that right!" They both laughed a little. Then Sonny tried again. "Anyway, about all that shit I said that night—"

Walker held up a hand. "Let it go, man. I have. Time you move on— and looks like you're headed in the right direction. I sure like your new lady."

"She's something, all right." Sonny grinned. "Here I am, damn near forty, and I just now got my first steady girl."

"Ain't so strange. The shrinks told me that people quit growing when they start abusing. How old was you when you really got to using?"

"Oh . . . White Tornadoes days. Barely fifteen, I reckon."

"Right. Just about the time when most folks find that first love." Walker tipped his hat. "Making up for a little lost time, is all you're doing."

"What about you? Back then you was getting high and drunk right alongside me. You started even younger than I did. Still, you always had a sweetheart."

"Sure I did," Walker grunted. "Me and Nancy Ruth? Getting blasted and screwing in secret before I could even grow a decent beard. I damn near ruined that little girl's life."

Sonny snorted. "You? I'm the one fucked her over."

Walker's face darkened. "I feel partly responsible for Otis, even."

"Why? Ain't no doubt who's Otis's daddy. You weren't messing around with her then."

"No. He's yours, all right. But I started her down that road. She was a born tease maybe, but that's all she was before she got with me. She really was a good girl, innocent, and a real fine student with a lot of ambition. No way she would have been fooling around as young as she did if not for me." Walker stood up, walking to the edge of the patio. He kept his back to Sonny as he went on. "Sonny, I never said nothing to you about this, but I was mad as hell about the way you treated her and Otis. It pissed me off even more after I got to know the boy.

He paused, letting out a sigh. "Except for Floyd, maybe, I don't think anyone else knows about what I'm going to tell you now. Some nights, after Vada and I got into it bad, I'd go over to Nancy Ruth's. This was before she and the Prof got hitched. I didn't do it to see her so much, and nothing wrong ever went on between us—by then we were just friends again. It was Otis I went to see. I'd go and play with him and stuff, and then sing the boy to sleep."

"You really did that?"

"Sure, I did. He used to love me tucking him in, singing to him. We been tight for years—been nuts about the kid since I first seen him. That's why I never understood how you didn't love the hell out of him."

I do now, Sonny realized. He'd die for Otis without a second thought. But he didn't say it aloud. Painful to picture Walker, holding his son, singing lullabies. Sonny felt envious about it, maybe a little pissed off—but grateful, too.

Walker sat back down beside him. "Long time ago Nancy Ruth told me how ya'll came to get Otis—her dancing naked for you that night? Ain't no doubt she was always wild about you. Really, you was just a wasted kid when that happened. I know that now. Besides . . . I'm real glad he's my nephew."

"Me, too, Walker."

Walker nodded, letting the thought hang in the air a moment. Then he cleared his throat. "Anyway, back to what we was saying about my women? Vada? I really did love her like crazy. But *crazy* sure is the right word for our time together. From the get-go, we was so much about booze and blow. Violent, crazy fights after bingeing. . . ." His voice broke and he dropped his face into his hands. "She's dead now, because of me."

Sonny laid a hand on his brother's shoulder. "Nah, it was her doing, Walker. It's not like you held a gun to her head."

"Maybe. But I was too gone to really help her. I ran like hell when it got too ugly. And where'd I run? Right to Cilla, fucking up her life." Walker coughed, quickly rubbing his eyes with the back of his fist. "Salome? She's still a child. We really didn't have much but N.A. in common. I was with her because I didn't want to be alone—not fair to the girl at all." Walker let go a humorless laugh. "Yeah, Sonny. Don't be envying my track record. Like you, I'm just now getting it together enough for that grown-up relationship. I just feel so blessed I got a second chance with Cilla, and that we both get a second chance for a child together. I know God's hand is in this. He meant this to be."

Sonny held out his coffee cup for a toast. "I know it, too. Here's to second chances, Squirt."

Walker clinked his mug to Sonny's. "Well, all right. And to third and fourth chances, if that's what it takes."

11.

THE PAY-PHONE RECEIVER hit the wall with a loud crash. A nurse, bigger-armed than Sonny was, stuck her head out of her station, scowling. She rumbled, "Watch it, Mister. You break it, you'll end up owning that phone."

Sonny opened his mouth to snarl back but managed to hold his tongue. The woman was just doing her job. He shouldn't be slamming around hospital property. But, goddamn, he shouldn't be here.

Walker was in New York City, at this very moment performing live on late-night TV. It was his last commitment before he took leave of the road and waited home with Cilla for their son's arrival. Cilla was huge with child now—swollen to the point of misery and pity. Hard to believe she still retained so much water, as much as she perspired, peed, and cried. When she walked, she waddled like a goose. She sure looked set to calve the kid.

She wasn't due for three more weeks, though. First babies are always late. They all swore this to Sonny. They were liars.

The rain had been relentless for the past two weeks. Though Walker's house had stayed dry on its perch above the bluffs, his driveway had often been impassable. Cilla's OB hadn't wanted her to travel with Walker and take a chance of going into labor on the road. Nor had she wanted to risk Cilla going into labor trapped at home by floodwaters. So Ruby agreed to take her in for Walker's last trip.

Then Ruby got the flu. She couldn't chance infecting Cilla and the baby. Annabelle and Julia Jean were at some conference for the Chamber over Houston way. Floyd and the Texas Sidewinders were opening for somebody, somewhere. Uncle Charlie and Aunt Lucille were on one of their many vacations. Ruby hadn't given Sonny room for argument. She bullied him into taking Cilla in for the night.

Sonny hadn't liked being left with her one little bit. The responsibility of watching over Cilla in such a helpless, delicate state was a bad thing. Though he tried to resist, Sonny felt deeply protective of her and the baby. It was an urge that seemed to him as primal in nature as was his sex drive. But this guard-dogish instinct was a lot harder to deal with than was lust.

Damned woman. Even in her condition, unable for once to make him horny, she still managed to cause Sonny's caveman hormones to flare.

Cilla bawled for an hour after Walker mournfully dropped her off at Sonny's. Her tears were finally stilled with Chinese food and spring training on cable. Sonny thought then they had it made—watch a little ball, check out Walker's set, then put her to bed in the guest room. Come morning, Walker, stale from the red-eye, would fetch her. Sonny could pass little mama back to her rightful owner.

All went fine right up until Sonny was doing the dishes. She'd cried out that her water had broken. Sonny hadn't known what she meant by it. He thought she'd dropped her drink on the floor. He was bringing a towel to mop up the ensuing mess when he saw liquid splattering onto his floorboards from under her skirt. He thought at first she was peeing on herself. Then he saw her expression—terrified, ashen.

"Stop that," he'd told her, and firmly, too. "You ain't having this baby on my watch."

But it looked like she was fixing to do just that. Sonny hadn't panicked—well, not too much. He'd called her doctor, followed her instructions. He'd picked up Cilla, a bath towel clutched between her trembling legs to soak up the fluid, and placed her in his Mustang to drive her to the hospital. He'd said reassuring bullshit to her the whole drive over. That should have been enough. No need to stay with her—hospitals creeped him out too much. The pros could take it from here.

But when he'd made to leave, the nurses wouldn't let him. "Mr. Blaine, you will not leave Cilla here by herself," a nurse had insisted.

"But ya'll are here. It's what ya'll do for a living here—help women have babies," he argued. He was starting to lose it. He could hear his own voice slipping into an unattractive whine.

"Sir, we have many other patients. We are nearly overwhelmed tonight—it happens every full moon. Someone needs to be with Mrs. Blaine at all times." She'd folded her arms, adding in a voice that brooked no argument. "You'll stay until someone else arrives."

A full moon? Like Cilla was a werewolf? A—what had Bonnell called them?—a fucking *loup-garou*? Now Sonny stood in the maternity ward hallway, wondering where to call next to get help. While the nurses were examining her, he excused himself and found the pay phone. He then started a futile round of calls.

Women were crying out their agony from the rooms all around him. The sound of them made him frantic with fear. He just couldn't face Cilla when she was in that kind of pain. But the way those nurses talked to him, they'd have security lock him in here, should he tried to flee. He had to get someone to relieve him.

First he tried his mama, hoping against hope she would be well enough to come and take over. But her phone was busy, no doubt off the hook until morning. When unwell, she made this a habit while she slept. She had been disturbed one too many nights fielding calls from her sons' faceless fans.

Next Sonny called Steven Taylor's home. Walker had given him his manager's private number for just such an emergency. Being Saturday night on the West Coast, it was still early. No one answered. He left a message, with Cilla's room number, begging Taylor to get a hold of Walker.

Next, he contacted the hotel where Walker was staying, leaving yet another message. Sonny knew it was too late to catch him in the room, as he checked his watch and did the time-zone shuffle in his head.

Sonny picked up the receiver again, finding it undamaged by his tantrum. Time to try and reach the TV show. After much finagling with New York's information operators, Sonny managed to get a number for the network. He reached only a recording, but it had the option of punching in an extension, to be connected directly to a given party. So Sonny started with 100, and kept redialing and punching numbers until he made contact with an actual human being.

Someone in security finally answered, thank Christ. After some fast and desperate talk, the guard on the line believed Sonny was indeed who he said he was. The man had not been able to get Walker directly, as he was right in the middle of his performance. But he did promise to let Walker know what was going on just as soon as he came offstage. Sonny hung up, praying the soul at the other end of the line was as competent as he sounded.

Sonny went into the smoking lounge and sucked down two cigarettes fast enough to make him lightheaded. Retrieving a cup of lousy coffee from a machine, he returned to Cilla's room to tell her the score.

He headed back into the room, gluing what he hoped was a comforting grin to his face. Cilla had been changed into a hospital gown, and the nurses had started an IV. A number of wires were running out from under the crisp sheets covering her bulge. She was hooked into what appeared to be some sort of bedside monitor. "Looks like they got you wired for sound, Cilla," he teased. "Maybe we can take them on as roadies next tour."

She looked at him solemnly. "You didn't reach him, did you?"

"I talked to someone who said as soon as he came off, they'd tell him." Sonny sat down in a chair near her bed. "He'll be calling us any time. Just stay calm."

She looked over at the monitor, tears filling her eyes again. "At least they feel J.R. is okay. He's not dangerously early."

J.R. was coming a damn sight too early to suit Uncle Sonny, he wanted to tell her. But instead he just said, "That's great news."

"Yes." She watched the blip on the monitor. "Sonny? I've been saying I couldn't wait for that first pain? I lied." She croaked out a little laugh.

"You'll be fine, girl." He did his best to pull forth a tempting smile. "You're all woman—got the ideal body for birthing sons."

She managed to grin. "Nice way of saying I have a big butt?" She reached for his hand. He let her take it, trying not to show how much he didn't want her touch. She squeezed, telling him, "I am so sorry, Sonny. I know you must hate every second of this. Let's face it, you aren't exactly the kind to volunteer to be a childbirth coach."

"That's putting it mildly. Only kid I ever had ... I didn't even see Otis's birth announcement until he was almost two. I didn't even meet him until he was in grade school." Sonny had never said that aloud. In doing so, he felt ashamed. The memory returned, seeing Otis for the first time. The boy had been holding Walker's hand in a busy rehearsal hall, gazing up at Sonny, still ignorant of what they were to each other. Sonny could still feel the cold shock of that moment, of seeing his own eyes in a child's face.

The memory stirred others—Nancy Ruth's tears when she told him she was pregnant, the result of a mindless night—countless other women's tears, too. He'd left a thousand desperate questions in his wake. Sonny cleared his throat, saying, "I never heard tell of other kids ... being born, anyway. But I always been a traveling man, so I can't be sure."

"How different it is for women," Cilla replied coolly, stroking her abdomen. "We can't have babies we don't know about."

"You ain't kidding," he exclaimed, eyeing her distended belly under the sheets. They smiled at each other for a moment. Sonny let go of her hand, walking over to peek out the blinds at the pouring rain. He said quietly, "Walker's going to be a good daddy. You're lucky there. I was afraid I'd be mean to my kids, like Daddy was to Walker and me."

He swallowed hard. He was unsure he even wanted to say what came out next. "Even if I'd married . . . and the only time I ever thought about doing that . . . well, you didn't think then you could ever have kids."

He felt her eyes on his back. After an uncomfortable minute, he dropped the blinds with a clatter. Walking back toward the monitor, Sonny intently studied the blinking numbers. He wouldn't look at Cilla. She stayed quiet. He watched the minutes leak by on the machine's clock.

"Did you really want to marry me, Sonny?" she finally asked him. Not just. . . ?"

He took his time answering, still watching only the monitor when he finally found his voice. "Just what? Fuck you?"

"Yes."

"Even the first time we met, girl, when I made such an ass of myself, I was struck deep by you," Sonny confessed. "Never left me, that feeling. I wasn't never just about fucking you, no matter what I said to you out of meanness since."

He turned his eyes back to hers. She was crying silently. She leaned forward with no little effort and grabbed both of his hands in hers. He permitted her to hold on. After a little while she quit weeping. She whispered, "Sonny, I swear I didn't set out to hurt you. I've always thought you were . . . something else."

"That's me, all right. Something else." Sonny tried to keep his voice light, but the words came out sour anyway.

Cilla squeezed his hands hard in her own. "Sweet man. I meant that in the best way possible—" She broke off suddenly, grimacing, turning him loose to clutch her middle. Sonny heard the monitor's beep increase in tempo, watched the numbers rise—then, gradually, descend. "Wow," Cilla breathed. "I think that was a contraction."

"I reckon that's what these numbers meant," Sonny said, trying to decipher the machine's information.

"That wasn't so bad." She let out a nervous laugh. "Worse to come!"

There was no hiding her terror. Sonny had to keep her calm somehow. "You're going to do fine."

"Glad you think so." Hesitantly, she added, "Um . . . I know I've already asked far too much of you."

"Sure enough approaching my limit," he admitted.

"Just for tonight, Sonny. Will you call me 'sugar' again? I'm so afraid. I need a little extra affection. You never call me that anymore."

Of course he didn't. She was the one woman who could never again be his "sugar." He looked into her frightened eyes and couldn't deny her. "Wish granted, sugar. But just for tonight."

The door opened, and a gray-eyed brunette, her slim body clad in scrubs, entered. "Hello there, Cilla. You two are jumping the gun a little. I hear your husband's away on live TV—" she checked her watch "—why, right about as we speak. Too bad it's on tape-delay here, or we might see Walker flip out as the news reaches him. That'd be one for the baby's video." She smiled, patting Cilla's shoulder as she checked the chart. "Little J.R. is causing his share of mischief already."

"You're right, Dr. Clark. He's certainly freaked out his uncle. Sonny, this is my OB, Dr. Clark."

Sonny extended his hand in greeting. The doctor glanced down at it, not taking it. She locked frosty eyes with him. "Oh, we've met."

"We did?" Sonny was clueless.

"It was years ago. Not surprising you don't remember."

The doctor opened Cilla's chart and pulled from it what looked like a yellowed prescription form, handing it to Sonny. "I had to go by home before coming into the hospital. My service told me you'd been the one to call in for Cilla. I pulled this out of an old scrapbook. Step into the hall and take a look at that while I give your sister-in-law a pelvic exam. See if it rings any bells."

Sonny did as he was told. He was amazed to see that the form bore his youthful autograph, back in the days before Icestorm was a part of it. As had always been his habit, he had scrawled the year he had written it: 1970. Printed on the piece of paper was the address of the old walk-in clinic that used to be on Congress.

Sonny remembered the clinic well enough. The place had treated anything for little or nothing. Sonny had been patched up after a bar fight or two, had snagged real cough syrup when his colds veered into bronchitis. They'd given him more than one shot in his ass to cure the clap, too. But this autograph? He'd given it to the woman who had taken care of Walker's injured ear, the day he had fled Mingus with Sonny.

The woman had come to see the Tornadoes play a few days after the chance meeting at the clinic. She'd made it a point to seek Sonny out at the break, saying she was checking in to make sure his jaw was healing okay. She'd been very businesslike as she first touched his face—a medical examination. He remembered still, how after a moment, the fingers on his jawbone had lost their professionalism, her touch morphing into something more like a caress. He recalled too his surprise when she'd told him then that she was not a nurse but was instead studying to be a doctor. Women doctors were still something of a rarity back then.

Intrigued by her, Sonny had bought her drinks that night in return for her concern, getting her pretty drunk. It hadn't been too hard to coax her into coming home with him after that show. He could still dimly recollect her shy, inexperienced enthusiasm. She'd confessed later that, what with her studies, she hadn't ever really taken the time for boys previous to that night. Stealing moments from her burdensome schedule, they'd shared a brief, smoky affair. Sonny couldn't remember now just how it ended—but he had no doubt it hadn't been pretty. It had almost never ended pretty back in his Tornadoes days.

It looked as though she had succeeded in her profession in spades. Sonny knew that Walker had Cilla under the best medical care that money could buy. Sonny felt the heat rise in his face. He was relieved that he could make out her first name on the autograph, because he would never have been able to dig it out of his memory. At this point calling her "Dr. Sugar" wouldn't be too cool.

She stuck her head out the door, motioning to him. "I've finished examining Cilla. You may come back in now, Sonny."

Sonny handed her back the autograph as he entered, giving her a swift kiss on the cheek. "Good to see you again, Maggie. Made doctor, I see. I knew you would. Plus, you're even prettier now."

Cilla's curiosity was burning in her eyes as she watched them.

"I think it's damned lucky for you that my name was on that piece of paper I just handed you," Dr. Maggie said, leaning away from Sonny. She handed Cilla the autograph to study.

He invoked his finest honey-dripper smile in return. Easy enough—she was a fine-looking woman, scrubs or no. "Lot of miles, and nineteen years, between here and 1970," he said by way of excuse.

"Oh, I know." Maggie Clark turned to Cilla, talking in the tone two girlfriends might use gossiping over lunch. "I was a resident back then, assigned to work unreal hours at that old walk-in clinic. Sometimes, off late, too wound up to sleep, I'd go to a club and catch a band. Even before meeting Sonny, I had a wicked crush." She turned a cool smile toward him. "Scads of long black hair back then, and far too pretty to be anything but trouble. Too young for me, too." The doctor chuckled. Cilla smirked at Sonny. Sonny wished he had a handy rock to crawl beneath. Maggie added, "Your brother Walker remembered me the moment we met again."

"I bet he did. Walker ain't about to forget the likes of you, especially since you doctored him that time."

"That's what Walker said, almost word for word," Cilla gasped.

Maggie nodded. "Then he made some silly comment about being surprised I had gone from looking inside ears to looking inside women." Sonny joined the women in their laughter.

Maggie pushed a chair toward Sonny. "Sit. I'll fill you in on Cilla's situation." He sat down obediently. "Cilla is in the early stages of labor. Usually, especially with a first child, it takes time. Hopefully, Walker will arrive before his son does. I don't suppose you have ever taken a childbirth class, Sonny?"

"Hell, no."

Maggie nodded gravely. "I was afraid of that. Cilla, you can get him through the early stages, I suppose. But later ... well, when things settle down a little, I'll see if one of the nurses can give Sonny a crash course."

He stood up, holding out a protesting hand. "Ladies, I can't do this."

Maggie smiled, something almost mean in her expression. "Oh, yes, you can, Sonny. As I remember, you're a man of many talents." She leaned in closer, whispering, "Ain't karma a bitch?" She headed for the door, stopping to add, "I'll be checking back with you shortly, Cilla. Remember your breathing, now. And, as a personal favor to me?" She shot a hard glance at Sonny. "Don't make this easy on your brother-in-law."

CILLA WAS SCREAMING, pretty much beyond words whenever a contraction took her. Her grip on Sonny's hand was ferocious. "No screaming, sugar—it don't help. You *breathe* through this." Thrashing her head wildly, she belted out another scream.

Sonny took his palm and popped her lightly on the cheek. "Focus, girl. My eyes, now," he commanded. She gasped at the slap, but turned her eyes to his. She began to pant like an overheated dog, her childbirth training bringing her back from panic. "That's the way, sugar," he cooed. "Doing so good. . . . It's waning now. . . ."

The contraction faded, releasing her from pain's vice. She fell back onto her pillow, moaning, eyes glassy with exhaustion.

Sonny could not believe the change that had come over her in the last few minutes. Her nurses had explained this was what was called transition, the intensely painful labor when the head crowned. Birth was not far off now. Her pains were topping out the monitor and coming on just a couple of minutes apart. Before transition hit, he was singing silly soul songs to her, to amuse her, to illustrate what kind of time was actually passing during the pains. But now the contractions were lasting longer than the length of an old 45. He had to be very stern with her to keep her from total meltdown.

A base creature had replaced the sublime Lady Mountbatton as she fought to give her son life. When it first started getting rough, she had reminded Sonny a little of a beast of burden at work. Now she had moved even beyond that, bringing to mind a machine with one sole purpose. He felt as though they had been at this terrible task for an eternity. Hell must be something akin to this.

"Sonny, it's starting again," she wailed, grabbing again his deeply aching hand.

"Okay. Look at me. Sugar? Look here, in my eyes. Short breaths. Concentrate on getting through just this one." Her fingers tightened on his picking hand to the point he was ready to join her in yelping. Before tonight, he thought playing five sets straight had been a workout on his fingers. Nothing compared with the brutal grasp of this laboring woman.

They panted at each other, eyes locked. As the pain started to wane, Sonny heard the door to the hallway open. He hoped it would be a nurse checking her progress. Neither looked away as the contraction released her. "Good girl. Now, cleansing breath," Sonny whispered. Cilla let out a long shuddering breath and dropped back to the pillows supporting her. He grabbed a damp cloth and sponged her face, humming a nameless soft tune.

With mind-boggling relief, Sonny recognized his brother's voice. "Just look at you, sweet darlin'. I'm so damn sorry. Glad I made it in time." Walker stood at the bed's end, staring with astonished eyes. He was drenched with rain, still wearing his outlandish stage clothes. Once the news had reached him, he'd frantically caught the first red-eye he could scrounge up, racing against nature to make it home for the birth.

In a hoarse voice somewhere between a cry and a laugh, Cilla called out Walker's name. Sonny motioned him over to where he sat, trading off to his brother's right hand her grasping fingers. "Well, you may not be *on* time, but you is *in* time. Now listen carefully, Squirt. You ever want to play guitar again, don't dare give her your fretting hand."

"Okay, Sonny," he replied, his eyes on Cilla.

"You're one tough lady, Mrs. Blaine." Sonny darted for the door, turning to see his brother kiss his wife, petting her matted hair with his free hand. He added, "Sure glad you could make it for the main event, Squirt. As usual, I get to be your opening act."

Walker turned toward Sonny, his expression scared and grateful. "Thank you so much, man. Words just can't express—"

Cilla screamed out, "Walker, it's starting again!"

"Time for you to get to work, bro." Sonny raced out of the room before he had to witness Cilla yet again contorted by a contraction. He could still hear her as he shuffled down the hall, letting the impact of the last few hours finally envelop him. He stopped just outside the smoking lounge. Leaning against the wall, Sonny slid to a crouch on the floor, burying his face in his hands.

Several minutes later, he heard soft laughter above him. "It looks as though Cilla amply demonstrated what women go through to give men children."

Sonny glanced up to see Maggie standing over him. She had on a different-colored set of scrubs from when he had last seen her, and a surgeon's mask hung from her neck. Her hair was coming loose from its bun, and black circles half-mooned under her eyes. Sonny said, in a voice that surprised him in its weakness, "Point me toward a urologist. I'll get myself snipped this second."

"Don't do anything drastic today." She shook her head, offering him a hand up. He took it, finding his legs weak when he gained his feet. "You went through the scary parts without getting to see the rewards of Cilla's labors. I'm sure she and Walker would let you stay, if you want to see your nephew be born."

He quickly shook his head. "Thanks, but no thanks."

"Well, at least wait until you've held and smelled the sweetness of that baby before offering yourself up to the scalpel." She rubbed her eyes with her fists, yawning. "Tonight alone, I've welcomed four little people into the world. Everyone is doing great, now sleeping peacefully with their mamas." She held up her pager. "From what the nurses just told me, number five, the impatient Blaine baby, won't be long now. I take it Daddy Walker made it back?" Sonny nodded. "Great! I better go do my part."

Sonny watched her hurry off toward Cilla's room, then he turned into the smoking lounge. The rain pounded on the picture window. A crack of thunder rattled the glass. He hadn't even been aware of the storm during the harrowing night. There was only one other person in the room, a young bewhiskered man, asleep in a most uncomfortable looking vinyl chair. Sonny lit up a smoke, thinking he better calm down a little more before braving the weather and driving home to bed.

After a few puffs the cigarette tasted shitty and was making him nauseous. He snuffed it out. A vinyl couch, mate to the chair the other man was using as a bed, beckoned him. Perhaps if he lay down for a few, he would feel much more like braving the slick morning streets. Sonny fell asleep before he was fully reclined.

He wasn't sure exactly how long he was drenched in slumber, but it wasn't nearly long enough. He slapped furiously at the hand attempting to shake him awake. Far away, he heard a woman's urgent voice. "Mr. Blaine, please wake up. Your brother needs you."

He started to come around, remembering where he was. He sat upright, his neck stiff from being cricked wrong on the atrocious couch. "What's up?" he asked groggily.

"It's your sister-in-law. There've been complications." The nurse they had sent to find Sonny told him J.R. had come into the world, howling mightily before he was even fully born. He had arrived not quite thirty minutes after Walker set foot in the hospital. The baby, good-sized and strong-lunged, was doing extremely well. Cilla was not.

They believed that some of the scar tissue due to her earlier tubal pregnancy had ruptured with the exertions of labor. She had begun to hemorrhage profoundly once she had given birth. She was now in surgery, fighting for her life.

Sonny felt the shock of the dismal news flow through him like a whiskey shooter. "She . . . can't die."

"They're doing what they can," the nurse answered solemnly.

"Jesus, no," he whispered, more prayer than curse.

The woman took Sonny's arm gently, leading him back toward the labor and delivery ward. "Your brother's waiting in another room. When no one answered at your house, he had me look for you."

She led him to the door of a private room, saying, "Help him get changed, will you? I'll update ya'll as soon as we know." Sonny nodded, thanking her, and let himself in.

Walker was collapsed into a chair, sobbing. He was dressed in scrubs that were splashed with blood. Sonny nearly fainted at the sight. He took a deep breath, managing to get a grip before passing out. He put on a strong voice, saying, "They found me, Walker. It's going to be okay."

Walker turned his bloodshot eyes to Sonny, voice full of horror. "She worked so hard. Then after one last big push, out came J.R. She got to hold him while I cut the cord, so happy . . . but then . . . blood. So much blood, just pouring out of her, everywhere."

"God."

"They took me away from her."

Sonny saw what needed doing. "They got work to do," he said. "They can't take care of the baby and her, and you, at the same time. You're my job, Walker. Now, come on." Sonny took Walker's limp arm, pulling him to his feet. "You need to get out of those dirty scrubs. They got some more Hawkeye Pierce duds for you, or do you got to put your tasteless stage getup back on?" He spotted some hospital clothes folded on the bed and handed them to Walker. "Here you go. Get in the john there, and get that blood . . . get washed up, hear? Can you manage by yourself?"

Walker meekly nodded, stumbling into the bathroom. He came out a few minutes later, clean but still ghostly pale, still crying. At least he wasn't covered in Cilla's blood. "Any word yet, Sonny?" he sniffed.

"Not yet. It's bound to take time, Squirt. Tell me about your boy, while we're waiting?"

"He's—he's just real pretty. I mean, he was all wrinkled and scummy, but he's perfect . . . he was howling, so pissed off." Walker laughed a little through his tears.

"Ain't that fine?" Sonny said, slapping his shoulder. Walker tried to smile. "We got us another soul shouter in the family. I better go make him some Bobby Bland and Johnny Copeland tapes, to start him out right."

"Right. They're going to bring him in to me in a minute, soon as he's cleaned up good and double-checked by his doc."

Soon a nurse did come in, holding a bread-loaf-sized bundle of white blankets. She smiled warmly, approaching Walker's chair. "Mr. Blaine? Your son's ready to see you again." She had Walker sit down and handed him the baby, showing him how to correctly support his head. Sonny watched Walker gazing wide-eyed at the swaddled infant.

Sonny felt his chest growing tight as he studied the two of them. A boy—Cilla's son and his brother's. Blood of his blood. He had to quit looking. He followed the pediatric nurse into the hallway. "Ma'am? Any word on his wife?"

"Not yet. And that's a good sign. It means she's still fighting." She sounded grave. "Ring the buzzer if he needs anything."

Sonny went back into the room. He went to stand over the two, peering at the baby's sleeping face. "Look at that head full of hair."

"Yeah." Walker stroked it, his heavy-veined hand covering the scalp entirely. "See how bright red it is?"

"Better be red, with ya'll for his folks. Them other babies in the nursery had little hats on. Why ain't your boy got one?"

"Because he's got enough hair to keep his head warm."

"Either that, or they didn't have a sombrero fancy enough to do your kid justice."

Walker pulled J.R.'s head close for a kiss. His teardrops wet the baby's silken red hair. "Oh, little man. Your mama's just got to make it."

"Just keep praying, hear?" Sonny said. Walker nodded, keeping his eyes fixed on the baby. Sonny took a seat again across from him, massaging his stiff neck. He had done more praying himself in the last eight-plus hours than he ever had in his life.

"You want to hold him, Sonny?"

"I ain't held a baby since—well, since I held you, when you and Mama first came home from the hospital."

"That so?"

"Yeah. I remember that clear as if it was yesterday. Don't Mama got a picture of that somewheres, me sitting on the couch, holding you?"

"Yeah. She's getting me a copy for that wall of photos I'm doing in my Guitar Room. Come on, Uncle Sonny. Go wash your hands. Get one of them robes off the bed, put it on. It's high time you held another baby."

Sonny washed up and put the sanitary gown over his chest. It was frightening, the idea of cradling such a tender life. Walker transferred his son carefully into Sonny's arms. The baby kept sleeping, his wrinkled red face peaceful, his mouth making phantom suckling motions. Sonny was amazed by his lack of heft, considering how big Cilla had grown before giving birth. He whispered, "Hey, you. Already messing with your Uncle Sonny's mind, huh, punk? Seeking revenge in your daddy's name, no doubt."

"That's my boy."

"You're pretty cool." Sonny brought him closer to his face. Maggie was right—he smelled so sweet, earthy yet new. Like nothing else Sonny had ever come across. "Don't he look like Winston Churchill, only with Cilla's red hair?" Walker nodded, keeping his eyes on his son. "You know your hair was this red when you was little, Squirt. God, how Mama and them went on about your damn hair! She'd do it up in spit curls and such. Me, just a straight black buzz cut. I was so jealous by all the attention you got. I was cock of the walk before you came around." Sonny chuckled, giving his brother the eye. "More things change, more they stay the same."

"They didn't keep calling me the pretty one for long, now did they?" Walker answered. To the baby he said tenderly, "Maybe you'll get lucky, J.R., and take after your lady-killer uncle."

They both watched the baby sleeping for awhile. Then Walker spoke, his voice serious. "Sonny? Got something important to ask. Cilla and I was going to ask you together, but I reckon I better now."

"So go ahead."

"If something happens to us, Cilla and me, will you take care of our boy?"

Sonny was beyond surprised. He couldn't even speak for a minute. "Walker, I'm flattered ya'll think that much of me, but I don't know shit about kids. It's like asking Scrooge to raise him up."

"That ain't so, Sonny. Just think about it, okay? I mean, if Cill pulls through—" Walker choked up.

"You mean *when* Cill pulls through."

"Yeah, when . . . with the way we make our living, all the travel, you know, there's lots of risks."

"Every job got risks."

"Ours are different. Look what happened to Roy Buchanan."

Sonny nodded. Roy's was already a legendary road story among stringers. He'd been one of the best of the D.C.-area Telecaster Masters. Always known as a strange cat, hard as nails, Roy had been found mysteriously "hung" in a Virginia jail cell.

"You believe those cops' story, Sonny?"

"Of course not. But he probably was shitfaced and gave them redneck pigs a hard time—and paid dearly for it. Maybe at one time, you could have been in the same spot. But now you ain't going to be out driving drunk."

"I reckon that's so. But when I'm traveling, sometimes I feel like I'll never make it home. The flying? I hate that shit."

"Walker, when you really think about how much we fly, you realize how safe it is. I ain't never even been on a plane that was in real trouble. When's the last time someone went down in flames like Buddy Holly?"

"Ricky Nelson," Walker shot back, a little too quickly. Sonny could see that he clearly dwelled on this. "Sonny, weren't you ever scared, flying?"

"Well, sure. Flying is the thing I miss least about the road . . . besides Bonnell." They both let out a loud laugh. J.R. jumped, pushing a little hand out of his blankets. Sonny rocked him, giving him a thumb to hold. He grinned, admiring his nephew's fingers. "Look at that, Walker. Got our hands, no doubt about it. How about his eyes? Are they that pretty green of Cilla's, or black like ours?"

"Just sort of a navy blue right now. They don't get their real color for a little while yet, the doc says. You mind if I hold him again?" Sonny carefully handed J.R. over to his daddy. "Thanks," Walker said. "Never liked holding babies much. But I could hold my boy all day."

"Good thing. I bet you spend a few nights walking the floor, doing just that."

"That's cool by me." Walker rocked side to side, crooning a little tune, and J.R. fell back to sleep. "Deepest thanks for all you did for Cill, Sonny."

Sonny tried to keep his voice light. "You owe me. Big-time."

"I know it." Walker paused. When he spoke again, his voice quavered with emotion. "I just can't imagine being in your boots. If I was you, I'd have dropped her off here then hit the closest bar and gotten smashed."

Sonny smiled. "I tried to do just that—these damn nurses wouldn't let me, though."

"You stuck by her, Sonny. . . . You. . . ." He started crying again.

A nurse, hair tucked up in plastic cap and mask loose around her neck, poked her head in. Walker scrambled to his feet, continuing to pat the baby. "Is my wife okay?"

"She's not completely out of the woods yet, Mr. Blaine, but Dr. Clark did want me to get word to you that she's stabilized." She smiled and was gone before the brothers could get more from her. As the door clicked shut, Walker really let loose the tears.

"Damn, you cry more than any cat ever!" Sonny said, gently punching his brother's chin. "God to millions of pickers across the land. Greatest who ever lived—but he'll bawl gallons at the drop of a hat."

Walker laughed, struggling to wipe his eyes while holding tight to the baby. "Now your uncle's spouting off quotes from the music press," he said to J.R. "He sure never thought I was such hot shit."

"Don't listen to him, J.R. If anyone knows your daddy's hot shit, it's me." Sonny knew he'd never have another chance like this. Too long he had not spoken of things that Walker needed to hear. "It's been hard on my pride, being your older brother."

"Man, I never meant for it to be."

"I know. You just did what you had to. What you was made to do, Walker. And me, too. There's nothing else I could think of doing in this life but play my guitar."

"We was both born for it, Sonny."

"I know it. And I'm proud, because I did it the way I wanted to. Didn't sell out and play some lame corporate shit just to pull in more bread. I could have. I don't mean to sound vain, but I got the looks and the chops to have been one of them big MTV video stars."

"You sure do, Sonny."

Sonny nodded. "But this blues we love so much, it's being married, ain't it? Like a lifetime thing?"

"Yeah. That's it exactly."

"And to hear you play . . . man, Walker, what a gift. What a special thing that is."

"You making fun of me?" Walker said, sounding a little sore.

"No, asshole!" Sonny laughed. "I mean this. You're it. One of those cats that only come around once. Like a Mozart, or a Da Vinci, or. . . ." Sonny grinned. "A Jimi Hendrix!"

"Now I know you're messing with me."

"Shut up and listen," Sonny ordered. He paused, running a hand through his hair. "Once, long time ago, I was talking with some UT music major babe. We got to talking about Mozart, and how he wrote his music? Do you know she told me old Wolfgang spit it all out in just one draft? No cross outs, no going back and reworking sections?"

"I didn't know that."

"Blew me away! But you know what this girl said about it?" Walker shook his head. "She said, 'It's not that amazing when you consider what he was really doing. He was just—' " Sonny pointed heavenward " '—taking dictation!' "

Walker nodded furiously. "I've felt it happen, Sonny. Not when I'm composing, because that's usually a real struggle. But when I'm actually playing, sometimes even I don't know where I'm going. But whenever it happens, I end up someplace amazing. It's like I'm using someone else's hands. It's plain scary. It don't feel completely right. It's almost like I'm messing with something that maybe people shouldn't. But, same time, it is the greatest thrill." Walker smiled down at his sleeping son. He hummed a gentle tune for a minute before continuing. "After I got sober, I was afraid I'd lose touch with that magic. Like, oh, hell, I don't know, maybe the drugs and all expanded my mind, like the hippies used to say." He shook his head. "But it ain't so. It's almost like I can zero in quicker and cleaner to what's out there, even better as I grow older and healthier." Walker looked up at Sonny. "You ever had that feeling, Sonny?"

Sonny was quiet for a moment, finally saying, "I don't rightly know, Walker. I don't think I have. I mean, sometimes I feel real inspired. I'm playing, and all of a sudden I feel something flow out of me that I know comes from a real place inside." He tapped his breast. "But you . . . I don't think what happens with you is entirely from inside you. Bonnell told me something about you once. . . ." He trailed off.

Walker frowned. "Bonnell? What'd that asshole say?"

"It don't matter. He's nuts."

"I hear that."

Sonny opened his mouth a couple of times, and closed it again. Finally, holding his hand spread out in front of him, he said, "There's one thing I know for sure, my heart of hearts. Ain't never going to be another Firewalker. Your talent runs so damn deep, wherever it comes from. It's like an onion is, just layers upon layers of skills. You got the speed thing, cold. You got a deep love of music. You always listened to all sorts of stuff, took it in, and digested it. When you play something by another guy, it's no cheap imitation. It comes out pure Walker Blaine, doing a killer version of whatever song it is. You just able like nobody to make stuff yours. And your tone is so rich and unmistakable."

Walker tapped his head. "That tone is right in here—been here as long as I can remember. I worked real hard to get the right techniques and gear to get it out like I hear it inside."

"I believe it. What you play sounds just like you, Walker. And who'd know that better than me?"

"Not nobody, Sonny. I—"

The door to the hallway opened. The brothers jumped to their feet. Maggie, looking exhausted but jubilant, came into the room. "Walker, Cilla has made it through surgery. Everything's going to be all right."

"Hey! That's the Otis Rush song from our record, Squirt," Sonny babbled. Relief and joy coursed through him. Walker handed J.R. to Sonny, and he gathered him to his chest.

Walker focused intently on Maggie as she explained that she had been forced to remove Cilla's uterus to stop the bleeding. She would not be able to have any more children. "But otherwise, she'll be perfectly fine," Maggie assured him. "It's great news. We were afraid of brain damage, frankly."

"Brain damage? Why?" Walker said, the joy draining from his face.

"Her bleeding was so intense, Cilla's blood pressure fell to nearly zero. We were worried about a lack of oxygenated blood flow to her brain. But she appears to be fine as she's coming around. She seems to know all she should. Mainly, she knows she's got a husband and son she needs to see immediately." Maggie smiled. "Are you ready, Walker?"

"Am I! I can take the little man with me?"

Maggie nodded. "You'd best, if you want to stay married. There's somebody waiting out in the hallway to take you in to see your wife. Ya'll won't be able to stay too long, because Cilla needs rest. But I imagine you boys do, too." Walker hugged her, thanking her profusely. Sonny handed over the sleeping child. Maggie and Sonny watched Walker as he darted into the hall, cuddling J.R. to his chest.

Maggie turned to Sonny, stretching her arms in front of her. "Oh, Sonny. That was a close one." She shrugged, her eyes growing distant. "So often nothing helps, when they start hemorrhaging like she did. Hysterectomy, transfusions. . . . Nothing stops it. They just bleed out on us."

Sonny studied Maggie's drained face. She was trying to hold on to her professional demeanor, but he thought he could detect her ripe lower lip quivering slightly. He went over and gave her a strong hug. At first she stiffened in his arms, but then allowed herself to return his embrace. He whispered, "Thanks, Maggie. My family will always be in your debt." He pulled back, giving her his patented grin. "You got any more babies to bring into the world right now?"

"No, thank God," she sighed. "Every time the moon's full, this place goes haywire."

"Them nurses said that about the damn full moon, too," Sonny said, laughing and rolling his eyes.

She shrugged. "Honest to God, it's true. Maybe it has to do with tidal flows or something. But while I still can, I'm going home, eating a tremendous breakfast, and sleeping for hours."

"How about letting me buy you that breakfast?"

She took his hands off her shoulders, stepping back from him. "I think not, Sonny."

"Maggie, I'm way more harmless than I used to be. Especially after last night. My girlfriend's going to have to work awful hard ever to get me within ten feet of her again." He was happy when Maggie laughed. "Consider this breakfast a thanks for what you done last night. And it's also my way of saying sorry for being so shitty to you all them years ago. I'm trying hard to change my ways. Okay?"

"Well, okay, I guess," she agreed. "But absolutely no hospital food."

Sonny draped his arm around her shoulder. "I'd never do that to you. I happen to know this little home cookin' diner, right around the corner."

"Sounds perfect."

"It is." Sonny laughed. "Hell, I just remembered something. I took Walker there the morning you and me met, right after you patched him up at the clinic."

"No kidding?"

"Yeah. He was the walking wounded, wearing one of my shirts because the only one he owned was bloody. A homeless punk, only my cast-off guitar to his name." The memory of it made Sonny laugh hard, feeling damn near delirious. Strange how often things turned out ass-backward from how you'd expected.

✷ ✷ ✷ ✷ ✷

13.

SONNY WAS STILL not ready for a full-blown tour, and Walker wasn't ready to be gone from his baby and bride for long stretches. But they were both road dogs at heart and agreed that a few festival dates during the summer might be just the thing. They could play short sets, see some old friends, and try out some of the stuff from the new record. The first gig that came up was one close to home. There was a Ranch Aid concert, with money earmarked for the recession- and drought-troubled ranchers between Abilene and Fort Worth. The ranch land it was to be held on was just an hour's slow walk from Mingus. The brothers agreed it would be ideal to start their tour with the Ranch Aid show.

The day of the show, Sonny and Walker retreated to their trailer to sleep through the afternoon heat. They weren't scheduled until nightfall. Sonny stirred awake to the sound of knocking on the flimsy trailer door. He slid off the small bed he was napping upon and hurried to answer before Walker was disturbed. He opened it to a burly Ranch Aid Festival security guard. "Icestorm, there's a dude out here claiming he brung Firewalker a car."

"A car?"

"Yeah. And it's one badass set of wheels, man."

"Firewalker's asleep. Let me see what this is all about." Sonny followed the big guy, scratching and yawning. There was a lot of commotion among the trailers as the gear and people were readied for the show. Despite the racket, Walker was snoring like a biplane on high pitch. Likely the first good sleep he'd had since J.R. had come home and taken over his parents' bed. "When he ain't sucking titty, he's sleeping, laid out, on my chest," Walker had admitted earlier. "He gets lonesome in his crib."

Sonny rounded a trailer and whistled low when he laid eyes on the machine. She was a debutante-model Ford Thunderbird, a 1955 type 40. The chrome and satin finish gleamed in the afternoon sun. She was at least as fine as when she rolled off the Detroit assembly line thirty-four years past.

As far as improvements, a state of the art Blaukpunt cassette/AM-FM radio had replaced the original Volumatic radio. The interior seats had been re-covered in the finest hunter-green leather, carpeted to match. As set up now, she had her white opera-windowed hard top in place. She came with a kit to change into a ragtop. Sonny couldn't resist getting in and starting her. The powerful V-8 sparkled, purring like a satisfied tigress.

Sonny wanted to drive the car right back to the trailer, but the area was too crowded with workers and gear. Instead, he grabbed the keys and trotted back to the trailer to get Walker. Sonny caught sight of himself in the mirror as he darted into the trailer. His usually perfect hair was going every which way, and he looked about as languorous and restful as an overfed lap dog. He grinned at the reflection, enjoying the sight of himself and that of Walker snoozing. Gone were the days of snorting up an eight ball and killing a fifth together before a show, driven to a razor's edge of madness. Now they both needed a nap prior to taking the stage. A sign of old age creeping over them but also of maturity—at long last.

"Hey, Squirt? There's a fucking dream machine out here that they say is yours."

Walker looked at Sonny, dazed for a moment. Then his eyes focused and he grinned. "Yeah? It must be Cilla's wedding present. I was hoping they'd have it ready in time to meet me here with it."

"Little late for a wedding present."

Walker splashed some water on his face from the sink and mumbled through the towel as he dried off, "Well, took some time to find her the perfect car. She's always wanted a T-Bird. I told my guy what I wanted—same cat who found and fixed up my 'Vette."

"Well, he found another 10. Just like your wife."

Walker was thrilled with the restoration, especially the satin finish. He and his car man had conferred with the Fender Custom Shop to get a green pigment identical to Cilla's favorite Strat. "Color sure seems just right, don't she, Sonny?"

"Sure enough does."

"Which mean it matches my girl's eyes, too," Walker added, running his hands over the surface.

"Some eyes," the trucker who'd driven the car from California commented to Sonny. "He's a lucky guy, your brother."

"Oh, that he is."

"I got to drive this thing," Walker exclaimed. He checked his watch. "Damn, we getting close to zero hour. Probably couldn't even get to the open road with all the audience traffic flowing into the place."

"You got that right. I had a hell of a time getting in from the highway," the trucker said. "People backed up for a long ways, trying to get in down the dirt roads into the ranches. You better wait until after your show, Walker."

Yeah, you're right," Walker said, peering under the hood longingly. He suddenly slammed it shut, eyes inspired. "You know what I'll do? I think I'll take her home to Cilla myself. Won't she be tickled?"

Sonny shook his head. "Walker, I know you want to drive her. Hell, I do, too. But it'll be real late by the time we get on the road. We got to do our show, then do our meet and greet. And all these folks coming in got to get themselves back out again, too. Just take the chopper out of here with the rest of us, head on back home via D/FW." He turned to the trucker, who was still at his side. "Look, we'll get you good seats, a backstage pass for this thing and pay your expenses to take it on into Austin for his wife. Okay, man?"

"Might as well. Drove her this far," the trucker replied.

"Come on, boys," Walker whined. "I need to take her out on the empty open road, cruise south under a million stars. You know how long it's been since I had a chance to do that, drive with the tape deck blasting without an entourage of yes-men or bodyguards in sight?"

"Too long, I'm sure, bro. But—"

Walker cut Sonny off with a slap to the fender. "I know. Let's you and me drive it home, Sonny."

"After the show, I'm going to want to get home to bed right quick."

"Shit, man. When's the last time we drove 281 together? I don't think we done it since that day I moved to Austin."

"No. The last time was when you and Vada got hitched. Look, I'm supposed to join Annabelle for some breakfast thing for the Chamber, way early in the morning. I'd better get a few hour's shut-eye before she shows me off to all her fat cats."

THE RANCH AID SHOW had ticket sales in the high tens of thousands. Definitely it was the biggest bunch of folks ever seen around Mingus parts. Several ranchers had donated the use of their overgrazed land. Pastures were packed with cars, food stands, portable johns, and people—tons of people, there for the music. The weather even cooperated—something that couldn't be taken for granted in these flood- and twister-whipped parts. Sonny had played quite a few big festivals in his day, but had never been involved in a fund-raiser of such Texas-sized proportions. He was pleasantly surprised by how smoothly things were running.

The bill couldn't be more impressive. The homegrown slant to the talent made it all the better. Floyd Montgomery and his Sidewinders were there. Eddie was again sitting drums for Floyd, making the group damn close to the White Tornadoes, back in the days when they'd ruled this part of the state. For the first time in years, Sonny got to catch up with Terry Joe McGowan, the country hippie bard whom he had recorded with back in the Sixties. Terry Joe had gone on to be a household name himself. He'd almost single-handedly changed the staid face of country music—not unlike what Walker had done with American blues. Terry Joe and Walker posed together for pictures in long hair and cowboy hats that no self-respecting local stomper would touch with fire tongs. At least Terry Joe was wearing his beans-and-jeans ensemble. Walker was sporting his gold crayon suit. Even in this crowd no one could miss him.

Bonnell and the boys, doing a crisp Rockets set, got the crowd to mov-

ing. Then nothing would do but to have the Texas Icestorm come in for
some foot-stomping encores. Sonny felt good, right, sitting in with his former bandmates. Gone was any bad blood that had lingered, leaving only the
joy that came from putting down some great, danceable blues. The Rockets'
current guitarist, young Buddy, was beside himself, playing on the same bill
with his hero. The chance to actually jam side by side with Sonny nearly
sent the kid into a full-blown fit. They tore into a long and tasty dual solo
on the old classic *Guitar Slim Boogie*. By the end of the song, Sonny was
mighty impressed with his successor.

Firewalker and the Salamanders took the stage after the Rockets, playing one song from each of their solo albums. Next Sonny joined them, causing a cacophony of screams from both the crowd and the assembled talent.
Then the brothers went to work on material from the new record. Sonny
honestly couldn't remember a time he'd had more pure fun playing. The
sheer size of the audience, a throng dancing and shouting almost as one, was
an awesome sight unto itself. And it was a choice thing to be backed by the
thumping, grinning Really Riley Goode and the thrash master Outlaw Jesse
James Goddard. No wonder Walker stayed true to them. If there were a
better rhythm section alive, Sonny had yet to hear them.

Sonny watched Firewalker playing beside him, taking his Texas fashion
excess one step beyond, his hat's red foxtail bopping in time. Hunched over
Goldie, his chin tucked into his shoulder, Walker's expression was nearly
pornographic. Walker wailed full-tilt with the rapture that gripped him. No
doubt he was channeling the fearsome mystery that only he could summon.
Tonight the power of his playing resonated in Sonny's very marrow—in
everyone's.

The Salamanders and Sonny left the stage after several encores and
curtain calls. The backstage celebs surrounded the sweat-drenched Walker,
piling on more applause. Sonny stood apart, pleased by the sight of his
brother toweling off, pounding down his bottled water, basking in the praise
of his peers. Suddenly he heard a voice croak in his ear. "Better watch your
back around your kid brother. Any time now, people'll take notice of how
fucking good he's gotten."

Sonny turned to see, swaying and grinning beside him, Kyle Reagan,
the unsinkable Bad Signs bad boy. "They already have, man." Sonny
replied, laughing. They grabbed each other in a fierce handshake. "How
you doing, Kyle?"

"I'm doing. Been recording in Dallas this week. When I heard about
this damn thing, I had to show. So, the kid snagged Pretty Priscilla. Who
knew, man?"

Walker, peering around the heads of the admirers, locked eyes with
Sonny and grinned, giving him a sharp greeting with a jut of his chin. Sonny
pointed to Kyle. Walker pushed his way over, bear-hugging the battle-

scarred old Brit. "Kyle, it's good to see you. My wife will be crushed she missed you."

"Your bloody *wife!*" Kyle yelped, pounding Walker on the arm. "Congrats, Walker. Seems you scored more at Jackie's long-ago party than a record contract. Thank God that girl married a fine Texas bluesman, instead of that arrogant dick I work with." The gathered musicians laughed.

"Well, I ain't arguing that point," Walker said, a proud and cocky smile on his face. "You and Jackie fighting again, Kyle? Maybe it's time the Bad Signs get a Fillmore Divorce."

"You know us. We're an awful old married couple that fights nonstop but couldn't live without each other. The Bad Signs will keep on keeping on."

"Yeah, despite the odds. Looky here, Kyle." Walker thrust a snapshot at him. It was a picture of J.R. that Walker showed to anyone he could corner. "Ain't my boy cute?"

"That he is," Kyle said, peering at the photo. "Ginger hair like his mum, too. There'll be one tempest after another in your house from now on."

"Excuse me? My grandson is as good as gold," declared Reg, surprising the assembled artists with his entrance.

"It's my daddy!" Walker said, embracing him. Reg winced theatrically at the words. Walker turned to their compadres. "That term of endearment's still pretty hard for Little Lord Mountbatten to swallow from the likes of me." The others rumbled with chuckles. More softly, Walker peppered Reg with questions. "You just get here from Austin?" Reg nodded. "How's Cill and J.R.? My boy ain't too fussy and driving little mama nuts, is he? Did you—"

"Relax, Walker," Reg told him, squeezing his shoulder. "They were both asleep in your bed when I left. Besides, your mum is there with them if either so much as stirs. Now—" Reg turned to address the surrounding crowd of musicians "—don't you think we should give that crowd out there some sort of an encore? They're going nuts while we sit back here gossiping with my son-in-law like a bunch of fishwives."

THERE WAS A PARTY vibe in the air after the all-star encore. The revelers split into two groups. The imbibers headed off for a most memorable shindig with Kyle Reagan. The clean crowd stuck with Walker and his family.

After socializing for awhile, Reg bid Walker farewell. "Since your heart is set on getting that car home to Cilla tonight, I'll go ahead and take the first chopper out and get on back. You'll ride easier if I do. I'll make some excuse to my daughter so as not to spoil the surprise of your gift."

"Okay, Reg." Walker grinned at Sonny. "I wish I could say she'd sleep through the night and never know I was taking the long way home, but she'll be up feeding that boy at least a few times. Why don't you and me say our goodbyes, too, and start rounding up our stuff in the trailer?"

"Sounds good to me, Squirt. I'm fading fast. Not used to this excitement anymore, I reckon."

In their trailer Walker stripped off his gold jacket, tossing it onto his pile of stuff by the door. He peeled off the sweat-soaked shirt and elaborate scarf he wore beneath, yanking on a sleeveless red T-shirt. He probably thinks he looks dynamite, tattoo on display and those Crayola-gold pants, Sonny thought, smiling and shaking his head. Seeking comfort for the flight home, Sonny changed from his sharp suit into old jeans and a swag shirt.

Putting his hat back on and pulling his peace symbol out from the neck of his shirt, Walker flopped onto a chair. "Man, wasn't that a gas, Sonny?"

"A real good time, Squirt."

"And I think they must have raised some bucks for the ranchers, too. Can't beat that. You sure I can't talk you into driving back home with me tonight, bro? Just think, you and me, two regular guys on a little road trip in that awesome T-Bird. We'll talk about old times and listen to great music." Walker picked up a cassette of *Storm Cellar Blues* out of a pile of tapes, holding it up for Sonny to see.

Sonny yawned. "I just want to get home to bed. Sorry I'm such an old fart. I'd be asleep before we hit Stephenville."

"It's okay."

"If you'd ride back on the plane with me, we'd have plenty of time to visit, riding them damn runways halfway to Houston and back." They both laughed. It had become a joke between them to set their watch once a plane touched ground at D/FW to see how long it took to reach the actual terminal. On holidays it often took longer than the entire short-hop flight to Austin. "You must be played out yourself, Squirt. How many nights has it been since J.R.'s let you sleep straight through?"

"Ah, it's like when I was all cokey. You get used to being sleepless after awhile."

"Right. And if J.R. wasn't enough to wear your ass out, you been out there tonight playing harder and better than you ever have."

Walker looked up at Sonny, real pleasure in his eyes. "You think so, Sonny?"

"Like you really got to ask?" Sonny shot back, grinning down at him.

Before Walker could answer, there was a knock on the trailer door. Sonny answered to a security guard. "The last chopper to D/FW's about to take off. Ya'll better grab it."

"You sure I can't convince you to come with, Sonny?" Walker asked.

"Not this time, Walker. Granddaddy Reg is staying at your place a few days, ain't he?"

"He sure is. Might act the cool one, but he loves snuggling his grandbaby."

"Okay. I'd like to catch up with Reg, and visit with my nephew some, too. I'll be at your place tomorrow, after I'm through with that thing that Annabelle's got us roped into. Think Cilla'll let me take her T-Bird for a spin then?"

"I reckon she will."

The security guy cleared his throat. "Icestorm—the chopper?"

"Go tell them I'm there," Sonny said to the guard. He turned to Walker. "Stop if you get tired, man."

"Yes, dear," Walker sang. As Sonny stepped toward the door, Walker added, "I love you, man."

Sonny nodded back at him. "Yeah. See you tomorrow."

Sonny followed the security guard toward the liftoff area. Right before he ducked behind an equipment semi, Sonny heard Walker yelling his name. He peered back at him. Walker was slumped on the hood of Cilla's car. He grinned, holding up the peace sign pendant.

As he had done that first time they had played together, at Sonny's eighteenth birthday party, Walker mouthed, "Thanks, Sonny."

This time, Sonny mouthed an answer back. "You're welcome." With that, he ran off to catch his flight home.

EPILOGUE: *KEEPER OF THE FLAME*

S ONNY FINGERED THE chain hanging from his neck. He could feel
Walker's peace symbol resting cool against the skin of his chest. A
young cop, a heartsick fan, had been thoughtful enough to save it from
evidence and sneak it to him. Sonny hadn't taken it off since, but he kept it
concealed inside his shirt. To wear it on the outside would be like crying in
public. He'd already done too much of that.

Sonny lit a cigarette, gazing through the kitchen window at the rose
garden that had once been a Sugar and Spice parking lot. This time of year
the blossoms burst forth like fireworks, in many shades. Looked just like
one of Walker's goofy kimonos. Sonny leaned heavily on the counter, listening as the radio continued to play nothing but Salamander songs.

U.S. 281 had always been a dangerous road, especially near Evant,
where it crossed Highway 84. As boys, riding the road with their folks,
Sonny and Walker had seen the bloody aftermaths of a couple head-ons.
Anymore, most travelers crossing the state's heart took I-35. Semis, dodg-
ing weigh stations, doctoring their logs, did still sometimes use 281. The
outlaw trucker who had killed Walker had been operating a rig overloaded
with some highly combustible and questionable shit, pushing himself hard
to get through to Dallas before morning. It seemed he had been behind the
wheel at least seventeen hours without sleep. Autopsies and investigations
would follow, but burnt remains of empty beer cans had been found in the
semi's wreckage. The trucker was likely on stimulants, too. Nothing unto-
ward had been found in the little that was left of the burned-up emerald
Thunderbird.

Too long, Walker had been a near vagabond, with no real permanent
residence. He'd always used Sonny's long-standing phone number for his
emergency information. Apparently he hadn't thought to change it over
when he'd bought the new house. Sonny had been the one the Highway
Patrol called in the predawn hours after the Festival. He'd taken it on himself to break the news to Cilla.

He couldn't remember driving to her. He did remember waiting a long
time beside his car, getting completely drenched by a cloudburst. Finally,
his teeth chattering, only in part from being soaked, Sonny made his way to
her door. Again he waited. A streak of lightning finally jolted him into
knocking.

Reg answered after a few minutes, taking Sonny's shock-slowed brain
by surprise. He had forgotten about Reg's visit. Sleep-saturated, Reg fum-

bled to put his spectacles on. He muttered, "Sonny? Why in hell are you here at this. . . ." His voice trailed off once his glasses were in place, expression changing instantly from irritation to concern. He reached out and touched Sonny's arm. "What's happened?"

Shaking violently, Sonny managed to rasp out, "A wreck, Reg. Walker's been. . . ." He stopped, holding up his hands in surrender.

Reg gripped Sonny's arm, clawlike, the color draining from his face. "Dear God. He's . . . hurt, then?"

"No. Not hurt."

Sonny hadn't seen Cilla behind Reg, listening in on the stairwell. She came at him howling curses of denial, her silk nightgown flowing miasmalike behind her. She knocked him to the porch and clawed at his neck, beat his chest and face with her fists. Sonny surrendered to the blows. He vaguely heard Ruby yelling from somewhere deep in the house, and the baby's cries. Reg pulled Cilla off him. Sonny propped up on his elbows and watched stupidly as she screamed Walker's name over and over again. She fought to break free from Reg's strong hands and tear at herself as she'd done Sonny.

In the kitchen, in the present, Sonny started to cry with the memory of it. He'd been so buried the last few days, wrestling with arrangements and legalities, that he'd almost succeeded in blocking that moment out.

To Sonny's surprise, Walker had carefully attended to his estate. He'd had a solid prenuptial agreement and will drawn up. Cilla kept the abundance that she had brought to the marriage, as well as the new house. Walker had seen to it that a trust fund had been arranged for J.R., made up of twenty percent of his father's music and licensed merchandise. Ruby was also left with a tidy little sum and twenty percent of Walker's future earnings. But the rest of Walker's estate—all his recordings, currently released or otherwise, and all the cash from various bank accounts and stock investments through Twelve Bar Records—had been left to Sonny.

Cilla had told him, "You were the one person Walker trusted most in all the world when it came to sound judgment about music matters. He very much wanted you to handle his legacy personally, if the need arose."

Sonny reluctantly accepted the responsibility, mostly as a way of making amends to Walker. Overnight he'd become an extremely wealthy man, growing more so hourly with the huge boost in record sales since Walker's death. In a way he'd never expected, Sonny now owned the music he'd spent most of his life wishing for. Sonny was slammed with remorse for the times he had treated his little brother poorly, times when he wouldn't even speak to Walker, except to wax cruel. But life was short, even when it was long. He had to somehow get beyond these feelings in order to do right by what had been left in his care.

Cilla's house had become a sanctuary to the inner circle in the days since the wreck. They'd hired tight security and were doing their best to steer clear of the press—and even more so of the dark rumors. People seemed to want to explain this tragedy in a supernatural fashion. Firewalker Blaine had died at the crossroads, the same kind of lonesome place where Robert Johnson was said to have sold his soul. Everyone knew he played like a demon. How could such unexplainable magic spring from an ordinary little man hailing from a no-count Texas town? Something unearthly happened when the kid with the Fender swaggered in, be it in a lowdown gin joint or a high-tone concert hall. Few besides Sonny knew that Walker's outward bluster hid deep insecurities. Fans didn't see the shy pain lurking just under the flashy hat brim. They saw a man to be reckoned with. No matter what Bonnell had once told him out in the swamps, what others were signifying now, Sonny knew in his heart that this death hadn't come from Satan taking what he considered his due. Senselessly, it came from being in the wrong place at the wrong time.

Sonny took comfort in the knowledge that Walker's musical hoodoo would tempt and torment players for as long as kids picked up guitars. His playing would stay a mark of excellence to those dedicated enough to learn what it took to make a six-string holler and moan. Sonny honestly believed what Daddy Jim had told him as a boy. Talent was God-given, but had to be coaxed into greatness by devotion, self-imposed patience and endless practice.

Reg entered the kitchen, dressed for the memorial service in a dark, conservative suit. "You holding up all right, Sonny?"

He made like he was coughing, turning his face away from Reg to wipe his eyes. "Yeah."

"You'd better go outside with that cig before Priscilla wakes up and smells it. You know how she feels about anyone smoking around J.R."

"Sorry. I just forgot myself." Sonny ran water over the butt, then opened the window and turned on the exhaust fan over the stove.

Reg cocked an ear and nodded toward the radio. "*Barroom Brawl*, isn't it? Listen to that solo. It's just an orgasm of notes." They both listened to the recording of Walker going for it, shaking their heads and exchanging sad smiles. "Where do you suppose he drew such inspiration from?"

"Guess we'll never really know, Reg."

They listened again to Walker working out the gold Strat. When the raucous vocals kicked back in, a smile flirted around Reg's mournful face. "I say. Don't you wonder if he was ever really in a fight of such epic proportions?"

"If one ever broke out when he was around, you can bet your ass he ran like hell. Never could throw or take a punch worth a damn."

"Says the voice of experience?"

Sonny dropped his head, feeling his eyes welling up again. "Shamed to say, yes."

"Please don't let that eat at you, Sonny. Your bullying never seemed to bother Walker. He held you in the highest regard." Reg let out a small laugh. "Lord, how he went on about you. It made the rest of us sick."

In silence they listened again. When the song ended, Reg took off his glasses and rubbed the bridge of his nose, saying, "I'll never forget the day Priscilla brought home that tape of the Salamanders playing for Jackie Higgins's birthday. A truck had been delivering her things from Jackie's place all morning long. But she didn't want to talk about that. She insisted I listen to that damned tape. I wanted some answers, and tried to give her a lecture about substance abuse, because I could see she was as high as a kite. I don't think she even heard me. I finally realized I had to listen to that tape if I was going to get through to her."

Reg paused for a moment. Sonny could see his friend's unfocused eyes going to that long gone morning. "Much like you, I was a blues prodigy, Sonny. By the time I'd heard Walker, I'd heard—hell, played—with them all. Them all! But he was . . . well, I simply had to get him signed."

"He was always real grateful to you, Reg. You and Cill, for putting Sterling onto him."

"It was a rare honor, to help such a talent make the big time."

"Had to be."

"Come now," Reg snorted. "You must know that you were more responsible for his career than all the rest of us put together."

Sonny felt a savage mixture of feelings flood him at Reg's compliment. All he could do was nod, turning to look back out the window before he lost it again.

Reg's voice cracked with emotion. "Walker was a fine man, too. Even though it was only briefly, I'm proud that I was able to call him my son-in-law."

He turned away, wiping a hand across his eyes before putting his glasses back on. Then he peered into the living room, at the Texas-shaped clock on the mantel. "The limo with Annabelle and the Montgomerys should be here anytime now. Are you ready?"

"As I can be, I reckon. Where's Mama?"

"The last I saw of her, she was out beside the creek. She's all dressed and ready. I think she just needed a moment to herself. I'll go and get Priscilla."

"Here I am, Dad," Cilla said, entering the kitchen. "I just put J.R. down in his cradle. Hopefully, he'll give Nancy Ruth an easy time of it." She looked unusually frail, dressed in widow's black instead of her customary jewel tones. She wore dark glasses and had her hair pulled up in a twist at the nape of her neck. She moved like she was walking underwater.

As she came in, Walker's version of *I'll Take Care of You* started to play on the radio. She smiled, looking toward it and saying, "I hear you, lover." To Sonny and Reg, she whispered, "This was the first song he ever did just for me. Did you know that?" They shook their heads, at a loss for words to comfort. She stood stock still for a moment, then removed her dark glasses with one hand. With the other, she rubbed her swollen, red eyes, shoulders shaking with silent crying. Sonny went to her and pulled her to him as the three of them listened to Walker sing the love song.

A few minutes later the limo arrived to take them to Lake Travis. Nancy Ruth came in to care for J.R. so that Cilla would not have to deal with the child at the public memorial. There would be a private ceremony that would include her later in the day. They rode in silence as they drove away from the property, the place that had become a haven in their grief. At the gate to the main road, the property-line fence was all but covered in wreaths and bouquets. There was also a special tribute to Walker, placed there by other players he had inspired. The entire road and drive beyond the fence was littered with guitar picks.

Being held at bay by the hired security was a brace of press outside the gate, training their cameras on the car. There would be even more at the service itself. Sonny realized that they simply wanted to record the service as the newsworthy event it was. That knowledge made the intrusion into their time of grief no easier to bear.

As they pulled into the secured area at the lake, and Sonny exited the limo, he saw a familiar face in the throng of press. Lurlene Luqadeaux, from *Texas Blues*, nodded to him with teary eyes. Lurlene was as close to a friend as he and Walker had in the world of reporters. She'd named them Ice and Fire in her first piece about them. Their careers had grown up alongside each other.

Fuck these other hacks. He'd only give Lurlene a statement. Still, what was there to say? Tell her, alongside the grief, how pissed off the family was? Not just family, of course. Everyone whose life he'd touched was smoldering with the randomness of Walker's demise. This wasn't supposed to happen—there was supposed to be time enough for everything. Years down the road he and the Squirt were supposed to sit on the back porch together, gnarled paws clutching their Fenders, mouths arguing their different approach to Texas Blues. They'd play for each other's pleasure, if no one else wanted to listen anymore. They'd debate the ice and fire that a good player could find inside the music. The fire had been snuffed out too soon, like others with too fine a thing for the mortal world to take more than a slight, sweet taste.

Sonny might even deny publicly that the devil had Walker in his vest pocket. He'd tell them how soulful and good Walker had been, as both person and player. After all, no one else could call Walker brother. Sonny would finally admit to everyone how much he loved him.

He glanced at Cilla. She touched his arm, whispering, "Please, talk to them for me."

"Of course. I'll be right back to sit with ya'll." He squeezed her hand,

and kissed Annabelle and Mama. Sonny approached the gaggle of press, glancing back at those he and Walker had loved. Their women: lover, Mama, sister-in-law. Their partners who'd shared their life of blues: the Tornadoes, the Rockets, and the ashen war orphans Real and Outlaw, who leaned against each other for strength. They'd all come together—for a boss, for a friend, for a son, and a husband—for the Firewalker, the true-blue Johnny B. Goode. Texas was a place where the natives really did things prouder, better, than all the rest. Walker had represented the best of the best. Too soon they had to lay him in this Texas soil—land of their birth, wellspring of their talents.

Sonny's own blood was now just another Lone Star tall tale. Time had come to say goodbye.

L.E Brady served for two years as contributing editor for *HHGI Online Guitar Magazine* and as local-music columnist for *Junction Magazine*. She regularly writes profiles and reviews for *Blue Suede News*, an American roots music magazine. Her short fiction has appeared in *The Mid-South Literary Review*. She currently resides in Ogden, Utah, with her husband, Steve, and children, Carmen, James and Lee. *Lone Star Ice and Fire* is her first novel.

ACKNOWLEDGMENTS

Without the kindness of many, this book would still be wandering around like a phantom riff inside my head. I'd be remiss not to thank at least a few.

Robert Dunn, my editor and publisher, has been unflagging in his support. His musical knowledge and literary vision were invaluable in helping me polish my manuscript. It does me great honor to work with this man. He has a heart and soul devoted to fine literature and music both. Thanks is also due copy editor Jill Jaroff and jacket designer Monica Fedrick for, respectively, smoothing out my last rough edges and bringing the Old Broad cover to spectacular life.

The late Lenel Moulds, my writing teacher, was stalwart in his encouragement and constructive criticism. I regret that he passed away shortly before I could share my joy with him that this novel was to be published. The news would have pleased Lenel to no end. Thanks are also due poet/fiction writers Bonnie Lee and Daniel Niemeyer for their invaluable guidance. Along with Lenel, they made up the Mission Inn Roundtable, my former writing group that met monthly to share work in the lobby of the storied old hotel in Riverside, Calif.

On the technical side, thanks are due John Page, former head of the Fender Custom Shop and current curator of the Fender Museum of Music and Arts in Corona, Calif. He was generous with his library of books featuring Fender's extraordinary instruments and ever patient in answering my gear-related questions. Howard Hart, a gifted musician-composer and my former guitar teacher, did his best to teach me a little of the magical language of the six-string and enlighten me about the hardware of his craft.

Humble thanks also go out to the many family members and friends who supported me in this project. They were ever gracious as I utilized them as sounding boards and readers. Many were called on to reread revisions, doing so without complaint. Extra kudos go to Elizabeth Frank, who not only read the very first draft and many revised chunks to follow but also gave me the brothers' names. I will always be thankful for this unique and selfless gift, as the handles fit these boys to a T.

I will also be forever grateful to my husband, Steve, and my children, Carmen, James, and Lee. Their patience allowed me the time and space needed to pursue this dream.

Last, but never least, I am indebted to the colorful and passionate men and women who play, write, and live the blues. Without their talents, sacrifices, and trials, there would be no such tales to tell.

Peace—
L.E. Brady